THE Tempted SERIES
COLLECTORS EDITION
VOLUME TWO
JANINE INFANTE BOSCO

Table of Contents

Reckless Temptations..4

Lethal Temptations................................251

Eternal Temptations.........................511

Bonus Chapters..785

Holiday Shenanigans..798

© Copyright 2018 Janine Infante Bosco

The Tempted Series Collection Volume two by Janine Infante Bosco

Reckless Temptations © Copyright 2016

Lethal Temptations © Copyright 2016

Eternal Temptations © Copyright 2016

All rights reserved. No part of this publication may be reproduced, distributed, or transmitted in any form or by any means, including photocopying, recording, or other electronic or mechanical methods, without the prior written permission of the publisher, except in the case of brief quotations embodied in critical reviews and certain other noncommercial uses permitted by copyright law.

Published by Janine Infante Bosco
Edited/formatted by: Jennifer Bosco
Cover Design by: Jennifer Bosco
ISBN: 9781717751706

RECKLESS TEMPTATIONS

JANINE INFANTE BOSCO

Prologue

Don't these bitches know who they're fucking with and who the fuck I ride with? Pretty ballsy move taking me—or any of the Satan's Knights for that matter. You would think after that shit went down with Jimmy Gold, people would realize we don't fucking play around. My club will come for me and when they do these motherfuckers will get down on their knees and tell me they love me. They'll beg my ass not to slit their throats—but I'll do it anyway because I'm nobody's bitch.

I heard a screech, like nails on a chalkboard, but that wasn't it. I knew that sound, someone needed a can of WD-40 for that garage door. Stupid fucks couldn't even spring for an electric door—that shit was still on a chain link.

Good, maybe these assholes will take the fucking bag off my head so I can spit in their faces and make them wish their mothers aborted their asses. Fuck that, I'd piss on them. Literally, these fucks took my cut, stripped me of all my clothes and tied my naked ass to a metal chair. I had to take a leak, and I was determined to take aim at one of these fuckers when the time was right.

"采取袋他的头."

Chinese, mumbo jumbo.

Great.

I would definitely piss on "Jackie fucking Chan."

The bag was lifted from my head and someone pulled a chain switch on a lightbulb dangling above me, temporarily blinding me as they said a bunch of shit I didn't understand.

These bastards ruined me. I used to love a good eggroll but after this shit, I'll never look at another one.

They exchanged more of their shit language before Sun Wu dragged a chair across the concrete floor and sat in front of me.

"Mr. Riggs, we meet again," Wu crooned, as he crossed a leg over his knee.

I wriggled my arms that were tied behind me, trying to free them so I could grab my dick and aim straight for his mouth, but it was no use.

"Fuck you, Wu," I sneered, as one of the Red Dragons' rammed his fist against the side of my face. I wasn't expecting the blow and bit the inside of my cheek, tasting the metallic flavor of my own blood.

"I expected more from you, something more original than fuck you, since you and your club have already fucked me over," he pointed out.

I turned my head, stared him in the eyes and swished the blood around in my mouth before spitting it at the *kung fu* warrior, which earned me another fist to my face.

"You have a sharp tongue Mr. Riggs," Wu said, lifting his head to meet the eyes of one of his men.

"Why don't we cut the bullshit," I said, spitting more blood from my mouth. "You got a hard on for me or something?"

"A hard-on," he scoffed, earning me a glare that could kill.

Fuck him.

"Explains why I'm naked as the fucking day I was born. You a faggot or something? I ain't bending over for you, "Jackie Chan." Ain't no fucking way," I growled.

"尊重," shouted the first asshole who punched me.

"Yeah, whatever the fuck that means! You jerk offs haven't realized I'm not fluent in your dick language," I spat, losing my patience with this game of cat and mouse. I turned my eyes back to Wu, "Why the fuck am I here?"

"You will tell me where my drugs are and why I'm burying three of my men and a bunch of whores." He held out his palm and one of his men handed him a leather whip.

What the fuck?

"Sounds like you bitches rang in the Chinese New Year early," I said, eyeing the fucking whip. "What are you people into? Like it rough, do ya?"

Sun Wu uncrossed his legs and stood, slapping the whip against the palm of his hand and crouched down in front of me.

"Mr. Riggs, I'm giving you a chance to save yourself right now and tell me what happened to my drugs?"

"I don't know dick about what you're talking about. If you're missing some of your drugs maybe you motherfuckers should turn on the news. That crazy mobster, Jimmy Gold, got caught with a shit ton of them. Maybe he's your guy," I snarled, cocking my head to the side. "Sucks for you though, that mofo is sitting cozy in the burn unit at Lutheran Medical. I heard his dick got singed off, maybe you can lend him yours…that's if you can find it," I said, winking at him.

I didn't have a clue as to where this guy was going or what he was fishing for—there was no way in hell they could've known it was us. I made sure I took the proper precautions before we ransacked their stash house—all fingers pointed to Jimmy Gold.

He snapped his whip against my shoulder and I yelped, more from shock than from pain.

"Don't fucking lie to me!"

I gritted my teeth, lifting my head to meet his slanted eyes.

"Jimmy Gold took your fucking shit, we don't ride with the mob no more, not since Victor went away. Now unless you have an issue with the gun deal I suggest you cut these fucking ties around me and let me go," I grunted. "You're only making it worse for you and the deal you have with our club."

"How's that?" He asked thoughtfully.

"You think the Bulldog will do business with you after you fucked our truce? You can kiss that deal goodbye after he finds out you took me," I roared.

"The Bulldog pissed, as you people put it, on our deal the minute you stole from me."

"Nobody took your fucking drugs," I hissed.

Three more lashes of the whip, three more marks on my flesh, secured the three bullets I'd put in this pricks head.

"Untie me and let me fight like a fucking man. Or are you Dragons too pussy to unleash me," I growled.

He laughed, cracking the whip and branding my chest with another fresh mark from the leather. I gritted my teeth through the fresh sting before glaring at him.

Give me more.

I'll take everything you got.

But I will come for you motherfucker.

"You have a lot of faith in your club. You think Jack will come riding to your rescue? You're nothing to him but a pee on that he uses to tweak his surveillance. You're the eye in the sky, someone who can be replaced. You're not his heart or his right hand. They won't come for you. They don't even know you're gone."

For a smart man, he made a pretty stupid move, using one of the oldest tricks in the book, trying to get me to turn on my club. Wu took the wrong brother, I'm no rat. I'll burn in Hell before I give up my family, before I give up the Satan's Knights.

Whip me motherfucker.

Give me all you got.

And so he did, him and his brothers took a chance a piece, cracking the whip and balling their firsts. My skin felt like it was on fire, I was bleeding from one of my eyes and spitting blood from my mouth.

Give me more.

"Enough," Wu ordered, before one of the Dragons could pound in my face a little more.

"This is how it's going to work, Mr. Riggs. You're going to tell me why my drugs are sitting in an evidence room. You're going to make me understand why Jack Parrish wants you dead," he insisted. "Because he does you know, sacrificing you and the rest of the club for a piece of pussy, that's some fearless leader you brothers have there," he continued. "Because if you don't I'm going to find everything and anything you love and I'm going to tear it apart. You know how it works and if you think what that stupid prick Gold did was fucked up, how he took Jack's vice president and his woman and made them pay for his sins, you haven't seen anything yet. When I'm through with you, you're going to sing to the Lord and beg for His mercy as you stare at the blood of those you love on your hands."

"You stupid bastard," I scoffed, laughing in Wu's face. "You took the wrong brother. I ain't got shit and as far as love goes—I only got love for the reaper on my back," I rasped, leaning as close as my confinements would allow. "I won't sing to the Lord but I'll rejoice with the Devil when I take your sorry ass down."

"Oh no, I've got the right brother," he assured, turning around and pulling back a curtain that lined the back wall of the garage, revealing a bunch of flat screen televisions.

"What the fuck is this, movie night?" I questioned, trying to figure out what he was up to.

"I'm a very patient man, Mr. Riggs, I will wait and bide my time but I'll always get my revenge. I will take back what is mine. The Knights took my product and they've killed three of my men—they owe me and I will collect. So, one last chance, one shot to tell me the truth or you and yours will be the first I take."

"We'll see about that motherfucker," I growled.

I'm going to come for you motherfucker.

Gonna give you all I got.

He turned around to face the screens and pulled a remote control from his pocket. He aimed it at the wall of televisions, bringing each of them to life. I peered at the screens with my good eye, slowly taking in each frame. I was thankful for all the red marks on my skin and the black eye because the blood drained from my body. The stash house was wired from the street to outside and back to the closets inside. Everything looked as it should. The time stamps all had the same date and time, every frame was perfectly adjusted to the footage we wanted them to see that day.

"Can you see what I see?" Wu sang.

My eyes scanned each frame slowly until they stopped and zeroed in on one, the one that showed Jack and me in the hallway.

Oh shit.

I cringed, closing my eyes as I lifted the ski mask and bared my face to the camera. Wu paused the frame, hit another button and brought the same image up on all the screens. He turned to me, his eyes meeting mine, and he smiled knowingly.

He had me.

"It's time to send your club a message," he informed me, as he looked over my shoulder at one of his boys.

He wasn't blowing smoke. I had fucked myself and royally too. Sun Wu had everything he needed to wage a war between the two clubs. He had everything he needed to be a man of his word and make us all pay.

I had no doubt that he'd start with me.

Then it dawned on me—his words, his threats, they all of a sudden had meaning.

One last chance, one shot, to tell me the truth or you and yours will be the first I take.

Lauren.

Pea.

One reckless move would change my whole life, actually two. One that changed my life forever and another that would ruin it.

I heard the sound of a machine vibrating before something crashed against my skull and everything faded to black.

Chapter One

Join an MC, it will be fun, they said. But no one mentioned babysitting a bunch of mobsters or getting smacked in the head with a frying pan by one of their mothers. This shit was worse than hazing. I knew I was a prospect, and I had to eat shit for a while before I became a patched member of the Satan's Knights, but this was fucking bullshit.

"Does your mother know you're part of a gang?" The Italian nutcase, Maria Bianci, asked as she climbed the stairs leading to her daughter's apartment. It surprised me that I hadn't killed the woman yet. I'm not going to lie, there was a time or two when I thought about it, but the bitch was mobbed up and I wasn't a patched member yet.

Her son, Anthony Bianci, was some wise guy in the mob and tonight he and his girl had been attacked. Bianci's chick was the daughter of mob boss Victor Pastore, or "Mr. Soprano," as I like to call him. Tonight, was the grand opening of some fancy club of his but instead of dancing and drinking the night away they dodged bullets. How the fuck I'm in the middle of this shit, I'll never know. Jack Parrish, the president of the Satan's Knights, ordered me to grab "Mama Leone" over here and her grandkid, or half a grandkid, I don't know the deal, but there was a kid and Bianci's mother was watching it.

I did as I was told, grabbed mommy dearest and the boy, delivered them safely to Anthony Bianci, only for him to take the kid and leave me with his maniac of a mother. Not even a thank you, Riggs. Say what you want about bikers, but these mob people were fucked. They were rude and their women were fucking violent. Imagine marrying one of these broads, she'd likely throw the fucking kitchen sink at you if you forgot to put the seat down after you took a piss. This one right here, would probably cut your balls off.

"Well? Does she?" She asked, glaring over her shoulder at me.

"I don't know lady, she's dead," I sneered.

My mother was very much alive, living the dream, married four times and all that but I wanted nothing more than to get the woman in front of me, who was busting my balls, to shut her mouth.

"I'm sorry," she said, pausing for a moment to stare at me. "She must be rolling in her grave," she continued, making the sign of the cross before knocking on her daughter's door.

See? Crazy. She was fucking crazy. Who says shit like that after you tell them your mother is dead?

The door swung open, and a girl stood there wearing nothing but a towel in the doorway. Finally, a light at the end of the tunnel.

The girl's eyes widened as she stared at Maria.

"Mrs. Bianci," she exclaimed, moving to stand behind the door to cover herself. "What're you doing here?"

"Mia, do you always answer the door in a towel?" Maria retorted.

"Um, no not usually," Mia stammered.

"You going to bitch about what the girl is wearing or you going to ask to be invited inside?" I chimed in, hoping to get a better glimpse of this Mia character.

"I'm sorry. He's right, come inside please. Does Lauren know you're visiting?" she asked politely, as she opened the door wider allowing us room to step inside.

"No. It's an impromptu visit she can thank her brother for," Maria said, looking around the apartment. "Where is she anyway? It's nearly three in the morning."

"Um...working," she smiled nervously.

"Can you give me a minute to throw on some clothes?"

Maria shooed her away with her hands before walking further into the apartment, picking up empty cups and paper dishes along the way.

"I'll just be a minute. Make yourself at home," Mia said, eyes bouncing anxiously between me and Maria. They locked with mine and she hastily turned on her heel and headed down the tiny hallway. Yeah, something was up and it wasn't my dick. Bummer.

"You can leave now," Maria said, glancing over her shoulder. "I wish I could say it was nice to meet you Rabbit."

"Riggs," I hissed.

"What kind of name is that anyway?" She asked, brushing me off and bending down to pick up a pair of shoes one of the girls had haphazardly left on the couch.

"It's my road name," I explained angrily.

"Well if that isn't the most ridiculous thing I've ever heard. What is your God given name?"

I shook my head in disgust and walked away from her, searching for the bathroom.

"Where do you think you're going?" Maria asked behind me.

That was it. A man can only take so much and I had had my fill of Maria Bianci.

"I'm going to go take a piss, would you like to come with me? Maybe hold my dick for me?"

I grinned in satisfaction when I heard her gasp behind me. One for Riggs, twelve thousand for Maria.

I walked down the narrow hallway, finding the bathroom and heard Mia talking in hushed tones in the room across from it.

"Lauren, you really need to answer your phone goddamn it! Your mother is here with some scary looking guy. Call me back."

I stopped outside Mia's bedroom door, peered through the crack and saw she was fully dressed. Double bummer. She was sitting on the foot of her bed, her fingers moving rapidly on her phone. I toed the door open with the tip of my boot and she quickly dropped her phone onto the bed.

"Problem?" I asked, checking over my shoulder to see if "Carmela Soprano" was anywhere near, then stepped further into Mia's room. She lifted her eyes to mine, sinking her perfectly straight teeth into her lower lip.

"Why would you ask that?"

I narrowed my eyes trying to read her. I didn't know what the hell was going on here but I was sure that my night wasn't over. I was starting to hate everyone with the last name Bianci.

"Where's Lauren?" I asked, crossing my arms against my chest. Her eyes zeroed in on my cut and I watched her throat as she swallowed.

"Who are you?" She questioned.

"I'm a friend of her brother's," I lied because Anthony was more of an enemy of mine at this point. She looked uneasy, I didn't know if it was because I was a strange guy standing in her bedroom or because she was hiding something. I lifted the skull cap from my head and ran my fingers roughly through my hair.

"Look, if Lauren's in some kind of trouble…" I started but my words trailed off the moment she stood from her bed and peeked her head out the door. She closed it softly and turned around.

"Lauren's been lying to her mother," she started.

I fitted the hat back onto my head and sighed. More Bianci bullshit was headed my way.

"Maria thinks Lauren is an intern at a hospital, a requirement for her nursing degree. The thing is, she kind of quit the program," she continued.

I lifted an eyebrow. "Mama Leone" was going to blow a gasket.

"So if she's not playing Florence Nightingale, where is she?" I questioned.

Silence.

Fuck my life. I stalked toward Mia, watching as she raised an eyebrow and walked backward until her back slammed against the door.

"Ouch," she muttered.

I narrowed my eyes, bracing one hand flat against the door over her head and leaned close to her.

"Where is she?" I repeated.

"She's working at a bar in town, near campus," she said, stepping around me to walk toward her desk. She ripped a piece of paper off a pad and scribbled something on it. "Here's the address. She's not answering the phone so you need to go get her before Maria starts asking questions."

"You're kidding right?"

Does the leather and tattoos not scare anyone anymore these days? These people are walking all over me like I'm some kind of jerk off.

"I don't even know what she looks like," I grunted, staring down at the scribbled address, wondering what kind of bar the Pink Pussycat was and what the fuck I did in life to deserve this shit.

Mia looked at me for a moment before turning around and grabbing a picture frame off her dresser. She held up the framed photo of her and what I assumed was Lauren. I dropped my eyes to the picture of the two girls, my eyes zeroing in on Lauren.

Big crystal blue eyes, framed by thick black-rimmed glasses, stared back at me. She had a killer smile, perfectly straight, white teeth, framed by full pink lips and a cute tongue since she was sticking it out the side of her mouth. Her black hair framed her face in waves, a stark contrast to her bright blue eyes. She was pretty, hot even, if you're into the girl next door type. Or nurses. I wouldn't mind being her patient.

I lifted my eyes back to Mia's and handed her back her photograph before turning around and pulling open the door.

"Are you going to go get her?" Mia called over my shoulder. I ignored her and brushed past Maria who was scowling at me from the bathroom door.

"Got lost on your way to the john?" she asked, crossing her arms and tapping her foot impatiently.

"No, when you wouldn't hold my dick for me I thought I'd test my luck with your daughter's roommate," I smiled, glancing over my shoulder at Mia. "Thanks, babe," I winked.

"What? No! I didn't…" Mia stammered.

These Bianci people were a pain in my ass but they sure were fun to fuck with. I turned around and shoved my finger in front of Maria's nose.

"I'll be back. Don't. Fucking. Move."

"Where are you going?"

"To pick up your damn daughter, because someone upstairs…" I pointed my index finger to the ceiling, "…wants to keep fucking testing my patience with you people."

It was her turn to shove her accusing finger in my face.

"You're going to the hospital to pick her up? Just…don't talk to anyone. I'm warning you, you better behave yourself and not embarrass her. Lauren has worked very hard to get where she is and the last thing she needs is some scoundrel like you, messing things up for her with your crude mouth and poor manners," she said.

Was this bitch serious?

"I'll try not to piss on the floors of the hospital and promise not to pick my nose in front of any hotshot doctors," I sneered, shaking my head in disgust.

She should only know how deep my manners go.

I stalked out of the apartment, slamming the door behind me and glanced at the address Mia had given me. Fucking bullshit.

I typed the address into the GPS of the cage I was driving because I was in the middle of Bumblefuck New York, full of winding roads and fucking deer. I was waiting for that to happen next because why not add killing Bambi to this wretched night.

I whimpered as I drove, feeling sorry for myself and slammed my hand against the steering wheel.

I just wanted my bike and the open road.

And maybe a blowjob.

That would be nice.

Lauren's pretty, pink lips, wrapped nice and tight around my dick and those blue eyes peeking up at me over the frames of her glasses. Shit. Where the fuck did that come from?

Get your shit together, Riggs.

"You've arrived at your destination," the GPS alerted, and I'm not going to lie, she sounded hot too.

I needed to get laid.

Or I needed to go to bed.

Something. Anything.

The Pink Pussycat was packed, people stood in line waiting to get inside even at three a.m., apparently making it a happening joint for the people of Bumblefuck. I moved to the front of the line and a big brut of a guy stood there, staring down at me.

"Line's back there," the beast said.

"That's nice, move aside," I replied, stepping around him but he mimicked my move and blocked me again.

I glanced at the heavens.

"Why?" I shouted into the dark sky.

No one answered.

Pussy.

Shit, I was probably going to hell for that one.

I looked back at the beast of a bouncer who raised an eyebrow at me, and was tempted to tell him he looked like Michael Clarke Duncan, but I needed to focus. I took a deep breath and opened my cut for him to see the gun I had tucked into my waistband.

"Listen, bud, I've had the night from hell and I'm ten seconds away from losing it, so move the fuck out of my way and let me do what the fuck I came here to do," I growled, reaching for the gun.

He crossed his arms, glanced at my gun, and shook his head completely unfazed.

"Pretty please, with sugar on top?" I tried. Nothing. "Fuck! The name "Tony Soprano" mean anything to you? Shit, I mean, fuck, what's his name…Pastore." The burley bouncer remained unmoved. That's it. I can't take anymore. "Bro, get the fuck out of my way, seriously, I have to get one of the girls that works here, I'm her ride."

"Who?"

"Lauren Bianci," I huffed. That fucking last name was nothing but trouble.

"Shit, man, why didn't you say so?" he pounded me on the back and smiled. "Lauren's my girl, love that chick, always makes me smile," he said, with an actual smile. "Go on in. She's working the bar tonight."

I think I muttered a thank you, I'm not sure, but I brushed past him and stepped foot into the loud bar that was packed beyond capacity. It took me five minutes, pushing my way through the crowd toward the bar that was surrounded mostly by men that were hooting and hollering.

What was the big fuss?

I squeezed my way between two jocks screaming for their turn to be next and caught a glimpse of what had every guy in this joint begging to be next.

The girl next door was on her knees, crawling the length of the bar, from one lucky bastard to another. She poured the liquor straight from the bottle into some lucky bastard's mouth.

"Marry me!" He shouted, and she threw her head back and laughed.

"Oh baby, I'm not the marrying kind," she said, blowing him a kiss before she rose to her feet and gave me a full view of her outfit. I started with the shoes that stomped across the bar, fucking sexy as hell. I'd make her keep them on when she wrapped her legs around me and wouldn't even mind those five-inch heels digging into my back. She was a tiny thing, maybe five foot two, if that, but those heels made her killer legs seem so long. Or maybe it was the short plaid skirt that gave every man at the bar a peep show. Her waist was tiny and her stomach flat, but her rack? Man, what I wouldn't do to shove my face in her tits. Her shirt knotted under her breasts and was open for all to see the black lace bra she was wearing. I squinted, hoping to catch a little peak of her nips but she was moving all over the place, dancing up a storm as she flirted and poured liquor into all the open mouths, waiting for a taste.

Lauren Bianci, the girl next door, rocked the naughty school girl bit like no one's business.

"What's the matter handsome? Why so serious?" she asked. Her big blue eyes, framed by those damn glasses, staring straight into mine. Every fucking thing went south, whatever common sense I had left, all my blood, it all went straight to my dick. She smiled wide, bending down and pulled my hat from my head before she ran her fingers through my messy hair and yanked my head back. "Open up," she demanded against my ear.

I looked into those eyes and was fucking lost. She could've demanded I run around the bar naked, barking like a dog and I would've done it. So I opened my mouth and let her poor the cinnamon flavored whiskey down my throat.

My dick was rock-fucking-hard.

Down boy!

She pulled the bottle away and swiped her thumb across my lips.

"Good boy," she cheered, turning her attention to the man beside me but I grabbed her wrist. Something changed in her eyes and she glanced around the bar, my guess in search of a bouncer. She probably thought I was just another schmuck that wanted to take her into a bathroom stall. I kind of did.

I leaned closer, hypnotized by her perfume and sniffed her.

"Show's over Lauren. Grab your things it's time to go," I said against her ear.

She tried to pull her wrist from my hand but my grip tightened and I turned my head a fraction to stare into those blue orbs again. Shit, they were pretty.

"How do you know my name?"

"Last call! Grab your favorite pussycat for a final round!" A voice said over the mic.

"Man, you had your fucking turn. C'mere pussycat," the guy next to me shouted. I let go of Lauren's hand and snapped my head in his direction and glared at the stupid fuck, shrinking him back down to his size. Napoleon complex bullshit.

"Fuck off," I growled, before turning back to Lauren. But she was gone. My eyes roamed around the bar looking for her but came up empty. Poof! Vanished.

Yep, it was official. I hated everyone with the last name Bianci.

Chapter Two

Last call was an hour ago and tips were split amongst all the pussycats. I hated that fucking name almost as much as I hated dancing half naked on a bar. Unfortunately, when you decide that you don't really want to be a nurse but have a shitload of bills…you have to do something. And running home to mommy isn't an option, at least not for me. Not because my mother wouldn't welcome me home with open arms. She'd do it and try to hide the disappointment in her eyes as she did so.

My mom was a single mom who sacrificed much of herself to give me and my brother a good life. We didn't want for anything and there was always food on the table because she busted her ass to make sure there was. When my brother got older he tried to man up and take the place of my dad and fell into the wrong crowd doing so. My brother broke our mother's heart when he became a *made* man. That's right, made, as in the mob. Anthony is an enforcer for Victor Pastore, a title that landed him in a jail cell for three years.

The day Anthony went to prison was the day everything changed for our little family or at least for me. I hated seeing how upset my mother was, how disappointed in him she was and most of all how she blamed herself for Anthony's lifestyle. It was me though, who finally got my mother to smile again, to believe she hadn't failed as a mother. All I had to do was show her my acceptance letter into one of the most prestigious nursing programs in New York State. The icing on the cake was the full scholarship I was gifted because of my good grades throughout high school.

So, while one child served time for a crime he didn't commit, Maria Bianci's other child busted her ass to maintain her scholarship.

Anthony was released a year or so ago, and despite my mother and his girl Adrianna's pleas, he fell back into his old life. And me? Well, I gave up. Gave up on being a nurse, threw away the scholarship, and gave up on being the prodigal child…gave up on everything. I didn't know what I wanted to do with my life but I was sure that changing bedpans wasn't for me. It was pretty silly to think the girl who hated the sight of blood was really contemplating becoming a nurse anyway. I gave up and kept that shit to myself. That's right, my mom and brother think everything is just dandy. Good little Lauren is hitting the books, making the grades, on her way to becoming the first person in the Bianci family to graduate college and make something of herself.

Lies. Big fat lies.

I shoved my slutty outfit, albeit it earned me a lot of tips, into my duffel bag and finished dressing back into my sweats. I walked toward the sink and stared at the girl reflected in the mirror. Taking a deep breath, I removed my glasses and washed all the make-up from my face.

Society was bullshit. I wonder, if I served drinks at The Pink Pussycat without a stitch of make-up on and a turtleneck, if I'd make a dollar.

Probably not.

Probably wouldn't even make enough to cover my cellphone bill let alone my rent.

I twisted my hair into a messy bun on top of my head and perched my glasses back on my nose. I was finally able to look like myself again, the good girl who just wanted to please everyone.

I slipped the strap of my bag over my shoulder and made my way back into the main room of the bar where everyone was getting ready to leave. I was hoping to catch a ride from Big Lou, the bouncer. My Toyota was out of commission and I didn't have the money to fix it yet. It's not even like it needed a lot of work but the brakes were shot and the tires were balled. Oh, and there was that little problem—it started whenever it felt like. See? Not much, easy job. A piece of cake…right?

"Hey Lou…" I started but was interrupted by my phone ringing at the bottom of my bag.

"What are you still doing here?" Lou asked me, confusing me. Where the hell was I supposed to go?

I grabbed my phone and my eyes widened when I saw it was my mother calling. My stomach dropped as I accepted the call nervously. It's never good news when the phone rings at four in the morning, and when your brother is a mobster? Well you get the point.

Please don't let him be hurt.

Please don't let him be in trouble.

"Mom?"

"Well, it's about time! Thank you, Saint Anthony," she shouted into the phone, causing me to hold the phone away from my ear. "I've been calling you for almost two hours. Is that hooligan there? He didn't embarrass you or cause you any trouble at the hospital, did he? Let me know, and so help me God I will smack him silly."

What in God's name was she talking about?

"What hooligan? Mom slow down…my shift just ended." I flinched as the lie came out of my mouth so easily.

"The biker boy!"

Yep, she's lost it. Although, I will not lie, I wish there was truth to this little story—motorcycles are hot!

Trying to concentrate on the phone call and my surroundings, I could hear a commotion going on at the door, and Lou yelling at someone.

"You again?"

"Get the fuck out of my way Duncan! I'm in no fucking mood."

Lou pushed the guy at the door back so I couldn't see him but the intruder started hollering.

"LAUREN BIANCI IF YOUR ASS IS IN THERE YOU BETTER GET IT OUT BY THE TIME I COUNT TO FIVE!"

"What is that? Oh, my God, he's not starting a scene in the hospital, is he?"

"Mom, focus, who is *he*, exactly?"

"One of your brother's friends. There was trouble tonight—"

"Is he okay?" I interrupted.

"Yes, he's with Adrianna and the baby but he sent this dope to come and bring me to your apartment. Your brother wants us both in the same place until things calm down. Fucking Victor Pastore, I could kill that man with my bare hands!" My mother said, sounding exasperated. "You know your apartment is a mess? And Mia, is she on drugs? The girl hasn't shut up since I got here."

"ONE!"

"Do you know this clown?" Lou asked me over his shoulder.

"Mom, did you send this guy here?"

"I didn't send him. Blame your damn brother, actually, blame Victor Pastore. It's all that son of a bitch's fault."

"TWO!"

"Lau?" Lou persisted.

"I've got to go mom, see you in a few," I said, quickly ending the call and hurrying to Lou's side before he broke Anthony's friend's nose and there was bloodshed.

I wonder which of the *dons* he sent this time.

"It's okay Lou, I didn't know my brother was sending someone for me," I answered, reaching up to kiss Lou's cheek. "I'll see you tomorrow."

"You sure you want to go anywhere with this guy?" he said, turning his attention to my ride, causing me to turn around and look at him too.

It was him.

The guy from earlier, the one who grabbed my wrist and I thought was just another creep trying to get in my pants. Only, instead of looking like sex on a stick, he resembled a mass murderer.

"Hiya handsome," I said, offering a smile as an apology for all the trouble I may have caused him.

He grunted.

So it would take more than a smile.

I had waited most of my teenage years for this moment. You know the one—when having an older brother finally has its perks because his friends are hot and not twice his age or mobsters. At twenty-one I had given up on the dream, but now I was staring at one of Anthony's friends—and he wasn't an old geezer. I leaned forward and stole a glimpse of the fingers he was cracking as he glared up at Lou. Nope, no pinky ring either! Score.

His eyes met mine, and holy fuck! He looked at me confused for a minute. It didn't take me long to understand why. It was because I had changed and I wasn't wearing six layers of paint on my face anymore. It was just little 'ole me, plain Jane, Lauren. I frowned, pushing my glasses further back onto my nose with my index finger nervously as I took him all in.

He was well over six feet and when I moved to stand closer to him, he towered over me. He had chocolate brown eyes that probably melted the panties off of any girl he ever looked at—I'd gladly throw mine away. The pair of well-worn jeans hung low on his hips and cut at the knee. He was wearing Timberland boots—(my favorite, but I was a sucker for fresh white kicks on a guy too), oddly the laces were missing from his boots. The heather gray thermal he wore stretched over his broad chest and shoulders, molded to his skin perfectly. He also wore a leather jacket type thing which had patches sewn into it declaring him a prospect, whatever that meant.

A real deal biker.

Thank you, Anthony.

"You're staring," he mumbled, taking hold of my wrist and dragging me away from Lou and The Pink Pussycat.

"Sorry," I shrugged. "It's just you're not like my brother's other *friends*."

"Thank Christ for that," he said, as he took big strides across the parking lot dragging me behind him. "Why'd you disappear from me before?" he grumbled over his shoulder.

"I thought you were a creep," I admitted honestly.

"You Bianci women really know the way to a man's heart," he hissed, pulling his keys from his pocket and unlocking the doors to a truck, shooting down my dreams of catching a ride on the back of a bike.

His phone rang.

"Why? Why can't this night just end?" he cried up to the heavens, before bringing his phone to his ear.

I think he might have a screw loose.

"Yeah, Prez," he said into the phone, nodding toward the passenger door. "Get in."

And his attitude sucked too.

"Yeah, I got the sister," he continued, to whoever was on the phone. "I'm dropping her ass off to her loony toon of a mother and getting the fuck away from anyone with the last name Bianci," he said, climbing into the truck beside me.

Well, that was rude.

He disconnected the call, throwing his phone into the console and glanced at me.

"What?" he demanded.

"You're kind of a dick," I commented.

"And you're a pain in the ass so we're even," he argued, starting up the truck. "It was supposed to be an easy job. Pick up the mother and the kid—take them to Bianci. That was it, the Bulldog said. But no, God wanted to fuck with me by adding to my misery—getting whacked with a frying pan by that lunatic of a woman, tying the bitch up and dragging her to Long Island just wasn't enough. I needed to get saddled bringing "Mama Leone" upstate to spend quality time with her daughter while the gangster son goes off the grid too. Fuck this shit!" He said, punching the steering wheel. "And instead of dropping off "Carmela Soprano" and running the fuck away from her, I get stuck in more Bianci family drama," he continued to rant, piercing me with a look. "Picked a fine time to become a stripper little girl," he hissed.

"I'm not a stripper!" I seethed.

"You're no fucking nurse, that's for sure," he retorted. "Fucking tease," he muttered

"Excuse me?" I asked, feeling my cheeks redden with anger. I wanted to throttle this asshole.

He grinned sarcastically and holy hell…his smile…there were no words. For one split second I lost my mind and wished we had gotten off on a different foot. I really wanted to see that smile again.

He's rude. He has insulted your family. Stop looking at his crotch.

"Stop smiling!" I demanded.

"I called you a fucking tease," he confirmed.

"I don't see—"

"Shouldn't slop all that shit on your face, you are way fucking prettier without it," he said, cutting me off.

Oh, wow.

That was kind of nice.

"So…which is the truth? Are you little Miss innocent or you some wild child looking for a good time?" he asked, diverting his eyes back to the road.

I thought about his question for a while and wondered if I should answer him truthfully. If I told him I was tired of being the good girl, tired of pleasing everyone and just wanted to live. I wondered what he would say.

I'm not saying I want to live recklessly, but would it be so bad to take chances? To experience life and find out what I really wanted from it?

"I liked the naughty school girl bit you had going on tonight, but this…" he said, waving his hand at me, "…this wholesome thing is pretty hot too," he complimented, shrugging his shoulders.

"Who are you?" I asked dumbfounded.

He looked back toward the road, driving with one hand and the other hand pointed to the name on his leather vest.

I squinted and peered over the rim of my glasses to read the name from his patch.

"Riggs?"

He dropped his hand to the shifter and nodded.

"Is that some sort of nickname?" I questioned.

He rolled his eyes in disgust.

"It's my road name," he said, through gritted teeth. "You know what a road name is don't you?" I remained silent, and he took that as his answer. "It's the name I use for my club."

"Like a motorcycle club?"

"Give her a gold star," he said sarcastically.

"What is your problem?"

"I hate your brother right now, and while we are getting to know one another and all that warm fuzzy shit, you should know I detest your mother too," he paused, eyeing me for a reaction. "The jury's still out on you," he continued.

"Touching," I said, rolling my eyes. "My jury came back with their verdict—you most definitely are a dick," I stated, turning my head to look out the window. "Stop the car," I demanded, grabbing my bag from the floor and reaching for the handle on the door.

"Cut the shit," he replied, hitting the lock button on his door, trapping me beside him.

I reached inside my purse looking for something I could use as a weapon…tampons, past due electric bill, lip gloss, ah ha! I wrapped my hand around the can, pulled it out and aimed the nozzle at him.

"I said stop the car," I ground out.

"Shit, not you too," he shook his head. "You people have watched *The Godfather* way to many times. I bet you're a dish thrower," he glanced at me. "Put the mace down, kitten," he said calmly.

"Then pull the car over and I will walk the rest of the way," I insisted, keeping my hand firmly on the mace.

"How come you don't have a car? Shouldn't everyone who lives in the middle of nowhere have a car?" he questioned, as he pulled the car over and dropped the shifter into park. He kept his finger on the lock and twisted himself around so he was facing me.

"Asked you a question," he reminded.

"None of your business," I hissed. "Look, I'm sorry I've been such an inconvenience to you but the longer you keep your hand on that button, the longer you're stuck with me," I said.

"I think I've lost my fucking mind," he whispered.

"Yes, you have," I confirmed. "Unlock the door," I demanded again.

"Why are you lying to your mother about quitting nursing school?" he questioned.

"How the hell do you even know that?" I asked exasperated, dropping the can of mace back into my purse and pressing my head against the seat. I closed my eyes and counted to three.

Re-opening my eyes, I was confronted by gorgeous, expressive eyes that belonged to the most annoying man I had ever met.

Yeah, not a fucking a dream.

"Don't tell your roommate if you ever off someone, girl's got loose lips," he replied.

"I have no idea why I'm even asking you this and I'm sure I'm going to kick myself in the ass but—you in some kind of trouble, kitten?"

Mia. I was going to *off* her. She was the reason this Riggs character knew my fucking life story.

I rubbed my temples, opened my eyes and fixed them on his.

"Stop pretending like you give a shit and just take me home, that way we both can be rid of one another," I said, turning my head away from him and staring out the window.

"I knew I shouldn't have asked," he mumbled, as he roughly put the car back into drive and peeled off the service road. "Fucking Bianci," he growled.

My mother was right.

This man was a hooligan.

A panty dropping, hooligan.

Five minutes later, he pulled up in front of my apartment and I climbed out of the truck, happy to be rid of him.

Even though he was easy on the eyes.

Despite he was a hot biker.

I slammed the door and marched my way toward my building, not turning back until I heard him call out.

"You're fucking welcome," he shouted out the window.

I spun on my heel, glaring at him over the rim of my glasses.

"I didn't fucking thank you!"

"Now there's an idea," he replied, giving me that grin one last time before he peeled away from the curb.

Chapter Three
Three Months Later

No fucking patch. I was starting to think my brothers saw me as a joke and had no intention of giving me my patch. Sure, I went on some runs with them, and every now and then things got a little out of control, but mostly they didn't even include me in the hardcore shit. The shit I signed up for in the first place.

I flipped open my laptop and my fingers danced along the keyboard. Might as well keep myself entertained as I waited for the next joke of a job to be thrown my way. Maybe today they'll make me clean the fucking toilets in this joint. I pulled up the four-frame on my computer and randomly selected one of the images.

Old man Gregursky, always came through when I needed a good laugh. I double clicked on the frame, enlarging the surveillance footage of his apartment to fit my entire screen. He was one of my neighbors, not that he even knew I lived next door to him. I kept an apartment in Brooklyn, but rarely ever spent the night there. It was more of a storage facility than anything else, home of all my gadgets and gizmos. I had an electronic fetish and was pretty fucking good at what I did. I could tap into phone lines, security systems and even trace 911 calls. I could get you social security numbers, credit card numbers, and if you needed funds, I could pull them from your bank account with a key stroke. I was the man.

I reached for my coffee mug on the nightstand and watched as Mr. Gregursky burnt his breakfast and used Poly Grip to glue his dentures into his mouth.

"Come on man, give me something good," I said to the screen as someone knocked on my door. I closed my laptop as Mr. Gregursky scratched his back with a spatula. I should've chosen the Chinese twins that loved threesomes.

"Come in," I said, throwing my computer onto the bed beside me.

Blackie, the vice president of the Satan's Knights, poked his head into my room.

"The Bulldog wants to see you in the Chapel," he stated, staring at me for a moment. Mr. Gregursky's moans filled the room. Fucking, Gregursky. "Were you slapping it to a porno?" Blackie questioned with a disgusted look on his face.

"What? No!" I said, jumping to my feet and glancing down at the offensive computer for a second before ushering Blackie out of my room.

"You're strange," he said pointedly.

"Yeah and you're grumpy," I replied, slapping him on the back. "We're one hell of a pair. So, tell me, any idea why Prez wants to see me?"

Jack 'Bulldog' Parrish, was the president of our club, a fierce leader and one badass motherfucker. Years ago, he lost his son, and the guys at the club, my brothers, say he hasn't been the same since it happened. Word around the Dog Pound is that our president has a dark side, one that would terrify a serial killer. Blackie and Pipe keep him on a tight leash, stop him from losing control, but one day that man is going to break and God help the poor bastard on the other end of that.

"No fucking idea," Blackie mumbled, as we walked down the stairs.

"Does that mean you assholes still haven't voted on giving me my colors?" I asked, as we walked through the common room. Blackie paused, fixing me with a cold stare. Yeah, did I mention he was a badass too? Fucking man was what nightmares were made of.

"You want to rephrase that?"

"Can't keep the president waiting!" I said, waving him off as I hurried around him and into the Chapel, closing the door behind me and leaning against it. I smiled sheepishly at Jack as Blackie pounded on the door behind me. "Should see about getting a lock on this thing and anger management wouldn't be a bad idea for the big brute out there," I suggested.

"I can hear you," shouted Blackie.

"What'd you do to piss him off?"

"I don't know…woke up this morning?" I said, kicking off the door and making my way toward the large wooden table that sat in the center of the room. "He's always on the rag that one," I added, taking a seat at the table. I turned to the man who beckoned me here and flashed him my signature grin. "So what's the deal, boss man? Finally, going to patch me in?"

I looked at him expectantly, flipping my baseball cap around as he stared at me. His dark eyes studying me, burning a hole right through me as he chose the words he would deliver.

"I like you Riggs," he said.

Gee, Prez. I like you too but not liking the warm fuzzy vibes.

"I like you a lot," he continued.

Okay, weird moment.

"And I feel your loyalty to the club but I'm not sure what makes you tick."

"I'm a real simple guy, Prez. I get high off of power and pussy," I answered.

His lips quirked momentarily. "Every man's last words," he said, leaning over the table and folding his hands. "Let me try this again," he countered. "You show a lot of loyalty and you're eager to be patched in—I have no doubt you'd wear your colors proud and live and breathe for your brotherhood. But we all got something in us, each member of this club, something else that drives us and that's heart."

"I've got a heart," I defended.

"Yeah, you do but what's your heart beating for? What inside of you is going to keep you level and keep you breathing? What's the one thing that will prevent you from being reckless? Because at the end of the day whatever makes your heart beat will be the thing that keeps you alive. For me, it's my daughter, for Blackie, it's the fear of dying and seeing his wife's tortured soul. Wolf keeps breathing for his boys and Pipe's got a young wife he's too jealous to leave behind. We've all got something," he stated. "What do you have?"

Well, fuck. Talk about crushing a man's dreams. What did I have? What would keep me from being reckless? My computer? No. I tried to think of something that would keep me from dying, something to live for. Definitely not my family, they probably thought I was dead already. I gave up. What the fuck is with this sentimental bullshit anyway?

"I don't expect you to answer," he added. "I expect you to find out what it is—when you know for certain, then and only then, answer me. I'll be waiting," he said, leaning back in his chair as he pulled a cigarette from his cut. "I've got a job for you," he offered.

I raised an eyebrow, happy to change the subject.

"Lay it on me," I said.

"I just came back from my visit with Victor Pastore," he continued, taking a pull from his cigarette.

Victor Pastore, AKA "Tony fucking Soprano." If I never heard that name or saw those people again it would be too soon. Crazy gangsters.

"He delivered me something that has been tearing me up trying to get. He gave me a gift and in turn I gave him peace of mind," Jack said, thoughtfully. "Man's going to rot away in that cell so his family could be free of his sins and he's still worried about them," he explained.

"Sounds like a real gem," I mumbled sarcastically. After that horrid night when I had to transport the Bianci family, a clan of nutcases, Victor turned himself in, confessing to a shitload of crimes. I didn't feel sorry for the mob boss, he's the idiot that turned himself in. Such an idiotic thing to do if you ask me. Man got away with every illegal thing he did for years only to confess like some sort of pussy. Word on the street is he did it to save his kids anymore pain caused by his lifestyle, they say it takes a lot of heart to do something like that…hmm.

Heart.

Then he delivered the blow.

"I need you to look out for Bianci, keep him and his family safe," he ordered, blowing out a stream of smoke. "A lot of moves are being made, power is being transferred from Vic's hand to his underboss, and with Bianci trying to be neutralized, he's fair game. So is his wife and kid, and that shit ain't going to happen on my watch," he declared angrily, before pointing his index finger at me. "Or on your watch, because you will be there making sure harm doesn't land on the Bianci's door step. They will be your heart for now until you find your own," he said.

"You're kidding, right?" I asked. "You want me to babysit those lunatics?"

"I want you to keep them safe," he corrected, flicking the ashes of his cigarette. "And don't you worry your pretty little head, his mother won't be around to fuck with you."

I whimpered.

Bianci.

At least his wife was smokin'.

Oh shit, the kid. I forgot about the little snot.

His bat shit crazy mother.

His hot as hell, crazy sister. I wonder how the little kitten and her rack are doing.

"Riggs?"

I shook my head, clearing my mind of motor-boating my little kitten's tits and looked at Jack.

"We good?"

Like I had a fucking choice.

"Yeah, Prez, we're good."

Anthony opened a boxing gym in his quest to become a legit, law-abiding citizen. What a crock of shit that was. The man had more ammo than I had underwear. I was a firm believer that underwear was overrated, just a nuisance really. Anyway, he spent most of his days at the gym trying to get it off the ground, so on my first official day reporting as Anthony Bianci's shadow, I parked my bike outside of Xonerated.

My eyes worked the gym, taking in the abundance of women working out in tight gym pants. A lot of ass to be had here. Maybe this gig wouldn't be so bad.

"Can I help you?" I dragged my eyes from the girl pummeling a heavy bag and focused on the blonde receptionist.

Why, hello there…the name tag plastered to her chest showed her name was Brittany.

I flashed her my smile and watched her eyes widen.

Yep, absolutely had its perks. Brittany would be riding my dick in the locker room by the end of the day. I was sure of it.

I winked at her, leaning over the counter.

"Hiya beautiful," I crooned.

"Riggs," a voice warned.

Fucking Bianci.

Add cock blocker to Mr. Legit's extracurricular activities.

"Lay off my employees," he growled, pulling me by the back of my vest like I was a little kid. I blew a kiss to Brittany and mouthed "later" to her.

I reached behind me, peeled his fingers from my vest and stood tall.

"Why the hell did you do that for? That was an easy score man!"

"Look, you and I are stuck with one another for a while which means we need to set some rules in place," he said, crossing his arms against his broad chest.

"Rules?" I scoffed. Neither of us did well with rules. This was a joke.

"Rule number one, keep your dick in your pants around my staff and my clients," he said.

I covered my mouth with my hand and tried not to laugh in the guy's face.

"I'm serious, Riggs," he grunted.

"I'll stay away from employees but clients are fair game," I said, eyeing the tight ass walking out of the locker room. "No negotiating," I declared as she bent over to tie her shoelace.

Goddamn!

"Jack says you're a loose cannon, that you fly off the handle," he started.

"I am not," I defended. "I don't take shit from people is all," I stated.

He smirked.

"What?"

He shook his head, his smirk firmly in place.

"Don't go there, bro," I said. "Your mother is the exception, that bitch is certifiable."

"That's my mother you're talking about," he said, his smirk faltering.

"Well if it's any consolation your sister is hot as fuck," I offered. "Makes up for your mom being a crackerjack."

His eyes narrowed, his jaw tightened as he advanced toward me making it obvious that Anthony had a soft spot where my kitten was concerned.

"Only gonna say it once," he said gravely. "Rule number two, the only one you better pray you follow," he added, backing me up against a wall. "Stay the fuck away from my sister," he growled.

Whoa. I held up my hands in mock defeat.

"Relax, bro, she lives in the sticks for crying out loud," I argued.

"She's visiting," he ground out.

My eyebrows raised and my cock perked up. Kitten was in town? Wonder if I can get the little kitten to purr.

"Stay. The. Fuck. Away. From. Lauren," he warned.

"Or what?" I taunted. "You'll sic your mommy on me?"

A vein bulged at his temple.

Okay enough poking the beast.

He's going to blow.

"Don't worry, she's not my type, and to be honest she's got the crazy streak you Bianci's all seem to have. Thanks but I've had enough crazy to last a lifetime," I patted his shoulder reassuringly. "Now, step aside big boy," I clasped my hands together and rubbed them excitedly. "Time to help hot pants over there with her work-out."

An hour later, two sets of digits and only one slap across the face, I was loving my new job. And Brittany? Well, she was dumb as a doorknob but she played drop the pencil a few times with me. I was about to drop it again, prepared for her to bend over and pick it up but I was distracted by the front door opening.

The pencil remained poised in the air as I locked eyes with Lauren.

The girl next door not the naughty school girl.

My kitten, not every man's pussycat.

I dropped the pencil for Brittany to fetch and rose to my feet, walking around the counter before leaning my back casually against it and shoving my hands in my pocket.

"Well look who dropped in for a visit, "nurse feel good,"" I quipped.

Her eyes widened, and she slapped my chest.

"Shh!" she hissed, looking around the gym for her brother. Guess she was still busy living a lie after all these months.

"Don't worry, kitten, your secrets safe with me," I promised, taking her hand in mine.

"What are you doing here?" she asked, pulling her hand free and dropping her pocketbook onto the counter.

"I work here," I said proudly.

"Of course you do," she said sarcastically, huffing and blowing the fallen strands of hair from her eyes. I reached out and tucked the crazy hairs behind her ears.

"Stop it," she hissed.

I traced my finger down the bridge of her nose before tapping the tip of it.

"Cute as a button, you are," I teased.

She rolled her eyes and smacked my hand away. She was a feisty little feline.

"Where's my brother?"

"Riggs, I found the pencil," Brittany cheered behind me.

I kept my eyes on Lauren, taking in her wide eyes as she looked over my shoulder at the dope holding a pencil.

"That's great sweetheart, but I dropped a pen this time," I said.

Go away, Brittany.

Blue eyes framed by those sexy fucking glasses met mine again and I grinned at her. The thought she was about to speak lost its way on her tongue and she snapped her mouth closed.

"How's school treating you? Bang any hot doctors lately?"

"You're despicable," she hissed, pulling her bag from the counter and throwing the strap over her shoulder.

"Oh baby, I love it when you talk dirty," I whispered against her ear.

"Kiss my ass, *Riggs*!" My name sounded like a curse on her tongue as she turned and stalked toward her brother's office.

"Anytime, kitten, anytime," I called out to her, eyes glued to her perfect ass and the way it jiggled in her jeans.

Yeah, this gig wasn't so bad.

"There's no pen under here," Brittany said, disappointedly. "Oh, but your friend left her phone here," she said, holding Lauren's phone in her hand.

I glanced over my shoulder at the phone and a mischievous grin worked its way across my mouth as I plucked the phone from Brittany's fingers.

"Stay the fuck away from my sister." Anthony's voice loomed in my ears.

I pulled a pocket light from my key ring and shined the beam onto the screen, picking up her prints I typed her passcode into her phone and called my own.

Easy as pie.

I added my number to her contacts, grinning as I typed my name into the requested field before taking my phone and storing her as "Kitten."

I placed the phone carefully onto the counter where she left it and laughed to myself.

Those Bianci's were a pain in the ass but they sure were fun to fuck with.

Chapter Four

I knocked on the door to my brother's office. Weird. I never thought Anthony would get out of the mob. I'm still not sure he is, but at least now he's like every other big-time gangster, with a legit business to cover his ass.

"Come in," he called from behind the door.

I opened the door and poked my head inside and instantly smiled. My brother was everything to me growing up. I knew he was a bad boy and although he scared all my boyfriends' away with merely a look, he was my idol. My best friend. Some girls measured every guy in their life to their father—me, I measured them to Anthony.

"Look at you, the boss man himself," I said with a smile, closing the door behind me.

He lifted his head from the papers on his desk and grinned at me.

"Hey you," he greeted, while standing and walking around his desk to peck me on the cheek. "What're you doing here? I thought you and Adrianna were going shopping with ma," he said, leaning against the desk as I took a seat.

"Yeah, I skipped out on that," I glanced at the security footage that covered every inch of Xonerated. "Everything looks great, Ant. I'm so proud of you," I enthused.

"Thanks," he said, crossing his arms as he stared at me.

Anthony had a gift at dissecting people with his eyes. I hated it and more so because I was lying to my entire family.

"What's going on?" he questioned.

Shit.

I turned my gaze to him and met his worried eyes.

"Nothing," I lied, as the pro I was at misleading the people in my life. After that first initial lie they seemed to drip from my mouth with no effort at all.

"Lau, it's me you're talking to," he coaxed, gently. "School getting to you?"

"Well, since you brought it up," I began, drawing out a deep breath. "We need to talk about Mom moving upstate," I said.

"What about it? She told me last night she loves it up there," he said.

"She's driving me bananas!"

"I know Mom can be difficult," he started.

"No you're not getting it," I interrupted. "She comes to the apartment when I'm not there. She's walked in on Mia and the guy she's dating. The other day she took my laundry with her and shrunk half my shit," I explained. "It's bad, Ant. She's bored shitless and to be frank, I will never get my nursing degree with her up my ass," I added.

I was going to hell for every lie I've told—that one right there, that's the one that bumped my ass to the front of the line. No purgatory for this girl.

"I'll talk to her," he conceded.

I lifted my eyes to his.

"Talk to her? Do we have the same mother?"

"Okay, what do you suggest I do?" he asked with a hint of amusement laced in his voice.

"I think she would be better off coming back here to live. Just think how much alone time you can get with your new bride if Mom was around to watch Luca," I suggested, nudging him with my elbow. "Possibly even get cracking on giving me a niece or another nephew," I hinted.

His eyebrows drew together looking as if he was contemplating my words before finally responding.

"Anything else you want to tell me?" he questioned.

"Nope that's it's," I confirmed cheerfully.

"Lauren," he said skeptically.

"Okay, okay, fine," I pouted, dropping back into my chair. "My car is fucked," I blurted out.

"What's wrong with it?"

"The thing starts when it wants, the tires are shot and the brakes squeak," I rambled.

"I'll take care of it when you go back home and send a tow for it," he promised. "You need anything else? Money? Books?"

I shook my head. It was one thing for me to ask him for help with my car, a desperate plea on my behalf, but I wouldn't take a cent from Anthony. After I quit the nursing program I had to give up the paid housing—a perk of having an all-expenses paid education. That's how I became Mia's roommate. I had to become an adult, and being an adult, well, it kind of sucked.

There was a knock on the door, pulling me away from my thoughts and Anthony away from his worried stare down.

"Come in," he bellowed.

The girl who was crawling around the floor in front of Riggs popped into my brother's office, waving my phone in the air.

"Sorry to interrupt Mr. Anthony," she smiled. Oh, poor thing she obviously hasn't met Mrs. Anthony yet. It might be worth extending my stay just to see Adrianna's reaction to this girl. She turned her eyes to me.

"How'd you get my phone?" I asked, stepping toward her and snatching my phone from her hand.

"You left it at the front desk," she bit her lip. "It keeps going off, someone named Tiger seems desperate to get in touch with you," she added sweetly, before turning to my brother and flashing him a smile.

I felt Anthony come up behind me and peer over my shoulder at my phone.

"Who's Tiger?"

I had no idea who Tiger was, but that was for me to find out not my overprotective, sometimes overbearing, older brother. I shoved the phone into my pocket, turned on my heel and rose on my tiptoes to kiss his cheek.

"Glad we had this talk," I said hastily, before turning and heading out of the office. "I've got to go."

"Lauren," he called out as I closed the door to the office and hurried through the gym. I made it out the door without a hitch, meaning no unnecessary run-ins with a certain hot biker. I didn't pull my phone out of my pocket until I was halfway down the block and sure my brother hadn't followed me.

My phone definitely was blowing up, eight unread text messages from...*Tiger*. I walked toward the train station as I opened the messages.

Tiger: Guess who?
Tiger: Do you need a hint?
Tiger: I'm a tiger in the bedroom.
Tiger: Not that you would know that. Yet. But you could imagine.
Tiger: Tell me Kitten, do you imagine the things I could do to you?
Tiger: I bet that's why you aren't answering me. Take your hand out of your pants Kitten, let Tiger do the job.
Tiger: Shit. I'm just joking.
Tiger: Sort of.

My lips quirked in amusement. Hot and funny...my dream guy. My fingers worked the keyboard of my phone to reply.

Me: How did you get my number and more importantly how did yours become saved in my phone?

The little gray cloud appeared, signaling that he was typing his reply and for some reason, unknown to me, that made me smile again.

Tiger: Wouldn't you like to know. A man never tells his secrets. Where are you?
Me: Maybe the right woman was never around to try.

I hit send, looked up to see what street I was on before typing a text in reply to his second question.

Me: 86th and 23rd Ave. Walking to the train.
Tiger: Why no car?
Me: It blew up.

I wished it had, at least then I'd have an insurance check to buy another piece of crap car.

I glanced up, looking both ways before I crossed the intersection and stopped in my tracks when I looked across the street and saw Riggs leaning against his bike with his phone in his hand and a devilish grin on his face. I'm pretty sure my ovaries exploded.

My phone chimed, and I tore my eyes from that sinful grin of his and read the last text message he sent me.

Tiger: Want a ride, Kitten?

My teeth sank into my lower lip and I lifted my eyes to his, managing to ignore the cars passing that threatened to obscure my view of him.

I wanted more than just a ride on the back of his bike.

I crossed the street, tucking my phone back into my pocketbook and watched as he shoved his into his pocket.

"Are you following me?" I said, standing in front of him, realizing he saw every one of my reactions to each text. He saw me smile and knew he was the reason for it.

"Me? Never!" he scoffed. "I'd never invade someone's privacy," he insisted with a straight face. He took the helmet hanging from the handlebars and offered it to me.

"What do you say? It beats having to ride the train," he said.

"Says who?" I replied, trying my best not to give away how much I wanted to take him up on his offer.

"Says any girl who ever wrapped their legs around me," he stated, fitting the helmet onto my head and tightening the chin strap. "Looks good on you, 'nurse make me feel good,'" he teased, before throwing his leg over his bike and glancing back over his shoulder at me. "Get on, Kitten."

I stared at him for a moment, watching as he revved the engine of the bike and how easily his foot kicked up the kickstand. It was so tempting, something I always wanted to do. I could argue, going for a ride with Riggs was just a check off my bucket list, but the more I stared at the man and not the bike, the more I wanted to because of *him* and not some silly fantasy.

"Are you always this crazy?" I asked, walking closer to him.

"I prefer the term colorful," he winked. "Place one hand on my shoulder and throw your leg over, then place your feet on the pegs but be careful of the exhaust pipe."

"I have virgin written all over my face, don't I?" I said, as I went through the motions. Once I was fully seated behind him, I wrapped my arms around his waist. He tightened my arms around him and glanced over his shoulder.

"Not exactly what I think when I look at your face, Kitten," he drawled. "Hang on," he added before pulling away from the curb.

I've done a lot of stuff that one might consider exciting, like parasailing in Cancun and the time I took skydiving lessons but didn't have the balls to jump out of the plane. But getting on the back of Riggs' bike, not knowing where we were going, evoked an adrenaline rush quite like no other I ever experienced. The wind in my hair, the sharp turns and fast ride…it was everything. And I never wanted it to end.

I clutched the leather of his vest tightly with my fingers and laid my chin on his shoulder. The smell of his cologne tickled my nostrils and gave me one more thing to add to the memory. I'd go back home, to my shit job, and my upside down life but when I was alone and trying to figure out where I went from there, something told me I'd remember the feel of the leather beneath my fingertips and the way he smelled so fresh.

He pulled into L&B Spumoni Garden's parking lot and killed the engine of the bike.

"I'm hungry," he declared, as we climbed off the bike. "And I hate eating alone," he added, taking my hand and dragging me toward the pizzeria so we could stand in line and wait our turn.

"So you're not going to tell me how you stored your number in my phone?" he grinned in response. "Okay, then are you going to tell me anything about yourself?"

"That depends," he said thoughtfully.

"On?"

"Are you going to tell me why a girl like you works in a place called The Pink Pussycat and not off saving lives?"

"Isn't that a bit dramatic?"

"Not really," he replied, shrugging his shoulders then holding up his hands in defeat. "Don't look at me like that, just a concerned friend," he explained.

"A concerned friend?" I questioned.

He threw his arm over my shoulders and brought me closer to him. The same way my brother used too. What a blow to the ego.

"Of course, Kitten. It's a bitch living two lives," he declared, stepping up to place our order.

The girl at the counter was a fan of Riggs', batting her eyelashes and scowling at me before she promised to bring our pizza to the table for us. She probably would poison me so she could slide into the booth with him.

I shook my head and dismissed her, bringing myself back to what Riggs last said.

"You speaking from experience?" I asked him, as we sat down across from one another. He took his hat off for a second to run his hands through his hair before he pulled the knit skull cap down again.

"Maybe," he said, leaning over the table. "You tell me your secrets and I'll tell you mine," he teased.

"You know my secret already. Which makes this friendship unfair as you have an advantage over me. We should be on common ground, so for the sake of our friendship you need to tell me some deep dark secret of yours," I said coyly.

His eyes dipped to my lips, and I reached out, lifting his chin with my index finger so our eyes could meet.

"Fine, what do you want to know?" he spread his arms wide in emphasis. "I'll give you anything you want," he grinned, glancing down at his crotch. "Anything," he confirmed.

The waitress dropped off our slices and Riggs went to work heavily shaking red pepper flakes all over his pizza. So he liked things spicy. Me too.

He took a huge bite, chomping away, when the thing I wanted to know most came to me.

"Your name," I said.

"What about it?" he replied, as he chewed, reaching for his bottle of water.

"Tell me what your real name is," I said, picking at the slice in front of me, still not sure the waitress didn't spike it to get to Riggs.

He swallowed the food he was chewing and stared at me quietly for a beat.

"You said anything," I reminded him.

"Robert," he hissed, as though it pained him to say. "Robert Montgomery the third," he finished, taking a big gulp of water, washing down the foul taste his real name left on his tongue.

I kept my face neutral, letting his name roll around in my head before I smiled, reached over the table and pinched his cheek.

"Robby, I like it!" I grinned before he flinched.

"Riggs, my name is Riggs," he insisted, eyes locking with mine. There was no playfulness when he looked at me this time and my smile faded instantly. "Robert is just a name written in ink on a birth certificate."

My eyebrows furrowed, but I knew when to leave something alone and remained silent as I wondered why he was so hell bent on forgetting who he was.

What a pair we made, huh? He was running to forget his life, and I was running to find mine.

"What's the matter, you don't like pizza? Isn't that like sacrilegious?"

I looked down at the barely touched pizza and lifted it to my lips taking a big bite. To hell with you, waitress. I chewed, watching the seriousness fade from his face to be replaced with the sly grin I was accustomed to. He picked up a napkin, reaching over to wipe the sauce from the corner of my mouth.

We finished our pizza, neither of us asked anymore real questions. The rest of our time together we kept light, mostly flirty banter back and forth. Afterwards he gave me a ride back to my brother's house and when I climbed off his bike and handed him back his helmet I felt disappointment settle in. It wasn't until I was inside the house, the door barely closed behind me when I heard the chime of my phone and knew Riggs and I weren't finished. We were just getting started.

Chapter Five

I lined up my shot, ready to sink this bad boy into a hole and collect my fifty bucks from Bones, when the door stormed open to the Chapel and broke my concentration.

"Bones, the Bulldog needs to see you," Blackie beckoned from the doorway.

I watched Bones place his beer down and grab his cut, slipping it on before he walked into the Chapel.

Lucky Bastard.

I averted my eyes back to the pool table just in time to see my ball roll into its respective pocket.

"You owe me a fifty spot!" I called out to Bones, only for him to flip me the bird as he stepped around the VP and into the Chapel. My eyes locked with Blackie's and I tipped my beer bottle to him before drowning my sorrows in my brewsky.

"You too, Riggs," Blackie added.

I nearly spat out the mouthful of ale but instead I swallowed and choked on it, resulting in a coughing fit.

"Oh, for fuck's sake, don't get all fucking dramatic. Get your ass in here," he ordered.

"Yes, sir," I replied while coughing up a lung and mock saluted him. I finally got myself under control, cleared my throat and tried not to grin like a banshee.

I took the only open seat at the large wooden table across from Bones and lifted my hand before I rubbed my index finger against my thumb.

"Pay up, bitch," I teased.

"Suck a dick, Riggs," he taunted back.

"Anything you earn the club gets half," Pipe reminded me. "You need help in collecting?" He asked, as he elbowed Bones.

"All right, if you assholes are done maybe we can get the fuck down to business," Jack growled from the head of the table. He waited for everyone to settle down, slamming his gavel down and bringing our attention toward him. "Need all hands on deck today," he began as he turned his gaze toward me. "Even you, Riggs," he confirmed.

"Aw, you're pulling Mary Poppins off of Bianci?" Bones joked, earning laughter from our brothers.

"Eat shit," I ground out.

"Just for today," Jack reminded me. He could eat shit too. I joined the Satan's Knights to be a man of honor, respect and loyalty. A man who wasn't afraid to break rules and shit for the greater good of his brotherhood and his club. I did not sign up to be a fucking babysitter. I didn't even like kids, not that Bianci was a kid, but well he had one, which made him guilty by association.

"Pipe has been working on a deal to get rid of the guns we have sitting over at Pops," he explained.

Pops was about a hundred and ten years old, well, not really but he was fucking old. Before Jack was voted president of the Satan's Knights, Pops son held the title, some guy named Cain. I don't know much about the man but I know he meant a lot to Jack because he inked his name onto his shoulder. Cain was a big drug guy back in the day, sold and sampled, used and abused, and even though he had hepatitis, I'm sure he used until his dying day.

The Satan's Knights had a shooting range up in Jersey but because each member has a rap sheet a mile long, and a mug shot on the wall, their names couldn't be on the paperwork. The government was funny that way and wasn't too keen on having outlaws run a shooting range so Pops ran the joint for the club. It was a pretty sweet deal, he did most of the dirty work, provided us a legit place where the club could house its weapons, all for a little kick back.

"Finally, got ourselves a buyer and a couple of g's over what we were shooting for," Pipe added. "No pun intended."

"Who's the buyer?" Bones asked.

"The Red Dragons," Blackie answered, as he kept his eyes on Jack.

"We're playing nice with the Chinese now?" Wolf questioned, genuinely surprised.

"No reason not to," Jack assured the sergeant of arms. "Our club doesn't stand for the shit it did when Cain held the gavel," he argued, wrapping his hand around the wooden object before it dropped onto the table with a thud. "We're not after their product nor are we interested in getting involved in their territory," he declared, crossing his arms against his chest and leaning back in his chair. "I know we want to keep the streets clean but the truth is, we never were too good at it, and if it wasn't for Victor Pastore helping to control the drugs coming in and out of the seaboard, we would've never accomplished as much as we have. Now, Vic's in jail, he's got pull, but not the kind that will stop the drug lords from polluting New York and without him and his crew aiding the cause, we're fucked. Don't need any more enemies, seems like we've got enough," he added. "So we let the Chinese do what they got to do, and as long as they don't interfere with our operations, we turn the other cheek," Jack enforced, turning to Blackie who seemed to be holding on by a thread. "We turn the other cheek," he repeated, mainly to the man sitting to the left of him.

"I heard you the first time," he grunted.

"Now, The Red Dragons are meeting us at Pops for the tradeoff. They are buying ninety percent of our supply so that's why we need all hands on deck," Jack continued.

"Wait a minute, ninety percent of our supply? What the fuck are we supposed to rely on if things go south for us? Water guns?" I asked. Maybe it wasn't my place to say anything, but fuck that. Things change in the blink of an eye, each of us knew that, so then what? We're left holding our dicks like a bunch of incompetent idiots. Albeit, my dick was impressive but it wouldn't fucking get me through a goddamn war, should the Chinese feel the need to rekindle their hatred for our club.

"Pops got word the new shipment will be in the harbor by the end of the week. We're good. We still have all the guns at the shooting range that are in the lockers. But no one here is expecting war, Riggs," he said, pausing for a moment before fixing me with a glare. Ah, fuck. "I appreciate the concern but next time you want to question my orders leave your vest on the table and haul your ass out the door," he growled.

Two steps forward, two-hundred steps backward.

"Anyone else want to add their two cents?" Jack asked the quiet room. "Good," he said finally. "Now saddle up, we've got to run," he ordered, slamming down the gavel and adjourning our meeting.

We all moved quickly, rising to our feet and ushering out to the parking lot. I straddled my bike, my engine purring to life as the adrenaline inside me kicked into gear.

This was the stuff I got off on, the shit that made my dick hard.

I secured my helmet as the sound of all our engines roaring in unison awakened the animal in me and was music to my ears.

I might not have my patch yet but I was a motherfucking Satan's Knight. I was a link in the chain of brotherhood and had finally found my place in the world, and was damn fucking proud of it too. Now, if I could just get the goddamn patch.

When we pulled up to the shooting range, Pops was standing out front waiting for us alongside the two dozen men that were a part of The Red Dragons. We dismounted our bikes and followed Jack toward the brood of bikers.

"Sun Wu, always a pleasure," Jack greeted, pushing his sunglasses on top of his head.

"Parrish, it's been a long time," the Sun Wu character replied. "Glad we could stand on common ground," he added.

I looked around, noting there were twice as many Red Dragons than there were Knights and while we looked like just a bunch of laid back men who loved Harleys and pussy, they looked like some serious fucking dudes that had a dildo shoved up their ass. They were like statues, perfectly still and eyes glued on us, watching our every move.

Jack and Wu continued to shoot the shit for a few minutes before we got down to business and made our way into the back shed out behind the range. Pops and Jack uncovered the crates of guns and "Jackie Chan" and his posse inspected everything. They talked amongst one another in mandarin, making this whole fucking thing like a scene out of *Rush Hour*. I was half expecting Chris Tucker to pop out of a crate and start singing "Can't Stop Until I Get Enough."

Finally, Sun Wu, handed over the suitcase and it was Jack's turn to inspect what he offered. Once the deal was closed, hands were exchanged and half the Dragons loaded their cage with the guns. Jack suggested we go back into the range and have a shot with Wu. It was a gesture of good faith, a plea to let bygones be bygones.

Jack poured Sun Wu and himself a shot before passing the bottle to Blackie who finished dispersing the alcohol.

"Salute," Jack said, lifting his glass toward Sun Wu.

"Gambier!" Sun replied, clinking his glass against Jack's before both presidents downed the alcohol. He placed the empty glass on the counter and looked at the surveillance cameras that hid beneath the desk. "That's a pretty impressive set up you have there," he said, motioning to my handiwork.

Jack nodded, throwing his arm around my shoulder and patting me on the back.

"Riggs only does the best work," he bragged. "This kid turned my house into Fort Knox," he joked—but it was true. The security system I installed in Jack's house, the one he never used because he always slept at the compound, blew this thing out of the water. Although, the best work I had done was definitely the clubhouse, that shit was locked up tight.

"Jackie Chan's" eyes met mine. "I've gained a new property I would need to have heavily secured with surveillance equipment," he started, turning toward Jack. "Is your prospect available for hire?"

"Kid talks for himself," Jack replied, turning toward me. "But since we're always in the business of helping *friends*, I bet he'll say yes."

I stared at Jack for a moment, assessing the words he implied, knowing that he wanted us to do whatever we could to make things nice between us and the Red Dragons. I turned back to Sun Wu.

"I have no problem taking your money," I answered.

"Come again?"

"Time is money, brother. You want a state of the art security system like that one right there, it will cost you," I declared.

Wu stared at me quietly for a moment before his lips spread into a grin and he turned toward Jack.

"You train them well," he mused.

Jack shrugged his shoulders and took another shot. "We all gotta eat, brother," he stated, moving to refill Wu's glass only for him to shove it aside.

"I'm good. Glad the Dragons and the Knights could work together, Parrish," Wu said, before pausing a moment and looking at me. "I'll be in touch," he said finally, turning to his men and snapping his fingers.

"Well that went off without a hitch," Pipe said, once they were out the door.

"Thank Christ," Jack hissed, slapping his hands against the counter. "Let's get the fuck out of here," he said, grabbing the suitcase as he turned his gaze my way. "Looks like you got yourself another gig."

I grinned at my president.

One step closer.

Chapter Six
Lauren

I threw back the shot of Fireball, sliding the empty glass across the bar to the hot bartender who bought one for me and one for Mia. She took the bus into the city and we've been bar hopping since happy hour, five bars, and two hours later...we were bombed.

"I think we should move to another bar, there's no hot guys here," Mia complained.

"The bartender's not bad," I said, squinting my eyes to get a better look, but I was blind as a bat without my glasses.

Mia giggled beside me.

"What?" I asked, turning to her. At least I could see up close.

"Where are your glasses?"

"I forgot them at my brother's house," I mumbled.

"Oh, that reminds me! Why haven't you mentioned that your brother's friends are fucking lickable?"

"Lickable? Really?" was that even a word? I picked the olive out of my martini and popped it into my mouth. "For the record, Anthony's friends usually aren't anything to write home about. They're usually twice his age and full of graying hair."

"That man who showed up with your mother was sex on a stick," she countered.

I brought my drink to my lips. Riggs was definitely sex on a stick and well...indeed lickable.

"Have you seen him since?"

"A couple of times. He works at the gym," I said, trying not to think of that smile or the way his eyes gleamed with mischief. He was trouble with a capital *T*, and not for the obvious reasons either. Anyone who ran in the same circle as my brother had criminal tendencies, but Riggs was trouble because he was hard to resist.

"You should get on that, or under it, whichever you prefer, but do something. It's your duty as a member of the female population," she declared.

"I couldn't," I said weakly.

"Oh yeah? Why the hell not?" she questioned, nudging me with her elbow. "I thought you were turning over a new leaf? What was it you said? Oh, yes, you would live for yourself and not everyone else. Seems the best way to start is by giving into your needs," she reasoned.

"Funny, I remember having this same conversation before I quit nursing school. I thought that was the start of the new me," I said sarcastically.

"Okay, fine, so this is the sequel," she laughed. "Stop worrying about everything so much. You're twenty-one, you're supposed to fuck up your life and do stupid things."

Words to live by.

She was an idiot sometimes.

"He gave me his number," I said, biting my lip.

"And I'll bet the next round you haven't used it," she surmised, treating me to an eye roll. "I love you, Lauren, but sometimes you're such a pussy," she added, climbing off the stool and pulling down her mini-skirt. "Seriously, you need to grow a pair." She downed the rest of her cosmopolitan, placing the empty glass on top of the bar. "Order me another, I have to go to the bathroom."

I sighed as she walked away and tried to make eye contact with the bartender, but for all I knew I wasn't even looking at the right guy. I'd just wait until he came closer to order the drinks.

I pulled my phone out of my purse, bored, I browsed my contacts until I came to his name.

Tiger.

I smiled instantly.

Fucking Riggs.

Fucking life.

And then I did what every normal twenty-one-year old with no direction in life would do…I texted him.

Me: Meow.

I hit send, immediately dropping my phone and covering my face with my hands.

I did not just do that.

I picked up my phone, wincing when I confirmed my stupidity.

Me: Delete that.
Tiger: Roar. LOL
Me: I said delete it. I meant to text it to someone else.
Tiger: Are your pants on fire, Kitten?

He should only know. I clenched my legs together and chose to ignore his question.

Me: What are you doing?
Tiger: What are you doing?
Me: You first.
Tiger: Watching the game with the guys.
Me: Out with Mia.
Tiger: You went back home already?
Me: Tomorrow. She came into the city for the night and we're going back home together tomorrow afternoon.
Tiger: Are you on the prowl?
Me: Maybe.
Tiger: Stay safe.

Huh? Okay, not exactly the answer I was hoping for from him. I decided to put my phone away before I did any more damage. Mia found her way back to me and instead of ordering another round, we took off to another bar.

The night was young.

And this "Kitten" was on the prowl.

RIGGS

"The Jets don't have a chance, not after Decker blew that touchdown," Bones said, shoving a handful of potato chips into his mouth.

"It's only the third quarter," I retorted, popping open my beer and glancing down at my phone. An hour and a half had passed since I texted Lauren back. I couldn't help but wonder what she was doing and what version of herself she was when she went out with her friend. Whether it be the good girl bit or the good girl gone bad. I'm sure she had guys dropping to their knees.

I leaned over, placing my beer on the table and texted her again.

Me: I should've brought my library card because I'm definitely checking you out.
Kitten: You got more game than half the men here.
Me: Where are you?
Kitten: Salty Dog.
Me: Bay Ridge? I thought you were in Manhattan.
Kitten: Bar hopping and borough hopping. I get around.
Me: As long as you're not bed hopping.
Kitten: Even if I hopped into your bed?

I froze, staring down at my phone as the images flooded my brain. I could picture her naked in my bed wearing nothing but her glasses. Yeah, I wouldn't mind that. Not one fucking bit. My dick agreed, hardening against my jeans.

Me: You can hop into my bed anytime, Kitten.
Kitten: You shouldn't say things like that to a drunk girl who needs a good duck.

What? She wanted a pet? Odd thing to say to a guy when he invited you to fuck.

Kitten: Duck! I meant duck!
Me: You want a duck?
Kitten: Yes.
Kitten: No! Ducking auto correct!

"Get off your phone, ass wipe! You're missing the game," Bones said, throwing a bag of pretzels at my head. "Who are you texting anyway?"

"What does ducking mean?" I asked.

"Ducking? Like you duck," he said, bending his head. "Like that, you get the fuck out of the way. You dodge the bullet. You duck and hide. Man, are we seriously having this discussion right now?"

"No, that's not it," I said, scratching the top of my head.

Kitten: Let's try this again. You shouldn't say that to a girl who needs a good lay.

"Fuck, she needs to fuck!" I cheered, typing my response.

Me: Happy to oblige, babe.

And this night just got a whole lot better.

Kitten: Oh yeah? You think you can make me purr?
Me: I'll make you fucking roar, baby.
Me: You still at the dog?

I was familiar with the Salty Dog, it was a popular bar mostly where firemen hung out. Lauren wasn't taking a ride on a fucking fire truck tonight, not if I had a say in it. I lifted my eyes to Bones who was staring at me like I had lost my mind.

"What?" I asked innocently. "I might need a wingman you game?"

"Depends what she looks like. I'm not taking one for the team, not tonight, when I can go riding and grab any piece of ass I want," he stated.

"Mia's pretty, killer bod, nice rack," I tried to entice.

"Mia?" he raised an eyebrow. "Wow, you know their names, impressive. That's a first for you," he teased.

"Stop being a dick, are you in or what?"

"When have I ever turned down pussy?" he said, taking another pull of his beer. "But then we're even, not giving you the fifty I owe you."

Me: Hello?

"Fine, fine, whatever," I replied. I'd eat the fifty bucks for a chance of having Bianci's sister in my bed. Oh, how sweet was that? I mean sure she was hot, but the fact she was off limits definitely sweetened the deal.

Kitten: Sorry. I was fighting with Mia. I could kill her right now.
Me: What happened?
Kitten: She left me! So much for girl code.
Me: I'll come get you.

"Well, are we going or not?" Bones asked annoyed.

"Change in plans, bro. One-man job," I said, grabbing my shit off the table. "You still owe me that fifty."

Kitten: No I'm going to take the train back to Ant's.

No. No. No.

I stalked toward the door, dialing her number instead of texting and listened as it rang.

"Can you believe that bitch?" she answered, slurring her words. "Leaving with the first guy that winks at her and buys her a damn drink."

"Hussy!" I replied, as I climbed onto my bike. "Listen, stay there I'm on my way."

"What? No!" she yelled into the phone.

"Why not?" I said, ripping the engine.

"Because if you come and get me there's no telling what will happen," she said.

"Oh, I know exactly what will happen babe, and you do too," I replied, loud enough so she could hear me.

"Riggs?"

"Yeah, Kitten," I said, kicking up the kickstand of my bike.

"I'm waiting outside," she whispered sexily into the phone, so low I barely heard her over the noise of my engine.

"Give me ten," I ground out, ending the call and slipping my phone into my jacket pocket.

Hang on Kitten, your Tiger is coming.

I almost crashed three times on the way there just picturing her naked. That round ass bent over as I pounded her first from behind. God, I hope she wore those shoes she had on at the bar. The second time I'd make her ride me and I'd bury my face in between those tits. Then I'd eat her pussy until she came all over my tongue. After a blowjob, I'd fuck her again nice and hard until she screamed my name.

I parked my bike in front of the bar and spotted Lauren leaning up against the brick wall talking to some guy. I threw my leg over my bike and readjusted my throbbing cock, then stalked toward her.

She laughed at something the schmuck she was talking to said, turning her head slightly her eyes locked with mine.

"Making friends?" I questioned, peeling my eyes away from her to the man leaning way to close to her.

"You know how it goes man," he laughed, running his hand down Lauren's arm. What the fuck was she wearing? My eyes traveled the length of her, taking in the jeans that molded to her legs like a second skin, ripped and shredded at the knees showing just a hint of her olive skin. The top she wore was see through and fell off her shoulder sexily. And then, there was the shoes, the ones that haunted my dreams. Thank you, God.

She smiled at me and that's when I noticed she wasn't wearing her glasses.

Wow. She was fucking gorgeous.

Her bright, blue eyes darkened making them appear navy as they stared back at me.

"Say goodbye, Kitten," I ordered.

"But," she started, turning to her new admirer. "We were just going to go back inside and have a drink," she squinted, snapping her fingers as she tried to remember his name. "What's your name again?"

"Tony," he said with a grin.

"Tony? Are you sure? I thought you said it was Tommy," she said, swaying on her heels. I reached out and wrapped my arm around her waist to steady her.

"Time to go, say goodbye Tommy," I said, glaring at the man looking at Lauren like she was a piece of meat, daring him to argue with me.

She spun around in my arms, her chest pressed against me, her mouth a breath away from mine, forcing me to glance down at her.

"I got bored waiting for you," she admitted, reaching up to touch my hat.

"Don't let it happen again," I said, liking the way she leaned up against me, and loving the way she felt. Even with heels she only came up to my shoulder. "You ready to get the hell out of here?"

Her perfect teeth sank into her lip as she nodded.

"Can I get your number?" Tommy/Tony asked.

"718-FUCK-OFF," I snapped, pulling my eyes away from hers to glance over her shoulder at the asshole who had the balls to just ask that.

Lauren giggled, dropping her head against my chest and gripping the ends of my jacket.

"That was so rude," she said, laughing into my chest. I took her hand in mine and led her toward my bike.

"Didn't that mother of yours teach you not to talk to strangers?" I hissed, as I strapped my helmet onto her head. "Get on," I ordered, patting the seat.

She grabbed onto my arm for leverage and straddled my bike. I shook my head as my hand automatically shot down to my pants to re-arrange my dick. How the fuck was I going to get on my bike like this? I'd fucking break my cock.

"Problem?" she asked innocently.

"You're a tease," I said, leaning close to her. "Gonna make you beg for it now," I promised, grunting as I maneuvered myself in front of her. Her arms wrapped around me, holding on tight as she leaned her chin on my shoulder.

"You just want to see me on my knees," she whispered against my ear.

"Lots of ways I want to see you, Kitten," I said, taking off quickly, hoping the ride sobered her up. Not completely though. Something tells me tipsy Lauren is a lot more fun than sober Lauren, and the odds of me getting laid are slimmer without the drunken fog.

I was such an asshole.

Don't be an asshole, a voice inside of me taunted.

Look at that, I didn't think I had a conscience.

That was new.

I never questioned myself when I was with a woman. I took what I wanted, respectfully, and let my partner take what they needed from me. It was obvious what she wanted, and I argued with myself that if it wasn't me it would be Tommy or Tony, whatever his name was, giving it to her. Still, something inside of me nagged to do the right thing, to think before I did something reckless.

What the fuck was wrong with me?

I chalked it up to Jack getting in my head with all his shit about heart and not being reckless. Then there was this little thorn in my side called Bianci. He'd fucking kill me, send me off to sleep with the fishes, if he found out I took advantage of his sister.

So, I decided I'd take her back to my room at the compound and we wouldn't go all the way. Christ, I sounded like a pussy. I was back to being a fifteen-year-old kid who settled for a friendly game of "just the tip."

I was fucked.

And not literally.

I could be the good guy, the one who did the right thing. I would. I'd be that guy tonight.

Tomorrow?

I'd fuck anything that walked and make no apologies about it.

Yep, that was my plan.

I turned off my bike and glanced over my shoulder.

"Where are we?" Lauren hiccupped.

"The clubhouse," I said, taking her hands and pulling her onto her feet. She freed her hands from mine and walked ahead of me, sashaying her hips and wiggling that ass with every step. God damn!

"Taking me home to meet your motorcycle buddies? Isn't that moving fast?" she laughed, tripping over her own feet and nearly falling flat on her face.

"Easy," I ground out, wrapping my arm around her waist. "What the hell did you drink?"

She lifted her finger in the air to begin listing her drinks but frowned and dropped her hand.

"Everything," she admitted, turning to face me. "You have alcohol in the playhouse?"

"Clubhouse," I said unable to hold back the chuckle. "And…I think you've had enough," I added, ushering her into the clubhouse. Thankfully, the common room was empty except for Blackie who was still sitting in the same spot at the bar.

"Oh, look! You do have alcohol," she said, motioning to the bar. Blackie lifted his head, his bloodshot eyes stared at Lauren for a minute before turning back to me.

"You're out of your fucking mind," Blackie stated.

"It's not like that," I said, waving him off. "Look at her, she needed a ride."

"I am looking at her," he replied, emptying the rest of the bottle of patron into his glass. "You better know what the fuck you're doing. This club don't need any bullshit with Bianci," he added, before throwing back the tequila.

"Don't worry about it," I insisted.

"Yeah, don't worry about it!" Lauren agreed, pointing a finger at Blackie. "But don't tell my brother I was here or you'll have bullshit with this Bianci," she warned, wagging her finger in the air.

Blackie's eyebrows shot up to his hair line as he stared at my ferocious little kitten, then turned back to me.

"Oh you're so fucked," he said smiling. My misery would be the one thing that makes the beast smile.

"Thanks, bro, love you too," I said, rolling my eyes, taking Lauren's hand and dragging her toward the stairs.

"Riggs! I can't run in these shoes," she complained.

I blew out an exasperated breath turned around and lifted her over my shoulder.

"Better?" I asked, as she yelped and I climbed the stairs.

"You have a perfect ass," she commented, slapping my ass.

I peered at hers out of the corner of my eye.

"Yours isn't so bad either, Kitten," I said, fighting back the temptation to sink my teeth into her cheek. I kicked open the door to my room and dropped her onto my bed, watching as she bounced against the mattress.

Oh, man.

She tried to sit up, throwing her black hair over her shoulder as she peered up at me with the "come fuck me" eyes.

Just the tip.

"Well now you've got me here, what did you plan on doing with me?"

Talk about a loaded question.

She threaded her fingers through the belt loops of my jeans and pulled me toward her, falling back onto my bed and taking me with her. I braced my hands on either side of her head so I wouldn't crush her and looked down at her. She pulled me closer, spreading her legs, so I fell in between them and pressed my erection against her.

"You want me," she declared with a smile.

"Yeah, I do," I said huskily. She had no fucking idea how much.

Just the tip.

I leaned down, pressing my lips to the tip of her nose, the right corner of her mouth then the left corner before slowly pulling my head back to gage her reaction.

Still drunk, but there was no mistaking that gleam in her eyes.

I dipped my head and covered her mouth with mine. Her lips were soft and wet as they parted for me, inviting me in to take what I wanted. I heard the groan rumble from low in my belly as I parted my lips and slid my tongue into her mouth. She tasted like cinnamon and mint, like Heaven and Hell, because there was no way I wasn't going up in flames for this one. No fucking way.

Her teeth grazed my lip as she tried to seize control. Feisty. I loved it. My lips latched onto hers and my tongue took its time stroking hers, feeding off her taste. I felt my dick strain against the denim and reached down to unbutton my jeans to give myself a little relief.

I pulled away from her mouth, drawing down my zipper as I watched her sit up and take a deep breath.

She reached for me as I went to pull my pants down and release my aching cock.

"You want it bad, don't you, Kitten?" I growled, kicking off my boots.

"Riggs," she whimpered.

Just the tip, I reminded myself, dragging my jeans down my legs and kicking them off as my cock sprang free.

Christ, she was hot.

I wrapped my hand around my cock giving it a stroke. I went to remove my shirt and she lurched forward startling me.

"I'm going to be…" She never finished her sentence as she threw up.

All over me.

All over my beautiful cock.

So much for "just the tip."

Chapter Seven
Lauren

I think I'm dead or maybe I'm in a coma. I'm most definitely not a functioning human right now. I wish I would've stayed in nursing school, at least I'd be able to diagnose myself. It's a scary thought, fighting with everything you have to open your eyes, not knowing why it's a struggle in the first place.

Then I remembered.

Alcohol. Lots of it.

Mia leaving me.

Texting Riggs.

Riggs showing up at the Salty Dog.

Riggs taking me back to his clubhouse.

Riggs kissing me.

And that's it, my last memory. It's a good memory too. He's a pretty awesome kisser.

Focus, Lauren.

I groaned as my eyes finally fluttered open. My head was killing me and I had a serious case of dry mouth. I tried to lift myself, to sit upright, but the room spun. Not really feeling like playing "Dorothy," I left my ruby slippers at home, I dropped my head back onto the pillow.

Something stirred beside me but before I could turn to see the critter moving, a hand wrapped around my midsection, pulling me across the bed. My eyes widened as I turned and saw Riggs beside me. He mumbled something into his pillow and I held my breath, waiting for him to open his eyes and release me but that never happened. Instead, he snored, and draped his thick leg over mine. His thick, naked leg, might I add. I pinched the edge of the sheet, about to lift it and peek under it to assess the damage when I felt something long and hard poke my thigh.

Oh, hello, little Riggs.

Although, little was the wrong word to describe the erection digging into me. I suppressed the urge to reach under the sheet and wrap my hand around him to size him up.

I closed my eyes and prayed for the coma to take me again. Yeah, no such luck.

Finally, finding the nerve I lifted the sheet and saw I was wearing a t-shirt that read "I'd Rather Be Naked." How fitting.

At least I had my underwear on.

"Go back to sleep," he mumbled, startling me and I snapped my head in his direction.

"You're up?" I asked, my voice squeaking like a chipmunk.

"No," he replied with his eyes closed.

"Riggs, you need to move. I have to get up. I have to get out of here," I rambled nervously.

"No, not moving," he grunted stubbornly, as his hands traveled under the hem of the t-shirt.

"Oh God," I groaned.

"You said that a lot last night," he murmured, as fingers grazed my belly.

My eyes widened and my cheeks felt like they were on fire.

"We didn't…I mean of course we didn't, right?" I asked, swallowing hard and praying for the right answer. If we had sex, and I didn't remember I'd hate myself.

I probably should've been thinking something nobler, something purer, like please God forgive me for having sex before marriage or something just as ridiculous. But me? I was kicking myself in the ass because if we had sex, and I forgot what his cock felt like inside of me, I'd never forgive myself.

His eyes opened halfway and locked with mine.

"What's the matter, Kitten? Can't remember?" he said, huskily.

I bit my lip, shaking my head silently.

"Want me to show you?" he asked as his fingers slid under the elastic of my panties.

Yes, please. Pay attention, Lauren. Don't forget this time.

"I remember kissing," I croaked.

His lips quirked and my heart stopped. Was it possible to come from a man smiling? I snapped my legs shut, trapping his hand between them, as his fingertips dragged along the seam of my pussy.

"You're soaking wet, Kitten," he growled against my hair, slowly sliding one thick finger between my lips.

"We kissed," he affirmed, pressing his mouth against my neck. "You tasted like cinnamon."

"I drank Fireball," I stammered, lifting my hips and moving against his hand.

"Mmm," he murmured against my neck, before his teeth grazed the spot just below my ear and he added another finger inside me. His fingers took slow, tantalizing strokes, sliding out and plunging back in as his thumb massaged my clit.

"You're very good at that," I commented breathlessly. "So we kissed and then this happened?"

"No," he said, picking up the pace with his fingers.

I was going to come in two seconds and I couldn't hold out even if I wanted to. I needed this. I needed him.

His thumb circled my clit over and over again, building up my release as his fingers curled inside of me. I arched my back about to fall over the edge when his thumb stilled and his fingers left me.

"Then you threw up all over me," he said, pulling his hand out of my panties.

"I'm sorry…what?" Did he just stop? I breathlessly turned to him, his smug smile firmly in place as he stretched his long body and propped his hands behind his head.

"It wasn't pretty," he added. "You made a mess of me and yourself. I threw your clothes in the wash but might want to consider throwing them out," he continued.

"So, we didn't have sex?" I asked, somewhat disappointed and somewhat relieved.

"No, Kitten but if you want to now, I'm game," he offered, treating me to an eyebrow wiggle.

I stared at him, mouth agape, as he stretched underneath the sheet, pitching a tent with his erection.

"What do you say?"

I snapped out of my trance, glancing over at the clock and my eyes nearly fell out of their sockets.

"Oh, my God, is that the right time?" I screeched, throwing back the sheet and jumping to my feet. Whoa, my equilibrium and my head apparently were not on the same page just yet. My head was spinning, causing me to sway on my feet.

"Please don't throw up again," he pleaded. "I ran out of air freshener," he said, sitting up.

That explained the funny smell in his room.

"Wait! Where did you say my clothes were?"

"In the washing machine," he replied, climbing out of bed, not one bit shy about his nudity. He turned around and looked up at me as I counted his abs.

"You have an eight pack," I stated, lifting my eyes to his.

"Thanks babe, I think you're pretty hot yourself," he winked, grabbing his jeans off the floor. "You sure you don't want to fool around?"

"I have to go," I repeated weakly, swallowing in an attempt to dampen my dry mouth.

"Why the hurry?" he questioned, pulling up his pants. No underwear. Hmm.

"Do you know where my phone is?" I said, trying to distract myself from him.

"On the nightstand," he supplied, walking to his dresser and pulling out a fresh t-shirt.

I had ten missed calls and five text messages from Mia. Three missed calls from my brother and one text from Adrianna. At least I know that if I ever should wind up abducted by crazy people, I had my own team of crazy looking for me.

I scrolled through the texts and quickly replied to Mia first, labeling her the worst friend ever then telling her I'd meet her at my brother's house in twenty minutes. We missed the early bus but if I hauled ass, we could still make the afternoon one.

"Shit," he said, staring at his own phone.

"What is it?"

"Your brother is looking for you, asked if I could meet him at the gym to give him a hand," he explained. Then he laughed.

I have no idea why he laughed.

I didn't really see anything chuckle worthy.

"Should we put the poor bastard out of his misery and tell him you're safe and sound?"

"Are you crazy?" I asked him incredulously.

"Relax, Kitten. I wasn't going to tell him I had my fingers inside your pussy. I'll leave that until Christmas," he said, with a shake of his head, mocking me—like *I* was the crazy one. He threw me a pair of sweats. "Here, throw them on and I'll give you a ride," he offered.

"I can't believe this," I said out loud. I went from being the good girl no one knew was in a room to a girl doing the walk of shame in hooker heels dressed in a biker's clothes. "And I didn't even get the happy ending."

Did I just say that out loud?

"I offered!" He defended.

I pulled his pants on and slid my feet into my ridiculous heels, vowing never to speak again. Once I was fully dressed we walked out of his room and down the stairs into the main room. Riggs disappeared into one of the rooms, promising to return with coffee and I started for the door, hoping to go unnoticed.

A young guy, probably around Riggs' age stared at me as I tried to make myself scarce.

"What's your rush, sweetheart?"

Shit.

"Sneaking out on Riggsy? I don't blame you," the cute biker said.

"Piss off Bones," Riggs called, walking into the room with a Styrofoam cup. Bless his heart.

Bones stepped closer to me, smiling lazily as his gaze worked over me.

"What's a gorgeous girl like you, doing with a guy like Riggs?"

"Bones," Riggs clipped.

"Why don't you ditch the zero baby and take a chance on the hero?"

Was there a handbook of cheesy pickup lines this MC abided by? That was just as bad as the library one Riggs delivered me last night. Oh, look, it's all coming back to me. Progress!

"She's already got the hero, don't you, Kitten?"

"Kitten?" Bones asked amused.

"That's me!" I said, waving my hand before I pointed my thumb toward Riggs. "And that's Tiger."

"Tiger? Oh, man, this is great."

"Lauren, walk!" Riggs ordered through clenched teeth, while pressing his palm against my lower back, forcing me out the door.

"Calm down, Tiger," Bones teased. "You never minded sharing before."

I stopped in my tracks and turned around.

"You two share women?" I asked, disgusted.

"Ignore him," Riggs commanded. "He knows dick about what he's talking about," he added.

"I'll flip you for her," Bones called out, as Riggs slammed the door behind him. He took my hand, mumbled some curse I couldn't make out and pulled me toward his bike.

"Contrary to what you may think, I'm not a slut," I blurted, snatching my hand back. "I wouldn't jump from you to him, willingly or otherwise," I said defensively.

I realize I was the epitome of an oxymoron, defending my lady-like capabilities while wearing five-inch heels and men's clothing. This had to be the most horrendous walk of shame in history, but then again, I always was an overachiever. My mother would be so proud. Not.

"Lauren, I'm only going to say this once, okay? So pay attention. You're the girl you take home to mom, not the girl you pass off to your friends. You're the type of girl that comes around and makes you grow a fucking conscience," he said, tucking a strand of hair behind my ear.

"You want me to meet your mother?" I asked, raising an eyebrow.

"Fuck no, and I don't ever want to see yours again," he replied, pressing his lips to my forehead. "Now get on the bike so I can take you home. The good guy act is threatening to expire," he added.

I wasn't sure what he meant by that. Riggs wasn't a bad guy, he was just crazy. Absolutely bizarre.

Everyone needed a little crazy in their lives, right?

RIGGS

She made me drop her off around the corner from her brother's house in case Bianci showed up. Ridiculous.

What was even more ridiculous was that I didn't want her to leave.

That was *fucking* ridiculous.

I didn't know when she'd be back for a visit, and with her car out of commission it probably wasn't anytime soon. Bianci still hadn't towed the damn thing to Xonerated. So, this was it, the end of Kitten and Tiger as we knew it.

All I had to hang on to was the memory of my fingers inside her. I shouldn't have been such a dick—at least then, I'd know what she looked like when she came.

I killed the engine of the bike as she climbed off and removed the helmet.

"Thanks for the ride," she said, extending the helmet to me.

"Anytime," I said before clearing my throat.

"I need to get going or I'll miss the bus. I won't tell anyone where I was," she rambled.

"I don't care if you do," I replied with a shrug.

Nothing happened.

"So, this is goodbye? I suck at goodbyes," she admitted. "I mean, it's pretty stupid isn't it? It's just a word. One word," she exhaled quietly. "Should I say see you soon? When I know I won't. There's always Christmas?"

"It's been real, Kitten," I said, with a smile. "Keep in touch?"

"See, that's so much better!" She replied. "Not final like goodbye. *Keep in touch* leaves a person with hope that there will be an opportunity for more," she added.

"More?" I asked raising an eyebrow.

"Yes, more," she said incredulously. "You owe me an orgasm," she accused. "I plan on collecting."

She winked at me and I was fucked. Fucked, because I temporarily fell in love with her, with those words, and the way she said them.

Temporarily.

I didn't do love.

"I always pay my debts," I replied huskily, crooking my finger, beckoning her closer.

She licked her lips, biting down on her lip before taking the steps to close the distance between us. I reached out and grabbed the hem of the t-shirt, my shirt, and pulled her against me, pressing my lips to the corner of her mouth.

"Let me know when you're ready to collect, Kitten," I murmured against her mouth, letting go of her shirt and inching back. "Go on, before we do something stupid."

I didn't tell her that by stupid, I meant asking her to stay, and her actually doing so.

She nodded, turned on her heel and walked away from me.

Smart move, Kitten.

I watched her walk away and contemplated what had just happened for a moment. I revved my engine and made a U-Turn, driving as far away from Lauren Bianci as I could.

But I wasn't as smart as her because she never turned around and looked back. I know this because I kept looking in the side-view mirror until I couldn't see her anymore.

Instead of going to the clubhouse I took a detour, jumping on the Belt Parkway and getting off at Fort Hamilton. I had an apartment with a killer view of the Verrazano Bridge but that's where it ended. An apartment with a nice view. No furniture, no television—hell, I didn't even have a refrigerator.

I should probably get one of those. I didn't even know what I was doing there, but I didn't want to go back to the clubhouse and hear Bones break my balls about Lauren. The truth was, I didn't trust myself around him, and if he said anything stupid I might just lay him out.

I moved to the window, crawling out of it and took a seat on the fire escape. I pulled half of a joint out of my pocket and lit it up, taking that first long pull as I stared out toward the bridge.

My phone rang as I blew puffs of smoke out of my mouth. Goddamn it, can't a man get high in peace? Jesus.

I glanced down at the screen and saw it was the Bulldog.

The bastard probably wanted to know why I wasn't holding the gangsters hand as he bid his little sister farewell. I rolled my eyes and answered the call.

"Talk to me," I answered.

"Yeah? That's how you answer the phone these days?" Jack questioned.

"Changing things up a bit," I said, taking another toke.

"Get your ass to the compound. You got a job kid, one that doesn't involve looking after anyone," he stated.

"Yeah? So what's it involve?" I asked, as I started to cough.

"Lo Mein," he quipped.

I guess "Jackie Chan" called and wanted to fork up the dough after all. This was a good thing because I needed a distraction, something to focus on. I needed to get my fucking patch too.

"Thank fucking God, because I'm starving," I ground out. "See you in twenty," I said, before disconnecting the call and clipping the joint.

Time to go do what the fuck I was made to do. No more sitting around dwelling on some girl. That shit was for pussy's not a fucking Knight.

Chapter Eight
RIGGS

I never waste an opportunity to bust Bianci's balls. I don't know what it is about the guy but it's so easy to piss him off—you just need to know which buttons to push. I happened to be an expert and thoroughly enjoyed fucking with the retired gangbanger. That was my excuse, and I was sticking with it.

Tormenting Bianci.

It was the reason I followed Pipe when he came to pick up Lauren's car from Xonerated. It was also the reason I offered to help with the tires, and it was most definitely the reason I robbed the keys once it was fixed and towed it back to her.

Not because I wanted to see her again.

Not because I was hoping she was ready to collect and beg me to fuck her.

And most certainly not because I've been jerking off to the memory of fucking her with my fingers.

I crossed the line when I got my dick sucked by one of the whores hanging around the Dog Pound. I actually asked her to put on some black-rimmed glasses, and if she was opposed to dying her blonde hair, black.

Not cool.

So fucking not cool.

I climbed out of the truck, lowering her car off the tow and parked before making my way toward her apartment.

I annoyingly knocked on the door, ignoring the calls of her coming, because that wasn't the way I wanted to hear her say the words. I had that shit planned out, and it definitely didn't involve her answering a door. Fucking her against the door? Different story.

"Riggs?" she half-screeched, half-stammered, very cute. So were the knee socks and sweater she was wearing. She lifted her hand to her head, attempting to control the nest that seemed to sit on the top of it.

"What're you doing here?" she questioned, pushing her glasses further onto the bridge of her nose.

I love those fucking glasses.

I held her keys up, dangling them like they were a steak and grinned at her.

"Good morning, Kitten," I said as my eyes worked her body over before they settled on hers. "I dig the hair," I teased.

She lifted her hand automatically to the bun on top of her head, causing me to chuckle as I stepped closer to her and wrapped one arm around her tiny waist.

So innocent, so goddamn innocent.

I bent my head, touching my mouth to her cheek.

"How did you get my car?" she asked, pushing me away so she could look at me.

"I stole it," I replied honestly. Pipe was probably combing the lot and flipping his shit because Bianci would be picking up the car in an hour. Lucky for me, I won't miss any of the festivities because I planted a camera in the lot before I left.

I wasn't stupid. That shit could be my ticket to winning America's Funniest Videos.

Been trying to win the grand prize for years now.

"You stole my car?" she asked confused.

I shrugged my shoulders, running my hand over my knit skull cap before narrowing my eyes in wonder.

"Aren't you going to invite me in?" I asked.

"Sorry! Of course," she stuttered. "I'm sorry…it's just I've barely spoken to you since I left and now you show up at my door claiming to have stolen my car. I need a minute to catch up," she explained, moving aside so I could walk inside.

The talking thing was bullshit but I let it slide. Sure, I didn't actually call her but I've been keeping it light and easy, sending her texts with funny memes and shit. She always LOL's right on back so she can't say she didn't get them.

"Your brother had Pipe pick it up from the gym so he could work on it. Being the prince, I am, thought I'd deliver it to you in person," I explained, with a smile before walking into her kitchen. I felt another pair of eyes on me and glanced over my shoulder to see Mia.

Good, glad she's home. I can finally give her a piece of my mind.

"Who's Pipe?" Lauren questioned.

"One of the brothers. It's owned by the Satan's Knights but Pipe runs the joint, it's his gig," I explained, rummaging through her fridge.

Oh, we'd never work. I may not have a fridge in my apartment but if I did, it would be fully stocked with all the gourmet things I've grown accustomed to. Like, those little packs of chocolate pudding, whipped cream, chocolate milk, of course beer and cold cuts for fancy dinners and such.

I would not have cottage cheese in my fridge. What kind of bullshit was that?

"Are you two on some sort of starvation diet?" I asked, slamming the fridge closed and tipping my head toward Mia, finally acknowledging her presence.

"Hey Mia, where's your towel?"

"Your towel?" Lauren asked, her curious eyes snapped toward her roommate.

"Last time your friend stopped in I was just getting out of the shower," Mia explained, looking back at me.

"Lucky towel," I said sarcastically.

"We have cereal," Lauren offered.

I bit the inside of my cheek, crossing my arms as I considered her offer but she was probably pushing some Kashi whole grain crap on me. I was more a Captain Crunch kind of guy.

"Get dressed," I said, finally.

"Why?"

"I drove two hours to bring you your car, Kitten, think the least you can do is accompany me to breakfast," I said, leaving out the fact I wouldn't mind a quickie in the bathroom either. I turned toward Mia. "You hungry towel girl?"

She shook her head.

"You two go ahead. I have to run out for boxes," she insisted, grabbing her own keys from the counter before smiling back at Lauren.

"You know, I don't know if I should thank you or tell you it was a really shitty thing you did, leaving your friend in a bar by herself," I called out to her.

"Riggs!" Lauren exclaimed, her fishbowl eyes narrowing at me, and I'm sure if I was in arms reach she would've smacked me.

"What? It's true. Doesn't make her a bad person, just makes her a selfish one," I turned to Mia. "No hard feelings, towel girl, I think you're great, a real catch, but that was foul," I said, raising an eyebrow, daring her to disagree.

"Mia and I discussed it, Riggs, and it's none of your business," Lauren scorned.

"I disagree," I stated, placing my hands on my hips. "It most definitely is my business, since I'm the one who picked you up and rescued you in your time of need," I objected, before looking back toward Mia. I was laying it on thick and I don't think either girl knew for sure if I was being serious or not.

"Don't let it happen again," I said, before reaching behind Lauren and squeezing her ass. "Hurry up, I'll wait outside."

I saw the flicker in my Kitten's eyes and hurried out of the apartment before she morphed into a ferocious kitty.

Lauren

"Do you always eat this much?" I asked, as I watched the waitress place Riggs' breakfast in front of him. Seriously, I think he ordered the whole left side of the menu.

"He's a growing boy," the middle-aged waitress teased, placing the final plate, stacked high with flapjacks, in front of Riggs.

He grinned up at her.

"Thanks doll," he said, with a wink before turning his gaze back to me. "She gets me," he added.

I reached for the pepper, shaking some onto my eggs as I peered at him.

"Your cholesterol must be through the roof," I commented, tipping my chin toward the five eggs he had in front of him.

"Aww, you're worried about me," he said, placing a hand over his heart. "I'm touched, babe."

I rolled my eyes and dug into my breakfast as my phone rang inside my pocket book.

"It's my brother," I said, swiping my thumb across the screen to answer it.

Riggs clasped his hands, rubbing them together excitedly, his grin firmly in place.

"Go ahead, answer it," he encouraged. "Put it on speaker," he added.

Crazy.

"Hi, Ant," I said, lifting a piece of bacon from Riggs's six plates and took a bite.

"Lau, listen, I got bad news," he started.

"Oh, yeah?" I asked knowingly, as I peered out the window into the parking lot and looked at my car.

"I had the car brought to a mechanic," he continued, as Riggs covered his mouth trying his hardest not to laugh.

"It's worse than we thought?" I asked, playing along. Because if you couldn't beat them why not join them.

Riggs, dropped his hand from his mouth, leaned over the table and kissed my lips quickly.

"Marry me and have my babies," he whispered, pleased with my eagerness to taunt my brother.

Crazier.

"Not exactly," Anthony said. "Your car is missing from the lot. I don't know how it happened and Pipe is trying to get a hold of Riggs so they can play back the surveillance cameras," he growled into the phone.

I could picture the veins bulging at his temple as he tried to hold his composure and had to admit, Riggs was onto something, busting Anthony's chops could be fun.

"That's funny, because I'm looking at my car right now," I said, smiling because it was hard not to when the man in front of me had such a contagious grin.

"Lauren, what are you talking about?" Anthony asked, annoyed.

Riggs leaned over and took the phone from my hand.

"Hey, boss man! What's shaking?"

"Riggs, what are you doing with my sister?"

"Just dropping her car off, runs like a dream. You should throw Pipe an extra hundred for doing such a good job. Or you could just give it to me when you see me, you know, for my services," he said, winking at me.

"Put Lauren on the phone, NOW," Anthony shouted into the phone.

"Oh, calm down, will you? And I will only give her back the phone if you promise not to yell at her," he antagonized, as he shoved a piece of toast into his mouth.

"PUT LAUREN ON THE PHONE RIGGS," he yelled again, causing everyone in the diner to turn around and look at what the commotion was all about. I grabbed my phone, hastily taking him off speaker and put the phone back to my ear.

"Ant, you're making a scene," I whisper-yelled into the phone.

"I'm making a scene? How am I making a goddamn scene?"

"I had you on speaker phone," I explained. "Look, I appreciate you fixing my car, Riggs was nice enough to deliver it to me as soon as it was done so I didn't have to wait. It all worked out so why are you going crazy?"

"What are you doing with Riggs?"

"Having breakfast," I said.

"Are you sleeping with him?" Talk about cutting to the chase. My brother didn't beat around the bush that's for sure.

"Ant!" I shouted, causing Riggs to raise an eyebrow. "Not that it's any of your business, but no I'm not. He brought me my car, that's it."

"Don't do it Lauren, he's not your type," my brother said softly.

"What's that supposed to mean? How do you know my type?" I questioned angrily. I really should've hung up the phone instead of taking part in this ridiculous conversation. But I wasn't about to let my brother dictate who I did or didn't sleep with. And what was this shit about Riggs not being my type? That burned my ass because my brother knew nothing about my dating life. He was in prison for the duration of my only serious relationship and never even met my crackerjack ex-boyfriend.

"Come on Lau, you know the type of guy I'm talking about. Riggs isn't the guy you're going to take home to mom for Sunday dinners. Shit, even if he was, they'd probably kill each other. You like things nice and orderly, and Riggs is chaos in its purest form," Anthony continued. "I don't want to see you get hurt."

"Thanks for your concern big brother, but I can handle my sex life without any help from you," I sneered.

Riggs started choking on his eggs and I handed him the water as I rolled my eyes.

"How about we talk about something of relevance—like if you've convinced Mom to move back to Brooklyn," I suggested, angrily, sliding out of the booth to pound Riggs on the back. Poor guy was coughing up a lung.

"You're on your own with that, I tried," he grunted. "She doesn't want to come back home, says she likes it up there. She promised to stay out of your hair while you studied for your finals, though," he mumbled miserably. "I've got to go, glad your car is on the road again. Stay safe," he added.

"Ant," I breathed, hating that he seemed mad at me. "I'm sorry I snapped at you. I really appreciate you fixing the car for me," I said.

"No problem," he clipped. "Bye," he added before disconnecting the call.

I stared at the phone in shock, dropping it onto the table before sliding back into the booth across from Riggs.

"He hung up on me," I fumed.

"That didn't go quite like I planned," he admitted. "In my head this whole thing was way funnier."

"He thinks we're sleeping together," I blurted.

"And you feel guilty because you're misleading him? We can fix that, Kitten," he joked.

"Is everything a joke with you?" I asked, lifting my eyes to his, seriously questioning him.

His grin disappeared and his eyes locked with mine.

"I'm sorry," I blurted. "I'm just stressed out and I think everything is finally catching up to me. I appreciate you bringing my car even if your ulterior motive was to fuck with my brother," I whispered and then I snapped. I felt my eyes fill with tears as the lies, the guilt of them and the stress of not knowing where I go from here all surfaced.

"I had a plan!" I blurted. "It was a good plan too, becoming a nurse, making a lot of money, making my family proud," I cried, not caring I was having a meltdown in front of Riggs. I couldn't hold it in anymore and he was there so—the poor bastard was invited to my pity party, hell, he was the only fucking guest. "It was a good fucking plan," I repeated. "And I could've done it too. I had the grades, I scored the internship at the hospital, even in pediatrics like I wanted," I sobbed, reaching to take the napkin he offered me and wiped at my cheeks. I'm sure tomorrow I am going to want to crawl into a hole for this but the dam was already broken and out of my control.

"So what changed?" he asked, surprising me with the sincerity I found in his voice.

"You ever see a baby born with his lungs outside of his chest?" I asked, lifting my eyes to his. "A little person, so helpless, relying on you and a team of doctors to help him make the twenty-four-hour mark. You don't even have a chance to process that you and your colleagues are playing God with this precious little baby's life. All hands are on deck and everyone has a job to do even the new intern. Granted, I was just assisting the registered nurses, but I was there, I was a part of that baby's team. I watched as his dad cried outside the room, wishing there was something he could do, something he could change, hating that we were the people who could help his son and not him."

I shook my head, closing my eyes, as the memories assaulted me. It was a game changer for me, the pivotal moment in my life, realizing I wasn't cut out for the life I thought I wanted. I wanted to believe in medicine. I wanted to heal. But I couldn't watch people die. And a doctor isn't God, doctors can't save everyone, sometimes people just die.

"My shift was over and by that time the baby was critical but stable. His mother still had yet to hold him and his father struggled to make the right decisions. The next morning, I returned to work, and the baby had passed away," I whimpered. "I cried for days, didn't go to school, and I called in sick to the hospital. I couldn't do it, Riggs, I couldn't become a nurse because I'm too weak. I'd get too close to my patients, and I'd lose it every time I lost one. It's inevitable, people die. We all can't live forever but that baby didn't even live one day."

"I don't know what to say," he admitted. "I'm sorry you lost a patient, Kitten. I'm sorry those folks lost their baby," he soothed, as he reached across the table and took my hand in his.

"Me too," I whispered. "I can't do it Riggs, I can't be a nurse," I confessed.

"Then don't be," he said simply. "So, you had a plan, plans change. Shit happens, Lauren, that's why there are things called detours. So take your detour and I promise you, you'll get where you're going eventually," he urged.

"I've made such a mess of things, Riggs. I've been lying to my mother and Anthony for months. On top of breaking my mother's heart—"

"Your mothers got thick skin, she'll get over it and if she doesn't…then it's her problem. I learned a long time ago you can't live your life pleasing others," he interjected. "You will have to tell them sooner or later, no reason to prolong it and drive yourself crazy. Babe, you'll be fine. Trust me, it all works out in the end.

"You sound so sure," I scoffed.

"I stopped traveling the path I thought I was supposed to be on and took a detour. It led me straight to the right road, the one I was destined for. Best decision I ever made, and I have no regrets. I'm sure I should have some, maybe even a little remorse too, but I don't," he said, shrugging his shoulders. "Not for my old life and not for the people I left behind. I choose who I let into my life, and those people accept me for the man I am. They are who I worry about, who I am loyal to and they are who I don't want to disappoint."

"Your club," I said, reading between the lines.

He nodded.

"Take the detour, Kitten," he coaxed.

He made it sound so simple. He made me wish I could. I just needed a little more time to figure it out. To plan what I would say. As much as I wanted to be a free spirit like Riggs, I didn't know how. I didn't know how to live life with no direction.

He dropped my hand and signaled the waitress for the check.

"I've got to get back to the city. I have a job I need to do, but we'll talk more, and if you need help throwing caution to the wind, I'm your guy," he said, seeing the apprehension in my eyes. He winked at me, enticing me to take him up on his offer.

Throwing caution to the wind with Riggs was probably a bad idea…a really bad idea but oh, so tempting.

Chapter Nine
RIGGS

Sun Wu was no joke, there was a reason he was named after a warrior. What? You think I would agree to a job without doing my homework? I had his blood type and his family tree memorized before I walked through the door. Nope, not just a pretty face, your boy Riggs has brains too.

He and the Red Dragons were big time players in the MC world. They weren't a threat to the Knights because we ran in different circles. Most of their operations were overseas, using the New York Harbor to move their weapons and their drugs back home to their pals in Beijing.

Wu wanted me to wire every inch of an apartment he kept over on Mott Street. He was vague about the details of the operation but he was adamant that every square inch of the property was secure. I ran wires through the walls, planted bugs on smoke alarms, and glass eyes in high hats. The place was suited up from the fire hydrant on the curb outside to the microwave in the kitchen.

Thanks to me, Wu had eyes everywhere.

And thanks to him I had a sweet envelope to deliver at Church.

I also had entertainment because there was no way in hell I wasn't tapping those wires. Sometimes binge watching on Netflix just doesn't hack it and I need an extra something, something. You know what I mean?

I was packing up my tools, shoving them back into my bag when I heard the roar of engines outside. Sun Wu and his boys started talking in Chinese making me wish I had paid more attention when my mother got me those fancy Mandarin lessons. Instead, I tried getting it on with my Asian Mrs. Robinson.

Wu pulled up the surveillance footage on his iPad and grinned at me.

"A day ago I'd be holding my gun out the window checking to see who was knocking on my door," he turned the screen around so I could see the Dragons dismounting from their bikes, clear as day might I add.

"You do excellent work, Riggs. I will be sure to tell Jack I appreciate him subbing out your services to the Red Dragons. If there is a way we can serve you in the future, I hope you won't hesitate to ask," he said, as he fingered the patch on his cut.

"I'm not the shy type, brother. If you got something I need, bet your ass I'm taking it," I said, zipping up my bag and throwing it over my shoulder.

I decided against asking him if he had an old lady that made fried rice. Homemade fried rice was the shit. I had an Asian nanny once, she made killer fried rice and her spare ribs were off the charts. Real authentic, none of that stuff you find at every Chinese takeout place.

If I ever take an old lady I might make sure she's Asian.

The door opened, and the Dragons walked in, signaling it was my cue to go.

"It's been real guys," I said, patting my cut to where the envelope was safely tucked away. "Pleasure doing business with you," I said to "Jackie Chan" and the

Ninja Warriors. Glancing around at the empty apartment one last time, I wondered what Sun Wu had in store for this place.

I pulled into the compound, killed the engine of my bike and found Bones sitting on top of a picnic table smoking a joint. I tipped my chin toward him before I took a seat on the table next to him.

"Pass that shit," I said, watching as he blew out a stream of smoke.

"How'd it go with Wu?" he asked, passing the joint.

I took the first pull, welcoming the burn of the herb and shrugged my shoulders.

"In and out, easy job." I thought about it—Wu, the Red Dragons and how over the top their operation looked. "The Dragons don't play, huh?"

Bones had been part of the Satan's Knights for a couple of years now, making him more knowledgeable when it came to rival clubs and how they worked. He had a better understanding of the history between the Knights and the Dragons too. He didn't need me to tell him that Sun Wu was a lethal bastard, he already knew that.

"No they don't," he affirmed. "It's good for the club that we make nice with him. You doing that job for him shows good faith. We don't want that guy or his club as an enemy," He said, taking the joint from me.

"I hear you," I said, staring at the bikes that lined the Dog Pound, noticing how everyone's bikes were parked, but the guys were nowhere in sight. "What are you doing out here? Where is everyone?"

He looked at me for a moment, silently, before he offered me the joint again.

"They're all inside," he replied finally.

"I'm good," I said, declining the joint and watching on as he took one last puff.

"I was waiting for you," he said, blowing out the smoke. He coughed slightly, and I reached over and slapped him on the back.

"Aww you missed me, brother?" I joked.

Bones and I went way back, a brotherhood before either of us ever knew of the Satan's Knights. His mother, Lorraine, was my family's housekeeper, the sweetest lady you'd ever have the pleasure of knowing. When we were kids, Lorraine would bring Bones with her on the weekends and we'd play together. We remained close through the years, and while my parents tried to shelter me, Bones was the one who enlightened me. He introduced me to sports, women and pot. And when I broke away from my family, he and his mom welcomed me with open arms.

Lorraine passed away two years ago around the same time Bones became a patched member of the Satan's Knights. He's led me on this detour, bringing me into the fold and introducing me to the club. He's the one who gave me my road name, and it's because of Bones, I've found my place within the MC.

I owe him a lot but he's never asked for anything other than my friendship. He's my brother, first and foremost. Always. Until we die.

"Riggs, you know I always got you, right?" he questioned me, both verbally and with his eyes.

"I know and that shit works both ways," I said, staring back at him, wondering where this was coming from.

He nodded thoughtfully as my phone chimed, signaling I had a text message.

"Everything okay?" I asked, as I reached into my pocket for my phone, glancing down at the screen to see Lauren's name. I swiped my thumb across the screen and opened the message.

Kitten: Hi…so, I've been thinking and I think I'm ready for that detour.

I smiled slightly, about to reply when I realized I was in the middle of a conversation with my friend and he looked all sorts of weird. I lifted my eyes back to Bones.

"Jack wants to see you. They voted on whether to patch you in," he said, solemnly.

Shit.

"You don't look too fucking happy. They voted against me?" I asked angrily. That was fucking bullshit. I've done everything asked of me and then some, I proved my loyalty and I fucking deserved my patch.

Bones jumped off the table and patted my shoulder.

"Come on, let Jack explain everything," he ordered.

Fuck that. Jack Parrish could kiss my ass. I shoved my phone into my pocket and hopped off the table. I'd go meet with my so-called brothers, but I wasn't about to listen to some bullshit excuse why they had voted against me.

"Calm down," Bones warned, quickening his pace to catch up with me as I charged into the Dog Pound.

"I am calm," I seethed. I very calmly was going to fucking flip their precious, fucking table upside down.

I charged into the Chapel, Bones on my tail, and peeled off my cut that labeled me a prospect, the fucking joke of the Satan's Knights.

"Riggs, don't—" Bones started.

"I'm done," I interrupted throwing my cut onto the table. "You got something you want to say?" I asked the man seated at the head of the table.

Jack raised an eyebrow, diverting his eyes back and forth between me and Bones. Then I heard Bones laugh behind me.

"What the fuck is so funny?" I asked, through gritted teeth as I glanced over my shoulder toward my friend.

They all started laughing.

Every single fucking one of them.

"What is so fucking funny?" I hissed, eyes on the Bulldog as he rose from his seat.

"The brothers and I thought it was time to vote on whether we patch you in," he explained, as I rolled my eyes. Was he really about to sugar coat this shit for me?

"It was unanimous," he added.

Blackie rose from his chair, walking toward the back of the room as Jack stood in front of me.

"Congratulations, you're officially one of the Satan's Knights," Jack declared, taking the leather vest Blackie offered him.

I looked at the leather cut in disbelief, running my fingers over the stitching of the patches and lifted my eyes to my president's.

"Are you fucking with me?"

Jack shook his head.

"Put it on," he said. "You've earned your right to those colors, wear them proud," he added, tipping his chin toward the vest I was clutching in my hand.

I glanced over my shoulder at Bones, taking in his shit-eating grin, and the pride reflected in his eyes.

"You're an asshole," I clipped.

"Stop! You're giving me goosebumps," he teased, taking a step closer to pull my hat off and tousle my hair. "What the fuck are you waiting for? Put your goddamn cut on! Wanted to tell you yesterday but your ass was nowhere to be found."

Pipe and Wolf started pounding their fists against the table as they chanted for me to put it on.

It was a surreal moment, a profound one, finding your place in the world. It was the first time in my life I felt like part of a real family. I slid the vest on, a perfect fit, and my brothers took a chance a piece congratulating me. Jack wrapped his arms around me and patted my back.

"Proud to call you a brother," he said sincerely.

"Thanks, Prez," I replied with a grin.

"You know what happens now don't you?" Pipe said, eyes full of mischief.

I turned my attention toward him as he threw something at me. I caught it just in time, starring at the box of condoms before grinning widely at him.

"Fuck, yeah," I agreed.

Blackie lined up shot glasses along the table, filling them with Patron before raising his own toward me.

"To brotherhood," he saluted.

"To Riggs," Bones added.

"Ay!" Pipe shouted.

"To being a Knight!" I chimed in, clinking my glass to theirs and shooting back the tequila.

"There's plenty more where that came from," Blackie promised, as my phone rang.

I pulled myself away from the high and lifted the phone to my ear.

"Hello?"

"Hi. Is it a bad time?" Lauren's voice filled my ear, reminding me of the text message I received before.

The guys started getting rowdy, re-filling their shot glasses and shouting their well wishes. I downed the shot Bones put in front of me, handing him back the empty glass and stepped out of the Chapel.

"Hey," I said hoarsely, the burn of the tequila working its effect on my voice. "Sorry, I got side-tracked," I explained, once I was in the common room. "I've got the best news."

"Really? What happened?" she asked, and fuck me, her voice did things to me. She actually sounded sincere, like she wanted to know. What was even more bizarre was that I wanted to share it with her.

"I got patched in, Kitten. They voted and I'm officially one of the Satan's Knights," I said excitedly.

"That's great, babe," she boasted, falling silent after the endearment left her lips.

"Yeah, waited a long time for this. They're having a party for me tonight at the clubhouse," I said, glancing over my shoulder watching Bones and Blackie stepping into the common room.

"I'm happy for you, Riggs," she whispered.

"Thanks," I said, stepping away from my brothers. "Listen, the guys are busting my balls but...why don't you come tonight?"

I'm an idiot.

I closed my eyes and slammed the palm of my hand against my forehead.

Really, there is no other way to describe me. I have no fucking idea why I asked her to come to my patch party.

"You want me to come to your party?"

Yes.

No.

Blackie handed me another shot. The man was on a fucking mission, I'll give him that.

"I've got to go but yeah, sure, why not?" I said in a hurry. "So maybe I'll see you later?"

"I don't know, Riggs," she said.

Good. Good. Maybe she won't come.

But a part of me, a real small part, actually wanted her there. I just had no fucking idea why. Not a clue.

"Detour. You come tonight and this could be it, Kitten," I said, realizing I got my patch and lost my fucking brains.

"I'll see. If I don't come, though, have a great night," she responded. "Bye Riggs," she said before ending the call.

"I just fucked up," I said out loud, staring at my phone.

"What'd you do this time?" Bones asked, lighting up a freshly rolled joint.

I snatched it out of his mouth and took a heavy pull.

"I just invited Bianci's sister to my pussy party."

I left out that the fact that if I had to choose between the club whores that would swarm this place tonight or my Kitten, hands down I would choose the girl next door with the gorgeous eyes and sexy glasses.

Glasses.

I thought glasses were sexy.

Yeah, I really lost my fucking mind.

Lauren

"What?" Mia asked, as I stared at my phone.

"He was patched into the club," I said automatically.

"Yeah, I don't know what that means," she counted, shaking her head.

I turned to her.

"It means he's a full fledge member. It means he gets a vote, it's everything to a man like him," I explained.

I remember when my brother became a *made* man. I remember the black suit he wore, the scent of his cologne, and how he wore entirely too much hair gel. But, what I remember the most, is the look in his eyes when he kissed my cheek before he left. They were full of pride, thinking he had made it in life, that he finally had everything he ever wanted. He didn't know every word of his oath was another piece of his soul he handed the Devil. Anthony didn't realize until he lost everything he ever wanted, until he lost Adrianna and their baby.

I didn't know if being a member of a motorcycle club was anything like being a man of the mob but if it was, if there was any resemblance at all, I hope Riggs knew what he was doing.

"Mazel to Riggs," Mia offered.

"He invited me to his patch party," I added, as I bit the inside of my cheek, trying to figure why he did that. I was pretty sure there would be a shitload of women there so why invite me?

"Did you say a party?" she asked, dropping her magazine on the coffee table.

"Yeah, but I don't think I want to go," I blurted.

"Oh you have to go! You'll break his heart if you're not there on his big night," she exaggerated.

"Mia," I warned.

"No, Lauren, you're an idiot if you don't go. It's not like you have anything better to do anyway," she pointed out.

Way to kick a friend when she's down. My best friend was better than yours. Not.

"I like Riggs, Mia," I said, feeling frustrated and honestly a bit naïve.

"More of a reason to go to his party," she suggested.

"No, more of a reason not to go," I argued. I knew enough about men to know the type of man Riggs was. He probably invited every girl he ever banged to his patch party. I wasn't stupid enough to think I was the exception, and I wasn't ready to face that truth head on. I didn't want to give up on Kitten and Tiger just yet and still wanted to hold onto the dream of us.

Maybe I was naïve.

Maybe I was just plain stupid.

"You're going to the party," Mia insisted. "And you will make Riggsy's head spin when he sees you," she said with a grin. "I have the perfect outfit for you!"

"Fine, I'll go but you're coming with me to make sure I don't do anything stupid," I conceded, knowing very well that deciding to go was the first of many stupid things I would do. But hey, life was about taking detours, right?

Chapter Ten
RIGGS

I leaned back against the back of the black leather couch, swigging tequila straight from the bottle as the blonde in front of me shook her tits in my face. She was one of many, a dime a dozen, just another piece of ass swapped by the brothers. She placed her hands on my thighs and fell to her knees, trying her hardest to smile seductively at me.

Her hands traveled up my legs, and I took another swig of tequila, feeling my dick jolt against the zipper of my jeans. I've been walking around with a hard on since the party began. It was a feast of nipples and ass galore, yet we were hours in and I still hadn't fucked anyone. Blondie over here was trying her hardest to be the one.

"You ready for me, tiger?" she purred, as she drew down the zipper of my jeans.

Wrong thing to say.

Because my dick died a little knowing it was the wrong girl asking, calling me a name meant only for her.

But my Kitten wasn't here. She never showed and all I had was blondie, a cheap imitation. Fuck, she wasn't even an imitation. She was the opposite of Lauren. They all were, every single whore that rubbed up on me tonight. I had blondes, redheads, even chicks with bright pink hair, but I stayed away from the brunettes purposely and I had no fucking idea why.

I grabbed blondie's face, leaned forward and crashed my mouth over hers.

It was all wrong. She was wrong.

My tongue darted in and out of her mouth as I reached around her waist and grabbed her ass cheeks.

"Thanks, babe," I said, pulling back and shaking the empty bottle of tequila in her face. "But it's time for a refill," I claimed, giving her ass a light smack, signaling to take what she was selling to another brother.

She stumbled onto her feet and looked at me dejected. I ignored her, brushing past her as I made my way through the sea of people toward the bar where I found Bones picking up his pants.

"Am I the only one who hasn't gotten laid yet?" I questioned disgustedly, as I reached over the bar and pulled another bottle from the shelf.

"What the fuck are you waiting for?" Bones asked, his breath ragged from pounding one of the usual bitches that hung around him like a hemorrhoid. I think her name was Sally, or maybe Suzy, fuck, I had no idea what her name was.

I glanced across the room at Brittany, the girl from the gym, getting tight with Pipe. Well, I didn't see that shit coming. I wouldn't have invited her if I thought she'd be on her knees sucking Pipe's dick and not mine.

"I need a brunette," I told Bones, taking the cigarette he just lit from his mouth and claiming it for myself.

"And what? You can't find one?" he asked incredulously, pulling another cigarette from his pack. "What about her," he suggested, tipping his beer across the room. "Pretty enough, if you bend her over and take her from behind. Her face is fucked but she's got an ass that makes up for that shit."

I squinted, trying to check her out but I couldn't see shit. I was piss drunk and seeing double of everything. I covered one eye and focused on the brunette in question.

"You boys want in on the bet?" Pops asked, walking up in front of me completely obscuring my vision.

It was fucking useless. I couldn't even fuck backward pussy.

I gave up, taking a seat on one of the stools and looked at Pops

"What're you talking about old man?"

"We're lining up some matches. Blackie is first up. He's going to fight one of the guys from another charter," he explained, holding out his palm. "Pay up."

"No one asked me if I wanted to fight," I said flatly.

"And chance messing up that pretty face of yours?" Bones quipped, handing over a fifty to Pops. "Fifty on Black," he told the old geezer.

If I couldn't fuck, I might as well fight. Get rid of some of this aggression somehow. I looked at my phone. Nope, no calls from Kitten.

"I want to fight," I declared, staring at Pops. "Set it up," I said, sliding off the stool. I grabbed my bottle and glanced at Bones. "And your money better be on me and not some other dick wad," I warned.

I spotted Blackie walking into the room with a smoking hot blonde on his heels and my dick stirred. Maybe I didn't need a brunette after all.

I took a shot of the tequila, placing the bottle down again, and left Bones and Pops to snatch Blackie's girl. Fuck that, it was my patch party. I should get first dibs on all pussy.

I cleared my throat, ready to lay on the charm in typical Riggs fashion. Blackie didn't stand a chance. Kiss your lay goodbye brother.

"This is the best fucking night of my life!" I shouted, moving to stand directly in front of the blonde bombshell who looked like a lost puppy. What the hell was wrong with me, and why was I comparing every woman I wanted to bang to a pet? Her eyes lifted to mine as I flipped my baseball cap backwards so she could check out my soulful eyes as I grinned at her. Go on baby, try to resist Riggs.

"Who are you, sexy mama?" I asked, as I reached out and ran my hand along her side.

"Riggs, she's here for the Bulldog," Blackie clipped.

Come on!

I dropped my hand from her side and she shoved a pie against my chest, forcing me to take it.

"I've got to go," she mumbled, spinning around, leaving me holding the pie.

No pussy.

I was going to get my ass kicked from some dope because I opened my big trap.

But I had pie.

I poked my finger into the crust and pulled it out covered in cherry filling. Sucking the cherry off my finger, I savored every flavor. Damn, it was good.

Heaven.

I ignored the fleeting thought that I probably looked a lot like Jason Biggs in *American Pie* and took off to the couches to enjoy it.

I found a seat next to the Bulldog, ignoring he was in the middle of getting his cock sucked by a brunette.

Oh, look, I found one!

I dropped myself onto the couch and dug into my pie.

Jack pushed the girl off his lap and she nearly took a tumble and fell face first into my dessert. I would've killed them both, but the broad found her footing and Jack zipped his jeans. All was well.

Happy Endings all around.

"Best fucking pie ever," I said with my mouth full, shrugging the whore's hands off my shoulders. I didn't want his leftovers especially when he had just blown his load in her mouth. Gross. I'll stick with my pie.

"You guys really went all out. I don't remember baked goods at any other club party," I said to Jack, licking the filling from my thumb.

"Where did you get that?" he asked, standing tall, looking at my lap like there was fire on top of it and not a pie.

I licked my lips, widening my eyes as he grabbed the pie from me, searching around the clubhouse—for what, I wasn't quite sure of. I don't know. The man is crazy. Like, literally, he's bipolar.

"Hey wait a minute, give that back, man!" I shouted angrily, reaching for the pie.

"Where. Did. You. Get. The. Fucking. Pie," he hissed.

"Some fucking hot blonde brought it by before she took off," I responded, holding out my hands for the pie. "Now give it back."

He glanced back down at the pie before shoving it back into my hands.

He was fucking lucky he did the right thing. I was about to throw down.

"Where is she now?"

I shrugged my shoulders, repositioning myself on the couch and took another taste.

"Blackie was on her like white on rice, bet he knows where the pie goddess is," I pointed out. "Do a brother a solid? When you find her ask her if she'll be my personal baker, will you?"

Hey a man could hope, right?

The Bulldog stalked off, in true tough guy fashion, but at least he left me his brunette and the pie. She was a persistent little thing, bending over giving me a prime view of her ass as her skirt hiked up. She looked over her shoulder, made sure she had my attention before turning back around and taking a seat on my lap.

She nodded toward the pie as she ran her hand up my thigh and cupped my cock.

"Can I have a taste?" she asked, stroking me through my jeans.

I lifted my fingers to her lips and watched her tongue slide out and wrap around them, licking them clean of the filling.

Fuck it!

I pushed the pie to the side and grabbed her hips, centering her so she had one leg on either side of me and gripped her hips. She leaned in for a kiss but I flipped her hair over her shoulder and pressed my mouth to her neck.

No mouth.

Not hers.

She ground herself against my cock and reached for my zipper as I sucked on her neck. She whispered dirty incentives into my ear as I arched my hips. My hands moved underneath her skirt, squeezing her ass before reaching between her legs to push her thong aside. She reached inside my jeans, pressing the heel of her hand against my dick. I pulled back, raising her off me to pull my pants down and bare my cock to her. She flipped her head back and for some reason, I lifted my head and my eyes locked with the pair of baby blues I had been searching for all night.

I blinked, pushing the broad off my lap and leaned forward to get a better look, to make sure my eyes weren't playing tricks on me.

My Kitten stared back at me for a moment. Her eyes wide behind her glasses but there was something different about them. They were done up with that eye crap girls put on when they want to give a guy the "come fuck me" eyes. Kitten most definitely stared back at me with the come fuck me eyes. My eyes took in the rest of her, noting her hair was loose, falling around her face in waves. I couldn't wait to pull it.

She was wearing a tight black dress that stopped mid-thigh and high on the neck. Her tits were completely covered, and I started thinking of the quickest way to get to them. I decided I'd pull the collar of her dress down her shoulders until the girls sprang free. It seemed like the quickest and easiest way to get my mouth on her.

I stood tall, pulling my pants up, ready to claim what was mine and give her what her eyes told me they wanted but she turned abruptly, grabbing Bones by his cut and wrapping her arms around him. That's when I saw the back of her dress was missing, exposing her creamy olive skin to me and every fucking guy in here.

Bones grinned at her, snaking his arm around her to place his hand against the small of her back, slowly working it up her bare skin.

I pulled the gun from my back pocket, not thinking, not fucking caring, just knowing no one's hands, other than my own, belonged on Lauren.

"Whoa, brother, what the hell are you doing?" Wolf asked me, stepping into my line of sight.

"Get the fuck out of my way, Wolf," I growled, looking over his shoulder as Lauren turned around and shimmied her ass against Bones. He grabbed her hips and moved with her, thrusting his hips against her to the beat of the music. She smiled, her eyes scanning the room until they locked with mine again, and then she narrowed them at me.

The come fuck me eyes were gone, replaced with fuck *you* eyes.

I pushed Wolf out of my way and stalked toward her, her eyes drifting down to the gun in my hand and widening before she spun on her heel.

They spun around together, Bones kept his back toward me as Lauren tried to hide behind him.

"What are you doing?" Bones asked her.

"Um…do you have a gun? Who am I kidding? You all have guns don't you?" she slapped her hand against her forehead. "It doesn't matter, listen, now might be the time to grab the gun," she rambled.

"You're one of those crazy chicks that wants to get fucked with a gun aimed at her?" he questioned, backing away from her.

"What? No! Girls do that?"

"Kinky shit, sure. Had a girl that wanted me to choke her. Shit ain't for me," he explained.

"Shit!" Lauren hissed, as her eyes locked with mine and I pressed my gun to Bones back.

"I didn't want you to fuck me with the gun, you dope! I was trying to warn you that if you didn't pull yours, he'd get to you first," she huffed. "Too late," she added.

"Kitten," I growled, holding the gun steady on Bones as I leaned over his shoulder. "You ever touch her again, I'll blow your dick off," I seethed, dropping the gun from Bones' back and stepping around him as I glared at Lauren.

"You ever pull your gun on me again and I'll blow *your* dick off, you hear me?" Bones whispered into my ear. "Pretty fine piece of ass you got there," he acknowledged. "I'll take her when you're finished," he said, patting me on the back before walking away.

Like fucking hell he would.

I mean it. I'd blow his dick off.

Best friend or not.

Lauren rolled her eyes and turned to leave. I wasn't going to let her go anywhere. I reached for her and caught her wrist, stopping her from leaving.

"Going somewhere?"

"Yeah, home," she sneered, tugging her arm free. I'd never seen her like this, so angry, so fucking hot. She turned toward Blackie, took his drink from his hand and threw the whiskey in my face before handing the empty glass back to him.

"Congratulations, you're a dick with a patch," she said, before turning and walking toward the door.

I sputtered whiskey from my mouth, lifting the hem of my t-shirt to dry my face, trying to ignore the surrounding chuckles.

"You better marry her because if you don't I will," Bones said, as he came up beside me and handed me a stack of napkins.

"Fuck off," I shouted, throwing the napkins up in the air like confetti before I took off after her. "Lauren," I shouted as I stepped outside. Scanning the grounds, I found her stalking through the parking lot.

I ran after her but Kitten had speed even in those heels she had on that threatened to take her down.

"Lauren, baby…Kitten," I called.

She froze in her tracks and turned around.

Hallelujah!

Oh, shit!

She bent down, removing one of her high heels and swung it like a Cy-Young pitcher, aiming straight for my head.

"Are you fucking crazy?" I shouted, dodging death by a high heel.

"Oh, you think I'm crazy?" she asked incredulously, looking every bit crazy. No question about it. "Maybe I am crazy! I mean, I must be because I'm here, right? Standing here in my little black dress, against my better judgement, because well, tonight was a big night for you and I…" she let her words trail off. "…I am crazy," she confirmed, shaking her head in disbelief.

"Kitten," I started, reaching for her.

She flicked my forehead with her fingers.

"Ouch! What the hell did you do that for?" I shouted, rubbing my forehead.

"There is plenty more where that came from, buddy!" She threatened, as she poked my chest with her finger. I had had enough of this shit. I grabbed her hips, hauling her up against me and maneuvered her legs to wrap around my waist. She didn't like that at all and yelped as I held her in place.

"Riggs, put me down," she yelled.

"You don't really want me to put you down," I ground out. My patience was gone, my nerves frayed. She kicked my back and I pinched her leg as I turned and slammed her up against the wall of the Dog Pound.

"Came here for a reason, Kitten, now it's time to tell me what that reason is," I whispered against her ear.

"It doesn't matter," she squealed, as I ran my hands up her thighs.

"I disagree," I argued, glancing down at her legs locked around my waist. "I like your dress," I said, sliding my hands underneath it.

"You should," she sneered, wrapping her arms around my neck. "I wore it for you," she rasped.

Sweetest fucking words I ever heard.

I felt the grin spread across my mouth, heard the whimper escape her perfect mouth as her eyes zeroed in on mine.

Without another thought, I crushed my mouth against hers, tearing her lips apart with my teeth. She parted her swollen lips, granting my tongue access to her mouth and tugged at my hat, pulling it off so she could run her fingers through my hair while I fucked her mouth.

She was so fucking hot, clawing at me, matching my desperation to claim her body, to taste and fuck every inch of her.

She arched her back off the brick wall, begging for more with her body. I reached under her dress, hooked my index finger beneath the lace covering her pussy and ran my finger along the center of her bare cunt.

"Jesus," I muttered against her lips, as I slid two fingers inside her drenched heat.

She fisted my cut in her hands, grinding her pussy against my hand, clenching around my fingers.

"You're so fucking wet," I growled, dipping my head to lick her neck.

She moaned then muttered something I couldn't make out. I leaned into her, securing her against the wall with my weight and pulled the front of her dress down. I heard a tear somewhere but didn't give it much thought as I exposed her bare breasts.

"No Bra?"

"Dress didn't allow it," she gasped, as I took her hardened nipple between my teeth.

The dress she wore for me.

If I didn't unleash my dick and get inside of her I was going to die. I was sure of it.

"Keep your legs wrapped around me," I ordered, reaching down to unzip my jeans and pulling my cock out. I tore the lace aside and guided my thick head toward her pussy. She clutched my shoulders as I braced one palm against the brick wall beside her head.

"Tell me this is why you came here," I demanded, as my dick teased her wetness. It took everything in me, all my will, not to drill my dick into her. I'd probably fuck her into the wall and break her if I did.

"I came here for you," she said hastily, as she pressed herself against me. "Riggs, give it to me," she demanded.

"Not until you admit you came here for me to fuck you," I insisted, the head of my cock sliding between her lips.

"I came here for you to fuck me, now do it already!" She cried out, her single shoe digging into my ass purposely, coaxing me.

"It won't be gentle," I warned.

"Gentle's for pussy's," she retorted.

I snapped, like a rubber band stretched to its capacity. Her words broke my resolve, and I slammed my cock inside of her. I should've realized her words were just words because I probably hurt her. She was so tight and my dick was three times its normal size—at least it felt like it was—there was no way I didn't tear her up with one thrust. But my girl hid the pain well, her tight pussy milking me, holding onto my dick as it moved in and out of her.

I like to think I was the one fucking her, but she fucked me harder, spreading her legs, her hands frantically grabbing for me, chanting my name—cursing it too. We fucked with no regard, taking what we wanted and needed.

It didn't matter we were in the parking lot of the Dog Pound, that I had her pressed against a wall, her legs wrapped around me, her tits falling out of her dress as I fucked her.

She bucked wildly, her only shoe falling from her foot as her legs flailed.

"Oh, my God, Riggs!" She gasped, dropping her mouth to my shoulder to hide the screams of her orgasm when she came.

Her legs locked around me, I felt her pussy tighten and I began to unravel. Two quick thrusts and I was done, growling her name as I released my load inside her.

"Christ, Kitten," I ground out, pumping her until she took everything I had to give.

I was balls deep in Lauren, her bare back against the brick wall and I made a list of things I hoped I'd remember come morning.

1. My Kitten was a screamer.
2. She came here tonight for me.
3. She wore that dress for me.
4. And when she came around my cock she owned me.

That last one was a scary thought, and I scratched it from the list. It must have been all the hype of the night, all the alcohol, the post orgasm was responsible for my temporary madness.

No one owned me.

I pulled out, setting her down on her feet before tucking my swollen cock back into my jeans. Lauren repositioned her dress, tugging the hem down her legs and shoved her breasts back in place. I looked down at her bare feet then lifted my eyes to hers as she pushed her glasses onto her nose.

She looked shocked, as if she had just woken up from a bad dream and didn't know where she was. I bent down, picked up one shoe and glanced around for the other. Then I remembered when and where she threw it at me. I stepped around the corner of the building into the parking lot and recovered the lost heel.

"Riggs! There you are," Wolf shouted across the lot. "Pops is looking for you. He found you a match in the ring," he hollered.

Oh fuck! I forgot about that.

"I'll be right there!" I yelled as I picked up Lauren's shoe. I straightened up and turned around. Lauren took the shoe from my hand and slipped it on her bare foot.

"Lauren," I started, not really knowing what to say.

"I've got to go," she interrupted, closing her eyes before pointing her finger toward the Dog Pound. "Mia is inside," she said in a whisper, looking all around the parking lot but not at me. "Can you please tell her I'm leaving? I don't want to go back inside," she pleaded softly.

I cupped her chin, turning her head so that her eyes were forced to lock with mine.

"Take a deep breath," I ordered.

She inhaled sharply, slowly releasing a deep breath.

"Very good," I encouraged. "We're good. It's just sex. We're still Kitten and Tiger," I reassured.

Lauren was a good girl. She's probably never had a fling, much less a cheap one on the side of a building. She was a girl you spooned not one you walked away from to go win a fight. She deserved more, but I wasn't the guy to give it to her so I did the right thing and calmed her down.

I lied to her.

We weren't still Kitten and Tiger.

We were nothing.

"Kitten and Tiger," she repeated, taking another breath before a smile worked her swollen lips. "Still friends," she affirmed.

"Still friends," I lied.

What a fucking night.

Join an MC, they said.

It will be fun, they said.

They were fucking liars.

Chapter Eleven
Lauren

So much for being the smart girl.

I was the biggest fool to ever walk the face of the Earth, or possibly the most inexperienced one. As much as I hated to admit it, my brother was right. In not so many words, he warned me that this would happen. But that's what you get when a girl like me plays with the big dogs. I should never have gone to Riggs' patch party. I should have been smarter. I should have realized I was way out of my league setting my sights on a guy like him.

But I wasn't thinking.

Riggs robbed me of my sanity that first night I laid eyes on him. He made me want things I had no business wanting someone like him. I was so jaded that I actually believe he liked me. Imagine that? A sexy guy like him, a patched member of a motorcycle club, a man who had women dropping to their knees with the snap of his fingers.

I didn't attract guys like Riggs, and even if I did, there was no way he'd stick. I was so angry with myself because I knew all of this, and still; I set myself up for the way I was now feeling. I just couldn't resist him despite the warning bells signaling he was all wrong for me.

Believing him when he said nothing would change, that we were still just Kitten and Tiger—that took the cake, labeling me the dumbest girl ever.

Stupid, stupid girl.

Sex changes things.

Sex in a parking lot, against a wall, destroys things.

And still, knowing that, I tried to analyze why things changed. He claimed it was just sex, making it sound so casual, like it was nothing. I went home that night and drilled those things into my head, making light of it because he promised we'd still be friends. I pushed the memories of him inside of me away, forgetting the way I felt alive, and for the first time I came with hardly any effort from my partner.

The next morning, I texted him like I usually did asking him how his first day with a patch felt. Corny? Maybe, but at least I didn't meow again. I still can't believe I did that.

Riggs never answered my text that morning, and I made an excuse, telling myself he was too hung over and probably had slept in.

So, I sent him another text later that night, securing the end of Kitten and Tiger, by declaring him my Prince Charming because he found my other shoe after I threw it.

Guess what?

Prince Charming didn't answer that one either.

I didn't text him after that for two days—every time I felt the urge Mia came through with a tub of tiramisu gelato. I think the first few days were just as rough on her but she redeemed herself as my best friend. She made a dartboard and taped a picture of a tiger to the bullseye. That was fun for a while.

Until it wasn't.

I lost my job at The Pink Pussycat and he was the first person I wanted to tell. And not because he and Mia were the only people who knew where I really worked, but because I knew he'd make me feel better about being laid off on top of everything else.

And so I called him.

It went to voicemail.

I hung up.

I called back and left a message then did the number one move every girl does when she's been shunted—I lied through my teeth.

"Sorry, I didn't mean to call you."

He would know it was a lie.

How many *Tigers* can one person have stored in their phone? I changed his name in my phone to dickhead after that.

Two more weeks went by and still not a word. One would think that I would've gotten the hint by now, but nope, I still stared at my phone hoping he'd have a change of heart. Things got progressively worse on my end and Mia and I needed to vacate our apartment.

The jig was up.

No job.

No place to live.

Mia was moving back home with her parents, and why not? She wasn't pretending to be someone she wasn't. Me? I had to come clean, once and for all. I had no other choice.

Anthony and Adrianna had asked my mother and I to come home for the weekend. This brought on my anxiety about bumping into Riggs. What would I do? What would I say? Then I drove myself crazy thinking about what he would do. Would he ignore me? Would he smile at me? Would he be with someone else?

I didn't have a broken heart, but I had a broken ego—I think that hurt just as much. The more I thought about it, the more my sadness turned to anger. I shouldn't care about seeing him, and I shouldn't give a shit if he was with another girl. I had bigger fish to fry. I should be concerned about telling my family about nursing school and the fact my ass was broke with no place to live. Instead, I was mulling over some douche bag who probably didn't even give me a second thought. A douche bag who stuck his dick inside any girl who would let him.

Stupid girl! You let him!

Yeah, I did, even after I saw him with some other girl five minutes before. I dropped my head into my hands and fought back the tears that threatened to spill.

Don't cry.

Don't give that bastard that kind of power.

He doesn't deserve your tears.

But it was no use, they poured from my eyes, three, almost four weeks of unshed tears.

Being the fool sucked.

I cried and cried, letting it all out as I sat alone in my empty apartment waiting for my mother. I cried because I lost my way. I cried because I thought Riggs would help me find it. I cried because I felt like an idiot. I cried because I lost my Tiger and I was no longer Kitten. Again, I was back to being plain old Lauren.

I used to like being plain old me.

What happened to that?

You wanted more, that's what happened, my conscience reminded me.

The doorbell rang, and I tried to pull myself together. It didn't do me any good because when you shut your feelings off for so long you become helpless to the emotions.

My emotions owned me.

I wiped at my tears, giving up on hiding my pain from whoever was on the other end of that door and opened it.

My mother's eyes widened as she took me in. Like so many times before, I saw my pain reflected in her eyes. I wonder if every mother and daughter had that kind of relationship. If they had a mom like mine, the type of mother that owned her daughter's pain as her own.

She dropped her bag onto the floor, opened her arms wide and I sobbed as I stepped into her embrace.

"Oh, my girl, it's okay," she whispered, hugging me tightly as she walked me back into the apartment.

My mother was always my hero and not because my father wasn't around and she had to be both our mother and our father, but because she knew all the right things to say. She knew how to heal and how to make me feel better. I was blessed with the best mom out there, one who loved fiercely and gave wholeheartedly. I don't think I will ever be too old, or there will ever come a time when I don't need her in my life. When the day comes that I have children of my own, I can only hope I'm half the mother to my children she is to me and my brother. One of the best gifts I'll ever be able to give my children is the gift of her as their grandmother.

She sat us on the couch and went to work on drying my eyes. She didn't ask questions or try to figure out why I was upset. She didn't tell me to stop crying but handed me tissues and told me to let it all out. We sat like that for a few minutes, me crying until there were no tears left, and her holding my hand as I sobbed.

"I'm sorry," I whispered, blowing my nose into the tissue before turning toward her.

"Are you ready?" she asked, with love and concern etched in her eyes, the eyes of a worried mom. The eyes of a mother that would always love her children unconditionally. I felt the familiar pang of guilt surface as I realized I should have never doubted my mother in the first place. She would always love me even if she didn't agree with me. She'd always be my biggest fan, my number one supporter.

"I'm ready," I whispered.

"Let's hear it," she said, squeezing my hand reassuringly.

"I don't want to be a nurse and I quit the program months ago," I blurted, blowing out a deep breath. I lifted my eyes back to hers and saw the confusion and shock settle in.

"I don't understand. What do you mean you don't want to be a nurse anymore? What happened?" she questioned.

"I can't do it, mom. It was one thing to memorize a text book and know the ins and outs of the human body, but it was another staring at a body trying to remember every single thing I've learned so I could help that person. It was too much responsibility, and it was too heartbreaking to lose my first patient on my very first day," I explained sadly. "Please don't try to change my mind," I started.

"Hold it, Lauren, right there," she interrupted me. "I would never, *ever*, try to sway you a different way," she declared. "You've made a decision about your life, and I, as your mother, need to respect your decision. It is not up to me to tell you what to do, you're a grown woman, and I made peace with that," she said.

"You're not going to tell me I made a mistake?" I asked.

"No, sweetheart, I'm not. Maybe you did, and maybe you didn't but that is for you to figure out, no one else," she stated, as she leaned forward and pressed her lips to my forehead.

"I'm out of school, forfeited the scholarship. I have been working in a bar until recently, but now I have no job and Mia and I have to move," I confessed, dropping the rest of the bomb and waited for her to explode with fury.

"Wow," she said, exasperated. "How long has this all been going on?"

"Four months," I admitted. "I've been lying to everyone. I tell myself it's because I didn't want to disappoint you but I think it's more that—I'm ashamed more than anything else."

"Lauren, I'm not disappointed in you," she objected.

"But you were so disappointed in Anthony—"

"Because I blamed myself for Anthony's choices," she interrupted "I thought your brother chose Victor's lifestyle because I was failing as a single mom and he figured he needed to step up to the plate. It killed me that your brother gave up on himself at such a young age. He could've been anything, he could've been a goddamn garbage man and I would've been proud of him," she paused, her eyes shimmering with tears. "I am proud of the man your brother became," she amended.

"I wish he would have valued his life more. Wish he hadn't lost three years rotting in a cell. Nobody wants that life for their child, Lauren. One day you'll have children and you'll understand. You will want them to have the best, you will want them to reach for the stars and be everything you never could. You'll watch them grow and you'll wish they were little, still clinging to your leg. You'll want to protect them from the world but you won't be able to. You'll learn to make peace with that too. You won't ever stop worrying about your children and you'll always want to take their pain away. You'll forever want to make their dreams come true and you'll hold their hand when their dream changes," she whispered, glancing down at my hand held tightly by hers.

"So you're not going to be a nurse," she stated, shrugging her shoulders. "Find a new dream to chase, Lauren. And if it seems out of reach, like it might never come your way, dream it anyway."

I let go of my mother's hand and threw my arms around her, holding her tight as I cried tears of relief.

"I love you mom," I whispered against her hair.

"I love you too, sweetheart," she said, squeezing me. "Promise me something," she requested, pulling back to look into my eyes. She smiled at me, brushing away the fallen strands of hair that stuck to my wet face. "Never be afraid to come to me with something. I'll always be here for you—whatever it is, no matter how bad, or how frightening we'll get through it," she said.

Then my mother said the words that would get me through the detour I didn't even know I was on.

"And when you feel like giving up, give more. Always hang on when your heart has had enough, and I promise you, it'll all turn out the way it was supposed to in the end," she vowed.

I didn't know it right then and there but I would learn that my mother's words would be what I held onto during the most trying times.

They'd get me through the detour.

Chapter Twelve
RIGGS

"I'm surprised Jack peeled you off Bianci for this," Bones said as he handed me another piece of wood.

We were working hard in a shed, behind Pop's shooting range for the last two days, building custom wooden crates to transport guns. Sun Wu reached out to Jack a couple of days ago looking for more guns. I don't know what that guy has going on, but he was up to something—probably protecting his ass from some kind of sudden death. He had enough ammo to fight Isis but still he made an agreement with the Knights to buy guns every two weeks, and now he was looking for bigger machines. The crazy motherfucker was in the market for sniper rifles and the crazier motherfucker, Jack, was off on the road, making sure we had them.

"Bianci went up to visit Pastore in the pen," I replied, drilling the screws into the wood, securing the hinge on the top of the crate.

I was thankful for the reprieve. These last couple of weeks have been hell on me. I thought I'd get off on having one up over Anthony, and one would think screwing his sister was a big advantage. However, I didn't feel the high I thought I would, and instead I felt like a big scumbag.

I should've kept my dick in my pants but I was a spoiled brat.

I wanted Lauren, and I always got what I wanted.

And it was everything I knew it would be.

I don't regret it even though I should.

See? Told you. Scumbag.

My only regret is that it wasn't longer, that I didn't take my time.

I should've fucked her with my mouth first, then I'd know how she tastes.

I know what she looks like when she comes and I'll just have to hang on to that.

My pretty Kitten.

I miss her.

I miss talking to her. I miss teasing her and getting her flustered.

I know I'm not the guy for her. I'm never going to settle down. I don't want an old lady. I just want to fuck around. I could do what I do with every other girl— I could fuck Lauren until I had my fill, but then what? Throw her to the side? Fuck another woman in front of her so she gets the point? Break her fucking heart?

It's better this way.

A clean break.

Maybe one day I'll be able to look at her and not want to bang her into next week.

Maybe then we could be friends.

"Who is after Bianci anyway?" Bones asked, as he opened and closed the crate I just finished assembling, testing it to make sure it was in working condition. He stamped "Heavy Automotive Parts" on top of the crate and set it aside to dry.

"Technically, no one, but what do I know about that mob shit. Now that the fuck with the fur coat is running the show I think "Old Man Soprano" is worried that he will clip his son-in-law," I surmised.

"Complicated shit," Bones said.

"Them Italians love to complicate shit," I added.

He smirked.

"What?" I pressed, placing the drill down and reaching into my pocket for my joint.

"I wonder how complicated things would get if Bianci knew you were banging his sister," Bones mused, as he took the joint and lit it.

"Banged," I corrected. "As in one time," I added.

"You're an asshole," he claimed. "You should've kept that piece around, real pretty to look at and feisty enough to make things fun," he added, thoughtfully.

"Don't think about it," I warned.

"Fair game, brother," he reminded me.

"You want my leftovers?" I asked angrily.

He shrugged his shoulders.

"Never bothered you before," he said nonchalantly, passing me the joint. "How was she anyway? She worth the ride?"

"Fuck off," I ground out, taking the joint from him. "She's off the table."

He shook his head.

"Don't work like that, Riggs, and you know it," he stated, kicking off the wall he was leaning against. "She's not your property, anyone can give her a go," he added.

"She's not club pussy," I seethed.

"Pussy is pussy, and if you're done tapping that, there are plenty of men lining up for it," he sneered.

"What're you doing?" I asked, narrowing my eyes at him. "You trying to fuck with me?"

"How many bitches have you fucked since your patch party?"

"You keeping tabs on my dick, Bones?"

"Just pointing out what you're too stupid to see," he countered. "If Lauren lived closer, you'd be all over that shit," he suggested.

"No I wouldn't," I argued. "I got what I wanted from her."

"Then you shouldn't mind if someone else, namely me, takes what I want from her," he continued.

I bit the inside of my cheek, my hands balling into fists at my side as I clenched my jaw.

"I don't give a fuck," I growled. "Are we going to talk about swapping pussy all day or are we going to get these fucking crates done?"

Lucky for me, Lauren lived two hours away. Two hours away from me and my dickhead brother who was itching for a taste of what was mine.

Mine?

Jesus.

After we were finished with the crates we rode back to the compound and met with Jack and Blackie. We were waiting on a call from Pops, to let us know when the guns would be ready to be packed up so we could make the delivery to the Red Dragons. There was tension between the president and vice-president and I surmised it was the stress of the deal—there was a lot riding on this. Wu was paying the Knights seven hundred thousand for this shipment and forking over another two for the next one. However, if any of us were caught by the cops with these weapons we were looking at life in prison.

Life.

That was no fucking joke.

The following day, Jack ordered me to resume my babysitting gig until the call came through from Pops, then all hands were on deck and the Knights had to roll. But for now, I'd watch Anthony teach a bunch of kids how to throw a punch.

I couldn't figure this guy out. The tri-state area feared this bastard for his reputation as Victor's enforcer, yet parents willingly signed their children up to learn from him. Who would've thought an ex-gangbanger would open up his own version of The Boys & Girls Club of America. The world was fucked—in a good way. It was pretty awesome of him to turn his life around and take the initiative to get neighborhood kids off the streets. And it was even more awesome that the people who once feared him, gave "Michael Corleone" a chance to do the right thing.

Only in New York.

Bianci was going off on the bag, doing what he did best, showing these kids there was an alternative to their anger and aggression. Watching him hit the heavy bag put me in a trance, like it did every time, and I didn't hear the bell sound as the door opened.

I felt a hand on my shoulder and I turned to meet Anthony's wife's smiling face. On top of being the neighborhood hero, Bianci scored the hottest wife this side of the Hudson. Adrianna winked at me before turning her attention toward her husband.

"How long has been at it?" she asked, as her smile widened, watching as Anthony held the chains of the leather bag and counted the jabs the little five-year-old was taking.

"About an hour," I replied, turning toward her. "He should be wrapping up any minute," I added, but I wasn't even sure she heard me. She blew Bianci a kiss, and that was my fucking cue to take a breather before I lost my lunch. These two could have you tossing your cookies with all their love bullshit.

I stepped outside the gym, lighting up a cigarette as I rounded the corner. Taking that first drag, I looked up and noticed some teenagers circling my bike.

Fucking, hell no.

"Get away from the bike," a voice shouted from the car parked on the corner.

I knew that car, towed that piece of crap upstate.

Shit.

"Make me," one of the little punks shouted.

The car door opened and my mouth dropped, the cigarette fell, nearly burning my lip off. Lauren stepped out of the car, calmly walking around to the trunk and popping it open. She slammed the trunk down and that's when I saw the baseball bat in her hand.

"I said…get the fuck away from the bike," she hissed, practicing her swing.

"Whoa, damn, girl…" another punk said, his eyes wide as saucers.

Me and my dick agreed with the punk.

Damn girl.

"You heard her," I yelled, walking up behind the kid, my eyes on Lauren as she held the bat over her head and stared at me.

"Sorry! We don't want any trouble," punk number one cried.

"Then I suggest you run because she looks pissed," I growled.

"Yeah, but she's not looking at us anymore, she's looking at you," punk number two pointed out.

Kid had a point; those blue eyes were glaring at me.

"Get out of here," she said, turning her eyes back to the two teens, rearing the bat back to take a swing.

They scampered away from my bike like a bunch of cockroaches, leaving me to deal with a very pissed off Kitten.

She watched as they ran down the block and brought the bat down to her side as she walked back toward the trunk of the car. I thought she'd turn my way that she'd say something but all she did was ignore me.

I pulled my hat from my head and ran my fingers through my hair, deciding on whether I should walk away.

I did it before and it wasn't that hard.

"Thanks for looking out for my bike, Kitten," I blurted.

Decision made.

I walked toward her car, watched as she popped her trunk and dropped the baseball bat inside, before slamming it shut again and snarling at me.

Whoa.

Pissed off Kitten was sexy.

"Don't call me that," she hissed, walking toward the driver's door.

"Don't do that," I objected, sighing as I walked around the front of her car. She pulled open her door and fixed me with a look.

"Get away from me Riggs before I grab the bat again," she warned.

"Kitten," I pleaded.

"I said don't call me that," she shouted, slamming the door closed before turning and closing the distance between us. She pressed her palms flat against my chest and shoved me backward.

"I'm not your fucking Kitten," she hollered. "And you most certainly are no Tiger," she added.

"What's that supposed to mean?" I asked, narrowing my eyes.

"You're a pussy, Riggs," she answered, dropping her hands from my chest. "Tell me something? Do you do that with all the girls you pretend to give a shit about? Fuck them and ignore them?" she shook her head, about to turn around but stopped, glancing over her shoulder at me. "Just tell me one thing…should I be worried?"

"Worried?"

She rolled her eyes.

"I don't go having unprotected sex all that often. Actually, ever. I never do that stuff. I know it's probably an everyday occurrence for you, so what I'm asking you is; are you clean?"

How fucked up was I that I didn't even remember not wearing a rubber? It happened so quick I wasn't thinking of covering myself up, I was just driven by the need to make her mine that night.

Then another thought crossed my mind. While I was off ignoring her, afraid she'd be a clinger, she was worrying I had given her an STD.

I owned the title of scumbag. Look it up in the dictionary, I bet Merriam-Webster had my picture next to the word.

"I'm clean, Lauren. I always wear a rubber," I said, as I stared at her, fighting the urge to touch her. "Always," I emphasized.

"Um, am I interrupting?" Adrianna asked, raising an eyebrow as she stood next to the passenger door of Lauren's car.

Great.

"No, we're done," Lauren declared, turning around and climbing inside the car, slamming the door closed.

I turned around and saw Adrianna still standing next to the car, her hand poised on the handle as she stared at me.

"What?"

"If I find out you hurt Lauren, so help me God I'll make my mother-in-law look like June Cleaver," she threatened, pulling open the door.

"I'm sure you will," I mumbled, stepping onto the sidewalk because I wouldn't put it past Lauren not to run me over.

"There you are," Anthony exclaimed, pointing his keyring toward his truck parked across the street and unlocking it.

Fuck my life.

"Come on, we're taking a ride," he declared.

Double fuck my life. Did he know? I watched Lauren's car peel away from the curb.

Fuck, he definitely knew.

"I'll take my bike," I said.

"Nah, leave it here," he said, crossing his arms against his chest.

"Some punk ass kids were just fucking around by my bike. I'm not leaving it here. Where are we going anyway?"

Please don't say the beach. I don't want to sleep with the fucking fishes.

"The Dog Pound," he said, narrowing his eyes. "You're sweating," he pointed out.

I reached up and swiped my hand across my brow.

Fuck, I was sweating.

At least he wasn't going to whack me.

Not yet anyway.

Chapter Thirteen
RIGGS

I fucked up.

No surprise there.

The only difference this time, was that I felt bad about it. I've walked away from a lot of people in my life and never once looked back. Hell, my own family might as well think I'm dead for all I know. Still, I don't feel any kind of way about that; it doesn't make me feel guilty, just indifferent. But the way Lauren looked at me that bothered me. It was one thing to be angry; I expected that much, but I didn't expect to see the hurt in her eyes.

I didn't want to hurt her. I should've realized she wouldn't just be angry like every other girl I've discarded. She wasn't like any other girl. She wasn't the rule, she was the fucking exception, and I was the asshole who thought rules were meant to be broken—to hell with the consequences. I realized I didn't just break a rule, I broke Lauren's ego, something that was already hanging on by a thread.

"Give us a minute, Riggs," Jack said, pulling me away from my thoughts. I forgot I was sitting around a table with Jack, Blackie and Bianci, waiting for Bianci to spill the reason we were there to begin with.

"Yeah?" I asked, looking confused.

"You okay kid?" he questioned.

Yeah, I'm fine, just grew a conscience.

"Kid's probably got the shits," Anthony surmised, suppressing a grin. "Just found out his favorite woman will be in town for a few weeks," he said, reaching over and squeezing my shoulder.

Then there was that.

We were waiting on Jack when we got here, apparently our Prez has a piece of ass tucked away, thinks it's okay to keep us all waiting on him while he gets his dick sucked. Anyway, I guess Bianci felt the need to pass time with me and told me that mommy dearest was moving back to Brooklyn. I was tempted to ask him if that meant Lauren would be too but he didn't give me the chance, sharing with me he and Adrianna had two houseguests until Maria found another apartment.

So I had two crazy women with the last name Bianci who wanted me dead. Three if you add Adrianna.

"You got yourself a woman?" Blackie asked.

"Fuck no," I protested, pointing my thumb toward Bianci. "This fucks' crazy mother is coming home."

Dread churned in my belly. I needed to get away from this psychotic family before they found out I fucked their princess and they tried to hang me by the balls.

"Think you can put someone else on babysitting duty? Me and "Carmela Soprano" don't exactly see eye to eye."

"The only eye she sees of yours is the black one she gave you," Jack added, laughing as he spoke.

Go on and laugh. It's fucking funny. I'm a clown here to amuse you. Oh, my God! I'm starting to sound like Joe Pesce. I needed out.

Stat.

"Don't stress it too much, kid. She'll be too preoccupied to pay much attention to you," Anthony insisted, glancing down at the table, a small smile worked his mouth.

Yeah, right.

"Adrianna's pregnant," he said.

Of course she is. Christ, they're expanding a family. More people with the last name Bianci. The matriarch was going to be a real basket case now.

"Mama "Leone" is going to be a grandma? Fuck, if I thought she was crazy before, she's going to be all sorts of bonkers now," I muttered, before shaking my head and glancing toward Anthony. "Congrats on the kid," I mumbled, before heading toward the bar.

I was retiring from life.

At least for today.

Yep, that's my plan. Get drunk and get stupid.

Lauren

"So, are we going to talk about it?" Adrianna asked, as we pulled up to the supermarket. We had left Luca with my mother and taken a couple of hours to have pedicures as well as doing some food shopping on the way home. Apparently, when you're married those two things go hand in hand.

I guess you learn something new.

I would never get married anyway. I took a vow of celibacy and decided the new dream I would chase was restoring my hymen.

"No," I said, grabbing the wagon because Anthony gave me strict orders she wasn't allowed to push anything or hold anything that weighed more than a lemon. These two had a long nine months ahead of them.

Lucky for me, I got front row seats to the "she's having my baby show," since my mother and I were staying with them until we found an apartment, or I got my shit together, whichever came first.

I was right about my mother jumping at the chance to be around her grandchildren. After my brother shared his news with us, I told him and Adrianna I was a nursing school drop out with an eviction notice on my door. They insisted we stay with them until we found some place else, some place close to them.

Now, here we are, food shopping with wet toes and Adrianna trying to get the goods on me and Riggs.

"I heard him, you know," she started.

"Forget what you heard," I said, shrugging my shoulders. "I've forgotten," I added.

Because what is one more lie on top of the thousands sitting on my shoulders already?

"I won't tell your brother if that's what you're afraid of," she coaxed.

I thought about her words for a minute. I wasn't holding back the twisted tale of how Kitten and Tiger got it on one night in an alley like a bunch of…well, alley cats. See what I did there? Cute right?

Did I mention I hate my life?

Take the fucking detour, he said.

I did.

It was a dead end.

Focus, Lauren.

I wasn't holding back the alley cat story because I was afraid of my brother finding out. He'd kill Riggs, and as fun as that might be to watch, the only one who would put that dope in the ground was me.

I was becoming very angry lately. Like, I might need help.

"I slept with him, okay?" I blurted.

Psychiatric help too.

She rolled her eyes as she picked out tomatoes.

"I know, I heard the whole "I wear a rubber thing,"" she exasperated.

"Yeah, he's a real catch," I said sarcastically.

Adrianna dropped the bag of tomatoes into the cart and lifted my chin with her finger.

"You fell for him, didn't you?"

"What? No? I may be going through a quarter-life crisis but I'm not that stupid," I said.

"You're not twenty-five," she pointed out.

"I always wanted to be older than I was," I stated and sighed heavily. "Look, I liked him a lot, that's it. I thought he liked me too, but I was wrong. All he wanted was to get laid. Which is fine, because hey, we all need to get laid every once in a while, right? I suppose I should thank him because I'm good now for like a year until the urge strikes again and I do something else incredibly stupid," I said, ignoring the lady picking out a bunch of bananas, staring at me like I just confessed to murdering someone.

I turned my gaze to banana lady and hissed.

You know what she could do with those bananas?

"What are you looking at? I'm having a crisis," I sneered.

Adrianna moved behind me and took the wagon from me, pushing it out of the produce aisle before I told banana lady to split.

Ha!

Banana split.

I burst out laughing.

"Oh, my God," Adrianna whispered, pausing mid-stride.

"What?" I asked, my laughter dying as I bumped into her.

"When did this happen between the two of you?"

"Like a month ago," I said, as I glanced at the fish counter. The smell got to me, making me nauseous, so I pinched my nose and guided Adrianna down a different aisle.

"Wait here, I have to go pick up my pre-natal vitamins," she said.

I shrugged my shoulders and took a seat on an Olive Oil display, waiting for it to cave on top of me because why not? I dropped my head into my hands and waited for my stomach to settle.

By the time Adrianna returned the nausea had passed, and I rose to my feet. She dropped a few more things into the wagon and stared at me.

"I'm fine," I said. "I don't think I ate today," I added, pushing the wagon into a clerk because I wasn't paying attention.

"Watch it!" the guy hissed, rubbing his side.

Actor, I didn't even hit him that hard.

"Well if you weren't taking up the whole aisle I wouldn't have hit you!" I hissed.

"I'm stocking the shelves!" He argued.

"Hormonal and crazy," Adrianna whispered beside me.

"Aww, A, it's okay you're supposed to be, you're pregnant," I said, wrapping my arm around her shoulders, diverting my eyes back to the clerk standing with his hands on his hips.

Road blocker.

"Move," I ordered.

"Yeah, and what's your excuse?" Adrianna asked beside me.

I turned to her in surprise and then let my eyes follow her finger as she pointed to the wagon. I leaned over and looked at the pregnancy test next to the tomatoes.

Oh, my God.

RIGGS

Getting drunk and stupid isn't very fun when you're by yourself. Blackie and Jack took off after the meeting with Bianci, leaving Pipe and Wolf in charge of our gun deal with Sun Wu. The guns were ready to go and tomorrow we were delivering them to "Jackie Chan." I took my tequila upstairs to my room, deciding that I'd watch Rush Hour until I passed out.

I settled onto my bed and grabbed my laptop to free-stream the movie and remembered Sun Wu's apartment. I bet that shit is more entertaining than watching a movie I'd seen a billion times. My fingers worked the keys on the keyboard, bringing up the surveillance footage of the apartment he had me wire.

The Red Dragons' bikes were parked outside the building and they had a man patrolling every corner of the hallway. I sat up, enlarging another screen and spotted Wu in front of the apartment talking to one of the guards.

That's a hell of a lot of man power to secure some dingy apartment. My first guess was that he had his mistress tucked inside trying to keep that pussy hidden from his old lady, but even that was extreme.

For some reason the mic wasn't working and I couldn't hear what they were saying. I fiddled around with the keys trying to retrieve the sound but it was no use. I wondered if someone cut the sound on purpose, but there was no way these guys were smart enough to find my bugs.

Wu opened the door, and I minimized one frame to locate the other frame that had him walking into the apartment.

Bingo!

I maximized it and holy shit! Naked Asians galore.

Seriously.

There was like ten of them.

Wearing nothing but a mask around their mouths.

Sun Wu and two of his Dragons walked to where the naked women were lined up, inspecting whatever it was they were doing.

I clicked on another screen and zoomed into the table that looked to be full of pure heroin. Someone else may have surveyed this shit and said it was drugs but my equipment was no joke top of the range, and my images were clear as day. That shit was in its purest form and these naked chicks were cutting and packaging it.

Sun Wu moved to the end of the table to inspect his product. Taking hold of the packaged heroin he lifted it for inspection. I leaned back as his eyes stared back at me. It was like he knew I was watching him.

Then the fucker smiled.

Right at me.

I was drunk.

There was no way he knew I was watching him. I was just paranoid and stupid.

Drunk, paranoid and stupid.

But this stupid drunk just uncovered The Red Dragons' stash house.

Chapter Fourteen
Lauren

"How long has it been?" I asked my sister-in-law as I sat on the toilet bowl while she stared at the watch on her wrist.

"We can check now," she said, lifting her eyes to mine. "Do you want to look or do you want me to?"

I guess I should put my big girl panties on.

I held out my hand, ignoring the fact that it trembled and waited for her to place the pregnancy test in my palm.

I can't believe this is what I'm doing right now. Talk about a detour. How's that for a fucking detour?

I grabbed the stick hastily, closing my eyes and taking a deep breath.

Please don't let it be...

I didn't even want to say the word because it felt wrong to say.

I opened my eyes, felt Adrianna's hand on my shoulder and opened my palm.

Two pink lines.

"It's wrong," I insisted, shoving the test back at Adrianna. "Give me another, two came in the pack, right? Fork it over," I demanded, as she took the test from my hand and glanced down at it.

I couldn't look at her, stepping around her I pulled the second test out of the bag and dropped my pants. Preparing to pee on another stick...in front of my sister-in-law, because I was fucking pregnant and two seconds away from crying.

"It's very unlikely to get a false positive, Lauren," she whispered. This is because I don't drink enough water. Tomorrow I was drinking a gallon of water and taking every goddamn test I could find.

Because I was pregnant.

Because I didn't want to be.

Because I was not ready for a baby.

Because the father was a dope.

Because my life was upside down.

Because I listened to dopey dad and took the detour.

Fucking Riggs.

Fucking baby daddy.

Oh God.

I picked up my pants and sat on the toilet bowl holding the second test in my hand and reached for the first one.

The two pink lines were still there.

"This can't be happening," I whispered.

Adrianna sat on the edge of the bathtub, taking my hand in hers and squeezed it.

"It will be okay," she reassured.

She was out of her fucking mind. It was NOT going to be okay. Nothing was okay about this. It was easy for her to say, she had her life figured out. She had everything she wanted, the man, the family, the life she dreamed about.

I had two fucking pink lines.

"I need to get out of here," I said, springing to my feet.

"Where are you going?" she asked, concern etched in her features.

"I need to be by myself," I declared, glancing down at the test before shoving it at her. "Do something with this, please."

"Lauren, you're upset you shouldn't drive," she cautioned.

"A, I need this," I stated, pleading with her, my eyes full of unshed tears.

She brought me into her arms and hugged me tight.

"I know it doesn't seem like it but I swear to you it will be okay," she whispered, talking from experience. She had an unplanned pregnancy when she and Anthony were younger but the circumstances were different. Anthony and A were in love, they were together, prepared to take on a family because it was something they wanted in the future. It didn't matter it came earlier than either of them expected, it was welcomed. They lost the baby, a baby that wasn't planned but one that was loved and mourned.

I pulled away from her.

"I'll be okay," I lied, before hurrying out of the bathroom and letting my legs take me as quick as they could out of that house, away from the happy family and the promise of something I would not have.

I got in my car and started it up, and as the engine came to life, the dam broke, and the tears cascaded down my face.

Aside from having a plan for my career I also had my family life mapped out.

I was going to get married, have one of those big fancy weddings and my brother would walk me down the aisle, giving me away to the man of my dreams. After, we would honeymoon in the South of France, we'd come home and go house hunting. We'd buy a fixer-upper and for the first two years of our marriage we'd rip apart every room in the house and remodel it together. Our house would be a Pinterest board, a result of my handy husband and the crafty person I am.

Once the house was perfect, and the dog was trained—a cute little Yorkshire terrier named Trouble, we'd work on our family.

He'd be there when I took the test, he'd be at that very first doctor's appointment and each one after that. He'd record our Pea's heartbeat on his phone and at night we'd listen to the recording in bed. We'd joke about the sex of our little Pea and argue over names. He'd be the doting husband, looking after his pregnant wife, making sure I drank water and ate vegetables. We wouldn't find out the sex of our baby because there were few surprises in life and that should be the best one.

He'd hold my hand as I pushed and when our little Pea took her first breath, we'd look at one another understanding we gave one another life's most precious gift.

We'd have three kids. Two girls, one after another and a year after that our little slugger would be born.

It was a good plan.

A beautiful plan.

One not meant for me to live.

The tears didn't stop, they kept falling, and so I sat in my car and cried. I cried because my plan went up in smoke just like all the rest of my plans did. I cried because I had a baby inside of me, an innocent baby that deserved a good life. I cried because I couldn't provide that life for my Pea.

My Pea.

Not Mine and Riggs.

Not ours.

Mine.

God, I didn't even know if I should tell him. What would I say? Hey you may not have given me an STD, but you put a baby in my belly? How's that for a parting gift?

Riggs wouldn't want a baby.

He didn't even want me.

Reality was harsh, and it was a bitch.

They say it takes two but how come in the end, when the shit hits the fan, there's only one person standing.

This was all on me.

And that sucked.

People have fought for women to have this right, to be granted the power of choice.

But all I wanted was for someone to decide for me, for a higher power to intervene and tell me what to do. Someone to tell me I'd be a good mom, that I might struggle for a while but I could do it. I needed someone to tell me that all a baby needed was love because I had a lot of that to give and could give it in spades.

Or I needed to be told I was doing the right thing by letting go because love only got you so far in this world.

I don't know if I can live the rest of my life knowing I'd ended a pregnancy by choice. I mean there has to be some sort of guilt that comes with that, right? Something that weighs heavily on you, that makes you constantly wonder, what if?

There was life inside of me.

That was something.

Something that maybe I should fight for and not against.

Maybe my Pea was the detour I needed to give me purpose. Maybe I could turn this around, if not for me, for my baby.

I could find a way.

My mother found a way, and she had two children.

I blew out a deep breath, bracing my hands on the steering wheel and glanced down at my flat stomach.

There was a piece of me inside there.

There was a piece of Riggs in there too.

There was life.

RIGGS

Me: #SheCameOutSwinging

I don't know why I texted her. Scratch that, I one hundred percent know the reason and it wasn't because I was drunk. I had slept that shit off and when I woke up I felt as fresh as a daisy. A wilted one, but whatever.
I text her because I wanted to fix what I broke.
I wanted her to stop looking at me like I hurt her.
Yes, I texted her a hashtag. Yes, I thought it was a good idea at the time. Yes, I stand by my decision because it might make her smile and she had a killer smile. I don't think she knows the power of her smile, or that she even has a beautiful one. She does it more often, maybe she'd understand how it affects people.
Like me.
I'm doing what I swore I wouldn't do.
I never rekindle things after I've blown out the flame.
But I'm doing just that because of her smile.
Because it's missing from her face and I might be to blame.

Me: Come on Kitten, talk to me.
Me: I thought we were friends.
That was a stupid move.

Me: #ImAnAsshole

Nothing.
Not even a thumbs up or an emoji.
She gave me a dose of my own medicine and she gave it good.
I chucked my phone across the room and gave up.

You can smell doom, it's the stench of death, lurking at every corner. The Dog Pound was reeking of doom and I wasn't the only one noticing it. We all kept our mouths shut because we had no idea what the fuck was going on. I might be new to the brotherhood but there was some kind of code being obstructed by our president and vice president.
The tension was mounting between Jack and Blackie and with my eyes on Wu, I knew it had nothing to do with the gun deal we had going on. They had something else brewing and whatever it was had Blackie hitting the bottle more than usual.

The man was still grieving his wife who died of an overdose, an overdose supplied on the product he was pushing before Jack became the head honcho of the Knights. Bones thinks Blackie's guilt will be the death of him if he doesn't get a handle on it.

I think he's dead already, just waiting for the reaper to call him home.

I parked my bike next to Blackie's, noticing it was the only one in the lot aside from the few cars. I hung my helmet off one handlebar and strode into the compound.

Bianci was off doing father-to-be crap and luckily for me I wasn't invited to that sort of shit. After the night I text Lauren, I kept my distance and respected she wanted nothing to do with me. Which sucked, because with the afternoon to myself all I wanted to do was take a ride on my bike with her. I don't know what the fuck was wrong with me. I guess it's the game of temptation, wanting what you can't have.

I stopped in my tracks when I heard a sob and turned around to see Jack's daughter running down the stairs. She froze, mascara streaking her pretty face, as she buttoned up her shirt.

Well, now.

"Lacey," I started.

"I was never here," she sniffled, straightening her back as she stared at me.

I raised an eyebrow. Daddy's little girl didn't fall too far from the badass family tree.

"I was never here," she repeated.

"Never saw you," I agreed, biting the inside of my cheek. She waited a moment, assessing me to be sure she had my word, before grabbing her keys off the bar and jetting out of the Dog Pound.

I think it was safe to say she wasn't visiting daddy looking for a handout.

I glanced toward the stairs and decided this afternoon just got a whole lot more interesting.

Who needs Kitten when you got a clubhouse full of demons?

I climbed the stairs, remembering the only bike in the lot was Blackie's and made my way toward his room.

If I had any brains whatsoever, I would've turned the fuck around and minded my own business. But I was bored and stupid. I've been doing a lot of stupid shit lately. I needed to get that shit under control, but not until after I saw why Lacey was running down the stairs crying.

I opened the door to Blackie's room and found him sitting on the foot of the bed with his head in his hands. He slowly lifted his face and the whites of his eyes were so red he looked like he had pink eye.

"Get out," he seethed.

"You the reason Lacey just ran out of here crying?"

"What's it to you?" he said, rising to his feet, stumbling a little as he did so. He was fucked up. No surprise there, but he wasn't drunk. He crossed his arms against his bare chest and that's when I noticed the fresh marks on his forearm.

I took a step closer, getting a better look at the bruises that marked his skin, and lifted my eyes back to his.

"You're using?" I questioned.

He uncrossed his arms and reached behind him for his gun before aiming it at me.

"Get the fuck out of my room, Riggs," he shouted, unlatching the safety.

The reaper was coming, and he was coming soon.

Chapter Fifteen
RIGGS

I wonder if the Psychic Friends Network is hiring. Dionne Warwick was dead, wasn't she? If not, the bitch had to be retired by now and I'm a perfect candidate to take her place.

It didn't take that long for the reaper to show up, ready to claim our souls. In fact, he showed the next day, getting our attention when Blackie's truck was blown to bits. The reaper has a name and his name is Jimmy Fucking Gold.

I knew these gangsters were nothing but trouble but now really isn't the time for "I told you so." Not while our club is on lock down. Not while Jack Parrish was in Bulldog mode, teetering on the edge of insanity.

I knew shit was heavy between Jack and Blackie, and for a hot minute I thought it was because Blackie might be banging Jack's daughter. But, this runs deeper than a little game of "just the tip." When Bianci showed up at the Dog Pound with Grace Pastore in tow it became clear that this was more mobbed up bullshit that found its way to the Satan's Knights doorstep.

It also became clear that Anthony had been working with Jack and Blackie for some time. Clearly, I was doing a bang-up job on keeping tabs on Anthony because I never saw this shit coming. But hey, the motherfucker was still breathing and I should get a gold star for that right?

I lifted my eyes from the beer I was holding as the compound door opened and Wolf pushed his three sons through the door. Pipe followed him with his young, hot piece of ass wife. I think she was one of those mail-order brides that married him for a green card. Gotta love America!

"They come back yet?" Pipe asked.

Blackie had gone to get Jack's daughter—no shocker there and Jack went to pick up his old lady, Reina. Everyone who ever mattered to a Knight would fill these four walls until this crap died down. At least then we could do our jobs and know the people who mattered most were safe.

Me and Bones? We had each other, no one else to rally together and bring here to keep safe.

The door opened again and crazy came barreling through the door.

Fuck my life.

Maria Bianci walked through the door holding the boy. Talk about déjà vu. All she was missing was her nifty little frying pan. I guess frying chicken cutlets wasn't on the menu tonight. Adrianna and Kitten followed, and I moved to make my way toward them but stopped myself. Anthony stepped inside, holding the door open for the next two stragglers. Adrianna's sister, Nikki and her boyfriend, Mike. It was a fucking party at the clubhouse.

For one fleeting second, I looked at the Bianci family and felt a sense of relief. I hadn't realized it, never wanted it, but these crazy sons a bitches had become my heart. I might detest some of them but they were mine to protect until I found what made me tick. Until I found my heart.

And they were here.
Safe and sound.
The whole crazy lot of them.
Plus a few extra.
My eyes locked with Lauren's as I brought the beer to my lips and watched her turn her back to me.
Lovely.
I was too busy staring at Lauren's ass to notice the door open again. At least her ass wasn't mad at me.

Wolf slapped me upside the head, tearing me away from Kitten and reminding me I needed to keep my head. I rose to my feet and followed him as Jack stared back at us, a grim expression on his face and Lacey at his side.

Lacey, not Reina.

"Where's Blackie?" Wolf asked.

"Gold has him and Reina," Jack said.

They were five words, representing a declaration of war. I had heard the rumors, listened to the guys tell stories, of times passed, wars fought and won but I had never been a part of one. I had never been a fighting Knight, but I was ready. Saddle me up motherfucker and put me in the zone.

Maybe it was a good thing I hadn't found my heart like Jack asked because there wasn't anything stopping me from fighting for what was ours.

We moved to the Chapel, Anthony and Mike too, because when you're down a brother and your woman's at the mercy of a crazy fuck, you need all the help you can get. I might give these gangsters a lot of shit but they earned my respect the minute they put themselves in our corner, willing to abide by our code and fight for a brotherhood they weren't even a part of.

Heart.

They had it in shitloads.

And they were still there.

Brothers not by blood but by choice.

The only type of brotherhood that was worth a damn.

"A couple of months ago Pastore asked me to take care of a problem he had. A Fed was sniffing around one of Jimmy Gold's bodies and they wanted me to make the Fed disappear. The Fed was my brother, Danny, and this guy over here…" Jack explained, pointing to Bianci who was leaning against the wall. "…was about to help me save my brother's life but we were too late. Jimmy killed Danny and set his house on fire. Reina, the woman I've been seeing was Danny's girlfriend, and she was in the house with Danny when he let the house go up in flames," he paused, making eye contact with each of us before he sighed and continued.

"I've been planning my revenge for months, figuring it was personal and so no need to bring it to the club. It's not personal anymore. It's not even about Danny anymore. Wolf, Pipe, you two have been around since Cain's days, you guys remember the G-Man, right?"

Pipe nodded.

"Remember going to a lot of funerals at his hand," he said.

"Yeah, well, long story short, Jimmy has been working with him since the days of Val."

Val was Victor's underboss and Mike's old man. He was murdered, and this Gold character took his place. Jack continued his story, informing us that Jimmy was involved in Val's death and every blow the Pastore's had taken over the last few years had been premeditated. Jimmy was working with our nemesis, the G-Man, since Jack took the gavel.

But that was just the tip of the iceberg.

Jack and Blackie cut a deal with Victor to set up Jimmy for all the shit he was responsible for. Val's death, Jack's brother's death, the demise of Victor's organization and the drugs polluting our streets. With Victor in jail and Jimmy running the show, the son of a bitch was going to run drugs through Vic's territory. He needed a supplier, and Jack and Blackie had it set all up, they would be the ones to get him the heroin.

I wondered if Jack knew Blackie was dipping into that shit.

I pushed the thought aside and continued to listen to our president, trying to make sense of this mess and figure a way for us to get through it.

Their plan was to get Jimmy hooked on their product and when he needed more they would tell him only large quantities. Jimmy was in the market for a quarter of a million dollars' worth of H—Jack had promised to deliver. They would set him up with the drugs and Victor Pastore would wait for him on the other side. But somewhere the plan went astray because it wasn't even about the drugs anymore.

We had no fucking idea what he wanted or why he took Blackie and Reina.

We were riding blind.

Victor knew something, tried reaching out to Grace, and that's why she was at the compound but we couldn't get a hold of him either because he got his ass thrown in solitary.

Blind.

"I'm sorry this shit fell on our doorstep. I'm sorry I didn't bring it to the table sooner. You can vote upon my poor judgement but not now, that will have to be done some other time because right now you have a choice to make. I'm going after Jimmy Gold, I will put him in the ground and I will plow through anyone who stands in my fucking way. You're either with me or you're not, but I got a brother to find and a woman to get back, and a cocksucking weasel to bury," Jack said, fire in his eyes, determination in his soul.

"Ay," Pipe said in agreement. "I've got you."

"We're brothers, that shit isn't temporary, it's a bond you take to your fucking grave. Now you may have forgotten that but I haven't and I will not let you forget it ever again. Got your back," Wolf said, pausing for a moment. "Always."

Jack turned to me, raising an eyebrow in question.

This was what I signed up for.

This was what I was born to do.

Ride or Die.

Motherfucker, I'm going to ride.

"I'm in but I want pie when your lady friend is safe and sound," I said, lifting my head to meet Jack's gaze as I brought my right hand over my heart. "And I'm not sharing it either," I warned, my words teased but my actions were my vow.

I've got you brother, and this club is my heart.

Bones sat beside me, slapping my back in agreement.

"Let's bring this fucker to his knees," Bones chimed in.

We sprang into action, doing what men like us did best, and prepared for war. Even, Anthony and Mike gave their share, contributing to our warfare. We were dispersing responsibilities to each man when Jack's phone rang.

Every pair of eyes were on him as we waited for him to clue us in. They say Jack's crazy. They say he's a loose cannon. I had never seen it first hand, not until I saw his eyes flicker and the darkness take over.

Crazy.

"Son of a bitch," he shouted, sliding his phone across the table.

"What'd he say?" Pipe asked.

"Nothing, just that he'll be sending me a video including his demands," he said, diverting his eyes toward me. "Get a wire on that thing and get it done fast," he ordered, before pushing back his chair and storming out of Chapel.

Everyone cleared out of the room and I grabbed the phone.

"Riggs," Bones called from the door.

"Yeah?"

"Whatever happens..." his words trailed off.

"Stay safe," I finished for him. "You too," I added.

He nodded in agreement before taking off with Pipe. I hurried up the stairs to get my equipment and work at tapping Jack's phone. Before I could even get started the message came through on his phone, missing the opportunity to trace it.

Strike one.

Shit.

I ran toward Jack's room and pounded on the door.

"Come in," he called as I opened the door.

"Message came through before I could get a tap," I said, handing him over the phone.

The moment he hit play, the stakes in the game changed. I actually wished I wasn't the only man in the room with him because I had no idea how to reel Jack in, but then again, he wasn't Jack.

Jack died when he played that message.

A more vicious man emerged from the ashes.

Now, he was the Bulldog.

Heaven help us all.

"Bulldog..." I started, mesmerized by the transformation. "Jack, man, come on, don't go there," I said, gripping his shoulders and twisting his body around so we'd be eye to eye. "You can't lose it, not now," I reprimanded.

We needed a leader.

He brushed my hands from his shoulders and shoved me out of the way.

"Get your hands off me," he bellowed, stalking out of the room.

I ran after him, fucking man was pushing forty but he was a goddamn machine. I needed to lay off the cigarettes…and the pot.

"Stop him!" I shouted, running down the stairs behind him. "Pipe! Wolf!"

"Get out of my way," he demanded, as they barricaded the staircase.

Thank Christ.

"Jimmy sent the video," I explained in a huff, trying to catch my fucking breath as I handed the phone to Pipe. Bianci switched places with Pipe, blocking Jack from making a move so Pipe could watch the video. The second Jimmy's voice sounded, Jack lurched for the phone and I grabbed the back of his cut as Bianci leaned his weight on Jack and we held him back.

How's that for teamwork?

"Jesus Christ," Pipe said, as Jimmy's voice sounded over the phone stating his demands and threats, a quarter of a million dollars in heroin or they die.

Ever see a bunch of bikers go into panic mode? Shit, ain't pretty.

Thankfully, Pipe was able to hold his shit together and forced us to pull our heads out of our asses and drag them into the Chapel.

"We have twenty-four hours to give him what he wants," Pipe informed everyone.

"We can't get the drugs," Jack hissed.

"I don't follow, you just told us that was the plan from the beginning. You were going to supply him with the drugs and set him up. What's the fucking problem?"

And there went Pipe, cracking at the seams. He was doing such a good job at holding it together…until this.

"The problem is that Blackie had the connection to the drugs with a club up north. He's been controlling the deal with them. There isn't enough time to go on a run, and even if there was, what are we supposed to carry the product in, our saddlebags?" Jack retorted.

There was no time.

No time and no drugs.

We were fucked.

Then I remembered my extracurricular activities and uncovering the Red Dragons' stash house. Those naked bitches were cutting mounds of heroin. There was an easy three mill in product over there, if not more.

The fucking place was wired with surveillance.

Thanks to me.

Good job, Riggs.

I could probably cut the feed but that would take time and with all this back and forth at the table it seemed like we were stretching these twenty-four hours thin. We still needed to grab the dealers and get Jimmy away from wherever he was keeping Blackie and Reina. And then, there were the guns. The plan was go to Pops and dip into the shipment we were preparing for Wu.

Poor guy, had no idea how hard we were going to fuck him up the ass.

"That leaves the drugs," Wolf said, and the room grew quiet again.

"I know where we can get the drugs," I said, breaking the silence and locking eyes with my president. "But if we do this, we might as well sign our own death certificates," I added, shoving the dildo up the Red Dragons' ass with my words.

How's that feel Wu?

"I'd rather sign my own death certificate than either of theirs," Jack replied.

The words signed to the doctrine, contracting us to fucking kill the truce with the Red Dragons.

A creed of bloodshed.

A creed signed by yours truly.

Love, Riggs.

Chapter Sixteen
Lauren

"Here, have a shot," Nikki offered, taking a seat next to me and placing a shot glass in front of me. She's been drinking and smoking since we arrived at the Dog Pound, taking the fact that we were on lockdown, in stride.

I want to be her when I grow up.

"A couple of these bad boys and I promise you'll be rapping like Biggie Smalls', "It was all a dream,"" she winked at me, filling the shot glass.

"She's not drinking," Adrianna said, shoving back the glass her sister put in front of me. "She took a vow to stay sober with me," my sister-in-law added.

"She's a better sister than me," Nikki replied, taking back the shot and downing the both of them.

"Yeah, she's a keeper," Adrianna said.

I mouthed a "thank you" to Adrianna, and she winked back at me. I don't know what I would've done without her the last two weeks. Since I found out I was pregnant she has been lending me her shoulder, and in true Adrianna form, she's making me realize I only have one choice.

I want my baby.

She's restored my faith in myself.

I am going to turn this around.

Because I can.

Because I want to.

Because I'm going to be a mother now and this heart of mine beats for two.

Now, if I could just find the guts to tell Riggs.

I've decided I will give him the benefit of the doubt even though he doesn't deserve it. I will let him know I'm having this child with or without him and he can either step up or step down—either way, I've got this.

My mother sighed as she scrubbed down the wooden bar, throwing the rag down in disgust and turning to Grace.

"What do we do?" she asked, causing Grace to raise an eyebrow in response. "Do we just sit here and wait for them to come back? This is all you sister, my husband walked out and never returned but you, you're the only one experienced in this kind of situation," she explained.

"Victor wasn't a biker, I have no idea what they do or what we're supposed to do," she replied.

"You used to cook a lot," Adrianna reminded her.

"Yes, they should have a meal waiting for them," Grace agreed.

"We're going to cook for these scoundrels?" Maria huffed and Lacey fixed her with a look.

"Those scoundrels are my family," she warned.

"What about the girl, and what's his name…" Grace started.

"Blackie," Lacey supplied.

"God only knows the last time they ate. We should cook for them," Grace offered.

"Fine, but try to find something in that refrigerator that isn't expired," Maria countered.

"Make a list of what you need and we'll send a prospect to the supermarket," Lacey said, looking between the two matriarchs. They may have had two decades on her but it was clear Lacey was the lady of the clubhouse.

The mention of food had my stomach turning, and I excused myself hurrying my ass to the bathroom before I emptied the contents of my stomach on top of the bar my mother had spent two hours scrubbing down.

I don't know how long I stayed in the bathroom, with my head in the toilet but by the time I was finished all I wanted to do was sleep. Another joy of pregnancy, when I wasn't throwing up, I was sleeping. I'll spare you the horrific truth of how a woman's breasts react to pregnancy.

I threw my hair up in a ponytail and stared at my pale complexion in the mirror. I tried splashing water on my face to hide the fact I looked like I was dying. I'd have to ask Nikki to do something with me because I was a mess.

I made my way out of the bathroom and Adrianna immediately walked up beside me.

"Are you okay?" She whispered.

"I'm fine...but why do they call it morning sickness if it happens all damn day?" I asked through clenched teeth while meeting her worried gaze.

I took in my surroundings and noticed the sternos that lined the bar and the tablecloth draped over the pool table.

"Jesus, what are they doing?"

"Please," Adrianna cringed. "Just go along with it."

I looked around the clubhouse, noting the prospects that guarded the door with their rifles strapped to their backs and Wolf's three boys who seemed unfazed by it all. I wondered if our situation was different, if me and Riggs were an actual couple, would this be our life. Reina was Jack's girlfriend, old lady, whatever you call it and Jimmy had taken her. What would stop someone from taking me?

Then there was Lacey who had declared these men her family. It was clear she feared for their safety and not just her father's but all of these men. I don't know if I could live like that. I glanced over at Grace who carried a tray of antipasto to the pool table and couldn't picture being that woman.

I turned to Adrianna.

"How did you do it for all those years?"

"How'd I do what?" she asked.

"Stand by while he risked his life doing God knows what?"

"It's not easy, Lauren," she said, wrapping her arm around my shoulders, dragging me against her side. "But these men, whether they are in the mob or this motorcycle club, were just little boys once. I might be the wrong person to ask, but as a mother of a little boy, if my son lost his way, and found purpose on the other side of the law, I'd still hope there was someone who loved him despite his flaws, despite his bad choices," she explained, pausing for a second as she looked around the clubhouse. "They're not bad men," she concurred. "Just good guys who lost their way and sometimes do bad things to protect their interests and the people they love. They're flawed and some of them are scarred but they have loyalty. I dare you to find one of them that doesn't look out for what is his. They have respect and honor, something half the law-abiding men in this world don't know the first thing about," she added.

"What're you talking about?" Nikki asked, as she joined us.

"Loving a bad boy," Adrianna said with a laugh.

"Isn't it fun?" Nikki asked with a mischievous smile on her face.

Yeah, loads.

They returned to the clubhouse an hour later but aside from Jack who took a few minutes to talk to his daughter, the rest of them were off doing whatever it was badass bikers do when on a mission.

"Lauren? Are you still finding yourself?" My mother asked as she took a sip of…was that whiskey?

"Uh, yeah, mom. It's kind of a process," I said.

She nodded.

"Do your mom a favor and don't join the ranks of Griselda Blanca. One career criminal in the family is enough," she said, throwing back the rest of her drink.

"Maria, the manicotti is done," Grace called.

"I'm coming," she shouted over her shoulder before mumbling under her breath. "Cooking Christmas dinner for a bunch of criminals wasn't how I saw this day going."

My mother was drunk.

This should be fun.

The door opened, the one some of the men had disappeared behind, and Riggs emerged strapping on a bullet-proof vest.

"Goddamn!" Nikki hissed. "I'm making Mikey buy a motorcycle."

Two weeks ago I would have had the same reaction but now, after knowing I was having his baby, all I felt was a huge lump in my throat.

What if he doesn't make it back?

He'll never know…

My feet made my decision as they walked straight toward him.

"Ink's dry, brother," Riggs told Jack, handing him a vest. "We gotta move," he added.

It's now or possibly never.

"Riggs, can I talk to you?" I asked, stepping in front of him.

"Can it wait?" he snapped, his eyes cold and uninviting, a side of him I had never seen before. "Don't really have much time to fight with you people on whether it's called sauce or gravy and I'm not in the mood to argue about my life choices, the ones you mob folk seem to love to criticize. So, no Lauren, not now," he said, fitting his helmet to his head and turning toward Jack. "I'll be outside," he stated, before walking out the door.

I didn't find my voice until the engines roared to life outside.

"No problem, just wanted to tell you to be careful because you're going to be a father," I said to no one.

"What did you say?"

Shit.

"Lauren?"

I slowly turned around and through my tears I stared into my mother's shocked eyes.

"I'm pregnant," I whispered.

RIGGS

Keep moving.

It was what we kept telling ourselves as we raced against the clock to get Reina and Blackie back. There was no time to think, when one of your own is at risk, you don't think anyway, you just act. We were high on adrenaline and the promise we would destroy Jimmy Gold.

It was our job.

It was our purpose.

Motherfucker, was going down.

The Satan's Knights would crucify that bitch.

We parked our bikes behind an Italian restaurant on Mulberry Street, strapped our guns to our bodies, ski masks firmly in place, not giving a fuck we were walking the streets of Manhattan with rifles hanging off our shoulders.

We needed to keep moving.

And that's what we did, moving our asses to Mott Street, like the pack of badass criminals we were. There was no trace of the men we were on a daily basis, the group of guys content on smoking weed and joking around in the Chapel.

We were unleashed.

Animals released from their confinements, free to stalk and capture their prey.

We rounded the corner, snapped ourselves into assailant mode, grabbed the guns that were draped over our shoulders and cocked them.

Locked and loaded, time to make our move.

The cut was easy to spot as the Dragon patrolling the front door to the apartment flicked his cigarette and turned around.

His eyes focused on the guns pointing his way.

He opened his mouth but the words never made it passed his lips.

Bang! Bang! Bang!

Jack popped bullets through his throat.

See ya!

He dropped to the floor, and we ran through the front door. The cocksucker would bleed out before we were finished.

Keep moving.

There was another Asian brother guarding the hallway. Poor bastard didn't have a chance to reach for his gun because Pipe put a bullet in his head. His body didn't even have time to hit the ground before we charged up the stairs. Bones blew the head off the one at the door, his brains splattered across the walls decorating the white paint in red.

We painted their walls with their own blood. Lucky for them red was their signature color.

Another one bites the dust.

I kicked open the door, and the mayhem continued. The naked women cutting the heroin screamed trying to take cover, and the two Dragons inside the apartment began to shoot.

"Go, I've got this," shouted Wolf as he crossed his arms, a gun in each hand shooting at anything and everything, no regard for life.

Keep moving.

"Get down on your knees," Jack hollered to the drug bitches. "NOW!"

I grabbed one broad looking to make a run for it, threw that bitch in a head lock and pressed the barrel of my gun into her head.

I don't play bitch.

"Pack the motherfucking drugs in the bags," I hissed against her ear.

She whimpered and I pressed the gun deeper against her flesh.

"NOW," I shouted.

Wolf took a break from shooting shit and helped us shove the kilos into a duffel bag. That man was a monster with a gun, a goddamn killing machine.

"Close your fucking eyes or I'll blow your fucking head off," Jack hollered to one girl crying under the table.

We handed the stuffed bags to Bones who zipped them and dropped them into the hallway.

I glanced at my watch.

Ten minutes.

Exactly how long we took to kill eight people, grab all their fucking heroin and sign over our lives to Sun Wu.

"We gotta get the fuck out of here," Bones shouted, grabbing a bag and heading for the stairs. I followed Jack and Pipe, tucking my gun away and grabbing two of the bags. We were half way out the door but Wolf was still upstairs playing God with the cutters.

"Wolf!" Jack called.

Strike Two.

Bang! Bang! Bang!

"Keep moving!" Pipe yelled.

"Not without Wolf," Jack shouted back.

Wolf emerged from the top of the stairs, his face splattered with blood.

"Let's go," he ordered, bounding down the stairs.

"You killed them?" I asked him, pulling my mask off to stare at Wolf in shock.

Strike Three.

"No, I played fucking Chinese checkers with them," he hissed, throwing the strap of one bag over his shoulder. I watched as he swiped his sleeve across his cheek, removing the drops of blood that painted his face.

We painted their walls and now our hands with the Dragons' blood.

Three strikes.

Three mistakes.

But no time to dwell.

Keep moving.

We ran as fast as we could, away from the faint sounds of motorcycles and sirens, away from the Red Dragons' territory and into Vic's old stomping grounds. We loaded up the cage with the bags and Bones jumped into the back as the prospect took off and headed back to the clubhouse. The rest of us took to our bikes and peeled the fuck away from the war we had just created.

There was barely any time to unload the cage when the call came through that Bianci had set up a meet with Jimmy through some drug lord. I didn't ask for details because anything that had to do with Bianci was like six degrees of separation. It was never an easy explanation with him. But that motherfucker always came through for our club.

We had an hour to do something with these fucking drugs before we hauled ass to Pier 33 to read Jimmy his last rights.

"What the fuck are we going to do with all these drugs?" Pipe asked, holding up the two suitcases.

"Oh we're taking them with us," Jack declared.

We all exchanged curious glances but none of us would question anything at this point. What was the use?

This was Jack's show now.

The Bulldog showed his teeth.

The Knights were gunning for blood.

It would all be over soon.

Keep moving.

At the pier we spread out, taking cover behind shipping containers and waited for Jimmy Gold. Bianci had set up the crazy mobster by luring him to the docks to meet with a drug dealer. Some guy named, Sanchez. It was easy to spot him; Anthony and Mike had worked that fucker for hours. He was a bloody mess with a laser bullseye between his eyes. My eyes followed the laser beam across the docks to where Anthony and Mike stood with their guns cocked and ready.

The sun was rising.

Time was almost up.

I turned around, spitting the toothpick I was rolling around between my teeth onto the floor. I reached for my gun as the fog lights of Jimmy's signature Escalade rolled into the shipping yard.

"We've got company, boss," I alerted Jack.

He stared at the headlights, watching as they closed in before turning around.

"Stand down," he ordered.

"What?"

"Jimmy is mine," he clarified. "But he won't be alone, you take care of whoever he's with," he said.

"I got you," I said, ripping back the safety as the truck rolled to a stop. The driver opened his door, and I moved to pop him, but Jack grabbed my cut.

"Do not make a move until I give you the word," he whispered, eyes glued to the Escalade.

"What word would that be?" I asked, wondering when we decided to use code before we started killing fuckers. If Jack started barking like a fucking dog, I was hanging up my cut. Two men flocked to Jimmy's side, and they started for Sanchez.

"Fuck it, just go," Jack said, releasing his grip on my cut.

"Thanks," I muttered, walking out from behind the crate. I eyed Bones across the yard and he nodded, stepping out from behind the container he was hiding behind.

Two shots.

One from my gun.

One from Bones.

Jimmy's men dropped and as the sick fuck looked at his men, Jack's fist wrapped around the gold chains on his neck and yanked him back.

See ya, motherfucker!

We kept moving.

Never stopping.

Not until we had Blackie and Reina.

I would be living off of cherry fucking pie when this shit was over.

We rode our bikes to Vic's club, Temptations, the fucking place where all this shit started, the same place it would all end.

Mike pulled Jimmy from the cage, spitting in the sorry fuck's face as Bianci unlocked the boarded up club and threw him inside.

"He's all yours," Anthony said, holding the door open for Jack.

A duffel bag on each arm, Jack glanced around at all of us before following Jimmy inside of the club.

"See you on the other side," he said, disappearing into the club as Anthony shut the door.

We waited outside while Jack got his revenge on that son of a bitch and prayed he wouldn't kill him before he got the location of where Blackie and Reina were. Jack took his time, making Jimmy pay for all his sins, and that bastard had many.

Slow torture.

It was the best kind.

The only kind.

Finally he emerged from the club, wiping the blood from his glove covered hands on Jimmy's beloved fur coat.

"I got the location. Give it a minute or two. When he screams put the fire out and leave the drugs next to his body. Then call Jones, he and his partner are waiting on word to make the arrest," he said, making his plan clear. He was setting Jimmy up to take the fall with the Red Dragons.

Smart move.

If only it worked.

"Tell Vic, a deal is a deal and when I give my word, I don't go against it," Jack added.

Ah, so "Tony Soprano" would be the one to deliver this fuck his fate.

Props.

"Riggs, gonna need a hand," he added, splaying the blood covered coat on the curb like the piece of trash it was and climbed onto his bike.

"I got you," I replied, as Jimmy's screams echoed off the walls of the abandoned night club.

Keep moving.

It's almost over.

Chapter Seventeen
RIGGS

The longest twenty-four hours of my fucking life but I was still going, still breathing, still fighting because I was a goddamn Knight and it was my duty.

I brushed my shoulders off and kept moving.

We arrived at the location and the shit was real bad, worse than I ever imagined. Jimmy had been shooting Blackie up with heroin, making him re-enact his wife's death. Sick fuck. I hope Jack gave him everything he deserved.

Reina was gagged and bound to a chair and the both of them looked like they were knocking on death's door.

I ran to Blackie who lay lifeless on the concrete floor while Jack ran to Reina. She'd survive but our vice president barely had a pulse.

"He's not breathing. What do I do?" I hollered over my shoulder at Jack who had untied Reina.

"Catch," he ordered.

I dropped Blackie's wrist and held my hands out to catch the vile and syringe he threw me.

"What the fuck is this?" I asked frantically.

"Naloxone, you need to inject it into his muscle and administer CPR," he explained, grabbing his phone. "Riggs, do it! He's going to die," he bellowed.

I took a deep breath, unpacking the new syringe and popping the top off the glass vile of the Naloxone.

"I need an ambulance," he barked into the phone before looking back at me. "Fill it to 1 CC," he instructed.

I did as he told me, filling the syringe and ripped the shirt from his bicep. I felt around for the hardest piece of muscle, and without hesitation slammed the needle into his flesh and released the Naloxone.

I pulled the empty syringe from his arm and looked back at Jack.

"Now what?"

"Breathe for him," he yelled.

It's funny how you don't think you're paying attention to things, like the CPR lesson I took ten years ago, but I guess some shit just sticks with you.

"Ambulance will be here soon. Just keep doing it," he said, glancing at his watch. "After two minutes he'll need another injection."

He dropped Reina's hand and moved toward us, falling to his knees on the other side of Blackie and re-filled the syringe.

"Stay with me, brother," he pleaded. "I need you breathing," he added.

I continued to breathe air into him until Jack pushed me off, so he could give him the second injection.

"Is this shit going to work?" I asked, before he pulled the syringe from him again and I went back to breathing life into Blackie.

Don't fucking die.

The paramedics arrived and pulled me off Blackie. They shouted things to one another, working vigorously to save his life, administering cardiopulmonary resuscitation. Jack informed them of the Naloxone we gave him and asked why it wasn't working.

Because he was already in cardiac arrest.

They rushed him to the hospital, and I followed the ambulance with my bike so Jack wouldn't have to leave Reina's side. They rushed Blackie into the emergency room and forced me to wait in the waiting room with all the other helpless souls.

I had gone from taking life with my own hands to standing by as one was taken from me.

Standing by, helplessly as I depended on doctors to take care of my brother reminded me of Lauren and her decision to quit nursing school. I was just a biker, nobody's hero, but the men and women in there trying to reverse the damage caused by Jimmy's hand—those people were heroes.

Kitten.

I dropped into a chair in the waiting room and waited for my brothers to arrive. Jack was the first one flying through the door with his banged up pie goddess tucked tight against his side. He urged her to get checked out too and disappeared into triage with her. I don't think he will let her out of his sight for a long time coming.

I didn't blame him.

Not one bit.

Again, I thought about Kitten and the rejection that took over her features when I blew her off.

I think it's safe to say she wouldn't be down to cuddle.

Sometimes a man just needed to cuddle.

Especially after the hell I've lived.

The rest of the club showed up as another ambulance and a cop car pulled up. Jimmy was burned badly, his body covered with a sheet as they wheeled him into the ER with the blue and whites glued to his side.

That motherfucker was going to rot in prison.

But first he'd rot on a gurney with his insides exposed because his skin was melted off.

Prick.

Hours passed before we heard word from the doctors. Blackie suffered a heart attack from all the drugs and he was in critical condition. The next twenty-four hours would be critical for him. They already had to give him another dose of Naloxone and he was in a coma. It was all a blur. I don't really remember if he was in the coma because of the drugs or if they had medically induced it, but he was out for the count. His body had been tried and tested and still he hung on a by a thread.

Blackie was a bull.

Jack ordered us all to leave, to go back to the compound and recharge our batteries before we took a chance a piece staying with our vice president. He kept a prospect with him until he himself could get back there after he got his woman situated and made good on a promise he made to his daughter.

By the time we pulled into the compound it was approaching dusk, making it way over the twenty-four-hour mark and pushing close to forty.

I was going to sleep for a fucking week.

At least that was my plan, but I was learning the hard way, plans changed.

By the hard way, I meant Maria Bianci charging at me, wielding a pool stick the minute I stepped foot through the door.

"You son of a bitch!" She shouted.

"What the fuck did you do?" Bones asked from behind me.

"Beats the fuck out of me," I hissed, reaching for my gun, because so help me God I was not in the mood for this woman.

"Ma," shouted Anthony and Lauren in unison.

Anthony was quick on his feet, wrapping his arms around his mother and holding her back before she could crack me with the stick.

"What the hell is your problem?" he shouted at her.

"Let me go! This son of a bitch took advantage of your sister!"

"Oh you have got to be shitting me," I shouted.

"What do you mean he took advantage of Lauren?"

"Lauren's right here you know!" Kitten argued. "And he didn't take advantage of me!"

"Oh no? Tell that to the baby you're carrying when he asks where his dad is," Maria shouted back.

Wait.

What?

"MOM," Lauren screamed, throwing her hands up in the air frustrated as she turned around and her eyes found mine.

"Shit. Duck!" Bones warned.

Anthony released his hold on crazy, pushing her to the side as he reared his fist back and punched me square in the jaw.

"You son of a bitch," he growled, flexing his fingers, debating if he should ball them into a fist and give me another shot to the jaw.

"I told you to duck," Bones shouted, moving around me to stand between me and Anthony.

"Anthony," Lauren screeched, stepping in front of me.

He must've clipped my lip too because it was bleeding.

"Move," I hissed.

"No," she challenged, as she glared at her brother. "This isn't any of your business. I don't need you punching him in the face and I don't need you..." she pointed to her mother, "...spreading my business around for the whole world to know!"

"I fucking warned you, Lauren!" Anthony ground out before turning his eyes back to mine.

"And I told you to stay the fuck away from her!" He added.

I blew out a ragged breath, losing my patience and ten seconds away from pummeling both Maria and Anthony.

I hadn't even had a chance to process what the fuck was going on.

And wasting time with these two clowns was pissing me off.

"You're in my fucking house now," I said, diverting my eyes between Maria and Anthony.

"My fucking rules. Now both of you sit the fuck down and let me handle my shit!"

My shit.

My shit being Lauren was knocked up.

"Oh, this I've got to see," Maria snarled.

"Shut up," Kitten and I yelled, causing us to look at one another. Her big blue eyes stared at me and shit, they were full of tears.

Now what?

I had no fucking clue.

"Shit, Riggs. You got a bun in the oven?" Wolf asked.

"She got your kid, she got you for eighteen years," Pipe added.

"Kanye West, Pipe? Really we're going to rap now?" Bones questioned.

"Fuck off," I growled, grabbing Lauren's hand. "Upstairs, now," I seethed.

She snatched her hand free, crossed her arms over her chest and stalked toward the stairs.

Like she had a right to be mad.

Like she was the one who just robbed a quarter of a million dollars' worth of drugs from a bunch of crazy Chinese people.

Like she had to breathe for her brother to save his life.

Like she walked a mile in my fucking shoes.

Like she came home with blood on her hands to be told, "Hey so there's this baby that exists and its half yours."

What the fuck?

Me a dad?

Get the hell out of here.

I followed her into my room and closed the door behind us. I placed my hands on my hips, standing as still as a statue, trying to figure the right thing to say.

This fucking blows, didn't seem fitting.

And I didn't want to upset her any more than she already was because…she was fucking pregnant.

Jesus.

"The veins in your forehead are bulging a bit," she said observantly. "I'm sorry, that wasn't how I planned for you to find out. I tried telling you before you left but…well you were there, you know how you stormed out of here," she added bitterly, and taking a seat on the foot of my bed.

"I had a momentary lapse of weakness and thought before you went out guns blazing like a cowboy you should know that you've got a kid on the way," she started, biting the inside of her cheek before she continued to ramble on. "I don't mean that having a kid should stop you from being who you are but, well, fuck! I don't even know what I mean anymore," she dropped her head into her hands.

I stared at her speechless, not realizing at first that I was pacing my small room. She dropped her hands and lifted her eyes to mine.

"I don't expect anything from you," she whispered.

I walked toward her and pressed my index finger to her mouth, silencing her. I felt more out of control in that single moment than I had in the last two days. Her eyes widened as I took a retreating step backward and she opened her mouth to say something else but I shot her down with a curt shake of my head.

Silence.

It was golden.

Especially when you were having a mental breakdown of sorts.

I peeled the bulletproof vest off and dropped it to the floor, kicking off my boots and disarming myself. I made sure the safety was on because clearly I was an advocate of safety.

What a fucking joke.

How's that for impending fatherhood?

I sighed, taking a seat next to Lauren and stared at the wall.

"How long have you known?" I asked, robotically.

"About two weeks," she replied.

I'm sure there was a protocol for this shit, like a list of questions I should've asked but the ones that came to me, sounded foul even inside my head. I wasn't going to ask her if she was sure the kid was mine. I may not know her very well but I knew her well enough to know what we had, that one night, was nothing but a detour.

Me and my big fucking mouth.

"I'm guessing you want to keep it," I said, grabbing my knees as I turned my head to face her.

She looked exhausted, drained, but still so fucking pretty.

She bit her lip and nodded.

"I'm keeping our baby," she insisted.

Our baby.

Wow.

That would take a whole lot of getting used to.

"Riggs," she started and again I lifted my finger to her lips.

"We'll figure it out, but I gotta tell you, Kitten. My brain ain't worth shit right now. I'm exhausted and honestly I'm not a hundred percent sure I've processed any of this."

"I understand," she said against my finger.

"You can't do it, can you?" I said, smiling half-heartedly.

"Can't do what?"

"Be quiet," I said, winking at her.

"Sorry," she whispered, breaking eye contact by turning her head.

I leaned over, cupped her chin and forced her to look at me.

"Can we figure it out tomorrow?"

"Yeah," she muttered.

"Kitten," I said hoarsely.

"Please don't call me that," she whispered, turning away again so I wouldn't see the tears in her eyes.

"You should probably get used to it if we're going to do this parenting thing. You will always be my Kitten," I said, taking her hand and tugging her against me. "Lay down with me?"

She lifted her head from my chest and looked up at me, blinking—her eyes full of unshed tears. Neither of us said another word as I pulled her onto the bed and wrapped my arms around her.

I closed my eyes, listened as she sniffled against my chest, and because I was a selfish fuck, I cuddled my baby mama.

Talk about a mind-fuck.

Chapter Eighteen
Lauren

Here we go again.

I removed Riggs' arms from me and hurried out of bed, making a beeline for the bathroom. Routinely, I dropped to my knees and pulled my hair back bowing my head surrendering to the nausea. I'm not sure how long this vomiting business can go on. At some point doesn't the baby need for me to sustain food to grow?

After the initial shock wore off, and I told the women I was pregnant, they tried to make me feel better and told me I was glowing.

I was most definitely not glowing.

But hey, thanks for trying guys.

I don't know what made me blurt the truth to my mother. I'm going to blame all my craziness on the hormones and pray that after I give birth they find some sort of chemical imbalance so I can continue the charade.

To say my mother went ballistic would put things mildly. Very mildly. She lost her shit, and rightfully so; I suppose. She hates Riggs.

But she didn't have to do what she did.

It wasn't her place to tell him.

Yet, as pissed as I am, I'd be lying if I didn't say I was relieved too.

I decided there was no right way to tell a man you slept with once, who blew you off and crippled your self-esteem, that you were having his child.

Now everything was out in the open and he had a choice to make.

I prepared myself for the blow, knowing very well he doesn't want a kid but he didn't outright say that.

Not yet anyway.

He didn't say much of anything.

I wonder if he even remembers. Oh, God, please let him remember. I don't think I could go through that again.

He knocked on the door as I flushed the toilet.

"I'll be right out," I called, making my way to the sink and rinsing my face. The cold water instantly made me feel better, but still, I wished I had a toothbrush. I grabbed the bottle of mouthwash he kept on the ledge of the sink and gurgled until the foul taste left my mouth.

I opened the door and spotted Riggs sitting on the foot of the bed, yawning as he ran his fingers through his hair.

"Hi," I said, leaning against the frame of the door, not really sure where we go from here.

"You okay?" he asked, tipping his head toward the bathroom.

"Yeah, I'm fine. I've gotten used to it," I replied, watching his face for some sort of reaction, not even sure what it was I was expecting.

He nodded, his eyes dipping down to my stomach momentarily before looking away.

This was going awesome!

"I should go," I stammered, pushing off the frame of the door.

"Go where?"

"Home, my brother's house. I'm assuming this whole lockdown thing is over with, right? I'm a free bird so I'll just fly away and get out of your hair," I rambled.

"Stop it, Lauren," he said, causing me to look at him.

"You're pregnant for Christ sake and you didn't get that way by yourself," he hissed, lifting his eyes to mine. "C'mere," he ordered, patting the empty space on the bed beside him.

I licked my lips and reluctantly walked toward him, sitting down next to him.

"You've had a helluva lot more time to digest this whole thing, so I'm assuming you being you, you have a plan?" he asked, reaching behind him and leaning over the bed to grab my glasses from the night stand. He sat up straight and pushed the glasses onto my nose. "Better," he said. "Now go on, tell me, what's the plan, Kitten?"

I felt stupid because he was right, I should've had a plan. But since every plan I make seems to go up in smoke, I decided to be reckless and just take it day by day. I say reckless because taking it day by day shouldn't be an option when you're responsible for another life.

"I don't have a plan, Riggs," I mumbled.

"Okay, no plan, then," he said, running his fingers through his hair which I decided was something he did when he was nervous. "You moved back here, right?"

"Yes, I'm staying with Anthony and Adrianna until my mother finds an apartment for us," I frowned. "That's temporary. I'm not planning on raising the baby with my mother," I added.

"You just said you don't have a plan," he pointed out.

"Well that much I know," I snapped. "I will not dump this on my mother's shoulders. She raised her kids and did it by herself. She did her time," I said defensively.

"Kitten, calm down," he said. "I don't want your mother raising the kid either," he declared. "And I don't want you not knowing where you will live. I have an apartment, it's got two bedrooms and not a stitch of furniture in it but we'll change that."

I leaned back and stared as if someone was performing an exorcism on him.

"Are you feeling okay?" I asked, because the Riggs I know wouldn't be instilling hope in a pretty hopeless situation. Yet, in his own way that's exactly what he was doing. Neither of us had a clue where we went from here, but he was taking the initiative and that was more than I ever imagined he'd do.

"I'm not even sure why I have the apartment, I sleep here every night, but it's there, and it's yours," he paused. "Lauren, I'm not going to lie to you, I have no idea how to be a dad and up until last night I never even thought about becoming one. But this kid, he's got other plans for me. So I'll try. I'll give you the best I got and hope it's enough," he promised. "And whatever it is you need, you tell me and I'll make sure you have it," he added.

I stared at him for a moment, unsure how to feel, desperately wanting to believe in him, to believe that Kitten and Tiger could do this. We weren't going to become some instant family and I could kiss my dreams of my perfect husband goodbye but we could be a team.

"I call the baby Pea," I shared.

He narrowed his eyes in confusion.

"Pea," he tested it out. "Okay," he agreed. "So you and Pea, you will move into the apartment, right?"

I let out a giggle because his patience was tattering and he was still trying to do the right thing. I stopped laughing and looked at him, seriously, eye to eye.

"If you're sure, I want you to be sure because I meant it when I said I will do this by myself. I know you didn't sign up for this—"

"Neither did you..." he interrupted. "...I'm sure," he continued. "I've got some shit to do for the club. Blackie's in the hospital and I need to get there but when I get back I'll take you to see the place," he said, rising to his feet.

"Okay," I agreed.

"So we're good?"

"We're good," I confirmed.

"All right, I'm going to head out. Do you need anything else?"

"No, I'm fine," I forced a smile as he looked like he was ready to flee. "Go ahead, do your thing," I encouraged.

He shoved his boots on, not bothering with the laces and grabbed his gun from the dresser, fitting it into the waistband of his jeans before he slipped his arms into his leather jacket and headed toward the door. His hand paused on the doorknob and he glanced over his shoulder at me.

I waved from the bed.

He nodded.

And then he hurried out the door.

Awkward.

RIGGS

Shit! Shit! Shit!

I ran the fuck away from that room, from Kitten and from Pea.

Pea.

I had a Pea.

The door across from mine opened and Bones stood in the doorway.

"Was wondering when you were going come out of hiding," he said, smugly. "You all right bro, you're looking a little green," he observed.

I pushed him aside and brushed past him as I walked into his room.

"Man, I'm fucked," I stressed.

He stuck his head into the hallway, looking from left to right before he shut the door and leaned his back against it.

"So congratulations would be the wrong thing to say?" He mocked.

"Laugh it up," I seethed, pacing his room, running my fingers through my hair tugging at the ends. "What the fuck am I going to do?"

He sighed, walking toward his dresser and opened a cigar box he kept on top of it. He pulled a perfectly rolled joint from inside, lifted it to his nose, breathing in the scent of the herb as he reached for a lighter and lit that shit up.

"You talk to her?" he asked.

"Barely," I confessed, watching him as he took the first toke. "I think she's just as fucked as me but hides it better," I said, reaching for the joint.

"So, she's going to keep it?"

"She's named it already!" I said, coughing up smoke.

Bones covered his mouth to hide the laughter.

Bastard.

"Seriously, man, I'm drowning here," I cried, taking a long drag of the joint. "My life isn't cut for a kid. I don't even have a car! What am I supposed to do? Strap a sidecar onto my bike?"

He took the joint from my hand and outright laughed at me. I glared at him and flipped him the bird.

"Look, you've got nine months to figure it out. Isn't that how long a woman is pregnant for?"

Nine months of freedom.

Nine months to live the rest of my life.

Nine months wasn't a very long time.

"It could be worse, bro," he said. "At least your baby mama is hot as hell," he took another puff. "That's a plus," he continued.

"Dude, I have a baby mama. Just stop right there," I sighed heavily. "Man, I don't want a kid. I don't know the first thing about being a father. My old man was never around, always chasing a dollar or a dream. He thought being a father meant handing me a trust fund," I explained. "I never had a dad so how the fuck am I supposed to be one?"

Bones crushed the joint into an ashtray and looked back at me.

"You do everything he never did," he urged. "You man the fuck up because twenty years from now you don't want your kid saying the same words you just did."

Twenty years from now? I couldn't think about twenty minutes from now.

"Don't do that shit," he criticized. "Don't be my old man."

Bones' dad skipped out on him and his mom before he was even born.

And then there was Lauren's dad who dipped out on the Bianci's.

I stared at Bones.

"You got a kid coming, man. That's huge. That's bigger than you, bigger than your girl, bigger than anything you've ever known. I know the club is everything to you right now and you worked real hard for your patch but this, you becoming someone's father? It's bigger than the club," he paused, leveling me with a stare. "Own that shit," he said, patting me on the back.

"You'll figure the rest of this shit out as it comes to you but get on board brother, because once that train leaves the station you will be sorry you missed it," he said, as he started for the door.

That was some deep shit right there. I thought about his words and wondered where they came from. Right now everything seemed out of whack and all I wanted was for things to get back to the way they were. Before Lauren. Before Pea. But his words, they rang in my ears, nagging me and making me wonder if one day I'd look back on this and regret everything.

I haven't lived a life of regrets and wasn't going to start now.

"Where are you going?" I asked.

"The morgue," he said flatly.

"What?"

"Jack's brother needs to be buried. I'm meeting the funeral director and setting it up for him. One last thing he needs to worry about."

"Any word on Blackie?"

"No change," he said. "You heading over there?"

"Yeah, after I go buy a fucking refrigerator."

"You're buying a refrigerator?"

"Yeah, and your ass is hauling it with me to my apartment," I demanded.

"I don't work for free, brother. It will cost you," he said, laughing as he walked out the door. "Oh, I forgot to tell you, Bianci's downstairs waiting for you,"

Of course he was.

Then I felt the color drain from my face.

"The brother not the mother, right?"

He laughed, ignoring my question as he kept on walking.

"Bones," I called out.

"Man the fuck up, Riggs," he shouted back.

I picked the joint out of the astray, lit it up and took another greedy pull before I faced the wrath of Bianci. He was sitting at the bar, his hands folded and his head down.

Was he praying?

I shook my head and pulled out the stool beside him.

"Where is she?" he asked.

"Upstairs," I replied, turning my face to meet his gaze.

"I should kill you," he pointed out.

I shrugged because it didn't seem like a bad alternative.

"You could do that I suppose, but I won't go down without a fight," I replied.

"Yeah? What would you be fighting for?" he asked, raising an eyebrow, daring me to answer.

"What do you think I'd be fighting for?" I asked incredulously. "World peace? My fucking life."

"Wrong answer," he said.

"Yeah, well, school was never my strong suit," I muttered.

"Pay attention, because I'm about to *school* you on something," he warned, twisting in his stool so he was facing me. "The next time I ask you what you're fighting for, you're not going to give me any wise crack remark and your answer won't be your *life* because your life don't matter no more," he continued, eyes sharp as they bore down on me. "You got a kid on the way, a kid that's my niece or nephew, and the only reason you will keep breathing is because I won't be the one who takes your life. I won't be the one that make's that kid grow up without a father, but if you turn around and decide not to be that kid's father all bets are off," he threatened.

I leaned into him and my eyes pierced his.

I was nobody's bitch.

"You forget I'm the one who stood by your side twenty-four seven, making sure you kept breathing," I fumed. "Don't fucking threaten me Bianci because I'll piss on your threats and shove them right back down your throat when I'm done.

Your mob card, your tough guy act, it won't work here," I ground out. "This shit between me and your sister, it's none of your business and until I ask for your goddamn input, stay the fuck out of it," I ordered.

He raised an eyebrow, crossing his arms against his chest before he nodded.

"Pretty strong words you got there, Riggs," he said, cocking his head to the side unfazed.

"Try me, Bianci and those words will turn to actions," I replied. "Your sister is a grown woman, stop fucking coddling her and let her be her own person. Give her that respect."

"What do you know about respect?"

"Fuck you," I ground out. "You think because I got your sister pregnant I disrespected her in some way—it wasn't like that," I explained.

Not that he deserved an explanation, but I was feeling generous.

I was losing my fucking mind.

"I've got respect for Lauren. I think she's great. I didn't plan on a kid, but shit happens," I argued.

"It's not about you, Riggs. It's not about Lauren, either. You're right she's a grown ass woman, and she needs to take control of her life, I'll give you that," he started, pulling out his phone, turning the screen toward me. "It's about that baby you created with my sister and it's about being someone that baby can depend on and look up to."

I glanced down at his phone and saw the picture of his kid, the one that wasn't even biologically his.

"I changed my whole life for this boy and there isn't an ounce of regret in me because he deserves it," he said, tucking his phone back into his pocket. "Your kid deserves the same," he added.

I should spit on him for telling me to change who I was.

I wouldn't, and more importantly I couldn't, because he was defending my kid. He was sticking up for my kid, fighting for Pea, and teaching me a lesson. I could learn a thing or two from Anthony Bianci.

He was a good guy to have in your corner and my kid was lucky to have him.

Not me.

Him.

That was pathetic.

It was wrong, and it made me want to prove to him I could be better. I could be more than just the asshole deadbeat dad they thought I'd be.

"I'm trying," I said.

"It's all I ask," he replied.

Yeah, Pea was damn lucky to have him as an uncle.

Pea needed a dad like that.

Pea needed me.

Bones was right.

I needed to own that shit.

Or at least try to.

For Pea.

Chapter Nineteen
Lauren

"I don't know why you're insisting on living here," my mother chastised.

For the millionth time.

After I explained to her that Riggs and I spoke and agreed to work together and co-parent, she started giving me shit. I can't say I don't totally agree with some of the things she's said, like, when she warned me about keeping my guard up. Or when she told me fairytales don't really exist and Riggs may say one thing now and do another later. I suppose she's jaded by my father and the way he left us high and dry. I wonder if she wasn't a woman scorned if she'd feel the same way.

"I don't trust that scoundrel, why keep an apartment if you're not going to live in it?" she asked, as she hung some of my clothes up in the closet.

I had Anthony take some of my things from the storage locker out this morning. There wasn't much, but I had kept my bedroom set, and when Mia and I went our separate ways, I won the sofa in the split. Actually, she told me to take it all because she wasn't planning on leaving her mom and dad's house unless she had a ring on finger. Mia didn't do adult very well. But hey, it works for me because I have a couch.

I plopped down on the couch and unpacked some of my clothes as my mother walked out of the bathroom.

"At least it's clean," she said, placing her hands on her hips as she fixed me with a look.

"You don't think he has a wife or a bunch of kids he's hiding and that's why he has this place do you?" she questioned, raising an eyebrow in an attempt to really drive her point home.

I rolled my eyes. My mother really was supportive in a crisis. She could make me feel better with all her reassuring words.

Not.

I heard a commotion from the door and jumped to my feet, peering through the peep hole to see Riggs shouting at someone down the flight of stairs outside our apartment. Our apartment. Fucking weird.

"What's going on?" My mother asked, nosily.

Shit.

"It's Riggs," I turned around and wagged my index finger at her. "Be nice!" I warned.

She scoffed.

Yeah, this was going to be fun.

Before I gave myself, an anxiety attack thinking about the next eighteen years of my mother and Riggs interacting over Pea, I turned around and pulled the door open.

"Go left," shouted Bones.

"We're not going to clear the wall," Riggs ground out.

"Well fuck you, next time pay for the goddamn delivery," Bones growled.

"Is everything okay?" I asked, stepping into the hallway and closer to the stairwell, noticing the refrigerator they were trying to maneuver up the stairs.

Riggs glanced over his shoulder, turned around slightly and leaned against the fridge.

"Hi, Kitten," he said with a smile, casually crossing his arms against his chest as he stared at me.

"Are you fucking kidding, man?" Bones called from down the stairs.

"Shit," he muttered, turning toward the fridge and taking some of the weight of it from Bones. "Sorry," he called down to Bones.

"Hi Bones," I said, peaking over Riggs' shoulder and down the stairs.

He lifted his hand and waved.

"Hiya, Kitten," he greeted.

"I'll drop the fucking refrigerator on you if you call her Kitten again," Riggs hissed as he maneuvered the fridge. "Push," he ordered, before glancing at me. "Make sure the door is open and step aside, I don't want you to get hurt."

Sweet.

I hated when he was sweet.

It made me hopeful.

I stepped aside, getting out of the way and kicked the door open wide, just in case they got that monster of a fridge up the tiny stairwell.

Bones pushed. Riggs groaned. They both cursed their lives, the refrigerator and life in general, and by some miracle of God they managed to get it up the stairs with only clipping off a part of the bannister.

"Who's the fucking man?" Riggs asked, grinning.

"Not you, asshole," Bones replied as they moved into the apartment.

"Riggs," I started, trying to warn him that his favorite person was sitting inside.

"Tell me I'm the man, Kitten," he winked.

"You're the man, but—" I was cut off.

"Well if it isn't "Johnny Appleseed" himself," my mother taunted.

"For fuck's sake," Riggs groaned.

"Mrs. Bianci, how are you?" Bones asked, wearing a shit eating grin.

My mother huffed as they pushed the fridge into its rightful spot in the kitchen, inspecting it for any damage.

"Does it meet your approval?" Riggs questioned, brushing his hands on his jeans before he plugged it in.

"You should've bought a Maytag," she snarled, grabbing her purse off the counter. She walked over and kissed my cheek. "If you need me, call," she said, glancing over her shoulder at Riggs. "And don't forget, you don't need this guy to do what you have to do," she turned her eyes back to me. "You've got your family," she said, giving me one more kiss and pressing her hand against my flat stomach. "I can't believe my baby's having a baby," she whispered, before she dropped her hand and started for the door.

"Always a pleasure," Riggs called out as she reached the door.

My mother paused at the door, lifting her middle finger to him before she walked out.

"I think she's warming up to me," Riggs said.

"Oh, yeah, definitely," Bones said, dropping onto the couch. "Looks good Lauren," he commented, glancing around the bare apartment.

"It does?" I asked, my eyes following Riggs as he inspected the changes to his apartment. I waited for his face to change, for the anxiety to set into his features but he remained indifferent.

"Still doesn't look lived in," Riggs added.

"She just moved in," Bones argued.

Riggs turned around. "You're going to need more furniture and I've got a few televisions I'll hang up," he rattled off, pulling off his hat and running his fingers through his hair.

"It's fine. There's no hurry to get anything," I started.

"I want you to be comfortable," he argued. "And when the kid comes, I want him to have a normal home," he declared, reaching into his pocket.

I wanted to ask him what his definition of a normal home was, because normal was what you made of it. Pea needed a loving home, not one stocked with flat-screen televisions.

He produced his credit card from his wallet and handed it to me.

"What's this?" I shook my head. "I mean, I know what it is but why are you giving it to me?"

"I want you to fix this place up however you want," he said.

I saw Bones shake his head out of the corner of my eye.

"That's very nice of you, Riggs. So is offering your home to me and Pea but that's where it ends. I'm not your charity case," I said, ignoring the card he handed me and stepping around him.

"What just happened?" he asked, turning around so he faced my back. "Kitten, I don't think you're my charity case," he argued.

I turned around.

"So what am I then?"

"Pea's Mom," he said simply, stepping closer. "Take the card Lauren, make this place look nice," he coaxed, taking my hand and opening my palm before dropping the card into it and closing it. He squeezed my closed palm and leaned down to press his lips to my forehead. "Let me do this," he whispered against my skin. "Make me feel useful," he added. "And not just like some asshole who turned your life upside down," he said, pulling back so he could glance into my eyes.

"I have a doctor's appointment tomorrow," I began, lifting my eyes to his. "You want to do something useful? Be there," I explained. "Adrianna says we'll probably get to hear the heartbeat," I added, smiling slightly.

I don't know what kind of childhood Riggs had but our child would not be bought. A dollar wasn't going to make up for a broken promise. He wanted to step up and do the right thing—that's great but I wouldn't allow him to throw money at a situation and think he's doing his share. Pea deserved better than that. Pea deserved a daddy.

He nodded quickly.

"Yeah, sure. I can do that," he said. "Shit," he sighed. "What time tomorrow? I've got Jack's brother's funeral and..." His words trailed off as Bones cleared his throat, causing him to look over his shoulder at his friend.

Bones coughed and muttered something that sounded like, 'own it', before Riggs turned back to me.

"What time is the appointment?" he repeated.

"Two in the afternoon. Dr. Heltzer is my doctor, his office is across the street from the hospital," I told him, looking down at the credit card. "I just want to remind you I don't want you to feel obligated," I said, cocking my head to the side as I stared at him. "I can do it without you," I paused. "I just don't want to," I whispered. "But I will if I have too."

He took my face in his hands, stepping closer, so I felt his breath against my lips.

"I'll be there," he vowed.

I wanted him to kiss me. I wanted to feel his lips on mine and be reminded of what kissing Riggs felt like. But the last time we did something reckless it resulted in two pink lines. He leaned down and kissed my cheek before dropping his hands from my face.

"I've got to get going," he said. "Text me the information and I'll be there," he reiterated as his thumb grazed my jaw.

I nodded, holding my breath as I stared into his eyes and saw the unmistakable flicker of desire. He turned around and snapped his fingers at Bones.

"Did you just snap at me?"

"Let's go," he exasperated.

"Don't you ever snap at me again," Bones warned, glancing at me. "See ya, Kitten," he winked.

"What'd I fucking tell you about calling her that?"

"You snapped your fingers at me like I was your fucking dog," Bones argued, as he followed Riggs out of the apartment, closing the door behind him. I heard them bicker back and forth for a few moments before I heard nothing at all. I walked toward the window and glanced down, watching Riggs straddle his bike. He fitted his helmet to his head, tilting his head back as he secured the chin strap. I would've sworn he was staring at me but I couldn't be sure as his sunglasses shielded his eyes and his facial expression was blank.

Hope.

It was going to break my heart.

RIGGS

It was strange seeing Jack with a woman. Well, not really, the dude had a lot of bitches at his beck and call but it was strange seeing him claim one. The sucker even put a ring on it. Not that Reina was a bitch or that Jack really was a sucker. He was a lucky prick, and she was a goddess. The pie goddess. That woman could throw down in the kitchen.

I wonder if Kitten can cook.

Jack wrapped his arms around Reina as he made his way down the hill from where his brother was freshly buried, back to where our bikes lined the road. Reina smiled, and I overheard her go on about stopping at the grocery store to get ingredients.

Because I was pissed.
Because I was due a pie.
And I wanted to collect.

Jack protested, and I started to argue when Pipe made his way over to us. He was grinning as he held the phone in the air and delivered us the sweet news that Blackie had finally pulled his ass out of the coma.

There was no question about it—the pie could wait.

We hustled out of the cemetery and drove our asses to the hospital, eager to see the brother we almost lost. The hospital tried to give us some shit about all of us not being able to visit him in the ICU but that didn't last very long and we did what we did best, disobeyed the rules and strode into Blackie's little cubical.

"There he is," Wolf cheered.

Jack was the first to make his way to Blackie, ignoring the tubes and pushing aside the machines they were attached to. He bent down, taking Blackie's head in his hand and kissed the top of his head.

"My man," Jack said, kissing his head again before he leaned back and stared at our vice president. "Left side of the table's been empty, brother," he explained hoarsely.

"I'm sorry," Blackie stammered.

"You got nothing to be sorry for," Jack replied. "I owe you everything," he reiterated. "You saved Lacey, and you kept Reina sane," he continued. "You sacrificed yourself for the club and that shit deserves a whole lot more than a thank you. Need you well, Black, need you to reverse this shit Jimmy has you strung out on, knocking on death's door," he growled. "Whatever it takes, we've got you," he insisted.

"Ay!" Pipe agreed.

"Did we get him? Gold is he…" Blackie asked.

"Oh, we fucking got him," Jack assured. "Lit that motherfucker up," he added.

"How?" Blackie asked.

Jack turned around and pointed his thumb over his shoulder at me.

"This son of a bitch right here, saved the day, your life and my sanity," he declared.

"And still no fucking pie," I added.

Blackie stared at me for a moment before looking back at Jack.

"What about the deal?"

"We made a new deal," he explained.

"You got the drugs?" Blackie asked, trying to sit up.

"C'mon man, don't worry 'bout that shit. You need to concentrate on getting off this shit and getting yourself good," Jack said, as he helped Blackie adjust himself in the bed

"I want to know," he insisted.

"We took the drugs from The Red Dragons," I offered. Apparently that was the wrong thing to say because Bones elbowed me in the gut and all eyes turned to me, glaring at me. I forgot that Blackie knew about the war with The Dragons, that he saw that shit, lived it and lost his wife in the middle of it. The guy wakes up from a coma to be reminded of the darkest time of his life.

Shit I'm a dickhead.

"You got the drugs from Wu? Are you out of your fucking minds?"

"Blackie, it's good. We're good. Jones arrested Jimmy at Temptations with the drugs," Jack explained calmly. "Everything went like we planned."

"We didn't plan to fuck the Chinese," Blackie said furiously, as he started to cough.

"It's fine, brother. Wu and the Dragons have no idea it was us. We have a meet with them tomorrow for another shipment of guns. We're good man," Pipe offered. "We're fucking good man, relax!"

Pipe turned, fixing me with a hard stare. "Tell him your news," he demanded.

"What news?" I asked bewildered.

"Yeah, give it to him. He's going to love this shit," Wolf agreed.

I rolled my eyes and clenched my jaw.

"Fine! I gave you mouth to mouth," I exasperated.

"Not that!" Jack said, shaking his head.

Bones leaned into me.

"Pea," he muttered.

"Shit," I sighed, feeling like a complete sack of shit for needing a reminder that Pea was my news.

My news.

My kid.

"I'm having a kid," I announced.

"Give him the good stuff, tell him who's the baby mama," Pipe said, wiggling his eyebrows to Blackie. "Wait for it," he told Blackie.

"Fuck off," I said, flipping the bird to Pipe.

"Riggs knocked up Bianci's sister," Wolf supplied.

"Come on guys," Bones started.

Blackie stared at me with a dumbfounded expression on his face, one I wasn't sure was due to the ordeal *he* had been through or the one I was going through.

"Glad I could amuse you fuckers," I grunted, as the door opened and Jack's daughter, Lacey, stormed into the room.

Now, I've been in a lot of awkward positions in my life, but that one right there, may have topped the cake. We all stared at her as she kept her eyes locked with Blackie's.

"You're okay?" She whispered, ignoring the rest of us as she walked toward the side of Blackie's bed. "You're okay," she repeated, this time her words surer than the first time she uttered them. I wanted to shout at the two of them that it was pretty fucking obvious this was no casual encounter. If I could notice the way she looked at him then everyone else could because we all know I'm not the sharpest tool in the shed.

Blackie turned his gaze away.

"I'm good, kid," he said, looking at Jack. "Going to want my gun back," he added.

"Yeah," Jack agreed, his eyes wandering back and forth between Blackie and Lacey.

Nice save!

"So a kid, huh?" Blackie said, turning back to me, his eyes pleading with mine to save his ass.

"Yeah, I'm going to be a dad," I said, the words sounding weird coming from my mouth.

Lacey took a step back, staring at Blackie like he'd slapped her across the face.

"Congrats, man," Blackie said, ignoring Lacey and the hurt expression on her face.

"I'm glad you're okay," Lacey whispered, turning on her heel and stepping out of the hospital room.

"Lacey," Jack called.

"Dude, speaking of Pea…" Bones started, glancing at the clock.

"Pea?" Jack asked, as he stared at the door his daughter closed behind her.

"Don't ask," I said, turning back to Bones.

"Didn't Lauren have the doctor's appointment today?"

Shit!

Fuck!

I pulled my phone out of my pocket and saw I had missed three messages from Kitten.

Kitten: I'm here.
Kitten: Are you on your way?
Kitten: I guess you're not coming.

The last message came an hour ago.

"Shit!" I roared, lifting my head as all eyes were on me. "I've got to get out of here," I said hastily, looking back at Blackie. "Glad you're awake, brother," I added before jetting out of the room.

I fucked up.

I tried calling Lauren but my call went straight to her voicemail.

I was off to a great start.

I was a contender for father of the year.

Pea was lucky to have me.

I pulled my hat from head and dialed Lauren again.

Nothing.

I didn't blame her.

I sucked.

Chapter Twenty
RIGGS

I climbed the stairs, carrying a bag of groceries as a consolation prize for letting down Kitten and Pea. Because stocking the fridge you bought and cooking dinner for your baby mama was as good as standing next to her while she listened to your kid's heartbeat for the first time right?

Yeah, I didn't think so either.

But it was worth a shot.

I paused at the door, reaching into my pocket for my key when I heard voices from behind the door. I leaned my ear against the door, sure it was Mama "Leone" lashing out about what a piece of shit I was but to my surprise Kitten had a different house guest.

A male one.

And not her brother either.

I set the brown bag of groceries on the floor and reached behind me for my gun, prepared to blow the head off the guy inside getting cozy with my Kitten.

I opened the door and stepped inside with my gun cocked and aimed that shit toward the man standing next to Lauren with his back toward me.

"Riggs!" She said, eyes wide as she stared at me.

"Kitten," I ground out, taking a step closer. "Want to introduce me to your friend?"

"Want to put the gun down?" She countered.

The guy slowly turned around.

"Whoa! What the hell man?"

"Who are you?" I growled.

"Put the gun down, damn it!" Lauren shouted, stepping around the guy and grabbing my forearm.

I glanced down at her.

"One more time, Kitten," I warned. "Who is your friend?" I asked, holding my gun steady on the guy.

"I'm just here to buy the car listed on Craigslist," he said, holding his hands in the air.

"What?" I asked, dropping my gun and turning to Lauren. "What's he talking about?"

She rolled her eyes, ignoring me as she walked toward the guy standing in the middle of the living room shitting his pants. "I'm sorry about that, he's just been released from the asylum," she began. "We're still working on a treatment plan for his irrational behavior," she began, batting her eyelashes at the douche. "I hope you won't let my ill brother interfere with your decision to buy the car."

"Your brother?" I asked incredulously.

"I think it's time for his medication," she added, dangling the keys in front of him.

He peered at me skeptically as I tucked my gun into the back of my pants and crossed my arms against my chest. He handed Lauren an envelope, and I watched as she peeked inside before handing him over the keys.

"Congratulations you're the proud owner of a used car," she winked.

One of my favorite things about my Kitten was the way she handled herself. She owned that guy with her smile and her sharp tongue.

She didn't need a prince to rescue her, she was her own hero, and that was the sexiest thing about her.

That and well, maybe, her ass. She had a killer ass.

He looked at Lauren, taking the keys she offered.

"Are you sure you're safe with him?"

Lauren didn't even look at me as she answered him.

"I'll be fine, once he's medicated he's a pussycat," she reassured him, as she led him toward the door. "Thanks for coming by and enjoy the car," she said.

"Thanks," the guy said, glancing over his shoulder at me again.

I moved to reach for the gun again but he scampered out the door before I could. Lauren glanced down at the bag of groceries I had left in the hallway, bending down to grab them before walking into the apartment and kicking the door closed.

She walked into the kitchen and dropped the bag onto the counter before walking past me toward the couch.

Kitten was pissed.

I bring out the best in her.

"Why'd you sell your car?" I asked.

She continued to ignore me as she flopped down onto the couch and grabbed her phone. I took a deep breath and accepted my fate as I sat down beside her.

"I know you're mad…" I began.

She threw the phone onto the couch and twisted around, pulling her glasses off her face and her big blue eyes narrowed at me.

"Mad?" She shook her head. "No, I'm not mad," she said.

"You're not?" I asked confused.

"I'm disappointed in you, Riggs," she informed. "Which is much worse than being mad at you. I get angry and then I get over it but once I'm disappointed in someone, I give up on them," she explained, shrugging her shoulders.

"I'm sorry I let you down, Kitten," I tried, reaching for her hand. I wanted to pull her onto my lap and erase the look in her eyes, the look that reflected all the ways my actions failed her.

"It doesn't matter, Riggs," she said, sighing heavily. "I'll get used to your disappointment, probably even come to expect it, but I won't let you disappoint Pea. I won't sit back and watch you make promise after promise to our baby, only to break each one. I won't throw you under the bus but I won't make excuses for you either, and then there will come a point where I won't tolerate it anymore," she declared.

It wasn't a threat, it was a promise, a promise that she would not let anyone inflict pain on our kid, least of all Pea's dad. While I was failing miserably at impending fatherhood, Kitten was becoming one badass mother.

"I didn't mean to miss the appointment, Lauren. After the funeral I was going to head straight to the doctor's office but Pipe got the call that Blackie woke up from the coma," I explained. "We almost lost him, fuck, I'm the one who found him half dead. I needed to see him alive and well, needed to erase that image of him dying from my mind," I continued. "I lost track of time."

Her eyes softened, and she cocked her head to the side. "Is he okay?"

I nodded. "Got a long road ahead of him, but he's a fucking bull. Blackie will pull through," I said, leaving out that he wouldn't actually pull through if Jack found out whatever the fuck was up with him and Lacey.

I didn't get that one. He was like twelve years older than her, but hey, who was I to judge anyone.

"How'd it go at the doctor?" I questioned, giving in to my urge to touch her and reached over and tucked a strand of hair behind her ear.

"Baby is good, perfect actually," she smiled widely. "I heard Pea's heartbeat," she said, biting her lip and shaking her head as if the words amazed her. "It's so strong," she whispered, her smile reaching up to her eyes.

I stared at her and I envied the look in her eyes, the pride and love reflected in them. Since I realized I had missed the appointment I had been feeling guilty but now, looking at Lauren I was actually jealous I missed a chance to feel the way she did. I missed out on something big and I was feeling it.

"I have a picture; do you want to see it?"

I nodded.

"Absolutely," I said, as she stood up and walked toward the kitchen. I followed her, surprised by how much I wanted to see Pea.

She pulled the sonogram picture off the refrigerator and I was never happier about a purchase than I was at the moment and I realized something else—furniture wasn't going to make this place a normal home.

But Lauren would.

Putting Pea's first grainy photo on the front of the refrigerator made these four walls a home.

I took the photo in my hand and tried to make out a head, two legs and two arms but all I saw was something that looked like a dot.

"That's Pea," she said, pointing to the dot. "And these lines, on this picture is the heartbeat," she added, showing me the lines that traveled up and down the photograph.

"Wow," I said, more to myself than to her, looking back at the dot, at Pea, before glancing over at Lauren. "Cute kid," I teased, winking at her.

She smiled at me and I stared at her for a moment, my eyes dipping to her flat stomach as I tried to picture what she'd look like in the next few months as Pea grew inside of her.

How fucking crazy was that? Lauren was growing a human inside of her.

Without thinking, I wrapped my arm around her shoulders and tugged her into the crook of my arm.

"I'm sorry I missed this," I said, holding up the photo. "But I won't miss anymore," I promised.

And I wouldn't.

Because I didn't want to.

Wow.

Funny, what one little picture could do to a person, how one little dot could mean so much.

I leaned down and kissed her forehead, dropping my arm from her shoulders and placed Pea's first photo back where it belonged.

"Did you eat?"

"No," she said, glancing at the bag of groceries. "What'd you get?"

"Sorry they were all out of cottage cheese," I lied. That shit was vile, and I wasn't about to subject Pea to that crap. I walked over to the bags and pulled out chocolate pudding, a gallon of milk, cookies, a rotisserie chicken, a tub of ice cream and lastly a jar of pickles.

All the necessities.

I may not know much but wasn't it some cardinal rule that all pregnant chicks craved pickles and ice cream? Tada!

"Riggs?" She asked, picking up the jar of pickles.

I did good, I knew the pickles would be a big hit and I smiled proudly.

This baby daddy thing would be a breeze.

"Yes, Kitten?"

"How about we order out?" She asked, placing the pickles back on the counter, covering her mouth with her hand.

I reached out and pulled her hand away and she giggled.

"What?" I asked.

"You bought me pickles and ice cream," she said through her giggles.

"Yeah, so?" I looked back at the ice cream.

"Nothing," she said, surprising me by wrapping her arms around my middle and hugging me. "Thank you, that was really sweet."

"But you rather order out," I said, wrapping my arms around her waist and glancing down at her.

"I want pizza," she declared, tilting her head back so she could look up at me.

Those eyes, man, they were pretty.

I hope Pea has her eyes.

"You want anything on it?"

"Sausage," she whispered, winking at me before she dropped her arms from me.

I knew that all these Italian's wanted the old sausage. Speaking of sausage, I wonder when the last time she had it was. Was I last the one?

Whoa, buddy. Don't go there.

The last thing I needed right now was to think about Lauren getting laid.

Still, I pictured her sprawled out on the floor, legs open wide, inviting me to devour that pussy. Nah, fuck that. I'd rather be on the bottom, have her sit on my face and ride my tongue. Now, that was a pretty picture. I'd grab onto her thighs as she went buck wild on my tongue.

Yes, please.

More of that.

A lot more of that.

"Riggs?" She questioned. "Are you okay?"

"Yeah, why?" I said as my eyes dropped to her tits. Had they gotten bigger? They looked tremendous right now in that t-shirt.

I wonder if I pretend to drop a glass of water on the front of it if she'll take it off and show me her nips.

I wanted the nips.

"You're sweating," she pointed out.

"Fuck," I growled. "I'm fine, just order whatever you want. I need to use the bathroom," I said, turning around to adjust my dick straining against the zipper of my jeans.

Down boy.

I went to the bathroom and for the greater good of Kitten and Tiger, I jacked off. There was no fucking way I'd be able to sit there and share a meal with Lauren with a hard on. I thought about asking her if this co-parenting thing involved sex but I decided not to rock the boat any more than I already had. Come to think about it, we already had a kid on the way, why not take advantage of the no rubber thing?

I guess we did that already.

But we should do it again.

And this time I'd eat her pussy while I was at it.

It didn't take long for me to come, and I was thankful for the fancy towels that were a new addition to the otherwise bare bathroom. When I emerged from the bathroom, Lauren's cheeks were redder than nail polish on her toes.

Cute toes.

I looked back at her face, her eyes wandering the room and her cheeks growing even redder.

She definitely knew I rubbed one out.

But why was she embarrassed?

Unless....

No, did Kitten have her hands down her pants too?

Ah, that's great.

I leaned back against the couch, spreading my arms across the back and stared at her knowingly.

She threw a pillow at me and I fell in love with her temporarily again.

We both burst out laughing.

When the pizza arrived, we had a picnic on the floor. I was kind of glad we didn't have a table yet because I had never been on a picnic before, outside or inside. Pea needed to go on picnics. I'd take him or her to Central Park and we'd have a picnic, just the three of us. Wow, two hours playing house with Lauren and I was turning into a bitch, making plans and dreaming of a family. What the fuck was wrong with me?

Time to go.

Run.

I grabbed my empty plate, moving to my feet and nodded toward hers.

"You done?" I asked.

"Yeah, thanks," she said, handing me the paper plate. I dropped them in the garbage as she packed up the rest of the pizza and brought the box into the kitchen.

"I've got to head out," I said, turning around to face her.

I saw the disappointment flicker in her eyes, kicking myself again because I was the reason behind that sad look in her eyes.

"It's better if I go," I explained.

"Yeah," she agreed.

Who says you can't bullshit a bullshitter? We fucking aced that shit.

I leaned forward and pressed my lips against her cheek, nuzzling my nose along her jaw because I was a greedy fuck and wanted to smell her. I wanted to go back to the compound with her scent on my face and pretend it marked me because of all the naughty things I did to her.

Her hand traveled the length of my arm and her fingers laced with mine, forcing me to pull back and look at her.

"Thanks for the pickles and ice cream," she said with a smile.

"Thanks for not cutting my balls off for missing the appointment," I replied.

"No problem, but next time you do, I might," she warned, dropping my hand and taking a step backward.

"Duly noted," I said with a laugh. "I'll call you tomorrow."

She nodded, following me toward the door and as I reached for the knob I remembered the guy who bought her car. I turned around and looked at her.

"Why'd you sell your car?"

She shrugged her shoulders.

"There are other things more important than a car," she explained.

"Like?" I probed.

"Riggs, I don't have a job. Anthony offered to hire me at the gym but let's be serious who would you rather see at the front desk Brittany or me? I'm going to start showing soon. I'll have a big belly and swollen ankles, not your ideal eye candy," she huffed. Besides, I lost my medical insurance after I dropped out of school, so for now I need to pay for my doctor's visits."

"Stop," I said, lifting my index finger to her lips. "I'm dead fucking serious, Lauren. I don't want you taking some job at the gym, and I don't want you selling your shit worried about paying for a doctor. I've got you," I said, then leaned close and repeated my words. "I've got you," I drawled. "That means whatever you need, I will make sure you have," I declared. "You should've told me about the insurance," I said, dropping my hand from her mouth.

"Why? What does it matter?"

"You're fucking car would still be parked on the street if you had just told me what you needed," I hissed.

"Riggs..."

"Nah, Lauren. I get you're uncomfortable with this shit, leaning on me and all that, but suck it up because we're doing this together. No more secrets," I ordered. "I'm serious, if you and Pea need something you come and tell me," I stressed.

"Fine," she sighed. "I don't like it but for Pea, I'll swallow my pride," she whispered.

I nodded.

"If you want something else to swallow, give me a call," I teased.

"You're a pig," she said, punching me in the arm.

I winked at her, stepping through the door.

"You love it," I quipped, turning around to look at her one more time. "For the record…" I shoved my hands into my pockets, pulling out my leather fingerless gloves and fitting them to my hands, "…if I had to choose between you and Brittany, I'd always choose you," I lifted my eyes, watching as her mouth opened slightly.

"Good night, Kitten," I said.

"Good night, Tiger," she whispered.

And just like that, we were Kitten and Tiger again.

I don't know why that made me smile.

Or why it made me feel better about things but it did. I walked away, running down the stairs and not because I was running away from Lauren but running to my bike, desperate for the open road to help me make sense of it all.

I stepped outside and turned to where I parked my bike and noticed it was missing.

You've got to be fucking kidding me.

I glanced around the street when I felt someone walk up behind me.

I didn't have time to turn around because whoever it was grabbed me, putting me in a headlock before they covered my head with a bag. My gun was lifted from my waistband and I went to elbow the motherfucker in the ribs but I was too slow, something crashed against my skull and everything went black.

Chapter Twenty-One
Lauren

The persistent banging on the door woke me up. I untangled myself from the blanket I had thrown on me and rose from the couch. I grabbed my handy baseball bat I kept hidden beneath the couch.

You never know when you might need one.

I stumbled toward the door, closing one eye and peering into the peephole to see Bones staring back at me. Well, not really. I dropped the bat, leaning it against the wall so he didn't think I was a maniac and proceeded to open the door.

"Hi," I greeted, pulling my sweatshirt together and zipping it up. "What's up?"

"Can I come in?" He questioned, looking past my head and into the apartment.

"Of course," I said, as I moved aside, giving him room to enter the apartment. I was about to tell him that Riggs wasn't there when my cell phone rang. I walked into the kitchen and pulled the phone from the charger, noticing Anthony was calling me. I lifted my eyes to Bones.

"Excuse me one second," I said before answering the call. "Hi," I said.

Bones moved closer almost as if he was trying to listen in on my conversation.

"Where's Riggs?" Anthony hissed into the phone.

"I don't know. Why?" I asked, covering the receiver and looking back at Bones. "It's my brother," I said, feeling the need to explain.

"Because his bike is parked in front of my gym and whoever he pissed off dumped red paint all over my door and his fucking bike," he growled.

"What? Hold on," I dropped the phone to my side and peered at Bones. "Why are you here?"

"Just a friendly visit," he replied, offering me a crooked smile as he took a step back. "Everything okay with your brother?"

"Riggs isn't here," I said, narrowing my eyes as I stared at Bones. "But you knew that already, didn't you?"

"Now I do," he said, before tipping his chin toward the phone. "You just going to leave your brother hanging like that?"

"You going to tell me why Riggs' bike is in front of my brother's gym covered in red paint?" I retorted, putting one hand on my hip as I gaged his reaction.

He remained neutral, shrugging his shoulders, and he pushed his hands into his pockets and stared back at me.

"Probably just a bunch of kids fucking with him," he suggested, biting the inside of his cheek. "So Riggs is at the gym?"

"No, he's not," I said, lifting the phone back to my ear as I recalled the teenagers I went after when I saw them circling Riggs' bike. "Anthony?"

"Who is with you?"

"Bones is here," I supplied.

"Put him on the phone," he demanded.

I extended the phone to Bones who stared down at it like it was a foreign object.

"He doesn't bite," I said, rolling my eyes.

"Like hell, he doesn't," he grumbled, taking the phone. "Bianci…no…yes…I have no idea…we'll figure it out…no…okay, I'll tell Jack," he rambled on, before finally disconnecting the call and handing me back my phone.

"Is Riggs in some kind of trouble?" I asked.

"Nah, he's fine," he assured. "He sleep here last night?" He asked as his eyes scanned the place. I don't know why, it's not like he'd find a clue here. These bikers could never be detectives, that's for sure.

"No. Okay, Bones, what's up?"

He looked at me blankly.

"Are you serious? You can't be serious. If something happened to Riggs I have a right to know," I demanded, but even as I said the words I wondered if I really had any right. Fuck that, of course I did. I was Pea's mom which gave me every goddamn right in the world.

"Where is he?"

"Lauren, calm down. I'm sure he's fine," he said calmly, placing his hands on my shoulders and smiled at me. "It's nice having company," he added.

I squinted.

"What's that mean?"

"For a long time, I've been the only one in Riggs' corner," he shrugged his shoulders. "Seems like I'm not alone anymore," he continued. "I'll take care of it, keep you posted."

It was his turn to receive a phone call and when he answered it he turned his back away from me.

Well fuck that, I made a mental note to do the same the next time my phone rang.

I tiptoed closer to him, trying to listen just as he had.

"Not here and Bianci called Lauren, yes the baby mama…"

I paused, fighting off the urge to take the phone and tell whoever was on the other end that was getting old.

I was Lauren Bianci not Riggs' baby mama.

But I was.

I sighed, accepting my title, or at least the one I'd carry with me for the next eighteen years and leaned closer to Bones.

"His bike is at Xonerated and apparently someone decided to fuck it up and poured paint all over it. Yeah, I know, he's going to blow a gasket," he said, turning around and raising an eyebrow at me.

Busted.

"I've got to go. Yeah, I know, well we can't afford to skip the meeting with Wu. We have to keep that deal in good standing. I'm on my way," he ended the call and looked back at me. "You're nosey."

"So are you," I argued.

He smirked.

"I like you, Lauren, think you're great for Riggs," he stated.

Wow.

Cue the violins.

Someone tell the poor guy we were just friends having a kid.

"Think you'll keep him on his toes and that's what he needs," Bones continued. "He's going to do the right thing and he'll be a good dad too, just have patience with him," he affirmed. "Don't worry, I'll bring him back to you," he said.

His words were meant to ease me but instead they instilled fear in me. What if he was wrong? If there was one thing I learned being Anthony Bianci's sister, it's that a man who plays on the other side of the law is a gambling man. You can't win every hand and one day you'll be forced to fold.

Bones started for the door and I stared at the patch on his back. The reaper stared back at me, warning me everyone folds eventually.

Hey Reaper.

Two words.

One finger.

And then Bones turned around as I held up my middle finger.

"Uh...that wasn't meant for you," I stammered, dropping my finger. Shit!

"Right," he said, cocking his head as he stared at me perplexed. "God she's perfect for him," he mumbled, turning around.

This time when I lifted my finger I gave it to Bones and not the Reaper.

I wasn't perfect for Riggs.

No, not at all.

Hope.

Fuck you hope.

I don't want you.

I locked the door, grabbed my bat and went back to the couch. Then I did what any good catholic girl did and prayed with my baseball bat tucked under my arm.

Because I was Anthony Bianci's sister.

Because I was having Riggs' baby.

Because everyone folds.

Because I was fucking pregnant and crazy.

RIGGS

I blinked against the darkness, unable to see. I wasn't sure if it was because of the bag over my head or the fact that one eye was swollen shut and the other was bleeding. My head was pounding and the left side felt like it was on fire.

I'm going to come out of this.

And when I do, I'm going hunting.

I'm going to torture and kill every fucking Dragon I can find.

I'm going to beat the fuck out of them until they're pissing blood.

I knew the moment I mentioned the Dragons' stash house to the Knights I was playing with fire. I was so sure that setting Jimmy up to take the fall would be key in saving our asses.

It would've worked too if I hadn't fucked up, but it's my fault I'm lying here beaten and bloody.

Jack wasn't kidding when he told Wu I was the best in the surveillance business.

I was.

I wired every fucking inch of Wu's building and in the process, I set myself up for my own fate. I'm the one who signed my death certificate the moment I took the mask off in the hallway of the stash house. I saw the footage with my own eyes. I was naked when I woke up from the blow to the head, handcuffed to a pipe and at the mercy of the Red Dragons. Wu played the video back for me and he played it over and over again, each time he did he struck me with a whip.

They maneuvered me into the back of a van, covering my head with a canvas bag as they drove me to wherever it was these fuckers thought they would kill me.

I may have made a mistake and been reckless but I wasn't going down without a fight.

I'd go "Jackie Chan" on their asses.

Jack was right about something else.

We all need heart, it's what keeps us from being reckless, keeps us breathing.

I needed to breathe.

For Kitten and for Pea.

I only wish I had found my heart before my mistake.

The van came to a sharp stop causing me to roll around the floor of the truck.

"Son of a bitch!" I screamed, as my welted body ached in pain.

This is it.

Time to fight.

I'm a motherfucking Knight, only Satan can drag my ass to hell.

Someone jumped into the back of the van with me, grabbing my arms and dragged them, tied at the wrists, across the floor.

"I will kill you, after I kill the woman who bore your pathetic ass," I hissed.

He shouted something in Chinese and then another voice replied in, surprise, surprise... Chinese! I was never eating Lo Mein again.

The van took off, speeding, and I felt the air wash over my naked body, figuring the door to the van was open. They shouted some more bullshit I didn't understand and then I heard the familiar sound of gunfire.

Music to my ears.

Then my body was thrown from the van.

What a fucking way to go.

"Shit. Riggs!" I heard Bones' voice over the gunshots starting to die down and the distinct sound of tires screeching against the pavement.

"Holy shit," Pipe, yelled.

Someone grabbed my body, forcing me to sit up and pulled the bag from my head. I brought my hands up to my face, trying to shield the sunlight that threatened to blind me with my tied hands.

"What happened?" Jack demanded.

"Bulldog, look," Wolf said, turning my head slightly.

"What?" I asked. "Shit, I have a hole in my head don't I? Someone untie me!" I shouted, trying to feel for the hole, my hands stilled when I touched my hair—it felt off.

I lifted my eyes to Jack as he crouched down in front of me.

"Who did this to you?" He asked calmly.

"Wu," I replied. "He knows we took the drugs it's on camera," I hissed.

He lifted his eyes to my head again.

"Jack why is my hair missing?" I asked hastily, looking around at my brothers. "Someone tell me what the fuck is going on," I demanded, before I reached for the pocket knife on Jack's belt and flipped the blade open. I lifted it to my head and with the eye I could open I tried to see the image reflected in the knife.

Someone decided to give my fine self a new do, and by that, I mean a fucking chop job.

I looked like one of those rappers that shaves his mama's name onto his head.

Bones held my head, turning it slightly to the right, so I could see what they were gawking at.

There was something I couldn't make out faded into the hairstyle, something legible if you had two working eyes.

"What's it say?" I demanded.

"Two hundred and fifty," Bones whispered.

Wolf turned my head around, inspecting it for anymore messages before glancing back toward Jack.

"They fucking carved a price tag to his head," he ground out.

That was a bit dramatic even for Wolf.

I ran my hands over my fucked up hair and scowled.

Jack straightened up, running his hands over his face before he turned to Pipe.

"The Dragons tried to slay a Knight, Prez, you know what that means don't you?" Pipe questioned.

"It means the fucking Chinese resurrected a war with us," Jack ground out. "It means, get your fucking saddle ready because we're going to ride 'til our hands are covered in Dragon blood," he vowed, fixing his eyes on me. "Means Riggs is going to show them who the fuck breathes fire. You with me, brother?" He asked.

"I'm with you," I said, numbly.

He cupped my chin, forcing me to look at him.

"Heart," he hissed, before dropping my chin and turning toward Bones. "Get him cleaned up and a goddamn cut," he ordered, before he turned to Pipe.

"I'm hungry," Jack said. "You hungry Pipe?"

Fine time for them to be talking about food while Bones hoisted my naked ass off the dirt road. I had a motherfucking price tag on my head and they were talking about their stomachs. Join an MC—it'll be fun—still waiting for the fun part.

"Starving," Pipe replied.

"Let me guess…you're in the mood for a little General Tso's chicken?" Wolf questioned, as he stepped into stride alongside them.

"Ay," Pipe agreed. "With a side of Wu," he added.

Time to hunt.

Chapter Twenty-Two

RIGGS

Once in the cage, Bones pulled his cut off and threw it onto my lap.

"Put it on," he ordered, turning the key in the ignition as the rest of the Knights straddled their bikes and peeled away from the scene of my drop off.

I looked down at his cut, wincing as I put it on.

"You don't happen to have a pair of pants lying around here somewhere, do you?" I asked.

He said nothing, keeping his eyes on the road as I glanced down at myself, my dick flailing around every time we went over a bump. Luckily for me, Bones and I have been close friends for years. So close as boys that we used to measure our dicks against the wall. If we didn't have that kinda friendship, this shit might've been awkward.

Boys who turned into men.

My brother.

The one person I trusted more than anyone.

I glanced over at him, noting his knuckles whitening as they gripped the steering wheel and how his jaw clenched as he worked his neck from side to side.

"I took my mask off," I said, breaking the silence between us. "When Wolf was still upstairs in the apartment I turned around and lifted the ski mask from my face," I explained.

"Why you telling me this?"

"Because Wu let me go," I said running my hand over the hair missing from my head. "You and I both know he only let me go to deliver a message. He'll be back, The Dragons aren't going to let me get away with that shit," I said, turning and glancing out the window.

"We'll handle it," he barked. "That chink fuck can try to do whatever he wants…we'll shut the motherfucker down," he added.

I nodded in agreement because he needed me to but I was realistic, there was a fucking price tag on my head, literally, and I needed to accept that shit. I'd fight alongside my club, fight to the death of me, but I needed to prepare myself in case I was fighting a losing battle.

"Need you to take care of something for me," I began, turning my eyes back toward him.

"What?"

"If this don't end my way, I need you to get my parents to give my money to Lauren," I said. His eyes turned to mine in a flash, anger reflecting in them at my request.

"Nothing is going to happen to you," he seethed, turning his eyes back to the road.

"Right, but if anything, ever should. Even if it has nothing to do with the Chinese, and ten years from now I get hit by a truck, I need to know you'll get her the money so she can take care of Pea."

"Do your parents even know about Pea?"

"No, and I don't want a fucking thing from them while I'm breathing but if something happens to me, then my kid deserves that money," I said, as we pulled into the Dog Pound lot. I glanced out the window and saw Bianci standing outside, next to my bike.

Shit.

I sighed and looked back at Bones.

"Can you do that for me?" I asked.

"Yeah," he hissed. "For Pea," he said through clenched teeth, before he pointed his index finger at me. "Don't fucking talk like that again, like you're going to get clipped and leave that kid fatherless," he ordered.

Pea was worming his or her way into everyone's life.

I shoved his finger out of my face and rolled my eyes.

"I'm not going anywhere, asshole. It will take a lot more than a pack of ninjas to take this guy down," I declared, reaching for the door handle and climbing my naked ass out of the van.

I squared my shoulders back, head held high as my dick flapped in the wind and strode toward the compound like the badass I am.

My demeanor dissolved when I saw my precious Harley covered in red fucking paint and Bianci standing next to it with a sponge.

"Step away from the bike!" I demanded, my one good eye assessing the damage before I looked back at Bianci, staring daggers at him like the one eyed bandit. Just call me Cyclopes.

"What did you do to my Bike?"

"What the hell happened to you?" He growled, ignoring my question, and me for that matter, as he turned to Jack. "What the fuck?"

"None of your business Bianci," Jack growled.

"The fuck it isn't," he pressed, diverting his eyes back briefly, taking in all the glory that is me.

"Go home, Bianci," Jack demanded. "Your ass don't belong here, this is club business, something you're not about. Now, I'll only say this one more time—go the fuck home to your wife and be the fucking upstanding citizen people fought hard for your ass to be," Jack ordered, turning around and eyeing the rest of us.

"Chapel, now," he bellowed, switching his gaze to me. "Get him cleaned up and checked out," he ordered, before moving toward the door that Bianci was standing in front of.

Guy had balls.

Or maybe heart.

Someone should give the poor sucker a patch—I think he misses the life.

"Riggs became my business when you put him on me and he's staying my business because of the kid he and my sister are having," Bianci ground out.

"Aww, you love me," I said mockingly.

Anthony diverted his eyes to me, silencing me with a glare.

"You people live for one another—me and my people live for family. So, you keep living for yours and I'll keep living for mine," he paused, pointing toward me. "I'll stand back, let you do your thing but a hair on his head gets harmed, all bets are off," Anthony warned Jack.

I guess he didn't catch my new do.

"Like I said before, Bianci…go home," Jack ground out, walking around him and into the Dog Pound.

Bianci stepped aside, and we all followed Jack into the clubhouse. When it was my turn to limp my ass across the threshold, Anthony reached out and cupped my chin, turning my head and staring at my dope haircut. I peered at him, watched his blue eyes darken in a way I'd never seen. Before I could say a word he dropped his hand and started for his car.

The Satan's Knights had a doctor on call for situations like this. Wolf had already made a call and the doctor was waiting for me when I stepped into the Dog Pound. I don't know if it was the adrenaline or the goddamn need for revenge but my injuries didn't bother me, I tried to make light of them. Even when the doctor had to stitch my fucking forehead. Good times.

My bike was fucked.

My cut was gone.

And I had a fucking haircut I didn't want.

Doc took his sweet time patching me up, making me look like Frankenstein. When he was done I hurried to put my clothes on and meet the guys in the Chapel. I didn't care if I had to ride bitch, since my bike was a fucking canvas now, I wasn't being left behind.

I grabbed a baseball hat, fitted it to my head and made my way down to Chapel just as they were walking out.

"What's going on?" I asked, watching as two of the prospects carried in one of the crates. The deal with Wu obviously hadn't gone down and now we had access to all the guns. Wolf pried the crate open and started dispersing the guns around the room.

"Sit this one out," Jack said to me, as he fitted his vest around his chest and draped a rifle over each arm.

"Yeah, no thanks," I said, snatching one of the guns from Wolf and turning to one of the prospects. "Give me the keys to your bike," I demanded, holding out my hand.

"What?" he asked, dumbfounded.

"Now," I hollered, as he glanced over my shoulder at Jack.

Jack sighed, shaking his head for a second before lifting his eyes to meet the prospect's eyes.

"Give them to him," he conceded.

I didn't know the plan, didn't even care what it was—I followed Jack with the borrowed bike, hell bent on revenge. The gory kind.

We pulled our bikes in front of a Chinese restaurant close to Mott Street and Wu's house of heroin. They weren't kidding when they said they were in the mood for Chinese. We dismounted, pulled out our guns and then Wolf announced our arrival by emptying a clip of bullets into the glass door. The glass shattered and Jack stepped through the frame of the door, his boots crunching the glass as he walked in.

"You should invest in bulletproof glass," he suggested, as the Dragons drew their guns on us.

They shouted in Chinese again and Wolf took another shot, this time his bullet shattered the fish tank that took up half the wall, the water pouring out everywhere. "Flipper" and his posse escaping confinement.

"Fucking English," he demanded. I guess all the Chinese talk was pissing Wolf off too.

I watched on as Jack stepped closer to the table where Sun Wu sat, sipping his fucking green tea, unfazed by this shit. A Dragon stepped closer, and I shot at his feet.

"Take another step and I'll make you dance motherfucker," I warned, and the bastard laughed.

Bang! Bang!

He yelped as the bullet pierced his shoe.

Dance motherfucker.

Make it rain!

I lifted my head and all the guns were aimed at me.

Ah, fuck.

"Damn it, Riggs," Wolf growled, reaching for his rifle.

"Should I add the glass to your tab?" Wu asked Jack in the middle of my quest for a rain dance and Wolf trying to save my ass. I think Doc hit me up with some pain killers because I was feeling loopy.

"You made your point Wu, now tell me what you want so we can put this shit to bed," Jack demanded.

Wu laughed, dabbing at the corners of his mouth with a napkin.

"That's funny," he said, rising to his feet, and walking around the table. He wasn't armed but remained calm as Jack cocked his gun and ripped back the safety. There was another Chinese exchange between him and his club. Jack kept his gun close as he narrowed his eyes, watching every move Wu made.

"You stole from me and now you expect me to close my eyes to that?" Wu shook his head. "I don't know who you're used to dealing with, maybe all your mafia handlings have made you forget your place…it doesn't work like that here, Bulldog," he stated, holding out his hands as one of his men handed him a leather cut.

He unfolded the cut.

My fucking cut.

"You see here, when you take from the hand that feeds us we expect a full payment," he explained.

"Yeah, I got your fucking message," Jack fumed. "I'll get you your fucking money but then it ends. This beef gets squashed, we're even because if you want to get down and dirty motherfucker, you marked one of my brothers and I don't take that lightly," he ground out.

"Your brother is lucky he's breathing, Jack, don't make the mistake of thinking I'm finished with any of you. I marked your brother but you've taken blood from me. I have three men to bury and a dozen whores to dispose of, we'll never be even." He affirmed.

Then he turned around and draped my cut over the table. He pulled a knife from his back pocket and dragged the blade along the seam of the reaper sewn into the back of my cut. He ripped the patch from the leather, turned back around to face Jack and threw my cut at me.

"You've taken three of my brothers, seems only fair I take three of yours."

"Don't threaten me or my fucking club Wu," Jack commanded.

"For now, my money will suffice, but the Knights and Dragons alliance is dead," he informed.

Jack advanced toward Wu and the Dragons turned their guns from our heads to Jack's, in return our guns moved across the room, from one Dragon to another, itching to pull the trigger.

Jack brought the barrel of his gun to Wu's lips, running it across the seam.

"Don't underestimate me Wu, I've killed for a lot less," Jack whispered, as he shoved the gun between Wu's lips. "If you ever touch another brother of mine again, I'll make you howl motherfucker, make you beg like the fucking dog you are," he hissed, reaching down and grabbing my patch from Wu's hand. He pulled his gun from his mouth and took a step back. "Don't underestimate me," he repeated.

"A quarter of a million dollars, Bulldog, or I'll shove that gun you had in my mouth up your ass, then you'll know what it's truly like to be fucked by a Dragon," Wu added.

Jack laughed, turning around to face us and handed me my patch before looking over his shoulder at Wu.

"I'll bring the lube," he sneered. "Let's go boys," he ordered.

We followed Jack out, walking backward through the restaurant with our guns held high in case one of these assholes decided to get stupid with us. We were halfway out the door when Wolf decided to send another message, walking back through the shattered door, the crazy fuck shot at the ducks that hung in the front window.

"You're fucking crazy, you know that?" Pipe asked him.

"Fuck you, the kid said he wanted to go hunting," he argued, pointing to me. "It just happens to be duck season," he said as he climbed onto his bike.

"Quack, quack, bitches," he called over his shoulder.

I loved Wolf, truly loved him.

Shit, that was kind of gay.

"Yo," Bones called as he revved his engine. "We need to get your ass home and I don't mean the Dog Pound," he said, daring me to argue. "Your girl's worried about you," he added.

My girl.

"She knows what happened?"

"Nah, but she knows something is up. When we couldn't get a hold of you I went to the apartment," he explained, kicking up his kick stand. "Dude, you fuck that up and you're the dumbest man on the face of the Earth," he continued.

"You got a thing for my Kitten, Bonesy?"

"Man, every man breathing wants a woman like your Kitten," he replied, peeling off in front of me.

Yeah, I imagine they did.

Chapter Twenty-Three

Lauren

I heard the doorknob jiggle and sprang to my feet, hurrying toward the door. It swung open before I could get to it and Riggs stumbled into the apartment.

"Oh, thank God," I said, rushing to meet him. Instead of over thinking everything like I usually did when it came to him, I did what I felt and wrapped my arms around him.

"Aww, Kitten, I missed you too," he said, wrapping one arm around my waist. I heard the sharp hiss escape his mouth and I pulled back, gasping as I took in his face.

"Riggs," I whispered, lifting my fingertips to his bruised cheek.

"It looks worse than it really is," he offered, kicking the door closed, dragging me against him and turning the dead bolt on the door.

I twisted in his arms and rose on tiptoe to inspect his eyes. They were mostly swollen shut and a butterfly stitch was placed in the corner of his right eye.

"It looks clean," I commented, cupping his face with my hands and turning his cheek to inspect the other eye. There was blood in the corner of his eye, hinting to a bleed but nothing too severe. I dropped my hands to his shoulders and ran them down his arms. I had never seen him in anything other than jeans—tonight Riggs was wearing a loose pair of black sweats and a gray fitted hoodie, looking less of a biker and more like a laid back trainer. I don't know where he had the time to workout but he definitely made it his business.

No one ate chocolate pudding and cookies and looked as good as he did.

I wanted to drag the zipper of his hoodie down with my teeth and trace his abs with my tongue.

I bit my lip and rubbed my sweaty palms against my thighs.

"Are you okay?" I asked, hoarsely.

"I'm fine babe," he assured, taking my hand and walking us toward the couch. He paused and bent down to lift the baseball bat that sat next to the couch. He winced again, sighing heavily in pain, before straightening up and glancing back at me with a smirk.

God, that smirk.

"Practicing your swing?" he teased, sitting down on the couch and pulling me onto his lap.

This was new.

"It's a precautionary measure," I insisted.

"Right," he laughed. "Little Miss Safety," he quipped, reaching up and pushing my hair over my shoulder. "Sorry I missed batting practice, Kitten," he said huskily, as his eyes dropped to my lips.

"I know enough to know I'm not supposed to ask questions but…" I wrapped my arms around his neck, "…it's kind of hard not to ask, looking at you like this," I said, as I ran my fingers up the back of his neck where the rim of the backward baseball cap rested.

"Lauren," he protested as I pulled the hat off his head. "Shit," he ground out.

"What the hell is this?" I demanded, moving the hat out of his reach as he tried to take it back.

"My barber got mad at me," he tried to cover, offering me his smile, knowing I was a sucker for it. But it wouldn't work this time. He usually wore a hat but the few times he didn't—I loved Riggs' hair. It was the perfect length to run my fingers through, and even though I hadn't done it all that often, if ever, some asshole with a razor robbed me of the chance.

"I hope you didn't tip him," I replied, playing along with my handsome…friend.

I hated that.

More today than yesterday and even more tomorrow.

He leaned back against the couch cushions and lazily stared back at me, watching as I cocked my head to the side to inspect the damage. I noticed the numbers shaved into his hairline and ran my fingertip along the fuzz, tracing the two, then the five and finally the zero.

"I can fix it," I said, turning back to meet his gaze. "Make it all even for you," I explained.

"Florence Nightingale is a hair stylist too?" he questioned, as his hands ran down my sides, playing with the hem of my shirt.

"I'm a jack of all trades," I replied, brushing the hair away from his face. "What do you say?"

"If I say yes does that mean you'll get off my lap?"

I nodded, holding back the frown that threatened my face—that was kind of a dickhead thing to say.

"Then, no," he said, treating me to a wink.

And there he went being sweet again.

I smiled widely at him, prying his hands off my hips and climbed off him.

"I promise to sit on you when I'm done," I said, pausing mid stride, knowing he was sitting there with a smirk on his face. I chanced it anyway and glanced over my shoulder to see his lips quirk.

"A promise is a promise," he warned.

"I said I'd sit on you," I called, as I fished through the drawers for a pair of scissors. "I didn't say what part of your anatomy I'd choose," I joked.

"I'm just going to throw it out there—I've had a killer day and could use a little loving," he hinted.

"Yeah? And?" I said, plucking the scissors from the drawer and turning around.

"And I'd really like if you sat on my face," he pointed out.

I should tell him that's what I wanted too, just to shock the shit out of him but my poor Tiger had had a rough day so I went easy on him.

"I'll be right back," I said, pointing my finger toward him. "Don't go anywhere," I warned, narrowing my eyes at him.

He held up his hands in mock defeat and I figured it was safe to grab a comb from the bathroom but by the time I found a comb in the cabinet under the sink, his body was hovering over mine.

"Jesus, Riggs," I croaked.

"Since you're giving me a haircut I thought it'd be easier if we did it in the bathroom," he suggested, as he sat on the toilet seat. He moved his arms and cringed as he drew the zipper down his sweatshirt and worked it down his arms.

I gasped when I saw the large red marks that covered his body and reached out to touch them but he grabbed my hand and I diverted my eyes to his. He shook his head.

"They're not there," he started. "Ignore them," he continued, throwing his shirt onto the counter before spreading his legs and pulling me between them, locking them around me. "How 'bout that haircut, Kitten?"

I swallowed, reaching across the counter for the spray bottle and misted his hair so it was wet, then ran my fingers through what was left of it. I heard the groan rumble low in the back of his throat, encouraging me to thread my fingers through his hair again, this time I tugged the ends and tilted his head back so he was looking up at me.

"Keep your head straight," I instructed, positioning his head so he wasn't looking up at me anymore and looking straight ahead. I ran the comb through his wet hair, snipping here and there.

"How was your day?" he asked after a few moments.

"Uneventful, until you came home," I replied.

"If it's okay with you, I'm going to start staying here with you," he said hesitantly.

"It's your place, Riggs," I reminded him. "If I get in your way—"

"Cut it out, Lauren," he clipped, interrupting me and tilting his head upward to look into my eyes. "I want you here," he added.

"Okay, then," I whispered, cupping his chin with one hand and forcing him back into position. "Stop moving," I ordered.

"Are you always this demanding?"

"Wouldn't you like to know," I teased.

"Yeah, I think I would," he answered immediately.

I ignored the comment, learning that reading too deep into Riggs would only hurt me. He was unattainable and the more time we spent together, the more he consumed my every thought. I was going to suffer a major heartache—his name was Riggs.

I continued to cut his hair in silence, willing myself not to look at the marks on his skin and happy that some of his tattoos covered the grueling red lashes. I ran my hand over his hair, checking each side to make sure it was even and there was no trace of the number some asshole decided to put on his head.

"I think we're done," I said, inspecting the crew cut he was now sporting.

"Thank Christ," he hissed. "I don't know how much more I can take," he stated.

"Anxious?" I asked, taking a step backward so he could glance in the mirror. He didn't move. He didn't get up or turn around to look at his new hair style, instead he stared at me.

"Had your nipples saluting me for the last twenty minutes, Kitten. I really appreciate the no bra thing but not when I'm horny as fuck," he rasped.

I didn't know words could deliver empowerment, but they did, giving me the courage to give into temptation. I took another step backward, watched as my poor battered Tiger peered at me with one lustful eye.

That look was all for me.

Maybe he did want me.

Or maybe he was just horny.

I was horny too so I decided to just go with it.

What was the worst that could happen?

Become pregnant? Ha!

Decision made.

I fingered the hem of my t-shirt, building up my courage and watching him intently. When his good eye glassed over and he growled, I pulled the flimsy fabric over my head. I balled it up and threw it on the counter with his sweatshirt.

I swallowed down my doubt. Doubt that this man wanted me the way I wanted him and rocked the confidence buried deep inside of me.

"How horny are you, Tiger?" I asked, arching an eyebrow as I stepped toward him. My breasts swayed with each step. They were bigger, heavier even, and my nipples always seemed to be erect and sore…so goddamn sore. My belly was still flat which only accentuated the flotation devises I had for breasts.

Riggs reached out, grabbing my hips and pulled me back in-between his legs.

"You giving me the green light, Kitten? Tell me you're giving me the green light."

I didn't even know what that meant but as his hand glided up my stomach and his thumb brushed one of my nipples, I didn't care to know either.

"Had a long day, didn't you, Riggs?" I said, throwing one leg over his thigh and taking a seat on his knee. "A man deserves to relax after a day like yours," I added, running my hands up his chest, wrapping them around his neck and pulling him closer so my breasts brushed against his chest.

"You're killing me," he gritted out, bowing his head to kiss the curve of my breast.

"I just want to make you feel better," I argued arching my back, pushing out my chest. "Think I can do that?"

I ground myself against his thigh as my teeth sank into my lower lip, I took his hands and worked them over my body until each hand grabbed a breast. Thatta' boy.

"My Kitten's a little tease," he growled, squeezing my tits. It hurt and felt like ecstasy at the same time, making me crave his mouth on them. I was hoping he'd use more than just his tongue and treat me to his teeth. There was an animal caged inside of Riggs and I wanted to be the girl who unleashed it.

"Maybe you're not the only one feeling a certain kind of way," I whispered, against his ear before taking his earlobe between my teeth.

"Say it, Kitten. Tell me how you're feeling," he demanded, rolling my nipple between his fingers. "Christ, your tits are perfect," he growled, pushing them together before burying his face between them.

"I'm just as horny as you," I panted, riding his leg, desperate for any sort of friction and frustrated that I wasn't getting what I needed. I pushed him back, climbed off his lap and grabbed his hands forcing him to his feet. "You sure you're up for this?" I asked, glancing at his nasty eye.

"You gonna send me to the couch with blue balls, Kitten?"

"Just making sure you're up for the ride," I said, taking his hands and wrapping them around me as I led him out of the bathroom.

"Who's riding who?" he asked, sliding his hands beneath the elastic of my leggings.

"Oh, Tiger, I'm riding you," I affirmed, turning around in his arms and walking backward into the bedroom. I shimmied the leggings down my legs, along with my thong, and kicked them off the rest of the way. I could see his erection bulging against his sweats and moved closer to him, palming his cock before circling his body.

Tight ass.

Broad shoulders.

My Tiger was easy on the eyes, that's for sure.

I rounded him and stared at his chiseled chest and the v that dipped into his sweats. I decided Riggs may not be mine forever, but he was mine for now, and for now I'd enjoy him. I pushed him toward the bed until the back of his knees hit the mattress.

"Lay down," I ordered, pushing down his shoulders until he was sitting on the edge of the bed. I slipped my hands inside his pants, dragging them down his legs. He was completely nude and his dick was pulsing for me. I positioned myself on my knees, placing a hand on each of his thighs and forced them wide open. I let my hands feel their way up and down his calves and thighs as I leaned into him and brushed my tits against his dick.

His hands fisted my hair and he pulled me back, forcing me to arch as he leaned down, his mouth finding the base of my neck. His teeth grazed the sensitive flesh before his lips worked it over, applying just the right amount of pressure to leave a mark. His mouth went to work, traveling from my neck, across my collar bone, down to the swell of my breasts, leaving his mark all over my skin

Riggs was branding me...

His Kitten...

His property...

All his.

Property of the Tiger. Little did he know with every mark he drew with his mouth, I drew one of my own. My branding may not have been visible to him but it was to me. Every touch, every sweep of my tongue against the bruises that marked his skin, branded him mine.

Mine to take care of.

Even if it was only for tonight.

I pulled back, trying again to take his cock into my mouth, to lick his arousal that glistened from his thick head, but again he forced my head back so my eyes met his.

"You wrap that sweet mouth of yours around my cock and this will be over before it even started," he grunted. "Get up here, Kitten, let me lick you," he said.

"I want tonight to be about making you feel good," I protested.

"Make me feel a fuck of a lot good, getting to taste that pussy of yours," he swore, as I stood up maneuvering myself so I was straddling him. He laid back against the mattress and stared up at me, reaching around to dig his fingers into my ass. "Fuck, you're pretty," he whispered. "Come on, give it to me, girl," he coaxed.

I bit the inside of my cheek and he grabbed my ass, dragging my body over his, my knees dipping into the mattress on either side of his head. He took hold of my hips, lifting me up before he raised his head from the mattress and pressed his mouth against my core.

He groaned like a starving animal, taking that first taste of his prey, and I lost my mind.

Gone.

See ya.

Everything faded, and all that existed was Riggs.

He moved his fingers to my lips, spreading me open and his tongue lazily lapped at me. I gripped the bars of the headboard and leaned over his face, my head hung low as I watched him devour me.

He sucked one lip before switching to the other and grazing it with his teeth. Two fingers dragged across my wetness before he plunged them inside me and flicked his tongue over my clit. I tried to be careful of his eye, of his stitches, but something told me Riggs didn't care if he went blind in one eye as long as he got me off, he'd deal with the sacrifice.

He was a keeper.

He ate pussy like a champ.

I might never let him go.

I think I might grow an addiction to his tongue.

His fingers moved in and out of me, stretching me enough to fit a third and that's when I lost myself. I didn't give a shit about leaning all my weight on him. I didn't care if I suffocated him. All that mattered was seeing what he could do to me and I started to ride his fingers.

He tricked me, removing his fingers, replacing them with his mouth. I rode his mouth just the way he wanted me to. His wet fingers travelling up my body to pinch my nipple was pure ecstasy.

"Come all over me, Kitten," he hissed, his words vibrating off my pussy. "So fucking good," he grunted.

I arched my back, braced one hand on his shoulder, the other wrapped tightly around the wrought iron headboard as my hips bucked. I was right there, just a little more... He gave me one lavish lick, nuzzled his nose against my clit and it was over. I fell over the cliff, my body convulsing against his mouth as he drove me to the single most gratifying orgasm I had ever experienced.

The rest of my body stilled as my pussy quaked with the aftershocks of my orgasm and I tried to catch my breath when I heard Riggs chuckle. My head snapped down and I glared at him.

"Are you seriously laughing right now?"

"Yes," he admitted.

I moved, trying to lift my leg and crawl off him but he grabbed me and rolled us over so I was on my back and he was on his side.

"I'm laughing because you're not what I expected. You're so much more," he explained, leaning over me and pressing his lips against my mouth. "Open your mouth, taste how fucking delicious you are," he dared, as his mouth hovered over mine. I pouted, trying to decide if that was a compliment or not. He sucked my lower lip into his mouth, forcing my lips apart with his tongue and did exactly what he wanted to, giving me a taste of myself. I spread my legs as he moved between them, his cock pressed against me, teasing me, taunting me until I lifted my hips and pressed up against him.

He broke the kiss, his lips lingering above mine as he gazed at me.

"Lauren."

"Yeah," I whispered.

"Just making sure you're real," he said, before he sank his dick inside me. I didn't remember much about our first time, but I don't think it was anything like this. I hadn't been paying attention to detail that night. Details like how I felt every inch of him. Details like how it felt to know what sex feels like without a condom. He was the first guy I didn't use protection with. The sex was so much better bareback, skin to skin, nothing but him and me.

I opened my mouth to speak but I couldn't find my voice and concentrated on moving with him. One deep thrust and I felt so full, wondering how I took him so easily that night at the compound and if it was possible he was bigger.

It was my turn to laugh as I imagined him taking penis enhancements.

He pinched my nipple.

"Ouch."

"New rule," he grunted, as he pulled out of me. I parted my lips but my objection died on my tongue as he pounded into me, harder, wilder, without resolve.

"No laughing when fucking."

"Harder!" I ordered, slapping his ass as he quickened his pace, his hips slamming into mine and flesh smacking against flesh. The noises we both made were so dirty and so sexy I could probably come again from them alone. Riggs had other ideas though, he worked me up to another mind-blowing orgasm with his magic stick.

Yes, that's right, his cock was a magic stick.

I usually have to work for my orgasms, will myself to come with my mind but I'm mindless right now, barely able to move and on the verge of coming again.

He pressed his lips to mine quickly, taking my hands and pinning them over my head as he rotated his hips and pushed as deep as he could go. I felt myself clench around him, my legs tightening around his waist as I tried to free my hands only for him to slam them against the mattress again. He buried his head in my neck and groaned my name as he came.

Breathless, sweaty, and sated we remained entwined in one another. It was bliss. Something I vowed to remember when it all went to shit. He slowly lifted himself from me, withdrawing his cock before flipping over onto his back, wincing as his back hit the mattress.

"Your mattress sucks, Kitten," he complained. "Tomorrow we're going shopping," he added as he raised his arm and stretched it over my head. "Come cuddle with me."

"I never pegged you to be one for cuddles," I teased, as I moved closer to him.

"Yeah, didn't peg the girl next door to be a wildcat in the bedroom either," he replied, wrapping his arm around me. "Guess we're both full of surprises."

That was for sure.

"Christ, your feet are like icicles," he said, lifting himself slightly to cover us.

"My feet are always cold," I replied, as I snuggled against him. He threw his leg over mine in what I think was an attempt to warm me. We remained silent for a few moments, my head resting on his chest as he lazily stroked my shoulder.

"I was worried about you," I admitted in the dark.

"Nothing to be worried about," he said automatically.

I traced my finger along one of the red marks on his chest wishing I could believe him, knowing I couldn't.

Chapter Twenty-Four

RIGGS

The best thing about getting your ass kicked by a bunch of crazy fucks is coming home to your girl and having great sex. It made up for my body feeling as if I had been hit by a Mack truck. I rolled over and reached for Kitten, hoping she'd be up for another ride on the "Riggs Express," but my hands grabbed air instead of titty.

I would have to talk to her about that. There were few things I required, at the top of the list was; no creeping out of bed without chomping down the morning wood. Major no-no.

I glanced down at my dick. Poor guy. I wrapped my hand around the length, giving it a slow pull as I pictured Kitten's mouth wrapped around it, her eyes peering up at me from the rim of her glasses.

She didn't wear them last night but it wouldn't have mattered anyway. I barely looked at anything but her tits and her pussy. That fucking pussy was sweeter than anything I've ever tasted. I could eat her twenty-four seven and never crave anything else. It wasn't such a bad idea, living off Kitten's pussy, at least I know I'd die happy.

My dick was harder than steel, all this talk about Lauren's pussy and I was sitting here with my hand wrapped around my cock. Fuck that, I climbed out of bed to find me some of the real thing. I didn't bother with clothes as I took my fine ass into the living room, spotting Lauren in the kitchen with her back toward me.

My plan was to sneak up on her, press myself up against her before I picked her up and laid her out on top of the counter. They say breakfast is the most important meal of the day, and eating Lauren would be the breakfast of champions.

She turned around, holding a mug in her hands and nearly jumped out of her skin when she saw me.

"You scared me!" She cried, as she set the coffee mug on the counter and stared at me. "You're naked," she accused.

"Yeah and you're not," I said, drawing my eyebrows together. "Why is that?" I'm pretty sure my lip curled as I locked eyes with the cock blocking pajama pants and t-shirt she was wearing.

"I...well...I figured," she stammered, nervously pushing her glasses further onto the bridge of her nose as I started for her.

"You figured..." I coaxed, closing the distance between us as I pressed my dick against her thigh and took hold of her hips.

"I figured it'd be like last time," she whispered, lifting her eyes to mine, challenging me to deny her words.

I lifted her up, turning around and placing her on the counter. I had no idea what she was talking about and rather than trying to figure it out I decided to have breakfast. She gasped at first as I pulled off her pajamas with my teeth and then she laughed. I loved Kitten's laugh.

"Riggs, wait!" She protested, as she wrapped her legs around my waist and I buried my face between her tits. I teased one perfect nipple before wreaking havoc on the other one.

How the fuck did I get so lucky?

She giggled again as I worked my mouth down her stomach, pausing for a second, realizing that my kid was inside of her, just hanging out while Kitten took care of him.

So, fucking lucky.

"Riggs, seriously, hang on a minute," she said as she cupped my face and tilted my head back so I was looking at her. "What are we doing?"

"Right now? You're stopping me from making you come," I pointed out, licking my lips for extra emphasis.

"I mean besides that."

"Kitten, you're losing me," I groaned, trying to rub myself against something…anything.

"You're not going to ignore me and pretend like I don't exist again?" she blurted the question, forcing me to give up on humping her leg and stare at her as if she had lost her marbles.

"Don't look at me like that," she warned. "Last time, you completely blew me off, and that's fine, you're not into repeats, okay, but that was before there was Pea," she explained.

Repeats.

No, I rarely did them.

And after the last time, I pulled away and turned my back on her because I wasn't a man who stuck with one woman. I wasn't the boyfriend type and wasn't ready for an old lady. I wasn't about that life.

But here we are.

And there's nowhere else I'd rather be.

No other girl I want.

I still wasn't about that life but a part of me wanted to be.

For Kitten.

For Pea.

I might not have my shit together, fuck, if I'm being honest my life resembles a fifteen-year-old kid who knocked up his high school sweetheart and just got jumped by a pack of thugs—but I wasn't going anywhere.

I owned my adolescent situation.

I owned Lauren.

And I owned Pea.

"Give me back my pants," she demanded.

"What do you want? You want me to go carve our names into a tree? Because I'm not about that—where I come from I give you my colors, you become my old lady and I'm not ready for that yet. To be fair, I don't think you are either but I'm here, and I'll keep being here because I want to be, because I want to see where this goes, and not just because of Pea but because of you. So, fuck labels, that's a bunch of bullshit anyway, let's just be who we are," I said, tucking a strand of hair behind her ear and leaning into her. "Be my Kitten and I'll keep being your Tiger," I rasped.

"You ever call me an old lady I might kick you in the balls," she said, as she brought her hands to my face. "I really want to be your Kitten," she whispered.

"So then let me show you how much of a Tiger I can be," I growled, my lips curving as she threw her head back and laughed.

That laugh.

God, I was fucked.

She wrapped her arms around my neck and hopped off the counter before standing on her tip toes. Her nose nuzzled my ear as her hands slid down my back and cupped my ass.

"Let's go Tiger, make me purr," she whispered against my ear, slapping my ass before she took my hand and pulled me toward the couch.

I watched as she spun around, her smile contagious as she worked her t-shirt over her head, throwing it onto the floor before she pushed me down onto the couch. I loved that she was so confident, that she took charge and showed me what she wanted.

She straddled me, rubbing herself against my cock as she held onto my shoulders.

"Kiss me," she demanded.

I was all about pleasing her so I leaned in to close my mouth over hers, but the tease she was, pulled back. I went at her again, but again she moved that mischievous smile away from me. I grabbed the back of her neck and pulled her to me, crashing my mouth over hers, capturing her, claiming her. I fucked her mouth, mimicking the way I'd fuck her pussy, promising my cock would give it to her the way my tongue did.

She moaned into my mouth as I reached between us and pressed my thumb against her clit. My fingers itched to tease that cunt of hers, to dip them into that pussy and pull them back, to suck her juice from my fingers and get drunk on her taste alone.

It used to be tequila that made my head spin, now it was Lauren.

"Riggs," she panted. I don't know if my name on her lips sounded like a prayer she wished for or the answer to all of mine.

"Yeah, baby," I said, taking her lower lip between my teeth. "Tell me what you want," I growled.

"I want to feel you, all of you…everywhere…now," she cried, pulling away and raising herself so she was lined up with my cock. I gripped her hips and arched my back, slamming her down onto my cock, rough and hard.

I kept one hand steady on her hip easing her up and down on my cock as she cupped her tits, her thumbs working her rigid nipples.

Thatta' girl, work those tits.

Get those nipples like rocks, give me something to suck on, something to bite.

"I'm going to come," she whimpered, as she quickened her pace, rotating her hips before she lifted herself off my cock. "Not yet," she panted. "Not fucking yet," she crawled off my lap, onto the floor and grabbed my cock with her hand as she peered up at me from the fringe of her lashes.

Sexiest fucking woman I ever had.

I ran my fingers through her hair as she took me deep into her mouth.

Holy fucking shit.

"You like the way you taste, don't you?" I growled, as she sucked the head of my cock, her tongue twirling around it, licking off the moisture covering it from being deep inside of her. Her hands moved to cup my balls as she pulled me from her mouth, her tongue taking a long sweep along the length of my dick. She wrapped her other hand around my shaft, lifting it so her mouth could replace the hand that cupped my balls and she took one sac into her mouth.

Every thought vanished from my head as I thrust my dick into her hand.

Talk about owning shit. Lauren owned me right then and there. She didn't even realize how she claimed me, ruining me for any other woman with that mouth of hers. That perfect fucking mouth.

Kitten gave good head.

Phenomenal head.

I take it back.

I'll go carve our names in every fucking tree in Central Park.

Right after I come in her mouth.

"Shit, Kitten, I'm going to come," I barked, as she jerked my cock one last time before dropping it. I think I whimpered, maybe I sobbed, but I didn't come.

She licked her lips, shaking her head as she stood up.

"Not yet, Tiger, not until you bend me over and fuck me from behind," she ordered. "Now where's it gonna be big boy? Over the couch or on the floor?" she panted.

Kitten was going to kill me.

But it definitely wasn't a bad way to go.

"On the floor," I hissed, moving off the couch on wobbly legs. My dick throbbing. I worried if I didn't get the fuck inside her I was going to combust. She laid down on the floor, rolling over onto her stomach and glanced over her shoulder.

"I'm waiting," she reminded me, lifting her hips and spreading her legs just enough so I could see her pink, swollen flesh beckoning. I got down on my knees, sinking my teeth into one cheek of that perfect ass perched high in the air.

She yelped.

"It's time I call the shots, Kitten," I ground out, slapping her ass and bending my head to allow my tongue one lap along her pussy. I should tease her, make her beg for it but I'd just be torturing myself. I took my time though, appreciating the view and ran my hands over the slope of her back. She glanced over her shoulder at me as I leaned over and took a fistful of her hair.

"Gonna fuck you hard, think you can handle it?" I asked, pressing my mouth to the back of her neck.

"Try me," she replied.

Dead.

But this was the sweetest Heaven I'd ever know.

She lifted her hips, urging me to enter, and that broke my resolve.

It was on. I knew it and she knew it too.

She laid her palms flat against the floor, bracing herself as I drove my cock deep inside her tight heat. I lost control, forgot about everything. All that mattered was filling her over and over again. She panted, she cried, and swore on everything holy and me? I fucked her like my life depended on it.

I was wild and reckless as I pounded her, slapping her ass and pulling her hair. It was rough, and I made no apologies about it. But Kitten didn't need apologies, she needed more, more of my cock, more of my vulgar mouth that whispered how sweet her cunt was, more of me. She took everything I gave her and begged for more. When she screamed out my name and thanked God, I knew I had met my match.

I don't even know what I shouted as I came and couldn't even be sure it was English. My orgasm raged on, and Kitten's perfect cunt milked every last drop of come I had. If she wasn't pregnant already, she would've been after this, because that was the mother-load of loads.

I chuckled.

Mother-load of loads.

"Riggs!"

"Shit, sorry," I said, still laughing. I forgot about the no laughing while fucking rule but I was pretty sure if she knew what I was laughing about she'd laugh too.

I leaned down and pressed my lips to her sweaty shoulder.

"You okay?"

She looked over her shoulder at me.

"That was good, Tiger…real fucking good," she said, still a little breathless.

"I love it when you talk dirty," I replied, giving her a quick kiss on that filthy mouth.

"I know you do," she said, winking at me. "Keep fucking me like that and I'll give you all the dirty talk you want," she promised.

I grinned, taking her mouth again and wondered how I ever got so lucky.

Chapter Twenty-Five
Lauren

I'm learning that sometimes life ends up differently than you expected, that I don't always need a plan, and sometimes I have to let go and see what happens. It's a pretty amazing journey, letting go of the things you thought you wanted and enjoying all the surprises *life* has to offer you.

In other words—I'm learning to like detours.

And Riggs? He's the best detour of all. I think I might be addicted to his dick. Is it possible to have a penis addiction? Hi, my name is Lauren, and I'm addicted to Riggs' cock. Don't sign me up for Dicks Anonymous, I most definitely will not go.

I'm perfectly content.

That thought alone should scare the shit out of me but it doesn't. Riggs is teaching me to roll with the punches, to ride the wave, and that's pretty fucking awesome, considering the only waves I've ever ridden are the ones in Mexico.

In all seriousness, it's not just his cock, it's everything. Riggs is everything I never knew I wanted.

And that's a hard thing for a girl like me to swallow because I usually know how to keep my feelings intact. I'm someone who likes to be one step ahead of the game, a girl who likes to know what will happen, before it even does, never allowing myself to get hurt.

Break my heart?

Give someone that kind of power over me?

Absolutely not.

Yet here we were, Kitten and Tiger, and no other label could compare. I didn't need him to carve our names into a tree because I had *him*. I had his word, his vow he wanted to see where we went, a promise he'd try.

It was enough for now.

It was everything.

He was pushing a wagon in a supermarket for Christ's sake and he wasn't even complaining, not one bit…and we were in the produce department too.

After we showered together this morning, he insisted we go shopping for a mattress. Riggs' bike was out of commission and since I had sold my car, we were walking the streets of Brooklyn. We stopped first at Sleepy's, where he insisted we roll around on every mattress they sold. Finally, he picked one perfect for us and it was being delivered the following day.

Afterward we walked along 86th Street when he turned and asked me to wait outside for a minute as he went into one of the many dollar stores that lined the busy street. I didn't question him, I loved that Riggs was full of surprises, and waited outside while he delivered the most thoughtful gift I had ever been on the receiving end of. Five minutes later he emerged from the store, his grin firmly secured to his face as he waved a bag over his head.

My face hurt from smiling so much.

He leaned forward and pressed his lips to mine before handing me the bag. I opened the bag and pulled out a pair of socks that had kittens all over them.

"You bought me socks?" I asked, looking back inside the bag to see it was full of all different kinds of funky socks. Some had kittens, some had superheroes; there was even a pair of Christmas socks in there.

"Make sure you wear them too," he said, draping his arm over my shoulders. "Can't have those feet of yours ice cold anymore, especially when you're rubbing them on me in the middle of the night," he added.

"You bought me socks," I repeated.

"So?" he kissed the top of my head and dragged me into the supermarket.

They were only socks to Riggs, not a big gesture in his book, but in mine they were the sweetest gift anyone had ever given me. He was taking care of me without even trying.

And how did I repay him? By forcing him to eat fruits and vegetables. I looked down at the celery in my hand then back at Riggs who appeared bored as he stared at the apples in the wagon.

"What's your favorite thing to eat?" I asked, watching his head lift and his eyes snap toward mine. He grinned mischievously at me and I laughed out loud. "Not what I meant," I said. "What's your favorite meal?"

"One could argue that what I had for breakfast this morning was in fact a meal," he pointed out.

"Food, Riggs. Tell me your favorite food," I clarified.

He took a minute to think about it, then straightened his shoulders and smiled at me.

"Spaghetti and meatballs," he said, smiling as he pushed the wagon.

Another surprise.

"Really? I took you more for a meat and potatoes kind of guy," I said, a bit bewildered as I bit my cheek. It just so happened that I made the best meatballs and while I preferred them fried, I could definitely throw together a little marinara sauce. "I want to cook dinner for us tonight," I blurted, throwing a couple of heads of garlic into the wagon.

I could feel him stare at me as I grabbed the basil and added it to the cart. When I lifted my eyes to his, I saw a slow grin work its way across his lips.

"You can cook?"

"Of course I can cook," I replied, feeling my cheeks redden I nervously repositioned my glasses on my face and looked back at him. "It's my God given right," I offered.

"Because you're a woman?"

"Because I'm Maria Bianci's daughter," I corrected. "I know she may not be your favorite person, but she can throw down in the kitchen," I informed him, lacing my arm through his as we walked through the supermarket. "Stop smiling at me like that, you're making me blush," I ordered. He continued to push the cart and I noticed from the corner of my eye he was still smiling.

"I like it when you blush, Kitten, like it a whole lot," he whispered.

RIGGS

I'm whipped.

And for lack of better words and all puns intended, I am one hundred percent pussy whipped.

The sickest thing of all was, I didn't give a fuck.

Lauren was my dream girl, sweet when she wanted to be, ferocious when she needed to be, and fucking wild in the bedroom. Plus she could cook. She made my favorite for dinner, something someone had cooked for me a long time ago, before Bones' mom passed.

I watched her from the living room, barefoot, pregnant and in the kitchen—I couldn't help but chuckle. Lauren didn't share my amusement and dragged my ass into the kitchen, insisting I help her. She taught me how to make the perfect meatball and I now knew Maria Bianci's secret ingredient. I wouldn't hesitate to leak that shit if that woman should find the need to piss me off.

Bones showed up as we were eating dinner and Lauren fixed him a plate. The three of us sat down like Three's Company and ate, forgetting all about the reason Bones was there in the first place. Jack was calling Church in an hour and my ass was needed at the compound. It was time to face the music and tell him the truth of how I fucked up, how all this shit with the Chinese was my fault.

I kissed Kitten goodbye and left with Bones. We were late walking into the Chapel, just as Jack slammed the gavel down.

"Nice of you two idiots to join us," he commented.

"Leave them alone, man. These two fucks were getting it on in the back of the cage," Wolf chimed in.

"You two dicks acting out a little Brokeback Mountain?" Pipe questioned.

"The fact that you even know what that is makes me wonder if that mail order bride of yours is just a cover," I growled. "Wolf here, probably does it for you," I turned to Wolf. "When you gonna make this bitch your old lady?"

Jack chuckled from the head of the table as Pipe stood, about to kick my ass but Wolf held him back, keeping his man in line and all that.

"All right, all right, enough. We have a lot of shit we need to cover and not a lot of time," Jack announced. "We want to keep breathing, we need to settle this score with Wu. We were desperate to get back Reina and Blackie and fucked ourselves by taking their shit. There's a reason we've been playing nice with the Red Dragons for all these years…them motherfuckers, they get down and dirty."

"Let them fuck with us, let them try, we can get down and dirty too," Wolf argued.

"I think you proved that point when you shot and killed those whores," Jack cited, grounding out his cigarette in the ashtray in front of him.

"God rest their souls," Wolf muttered, making the sign of the cross.

"You're sick," Bones declared, as he watched Wolf bow his head and pray for the souls of the whores who made a living cutting heroin.

I wasn't a church man but something told me they needed more than a prayer to cleanse their souls, but then again so did we.

"Pipe, where we at with our finances?" Jack questioned.

"Wait, we're seriously going to pay these rat bastards?" Pipe asked, turning his attention toward Jack.

"We pay them what we owe them because I don't want them taking another one of my guys," Jack said. "Now, I asked how our finances are and I expect an answer," he barked.

"We don't got much to work with, most of the clubs money has been tied up in the guns, but hey, we got a shitload of guns now," he informed.

"What if we got another buyer?" Bones asked.

"Not enough time," Jack answered. "There's no money coming in from our dealings with Victor either, not until I get my ass up there and figure out where we go from here. What about the Corrupt Bastards, they paid their debt?"

"Yeah, they paid for the run we made up north with them—a whopping fifty grand. We're right there boss," Pipe said sarcastically. "I can pull about seventy-five grand from the garage but how we going to get the other half?"

"I'll take the rest of the money out of my house," Jack declared, diverting his eyes to Wolf. "Tell the Chinese prince we're coming for him, to set the fucking table," he grunted.

"I can't let you do that," I said, raising my eyes to meet Jacks. "We leave the clubs money alone and you don't touch one red cent of the equity in your house," I stated.

"Not your call to make, Riggs," Jack bit back.

"Too bad," I leaned back in the chair and glanced around the table at my brothers. "This is my fault, I'll pay the debt." I declared.

"If you didn't give us that intel we wouldn't have had the drugs. It was pure luck we got Jimmy the way we did, if things went differently and we didn't have the drugs to bargain with Reina and Blackie would both be dead," Jack explained. "You did good, kid."

"You want to know why Wu came after me," I asked, as I turned around and looked at him. "Why he didn't put a bag over Pipe's head, or put a price tag on Wolf? Because I'm the one that fucked up."

I watched as Jack narrowed his eyes in confusion and the table grew silent.

"When you gave me the green light I switched the camera feed on Wu's stash house and replaced the live feed with the recordings of the day before. So when we got there and Wu checked his cameras he wouldn't see shit."

"Smart man," Jack commented warily.

"Yeah, except I missed a frame, one frame out of a forty-five. I had no idea, even after he took me I didn't know why he did, and then he showed me," I pulled my hat from my head, displaying my new haircut to my club. "The frame I missed was the camera in the hallway. I may be good-looking but I'm not very photogenic," I turned back to Jack. "When we were calling out for Wolf I turned toward the camera and lifted my mask. That's how Wu knew it was us…knew it was me," I confessed.

"Shit," Pipe mumbled, swiping his hand over his face.

"It was a slip up Riggs, doesn't mean this shit should lie on your shoulders. We were racing against the clock and anyone of us could've made a mistake," Jack began. "We could vote on it but it'd be a waste of time."

"Appreciate that boss but I've got the money and I want to be the one who pays," I insisted.

"You got a quarter of a million dollars just hanging around?" Pipe questioned.

"Ever hear of Montgomery Oil?" I asked the club, glancing over at Bones who shook his head.

I never wanted the club to know where I came from, mainly because if they knew the truth they probably wouldn't have patched me in. I was the heir to a fortune, a spoiled brat who turned his back on his family and their millions to be a fucking criminal. It was the shit FX movies were made of. To be fair though, my family wasn't worth my piss, they didn't give a damn about me. I was just a dick that would carry their name and hopefully produce more dicks for them. Long live the Montgomery's and all their glory. Bullshit.

My mother reached out to me a couple of times after I left, only because my old man cut her off. It didn't matter that they were divorced, that she had been re-married three times since their divorce, Robert Montgomery owned that bitch with a fat checking account. She jumped at his command. When he told her to reign me back in or he'd cut her flow of money, she tried her damnedest to be the doting, loving mother she never was when I needed one. Fuck her too.

I didn't need them or their money.

Montgomery was a name inked to a piece of paper.

Riggs was a name I chose for myself and the Satan's Knights was the name of the family I chose.

I may not need them or want them but I took what was mine to take. What I fucking earned. Twenty-one years I gave them fuckers, being the son they pawned on babysitters and hired help. I deserved every dollar of that trust fund.

They could keep their fucking empire.

I was sitting at the table of a different kind of empire.

One where family mattered.

"What about it?" Jack asked.

I lifted my hips, pulling my wallet out from my back pocket and took out my license, throwing it onto the table.

Pipe reached out and lifted it up to his eyes.

"Fucking ay!" He hissed, handing it over to Jack. "Got ourselves a rich one, don't reckon ever having one of those before," he mused.

Jack looked at me for a moment, meeting my stare before his eyes dropped to the name on my license.

"I've got the money," I repeated, causing him to lift his eyes to me. "Give me a day to pull it all out and then set up the meet with Wu."

"You realize that you might be pissing away your daddy's hard earned cash, don't you? Ain't no guarantee meeting Wu's demands will make him go away," Jack enlightened. "The last time the Knights and the Dragons were at war there was a whole lot of bloodshed across these streets and all the money in the world wouldn't have made it disappear."

"I've been pissing on my father since I walked away from him," I declared, slapping my palm against the wooden table. "It's the least I can do, man."

Jack stared at me long and hard. He could tell me to take my money and shove it up my ass but tomorrow morning I'd go to Wu myself and pay the clubs debt off, with or without them behind me. His words rang in my ears, the promise of more shit heading our way because of my mistake, and I realized I would do whatever I had to, to keep this shit at bay.

"Fine," he said finally.

"Get the money," he tore his eyes from me and looked at Wolf. "Get that meeting set up."

"You got it, boss," Wolf agreed.

"Good," I said. "What happens next?"

"We wait," Jack said. "This club needs to make as much money as possible to fund our asses when Wu comes calling again, and mark my words that bitch will call," he continued. "We're going to need all the ammo and all the allies we can get," he added. "With Blackie still in the hospital, I will reach out to the Corrupt Bastards myself and see if we can work something out with them. They've carried us before, if the deal is sweet enough they'll do it again. I'm heading up to see Vic next week, finish up this shit with Gold and feel him out for who's got the power now. If his organization has any life left I'll make sure they're in our pocket, ready to roll when the storm blows through."

"Look around, Jack, this club ain't ready for a war. We've barely got a pulse right now," Pipe cautioned. "Our vice president is on a methadone drip trying to get clean. We need more men, another charter or something. The only reason we're still standing is because Bianci and Val's kid pitched in with the Gold situation."

"You think I don't know that? You think I'm fucking blind?" Jack roared. "But I ain't bowing down to no Dragon and neither is this club," he spat. "So protect your interests, hold tight to those you love and make it count because we're living on borrowed time."

Those were his final words before he adjourned our meeting, final words that had a whole lot of meaning. One of the prospects had fixed up my bike, and I didn't need Bones to drive me back home.

Home. What a joke.

My home was here at the Dog Pound, away from Lauren.

Where it should be.

If Jack was right, and he usually was, every moment I spent making it count was another moment I put her and Pea at risk. Jimmy took Reina partially because she meant something to Jack. That sick fuck tried to grab Jack's daughter and would have if Blackie hadn't of sacrificed himself.

An enemy didn't care about the people that mattered most in your life, it wasn't about them, they were just a pawn they took to make you suffer. I understood the concept, there was no greater torture than being helpless as someone you cared about suffered for your sins. I wouldn't hesitate to do the same thing to one of my own enemies.

Make it count.

Borrowed time.

Jack's words repeated over and over in my head but they didn't stop me from going home to Kitten. His words should've been a wake-up call, a warning, but all they did was push me closer to finding my heart. The thing that keeps me breathing.

It was late by the time I got home and all the lights were out. Lauren was sound asleep in our bed with a book resting on her chest. I walked around the bed, glancing down at her feet curled under her and saw the socks she wore. I felt something squeeze inside of me and I brought my hand up to my chest trying to rub it away.

I carefully took the book from her chest and closed it, turning it over to see what she was reading.

What to Expect When You're Expecting.

My lips curved slightly as I placed the book on top of the nightstand and my eyes wandered to her stomach.

Still no sign of Pea.

Still a chance for that kid to be spared the hell my life would inflict on him or her.

Then I looked at Lauren and remembered I promised her I'd stick around. She'd hate me if I left but she'd hate me more if something happened to her or the baby.

I turned around and walked out of the bedroom, deciding that I couldn't walk away just yet and knowing with every fiber of my being I was doing the wrong thing. I kicked off my boots and told myself sleeping on the couch was at least putting distance between us but before I could lie down, Lauren padded into the living room.

"What're you doing?" She asked softly.

"I didn't mean to wake you, go back to sleep, Kitten," I said huskily.

"Okay, then come with me," she replied, holding out her hand as she cocked her head to the side and stared at me.

My hand moved up to my chest again, rubbing away that ache as I stood up and walked over to her. She pressed her lips to mine quickly before turning around and taking me to bed.

It was painfully obvious that I couldn't say no to Kitten and more importantly I didn't want to, so I yielded Jack's advice and made it count.

Chapter Twenty-Six

RIGGS

    We met Sun Wu at Pop's shooting range the following day to give him back the money for the drugs we stole. I underestimated Jack, maybe because that shit Wu spewed when he took me was stuck on repeat in my head. I assumed he would try to forge a new truce between the clubs. Jack didn't do anything like that, he gave that motherfucker his money and assured him he'd be waiting for him. He didn't back down from the inevitable threat but welcomed it instead. He was a sick fuck.

    Three months had come and gone without one word from Wu. Three months, living life, looking over our shoulder waiting for the bloody war to begin. But it never did, the Red Dragons didn't strike and so we kept on breathing, waiting for the moment when the air would be robbed from our lungs.

    The club was in a bad place financially and worse; we were weak when it came to our man power, making us vulnerable. Blackie had been released from the hospital and joined a state funded methadone program, which only substituted one high for another. He needed to get himself checked into a rehab but refused, mainly because of the impending war with the Chinese but also because he had a death wish. Every day out of rehab, was another day he suffered, and that man loved living life waiting for it to end. He promised Jack he'd go to rehab when this shit died down. Nobody knew when that would be and we all feared he'd succumb to his demons before that.

    Jack busied himself with tying up any loose ends with Jimmy Gold, that crazy fuck was getting his ass carted to Otisville once the hospital cleared him for discharge. Over the last few months he and Bianci made a couple of trips up to see Victor Pastore. Aside from sealing Jimmy's fate, Jack was trying to get in with another family. Victor's organization was dead on the streets and he turned most of his interests over to another local mob boss, Rocco Spinelli and his crew. With our Chinese deal off the table, Jack was looking for a new buyer and Rocco was the top of list.

    Pipe was expanding the garage, he hired a few new guys who specialized in custom bikes, hoping to generate more business for the club. Wolf went off the grid for days at a time, going on runs, hoping to sway nomads that didn't belong to a charter to come sit at our table. So far the poor bastard hadn't recruited one. Can't blame them though, it's like signing up for the military after our countries had been attacked but there's no fucking purple heart to be won here.

    Bones hasn't had much going on other than his mission in life to annoy the fuck out of me. After the whole thing came to light, and I explained to Jack and the rest of the club it was my fault this shit went south, I tried to put distance between me and Kitten. I wasn't doing it because I was freaking out about being tied down or even because we were having a kid; I was doing it because for the first time in my life I didn't feel like being selfish. For the first time I had people in my life that were worth a damn and deserved better than I could give them. But every time I thought I could do it, thought I could turn my back on them and sacrifice my promise to Kitten so she and Pea could have a life without fear...Bones was there reminding me I was more than capable of taking care of what was mine. *Own it* became two words I contemplated tattooing to my body.

It's not a hard thing to do, owning my responsibilities, it's something I'm happy to do. You would be too if you had Lauren every night waiting in your bed, ice cold feet and all, she was my favorite person.

At nineteen weeks pregnant, she was the prettiest, sexiest creature I had ever laid eyes on. About six weeks ago, Pea decided he or she didn't want to go unnoticed anymore and Lauren's belly started to round. Each week since, it seemed to get bigger and bigger, all signs that our kid was growing and gearing up to make his big debut. Kitten was almost at the half-way mark and everything was smooth sailing. I hadn't missed another doctor's appointment since that first one when I fucked up. Our refrigerator now proudly displayed grainy black and white pictures of Pea, a souvenir from every visit.

Jack walked up beside me, handing me a beer and tipped his head toward Lauren.

"When are you two going to do one of these things?" he asked, studying a pink and blue napkin in his hands before shaking his head. It was quite comical that the Bulldog was at a gender reveal party. Fuck, if we're being honest it's pretty crazy that either of us were here. If someone would've told me six months ago I would be sitting in Bianci's house, with his mother ten feet away, waiting for his kid to pull the tape off a box and let us all know if they were having a boy or a girl...well, I'd tell them they were fucking bat shit crazy.

Yet, here I was.

And Jack was standing next to me guzzling a beer.

Join an M.C. they said... Ha.

"Lauren wants to be surprised," I answer Jack finally, taking a greedy sip of the beer he offered me.

"I can't believe you're having a kid with Bianci's sister," he mused.

"Yeah, it kind of threw me for a loop too," I replied sarcastically.

"Noticed you're not sleeping at the Dog Pound anymore, guess things are working out for you two," he coaxed.

"Just trying to do what's right," I said automatically, running my fingers through my hair that had grown back.

Whatever the fuck that is anymore.

I stared at Lauren from across the room, our eyes meeting and she smiled widely. I stopped myself from walking over to her, from wrapping my arms around her and claiming what was mine. I've been doing that a lot lately, slamming my foot on the brake every time I wanted more from her. It wouldn't be fair to take more, not now, not with this threat looming in the air.

I battle with myself on a daily basis, thinking I'm doing the wrong thing by staying with Lauren, getting close to her and actually learning what it is to be a dad. I argue that she and the baby need me that I can save them from the unknown but when I'm alone I know the truth. I look at Blackie struggle with his wife's death. I look at Jack, constantly worried something is going to happen to Reina or

Lacey and know every minute I'm with Lauren is a risk, a gamble I'm taking with her life.

But still, there's a shred of hope inside of me that overpowers the truth, and I tell myself it's okay. I can protect her. I can protect Pea.

I love my life.

Or I did.

I thought being a part of the Satan's Knights was my calling, my destiny, a goddamn saving grace.

I guess that was before I had something to lose—before *them*.

"Twenty bucks says it's a girl," Jack said beside me, as everyone shouted pink or blue and little Luca pulled the tape from the box.

Anthony crouched down beside his son, helping him as he opened the box and a bunch of pink balloons escaped. He pulled Luca into his arms and reached for Adrianna.

He did it.

He got the girl and the kid, even managed to keep them.

"Fork over your money, Richie Rich," Jack teased, holding out his palm as he polished off the rest of his beer.

"The rich kid jokes are getting old man," I complained.

"Hey," Lauren said as she laced her arm through mine. "Mind if I steal him away for a minute?" she asked Jack.

"He's all yours, girl. Good luck with that," he winked, chuckling to himself as he walked away from us.

"Congrats," I said, taking Lauren's hand in mine. "A niece."

She sank her teeth into her lower lip, staring at me thoughtfully before she shook her head and blinked.

"Thanks," she muttered, as she glanced around the room and led me away from the crowd.

"Where are we going?"

"I can't take it anymore," she hissed.

"What's the matter?" I asked curiously, as we walked through the kitchen, turning into a hallway. Lauren glanced around, a mischievous smile on her face as she opened the door that led to the garage and pushed me through before closing it behind her.

"Kitten," I started, unable to help the smile that formed on my mouth as I stared at her.

"No time for small talk, Tiger," she whispered, taking my hand and leading me toward the car parked in the center of the room.

Did I mention pregnancy was the best thing ever? Lauren was insatiable, wanting my dick morning, noon and night. How could I ever deny her?

She hopped onto the hood of the car, spreading her legs and crooked her finger.

"Whose car is this?" I asked, as I walked toward her.

"Victor's, the man has no use for it where he is and I always wanted to take it for a ride," she whispered, grinning as she gripped the ends of my cut in her hands and pulled me between her legs. "So, I've got this fantasy…one that involves this car, you and me."

She leaned in, peppering my lips with kisses as her hands traveled down my chest.

"Kitten, you're going to be the death of me," I whispered huskily, as I gripped her hips and pulled her further onto the edge of the car. She locked her legs around my waist and I groaned.

"Would that be so bad? I mean there's worse ways to go, right?" she cupped my face and those crystal blue eyes stared into mine.

Shit.

I was lost.

In the abyss known as Lauren Bianci.

I wish I had seen her coming.

Maybe if I had had a warning, I would've stood a chance.

"No I guess not," I replied.

"Ask me about my fantasy, Riggs," she ordered, her hands still holding my face.

"What's your fantasy, Kitten?" I urged, my voice sounding gruff.

She leaned her forehead against mine.

"Don't look at me like that," she pleaded, her voice barely audible.

"Like what?"

"Like I'm a dream," she whispered.

"Starting to wonder if you are," I admitted, pushing back the threats, the bad vibes, all the things that could turn this thing we had into a nightmare. I pushed back the truth because the lie was the dream.

"You know what dreams are don't you, Riggs?" she questioned, as she unbuttoned my jeans and drew down the zipper. Liking where this was going, I reached behind me and retrieved my gun from the waistband and laid it gently against the roof of the car. "They're the things you're too afraid to go out and grab. A dream is a subconscious plea, it's a taunting voice telling you to grab your balls and take what you want," she explained, lifting her eyes back to mine. "Do you ever dream?"

Christ, shut up. Please.

I was two seconds from getting down on my knees and not to get a taste of the thing I craved most but to beg her to stop talking.

Every word she said I fell deeper into the abyss.

I'd never be able to get out.

She palmed my cock and whispered against my ear.

"Dream with me," she said softly.

I lifted my hand to her cheek, turned her slightly and took her lips, silencing that mouth before it ruined me. My fingers threaded her hair as my lips worked hers, slowly, achingly, before the brutal assault of my tongue and teeth. She met my demands, played right into my hands or maybe I played into hers, this was her fantasy after all, either way she parted her lips and invite me inside.

Her tongue greeted me, welcoming me home, just like she did every fucking night I walked in the door.

Home.

Dreams.

Everything I never wanted.

Everything I had wrapped around me.

She pushed me back, lifting her skirt, letting the stretchy material pool around her belly, and lifted her hips as she shimmied her panties down her legs. I watched as she bent her leg and pulled her panties from her ankle, twirling them around her finger with a smile on her face.

"Dream with me," she repeated, only this time there was no soft whisper of the words and instead a bold demand. She spread my cut open, reaching inside and tucking her lace panties into the inside pocket. "I promise they'll be good dreams…every single one," she whispered, before pulling me back to her and wrapping her legs around my waist.

I knew every dream we shared would be beautiful in their own right. Every single one, starting from the one we were in the middle of sharing right now, to the one growing inside of her. I gave into her like I always did because I have no fucking idea how to say no.

And I didn't want to.

As God as my witness, I never want to say no.

I'm going to Hell.

I grabbed her face and crushed my mouth against hers as she worked my boxer briefs down to release my cock. I blocked out her words, her goddamn quest for a dream and turned a heavy moment, a moment I'd go to my grave thinking of, and turned it into just sex.

Just sex.

Something I knew.

Something I wasn't scared of.

Something I wasn't afraid of losing.

I reached down, dragging my fingers along her wetness. Kitten was always drenched for me, always taking my cock like she was made for me and only me. I parted her lips, wrapping my hand around my shaft and brought my thick head, glistening with her dreams and her promises, to her pussy.

I cupped the back of her neck with one hand as my other hand fell to her hip and I pushed inside of her. Keeping my eyes on hers as I succumbed to the abyss, inch by inch, each beat of my heart, each beat of hers.

"Riggs…" she moaned, as I filled her.

I was balls deep in Kitten, surrounded by everything I wouldn't allow myself to dream of and my hand moved subconsciously, like a dream, to her stomach.

She ran her index finger down my cheek, lifting my chin so my eyes found hers.

"Tiger," she whispered.

"Kitten," I growled, snapping out of it. I leaned into her, splaying my palms on the hood of the car as I rotated my hips, making her feel me and how deep I was inside of her. She grabbed onto my shoulders, lifting her ass off the car and pressing herself into me.

"Doesn't get any deeper than this baby," I hissed, bending my head to graze her neck.

"No, you're right it doesn't," she whispered. I lifted my head and my eyes bore into hers and I began moving, in and out, slow and fast until the fire inside me built to an uncontrollable need. It was then I gave into the temptation and recklessly fulfilled the dream.

Her pussy tightened around my cock, her body went from writhing wildly to being completely still as she came. Her back fell against the hood of the car and she arched one final time before I started coming deep inside of her, giving her everything, everything I didn't even know I had in me to give someone.

I dropped my body over hers, taking her arms and pinning them over her head before pressing my mouth to hers.

"You're ruining me, Kitten," I said against her mouth.

"How so?" she panted.

"Just trust me, you have fucking sunk your claws so deep inside me I'll never recover," I declared, slowly lifting myself off of her and pulling out.

She sat up, her eyes watching intently as I tucked myself back into my jeans and carefully zipped them back up. She hopped off the hood, tugging her skirt down her thighs before pressing her hand over my chest.

"Keep the panties," she smirked.

"My gift to you. A reminder that dreams come true," she patted my cut where her panties were safely tucked away and turned toward the door. I grabbed my gun from the hood of the car, pushing it into the waistband of my jeans and watched as she walked away. Her hips had widened a bit, her ass slightly rounder, all the makings of a pretty fucking spectacular view.

I felt the grin spread across my face until she froze.

"Oh, my God," she said.

"What? What's the matter?" I asked, as I strode to her side. Her hands falling to her stomach, as she looked at her belly. "Lauren, what's the matter?" I asked, something in the pit of my stomach dropped as I stared at her.

Her eyes widened and then a smile spread across that perfect mouth of hers.

"She kicked!" she turned, grabbing my hand and pressing the palm against her stomach. "Oh, my God, Riggs, Pea kicked," she exclaimed, moving my hand all around her belly.

I diverted my eyes to her stomach, holding my breath as I waited to feel our kid.

"There, did you feel it?" she lifted her eyes to mine.

"I don't feel anything," I whispered, drawing out a deep breath as my eyes met hers.

"The book says the mom usually only feels it at first," she said with a frown, laying her hand over mine. "I'm sorry."

"Nothing to be sorry for," I replied, lacing our fingers together and moving to open the door. "Just something to look forward to," I said, realizing I meant the words as they left my mouth.

I wanted to feel Pea.

This dad shit was one surprise after another.

We walked out of the garage as my phone rang. I glanced down at the screen, drawing my eyebrows together when I saw it was Jack. He was just fucking here…somewhere. I lifted the phone to my ear.

"Hello?"

"Put your dick in your pants and meet me outside," he snapped, disconnecting the call.

"Everything okay?" Kitten asked as we walked into the kitchen. I turned around and looked at her, watching as she sipped a bottle of water. Her cheeks flushed, her hand still on her belly hoping to get another feel of Pea.

"I've got to go," I said, leaning in to kiss her cheek.

She pulled the water bottle from her lips and looked at me.

"Oh, okay," she placed the water on the counter and turned to me.

"Give me a kiss," I ordered, hating the disappointment reflected in her eyes.

She reached up on her tip toes, wrapping one arm around my neck and placed her hand against my cheek as her lips glided over mine.

"Be careful," she said against my mouth.

"I'll see you later," I replied, giving her ass a soft smack before winking at her and slipping out the back door, avoiding the bunch of crazy Italians that were probably fighting over godparent rights.

I walked around to the front of the house and saw Jack straddling his bike.

"What's the big emergency?" I asked, walking up to him.

He lifted his head, his facial expression grim as he stared back at me.

"Wu sent a message," he clipped.

Four simple words.

Words that turned any short-lived dream into a nightmare

Chapter Twenty-Seven
RIGGS

"Shit," Jack growled, as we killed the engines of our bikes and assessed the damage at Pop's shooting range. I stared at the front of the building, riddled with bullets, as Jack pulled off his fingerless gloves, taking casual strides toward the dozens of cops swarming the joint.

"Sorry fella's we're fresh out of donuts," Jack said, shoving his gloves into his pockets. He leaned back on his heels as he eyed a group of blue and whites. "But gotta tell you, got this warm fuzzy feeling…" he pounded his fist against the center of his chest, "…up in here. We're touched all you rat bastards showed up in our time of need. Isn't that right, Riggs?" he asked, keeping his eyes steady on one particular cop.

"Right," I agreed, sizing up the situation. The cop Jack was staring at narrowed his eyes at him.

"Just doing our jobs, Parrish," he replied. "Putting away the bad guys and all that shit."

Blackie, Bones, Pipe and Wolf walked up behind us, all of them glaring at the men in uniform. The cop lifted his head and raised an eyebrow in Blackie's direction.

"Well, look who it is," he taunted, stepping around Jack and closer to Blackie. Jack was quick on his feet and stood in front of the vice president.

This was new, usually the cops we deal with are on the payroll, not these guys. They were out for blood, and by the looks of it Blackie's was what they were thirsty for.

"Relax Bulldog, no need to get possessive over a junkie," the cop ground out, flexing his jaw. "Scum like that not worth the effort," he added.

"You would know right, Craig?" Blackie clipped, as Jack placed his hand on his chest, holding him back. "I'm good," he told Jack, shoving his hand off his chest.

"Instead of taunting my brothers why don't you assholes do your job and find out who shot up Pop's business," Jack suggested.

"We intend to," Craig promised. "Who'd you piss off this time, Bulldog?"

"Don't bust my balls. Do your job or get the fuck out of here, put all those hard earned tax dollars to use," Jack hissed, turning around to face the rest of us and nodded toward Pops.

"You people probably never paid taxes a day in your life," he sneered.

Jack ignored him and we walked away from the tribe of officers when Craig called out to us.

"Hey, Blackie, I'd watch my back if I were you. It'd be a shame if you suffered the same fate as Christine," he crooned.

Blackie spun around.

"Fuck," Jack hissed, as Blackie charged for the cop.

"Keep her name off your fucking tongue or so help me God I'll slice that thing right out of your fucking mouth," Blackie growled, as I grabbed him by the back of his cut and pulled him back.

"Sounds like you just threatened a police officer," he tormented.

Blackie shrugged me off of him and took another step toward Craig.

"You got a hard on for me, motherfucker?" Blackie whispered, extending his arms outward and crossing one wrist over the other. "Go on, lock me up," he hollered.

What the fuck was going on?

I glanced at the name on this Craig character's badge, Brantley. I think Craig Brantley needed to get locked out of his bank accounts, or maybe he needed a profile on a gay dating website, shouldn't be a hard task, for a mastermind like me. I'd be all over that shit.

"Pussy," Blackie hissed, dropping his hands to his sides and turning back to face us.

"You okay?" Jack questioned.

"I'm fine," he confirmed, tipping his head toward the ambulance rolling into the parking lot.

"Pops?"

"No, the kid working," he informed us, leading us to where Pops was crouched down on the ground over the young worker's body. "Took a shot in the leg but he should be fine. Pops on the other hand, he's feeling some sort of way," Blackie added.

"They took the guns," Pipe confirmed.

"We're sure it was Wu?" I asked, knowing the answer.

"Yeah, they didn't even try to hide their identity, sending their message loud and clear," Wolf said as he lit up a cigarette. "Those fucking Dragons, man," he took a puff, turning toward Jack. "Give me the green light, make them watch as I fuck all their mothers," he offered.

"Christ, Wolf," Bones snarled. "What the fuck did their mothers do to you?"

"Them bitches brought those fucks into the world," he insisted.

Wolf was a maniac.

I loved him.

Jack walked over to Pop and I decided to follow him, my eyes zeroed in on the kid on the ground, no more than eighteen years old.

"You're going to be fine, boy," Pop assured the kid wailing in pain, as he lifted his eyes to Jack.

"Christ," Jack muttered, running his fingers through his hair.

"He won't help you now son," Pop said through gritted teeth. "Hope you know what you're doing because these bastards aren't playing games."-

"You okay?" Jack asked.

"Going to take a lot more than a bunch of amateurs to take me down, but this kid here? He didn't deserve to get stuck in the crosshairs of whatever it is you have going on with the Chinese. He didn't sign up for that, and quite frankly neither did I," he glanced over his shoulder at the building behind him. "Got a fine mess here to clean up."

"I'll take care of it," Jack vowed.

"Yeah, you will," Pop announced as the paramedics pushed him aside to work on the kid. "Don't feel like revisiting history son, did my time, buried enough innocent lives to last a lifetime." He rose to his feet, brushing the dirt from his pants and stepped closer to Jack.

"You need to get a handle on these bastards before they draw more blood," he demanded.

"I said, I'll take care of it," Jack seethed.

"Pop, you should go to the hospital, get yourself checked out," I suggested, noticing the blood on the old man's neck. "Were you hit?"

Pop turned around, lifting his hand to his neck, bringing it back to stare at the blood on his fingers before he turned to Jack.

"Just a nick," he declared, holding Jack's stare for a moment before turning back to the paramedics. "I'm riding with him," he told them as they lifted the kid onto the stretcher.

I watched as they ran the stretcher to the back of the ambulance, one paramedic applying pressure to the wound as the other opened the ambulance doors. They lifted the stretcher into the back of the ambulance and Pop climbed up, taking a seat on the bench beside the kid. The paramedic closed the door before running around to the driver's side. The sirens sounded, and lights flashed as they peeled away from the scene of the crime.

That kid would be fine.

But Pops was right.

More blood would be shed.

More innocent lives were at stake and would pay the price for what we did.

I was the one behind the plan. Wu knew I had orchestrated this whole thing—there was no doubt he had let me go because the motherfucker had a bigger plan for me. I get it. I'd do the same fucking thing. I'd let the bastard suffer, make him wonder when I was coming, and then I'd make him watch helplessly as I took everything he cared about.

I got it.

It's exactly what I would do.

I put myself in the enemies' shoes, calculating what my next move would be if I was him and Lauren's face flashed before my eyes.

"Riggs," Jack said, pulling me away from my Kitten's innocent face and I turned to him, blinking as I tried to mask the fear in my eyes.

"Yeah," I rasped.

Jack stared at me thoughtfully and opened his mouth to speak but Blackie interrupted.

"What are we going to do here?" he questioned, rolling a toothpick between his teeth and tipped his head back toward Brantley and his posse. "You know they're going to be riding our asses now," he added.

"Fuck 'em," Jack hissed, blowing out a heavy sigh.

"Gladly," Blackie gritted, spitting the toothpick onto the ground. "We putting this club on lockdown?"

"No, not yet," Jack said, surprisingly. "For now, round up the prospects, put them on Reina, Lacey and Lauren," he ordered, turning his eyes to mine. "That going to be a problem?"

"No," I said immediately. The fact that Kitten was lumped in the list of priorities along with Reina and Jack's daughter, scared the fuck out of me. "Jack," I started, losing the words on my tongue.

"It's a precaution, Riggs," he answered, taking in the worried look in my eyes. "We need to bide our time and keep our heads. We can't keep our heads if we're worried about our women. You feel me?"

"Yeah," I agreed, nodding my head.

"You trust me?" He asked.

"Of course," I declared.

"Then trust me when I say we will get these motherfuckers," he declared, as he cupped my shoulder. "We always win, even when it looks like it's impossible. You know why? Because I've lost too much to let anyone else ever take a goddamn thing from me and mine," he fixed his eyes on me and patted my cheek. "Get that look out of your eyes, Riggs," he ordered. "Looks like you found your heart, kid. Now, you have to hang on to it."

I should've freaked out with the first part of that sentence but it was the last part that threw me for a loop.

I knew Lauren had become my heart and if I'm being honest I've known for a while. I didn't fight it very hard, a part of me wanted her to be the person I lived for, for her and Pea to be my purpose.

A big part.

But the small part of me knew having them in my life could hurt them. That was the part that was winning now, trumping everything else.

How do you hang on to someone knowing it's better if you let them go?

What kind of man would that make me if I kept Lauren around just for my benefit? Sure, I could throw a prospect on her but that wouldn't ease my conscience.

Hang on for what? Purpose? A reason not to be reckless?

Something happens to them, God, if something happens to them I'd really lose my heart. Then, and only then would I lose my purpose.

I turned around, striding toward my bike, ignoring Jack and Blackie's calls and grabbed my phone from my pocket, dialing Anthony's number.

"Yo," he answered. "Where'd you guys go—"

"Don't tell anyone it's me," I interrupted. "I know you've got company and shit but think you can sneak out and meet me at the gym?" I asked, as I straddled my bike. He was silent for a moment. "It's important, Bianci. I wouldn't ask you otherwise—it's about Lauren," I confessed, my own voice sounding very unfamiliar to my ears.

"Give me an hour," he said.

"Thanks," I muttered before disconnecting the call.

Bones ran up beside my bike, placing his foot on top of the wheel and gripped the handlebars.

"Where are you running off too?"

"Get out of my way," I snapped.

"Riggs, I know that fucking look in your eyes. Don't do something stupid," he ordered.

And for the first time I wasn't doing something stupid or reckless. I was doing something worth a damn.

"I've got no issue running your ass over," I shouted over the noise of my engine. Bones knew me well enough to know that when I had something in my head, no one could sway me another way. He grunted as he removed his hand and foot, standing to the side as I peeled away from the mayhem and headed straight to Hell.

The Hell where Kitten wasn't mine.

I sat on my bike parked in front of Xonerated and waited for Anthony to arrive. I reached into my cut, desperate to take the edge off and pulled out a perfectly rolled joint. I searched the inside pocket of my cut for a lighter and my fingers gripped the lace of Lauren's panties.

My gift to you. A reminder that dreams come true.

What a fucking nightmare.

I left the panties in my pocket and pulled out the lighter, flicking a flame and lighting up the paper, taking a greedy hit as it burned. I took it from my lips, holding the smoke in, letting it ferment within before exhaling and staring down at the joint in my hand.

Funny how it used to work, how it used to take the edge off and calm my restless ways.

Not this time.

It's pretty fucking crazy how I went from living life without a care in the world to this shit.

Soon enough my life would go back to the way it used to be.

A life with no worries.

No responsibilities.

Free to do whatever the fuck I wanted, whenever the fuck I wanted.

A life I thought I was meant to live.

One I wanted.

I chose my path.

And here I am, wishing for a motherfucking detour.

Wishing for another way.

Another life.

Regrets?

I had them in spades.

Dreams?

I had those too.

Nightmares?

I'm pretty sure I'm living one right now.

Anthony pulled up in front of the gym and I took another long hit of my joint as he stepped around the car and made his way to my side. I glanced at him from the corner of my eye, clipping my joint before tucking it away in my pocket.

"What's up?" he questioned, crossing his arms against his chest as he scrutinized me.

"Some shit went down today," I began, blowing out the smoke I held hostage in my lungs.

"Figured that much," he cautioned, cocking his head to the side, trying to figure me out.

Good luck, brother.

Let me know what you find.

"You sat at that table when everything was going down with Gold. You know it was me who offered up a way to get the drugs to save Blackie and Reina. What you don't know, and I'm not even sure I should tell you, is who we took them from," I paused, deciding it didn't matter.

Anthony was better off not knowing, one less casualty when the dust settled, and I needed Bianci breathing. I needed him to be there for Lauren and to be the man in my kid's life. I had no doubt he'd be there for Pea. It was a good thing I spent all those months keeping him safe, keeping him out of the enemy's line of fire.

Time to pay it forward Bianci.

"They know it was me who gave up their stash house. They know it was the Satan's Knights who robbed them and it doesn't matter that we've paid them back because we killed their men. They won't quit until they've settled the score, until they've taken our blood."

"Jesus, Riggs," Bianci hissed, taking a deep breath before he shrugged his shoulders.

"So what do you want me to do? Jack wants my help?"

"Jack doesn't know I called you," I said, lifting my hand to rub that ache away from my chest, the one that seemed to keep nagging me.

"He's putting prospects on Reina and Lacey until he figures what our next move is. He wanted one on Lauren too but…" I shook my head and paused, "…I'm not about to put her life in the hands of some little shit who doesn't have a patch," I said, looking away from him.

I hadn't expected this to be so hard.

I hadn't expected for it to hurt.

"I need you to look after Lauren," I whispered, lifting my head to meet his wary stare. "I need you to keep her and the baby safe."

"Riggs, I don't like where this is going," he started.

"C'mon man, you fucking owe me and I'm collecting. You love your sister, hell, you even love that kid she hasn't given birth to yet. No one will look out for her like you will. No one will protect her and make sure this shit doesn't land on her."

"And you? Where does that leave you?"

I shrugged my shoulders.

"I want you to take Lauren back to your place, keep her close until everything dies down. She's going to be upset, so make sure she doesn't get herself worked up," I pleaded. "It won't be good for Pea if she's sick," I rasped. "Anything she or the baby needs, you come to me and I will make sure they have it."

"Got it all planned, huh?" he questioned. "You still didn't answer me. Where does that leave you?"

"It doesn't matter, bro. I've got to do the right thing by them and being away from them, making it like they don't mean shit to me, it's the only way I can fight for them. They probably know about her already but if I end things now, if I prove to the world she's nothing to me, no one will hurt her. She'll be old news and they'll be looking for another way to hurt me, another way to get to me," I removed my hat and nervously ran my fingers through my hair.

"You're going to break her heart," he said.

"I'm going to save her life," I countered. "She'll bounce back from a broken heart, can't bounce back from death," I choked out.

"I did what you're doing, you know? I stayed away from Adrianna and Luca, told myself I'd only poison them with my lifestyle—"

"Stop!" I interrupted. "Don't try to give me hope because I'm not like you. I know you think we run in the same circles, but we don't, brother. This shit isn't the mob, it doesn't go away because your boss goes up the river and spares your life. This is an oath, it's a way of life. It's my life and a choice I made long before I knew Lauren existed. Would I take it back? I can't even ask myself that question because I'm a Satan's Knight and I will ride to my death," I argued. "But I won't take Lauren on that ride or my kid. Now do I have your word?"

He remained still for a moment as he absorbed my words and stared at me. It took everything in me not to turn my head and pretend like I didn't just hand over my *heart* to this man.

Anthony slowly nodded in agreement but it wasn't enough.

"Man, need your word, not just a shake of your head. This is my…" I paused, taking a deep breath before I continued. "… we're talking about my kid. My flesh and blood. Gonna need the words for this one," I said, my voice sounding more like a plea than an order.

"I'll take care of them. I'll keep them safe," he promised.

I nodded before I bowed my head and swiped my hands along it.

Goodbye Kitten.

Goodbye Pea.

Be safe.

Chapter Twenty-Eight

RIGGS

I stormed into the clubhouse, headed straight for the bar and ignored everyone that was watching me. I pulled the strongest bottle of poison I could find from the shelf and grabbed a glass. Blackie stared at me with his signature beady eyes as I poured myself a shot and took a seat beside him.

I threw the shot back, letting the amber liquid worm its way down my throat and into my belly. I had hoped that the burning sensation in my chest would dull the ache that wouldn't leave me.

"Tell me I did the right thing," I demanded of Blackie, as I refilled my glass.

"I don't even know what you did," he muttered, eyeing the bottle I was clutching.

"It don't matter, just tell me what I need to hear," I said, downing another shot.

"You did the right thing," he appeased. "You looking to forget? That shit won't do it," he informed me as he passed me the bottle he had half emptied.

Great, now I was swapping bottles with the club drunk. My life really had turned to shit.

At this rate, by the end of the night I'll have a fucking needle sticking out of my arm.

That was fucked up.

But I was in a fucked up mood.

"I'm sorry," I grunted, apologizing to him for my inner thoughts. Luckily, he paid me no mind, a combination of not giving a fuck and being sloshed.

"You have a fight with your ol' lady?"

"I don't have one of those," I replied.

"Right, the baby mama then," he corrected himself, as he pulled a bud of pot from his pocket and broke up the herb on top of the bar.

I ignored his question, not ready to admit out loud that I didn't have a baby mama either. I had nothing.

Gave it all away.

Because of the fucking Red Dragons.

If I was a holy roller, I'd swear on a stack of bibles I would kill every Red Dragon from here to California.

I wasn't a holy roller.

I wasn't even a sign of the cross type of guy.

"What was that shit with the cops earlier?" I asked, changing the subject as I watched him dump the ground up weed into a rolling paper.

"Ah, me and officer Brantley go way back," he slurred, as he rolled the joint perfectly, bringing the end of the paper to his lips to lick and seal it. "I don't know who gave that piece of shit more of a hard-on me or Christine," he added, passing me the tight joint as he lifted his eyes.

Christine, his wife, the wife he barely mentioned, much less ever used her name. I raised an eyebrow and flicked my lighter and blazed up the joint.

"Never heard you talk much about your wife," I said, inhaling sharply. "So, this rat, the cop, he's been itching to put you away for a while?" I thought about it for a second. "And Christine? He wanted to arrest her too?"

Blackie laughed, a low rumble that sounded more scary than jolly.

"Nah he didn't want to arrest her," he said before taking a toke. "Christine wasn't some low-life junkie, Riggs," he seethed.

"I didn't say she was," I replied, as I poured us both a shot.

"It's what you think because it's all anyone in this fucking place ever talks about. You've got this image of Christine, a woman you never met, lying face down in a bathtub with a fucking needle in her arm but that's not the woman I married. Everyone in this club assumes I drink because I feel guilty she overdosed with the shit we were selling, but they're wrong, so fucking wrong."

"So why do you do it?" I asked, watching as he downed the shot I placed in front of him and he passed me back the joint.

"Sure, it's got something to do with it. If I wasn't dealing heroin she wouldn't have been able to get her hands on it. But, Christine would've found some other way to end the nightmare she was living," he revealed, staring down at his left hand, his fingers running along his ring finger.

"I was a shitty husband," he admitted. "I put this club before her. I put the drugs, the money, the goddamn patch before the sweet girl I fell in love with when I was fifteen years old. See, she knew me before the club, before the corruption and the mayhem and she had to watch me morph into a Knight. It was all good when I was just a prospect, still had time for my girl and the crazy shit we used to do."

He smiled faintly before glancing back at me.

"I don't know Lauren all that well, ran into her a few times since you two started up, but she seems spunky. Christine used to be spunky. She used to love life, and more than life, she loved me. She loved me hard, felt that shit down in my bones."

I swallowed hard, blaming the burning sensation in my throat on the weed but it was his words, his comparison of his woman to mine. It was hearing Blackie recall the love he remembered Christine had for him, knowing I'd never know that with Lauren.

"After I patched in, Cain pushed me to the front lines. I was eager to earn, eager to prove I would do anything for the club," he cocked his head to the side. "Sort of like you," he pointed out. "In our time of need you stepped up and became a front runner. That isn't lost to the club, Riggs, and you don't have to keep proving your worthy of your patch," he added.

"I'm not," I contested. "I'm just doing my job."

"I thought the same thing and kept doing my job. I ran drugs, guns, women…whatever made the most profit and never looked back. I forgot about the love I had at home and what it felt like to go home to a warm body. I pushed the thoughts of how fucking good it felt to crawl into bed and have the sweetest woman wrap her legs around me. She didn't know what I did, and if she did, she didn't care. I could've killed a man, sometimes did, and she still welcomed me home, into our bed, night after night."

"So how did it all change?"

"I started pushing her away. Cain made a deal with the G-Man and we moved more drugs, became the biggest operation on the east coast."

"The G-Man is the guy Jimmy Gold was working with to push Pastore out, right?"

"Yeah," he confirmed, taking another shot. "Anyway, there is only so much bad shit you can do before it catches up to you and changes who you are. It didn't bother me at first, I had shoeboxes full of money and in my head I was doing it for a good reason. I would buy Christine her dream house, make sure my woman had everything she wanted, the best of everything. I told myself I was doing it for her, making up for the douche bag I was on a daily basis. I didn't have a conscience I only had a goal, but I didn't plan on being the reason two seventeen-year-old kids died," he confessed.

I stared at him dumbfounded for a moment, realizing Blackie had lived a whole lot of life and I really had no idea how deep his wounds went.

"It changes you," he repeated. "Knowing that two kids, who had their whole lives ahead of them died, so you could make a quick buck—it fucking wrecks you, man. That was the beginning of the end for me and Christine. I stopped going home, started staying here every night. I couldn't look at her; I couldn't let myself have something as good as her when all I ever did was take the good from other people."

He sighed, pushing away the bottle of alcohol.

"She thought I was cheating on her and that's when Brantley came around. He was a rookie then, looking to make a name for himself and thought he'd start by taking down the Satan's Knights. He's smart, I'll give the son of a bitch that. He looked for the weakest link, found it was me, and used my wife as bait."

I didn't know what to say and wasn't sure I could find my voice even if I had the words to give him. So, I gave him my ear and let him continue with his story because he was a drunk, immune to alcohol. It doesn't give him peace anymore, and he's running out of ways to escape his grief.

"He gave Christine all the attention I wasn't giving her anymore, made her feel things I gave up on making her feel, and promised her all the things I couldn't. He used her, played on her broken emotions and convinced her I would wind up dead because of the club. I found out they were having an affair, put two and two together and confronted her but she had already made a deal with him. She would get the drugs from me and prove I was dealing the shit that killed those two kids," he said, solemnly. "Instead of giving me up she gave up her life."

He covered his face with his hands and I reached out and patted him on the back. He let out a groan and dropped his hands before piercing me with his tortured eyes.

"Jack's been trying for a long time to get this club on the right track, to give us some peace. He thinks he can turn us into a legit club and make us proud to call ourselves the Satan's Knights—but he's in over his head. We're in too deep, and every time we think we are pulling ourselves out of the hole, some other fucking threat comes along. Whether it's a man in a fur coat or a fucking Chinese emperor, there will always be a fucking cancer that will drag us down."

He held up his tattooed hands, turning them over and displayed his palms.

"See these hands? They have a lot of blood on them and that's all I see when I look at them, all the blood and all the faces of the people who bled from these hands."

"Blackie…" I started.

"You got something good with Bianci's sister, stop trying to prove yourself, man, you paid your dues. Now, take a step back and don't let that girl doubt she has you because when *you* don't have her anymore you're going to feel it," he vowed.

"It's too late for that," I said, looking away from him.

I meant to get drunk tonight, to forget that I had handed Lauren and Pea over to Anthony, making her brother be the one responsible for her safety and their well-being. But, sitting here with Blackie, listening to his story only affirmed that I had made the right choice by ending things now. I didn't want to be sitting here one day, the way Blackie sat here, and think of all the ways I failed her. I didn't want to look at my hands and see her blood.

I made my choice.

I had to own it.

Lauren

Twenty-eight calls, twenty-eight voice mails, not to mention the thirteen text messages and I didn't even care I looked like a desperate stalker.

Something was wrong.

I felt it deep down with every fiber of my being. It wasn't like Riggs to ignore my calls. The last few month's things had been great. We weren't officially anything more than who we were, just Kitten and Tiger, Pea's parents, and dare I say…two people who were making it work. Making it work sounds like it was an obligation but it wasn't, we were making it work because we wanted to and not because we needed to.

Something was wrong.

I placed my hands over my belly and relished in the flutters Pea was making inside of me when there was a knock on my door. I smiled instantly as I rushed to the door.

Daddy's home, Pea.

I pulled open the door as my brother turned around to face me. The smile fell as quickly as it was born as I stared at the torn expression on Anthony's face.

No.

"What're you doing here?" I asked, hoarsely

"Can I come in?" he said, as he shoved his hands into his pockets and rocked back on his heels, looking anywhere but at me.

I swallowed the lump in my throat and robotically stepped aside to let him in. I slowly closed the door, gripping the doorknob, hanging onto it as if it was my salvation and touched my forehead to the door.

How does someone prepare themselves for the words I was about to hear? A million thoughts ran through my mind as I feared the worst.

Please don't let him be hurt.

Slowly, I turned around and lifted my eyes to Anthony's.

"Is he okay?" I whispered.

"He's fine," he confirmed.

I let out a sigh of relief as I closed my eyes briefly.

"Thank God," I said.

"Lauren—"

I held up my hand to stop him from saying whatever it was he was about to say.

"No, don't," I ordered. "I don't want to know," I explained. "Something happened, he left with Jack but he said he'd come home. He told me he'd come back home."

"Something did happen, and that's why I'm here. Pack a bag, you will be staying with me until whatever this shit is…until it dies down," he grunted.

"What? No!" I shook my head. "Why would I do that?"

"Because you don't have a goddamn choice," he growled, swiping his hand across his face. "Lauren don't make this harder than it has to be. They have something going down with the club. I don't know the details but after what happened with Reina and Blackie I'm not taking any fucking chances with you. You're coming home with me," he demanded.

I don't know who he thought he was talking to. I might be his little sister but I wasn't a child. Sure, I've run to him in the past, asking for his help with whatever mess I got myself into but I wasn't that girl anymore. I was a woman finding her place. I was a mother. I wasn't a little girl who needed protecting. I was the one doing the protecting, taking care of myself and my child.

"I'm not going anywhere, Anthony. This is where I live, this is where I belong," I declared. "If there was some kind of threat then Riggs would be the one who took care of me."

"Riggs can't take care of you, Lauren, he can barely take care of himself," he seethed.

"Don't do that. Don't talk about him like he's not in your category, like he's some incompetent asshole," I yelled.

"Pack a bag," he ordered.

"I don't take orders from you, Anthony!"

"I'm telling you something goddamn it! Grow the fuck up and listen. You want to put your life at risk? Your kid's life at risk because you're stubborn?"

"Get out," I screeched. "Get out of my house!"

He ran his fingers through his hair, tugging at the ends as he took a step closer and pierced me with a cold stare.

That shit didn't work with me. I wasn't some street thug who he could scare with one look. I was his goddamn sister. I was his blood. I knew him better than most people did and that look, it meant nothing. I could stare right back at him, give him the same look because I learned from the best. I learned from him.

I learned a lot from my brother.

I learned not to ask questions.

I learned to stand by the people you care about even when the things they do are unethical.

I learned to defend myself because he went away for three years, leaving me to fight my own battles.

I learned how to fight for what I wanted because he never gave up on what he wanted.

I bet he's sorry he taught me how to be a strong woman.

"He asked me to do this, Lauren," he said hoarsely. "He asked me to take you away from here and to be the one who watches over you and the baby."

I shook my head.

"You're lying," I whispered, the words settling in causing my eyes to fill with uncertain tears. I stared at him, waiting for something, some kind of sign he was just blowing smoke at me to get me to go with him but it never came.

"He's not coming home, Lauren."

"No, stop it," I demanded, wiping away the tears that fell down my cheeks. Stupid hormones! I took a deep breath, trying to collect myself before I looked back at my brother. "Riggs wants me to move out? He wants to pawn me off on you? Because there is some bullshit problem with his club. That's what you're telling me?"

He didn't answer me.

"Fine, then you're going to take me to wherever he is, and he's going to have to tell me with his own mouth."

"Lauren, you don't want that," he said.

"No, what I don't want is my brother coming here to collect me like I'm some piece of baggage," I croaked, as my voice cracked and the tears fell again. "So, if Riggs wants me gone, then he will have to look me in the eye and tell me himself. He will have to be man enough to break my heart this time."

I turned around, grabbed my purse from the counter and started for the door. Anthony remained where he was, just staring at me.

"Now!" I demanded.

"Don't do this," he pleaded one final time.

"I didn't do shit," I hissed as I opened the door.

He sighed heavily before walking toward the door, pausing in front of me and taking my hand in his. I glanced down at our joined hands before lifting my eyes back to his. He squeezed my hand as his eyes silently apologized for his words.

Something was wrong all right.

And my heart wouldn't survive it.

Anthony brought me into his arms and held me as I cried against his chest. I prayed for it to be a lie, but in the back of my mind I feared that it was the truth.

Kitten and Tiger were the lie.

Chapter Twenty-Nine
Lauren

"Are you sure you want to do this?" Anthony asked, as he turned off his truck and glanced at the Satan's Knights clubhouse.

The only thing I was sure of was that I was a mess. My emotions were all over the place, one minute I was upset, the next I was angry wishing I had grabbed my baseball bat before leaving the house. I've cried more tears in the last twenty minutes than I have in the last twenty-one years.

"Lauren?"

I ignored my brother as I found the strength to open the door and climb out of the car. I stood in the parking lot, my eyes diverting to the side of the building where Riggs first took me, and I closed my eyes.

I've come full circle.

I balled my hands into fists as I drew in a deep breath and marched my ass across the pavement. Anthony slammed his door closed, and I heard him curse as he tried to catch up. Bones stepped in front of the door, blocking my path and stared at me for a moment with concerned eyes.

"Lauren, what's the matter?" he asked, taking in the train wreck I could only assume I looked like.

"Out of my way, Bones," I demanded. He lifted his eyes and glanced over my shoulder at Anthony.

"Let her go, man," he said defeated.

Bones stepped aside, warily staring at my brother as I brushed past him and charged into the Dog Pound. My eyes scanned the common room as my heart lurched in my chest. I hadn't prepared myself, hell bent on confronting Riggs I didn't take into consideration I could walk into something I didn't want to see. Blackie stumbled out from the room they congregated in as a club, clutching an empty bottle of tequila. His jeans were unbuttoned, and he was shirtless, displaying a chest covered in tattoos and two nipples that had barbells through them. He lifted his eyes, peering at me and the posse I had behind me before he groaned.

"Shit," he hissed

"Where is he?" I shouted.

Two naked girls stepped out of the room and stared at me as if I wasn't part of *their* plan.

Hell-fucking-no!

A glass fell to the floor, shattering into a million pieces, mimicking my heart. The sound forced me to turn around and met Riggs' shocked expression. He was standing behind the bar and quickly glanced down at the glass he dropped before lifting his eyes back to mine.

I looked back at the two naked girls, one raising a cocky eyebrow at me while the other one gaped at my belly.

"Kitten," Riggs called.

I snapped.

Really fucking snapped as I walked over to the pool table, taking one of the pool sticks that had been abandoned on the felt tabletop. I swung it over my head as I stalked toward the two fucking whores that stared at me wide-eyed. The one who smiled at me cockily, stared at me dumb-fucked and the other who looked at my stomach in disgust—what a bitch.

"Get the fuck out of here," I shrieked. "GET OUT!"

Anthony ran up behind me, trying to pry my fingers from the stick.

"Riggs, get a handle on your woman," Blackie ordered.

"Fuck you," I hissed, turning around on my heel, pulling the stick away from my brother and glaring at Riggs. "I'm not his woman," I seethed. "Isn't that right?"

"Put the pool stick down, Lauren," Riggs reasoned calmly, as he stepped out from behind the bar. His eyes turned to Anthony's. "What the fuck is this, huh?"

"I'm right here!" I yelled, throwing the pool stick onto the floor as I stared at him. "Stop looking at Anthony and start fucking looking at me," I demanded.

He averted his eyes back to mine, shoving his hands into his pockets.

"Give us a minute," he told the room.

"I'm not leaving her," my brother said.

"I said give me a fucking minute, Bianci," Riggs shouted over my shoulder. Our eyes remained locked as the room cleared out, leaving us alone with the truth lingering in the air.

"You sent my brother to our apartment to give me the kiss off?"

"It's best if you stay with him. I'd tell you to stay at the apartment but someone needs to protect you and it would just be easier if you were with him," he argued.

"You are supposed to protect me, not Anthony. YOU."

"Look, it's too much," he shouted. "It's just too much," he insisted. "I never wanted any of this shit, Lauren! I went from being a guy whose biggest worry was his fucking bike or which broad he would screw for the night to having an old lady and a kid on the way. Like you had a fucking plan, so did I, and it didn't include a family! I never wanted any of this and now I'm stuck with it. My life isn't set up for you and a baby, Lauren."

He pointed to the Satan's Knights logo painted on the wall, the reaper that stood in the way of everything.

"That, that right there is my life," he declared, tipping his head toward me. "Not this. I don't know how to do this and I never really wanted to."

"You're lying," I insisted, searching his eyes for the truth. He may not have planned on this but over the last few months he gave me his best. His greatest attempt to make this work and I saw truth in his actions. He didn't know how to be a dad or the main man in someone's life but he wanted to learn.

The man in front of me now. He was the lie.

Wasn't he?

"Ah, shit, don't cry, Lauren. You know I'm right," he exclaimed, as he ran his fingers roughly though his hair. "You know it's the truth."

I pinned him with a gaze and wiped away my tears.

I won't cry.

I won't give you any more of my tears.

"You people pride yourselves on being these badass men. You." I pointed an accusing finger at him. "You call yourself a Satan's Knight, a goddamn soldier of the devil, but all you are is a fucking coward with no backbone. You preach about loyalty and honor for your club but you don't know the first thing about what either of those two things mean. Loyalty is about support, a strong devotion to something or someone. It's a pity your loyalty doesn't rest with your child."

"Lauren," he interrupted.

"No, I'm not done. Honor? Honor is having great respect for someone and that honor should be with me. I am the one giving you a son or a daughter," I tipped my head back to the reaper on the wall. "He won't give you a family. I know you think he already has, that these men are your brothers, and that's all that matters but your brotherhood won't keep you warm at night. Your brotherhood won't give you the joy you'll be missing out on by throwing your child away. So, fuck you, Riggs. Fuck your club and seriously fuck your patch."

"Shut up," he growled. "You don't know what the fuck you're talking about, Lauren. You have no idea how fucking loyal and honorable I am. And that's okay, you don't need to. You just need to stay away from me," he hollered.

I took a step closer to him, the anger that consumed me faded and was replaced with determination.

I may have fallen, but I needed to get back up.

I need to fight.

A part of me wonders if he realizes how much of a fighter I truly am. Doesn't he understand I would've fought for him too? But he lost that right. I won't fight for him but I'll fight against him. I'll fight for Pea because someone had to.

"I can't even say I'm sorry I ever met you because without you there is no Pea. I will always have Pea. So, thank you for that. Thank you for giving me something you'll never enjoy. You're the one who loses. You're the one who has to live every day knowing you walked away from something great, something bigger and better and more rewarding than some pathetic patch."

I walked to the bar, grabbed the empty bottle of liquor and turned on my heel as I wailed it across the room and it crashed against the reaper on the wall.

"Hope it was worth it," I called over my shoulder, as I stalked out of the club.

I walked away from Riggs that night, chin up, head high but my heart shattered like all the pieces of glass that decorated the floor of the Dog Pound.

RIGGS

I stared at the reaper on the wall, the glass of the bottle crunching under my boots as I made my way to the wall. I ran my fingers over the paint that declared this the home of Satan's Knights and then I reared my fist back and screamed as it connected with the wall.

I heard the door open behind me but I was too engrossed in demolishing the reaper, an image of something I thought I was supposed to live for. So why did it feel like the reason I was living just walked out the door and straight out of my life?

I felt strong hands wrap around my arms and pull me back, pulling me away from wreaking havoc on the devil that stole everything from me.

"What the fuck are you doing?" Blackie hollered, as he slammed my back against the wall.

"Let me go," I seethed.

"Like you let her go?" Bones added, walking up behind Blackie. "What is wrong with you, man?"

I pushed Blackie's hands off me causing him to stumble backward and scowled at Bones.

"You're an asshole, you know that?" Bones taunted. "You just threw away the best fucking thing that's ever happened to you and for what? Because you're a pussy!"

I charged at him, rearing back my fist and letting it connect with the side of his jaw.

He gripped my cut, and slammed me back against the wall, his fist pounding against my ribs.

"Truth hurts, brother," he hissed, as I pushed him off me and punched him again, aiming for his nose this time.

"Thought you'd be happy, me out of the way you're free to claim her for yourself. That's what you want isn't it? Been dying to stick your dick in my girl since the moment you laid eyes on her," I roared, as I threw him onto the pool table.

He kicked off the table, charging his head into my stomach and pummeled me to the floor.

"Someone will claim her, douche bag," he clipped. "Girls like that will bounce back, move on and fall in love. Some other man will gladly grab what you threw away, only he'll hang on tight, and that kid of yours? He'll call someone else daddy," he barked.

I lifted my head from the floor and drilled him with a cold stare.

"Looks like you're applying for the job," I spoke through clenched teeth.

"I would in a fucking heartbeat but you're my brother, and that shit means something to me," he said, releasing his grip on me. "Wake up, man. Whatever it is you think you're doing, I'm telling you you're doing it all wrong. Don't do this, don't let them go."

"I'm no good for them," I growled, trying to sit up.

"Then make yourself better," he demanded, holding out his hand toward me.

I took his hand and pulled him down beside me, wedging my forearm against his throat as I leaned over him.

"Mind your fucking business, Bones. And do yourself a fucking favor and don't bring this shit up again, because so help me God, next time you do I'll cut you, *brother*," I promised, as I dropped him onto the ground and stepped over his body.

I know why Blackie tries to numb himself from the hell he lives.

The pain is unbearable.

The dull ache in my chest that had been haunting me, turned into a sharp spear, twisting and turning a hundred times over.

I lost my Kitten.

I'll never know Pea.

And I just pissed on some twenty odd years of friendship with Bones.

I was on a roll.

I had walked away from a lot of people in my life, gave up my birth right, but none of it hurt the way walking away from Lauren and our baby did.

I hadn't lied when I said I never wanted to be someone's man, or someone's father. Now that I held those two titles, even for a short while, was everything to me.

Everything I no longer had.

But losing them, kissing goodbye my rights to my child and Lauren, would be worth it because they'd be safe.

Safe from me.

Safe from my enemies.

Safe from the reaper.

Chapter Thirty

RIGGS

Jack slammed the gavel repeatedly against the wooden table trying to reign us in but we were congratulating the nomad's that had just patched into our charter. After the Red Dragons attacked Pop's shooting range, Jack sent Pipe and Wolf back into the field, ordering them not to come back to the Dog Pound without nomads worthy to wear the Brooklyn patch on their cut. Deuce, Stryker, Linc and Cobra were officially voted to sit at our table, and not a moment too soon because aside from the vote on whether they should wear our patch or not, Jack called Church to discuss how he planned to retaliate against the Chinese.

"For the love of God, would you bitches shut the fuck up so we can discuss business," Jack grunted, throwing the gavel across the table and rubbing his temples.

That got our attention, and we fell silent as we gave our pissed off president our undivided attention.

"I swear to God, I question if you jerk offs even have dicks," he muttered.

Wolf grabbed his crotch in defense.

"Want me to whip out the old anaconda?"

"You do that and I'll shoot it off," Jack hissed, before glancing at our new members. "Pipe and this clown..." he pointed his thumb toward Wolf as he spoke "...have filled you guys in on the war we have going on with the Red Dragons, so no need for me to rehash the reason behind what we're about to do."

He reached into his cut for his pack of Marlboros and picked one out with his teeth as Blackie slid a lighter across the table.

"Been working on a way to retaliate against them for the guns they stole and the bullets they pumped into Pops place. Rienzi, who's a longshoreman, one of Vic's guys, came through with a tip. Seems like our friend Wu is receiving a shipment tonight from Beijing," he clarified, flicking his ashes into the ashtray. "Saddle up, boys because we're going to intercept their shipment."

"Do we know what it is?" I asked, as I took the toothpick I was chewing on out of my mouth.

"It don't matter what the cargo is, I don't want their shit. I want to hit Wu were it really hurts—his wallet. We'll unload the container and dump that shit right into the river, sending a message back to our friends. They fucked with us, now it's our turn to fuck them ten times harder," he growled.

"Ay," Pipe agreed.

"It's about time those Lo Mein eating motherfuckers get a dose of my cock," Wolf added.

We all turned our eyes to Wolf, and he shrugged his shoulders.

"What?" he asked innocently. "You said fuck them hard, only trying to do my part for the cause," he claimed.

"You're a sick fuck," Bones added.

"Welcome to the club, boys," Jack said sarcastically, earning a few laughs from our new additions.

"Nothing we haven't seen before, Bulldog," Stryker replied, his lips curving slightly.

"There is just one more thing I want to discuss before we get our asses in gear." His eyes drifted toward me then to Bones who sat across from me. "For the last month you two have been acting like a bunch of bitches in a cat fight," he ranted. "Time for this lover's quarrel, or whatever the fuck it is between you two, be put to rest."

I averted my eyes to Bones who met my blank stare with one of his own. It was true, since Kitten stormed into the clubhouse, handing me my ass and walking out of my life, Bones and I haven't been the same. I know him well enough and long enough to realize he gave me a pass. No one gets away with putting their hands on Bones. They don't live to tell about it, but here I was breathing.

I also know that he'd never disrespect me and go after Lauren. His interference came from a good place, a place where he knew what I was sacrificing and had remorse for my decision. I wasn't ready to hear him say what I felt in my heart. I didn't want to face facts that walking away from Lauren and the baby was a shit thing to do and Bones wasn't about to let me forget it.

"We're all brothers here but you two are in a class of your own, one of you gets wounded the other one bleeds, so bury that shit and bury it deep," Jack emphasized.

"Yeah girls, why don't you kiss and make up," Wolf pleaded.

Bones uncrossed his arms, keeping his eyes steady on me as he reached across the table and offered me his hand. I took a deep breath, apologizing to my best friend with my eyes instead of my words as I took his hand and shook on it solidifying our brotherhood.

"Can I get an Amen?" Pipe quipped.

"Amen," preached Wolf.

"Amen," chanted Stryker.

"Praise be to God," Linc added.

"Hallelujah," Blackie mused.

"All right, all right, go in peace my brothers," Jack said, bowing his head and making the sign of the cross.

God was going to strike us all dead, luckily, we weren't relying on him to welcome us at the pearly gates. We were destined for the flames and the only one waiting for us in the end would be Satan.

We pulled our bikes into the shipping yard, locked and loaded, ready for mayhem, thirsty for blood. We weren't the weak ass motherfuckers the Red Dragons assumed we were. We had Blackie back, and as fucked as he was he was crazy too, and now we had four more men, ready to make names for themselves within the club.

Cutting our engines, we dismounted our bikes before pulling our weapons and crouching down as we ran up the pier where the vessel docked. Sun Wu and the Dragons were nowhere in sight, not scheduled to unload their shipment for another hour. Jack led the pack, pausing at the container and forking over an envelope to Rienzi before he snapped the plastic seal off the doors giving us access to Wu's merchandise.

Wooden crates stacked from the floor to the ceiling, filled the entire container. It would take more than an hour to unload this thing.

Stryker and Deuce charged in first, tucking their guns away before Stryker got down on one knee, placing one palm over the other while Deuce put his boot clad foot onto Stryker's hands before he hoisted him up. Deuce pulled a crate from the top and dropped it onto the floor beside us. Together Stryker and Deuce demolished the first row of crates.

The last crate fell onto the others, busting open and Wolf, the nosey fuck he was, sifted through it.

"Well, well, looks like Wu wanted to get fucked after all," he mocked, as he held up a pink dildo.

I walked over to the crate, pushing around the contents, and sure enough it was full of sex toys.

"I bet this one is labeled butt plugs," Pipe said, prying open the top of another crate.

"Dump it," Jack ordered.

Pipe raised an eyebrow, questioning Jack.

"You sure about that, boss? Bet we can turn this shit for a pretty penny," he countered.

"Dump the fucking shit," Jack barked, as he lifted a crate over his head and threw it into the water.

Sweat poured from our bodies as we hustled to empty the container, finally hauling the last crate into the river, creating a sea of vibrators. The Hudson River looked like a goddamn nympho's paradise.

What a fucking sight.

"Pack it up," Jack demanded, as he reached into his back pocket and produced a can of spray paint. I turned to Bones, my eyes questioning his, but he merely shrugged his shoulders and we both turned back to watch as Jack nodded toward Rienzi.

Rienzi closed the container, locking it up with a new plastic seal before taking a step back and letting Jack do his thing. He pulled the cap off the bottle, throwing it into the water before putting his finger on the aerosol can and writing a message to Wu.

Fuck you.

In bright red letters across the door.

Jack took a step back, admiring his handy work before dumping the can of paint into the water and turning around to face us.

"Clear enough?"

"Still think we should've fucked him with one of his toys," Wolf clipped.

"Message is clear," Pipe confirmed, smacking Wolf upside the head.

Jack slapped each of the newbies on the back, impressed with their efficiency as we strode down the dock, pretty fucking pleased with ourselves that we pulled it off with fifteen minutes to spare.

We were half way down the dock when we heard the roar of the Red Dragons engines.

"Shit, we've got company," Blackie declared, reaching for his gun.

Time stopped after he uttered those words and everything moved in slow motion. It didn't matter we were running down the rickety wooden pier, guns drawn and lighting the shipping yard a blaze, to me we were just standing still.

I glanced down at my feet then lifted my head and watched as my brothers ran forward, shooting their way back to their bikes and I remained still.

They ran.

They fought.

I stayed still, taking it all in before something clicked inside of me and I took my other gun, crossed one arm over the other and fired both guns.

One down, then another, and another. I didn't know if they were dead or not but I told myself they were.

It wasn't enough.

I needed more.

I took my time, walking the rest of the pier, firing one gun then the other. Another two dropped to the ground.

Still, not enough.

I wanted Wu.

I wanted to decorate my hands with his blood.

I wouldn't stop until I did, and I continued to pop any Dragon that stepped in my way, full of lead.

I heard my brothers shout out to me.

But I tuned them out.

I didn't give a fuck.

Let them tell me I'm reckless.

Let them tell me I have no heart.

I don't.

This motherfucker was the reason I won't see my kid being born, or hold Lauren's hand as she brings him into this world. This son of a bitch took my family from me with his threats.

I don't make threats.

I make promises.

I promise to take that bastard's blood.

I solemnly swear to make it my mission in life.

I reached the end of the dock as another Dragon neared and I pulled the trigger, emptying my clip into his head. One of his brothers came up behind me, shouting in Mandarin as he watched the blood of his brother pour from his eyes and drop to the floor. I turned around, fired a shot and clipped him in the shoulder. I went to finish the job, but I ran out of bullets. He screamed, spewing Chinese bullshit as I tucked my guns away and rolled up my sleeves. My dick got hard from the look of fear in his eyes and it was all I needed to finish him. I grabbed him by the neck, smiled at him as I leaned into him and spit in his face before I snapped his neck and dropped his head to the ground.

"Jesus Christ," Bones hollered, pulling me to my feet. "C'mon, man, what the fuck are you doing?" he fumed, as he stared down at the slayed Dragon. I followed his eyes and looked at the man at my feet, feeling unsatisfied as I gasped for air. Bones looked at me, muttering something under his breath before he bent down and grabbed the guy's feet, dragging his bloody ass to the end of the pier before he kicked him into the water.

He grabbed the back of my cut and pushed me forward.

"We gotta get the fuck out of here," he ordered. "Now, Riggs."

I stared at him blankly before glancing down at my hands, recalling how Blackie lifted his hands and spoke of the bloodshed his hands were responsible for.

My hands weren't clean anymore.

But they weren't nearly as dirty as I wanted them to be.

Not until I had Wu.

I was going to get that motherfucker.

Mark my words.

Lauren

I was six months pregnant, more than a month had passed since I had seen Riggs. The first few weeks were rough, I went from having so much hope to having nothing at all. I felt like I was crawling out of a hole, desperate to get above ground. I'm still not there yet, and I may never be, but I'm moving forward.

I have no choice.

After I left the clubhouse Anthony took me to the apartment so I could pack my things before bringing me to his home. I feel bad for the hell I've put my brother and Adrianna through. It should've been a happy time for them, they should've been enjoying Adrianna's pregnancy but instead they listened to me cry myself to sleep and put off painting their daughter's nursery in fear it would upset me.

They tiptoed around me, but I'd catch things here and there, like when they were laying on the couch together and Anthony dropped his head into Adrianna's lap so he could talk to the baby. Or the several times he placed his hands on her stomach when their little girl kicked.

Pea kicked a lot.

But there was no one to lay a hand on my belly other than me.

I was happy for my brother, really I was, but I didn't like feeling envious so when my mother suggested I move in with her, I jumped at the chance. Of course, Anthony didn't like the idea, he was my shadow these days and me living with our mom, made his job harder.

I got a job, working from home, billing and coding for a doctor. It wasn't a great job but it would get me through until I had the baby. Then I really needed to figure out what I would do to support us.

I think of Riggs all the time. I hate myself for it but I can't help it. I wonder if he regrets what he did or if he's happy to be rid of the burden.

I'm dreading going to the doctor tomorrow, and not because I can't wait to see how the baby is doing, but because Riggs won't be there to hold my hand and whisper jokes in my ear. He won't be there trying to put his own legs in the stirrups like he did the first time he came to a doctor's appointment with me. He won't be there trying to convince the doctor he has super sperm and that our baby will be a genius. He won't be there to rob hospital gowns intending to play doctor when we get home.

He's gone.

It's like he's dead.

And if I'm being honest, there are days when I tell myself he is.

Rest in Peace, Riggs.

You'll forever be in my heart.

Chapter Thirty-One
RIGGS

I started staying at the apartment almost immediately after Lauren left, partially because of the feud with Bones, but mainly because I wanted to hold onto my brief time with Lauren and Pea. The first few days it took all the willpower I could muster up not to break every piece of furniture. The couch, the bed, hell, even the refrigerator reminded me of what I gave up.

I had to keep reminding myself that I was doing the right thing even when my conscience tried fucking with me, whispering in my head words of doubt.

I could've protected them.
They would've been safe with me.
It was my responsibility to watch them.
Not Anthony's.

And when I pushed those thoughts out of my head all I saw was Wu's face as he promised to go after me and mine. It's real clear that this shit won't die until one of us does. Throwing a bunch of dicks, literally, well, fake dicks, into the river wouldn't do anything to end this war. Jack says intercepting their shipment sends a message—we aren't weak, we won't sit back and let them attack us.

It's all bullshit.

He will strike.

We'll strike back and so on and so forth.

We don't have a common goal with the Dragons, no truce to iron out.

It's either their blood or ours.

Me, personally? I don't want to sit back and wait for them to draw our blood. I say we take them out, starting with Wu. But I don't call the shots and everyone thinks I'm a mad man these days.

I placed the roller in the tray when I heard someone knock on the door and took a step back to admire the paint I had chosen. The clerk at the paint store recommended either yellow or green, something neutral…something gay. I painted one wall gray and the other three white. If Pea was a girl then we could add a ton of pink shit but if he's a boy, then we'd add a ton of blue.

Who was I kidding? Pea wouldn't see this room.

But still I'd continue painting these walls. I'd buy a crib, and whatever other shit a baby needed because I'll always be his dad. Even if he doesn't know it. Even if this is just for me to feel like I'm someone's dad.

I walked out of the room, wiping my hands on my t-shirt before I pulled open the door to find Bones leaning against the doorjamb. I stepped aside as he kicked off the wall and walked into the apartment.

"Painting?" he asked, as he sniffed the fumes.

"Yeah," I said, as I grabbed two beers from the fridge and popped the tops off them, offering him one. "Thanks for coming," I added.

He nodded, taking the beer I offered him and placed it on the counter.

"I figured you wanted to talk about last night," he started.

"Why would I want to talk about what went down last night?" I asked, narrowing my eyes in confusion.

"Dude, you snapped that guy's neck," he reminded me as he widened his eyes.

I shrugged my shoulders, taking another guzzle of the beer.

"One less motherfucker roaming the streets, one less man looking to kill us. He had to go. They all have to go. It shouldn't matter how I killed him, whether it be a bullet or my hands, he's dead. Job's done."

"The goal wasn't to partake in a massacre on the docks."

"There is no goal, Bones. Don't you realize that? Jack's big plan to intercept their shipment was a pussy move, so was Wu's when he cut me loose, roughing me up with a haircut. It's just prolonging death because that's the only way this ends, one side dies."

He studied me for a moment before he nodded in agreement.

"Is that why you asked me to come here?"

"No, but I'll get to that."

I placed my beer on the counter and braced the edge of it, collecting my thoughts before I whipped around and pinned him with a gaze.

"I'm going to kill Sun Wu," I declared.

"What?"

"You just agreed that this won't end until either our club goes up in smoke or theirs does. I'm making the choice and I chose them," I hissed.

"You can't do that Riggs, and you know that. Nothing goes down without a vote," he scolded.

"I don't give a fuck about democracy anymore. You weren't there, you didn't hear his threats, every time he promised me and mine would be first, all I could picture was Lauren's face and the face of a kid I hadn't even meet yet but dream about all the time."

"You go after Wu on your own you might as well commit suicide," Bones shouted.

"Feels like I did that already," I muttered, glancing around the empty apartment. "Look, I'm not asking for your help, your permission or even your opinion. I asked you here for a favor," I said, walking around the counter and opening a drawer and pulling out a check.

"Here's a blank check," I said, extending it over the counter to him. "I need you to go to the hospital and settle up Lauren's medical bills. I wrote the account number on the memo of the check, it should be the same account as in the beginning but I haven't received a bill since she moved out."

"She still staying with Anthony?"

"No, he told me she moved in with her mother," I said, watching as he folded the check and shoved it into his back pocket.

"You sure this is what you want?"

"I don't want any of this but as long as Wu is out there, Lauren isn't safe with me."

"Let's talk hypothetical's and say this whole war ends, Wu gets what he has coming to him and we walk away the winners, then what?"

"Then I go get my Kitten and my Pea and beg her to let me be in their lives," I said automatically.

"You love her," He stated.

"Yeah, I do. Go figure," I said, huskily. There was no point in denying it. I loved Lauren Bianci more than I ever imagined possible. I loved her for the woman she was, the crazy bat swinging girl next door who stormed into my life, turning it upside down as she gave me everything I never knew I wanted. When I first met her I kept telling her to take detours, to go with the flow and see where she wound up, not expecting she'd take me on my own detour.

Greatest fucking detour ever.

"I'll make sure I go to the hospital first thing in the morning."

"Thank you," I said, with a nod.

"No problem," he said, turning around and heading toward the door. He paused mid stride, glancing over his shoulder at me. "Please, don't do anything stupid. Don't make me be the guy who tells her you're dead. Just hang on and we'll figure it out."

He waited for my response but it never came. I'd make no promises other than the one I made to myself to protect my family.

Whatever it takes.

Whatever it costs.

Even if it's my life for theirs.

It's worth it.

They're worth it.

Lauren

I hurried down the corridor of the hospital where my OBGYN, Dr. Goodwin, was located. I was already late for my appointment and smacked into a hard wall of a person. I placed one protective hand over my belly as I lifted my eyes to apologize to my poor victim and to my surprise the poor bastard I body slammed, or bump slammed rather, was Bones.

"Lauren...are you, all right?" he asked, his eyes instantly dropping to my belly before lifting to mine.

"I'm fine, sorry. I'm late for my appointment and I wasn't paying attention. What are you doing in the gynecology wing of the hospital?"

Talk about a fish out of water.

"Shit," he hissed, looking up at the sign that read Obstetrics and Gynecology. "Is that where I am? I must've made a wrong turn somewhere. Jack sent me to check on Jimmy Gold's status and somehow I wound up here," he explained.

I raised an eyebrow questioning him but then my eye caught the clock on the wall.

"Dammit," I said.

"I'll walk with you," he offered. "At least I won't look like a moron if I'm accompanying someone who belongs in this part of the hospital."

"Okay," I said, standing there for a moment before pointing behind him. "My doctor is down the hall."

He fell into stride beside me as we walked down the corridor.

"How do you feel?" he asked.

"Pretty good," I said. "The baby kicks a lot now, keeps me up most of the night," I added with a smile. "I keep thinking to myself I can't wait for him or her to be here and then I stop myself because it'll be over before I know it and then I'll probably miss feeling her inside of me."

He smiled.

"You sound pretty confident it's a girl," he commented. "Do you have any names picked out?"

"No names yet," I admitted but left out the reason I hadn't chosen any names. I hated that Riggs wouldn't be a part of choosing Pea's real name. As silly as it sounded, I sort of hoped I was having a girl because then I could really name her Pea, something Riggs and I both called her. If it was a boy, well I didn't want my kid growing up with a permanent "kick me" sign on his back so Pea would be out of the question.

We reached Dr. Goodwin's office and I looked through the glass door, spotting the three couples in the waiting room, the women just as far as long as me, if not more. There were a few other women in the waiting room but they were probably there for routine check-ups. I glanced back at Bones.

"It'll probably be a few minutes before they're ready for me…would you keep me company while I wait?"

He rocked back on his heels for a moment before nodding slightly and reached around to pull the door open for me.

"After you," he insisted.

I smiled and walked into the office, checking in with the receptionist as Bones slipped into one of the seats and immediately buried his face into a Parenting magazine. I laughed slightly as I made my way toward him, taking the seat beside him.

"Preparing yourself Uncle Bones?" I asked, taking the magazine from him.

"Uncle Bones," he repeated thoughtfully before smiling. "I never thought I'd be anyone's uncle," he said, more to himself than me but when he turned his gaze to mine he explained. "I'm an only child."

"Is it okay then if Pea calls you Uncle Bones?"

"It's more than okay," he winked.

"So how is everyone else doing? You know, Jack, Pipe, and the rest of the crew?" I asked nonchalantly as I smoothed my shirt over my bump. "Any wild and crazy clubhouse parties?"

"You want to know how Jack and Pipe are?" he questioned, and I heard the amusement in his voice.

I didn't say anything, pleading the fifth, knowing very well Bones knew I was fishing for information on Riggs.

"He's miserable," he said finally.

I snapped my eyes to his and stared at him as he blew out an exasperated breath.

"He's not staying at the clubhouse either, goes home every night to the apartment," he revealed.

I was torn on how I felt about that, knowing he wasn't staying at the Dog Pound but choosing to go home, *our* home, gave me that false hope I've come to associate with Riggs. Then I wondered if he was bringing other girls to *our* home and that shit didn't fly with me.

"Lauren, he thinks he's protecting you and the baby. He thinks if stays away from you then no one will ever look to hurt you guys. Jack wanted to put a prospect on you until this club business blew over but that wasn't enough for Riggs. He asked Anthony to watch out for you because he knows he's your brother, that baby's uncle, and he wouldn't think twice about stepping in front of a bullet for you."

I glanced down at my lap as tears welled in my eyes.

Hope.

Don't fall for it again.

Hope.

Stay strong.

"He should be the one protecting me," I whispered, lifting my eyes to Bones, fighting to hold back my tears. "I know he wouldn't let anything happen to me or Pea. I know he wants to keep us safe, that he wanted to do the right thing, but he lost his way somewhere. He lost that self confidence that he could do right by his family and instead he gave up on us. I saw past the club, I saw the man behind the patch and I wanted him so much more. It was beautiful to watch him go from a man with raw uncertainty of his ability to be a good dad to learning he wanted to be one, and he wouldn't let his fear dictate the type of father he was to Pea. He changed Bones, I saw it with my own eyes. He wanted Pea, but he gave up the minute things got messy, the minute life threw *him* a detour. I don't know what's going on with your club and I don't care but I'm mad as hell he chose that club over us. He should have spat in the face of his enemy and fought ten times harder for what he was hanging on to but he didn't. He gave up."

Bones said nothing. He probably didn't know how to respond but his silence also was a sign of his loyalty to his brother.

"Miss Bianci? Dr. Goodwin will see you now," the receptionist called.

I gripped the arms of the chair and rose to my feet.

"Lauren, I know you're mad and you have every right to be," he said, standing as he spoke. "And I also know he probably doesn't deserve it but I'm going to ask you anyway…"

"Ask me what?"

"Not to give up on him."

"Too late for that Bones," I answered. "Do you see him here? Where his place is? No you don't. Look around the room," I whispered. "I'm the only one alone here," I added, my voice cracking with emotion.

I continued to walk toward the receptionist when she smiled over my shoulder at Bones.

"You too, Dad," she said, cheerfully.

Bones opened his mouth to correct her and then I followed his eyes as they roamed around the room, pausing to stare at the couples I had pointed out.

"I wouldn't mind not being alone," I croaked.

He bit the inside of his cheek, shoving his hands into his pocket before he nodded.

"Uncle Bones is happy to help," he said, winking at me and following me into the exam room.

He took a seat in the corner of the room, fidgeting about as the nurse weighed me and took my blood pressure. I stepped onto the exam table and lifted my shirt, exposing my round belly and waited for the doctor to join us.

I turned to Bones, watched as he stared a hole into the wall beside me and giggled. The big bad biker was uncomfortable, but I relished in his company, the support of another human being beside me.

"Do you want kids, Bones?" I asked, forcing him to look at me.

"Yeah," he said automatically. "Someday."

The door opened and Dr. Goodwin stepped inside, smiling at me before looking back at Bones with a confused look.

"Dad couldn't join us again?" she asked.

"No, so Uncle…Eric, is stepping in just for today," he offered, looking back at me and winking.

"How nice," Dr. Goodwin replied as she looked over my chart.

I stared at Bones wide-eyed.

"Uncle Eric?"

"Figured it was better than explaining why the kid had an uncle named Bones?" he explained, in a hushed tone.

I smiled at him before Dr. Goodwin squirted the cold gel like substance onto my belly. Bones' eyes diverted to the screen as the doctor moved the wand around my belly, until Pea appeared on the screen.

My perfect little baby.

That image would never get old.

I listened as Pea's heartbeat sounded, strong and healthy and I couldn't wait to hold her in my arms.

I couldn't wait to meet the love of my life.

Bones looked amazed by it all and smiled when Dr. Goodwin pointed out Pea's features, freezing the image of her perfect profile. After the sonogram was over, the doctor printed out several photos of the baby and handed them to me. She instructed me to make another appointment for next month and informed me that Pea was progressing wonderfully and was right on track.

I wiped the gel from my belly and pulled my shirt down, turning toward Bones.

"Thanks for getting lost and sticking around with me. It was nice not to be alone," I said, as he walked with me to the door. "Eric," I mused.

He nudged me playfully.

"Bones," he corrected. "Anything for Pea, even if it means giving up my real name," he joked.

I folded one of the sonogram photos and ripped it off the strip before handing it to him.

"A gift from Pea, to say thank you," I offered, holding the picture out for him.

He glanced down at the black and white grainy photo before slipping it into the inside pocket of his cut.

"C'mon, I'll walk you out," he said.

Of course I took him up on his offer because hanging out with Bones made me feel closer to Riggs. I wanted to say something, give him a message for Riggs that we were still here if he had a change of heart. But I knew that would only break what was left of my heart if he didn't take me up on the offer.

Stay strong, I reminded myself.

You've got this.

It's his loss.

But each day that passed was another piece of my heart lost to Riggs and the dreams I thought we could make come true.

Dreams.

What a joke.

Chapter Thirty-Two

RIGGS

I had to get out of this apartment. I was going crazy sitting here drinking myself into oblivion, staring at my three white walls and one gray one. I ordered a crib today. A mattress too, and one of those fancy rocking chairs for when the baby wakes up in the middle of the night.

I know.

I'm losing my mind.

I rode my bike to the Dog Pound; even though that was the last place I wanted to be. I found the guys on their way out, headed to some bar in Bay Ridge. I wasn't much company but it was better than wallowing in my self-created Hell.

The new guys were alright, Stryker was a pool shark, and by the second round he had half the bar lining up to try and beat him in a game. He couldn't lose, so Cobra made things interesting and started placing bets on his games.

It was obvious Cobra was an earner. There probably wasn't much he wouldn't do to make a dollar. Jack was going to love him.

Linc was quiet, more reserved. He sat at the bar, eyes glued to whatever game was on the flat screen. Why was it that women always gravitated to the brooding types? The bar was more or less empty but every girl who stepped up to order a drink made sure they cozied up to Linc. He was a pussy magnet.

Deuce was young and chasing tail, reminding me a lot of the old me. The reckless Riggs who only cared about his bike and his dick.

Blackie pushed a shot of tequila toward me.

"You look like shit," he muttered.

"Thanks, bro," I replied sarcastically, wondering if he knew how bad he looked. The two of us made quite the pair, looking like two drunk bums instead of two badass bikers.

I threw back the shot.

"Oh, look, here comes your girlfriend," Blackie mocked. For a moment I thought he was referencing Lauren. I quickly turned around to see Bones walk through the door, making eye-contact with me as Stryker grabbed his arm and led him to the pool table. I snarled, swiveling around in my chair when my eyes latched onto the unmistakable dark eyes of a girl. I laughed, nudging him as that bitch *karma* made her presence known.

"Yeah, and there's yours," I mused.

He turned in his chair, his eyes following the direction of mine and collided with Lacey's.

"Goddamn," he hissed, quickly turning back around.

I waved at Lacey and received a scowl in return.

"She looks pissed, guess her date isn't doing it for her," I observed. Blackie ordered another round of shots while glancing over his shoulder at the guy who was getting cozy with Jack's daughter.

He shook his head before turning back and staring down at his drink.

"Stop looking at her," he growled.

"Shouldn't you be saying that to the guy with his tongue in her ear?" I asked incredulously, as I turned around and minded my own business—kind of. "C'mon man, I know you have a death wish and all that, but Jack's daughter?"

"It's not like that," he growled.

"Right and Michael Jackson didn't think he was Peter-fucking-Pan," I retorted.

"What?"

I rolled my eyes, about to call him on his shit when Bones came up alongside me and parked his ass on the stool next to mine and ordered a beer.

"Hey," I greeted, looking at him expectantly. I had called him earlier to ask if he went to the hospital to pay Lauren's medical bills and he told me he'd meet me here.

"It's all taken care of," he stated. "She's paid in full until next month—I guess when she sees the doctor again," he added.

I nodded in response.

"I ran into her at the hospital," he said. I turned, pinning him with a stare. "Relax, she didn't know why I was there. I told her I got lost," he stated, shrugging his shoulders. "She seemed to buy it. Anyway, everything's good with her and the baby, moving along just as they should be," he informed.

"Good," I said, turning back to Blackie, stealing the shot he was about to bring to his lips and claiming it as my own. I flinched as the liquid burned my throat. "Thanks for doing that," I croaked.

He slapped his hand on the bar.

"Go easy on that shit," he said, lifting his hand and leaving a black and white photograph of Pea.

My Pea.

I reached for the photo, mesmerized by how much he had changed since I last saw him.

"Kid's got your nose," he added, before slapping me on the back and strolling out of the bar.

"He does," I whispered out loud, as I traced my finger over my kid's nose, the same nose he shared with me.

I swallowed the lump in my throat and reached into my pocket, pulling out a couple of bills and dropped them onto the bar. I took Pea's photo and slipped it into my back pocket.

"I'm getting out of here," I told Blackie. Without waiting for a reply, I walked out of the bar and climbed onto my bike. I revved my engine and drove aimlessly around the streets of Brooklyn with the image of Pea's profile fresh in my mind, burning a hole in my heart.

My nose.

Lauren's lips.

I wasn't sure about his chin but it was still a handsome chin.

I hope his eyes are just like his mother's.

I wanted to drive to Lauren's apartment, I doubt Maria would've let me in, but I wanted to see her. I could really use a cuddle right now. I needed Kitten to wrap me in her arms and fill me in on everything I've missed. Knowing her, she probably had a scrapbook full of Pea's pictures. Maybe I would get a chance to feel the baby move. That would be epic.

I didn't do any of those things; instead I drove my ass to the Red Dragons' clubhouse and sat across the street from their compound with my hand wrapped around my gun. I thought of a million different ways I could get through those iron gates and twice as many ways I'd kill the motherfucker. I didn't want them all. I wasn't greedy like that. I'd just take Wu.

But I knew Bones was right. It was suicide. If the Dragons didn't kill me for offing their president then Jack would kill me for going against him. Brother or no brother, that shit was wrong.

I resigned, tucking my gun away, deciding Wu and I both got to live another night and peeled away from the curb, making my way to my apartment. Maybe I'd put another coat of paint on the walls, or finish that bottle of whiskey I had been working on. The first thing I'd definitely do when I walked in the door was put Pea's picture where it belongs...on my refrigerator.

I reached for my keys as I climbed the stairs to my apartment, pulled them and the photo out of my pocket, jingling the keys in my hand as I stared at Pea.

I was still shocked that me and Lauren made a kid.

I reached the landing and turned my head when I heard footsteps, stopping in my tracks as my eyes met Lauren's briefly before they dropped and zeroed in on her protruding stomach.

My God.

She'd gotten so much bigger since the last time I saw her.

There was no question that she was pregnant, that round belly said it all. The club always talks about branding their women, making their women their property, they give them their colors and stamp them as their old lady.

I made Lauren my property, claimed her as mine, the sweetest way imaginable the night I put Pea inside her. That bump was her brand and it made her mine forever.

I lifted my eyes back to her face, noticing her cheeks reddening ever so slightly. I moved around her to open the door. Silently, she stepped inside and I followed her, closing the door behind me.

She stared at me for a moment before looking down at the photo I clutched in my hands.

"Funny thing happened today," she started, taking the picture out of my hand and walking into the kitchen. She pulled a magnet from the side of the fridge and placed Pea's photo front and center on the refrigerator door before she turned around and looked back at me.

"Actually, a couple of things happened today. I went to my doctor's appointment and guess who was there?" she asked, walking closer. "Bones. Picture that. He said he was lost and I believed him. You've made it clear that you guys aren't really the brightest bulbs," she said, her lip curling slightly. "Anyway, after my appointment he walked me to my car and took off but I forgot that I didn't make my payment with the doctor."

I should've turned around and ignored her but I couldn't take my eyes off of her.

"Are you ready for the funny thing? I went to make a payment and the receptionist told me that the man I was with came in a little before me and paid my balance in full."

"That Bones, he's a good guy," I said hoarsely.

"Yeah, he is," she agreed. "Some might say his friend is too," she added, crossing her arms under her chest. "Why did you pay my doctor's bill, Riggs?"

"It's not a big deal, Lauren," I argued.

Fiery blue eyes pierced me as she stalked toward me, closing the distance between us and shoving the palm of her hand against my chest.

"It's a big deal to me! So is watching you walk up the stairs holding our baby's picture in your hand. It's huge for a woman who thinks she's all alone and the only one who wants this baby."

"What do you want me to say? You want the truth? It's not going to change anything. It's not going to make all the bad shit disappear, Lauren."

"For once can we just stop talking about the club and all the bad things that can happen? I'm so sick and tired of letting that patch dictate our life," she reached out and placed her palm against my chest.

"Just tell me what's in here. Please," she whispered. "It's just us, just the three of us, give me this Riggs. I promise I won't hold you to anything. I just need to hear it. I need to know that it all wasn't lies."

"The three of us," I repeated hoarsely, laying my hand over hers. "Let me look at you, Lauren," I said, as I took a step back and let my eyes travel the length of her, taking in all her changes, all her beauty.

"You're so goddamn pretty," I said, lifting my eyes back to hers. "Pea has your mouth," I whispered.

"And your nose," she replied.

I stepped closer to her, mindlessly taking her face in the palms of my hand and bent my knees so we were eye level.

"Thank you," I said sincerely.

"For what?" she replied breathless.

"For being a great mom to Pea. You're doing a great job, Kitten," I whispered, as I touched my forehead to hers.

"I miss you," she blurted. "I know you love Pea, Riggs," she insisted.

Love?

The word wasn't close enough to what I was feeling.

"For the first time in my life, I've got people that depend on me, and not just for support but for protection. Lauren, I can't deal with that pressure. If something ever happens to you or the baby because of me—"

"Nothing's going to happen," she interrupted, placing her hands around my wrists. "Riggs, we're okay, we just want you.

The last words she spoke were the ones that broke me; split me in two. I picked the man who loved Kitten and Pea, the man who wanted the family over the monster who sought vengeance. I covered her mouth with mine, giving us both what we wanted and damning everything else to Hell. She tasted like all the good things you wish for but don't think you'll ever have.

Her arms wrapped around my neck, pulling me closer, her belly pressing against me as she struggled to get us as close as possible. I pulled my lips from hers, letting my tongue taste her lips one last time before I lifted her into my arms.

"What're you doing?" she whispered, as I cradled her, carrying her to our bedroom.

"Proving to you nothing was a lie."

It was the only truth I knew.

Lauren

I followed my heart to Riggs' doorstep, knowing I'd probably lose it—but if there was the slightest chance I could get him to admit the truth, then it would be worth it.

Wouldn't it?

He set me down on the foot of the bed and kneeled before me, spreading my legs apart as he moved between them and ran his hands up my thighs.

"Let me see you, Kitten," he said, for the second time since I came here. I looked into his eyes and saw the desperation reflected in them and knew I'd never be able to deny him. Aside from that, I wanted this just as much as he did, if not more. I hated being alone, I hated not having him. I didn't only miss him emotionally, but physically too. I craved his touch, his comfort, his existence.

There was no sexy way to undress for him. I lifted my maternity shirt over my belly, revealing the blue stretchy material of my jeans that covered my bump before I finally pulled it over my head. He stared at my breasts that were straining against my lace bra. I was a whole cup size bigger than the last time he saw me like this. He licked his lips, slowly, tantalizingly before reaching down and cupping his dick.

Clearly, he enjoyed the change.

And that gave me the confidence I needed.

I slipped my fingers beneath the stretchy fabric of my pants and lowered the band, exposing my belly. I lifted my hips and pulled the pants down to my thighs, knowing it would get awkward and I'd have to lift my leg to get the pants off.

Riggs laid his hands over mine and stopped me from going any further.

"Can I?"

I nodded thinking he was asking to finish removing my pants but he lifted his hands off of mine and splayed them across my belly.

"Oh, wow," he whispered, lifting his eyes to mine. I was taken aback by the emotion conveyed in his eyes, something I thought Riggs was immune to.

Then he broke my heart.

Or maybe he picked up the pieces.

I couldn't be sure.

But when he pressed his lips to my belly, my heart ached for the time he missed and the time he still might.

Please choose us, I pleaded.

A message from my heart to yours.

I reached behind me and unclasped my bra, letting my breasts fall from their confinements of the lace, giving him another piece of myself. He reached up and cupped the back of my neck, pulling me closer and pressing his lips against mine.

"You're beautiful, Kitten. So fucking beautiful," he whispered against my mouth.

His mouth left mine as he took my shoes off and maneuvered my pants down my legs. I tucked my thumbs into the waistband of my underwear but he pushed my hands away and brought the silk down my legs.

"Lie down, let me look at you," he said huskily.

I was completely nude, everything on display for him to see and still he asked me for permission to see it all, to take everything in, all the changes in my body. This moment we were sharing, the truth…we'd always be Kitten and Tiger.

"Aren't you a little over dressed?" I rasped, leaning back on my elbows. "Take your clothes off, Riggs. I want to feel you."

I wanted him pressed against me, skin to skin, chest to chest, one broken heart beating against another.

He reached behind him, pulling his shirt over his head and throwing it to the floor before he unzipped his jeans and dragged them down his legs. I let my eyes greedily travel the length of him, taking every inch of him in.

I missed him so much.

I inched back on the bed until my head rested on the pillows. His hard, thick, cock stood between his legs as one knee dipped into the mattress and then the other. He ran his hands, ever so slowly, up my calves, then the inside of my thighs, finally spreading me wide for him to enjoy.

I bit down on my lower lip, watching as he touched and spread me—loving the feel of his hands on me. He positioned himself between my legs, his face merely inches from my pussy.

"This is mine, been too long since I staked my claim," he hissed, before his mouth went to work. I closed my eyes as my head sank into the pillow and his tongue sank inside of me.

I should've put up more of a fight, demanded his cock and not his mouth, but Riggs' mouth was magic and pregnancy had made me a hormonal, sex crazed lunatic. I'd take whatever I could get.

Quite preferably his mouth more than once and then his cock. Actually, I wasn't picky. He could use his mouth now, fuck me and then eat me again. I'd be perfectly okay with that as long as I got my trifecta of orgasms.

And I most definitely did.

We made up for lost time, reacquainting ourselves with one another's bodies. I thought I would have been more self-conscious over my body and the changes; the wider hips, the curves that weren't there the last time and the six pounds I gained on my ass alone. Riggs looked at me and loved me all night like I was the most beautiful girl he had ever laid eyes on.

I never wanted the night to end, too afraid of what tomorrow would bring. Eventually I fell asleep in his arms with his hands resting on my belly.

Just the three of us.

Chapter Thirty-Three

RIGGS

We didn't stop until the early morning, when both our bodies were spent. Even after all that, I still couldn't get enough of her or satisfy my need to hold her. She was fast asleep when I pulled her into the crook of my arm, resting her head against my chest. Her stomach wouldn't allow her to completely rest on me, so she lay on her side—that perfect belly tucked against my side.

I was exhausted but I wouldn't let myself go to sleep because I didn't want to miss a thing. I rested my hand against her belly, careful not to disturb her.

"Hey, kid, it's your dad," I said, feeling a little like a jackass, wondering if Pea could even hear me. And if he could, he didn't have any clue who I was—that was just downright wrong.

I felt something push against my palm.

No way.

"Pea is that you?" I asked, glancing back at Lauren, looking for her to confirm I had just felt our kid kick her, but she was out cold. Too much sex. See you next week, Kitten. I chuckled to myself and then I felt it again, stronger this time, I moved my hand to stare at Lauren's stomach, and sure enough, saw movement.

I quickly put my hand back to where Pea was kicking a field goal.

"Whoa, you're a strong one aren't you?" I asked, gently rubbing the area he continued to kick. "Take after your mama, that's for sure," I said, smiling as I pressed my lips to her forehead.

I closed my eyes and finally let myself fall asleep with my family in my arms. I don't know how long we stayed like that before the devil awakened us, and by the devil, I meant the pain in the ass soldier, Jack.

I untangled myself from Kitten and climbed out of bed to search for my pants and grab my phone.

"Hello?"

"Where the fuck are you?" he growled into the phone.

Great, I wasn't in the mood for some bullshit, not when I had Lauren stirring awake, probably ready to go another round.

"I need all hands on deck, Blackie got into some trouble last night," he hissed angrily into the phone.

"What kind of trouble?" I asked, running my fingers roughly through my hair.

"The kind that involves a fucking lawyer. Not going to say it again, get your ass to the Dog Pound," he ordered, disconnecting the call, leaving no room for argument.

I turned around and Kitten was busy covering herself up with the blanket.

"Hey," I said softly, walking over to her side of the bed. "I've got to run to the clubhouse but I want you to stay," I requested, sitting on the edge of the bed.

She looked at me warily.

"We'll talk when I get back, figure everything out," I said reassuringly.

"Okay," she replied after a moment.

I pressed my lips to hers, letting them linger for a moment before pulling back.

"Go back to bed. I won't be too long," I promised, before pulling my clothes on, grabbing my gun and my phone and heading out. The quicker I got my ass to the compound, the quicker I can get back home to Lauren.

I didn't know what exactly I had intended to tell her when I got back. Could I just forget the reasons we were apart in the first place? The more I thought about it the more I knew I needed to get my hands on Wu, take him out and take back my family.

The MC will get over it.

Or they wouldn't.

But Kitten and Pea would be safe.

And I'd be the one who made them safe.

The clubhouse was packed when I stepped inside but Jack stood from his chair and stalked over to me immediately.

"What's the big emergency?" I questioned, ticked off that I had been summoned here in the first place.

"Blackie got arrested last night," Jack ground out.

"For what?" I asked incredulously. Shit, he probably got a DUI.

"Brantley arrested him. It's not good," Jack said, swiping his hand across his face. "The kid he beat up is nearly dead."

"The kid..." I said, recalling the guy with Lacey.

Oh, for fuck's sake.

"Yeah, Riggs, the kid that nearly raped Lacey in the parking lot," Jack said, through clenched teeth.

"Blackie was leaving and caught Lacey struggling in the parking lot. He beat the fuck out of him. Brantley showed up and slapped cuffs on him. If that piece of shit dies, Blackie is looking at murder," Jack explained, shaking his head. "I can't believe I'm actually saying this, but I pray that little shit lives," he grunted. "He lives, I'll cut his little dick off but at least then Blackie is looking at assault in the first degree and attempted manslaughter. With his priors he'll serve about five years."

"And that's the best case scenario?"

Jack nodded.

"Blackie's doing time, either way, let's just hope it's five years and not twenty to life," he sighed.

"Christ. I had no idea man, everything was cool when I left," I paused. "How's Lacey?"

"Stryker took her to my house. She was shaken up but she's blaming herself for all this shit," he paused.

"You're probably going to think I'm crazy but I've got this feeling…" he said, as he reached around and cupped the back of his neck. "…I think Lacey has a crush or something on Blackie."

Ah, fuck this.

Why me?

I shrugged my shoulders and tried my best to act clueless.

"Why, because she feels bad? I'd fucking feel bad too if Blackie saved my ass and got arrested for it," I said, shoving my hands into my pockets.

"Right," Jack agreed warily. "So, you didn't see anything strange between the two of them at the bar?"

"I saw Lacey on a date with some douchebag and Blackie being Blackie at the bar wallowing in his shit. They didn't even acknowledge each other and when I waved at Lacey she stared daggers at me."

It was somewhat true.

"I've got to go to the courthouse. Bones is staying with Lacey and Reina at my house, think you can swing by the hospital and get an update on the kid?"

I sighed.

"Yeah," I said, deciding I'd make a quick stop at the hospital then head straight home. Unfortunately, I'd have to wait to discuss a plan for Wu with Jack. If he didn't give me the answers I needed, a solid course of action to bring this motherfucker to his knees, I was taking things into my own hands.

I felt my kid kick for the first time today.

I missed months of that.

I wasn't going to miss one goddamn moment once he was born.

So this war? It had to end before Lauren gave birth.

Either I would end it.

Or the Satan's Knights would.

But Wu's days were numbered. I wasn't letting that stupid fuck rob me the chance of being a good dad. He got his fucking money, that should've been enough but he was a sick fuck who would fight until he got whatever satisfaction it was he was searching for.

Not on my fucking watch.

Lauren

I quickly dressed, gathered my belongings and tried to make a beeline out the door before Riggs came back. He wanted me to wait, said we'd talk but that was hours ago. One call from Jack, God only knows what happened this time, but whatever it was it took Riggs away from me again.

He'd come back.

But I wasn't sure which man would be back. The one from last night, or the Knight cloaked in leather. I wanted so badly for him to come home and make things right for our little family but I couldn't stand anymore heartache.

I shouldn't have come here last night.

I shouldn't have given into my desires.

I shouldn't have let the dreams we shared get the best of me.

And I most definitely shouldn't have looked for hope in a hopeless situation.

I stopped in front of the closed door next to our room, the room we were going to make Pea's room. I curiously put my hand on the doorknob, wondering why he kept it closed but stopped myself from opening it. I didn't need to know what was behind that door.

It didn't matter.

I walked to the front door and did what I did best, gave Riggs an out and spared myself the words he'd come back and tell me.

Or maybe I gave him too much credit. He probably wouldn't come back at all and send either Bones or my brother to remove me from his life.

I opened the front door, glancing over my shoulder at the apartment one last time.

Don't worry, Tiger. I'll be gone before you have the chance.

I shut the door, both the physical one and the one to my heart.

Chapter Thirty-Four
Lauren

I was twenty-eight weeks pregnant, just starting my seventh month, finally in the home stretch. I feel like I had been pregnant for a year—it's been the longest seven months of my life—I keep reminding myself it will all be worth it soon enough. Soon enough I'll get to meet Pea.

I even began to think of names. I'm torn between Ashley and Aubree, everyone I tell them to hates both equally. I remember Riggs telling me his real name was Robert and tried thinking of similar names that I could name our daughter, However, I'm not willing to call my daughter Berta.

After I left his apartment last month he didn't come looking for me. He sent me a text message thanking me, actually. He claimed I did him a favor by walking away.

My guess is that I saved him the hassle of doing the walking himself.

For the past four weeks I've been struggling not to overthink our situation or look for some fictional light at the end of the tunnel. I'm pushing forward, you might think I'm not as I just finished telling you I was contemplating naming Pea after him but I just want her to have something of him.

I know he loves her despite his actions.

Riggs doesn't have a phony bone in his body. He's not a man that has a filter either. He says and does what he wants and makes no apologies for it.

I saw how he was with me that night, how amazed he was by our baby growing inside of me. There was nothing fake about that.

It's just sad, the whole thing is just so sad.

But there's no time to cry.

Time to move forward. I found the path I was meant to be on, the one that included Pea. Now I needed to prepare for that road.

"What about this one?" my mother asked, as she began to push a stroller. "It's light and rides nice. See if it closes easily. When Luca was a baby Adrianna bought one of those fancy strollers and needed to google directions on how to close it."

I took the stroller from my mother and started to wheel it around the store. She insisted we take a trip to Babies R Us and make a list of things we needed for Pea.

"I like the other one better," I said, pointing to the gray one. My mother zapped it with some little gadget the store gave us to help create a list. One thing down, twelve thousand to go. A baby needed a ton of things, things I didn't even know existed. What the hell was a diaper genie anyway? Or a wipe warmer? I'm pretty sure my mother didn't warm my wipes before she wiped my ass and I survived.

"Did you give anymore thought about what we talked about?" my mother asked nonchalantly, as we strolled down the bottle aisle.

My mother also suggested a week ago that I should speak with an attorney. She argued that the baby would be here before I knew it and I needed to decide if I was going to give Riggs any legal rights to Pea. She also mentioned that he is responsible for child support and I shouldn't let him get away with that. I needed to protect my baby and stop worrying about my pride. Her words not mine.

She had a point.

I texted him this morning asking him if we could meet up to talk about Pea. He didn't respond right away but when he did he said he was on a run and would be back at the clubhouse this afternoon. So after this shopping excursion I was going to head over to the clubhouse and ask him what he wanted to do.

"Yes," I finally said to my mother. "I'm meeting up with him after here to discuss it."

"Good, girl," she said. "Even if he doesn't want to be a full-time dad, he should still have to support that baby," she added with a scowl.

A part of me wondered if she was projecting all the hatred she had for my father onto Riggs. They weren't the same people, my dad turned his back on us and never looked back. Riggs turned his back and kept looking over his shoulder.

There I went being hopeful again.

RIGGS

I was fucking beat by the time I pulled up to the Dog Pound, being on the road ten days will do that to you. Jack ordered me to ride up north with Wolf to secure our connections with the Corrupt Bastards MC. They usually dealt with Blackie but with him at Ryker's waiting for trial, they'd be dealing with me from now on. The kid Blackie pummeled into the asphalt survived so they weren't charging him with murder but they had a solid case against him. The surveillance from the club aiding in their mission to declare Blackie a maniac. He's looking at five years, best case scenario, and that's with all the club's money backing a fancy hotshot lawyer from Manhattan.

I smoothed things over with the Corrupt Bastards and even scored a potential deal with them that I would bring up at Church.

"Well it's about time you two bitches came home," Pipe called, walking across the parking lot toward us. "Just in the nick of time too, you can help unload the trucks."

"What trucks?" Wolf asked.

"While you two were off riding the wind, I got a maintenance job, restoring all the Atlantic Express tour buses," he grinned proudly. "The yard is full with buses and I had no room for the parts I had to order so I had them shipped here," he glanced down at his watch.

"They should've been here already."

"I need a shower before I do anything," I said, removing my helmet.

"Showers going to have to wait," Pipe said, tipping his chin across the lot to where Lauren was parked in her mother's car.

"She been here long?" I asked, hanging my helmet on one of the handlebars.

"About ten minutes or so," he replied. "Asked her if she wanted to come in but she said she'd wait out here for you," he added.

"She alone?"

"Afraid mommy dearest is with her?" Pipe smiled before he howled with a hearty laugh. "Relax, Riggs, she's all by her lonesome," he assured.

I was relieved to know that Lauren was on her own. I watched as she opened the driver's door and stepped out. At the same time the rusty gates opened and the prospect guarding the gate hollered over his shoulder.

"Incoming!"

I slapped Pipe's back and grinned. "Looks like your shipment is here. You guys can handle this can't you?" I laughed.

"Fuck you," Pipe said, turning to Wolf. "And where do you think you're going?"

"To take a fucking piss. Your goddamn parts can wait, my dick can't," Wolf snickered.

I laughed to myself as the two of them exchanged insults. In that moment, I lifted my head and locked eyes with Lauren. I raised my hand to my chest rubbing that ache that instantly came every time I looked into those eyes, the familiar sense of longing washed over me as it always did when she was around.

Around.
But just out of my reach.
She was my goddamn unicorn.
A mystical creature I could never capture.
But that was only because I didn't allow myself to.
Because in my head I thought loving her from afar was better for the both of us.
Loving her.
I loved Lauren.

That was the ache in my chest knowing I was in love with her and not being with her, not telling her how I felt, how she took a reckless biker and made him a man.

She gave me purpose and my purpose was to love her.
She brought me back to a place where I believed in dreams.
Because fuck me, she was a dream come true.
She was my Kitten.
My Kitten that was giving me a little Pea.
Dreams.

They were real and they were wrapped in the blue-eyed girl who came charging into my life. I thought she was a detour, that we were a detour, but we weren't, we were one another's path. The only path that existed.

We were Kitten and Tiger.

I smiled at her, watching as she pushed her glasses further up her nose and stared back at me.

Smile at me.
Give me something.
Tell me it's not too late.

She took another step away from the car, tucking her hair behind her ears and then smiled back at me.

I love you, Kitten.
Gonna show you just how much.

It's me and you against all this shit.
You just need to give me one last chance.

"Park the truck over here," Pipe hollered to the driver. "Over here!" He demanded. "What the fuck, are you assholes deaf? Park the fucking truck over here," he shouted

Life was too short to live it running scared. It was too fucking precious to live in the shadows of a threat. I gave Wu too much power over me. It was time to own my love, my heart and take back what was mine. I'd hang on tight and never let anyone take my family from me.

My family.

Wow.

"Shit! Get down," Pipe shouted.

Lauren's eyes widened and I followed them to where Pipe was shouting, waving his hands and shaking his head.

Everything went silent.

I didn't hear the shouting.

I didn't hear the gunfire.

I watched as the back of the truck lifted open and the Red Dragons appeared firing machine guns. The guns they took from us. They shot at us with our own fucking guns. I reached for my gun as the rest of the Knights appeared from the clubhouse and we started shooting back.

"Lauren, get down!" I screamed over my shoulder.

"Riggs!" She shrieked.

"Get down," I yelled, as I ran backward, shooting my way toward her.

"Get your girl," ordered Jack, coming up beside me and firing his AK-47 at the targets I was aiming for.

I turned around to where Lauren was but I didn't see her. I frantically searched the lot and saw her running toward the clubhouse.

"No!" I screamed, the shrill sound of my cries vibrating through my ears as I watched the bullet fly through the air, headed straight for her.

I started running, my eyes widening, my heart dropping as the bullet struck her.

"NO! NO! NO!" I screamed. "Lauren!"

She turned, her eyes widening as she lifted her hand to her chest and stared at the crimson that painted her fingertips. I shook my head, tears falling down my face as Bones jumped in front of her, as two more bullets flew in her direction.

I skidded to a stop on the asphalt just as the two bullets pierced my best friend. I watched as his gun dropped out of his hand and his body lurched back from the impact of the bullets. His eyes met mine before he dropped to the ground beside Kitten.

My gun fell to the ground as my whole world crumbled before my very eyes.

Chapter Thirty-Five
RIGGS

I dropped to my knees between Lauren and Bones, the gunfire muffled by the sounds of my own desperate pleas.

There was blood everywhere.

His.

Hers.

So much blood.

I reached out, my hand trembling as I pushed her hair away from her face.

"Riggs," she whispered, her lip shaking as she spoke my name.

"Shhh," I sighed, bending over her and kissing her. "It's going to be okay. It's going to be okay," I chanted. I lifted my head and stared at the blood saturating her shirt, trying to locate where the bullet hit her. "You just have to stay with me, okay, Kitten? You need to stay with me," I begged, lifting her head into my lap. "Please stay with me."

I lifted my head and saw Jack rushing toward us.

"Call an ambulance," I screamed.

"The baby," Lauren struggled and I peeled my eyes away from Jack and glanced at her stomach, reaching over her and placing my hand that was covered in her blood, over her belly.

"Pea's going to be okay but you need to hang on for her," I said, my voice rattling.

"Her," she whispered, closing her eyes.

"No, don't close your eyes, Lauren!" I cupped her face with my hands. "Lauren, look at me," I ordered.

She fought to open her eyes, the color draining from her face as she bled in my arms.

"Kitten, please," I cried, lifting her head against my chest and rocking back and forth. "I was going to tell you how I felt."

"Riggs," she whispered, forcing me to look down at her. "If it's me or the baby," she gasped, short of breath. "Promise," she struggled.

"No, stop, don't talk like that. You're both going to be fine. You hear me? You're going to be fine and so is the baby!"

"Choose Pea," she rasped, tears falling from the corners of her eyes as they looked up into mine begging me to do as she asked.

"I choose the both of you…always, forever," I bent down and kissed her lips softly. "I'm sorry, Kitten. I'm so sorry," I murmured, pulling back as her eyes drifted closed. "Lauren? Lauren! No!"

"Riggs, the ambulance is here. You gotta move out of the way so the paramedics can do their job," Jack said from somewhere close. I lifted my head as the sirens sounded and the ambulance pulled into the lot. The paramedics jumped out, one grabbing a medical bag, the other pushing the stretcher toward us as the second ambulance pulled in.

"Her first, she's pregnant," Jack demanded. That's when I saw him crouched down next to Bones, his hands covered in his blood as he tried to apply pressure to his wound. "Stay with me Bones. No one's dying on my watch, you hear me," Jack growled. "No one."

"Sir, you need to step away from her so we can work on her," one of the paramedics said to me.

"Please help them," I pleaded, kissing Kitten one last time before gently sliding her head from my lap.

"How far along is she?"

"Uh…" I tried to think, running my fingers through my hair. "Seven months," I answered.

"We have to hook her up to a monitor immediately. She's losing a lot of blood," the other paramedic shouted. "We have to get her out of here," he continued.

I watched for a moment as they worked on Lauren, cutting her shirt open to find the wound and then turned back to Jack who was standing near Bones covered in his blood. I watched as they lifted my brother onto the stretcher before I stepped toward him. I glanced down at Bones as he gasped for air.

"Thank you," I whispered, placing my hand over his and squeezing it slightly.

"Own…it," he said, barely audibly before the paramedic covered his face with a mask and raced with him on the stretcher to the ambulance.

He shouldn't be riding alone.

He never let me ride alone.

Not once.

"We're ready," the paramedic said behind me and I turned to Jack.

"Go, I'll ride with Bones," Jack said, reading the guilt on my face as he wiped the blood covering his hands onto his shirt. I nodded before following the paramedics running with Lauren to the ambulance.

I sat helplessly on the bench inside the ambulance. I couldn't even hold her hand, forced to sit there and watch as a stranger fought to keep Kitten and Pea in my life.

I closed my eyes and everything hit me like a ton of bricks.

Every single memory.

Every single dream.

The first words she ever said to me.

What's the matter handsome? Why so serious?

All the times I teased her and all the ways she gave it right back.

You're despicable.

Oh baby, I love it when you talk dirty.

Kiss my ass, Riggs.

Anytime, Kitten. Anytime.

That first night I brought her to the clubhouse and brought her into my world.

Well now you've got me here, what did you plan on doing with me?

If only I knew we'd end up here…

I'm sorry, Kitten.

The night we made a baby.

Came here for a reason, Kitten, now it's time to tell me what that reason is.
It doesn't matter.
I disagree. I like your dress.
You should I wore it for you.
Finding out we made a baby.
I'm guessing you want to keep it
I'm keeping our baby.

Pea.
I call the baby Pea.
The first time I took my time with her.

Lauren.
Yeah.
Just making sure you're real.

When I realized I had dreams and they were all of Kitten.

Don't look at me like that.
Like what?
Like I'm a dream.
Starting to wonder if you are.
The last words she said to me.

Choose Pea
I watched as Kitten and Pea were wheeled away from me and into an operating room that was waiting for them, one last memory burned into my brain and to my heart.

A doctor introduced himself to me, but I couldn't tell you his name if my life depended on it. Nor could I tell you everything he said as I heard every other word.

She lost a lot of blood.
Too much.
Your wife is going into shock.
Your baby is in distress.
Emergency C-section.
Remove the bullets and stop the bleeding.

All the dreams turned to nightmares.
The dream of Lauren.
The dream of Pea.
The dream of us.
It all hung in limbo along with their lives.

Chapter Thirty-Six
RIGGS

I was never afraid of dying. Granted, I never gave death much thought, figured it was just an end to a cycle but right now, death scares the fuck out of me. And still, not for myself, not because I'm afraid to die but because I'm afraid to live. Live without them.

For all I know, they could be gone.

You've taken three of my brothers, seems only fair I take three of yours.

Kitten.

Pea.

Bones.

Three lives.

Wu had his three bodies. It didn't matter that only one wore a patch, they all belonged to the Satan's Knights. They all belonged to me. Everyone I cared about, everyone I loved was fighting for their life right now while I sat here in a waiting room, helpless and wishing I'd chosen God over the Devil. You can't pray to the Devil to save those you love. That crazy fuck gets off on this shit.

The hospital's automatic glass doors opened and the Bianci's came running in, stopping just in front of Jack. Maria lifted her hand to cover her mouth as she gasped, taking in the blood that covered my clothes, while Anthony stared at Jack expressionless.

"Oh, my God!" She wailed, her eyes diverting back and forth between Jack's blood stained clothes and mine. She lifted her grief-stricken face, her eyes crazed with anger as they peered into mine. She reared her hand back and slapped me across the face.

Anthony grabbed her but she snatched her arm free and started to pummel my chest with her fists.

"You son of a bitch. Look at you!" She shoved her hands against my chest. "How does it feel to have your child's and my child's blood all over you?"

"I'm sorry," I rasped, welcoming the sting to my face, wishing she'd inflict more pain. I deserved to feel it but knew it wouldn't be enough. I'd never feel the pain any of them are feeling.

Anthony pulled his mother back.

"This isn't helping."

"Nothing he does helps, he's poison!" She hissed, glancing over Anthony's shoulder at me. "If anything happens to my daughter or that sweet innocent baby, so help me God, I'll kill you with my bare hands!"

"Get a hold on your mother, Bianci," Jack seethed. "You want to blame someone lady, blame me, not him. While that may be your daughter fighting for her life in there, it's also the woman *he* loves. It's his child, not just your grandchild, not to mention his brother who stood in front of your daughter."

"Jack, stop," I interrupted. I deserved Maria's anger, her blame, every fucking word was true. I did this to the innocent girl next door that came out swinging. I did this to the baby she was going to give me.

"No, fuck that. You're entitled to your grief, Mrs. Bianci but the way you're feeling, so is Riggs. It's his eyes that watched them fall to the ground. It's *his* hands that tried to stop the bleeding and it's his goddamn heart that is bleeding now. So you need to pass the blame, blame me, because I allowed this shit to happen," he growled.

She wiped furiously at the tears that streaked her face before throwing her hands up in the air and shaking her head.

"I blame all of you," she pointed a finger at her son. "Including you, goddamn it."

"Maria, come on, let's sit," Adrianna tried, taking her mother-in-law's hand and guiding her across the waiting room toward a row of chairs away from the one's we occupied.

"What happened?" Anthony looked at me. "Why was she there in the first place?"

"She wanted to talk about the baby. I figured she needed something or hell, I don't know I was just fucking happy she called and told her to meet me at the compound," I explained, running my fingers through my hair. "Man, I didn't want any of this. You know that," I emphasized.

"I know," he said, turning his eyes toward Jack. "I don't give a fuck about your goddamn club business. This shit is personal to me now. That's my fucking family in there, my blood and your *family* ain't keeping me at bay anymore. You hear me, *brother*?" he snarled.

Jack held Anthony's stare but remained silent as I brushed past them, needing a break from everyone. I made my way through the parting doors, taking big greedy gulps of air as I ignored the stares of people outside watching me. I leaned against the wall, propping my boot against the bricks and watched as a man pulled his SUV up to the entrance. He walked around the car, opened the backseat and removed one of those infant car seats. He wore a big grin on his face as he slammed the door of his car and told the security guard he'd be right down, he was taking home his newborn daughter today.

A great day.

One that man would never forget.

It's amazing how one man's life can be complete while another man's falls apart.

I don't know how long I stood out there waiting for the man to come down but the moment I saw him wheeling his wife out of the hospital, I knew that's why I stood outside and waited. I wanted to catch a glimpse of the happy family, and happy they were. Both mom and dad beamed from ear to ear as they worked their precious bundle of joy into the car.

I never wanted any of that. Standing here watching that couple, knowing I could've had that and not sure if my family will live to see a day like these people were sharing…well, now, it's all I wanted.

I thought of Pea entering the world alone.

I hope he isn't scared because Mommy and Daddy would make it okay.

We will.

Just give us a chance.

Hang in there Pea, Daddy loves you.

So fucking much it hurts.

I watched the family drive away from the curb before finding my way back into the hell that was now the waiting room of Lutheran Medical.

The doors opened and two doctors walked out, one lifted his eyes, pulling off the mask as he searched the room. The other doctor pointed to where we were sitting as they made their way to us. My eyes locked with the first doctors and I tried desperately to read his expression, to prepare myself for what he was about to say but he remained neutral. I kicked off the wall I was leaning on and started toward him, my brothers rose from their seats, flocking around me.

Anthony and Maria who were sitting across the waiting room, gravitated toward me, fear in their eyes as they stared at the doctors.

I felt someone take my hand and when I looked down, Maria's hand was wrapped tightly around mine. I lifted my eyes but she looked straight ahead at the doctor. I don't know why she took my hand, maybe she did it for selfish reasons, maybe she did it for me, or maybe she did it because Lauren would've wanted her to. Whatever the reason was, I was glad she did and I squeezed her hand back. I vowed to prove to this woman how much I loved and respected her daughter. And with that vow, came the realization that Lauren didn't even know how I felt about her.

What if I never get the chance to tell her? What if I never get the chance to thank her for taking the detour and storming past the roadblock that guarded anyone from getting close?

"Are you the family of Eric Nicholson?"

Bones.

The other doctor opened the chart, glancing at it.

"He has a Robert Montgomery, listed as an emergency contact."

"That's me," I croaked.

"Is he okay?"

Jack walked up beside me, placing one hand on my shoulder as he and the doctor exchanged a look.

"What? What is it?" I asked, as I diverted my eyes back and forth between Jack and the duo of doctors.

"I'm sorry, Mr. Montgomery. One of the bullets hit his lung and the other pierced through his heart. We couldn't get the bullets out because we couldn't stop the bleeding. We tried everything we could to save him but the blood filled his lungs."

"No!" I shouted, trying to absorb what he was saying. "He's dead?"

"I'm sorry for your loss," the doctor said, offering his condolences as the other doctor bowed his head regretfully.

Jack gripped my shoulders, turning me around to face him.

"Bones is dead? Jack, Bones is dead," I rambled, as he grabbed a hold of my shoulders and stared at me solemnly

"I'm so sorry," he muttered.

"Bones is dead," I repeated. "And I didn't get to say goodbye or thank him," I pulled away from Jack. "He jumped in front of those bullets, trying to save Lauren, trying to save my kid."

I took a step backward, running my fingers roughly through my hair as I glanced around the waiting room at my brothers and the Bianci's.

"He died trying to save my family and he was alone when he died, no family, no brother. I didn't get to say goodbye, and thanking him while he bled out on the ground isn't enough. It's not enough," I shouted angrily, turning around to the doctors. "Can I see him?"

One of the doctors nodded.

"We've closed him up already. Give us a few minutes and we'll take you downstairs," he explained.

Downstairs.

The morgue.

My best friend was just another lifeless body in a freezer.

"What about my daughter?" Maria asked.

"I'm sorry but we haven't heard anything on the other woman," the second doctor informed us. "Just give us a few minutes. We will take you down, sir and hopefully get another doctor to give you an update on the young woman," he offered, before turning around and leaving us.

Maria's lip quivered as she glanced at Anthony.

"Why haven't we heard anything?" she screeched frantically.

I didn't know if that was a good thing or a bad thing. First getting word on Bones and being told he didn't make it, made me slightly relieved we hadn't heard anything on Lauren or the baby.

No news is good news, right?

Say I'm right.

One of the doctors returned a few minutes later, informing us that his colleague was still trying to get information on Lauren and asked me to follow him. I stepped onto the elevator, along with the doctor and watched as the doors closed.

The memories hit me hard, and as the elevator dropped so did my heart. We went from kids, to rebellious teenagers, finally becoming men we were proud to be.

I'm a prospect, earning my keep, going to be a Knight one day, Rob.
Why do they call you Bones?
Because I was born to break bones.
Well I need a nickname too.
A Road name. How about Riggs?
Riggs?
Because you were born to walk away from the oil rigs and all that shit that comes with being a Montgomery.
Riggs, no last name, kind of like Eminem. I like it.
You got a kid coming, man. That's huge. That's bigger than you, bigger than your girl, bigger than anything you've ever known. I know the club is everything to you right now, you worked real hard for your patch but this, you becoming someone's father? It's bigger than the club. Own that shit.

His last words to me.

Own it.

The elevator doors opened and I followed the doctor down a hall to another room, he nodded at the lady behind the counter and pushed open another set of doors, leading me into a sterile room. I saw him immediately, laying on a gurney centered in the room, with a sheet covering him up to his chin.

I've seen death a thousand times, always in the eyes of an enemy. I've never lost anyone close to me, and now here I stood in the morgue, staring at my dead best friend wondering if the girl I loved and my kid would be the next two bodies I saw in this room.

"We'll give you a moment," the doctor said, before walking out of the room, leaving me alone with Bones' body.

I stepped closer to him, my boots pounding across the linoleum, muffling the groan that left my throat as I stared down at his face, pale, and lifeless. His lips already gray, matching the skin unmarked by tattoos.

This was the last time I'd see him, the last chance I had to look at him and speak, from this point forward I'd talk to a headstone, and even knowing that, my words still got lost on my tongue.

I knew what I felt and what I should say, yet I couldn't do it. I couldn't stand there and say goodbye. I couldn't thank him for being a brother to me, not the kind that wore matching cuts, but the type of brother that guided me through life. Jack preaches about heart and that it keeps you from being reckless but most of my life it was Bones who kept me from being reckless. I didn't need heart when I had a friend that could always reign me in, guide me away from the peril and put my ass on the right path.

He's been my voice of reason, the one pulling me back from the edge for years. Sure, I could stand here and tell him how lost I would be now without him but he'd given me so much throughout the years it was time to give him one final thing in return. One piece of truth his soul could take with him on his journey.

I laid my hand over his chest, feeling the cold beneath the sheet against my warm hand.

Life and Death.

Such a fucked up thing.

"I promise you I'm going to own my responsibilities. I'll be the father you always wanted for yourself and the one you wanted to be some day. It's only fair since you lost your life, I will do everything in my power to do something the both of us wanted. I may not have known it right away, because you were always quicker to learn what you wanted out of life than I was, but usually we shared the same goals. I'll be the father both of us never had and every day I look at my kid, God willing, I'll think of you and the ultimate sacrifice you made for me," I said hoarsely, hoping God didn't make me out to be a liar.

Please let Pea survive.

"My kid will always know who you are. Always," I vowed as my voice caught in my throat. "And any good I get to teach him is because I've learned it from you. Got one more promise for you, and it's big so, listen up…" I said, drawing in a shaky breath as I leaned over his body. "I'm going to make the motherfucker who did this pay. I promise you. I fucking promise you with everything I am, I will get him. I will be his judge and his jury and I will make him pay for every sin he's committed, starting with your death."

I straightened up, patted his chest one final time before shoving both hands into my pockets and taking a step back.

I'll never forget this moment.

I'll put men in the ground remembering this exact moment.

I turned around to walk away and leave him to rest but something nagged inside of me. I didn't want to ask anything of him. He's given me so much and still I turned around to ask him one last favor, because I'm a greedy fuck. A terrified, greedy fuck.

"If they don't make it, please take care of them," I whispered to my friend. Turning once more, I made my way out of the morgue; glancing over my shoulder to catch one last glimpse of the man I was always proud to call my brother.

"Love you, my brother. See you soon," I rasped, before closing the door behind me and coming face to face with the doctor again.

"These are his belongings," he said, handing me a clear bag. I opened it and pulled out his leather cut stained with his blood. I fisted my hand around the leather and glanced at the rest of the stuff in the bag before handing it back to the doctor.

I walked to the bank of elevators clutching Bones' cut, stepping inside the first one that opened and when the doors closed I drove my fist into one of the walls, my scream echoing off the walls of the elevator.

Chapter Thirty-Seven
RIGGS

I turned the corner, lifting my head to see Jack and the rest of the club flocked by police officers, namely officer Brantley. As I made my way further into the waiting room I could hear Jack and the cop arguing. I'm sure the cop was having a chubby over the massacre that took place in the parking lot of the compound.

"Now isn't the time to gloat Brantley. We're one man down and waiting on word on an innocent woman and her child, so instead of you busting my balls and picking apart my club, why don't you go find who the fuck is responsible for the bloodshed?" Jack growled.

"You're partially responsible for this bloodshed and you know it Parrish," Brantley countered. "The Satan's Knights have been taking the lives of innocent women for years. It doesn't matter if that girl in there lives or dies. She's better off dead," he seethed.

I charged at him but I was too slow as Anthony got to him first, slamming the cop in uniform up against the glass window of the hospital.

"Anthony!" Adrianna shrieked.

"That's my sister in there you pig," Anthony seethed, slamming his body against the glass.

"You're assaulting an officer," Brantley warned.

"Then fucking lock me up, douchebag," Anthony gritted, releasing his hold on Brantley.

"Excuse me?" a doctor said, speaking over the commotion. "Are you the family of Lauren Bianci?"

I turned on my heel and looked at the doctor, watching as she removed her paper mask and glanced around at us until her eyes focused on mine. She glanced down at my clothes before lifting her eyes back to mine.

I'll never forget the worn and drained eyes that stared back at me sympathetically. And I'm even more sure I wouldn't forget the words she was about to deliver.

"I'm her mother," Maria declared. "Please, is she okay?"

The doctor turned her attention to Maria.

"She's still in surgery. I'm the resident OBGYN and this, is Dr. Meadows, the head of Pediatrics," she explained, motioning to the doctor standing off to the left of her, a man I hadn't even noticed was there.

"Pea," I whispered, looking back and forth between the two doctors who were about to tell me if mine and Lauren's baby had survived. It was that moment I became a father first and foremost, when I understood what it was to be a parent. I was terrified that they were going to tell me that Pea didn't survive. The old me would've walked away just like I always did when something threatened to hurt me and not in the physical sense. Physical pain I could live with. The pain that slices through your heart? That shit was different, and as tough as I claim to be, as brutal of human I am, I usually run scared when it comes to the heart.

But I'm someone's father now and that someone comes before my fear. That someone is my heart. The reason I have one, the reason it beats.

"I'm the father," I said, walking up to them.

"As you know the baby was under distress and before they could operate on Ms. Bianci we needed to perform an emergency cesarean to deliver the baby," she paused for a moment.

"Ms. Bianci successfully delivered a baby boy, weighing three pounds, one ounce and I believe fifteen inches in length. I closed and the surgeons took over. I don't have an update on her status but while I was performing the C-section she was stable and I delivered the baby in under two minutes," she explained.

"A boy," I said. "I have a son."

He was born weighing three pounds, one ounce but his birth caused my heart to weigh a ton. Who knew such a revelation could make my heart feel so full? Not me. Not me at all.

"Is he okay?"

Dr. Meadows stepped up.

"I took over for your son once he was delivered and immediately began working on him. His lungs aren't fully developed so we needed to place him on a ventilator. He is in the NICU right now, stabilized with the machine breathing for him. We also inserted a feeding tube in him and are carefully monitoring him."

"But he's okay? I mean, he's little and all but he's going to make it, right Doc?" I asked, unable to recognize my own voice.

"Mr. Bianci is it?"

"No, Montgomery."

"Mr. Montgomery, your son was born twelve weeks early, aside from Respiratory Distress Syndrome, your son is still very much considered to be in critical condition. We are working to determine if there is an intraventricular hemorrhage, which is a brain bleed. If there is we need to monitor it very closely but they usually dissolve on their own accord. However, there may be lasting side effects that we won't be able to determine right away."

"Such as?" I asked, turning to Maria. "Please, listen in case I forget anything," I pleaded.

She nodded, tears falling down her cheeks as she listened along with me as the doctor explained Pea's condition and the illnesses he may face.

Cerebral Palsy.

Mental Retardation.

And that was just if he had a brain bleed.

I think.

All I knew was he spoke of things no parent wants to hear.

"Can I see him?" I asked, interrupting him as he went down the list of possible occurrences. Pea wasn't going to get any of those things. I was sure of it. He was half Lauren and half me. He was his mother's son and he was a fighter. He'd get through it.

Dr. Meadow's eyes assessed me before he sighed.

"I'm going to get a nurse to give you some scrubs and get you out of these clothes. The NICU is a very sterile environment. You'll need to scrub down and then of course you may see your son," he said, turning toward Maria and Anthony.

"The rest of you may see him from the window but at this time we're only going to allow the father inside the unit."

Maria nodded, turning to me.

"You tell that little boy he has a lot of people who love him and can't wait to meet him. You tell him his mommy is the number one person on that list, okay?"

I nodded, pushing down the lump in my throat as I stared at her. I get it now...what family is. It's the people you laugh with, the people you cry with, the people who stand by your side through the good times and bad. You fight and make up, or maybe you don't, maybe you go months, sometimes years without speaking but then something happens and it erases all that negative shit that kept you from being family. One circumstance is all it takes to bring a family together. If you're lucky it's a birth or a wedding, some warm, fuzzy shit that everyone wants a piece of. Other times, times like now, it's when everything falls apart and things are so far out of control, they're so fucked you can't help but turn to one another for support. It's times like these when families become stronger.

"We'll go get you some clothes," Pipe spoke up. "Anything else you need?"

I reached into my pocket and threw Pipe my keys.

"There's a bag on my kitchen counter can you bring that too?"

"Aye, of course," he agreed.

I thanked him, tipped my chin to the rest of them and squeezed Maria's hand reassuringly before following the doctor through the doors and into the elevator. I was taken to the eighth floor and a nurse handed me a pair of scrubs, pointing to a vacant room and instructed me to change my clothes. I pulled the shirt over my head, laying it flat on the chair and stared at the dried up blood, a nasty mix of red and brown painted the once plain white t-shirt.

Lauren's face flashed before my eyes.

Choose Pea.

Our son.

I twisted the shirt in my hands and shoved it into the waste basket before I continued to peel the clothes from my body. I changed into the scrubs and met the nurse outside the door. She took me into another room and I started to feel anxious as she handed me a bar of soap and instructed me to wash my hands and forearms. I vigorously scrubbed my skin, watching as the water in the sink mixed with the blood on my hands and swirled down the drain.

Once my hands were sterilized I followed her into the NICU, my heart beat rampantly inside my chest as my eyes scanned the room, looking at all incubators and wondering which one held my son until the nurse came to a stop and turned around to face me.

"Are you ready to meet your son?" she smiled warmly, as she stepped to the side. "He's been waiting to meet his daddy," she continued.

My eyes dropped and rested on the little miracle fighting for his life. I heard the gasp escape my lips as I took a step closer, cocking my head to the side as I stared at the tiniest human I had ever laid eyes on. He looked so frail, so fragile hooked up to all the machines. Aside from the respirator and the feeding tube, his skin was decorated with tiny little stickers that connected more wires to him.

But I saw past the wires and ignored the sounds of the machines, focusing on the beautiful little boy that was half Lauren and half me.

"You can't hold him just yet but you can stick your hands through the holes and touch him," the nurse stated. "It would be good for him to feel you," she encouraged.

"Can he hear me?" I asked hoarsely, running my hand over the top of the incubator.

"Of course he can," she smiled. "He already probably recognizes your voice from in utero."

His eyes were closed and because of the feeding tube and the ventilator I couldn't assess his features, but still, I knew he had the most adorable face.

After all, I was his dad.

And his mom? She was pretty hot too.

I lifted my hands from the incubator, hesitating as I brought them to the circular holes for my arms to slide through.

"You sure I won't hurt him? I can't like pull a wire or anything like that, right?"

"I'm sure," she said calmly.

I drew in a sharp breath, turning my gaze back to my son, thinking how strange it was that it felt perfectly normal to be calling this little guy my son. That wasn't something I expected to feel. I thought it would feel strange at first, constricted and forced but one look at him and it was the most natural feeling I had ever had.

I was always a sure shot, a steady hand and a perfect eye. My hand never once quivered when it was wrapped around a gun but my hands trembled as they slid into the incubator and my fingertips touched my son's skin for the first time.

"Oh," I whispered. "You're really here," I said, softly caressing the top of his hand with my index finger.

He's so tiny, making my hands look so much bigger than they really are.

"Hey, little guy, I'm your dad," I introduced myself, crouching down so he could hear me better and I could see him more clearly. "It's okay, Daddy's here, you don't have to be scared. I know it's a big deal, coming into the world and all that. It's terrifying to go from being safe inside your mom to the ugly world that ripped you from her but I promise you, you don't have to be afraid anymore," I vowed, drawing circles on his tiny hand with my fingertip.

"You know I'm already the proudest dad in this place. Just look at you being such a strong boy, fighting hard like a little bull—you get that from your mom. She's a fighter and right now she's fighting with everything she's got because she wants so badly to meet you, to hold you and to kiss you. She's loved you since she first found out you were just a little pea inside of her," I whispered, feeling the sting of unshed tears assault my eyes.

I blinked, tears escaping the corners of my eyes but I didn't take my hands out of the incubator to dry my eyes. I wanted to touch him for as long as I could, to comfort him. I wonder if he realizes I'm here. Does he recognize my voice? Probably not.

"Do you have a name picked out for him?"

I turned my gaze to the nurse and shook my head.

"No, but I bet his mom does," I said, turning back to glance at my boy. "I'm sure it's a good, solid name, perfect for you."

I pictured Kitten holding our son for the first time, looking up at me and telling me what the name she chose for him was but then another thought invaded my mind.

What if she doesn't make it?

What if she doesn't get to meet our son?

What if he doesn't get to know what a great mom he has?

What if she never gets to tell us what his name is?

I felt myself teetering on the edge, ready to lose it and succumb to the grief of it all. The grief of losing Bones, of not knowing if Lauren will live or die and standing here watching as a machine breathes for my newborn child.

And then the most amazing thing happened.

A tiny hand wrapped around my finger.

I stared at my son's hand, his small fingers wrapped around my index finger and I was undone.

I thought I had the perfect life, that I had everything I wanted and wasn't missing anything. But it wasn't until that moment, when my son held onto me that, I realized I didn't know the meaning of life…until him. Kitten and Tiger may have given this boy life, but he gave me a reason to live mine.

Heart.

It was right there, three pounds one ounce of the purest love I'd ever know.

Thank you.

"Oh, kid, you're already wrapped around my finger, but thank you," I whispered. "I love you, Pea," I whispered.

A knock on the glass window startled me, pulling me away from the most precious gift I had ever received and when I glanced over my shoulder my eyes met Anthony's. His eyes dropped to the incubator before they closed briefly then finally lifted back to mine.

He crooked his finger and I read his lips as he uttered the name that made my world stop for just a second.

Lauren.

Chapter Thirty-Eight
RIGGS

Anthony filled me in as we walked toward the elevators, riding it up to the twelfth floor where they were moving Lauren to an ICU recovery room. She survived surgery but her body was in a state of shock. The doctors were able to stop the bleeding and remove the bullet that missed her heart but nicked her lung, causing it to collapse. Once they had the bullet out they had to repair the damage to her lung which was why the surgery took longer than the doctors had anticipated.

She was unconscious, and like her son, she was on a respirator because her lung function was too weak. The next twenty-four to forty-eight hours would be critical for her. As we stepped off the elevator Anthony became quiet, causing me to turn around and look at him.

"What is it?"

"The doctor said if the two bullets Bones took had hit her, she would've died on the spot," he said, lifting his eyes to mine. "I don't know him but I'll always be thankful to him," he said, sighing heavily.

"Yeah, that makes two of us," I said somberly.

"How's my nephew?"

"He's tiny but he's going to make it. I know he is. That kid wrapped his finger around my hand, and as small and fragile as he is, he has some grip," I replied, proudly glancing around the intensive care unit. "Where is she? I need to see her," I demanded.

Anthony led me around the nurse's station, stopping in front of a large glass wall. I spotted Maria first and then I let my eyes travel to Lauren. Again, I wasn't prepared to see her like that, hooked up to several machines, lying perfectly still as the life support kept her breathing.

Maria lifted her head, made the sign of the cross, before turning around and meeting our worried gazes. She rose to her feet, bending her head to kiss her daughter's hand before slipping out of the room. Before she could ask me any questions, I brushed past her and walked into the room, sliding the glass door closed behind me.

I stood there, my feet firmly planted on the floor as I stared at my Kitten. The sound of the machines she was hooked up to was the only noise in the room, reminding me they were keeping her here with me. Finding the courage inside of me, I moved to the side of her bed and looked at her beautiful face. I would do anything to see her smile at me, hell, she didn't even have to smile. She just needed to open those beautiful blue eyes and I'd even welcome a snarl, or one of her snarky remarks.

I just needed to know my Kitten was going to be okay.

I tore my eyes away from the tube that ran all the way down her throat and stuck out between her lips and looked at the machine and the slinky looking thing compressing the air into her lungs.

I pulled the chair closer to the bed and sank into it as I leaned over the bed and reached for Lauren's hand, careful not to disturb any of the wires as I interlocked my fingers with hers.

"Hey, Kitten," I whispered, as I looked up at her, trying to make sense of all the things going on in my head, all the things I knew I needed to say, all the things I felt down in my soul.

"I'm so sorry it came down to this," I began, hoarsely. "I'm so sorry you're lying in this bed and not me. Every move I made, every attempt to push you out of my life was to prevent you from being exactly where you are. I thought by staying away from you I was protecting you but all I did was waste time, time I could've spent showing you how much I wanted you. How goddamn grateful I was that you came into my life and how excited I was for you to make me a dad. I thought the best title I'd ever hold was being one of the Satan's Knights but it pales in comparison to being Pea's dad. That's the best title, the only one worth a damn," I expressed, pausing as I brought her hand up to my lips and kissed her knuckles.

"You need to wake up, Kitten, you need to find your strength and you need to pull through because there is a little boy sitting in the NICU who needs his mommy. He's beautiful, Lauren, so beautiful. You did such a good job, baby."

I swiped my free hand across my face, fighting back the emotions threatening to surface. I was starting to cry more than a goddamn bitch in a soap opera but I owned that shit too, proud to cry, proud to know I was capable of some sort of feeling. Proud because every tear that threatened and every single one I exposed all meant that I was owning my feelings of how much Kitten and Pea meant to me.

Bones would be proud.

"I love him," I whispered. "It's the craziest thing I ever felt and nothing compares. I mean it Lauren, one look at that little boy, knowing he is ours, did something to me. He filled all the parts of me that were empty. He's everything I never knew I wanted, everything I never knew I needed. He's just…he's everything," I wiped my cheek, and switched the hand that held hers. "Thank you, Kitten. Thank you for giving me my heart."

I gave her hand a soft squeeze before reaching up with my free hand and smoothing back her dark hair that fell over her forehead.

"Guess what else I realized?" I paused, unable to tear my eyes away from her. "God, you're pretty. I don't think I'll ever get tired of looking at your face. Even when we're old and you have lines on your face and you're jealous because I don't," I teased, desperate for us to be Kitten and Tiger again.

"All kidding aside, I realized I have loved you for a long time. I love you so much more than I ever knew I was capable of loving someone. But it's you Lauren, it's all you, all my love is yours. I'm not a second chances kind of guy, they don't come around that often for me but that won't stop me from asking you for this second chance. Wake up, Kitten, give me another shot and I promise you I'll never need another one. I'll be the guy you deserve, I'll be the family guy first and the motorcycle man second," I declared, brushing my lips back and forth against her hand.

"Wake up so I can make all your dreams come true," I murmured against her skin.

A knock sounded on the glass door causing me to look over my shoulder toward Jack who held up a bag. I looked back at Lauren, kissed her hand before gently placing it back on the bed.

"I'll be right back," I promised, as I stood up and slid the door open and stepped out of her room. "That my stuff?" I said, tipping my head toward the duffel bag he was holding.

"Yeah, Pipe put everything in there," he explained, glancing over my shoulder at Lauren.

"How is she?"

"Hanging in there," I said, taking the bag from him.

"I saw the baby, the nurse says he's doing good," Jack continued, before he pinned me with a sharp gaze. "I know your head is focused on your family, as it should be but I want you to know I'm taking care of this, going to make them all pay, every last motherfucker that has a dragon tattooed to their back."

"We should've taken them out before they had a chance to ever touch my family," I said, knowing my voice sounded bitter but I wouldn't apologize for it either. "You and the club can go buck-fucking-wild on the Dragons, but Wu—he's mine, not the clubs. This shit is personal," I said, glancing over my shoulder at Kitten, driving my point home before turning back to Jack. "You understand personal don't you?"

"I do," he agreed.

I took the duffel bag from him.

"Then I have your word that you don't strike until I can leave here and do what I gotta do," I clarified.

"If that's what you want, man, but I'm telling you I've got this," he protested.

"No, Jack, you don't," I cut him off, turning around and leaving no room for him to argue with me as I walked back into Kitten's room.

I dropped the bag onto the chair, unzipping it and digging around until I pulled out the black plastic bag I had asked Pipe to get. I took what I wanted, walking to the foot of the bed and lifted the sheet, exposing Lauren's toes that were painted bright pink. I wrapped one hand around each foot and shook my head.

"Your feet are always so cold," I said, taking the socks I had removed from the bag, the ones that had kittens all over them, and pulled them onto her feet.

"There," I said, bringing the sheet down over her feet before walking back around to her side. "Those should help keep you warm," I whispered, sitting down in the chair before I laid my head on her bed and clutched her hand with both of mine.

"Please wake up, Lauren," I murmured as I closed my eyes and brought her hand to my lips. "I need you."

I must've fallen asleep because the next thing I remember is a nurse waking me up and telling me they needed to check Lauren's vitals and change her dressings. There was still no change, no sign of improvement and so I left her room and let the doctors do their jobs while I checked on the baby.

I stopped in my tracks when I spotted Maria standing in front of the glass, her hands covering her mouth as she sobbed. My heart dropped, immediately looking for my son and spotting him in the same position I had left him. I breathed a sigh of relief and glanced around the empty corridor in search for Anthony or Adrianna but they were nowhere to be found.

"Maria?"

She turned to me, wiping her face as she did. "Is she okay?"

"She's the same," I confirmed. "They asked me to leave so they can change her dressings and check her out, so…I figured I'd check on this little guy," I said, turning my attention toward my boy. "I feel like I'm failing them. When I'm not with her it feels wrong and when I'm not with him it feels the same but how do I choose?"

"You're doing a good job," she said, taking me by surprise.

I turned to meet her sincere eyes.

"I never expected to like you," she said deliberately, blowing her nose into a tissue.

"Yeah, neither did I," I retorted.

"But you surprised me Rabbit," she teased.

"Riggs," I corrected, earning a wink from her as she laced her arm around mine.

"Come with me," she coaxed, leading me down the corridor. It was almost a year ago that I first met Maria and she knocked me in the head with a frying pan. Up until a couple of hours ago, or maybe days, I don't even know how long this shit show had been going on, I wouldn't have followed her anywhere too afraid she'd whack me.

We rounded the corner and she brought me inside the hospital chapel. I didn't tell her the only chapel I was familiar with was the kind where Jack was the reverend and instead of saying prayers we voted on who dies.

She slid into the first pew and I followed behind her, staring at the altar and the candles that were displayed, some of them lit some of them not.

"Do you pray?" She asked, making the sign of the cross before she folded her hands.

"No," I admitted. "Do you think it will help?" I asked, sounding half like a moron, half like a man running out of options but desperate to do whatever it takes to fix this situation.

"Yes, now pray with me," she ordered.

"I don't know how to pray," I whispered, scratching the back of my head, waiting for nice Maria to morph into bat shit crazy Maria.

She shook her head, grabbed my hand and laced our fingers together.

"Heavenly Father, please hear our prayer," she began. I thought she'd go on to recite a bunch of prayers, a few Hail Mary's and whatever else there was but she prayed to God by talking to him. She explained Lauren's situation, the baby's and how they both needed his help to fight their way back to us. She promised she'd be a good servant of the Lord and drag my ass to church every Sunday if need be. Yeah, she told God she was going to drag my ass. When she was finished she taught me the Our Father, and then we both made the sign of the cross before walking over to the candles and lighting one for Lauren and one for Pea.

By the time we made our way back to the NICU, Maria offered to sit with Lauren while I spent some time with the baby. I tapped my knuckles against the glass, signaling to the nurse that I wanted to see the baby. She held up a finger telling me to wait a moment and then met me outside.

"Dr. Meadows came in and assessed the baby, he was able to take a few breaths on his own and suggested that we try the Kangaroo Care," she said, leading me to the room where I scrubbed down before.

"Kangaroo what?" I questioned, taking the soap she offered me and started the scrubbing ritual.

"Studies have found that when premature babies have skin to skin contact with a parent they thrive so we're going to have him lay on your chest," she explained.

I froze in the middle of soaping up my hands and stared at her.

"You mean I'm going to be able to hold him?"

She smiled widely as she nodded. It took a moment for that to settle in before I continued to sterilize myself. I was anxious to hold him but a part of me felt guilty that I'd be holding him before Lauren. She already had missed some of the things I knew she was looking forward to, and this, the first time he's held, well, it should be her arms holding him. She deserved that.

I followed the nurse and sat down in the chair next to my son's incubator and did as I was told to prepare myself for this moment. I watched as she disconnected some of the wires that were attached to him and opened the top of the incubator, maneuvering his little body into her arms. I reached behind me, nervously pulling my shirt over my head before she turned around and faced me. I held out my arms, not sure where to hold him and not wanting to hurt him or pull any of his wires.

"Lean back," she instructed, and as my back rested against the chair she laid my son against my chest, transitioning my hands where hers were.

I inhaled sharply as her hands left his tiny body and mine kept him curled against my chest.

Words failed me.

None could ever justify the feeling of him in my arms.

My palm covered nearly most of his body as I splayed it over the blanket covering his back and felt the rise and fall of his chest.

He took one breath at a time without the help of the machine.

That's my boy.

I closed my eyes and held him close.

Dreams.

Maybe they did come true.

Chapter Thirty-Nine
Lauren

I glanced at the side-view mirror, watching as Riggs hung his helmet on one of the handlebars of his bike then turned his eyes in my direction, giving me a glimpse of that face, I missed waking up to.

Most girls in my situation would hope their baby didn't look anything like the father, but I was the opposite. I wanted Pea to look like Riggs. I wanted the reminder of the happiest few months of my life. I know my baby will fill the void of Riggs, and once I lay eyes on him or her, this pang in my chest will melt. I'll be so overwhelmed with love for Pea, I'll forget about the love I lost.

I'll forget all about Kitten and Tiger.

I opened the car door, preparing myself for the awkward discussion we were about to have as I stepped out of the car. I walked around to the back of the car and leaned against the trunk as I waited for him.

He laughed along with his brothers, breaking my heart with every chuckle.

His laugh.

His smile.

They were the things that tugged at my heart strings, the things that first hooked me to the hooligan that came looking for me one crazy night in a bar. The same hooligan that told me to take a detour, to trust him because I'd end up exactly where I was supposed to be.

Here I am.

And he's walking toward me.

Exactly where I'm supposed to be.

With him.

I pushed off the car, my feet making the choice, siding with my heart and not my head as I started for him.

A truck pulled into the lot, distracting me momentarily and I froze in my tracks, watching as Pipe started shouting at the driver.

"Park the truck over here," Pipe hollered to the driver. "Over here!" He demanded. "What the fuck, are you assholes deaf? Park the fucking truck over here," he shouted.

"Shit! Get down."

I felt my heart lurch into my throat and my eyes widened as Pipe tried to warn us of the danger before the back of the truck opened and men started firing machine guns.

"Lauren, get down!" Riggs, hollered.

"Riggs!" I cried, knowing he probably couldn't hear me over the gunfire.

No. This can't be happening.

My eyes darted around the property fearful of what was happening.

There was nowhere to turn, nowhere to hide and it was pretty damn impossible to stop, drop and roll with this belly.

"Get down," Riggs shouted.

I crouched down as low as I could get and tried to run toward the clubhouse. I stopped in my tracks and turned to look at Riggs.

"NO! NO! NO!" Riggs screamed. "Lauren!"

I never thought I'd die young, but we already know all the plans I've made for myself have been a joke. Maybe that was why they all went astray, not because God was a prankster and I was his victim, but because he knew I was going to join him and never be able to fulfill any of my plans.

He had a greater plan.

One that didn't include Kitten and Tiger.

One that didn't include Pea.

Or maybe that was his plan, maybe I was the detour, the unexpected turn in Riggs' life. I was just a means to a cause. I was here to unite Riggs with Pea and that's it.

God's plan for me was to give them to one another.

As I pulled my hand away from my chest and looked at the blood coating my fingertips I was certain of it.

I felt the burning sensation in my chest; my heart physically felt as if it was being torn apart by the bullet and knew this was my ending and their beginning.

I love you Riggs.

Mommy loves you, Pea.

My eyes locked with Riggs' before Bones came into my view charging at me and throwing me to the ground.

Heaven.

It's not some grand garden, or a blissful oasis of clouds and I must've missed the pearly gates because it's pretty dark where I am. I feel like I'm under water as I strain my ears to listen to the muffled sound of a baby crying.

Pea.

The cries are louder and this time I hear someone else's husky voice cry my name.

Riggs.

They need me.

Me.

RIGGS

We passed the forty-eight-hour mark hours ago and Kitten still hadn't opened her eyes. I've been going back and forth between the NICU and ICU, and I'm starting to lose it. Every time I look at our son, or hold him in my arms, I'm crushed because these are moments Lauren's missing, moments that were robbed from her by a fucking bullet.

It wasn't fair.

It was fucked up, so fucked up.

I paced her room, staring at the ventilator from the corner of my eye wishing like hell she'd wake up and that fucking noise would stop. It's a noise that will haunt me for the rest of my life—that along with every fucking minute of the last few days.

I rubbed at the scruff that lined my jaw, knowing it was more like a premature beard than a five-o'clock shadow at this point.

"C'mon, Lauren," I hissed. "Where's the girl with the bat? Open those eyes of yours baby, come out swinging for me," I pleaded.

Nothing.

Just that fucking machine.

I took my place beside her bed, dropping my head onto the mattress as I wrapped my hand around hers, trying to think of something else to say that would get her to come back to me. I've told her about the baby, I've told her how much I love her and I gave her a hundred different dreams we were going to fill when she woke up, and still I didn't get to stare into those blue eyes that *owned* me.

Then it came to me.

I lifted my head, reaching into my pocket for my phone and quickly thumbed through my camera roll to the videos. After Pea was fully taken off the ventilator and only had the feeding tube, I started videoing little things here and there so Lauren wouldn't miss these moments. Like when he opened his eyes or when I caught him yawning and my absolute favorite was his cry. It was the most adorable sound my ears had ever heard. I brought my phone close to her ear, raising the volume before I pressed play.

Pea's little cry filled the room and hopefully Lauren's ears.

"Lauren, do you hear that? That's your son, Kitten, your little boy," I said, replaying the video again.

"He needs his mom," I added.

"So do I…please, wake up, Lauren," I begged. "Listen to him, listen to me, we need you, Kitten," I rasped, watching intently as her eyelids twitched in response. "Lauren?"

My eyes traveled the length of her looking for another sign of movement. I took her hand in mine before diverting my eyes back to her face.

"Come on, Lauren! Damnit, please wake up," I cried.

She squeezed my hand. Startled at the movement, I glanced down at our joined hands and saw her squeeze me again. My eyes widened as I lifted them to her face just in time to watch her eyes slowly flutter open.

I blinked, unsure if my eyes were playing tricks on me but when my eyes re-opened they found Lauren's.

I dropped my phone onto the side of her bed and lifted my free hand to the side of her cheek as I hovered over her, staring into her wide eyes.

"There's my girl," I whispered hoarsely, swallowing hard against the lump in my throat, trying to smile at her. I wanted to look into her eyes, touch her all over, just so I knew she was real and not a figment of my imagination.

I can admit it now, looking into her eyes, but I was beginning to doubt I'd ever look into the eyes of the girl I fell in love with. I was nervous she wouldn't ever know how I felt about her or how grateful I was for all she's brought to my life. And most of all I was heartbroken she wouldn't get to see the boy she brought into this world.

But there she was, looking back at me with uncertainty in her eyes, my ferocious kitten. She came back to me.

To us.

She reminded me that she wasn't a quitter, sure, she gave up on the whole nursing school gig but that's because she was meant to be something more than being another face in the ER, she was meant to be *my one and only*. In a world full of faces, hers would always stand alone in a crowd; those eyes would always find mine and remind me of a dream that came true, one I never even knew I wished for.

"You're really awake," I stated, attempting to hang onto this moment for as long as I could before I had to share her with everyone else. I bent down, pressing my lips to her forehead, careful of the tubes and wires, pulling back to look at her some more. "I knew you'd come back to us," I rasped.

"She's awake? Why didn't you call us?" Maria questioned from the door. "Nurse! Get the doctor. My daughter is awake," she shouted over her shoulder before she charged into the room, toward the other side of Lauren's bed.

"She just woke up," I explained.

"Oh, thank you, Saint Anthony," she exasperated, making the sign of the cross ten times before she leaned over Lauren and kissed her. "We were so worried about you."

Lauren's eyes shot back to mine, still wide but not with confusion as she slowly lifted our joined hands, bringing them close to her stomach. The machine beside me started beeping, causing me to glance over and see her heart beat spiked.

I turned back to her, squeezed her hand as I leaned close to her ear, nuzzling her slightly.

"It's a boy, Kitten, we have a son," I whispered, giving her the answer to the unasked question shining in her scared eyes. I pulled back, staring at her as tears escaped the corner of her eyes.

"He's small but he's perfect. Really, perfect," I said. "Thank you," I added as I winked at her before turning to Maria. "Tell her, grandma, how great our little guy is," I urged Maria, as I bent down and kissed Lauren's hand.

"Oh, my God, he's beautiful, Lauren," she said, as she ran her hand over Lauren's head. "And this guy here, has been taking good care of him, waiting for you to wake up," Maria said, meeting my eyes.

"Thank you," I mouthed to the crazy woman that I was beginning to like as two nurses and a doctor charged into the room.

"We need you both to step outside for a moment," the doctor ordered, walking to the machine reading Lauren's stats.

I tore my eyes from Maria's to Lauren's and shook my head.

"I'm not leaving her," I growled over my shoulder at the doctor.

The doctor proceeded to insist I was in the way and that he needed to thoroughly check Lauren out. I knew logically they weren't requesting something so crazy and that they could have my ass kicked the fuck out of her room by security but I didn't want to leave her. I just got her back and maybe a part of me still didn't believe she was really awake.

The funny thing about dreams is once you believe in them you don't know when you're dreaming or when you're really living the dream.

Especially, when your dreams are Lauren and you know she's too good to be true—and a man like me doesn't deserve goodness like her.

But I'll take it anyway, I'll take all the goodness that comes with Lauren and work my ass off to be worthy of it.

Lauren…

The girl next door with the killer rack and pretty eyes.

The girl who took a chance on a guy like me.

My Kitten, who took the detour and got reckless with me.

One reckless night that resulted with the most perfect boy.

The girl who gave me my heart.

Lauren, the good girl who completed this bad boy.

For a man who never stepped foot inside of a church and had to be taught how to pray it was pretty ironic that I found myself back at the chapel, in front of God and not Satan. I made the sign of the cross as I slid into the first pew and stared up at the altar.

We may not be the best of men, me and my brothers, and Lord knows we all have our sins but I like to think that God took Bones and spared him Hell. I want to believe that saving Lauren's life and the baby's life earned him a ticket to Heaven and washed away his sins. I wanted to think that sitting here in the chapel, where people pray and talk to God and their loved ones, was where I could go to talk to Bones because right now he was the only person I wanted to speak to, the person I wanted to run to and tell that Lauren was okay and so was Pea.

Thanks to him.

Thanks to his sacrifice.

And I wanted to ask God to forgive me for all I was about to do.

I walked to the candles and lit one for Bones and one for my soul before I made one last bargain with God, asking him to watch over my family and forgive me of my sins.

I walked out of the chapel, checked in on Pea, and on my way back to Lauren I made the call to Jack.

"Parrish," he answered.

"It's me. I'm hungry, Jack," I clipped, as I stared through the glass window at Lauren.

"Yeah, I bet I know what you have a hankering for," he replied.

"Make it happen," I ordered, before disconnecting the call and shoving my phone back into my pocket.

Heart.

It keeps you from being reckless.

Heart.

I wouldn't be reckless but I was going to fucking settle the score. *My way.*

For Bones.

Chapter Forty
Lauren

I was shot...in the heart. I had a baby, a little boy I have yet to meet because...I was shot. But there was a silver lining and that was Riggs. He turned from the hooligan my mother hated to her best friend, but more importantly he went from a man who didn't know he wanted kids to the best father I could've imagined.

Pea was lucky.

We were still calling him Pea until I got to see him, then when I looked into his eyes I'd know his name. I'd know if he was a Robert or an Anthony, or maybe a Joseph.

And today was the day.

The day they took the tube out of my throat since I was able to breathe on my own. I was finally able to meet the boy who stole his daddy's heart and claimed mine without ever meeting him.

With the help of a nurse, Riggs situated me into a wheel chair and pushed me through the hospital to unite our little family once and for all.

"Riggs?"

"Yes, Kitten," he said, pushing the elevator button.

"You never told me how Bones was doing? Can we see him? I'd like to thank him for well...everything," I said, looking up at him, watching as he turned around and stared back at me.

"What? Did they discharge him already?" I asked, but as the question left my mouth I had an unnerving feeling that I knew the truth. If I was still here there was no way Bones had been discharged before me. I felt dread wash over me as I saw the solemn expression take precedence over Riggs' features.

"Lauren," he began, bending down so he was eye-level with me and his hands were braced against the arms of the wheelchair.

"No," I whispered, shaking my head, as I brought my hand up to my mouth. "Don't say what I think you're going to say."

"I'm sorry," he whispered, as his eyes glistened back at me. "Bones didn't make it, baby," he added, confirming the horrible truth I knew already.

What's that saying? Some people come into your life for only a short while but they leave footprints on your heart forever? I think that's it.

Every breath I take is because of him. Every beat of my heart is a gift from him.

Every breath my son takes is because of him. Every beat of his heart is a gift from an Uncle he'll never meet.

Footprints?

He left more than footprints—he gave me and my son our heartbeats. He gave us life.

Tears fell from my eyes as Riggs kneeled down and reached out to wipe my tears with the back of his hand.

"I'm sorry, Riggs. I'm so sorry. I know how close you were," I cried, reaching up and wrapping my arm around his wrist.

"Bones will always live here," he said, as he took his hand and beat it against the center of his chest. "And here," he added, taking that same hand and lifting it to my face before he leaned into me and pressed his lips gently against mine.

The elevator doors opened and he pulled away from me, glancing over my shoulder at the empty elevator before his eyes found mine again.

"You know how we can honor his life? By giving our son the best life we can. Let's go hold our boy and make losing him mean something," he said huskily.

I nodded and he rose to his feet before he wheeled me into the elevator. I'd never get to thank him or say goodbye. Riggs was right though, the best way to honor him was by giving Pea a great life, a life where he grew up to know the uncle he missed out on knowing.

I was still reeling from the blow of losing the unexpected friend I found in Bones as Riggs brought me into the NICU. The nurses smiled at us, and the one specifically appointed to take care of Pea introduced herself to me as she led us to our baby. He was still in the incubator but didn't need the ventilator anymore.

"Someone is anxious to meet his mommy," the nurse enthused, as she opened the incubator.

Riggs helped me stand up, moving the wheelchair out of the way as he laced his arm through mine and brought me to the chair next to the incubator.

"Are you good? Comfortable?" Riggs asked, as he eased me into the chair.

"I'm fine," I assured him, turning my eyes to the little bundle the nurse was holding and felt my breath catch as I positioned myself and waited for her to place him into my arms and reunite me with Pea.

"Oh, my," I whispered, as I held him for the first time, staring down at his face, memorizing all his features. "Hi, my angel, I've been waiting for this moment since I found out about you." I bent my head and kissed the tip of his tiny nose. "I love you so much," I whispered to him.

I've experienced love. I love my family. I love Riggs. But I never knew the true extent of my love and how much someone could mean to me until that very moment. I glanced at Riggs as he took photo after photo with his phone.

"He's perfect," I said.

"Isn't he?" he smiled and my heart grew even larger. Everything I needed was right there. Riggs and Pea.

This was where I was supposed to be.

This was the plan.

And such a sweet plan it was.

Thank you, God.

Thank you, Bones.

I nuzzled my baby, brought him as close as I could, careful of the incision on my chest, and kissed the top of his head as I looked back at Riggs.

"Thank you for telling me to take the detour, getting here, it was a wild ride but the best one," I whispered.

He opened his mouth to say something but I shook my head silencing him.

"I know his name," I said, diverting my eyes back to our baby for a moment, fitting his name to his face...a perfect match. I lifted my eyes back to Riggs.

"What do you think about Eric?"

He stared at me for a moment, realization settling across his features.

"That's Bones' real name," he said, his voice thick with emotion.

"I know, he told me the day I bumped into him at the hospital," I said, looking back at my son. "Eric Robert Montgomery, after his uncle and his dad, the two men I hope he grows up to be just like."

"Eric," he whispered, kneeling down before me, reaching out to take Eric's hand. "It's perfect," he agreed.

I smiled up at the nurse, tipping my chin toward the name on his incubator "Baby Boy Bianci."

"Can we change that?"

"Absolutely," she said.

"Kitten," Riggs called, forcing me to turn and watch as he went from kneeling on both knees to one.

No.

Please.

Yes.

God, is this a dream.

"Count his toes," he said, nodding toward the baby.

"What?"

He grinned, winking at me before he unraveled the blue blanket from the baby.

"Count his toes," he repeated.

I looked at the nurse and noticed she wasn't the only one staring, but all of the NICU nurses had gathered around and were watching us. I looked back at Riggs and saw my mother and brother standing behind the glass window witnessing this moment.

"Go ahead," he urged.

I unwrapped the blanket from Eric's feet, blinded by tears that I tried to blink away before setting my eyes on the ring that dangled from my son's big toe.

"Oh, my God," I whispered, looking back to Riggs. "Is this what I think it is?"

"I'm going to make a hundred mistakes, but I promise I'll fix them. I'll always fix them. I know I'm not your plan, but I'll make the detour worth it. We'll make new plans, and you'll dream...please keep dreaming. I want to make all your dreams come true, starting with a family. We already are a family but I want to make it official," he insisted.

"You want to make an honest woman out of me?" I joked through my tears.

"I want to make you *my* woman," he corrected. "Marry me, Kitten, be Mrs. Tiger," I laughed, earning another smile, the kind that reached his eyes...my favorite one.

"I love you, Lauren Bianci, so goddamn much," he added.

"I love you too," I replied, watching as he gently lifted the ring from Eric's toe, laughing when the baby curled his toe and held the ring hostage for a second. He slipped the ring onto my left hand before he looked back at me.

"Tell me it's a yes."

"Yes! Of course," I exclaimed.

"I knew you'd say yes," he grinned, pointing his thumbs toward himself. "How could you say no? This is all yours now."

"I got news for you, Tiger. It was always mine and it would still be mine with or without the ring." It was my turn to wink and grin back at him. "But the ring is a nice touch and the baby? Is the best bonus."

"Good, glad you feel that way. I want more," he said seriously, as he rose to his full height. "I'm thinking five or six."

"Five or six kids?" I questioned. My eyes widening in disbelief—I'm pretty sure my uterus twitched violently at the thought.

"Yeah," he tipped his head over his shoulder toward my mother. "Think she'll move in and watch them when we need alone time? You know, when we feel like playing drop the pencil or just the tip?"

"You want my mother to move in?"

He waved at my mother and brother through the glass, giving them a thumbs up.

"Shit, Kitten, I'm joking. You Bianci's are a shitload of fun to fuck with," he said with a chuckle, turning back to me and kissing me softly. "Who would've thought I'd be marrying a Bianci?" he whispered against my mouth, pulling back to kiss Eric's head.

"I bet Bones did," I whispered.

"He'd be so fucking proud right now," he said, as he looked down at our son. "Best thing I ever did was listen to him."

Thank you, Bones.

The End.

Epilogue

RIGGS

The thing about finding your heart is knowing that you now have something valuable, something worth more than any dollar in a trust fund, and with that knowledge comes the urgent need to always protect your heart.

One month ago Sun Wu tried to take my heart from me.

Stupid fucker.

But tonight, he'd be a dead fucker because tomorrow my family was coming home and before they step foot outside that hospital it's my job to ensure their safety.

To settle the score once and for all.

For the first time since the shooting, I parked my bike in front of the Dog Pound and killed the engine before removing my helmet. I glanced over to the spot where both Bones and Lauren had been shot and the memories came rushing back. Her frightened eyes as she begged me to choose Pea, and Bones' short breaths as he bled out beside her.

The memories gave me a burst of adrenaline, making me even more certain that tonight was the night I'd live up to the promise I made to Bones.

I shook my head, trying to shake the memories as I pulled opened the door and heard the boisterous sounds of my brothers as they prepared for war.

I missed that fucking sound.

"Get your dick out of your ass, boy, and suit up," Wolf told Stryker, slapping him upside the head before dropping a bullet-proof vest on his lap.

"Well, look who it is," Pipe shouted over their voices as his eyes met mine.

The room grew silent as they all turned around and looked at me as I walked further into the clubhouse, my eyes catching the cut that hung behind the bar in a frame.

I didn't have to look at the patch to know it was Bones'—the blood still stained parts of the patches. I locked eyes with Jack, who stood behind the bar, lining up a row of shot glasses.

"Nice to see your pretty face," Pipe said, breaking the tension that filled the room.

I tore my eyes away from Jack and looked back at the rest of my brothers.

"I know you bitches missed me," I said, grinning.

"Pipe cries himself to sleep night after night. Keeps a photo of your naked ass under his pillow," Wolf chimed in, walking over to me and patting me on the back. "Glad you're back, kid. You ready to hunt, motherfucker?"

"That depends what's on the menu," I said, looking back at Jack.

"Peking-fucking-duck," he growled.

"With a side of Wu," Wolf added.

Jack walked out from behind the bar, stood in front of me as he crossed his arms and assessed me.

"Only going to ask you once—" he started.

"You don't have to ask at all," I interrupted. "Let's do this."

Jack remained quiet for a moment before he bit the inside of his cheek and nodded. He knew all about revenge, got his and now it was fucking time for me to get mine.

"One thing before we hit the road," Jack said, turning back toward the bar.

We all followed and took the glasses he offered us before lifting them to his.

"To Bones," Jack cheered.

"To Bones," we all said in unison before shooting back the liquid fire.

Time to make it right.

We slammed our empty glasses down onto the wooden bar and started marching for the door like the devil's soldiers that we are. Jack grabbed my arm and slapped a vest against my chest.

"Don't be reckless," he ordered. "Stick to the fucking plan, you hear me?"

Plans.

I wasn't big on plans.

"Right," I agreed. "Stick to the plan," I said, bringing my fingers to my forehead and saluting my president.

We walked outside, mounted our bikes and the roar of our bikes was deafening throughout the lot. Jack peeled out first, followed by Wolf and then Pipe. Bones would've been next but his bike remained parked across the lot. I glanced over at it before gripping the throttle on my bike and tearing out of the lot taking his spot in our line-up. The nomads came up behind me and then the prospects were last to take to the rode as our pack rode against the wind on a mission to take back life lost from our club.

This will always be a part of my life but it wasn't what gave me purpose anymore. I'll always be a man who loves the road, his bike and the wrong side of the law. But, I ride second, and love first. I owned my place in the world.

I sped up, whipping around Pipe's bike and made my way next to Jack.

"What are you doing?" he shouted against the engines of our bikes and the sounds of the city.

"Taking a detour," I hollered back, turning right as they turned left and pushed my bike full speed ahead.

They had a plan.

They were going to raid the Red Dragons' clubhouse on a night they planned a patch party. It was a very well executed plan and I had no doubt that my brothers would take out every motherfucking Dragon and whore that populated that party.

But I had a plan too.

And my shit was personal.

Wu killed my brother.

He put a bullet it my woman.

He forced my son to be born before his time.

It didn't get more personal than that.

I pulled up to my destination, my boots chomping at the wooden planks as I made my way to the warehouse on the pier overlooking the Hudson River. The same pier Sun Wu used to transport his shit to Beijing. I came up to the door and greeted Michael Valente, Anthony's soon-to-be brother-in-law. When I had first decided on how all this would go down, Anthony suggested Michael as the man for the job, the job being kidnapping Wu on his way home from the Red Dragons clubhouse.

"Thanks for doing this," I said.

"It's all good, man," he replied, opening the door to the warehouse. "He's all yours," he said, as he moved aside and allowed me room to step inside. "I'll be right here," he added, before stepping back out into the night and closing the door behind him.

I turned around, flicked the lights on and spotted Sun Wu on the floor with his ankles tied together and his hands handcuffed behind his back. He was gagged with a....pink dildo?

Jesus Christ.

Then it occurred to me he wasn't even gagging—this motherfucker must've sucked a lot of dick. The Red Dragons' own personal club whore was none other than their president.

I laughed.

That would explain the sex toys.

And the fake dick he had in his mouth now.

Good job, Mikey.

I stepped closer to him, pinning him with my eyes as I pressed the steep tip of my boot between his legs.

"Hey motherfucker, remember me?"

I pressed harder as I crouched down and pulled the duct tape that kept the dildo lodged in his mouth.

"Does your wife know you can deep throat a cock like that? Or just your brothers?" I questioned, as I pulled the cock from his mouth and threw it to the side.

"Fuck you, Mr. Riggs. You're a dead man," he hissed.

"I wouldn't be making threats, "Jackie Chan." You, motherfucker, you're in my fucking house now and I'm the one cracking the whip," I ground out, digging the tip of my boot into his crotch just to hear him wail like a bitch.

I pulled out my phone from the back of my pants and started swiping my fingers across the screen until I pulled up exactly what I needed.

"You couldn't leave well enough alone, could you? You got your money for the drugs, you shot up Pops warehouse and took our guns and still it wasn't enough," I reminded him, still toying with my phone.

"You killed my men! Money can't replace lives, you know that, now don't you? You were particularly close to the Knight that died, weren't you?"

He tried to taunt me but it wouldn't work. I remained in control. I stuck to my plan and I did what I came here to do.

"How's the surveillance on your house these days, Wu?"

"What the fuck do you care?"

"I don't care," I said, as I looked him in the eye. "But I feel it necessary to tell you it's pretty shitty and your alarm system is bootleg. Maybe I should thank you for that, you made this so much easier," I pointed out, as I sat down beside him.

"What are you talking about?"

"You see a funny thing happened when you and your club shot up the Dog Pound. Yes, you killed my best friend but only because you almost killed the mother of my child and my child. If Bones didn't die, they would've. They almost did die. You have a daughter and a son, not to mention the "Yoko Ono" wanna be wife of yours."

I felt his gaze wander to me but chose to ignore it as I brought the phone between us, so we both could see the screen when I pressed play.

"Imagine not knowing if they are going to live or die. Imagine knowing they may die and there isn't a fucking thing you can do about it."

I turned and met his eyes.

"Ever feel so helpless in your life?"

"Keep my family off your tongue," he seethed.

"Or what? You'll kill me or maybe you'll have your club kill me?" I shook my head. "That's not going to happen, Wu because right now my club is desecrating the Red Dragons, right now your brothers are dying and mine are the ones taking their lives," I cocked my head as I studied him.

That's right, my house, motherfucker.

My rules.

"How about a little entertainment? Get your mind off the bloodshed?" I nodded. "Sorry I forgot the popcorn," I added, as I brought up the surveillance footage of his house. Anthony was dressed in black, with a ski mask covering his face and shielding his identity as he stared into the camera, reaching up and turning the lens toward the three people tied to chairs in the center of Wu's living room.

His wife.

His daughter.

His son.

They were gagged and bound.

Helpless.

Just like Lauren and our son were.

I turned back to Wu as he shouted something in Chinese, turning to me with desperate eyes, or maybe they were vengeful. I wasn't sure.

I didn't give a fuck either.

"Let them go. Now! Please, don't hurt them. They're innocent," he pleaded.

"You're right, they are, just like mine were. So now here's the part where you become me. Where you have to sit there and know there is nothing you can do to save them but there is one difference," I stated, handing him the phone as I stood up. "I wondered for nearly three days if my family was going to live or die, you'll wonder for eternity."

Anthony stepped into the view of the camera and slowly pulled a gun from his back pocket just as I drew mine and aimed it at Sun Wu.

He screamed as he watched Anthony lift the gun and aim it at his wife just as I aimed mine at his chest.

Bang!

One shot to the heart.

That's for Lauren and Eric.

Bang! Bang!

Two shots between the eyes.

That's for Bones.

My phone dropped from his hand as Satan came and claimed his soul.
See ya motherfucker!
This shit was personal.
I glanced down at my phone and watched as Anthony cut the wires to the feed, killing the image on my screen.
It was all part of the plan.
I took the burner phone out of my cut and called 911. They would send the cops over to Wu's house and cut his family loose and find the ransom note that we left behind, staging this whole thing to look like he pissed one of his trade partners off. Eventually, they'll find his body in this empty warehouse where he conducted business overseas and the story will all match up.
Plans.
They don't always go astray.
Some things are just meant to be.
"911, what's your emergency?"
"I'm calling to report a home invasion at two-thirty-six Cromwell Ave," I said, before disconnecting the call and stepping outside to meet Mike.
"We all good?" He asked.
"Yeah, we're good," I confirmed.
Revenge was sweet.

LETHAL TEMPTATIONS

JANINE INFANTE BOSCO

Prologue

BLACKIE

"I'm getting out of here," Riggs said, throwing a few crisp bills on the bar. I nodded, a delayed reaction to his departure, and lifted the shot glass to my lips, welcoming the smooth poison down my throat. Unsatisfied and insatiable I flicked the empty glass across the bar.

"Another, boss?" the bartender asked.

I shook my head, pushing back my stool and slowly rose to my feet. The alcohol wasn't making me numb like it usually did and the methadone doesn't bring me to the state of oblivion I crave. I tried not to take anything today. I tried to be better than yesterday and the day before that.

But once a junkie always a junkie.

And I make no apologies for it.

This is who I am, or what is left of who I used to be, depending on who you ask.

I feel her innocent eyes on me, burning a hole into my back, setting my black heart on fire. I won't turn around, I won't even acknowledge her because I have enough demons and don't need those dark, sad eyes haunting me anymore than they already do.

I told myself I was just coming to the bar to make sure she was safe.

I wanted to see her one more time.

I got what I wanted.

I walked into the crowded bar and found her amongst a sea people. Her face stood out and those eyes of hers… they were almost as black as the leather on my back and held me captive. It was impossible to turn away. She laughed and when she laughed she lit up the whole room.

Fuck, she lit up the whole world.

Turned on the lights and drew me out of the darkness I've been wallowing in.

Some people think I have a death wish, that I'm on a mission to end this nightmare I call life, and maybe for a while I thought they were right. A part of me wanted to join Christine, to see her one last time and make right all the wrong I did to her. But when I nearly died, my body didn't succumb to the darkness and fought against it. Jimmy Gold pumped me with enough drugs to kill me two times over but it was Reina, my president's girlfriend that made me realize I wanted to live and I wanted to live for those dark eyes that she had pinned on me.

Leather.

Lace.

Me.

Her.

A temptation so lethal, neither of us would survive.

Maybe I had a death wish after all.

I stumbled into the bathroom, locking the door behind me, before I turned around and glanced at myself in the dirty mirror. Staring at my reflection in the mirror, I wonder why she ever looked at me in the first place. Someone as innocent and pure as her doesn't belong with a poisonous bastard like me.

I reached into my pocket, pulled out a plastic baggie filled with five Xanax pills and slapped the bag onto the counter. I diverted my eyes back to the mirror, glaring at the piece of shit staring back at me.

"Fuck you," I growled, hanging onto the feeling of self-loathing, welcoming it and encouraging it to overcome me as I slammed my fist against the baggie on the counter. I pounded it over and over again, crushing the pills until they turned to dust. Then I emptied the contents onto the counter, not giving a fuck how dirty and disgusting the bathroom was because, all that mattered was getting my fix.

I was in the zone, anxious for the high that hopefully will come and wash away my thoughts of *her*.

She is my savior and my assassin.

The one that keeps me from ending it.

And yet, right now I'm slowly killing myself trying to escape the thoughts of her.

Lacey Parrish. Jack's daughter. His fucking nineteen-year-old daughter who wasn't even legally allowed to order a fucking drink so why the fuck was she in some bar.

I fought long and hard not to see her as a fucking woman, not to take what I so badly wanted. But like everything else in my life…I take and I take until there is nothing left.

She was so innocent, so pure, so untouchable and untainted.

I'm the filth that took her innocence, who touched her and tainted her.

But it wasn't enough.

I kept going back for more.

I rolled the twenty-dollar bill, leaned over the counter dragging the bill across the powder and snorted the drugs up my fucking nose.

One rip.

Another.

Three rips later, I licked my finger tips and swiped them across the counter top, before popping my fingers into my mouth and sucking any residue of the pills from my skin.

No waste.

A true junkie.

I sniffled, wiping the excess powder from my nose before I turned around and unlocked the door, waiting for the numbness to inebriate me as I stepped out of the bathroom, colliding with the soft body I used to worship and called mine.

I stared into her sad eyes, knowing I was the reason she looked broken, just a shell of the girl she was before I touched her.

I ruined her just like I ruined Christine.

Everything I touch I destroy.

"How long are you going to pretend I don't exist?" she finally asked, her voice just an octave above a whisper.

Pretend she doesn't exist? She's the only fucking thing that exists in my head. She's the face I see when I wake, when I lay my head down and when I pass the fuck out from whatever poison I consume trying to forget that she *does* exist.

I shoved my hands into my pockets, took a step closer to her, the scent of her worked its way through my raw nostrils, more intoxicating than any drug I could ever snort or shoot through my veins. I leaned closer, closing my eyes and got high off her.

My sweet Lace.

So damn pretty.

So fucking innocent in all this.

"Until you disappear once and for all," I said, opened my eyes and glared at her.

Go away Lacey.

One day maybe you'll know why I did it.

Why I broke your heart and killed my soul.

I pushed past her, leaving her alone in the hallway, knowing her eyes were full of tears that my words caused.

Cry.

Hate me.

I'm no good for you.

Run.

I ordered another shot, made it a double, and knocked it back. I placed the empty glass on the bar and from the corner of my eye I watched as she took her date's hand and begged him to leave.

Thatta' girl.

Get the fuck out of here.

"This one's on the house," the bartender offered, sliding me a refill.

"Thanks," I muttered.

"The bill is on the table," someone said from behind me, causing me to glance over my shoulder and look at the kid holding Lacey's hand.

Treat her good.

She didn't look at me, keeping her back towards me as she followed him out the door and disappeared like I asked her too.

She should only know I'd spend the rest of the night thinking about her, that she'd never fucking disappear because *she* owned *me*.

Every moment we shared haunts me.

Starting with that first night when her hands trembled as she reached for my body and the way I took hers. The tears she cried that night and the words I wounded her with.

That was just the first night where lines were crossed but, there were a shitload more incidents I wreaked havoc on Lacey. But that night? That was the night I claimed her. In my dark world of self-destruction and mayhem, I selfishly took Lacey, branded her mine, and I continued to brand her and mark her with my actions and my words.

And then I fucking fell in love with her.

Don't think for one second that the few words I said to her tonight wasn't a mark, purposely branding her, scarring her, ruining her for any other man. Others piss on their territory, I destroy mine. For all the track mark on my arms, she has a matching one on her heart.

Lacey was still mine and always will be.

Even when she gets over me and thinks she's giving herself to someone else. She'll still be mine.

And any man who ever loves her will know who she belongs to. She won't be able to give them all of her because I've taken most of her and I'll never give it back.

I can't have her but no one else can either.

I'm a selfish motherfucker.

A greedy son-of-a-bitch.

I'm a junkie and when drugs no longer do it for me I'll get high on pain and suffering. My own.

Hers.

And all the faceless men that will one day try to take her from me.

I finished my drink, paid my tab and walked over to the nomads hanging around the pool table, a new group of brothers' that were patched into our charter of the Satan's Knights. My eyes zeroed in on Stryker's as his peered back at me questioningly, trying to figure me out. The poor bastard had no idea what he signed up for. None of them did. I said my goodbyes and made my way out of the bar, letting the cool breeze blow over me as I walked towards the parking lot.

I could feel the high start to work me over as I strode to my bike and thought the drugs were finally kicking in but it wasn't the manufactured shit that called to me.

It was her.

Her voice.

Her cries.

I closed my eyes as they consumed me, pulling me away from my surroundings and into a world where only she existed.

"Get off of me! Please! Someone help!"

So real.

I opened my eyes.

"Fucking bitch. Get the fuck back here!"

So fucking real.

My eyes drifted across the lot to where the sounds were coming from and the sobering image of my Lacey struggling to crawl out of a car, screaming into the dark parking lot for someone to help her.

Fuck no.

Hell motherfucking no.

I felt my fists clench at my sides, my breath quickens and my heart rocket against my chest cavity as my boots pounded the tar of the parking lot. I reached the driver's side of the car, yanked opened the door and reached for the cocksucker leaning over the console, pulling Lacey's hair. His fucking pants were around his ankles and his dick was hard when I pulled him off her and slammed him against the side of the car.

"What the fuck?" he sneered.

"Motherfucker, you know what *no* means? Huh?" I shouted as my fist collided with his jaw. The adrenaline soaring in my veins as I pummeled his face with my fist.

"No, stop!" He cried. "Shit, I'm sorry! Help!"

I grabbed him by his ears and threw him onto the ground, wedging my boot between his legs, crushing his balls.

"Blackie!" Lacey shouted.

"C'mon motherfucker, cry for me. Cry like the bitch you are," I demanded, grabbing his hair and slammed his skull against the pavement.

"CRY!" I shouted, lifting him by the ears and crashed his head against the ground again.

"WEEP MOTHERFUCKER!"

Blood poured from his mouth, his nose and the back of his head as his eyes stared back at me wide with terror. I tugged his face close to mine, his blood dripping onto my hands as I leaned close and looked into his eyes that were half closed.

"Open your fucking eyes. Look at me!" I ordered.

"Blackie, the cops are coming! Please stop!" Lacey shrieked from somewhere behind me.

"Blackie man, you need to get the fuck out of here. Let's go," Stryker called.

Voices surrounded me, yelling at me, warning me, but I ignored them all.

"LOOK AT ME!" I shouted, yanking on his ears until he struggled to meet my gaze.

"You see this face? Remember it. I'm the one who fucking did this to you," I hissed, before slamming the back of his head against the ground.

The voices faded.

The sirens faded.

All I heard was the sound of bones shattering and the cries of a man dying.

Someone grabbed me from behind, pulling me off him and yanked my hands behind my back. I tore my eyes away from the body on the floor and took in my surroundings as I felt the cold metal tighten around my wrists.

"Dominic Petra, you are under arrest," Officer Brantley's voice sounded in my ear. "You have the right to remain silent. You have the right to an attorney…"

He continued to read me my rights as my eyes locked with Lacey's.

Dark and dull, wrecked and ruined. My beautiful innocent Lacey tainted by my selfish sadistic ways, stared back at me. I watched the tears fall down her cheeks, each droplet another mark. Those tears were as much mine as everything else about her was.

Mine.

Always mine.

Leather.

Lace.

Me.

Her.

So fucking tempting.

So fucking lethal.

Chapter One

BLACKIE

7 Months ago

I'm a masochist, a man who gets off on inflicting pain on himself. I'm my own worst enemy. I've fucked myself more times than any rival club or gangbanger ever could. I had a shaky past with drugs, been trading one fucking addiction for another since I was a rebellious teenager. So when I offered to be the drug man in an operation Jack Parrish the president of the Satan's Knights orchestrated with a psychotic gangster, I knew I was sealing my own fate.

"I might not have him where I want him but there's one advantage I have over him, over you, over everyone in this goddamn club. I know drugs, man. I know their worth and their consequence. I know how to make them desirable and I know how to make them your enemy. I will have Jimmy Gold high on my promise before he or his streets are high on the product."

What I didn't expect was that it would all come crashing down so soon. The reputed mob boss, Victor Pastore, got himself carted off to prison, doing a lifetime bid, and the sick fuck sitting across from me was now in charge of all Vic's operations.

Jimmy Gold.

The scrawny bastard covered in tattoos, wore a long fur coat, pairing it with perfectly tailored pants and a white wife beater tank top. He had a dozen or so chains dangling from his neck and when he smiled his top two front teeth matched those gold chains. He looked like a fucking asshole.

It was hard to look him in the eye and not want to kill him on the spot, especially since we knew for a fact this prick killed Jack's brother. Danny became some federal agent thirteen years ago and recently changed his name as he went to head the agency in a RICO case. Danny was sniffing around one of Jimmy's bodies and threatened to take him down. The Golden Nutcase in front of me decided he wasn't going to go down like that and murdered Danny.

That was partially why this motherfucker was sitting in front of me, the other reason was he was working with the G-Man. Cain the former deceased president of the Satan's Knight used to get his supply from the drug lord and forced the rest of us to deal it on the streets. It didn't matter if you were a kid, pregnant or somebody's innocent wife…we fed your habit and took your money.

Or in Christine's case we drove you to your own death.

Not we.

Just me.

That shit was all on me.

And this, right now, this was my chance to make things right for *her*. I will take this motherfucker down, and after I bury his ass we will end the G-Man once and for all. It doesn't matter he's rotting in a cell…when you want something badly enough, you find a fucking a way. Prison bars won't stand in the way of revenge.

A revenge so sweet and one that was all mine for the taking.

I'd start by playing this prick like the fool he is. This guy thinks he's the fucking boss but I'll show him who the fuck runs these streets.

"Victor tells me you're familiar with the business, that you used to be one of the biggest players in the game," he raved. "That makes me wonder why you would ever stop," he questioned.

"Who said I did?" I bit out, leaning back in my chair as I pinned him with a glare.

The thing about guys like us, bikers, and mobsters—we're all the same in one regard. We are all street thugs and you might be able to pull a man off the streets but you can't take the streets from the soul of the man. That shit sticks with you until you die.

The same way being an addict does.

Jimmy didn't need to know that since Christine's death I've substituted one addiction for another, using alcohol to numb me—a last ditch effort to honor the woman I helped bring to her death. I thought if I swore off the drugs, kicked the heroin, I was honoring her in some way.

"Your boss wanted to keep his streets clean, made it real hard for us to do business, so I took my product elsewhere," I said, drumming my nails against the table as my eyes locked with his. "Make no mistake about it Gold, I am the biggest player in the game. Always have been, always will be," I assured him.

And that was true. I'd put my fucking game face on and be the drug dealing degenerate I tried to bury, the worthless man who lost his wife because of his greed. The legend on the streets. I told myself I was doing the right thing, resurrecting the demon inside of me, because bringing down Jimmy and the G-Man would finally bring me closure on Christine. It would bring me peace to know the men who fed my palm the shit she overdosed on would finally pay.

"Confident," he stated. "I like it, but as confident as you might be, I don't trust you," he added. "And I don't do business with anyone I don't trust."

"Smart man," I countered as I leaned closer to him. "Then why the fuck you wasting my time?"

"Well," he started, diverting his eyes to Reina as she placed a bottle of beer on the table, playing the role I quickly dumped on her. When we saw Jimmy and his goons prance through the parking lot on the surveillance feed, I told Jack's woman to follow my lead. I didn't trust this scumbag. He'd already fucked with the president's brother there was no telling what he'd do if he got wind that Jack had an old lady. I told Reina to get down on her knees and she followed my lead, aiding in making this fool think she was nothing but a whore, a piece of pussy we shared. A worthless cunt.

I turned my attention toward Reina. "Thank you, now go upstairs and take your fucking clothes off. I'll be right up," I ordered, watching as she snarled before disappearing into the hallway and out of sight.

"As I was saying, my mind may be swayed if you provide me with an example of good faith," Jimmy purred. "I'd like to think a man like you knows his product, enjoys it even, won't you have a taste for me?"

"You want me to shoot it to prove what exactly?" I narrowed my eyes at him.

"That you're not selling me shit for one," he said.

"I don't know how you do business Gold, but usually you or one of your own test the product they are buying," I informed.

"Of course that's why I brought Carmine, but I'm not stupid Blackie, you are going to shoot the same sample you're giving me. If it's good for your own veins then it should be good for Carmine's," he sneered. "Those are my conditions, take them or leave them," Jimmy added.

It's been years since I've used heroin, fucking years since I did any drug other than pot. That doesn't mean I haven't been tempted. Fuck, there's been so many times I've filled a syringe and tied a rubber around my arm but it's been five years since I've felt the prick of the needle. Five years since I felt the heroin swim in my veins and take control over me. I stopped myself every time because I saw her face. I remembered pulling her out of the bathtub and untying the rubber band from her arm. I could still feel the weight of her lifeless body in my arms.

I stared back at Jimmy.

I couldn't deny his demands, Jack was depending on me to bring this shit home, to end this motherfucker—if I bitched out now then we'd never get him or the G-Man.

What's one more time?

Just one more taste.

I pushed back my chair and left him to stare after me as I walked into the Satan's Knights chapel, straight toward the safe in the wall and punched in the code.

After, we decided we would pose as Jimmy's supplier, I needed to get my hands on the drugs so I went up to north to the Corrupt Bastards MC and ironed out a deal to get the heroin from them. The plan was to give Jimmy a taste of their product, let him think it was ours, and get him hooked on the profit. Once he was polluting the streets with the smack we would cut him off, tell him he needed to buy an obscene about if he wanted to keep the connection. Then when we delivered we would set him up with the cops. Jimmy would get arrested with all the drugs on him and with all Vic's connections, eventually the bastard would wind up in the same prison as his former boss. Vic was itching to kill this motherfucker.

I grabbed the leather pouch and shut the safe before walking back out to find Jimmy exactly where I left him. I threw the pouch on the table before sitting back down and stared back at him.

"Fine, let's get this over with," I seethed.

Just one more taste.

"Wonderful" Jimmy exclaimed, pulling out his phone and quickly making a call, instructing whoever it was to come inside. Jimmy ended the call and reached for the pouch, unzipping it and pulled out a vile of heroin. Carmine walked into the clubhouse, taking a seat between us and we both watched as Jimmy filled one needle and then another.

Carmine rolled up his sleeve, exposing the track marks on his arm, searching for a vein that wasn't collapsed from all the use. I watched him stab the needle into his flesh and close his eyes as he drained the syringe into his bloodstream.

Jimmy extended the second needle full of smack toward me and my eyes met his.

"Whenever you're ready Blackie," he crooned.

I reached for the band, tying it tightly around my bicep and turned over my forearm, slapping at it until a solid vein bulged beneath my skin. I took the syringe from him, forcing my eyes to stay open, knowing if I closed them now all I'd see was Christine.

I'm sorry.

So, very fucking sorry.

The needle pricked my skin and my thumb pressed down on the top as the poison began to fill me. "There you go," Jimmy taunted. "Just a little more," he coaxed as I emptied the syringe into my vein. "All done."

Carmine pulled the needle from his arm, dropping it onto the floor and it rolled across the laminate flooring. I left the needle in my arm as I stared back at Jimmy, struggling to fight against the shit swimming in my bloodstream.

"All good," Carmine drawled, already feeling the effects of the drugs.

"I'll be in touch," Jimmy said, satisfied as he pushed his chair back and rose to his feet. He snapped his fingers, muttered something under his breath as he pulled Carmine to his feet and strutted out of the clubhouse. I heard the door close behind them, signaling I was alone and then I allowed my eyes to close and saw her face. A moan escaped the back of my throat as I vividly recalled the way I stared into her dead eyes and cradled her body in my arms before pulling the needle from her arm. My cries repeated over in my mind, begging her to wake up, for it all to be a dream and then I remembered lifting my hand to her eyes and closing them gently.

"Blackie?"

For a moment I thought it was her sweet voice calling my name but when I lifted my head, struggling for my eyes to focus, I saw it was Reina.

"Oh my God," she said, rushing towards me. I tore my eyes away from her and glanced down at the offensive needle sticking out of my arm.

I spent the last few years desecrating my liver to save my veins only for it to come full circle. I kept myself alive but numb, telling myself the only reason this life was worth living was to have a chance to right all the wrongs I had done but staring at that needle solidified that I'd never be able to get the penance I craved.

I bent my head, opening my mouth around the needle and pulled the fucking thing out with my teeth before spitting the empty syringe on the table and untying the band around my arm. I lifted my watering eyes to Reina's, not giving a fuck if she saw the pain I tried to numb myself from.

Let her know.

Let the whole world know how fucked I truly am, how every goddamn thing I do turns to shit.

Masochist.

"Earned your keep, Reina," I slurred, swaying slightly in my chair as I lifted my hips and pulled my keys from my back pocket. "My car is out front, Ford Expedition. Go find your man," I said, throwing the keys in the air.

"What about you?"

"Just go," I mumbled, leaning back in the chair and closed my eyes. I surrendered to the heroin, welcoming the numbness, and accepting the fact my life had been over a long time ago.

Chapter Two

Lacey

There is a little boy who lives in my dreams and forever in my heart, a little boy named Jack Parrish Jr. He was my little brother and I was five years old when I watched him die. Literally, I stood there and did nothing as he ran into the street. I thought I would forget that someday the memory would fade as I became older—yet it seemed to only grow more vivid with every year I aged and he didn't.
Lala.
That was what he used to call me because he couldn't say Lacey.

"Lala," he cheered as his wobbly legs ran out the front door.

I was only a kid myself but I knew that he shouldn't be outside without an adult and more than that I knew he could get hurt. I tried to get my dad's attention, telling him to help me get Jack back inside the house but he was too engrossed in the madness that consumed him. I had never seen my dad like that before, so out of control, so far away in his own mind that my cries went unheard.
I ran outside as my father repeatedly beat down the walls of our home. I can recall him shouting about bugs but I thought he was looking for creepy little critters; the ones I would shout for him to stomp on. That wasn't the case, and I learned later on that my father was looking for the bugs the Feds plant when they are looking to send your ass to jail.
That was the first of many memories I have of my dad losing his battle with his *maker*. His maker is his mind, and it reigns over everything. My father is Jack Parrish, president of the Satan's Knights MC and he is a manic-depressive.
He didn't know at the time of Jack Jr.'s death he was mentally ill, and it wasn't until after my little brother was buried six feet in the ground he sought help and was diagnosed.
He blames himself for his death but it wasn't his fault.
It was mine.
I stood there as Jack Jr. smiled and pointed at me.
"Lala, look!"
I should've run after him.
I could've asked a neighbor to help.
Something.
Anything.
Nothing.
Instead, I stood there listening to my father shout at the demons in his head and watched as the car sped down the street.
I want to believe that I called out to him, that, I shouted at the driver to stop but I remember nothing other than standing there and watching as the tires skidded across the tar and over my baby brother. I try to block out the last sound he made a shrill cry that rings over and over again in my ears until it fades to silence. The

silence is worse though because it reminds me that when his cries faded so did his life.

My father snapped out of it too late and when he made his way to Jack, he fell to the ground and cradled the child he lost.

His maker won that day.

And *mine* was born.

Today would've been Jack's fifteenth birthday. It's also the one day a year my father goes off the grid, a day when he struggles to find the courage to end his life and be reunited with his son.

It doesn't matter I'm still here.

And I suppose it shouldn't.

Because I let him die.

I'm the reason my dad didn't get to watch his little boy grow into a man.

I'm also to blame for why my mom will never dance with her son.

It's my fault I'll never hear him call me Lala again.

I usually let my father have the day as I wait in agony for the moment one of his brothers comes knocking on my door to tell me that it's over. Jack Parrish the toughest man I'll ever know, has finally succumbed to his maker and is now at peace.

Not today.

Today I foolishly want to be enough. I wanted what I suppose any surviving child would want, and that was for him to look at me and realize I am still here and that I have been here for the last thirteen years wishing to be enough for him. Just once I wanted him to see me, just me.

You're selfish.

You're foolish.

He'll never see you.

All he sees when he looks at you is the boy he lost and the girl he was left with.

I lifted my eyes to the rear-view mirror and stared at the dark eyes reflected at me. I had my father's eyes, identical in color and when you looked closely the pain in his eyes were mirrored in mine.

I tore my gaze away, glancing out the window and stared at the Dog Pound, the Satan's Knights clubhouse, the place where my father spent most of his days and nights. I slid out of the car, slamming the door behind me and beeping the alarm as I started for the compound. The parking lot was mostly empty, and I didn't see my dad's bike but my eyes zeroed in on the Harley parked in front of the clubhouse.

The bike was as badass as its owner and just as beautiful too.

Blackie, the tortured soul with a patch declaring him the vice president of the Satan's Knights.

My father's right hand and his best friend.

His *brother*.

Blackie.

He'd make me feel better.

He always did.

Always.

BLACKIE

I ripped the line of coke like a motherfucking champ, desperate to reverse the effects of the heroin. If there was any justice to be had, I'd suffer a fucking a heart attack as a result of mixing the uppers and downers but I wasn't that lucky. There was a higher power that had my destiny all mapped out, he'd let me beat all the odds, keep me breathing just to torture me more.

I pushed the remaining coke with a credit card, forming another line before I bent my head, pressing my index finger to the nostril I used to rip the first line and snorted the second.

I lifted my head, stumbled back as the door opened and I turned my head, lifting my hands to push the hair away from my eyes as they locked with Lacey's.

Shit.

I didn't need this now, another fucking temptation I wasn't strong enough to beat. I shook my head, wishing she'd disappear, but she was there, staring at me with innocence radiating from her dark eyes. She looked at me like I was some goddamn mythical warrior.

"Your old man ain't here, go home," I clipped, peeling my eyes off of her as I walked around the bar, sniffling from the coke and itching for a drink. I pulled a bottle of whiskey from the shelf before reaching for a glass and filling it with the amber liquid. I placed the bottle on top of the bar and lifted the glass to my lips, knocking back the liquid in three gulps.

I set the empty glass down and she was in front of me, her eyes bored into mine and as much as I wanted to look away I couldn't.

"Lace, I'm not in the mood, so why don't you go on and tell me what you need that way you can get the fuck out of here," I slurred, watching as her eyes widened at the tone I took with her.

Fuck.

I ran my fingers roughly through my hair, teetering on the edge of insanity, hating the way she was looking at me.

Quit looking at me like I'm something when I'm nothing.

"What's the matter, Lace? You didn't know your favorite Knight got down like this?" I sneered.

"Oh, I knew," she quickly said, pulling out one of the stools before she took a seat.

Great, she was sticking around.

"I never saw it firsthand before is all," she added, softly as her teeth dug into her bottom lip and continued staring at me.

I leaned over the bar, so she could get a better look at me and see how truly fucked I was. I wanted to scare her, to make her run the fuck away from me before I lost the little control I was hanging onto.

"Get out of here Lace, run the fuck away and don't turn back," I warned her, leaning back and refilled my glass.

"I have nowhere else to go," she whispered.

Her broken voice and the words she uttered forced me to look back at her and through my hazed eyes I noticed the pain in hers. Lacey was the girl who lit up a room with her smile but, staring at her now, seeing how tortured her eyes were, made me wonder if the smile was a mask. And then Jack's voice worked its way inside my head, reminding me that today was Jack Jr.'s birthday and he went off on a mission to wallow in his own misery.

If Lacey comes around or calls...

"Shit," I mumbled. "Buying her an ice cream cone and pretending the world is a giant playground don't work no more for her."

He smiled proudly. *"Girl's all grown up."*

"Yeah," I whispered.

God or whoever the fuck was responsible, made it real fucking hard for me to ignore Lacey had grown up. He gave her a fucking body that made you want to drop to your knees and worship. Jack would've shot me dead if he knew the thoughts that sometimes ran through my head or the way I couldn't help but look at her.

She was fucking beautiful.

And sweet, so goddamn sweet.

Fucking lethal was what she was.

Wasn't that what I was looking for?

"Your pretty little face doesn't belong here," I grunted, reaching across the bar to tuck a strand of her brown hair behind her ear.

I was jonesing.

Not for drugs, not even alcohol.

I was jonesing for her.

For Lace.

I snapped my hand back, tore my eyes from her as I walked around the bar, taking a seat next to her. She lifted my glass to her lips and took a sip, cringing immediately.

"How do you drink that?" she asked in between coughing, shoving the glass back at me.

"Why the sad eyes?"

"Do you always answer a question with a question?"

"Cut the shit," I clipped, reaching out for her again, this time lifting her chin with my index finger.

Touch.

I wanted to touch her.

I *needed* it.

I shook my head, raging against the need, trying to convince myself that it was the drugs fucking with me. I wanted to believe that deep inside me I was a good guy, that I had morals, maybe not many but enough to know touching her was fucking wrong.

So fucking wrong.

"You know what today is don't you?" she asked, looking away for a moment before she turned back

"Yeah," I muttered, staring at her lower lip as it quivered slightly. "I know. Is that why you're here? Checking in on your old man?"

She lifted her eyes to mine.

"No," she whispered.

"Then tell me why."

She remained quiet as she studied my features. I opened my mouth to speak, but she shook her head, cocking it to the side as she laid her hand on my thigh and leaned close.

"Does it ever go away?" she asked barely audible.

I glanced down at her hand and closed my eyes as it burned a hole in my jeans, lighting my whole body on fire.

Drugs man, they'll fucking ruin you.

Wreck you.

Destroy you.

I shoved her hand away, narrowing my eyes at her.

"What are you doing, Lace?"

"I asked you a question," she said, her hand closing over my wrist. "Does it ever go away? Tell me it goes away Blackie, tell me this isn't it," she whispered, her eyes pleading with mine.

"Does what go away?"

"The pain," she replied, tightening her hold on my wrist as she peered at me. "It doesn't," she said, answering her own question. "Look at you," she added. "The pain never left you. It's written all over your face, it's there, alive in your eyes but the rest of you is dead."

"You in pain, Lace?" I asked hoarsely. "Came here looking for someone to make it go away?" I ground out.

She shook her head.

"I came here, hoping someone, anyone, would see *me*."

"I see you," I said as her hand dropped from mine.

"You see what I allow you to. No one sees the real me," she whispered.

She was going to fucking bury me.

"Show me what you're hiding," I coaxed. "Take off your armor, peel back your mask and let me see you. Otherwise you're going to let that shit tear you down. Pain is a bitch and it'll swallow you whole if you let it."

"Like you did?" she snapped. "You haven't let anyone in, never 'peeled back your armor', you never gave anyone your pain, never gave anyone a chance to take it away from you. You hang onto it like it's an organ you need to survive." She paused, sucking in a deep breath. "We're not that different, Blackie. You and I, Leather and Lace, on the outside we're total opposites but inside, deep down inside, we're the same."

"God, I hope not," I said, twisting in my stool as I stared at her.

I wanted to hang on to the belief that there was still good in this world, still purity and it was there looking back at me.

Then I saw her.

The Lacey she hid behind, the fractured soul that was tortured by the pain no one knew existed in the sweet girl with the pretty smile.

I saw her.

And I wish I hadn't.

She wouldn't just bury me.

She'd own me.

She'd make me wish I had given up the pain.

She'd make me wish I was a better man.

Someone who could take away her pain.

A man fit to rescue her from her demons.

She'd make me wish I wasn't a fucking junkie with a death wish.

She moved off her stool, stood in front of me and took one dangerous step closer toward me and then another, until I felt her breath against my face.

"Don't," I said.

"Look at me," she whispered.

The addict in me surfaced, and I was drawn to her like any other toxic substance, lifting my eyes to hers.

"Do you see me, Blackie?" she asked, taking my face in her hands, her fingertips brushing over the scruff hiding my face.

She leaned closer, her lips just a breath away from mine.

"Say it," she demanded, as she pressed her lips to the corner of my mouth.

I pushed back my stool, the legs dragging across the floor as I stood. Her eyes widened and her lips parted as she took a retreating step, backing herself up against the bar.

Bury me, girl.

Make it end.

I braced one arm on either side of her and gripped the edge of the bar as I caged her in.

"I see you," I said huskily. I was about to add that I wished like hell I didn't when her arms wrapped around my neck and her mouth came crashing down over mine. Her lips were frantic as they worked mine, begging me to respond, to give in to her and give her what she needed.

I lifted my hands to her face, heard her moan against my mouth and then I did the one thing that would secure my place in hell and bring me there soon… I gave into the lethal temptation that was Lace.

I slid my fingers roughly through her hair, tugging at the ends, forcing her to angle her head back and watched her eyes flutter open and look up at me.

Bury me.

Make it end.

I crushed my mouth over hers, my tongue slid out and ran along the seam of her lips demanding entry. She opened for me and the high I was on from the drugs faded away and was replaced by a high induced by her taste. There was nothing sweet and innocent about the way I kissed her, or even how she responded. We kissed like we needed to, like it was our survival and maybe it was for her. But for me kissing her, it was my desperation to ruin myself.

I had finally found a way out of this misery and it was wrapped around me, asking me to take away her pain. I grabbed her hips and lifted her up, her legs wrapped around my waist and her tits against my hard chest, awakening the beast inside of me.

I fucked her mouth, creating a rhythm she easily adapted to as I started for the stairs. Her hands were everywhere, exploring my body over my clothes, before she threaded her fingers through my hair and pulled.

Driven by the need to take her pain, to claim her as mine and secure my hell, I made my way up the stairs, slamming her back against the wall once we reached the landing. I squeezed the back of her neck and kissed her so deep, so fucking hard that she forgot whose air she was fucking breathing.

My hands slid down her throat, over her tits, cupping them in my hands before snaking around and grabbing her ass and bringing her body flush against mine again. I stumbled back, find my balance and carried her down the hallway to my room. I kicked the door open with my boot and stepped inside, balancing her with one arm I swiped my free hand across the desk and set her down on top of it.

I pushed my hair back from my face and stared at her, my dick straining against the denim as my eyes dipped to her chest and watched as it rose and fell with each exasperated breath. She reached out, taking my shirt in her hands and pushed it over my chest. I reached with one arm, behind me and pulled the shirt over my head, letting my messy hair fall back into my face. Her fingers ran down my chest, over each tattoo that marked my skin, stopping to flick the barbell pierced through one of my nipples.

I lifted my hands to the neck line of her shirt and pulled it apart, exposing her lace covered tits. I bent my head and closed my mouth over the lace, dragging the flimsy fabric down with my teeth until I freed one of her nipples.

I took it between my teeth, sucked on it before running my tongue over it, as my hands dragged her pants down. I grazed her nipple one more time before leaning back and removing her pants completely. She was wearing a skimpy thong that barely covered her and when I leaned back to stare at her, really taking her in, she hooked her thumbs beneath the waist band and dragged the underwear down her legs.

She would be my death.

But I'd remember her in the depths of hell.

The innocent girl with the sad eyes that begged me to take her pain away.

I wasn't sure if it was the drugs or my head playing fucking mind games with me but as I walked towards her, unbuttoning my jeans and freeing my throbbing cock, my eyes locked with hers and the pain faded from those dark eyes and was replaced with desire.

I reached for her hips, pulling her to the edge of the desk and positioned myself between her legs. My head spun, my conscience resurrected as I wrapped my hand around my cock and peered at her through the hair that covered my eyes.

What the fuck was I doing?

Committing suicide.

She lifted her hand to my face, brushing my hair away from my eyes and forced me to look at her.

"Leather and Lace," she whispered, covering my hand with her own.

The thread of control I was grasping, finally frayed, and I grabbed her hands, pinning them to her sides as I closed my eyes and drove my dick deep inside of her. She screamed out, her head falling onto my shoulder as she remained perfectly still. I couldn't move either; her fucking pussy was so tight. I turned my head just as she did and saw the tears in her eyes.

Shit.

I removed my hands that kept hers flat against the desk and started to pull out when she lifted her arms around my neck and held me close.

"Don't stop," she pleaded.

I slowly pulled out and more carefully charged back in, repeatedly until I stretched her enough that I could slide in and out without killing us both. She arched her hips, and that was all the encouragement I needed to drive home, still, I restrained from all I wanted to do to her. I could fuck her until the sun rose, every which way, with my mouth, my cock and my fingers.

Never stop fucking her.

Because I was an addict, and I realized, balls deep in the sweetest, tightest pussy, I ever had wrapped around my dick, Lacey was my new drug.

I'd never get enough.

I wanted to stay high on her all the time.

Until I fucking died.

Bury me, girl.

End me.

I lost it. I fucking lost my mind and my control as I gripped her hips and pumped her harder and harder with each stroke until she was gasping for breath and I was coming. I heard the moan escape my lips as her pussy milked every drop from my dick.

I fought for control, for breath, and for clarity. I felt her hands travel up my back to my neck and toy with the ends of my hair.

Clarity came first.

I had just fucked the girl I always tried to protect, to shelter from the darkness and now *I* was her darkness. I crossed a line in my quest to end my pain and took something I had no business having. I told myself I did it because I was searching for the end, the end of my life, the end of the suffering I liked to inflict upon myself. But, this, having her, taking her, it was just the beginning.

I lifted my hands and pulled hers away from me.

Breathe.

I took a deep breath and pulled out of her and looked down at my cock, covered in my release and her blood, her fucking innocence.

I lifted my eyes to her as she stared at my dick before meeting my gaze.

"Blackie," she started.

The control never came.

She didn't have to say the words, the evidence was on me and reflected in her eyes.

"You need to get the fuck out of here," I growled, angry with her for not telling me, livid that I didn't realize it first, disgusted by the realization I polluted the purest thing I had ever known.

"It's okay," she struggled, as I backed away from her and she hopped off the desk. "I wanted that to happen. Blackie, don't do that, don't shut me out," she begged as she reached for me.

"Get dressed," I ordered.

"But—," she argued.

"GET DRESSED!"

I turned my back to her, bending down to pick up my shirt and wipe the evidence of her and me from my cock before pulling up my pants. I didn't turn around and look at her. I heard her sniffle, and shuffle around the room collecting her shit as I walked to my nightstand and grabbed a vile of heroin and a syringe I kept tucked away in my drawer.

I filled the syringe before knotting the band around my arm and searched for a vein.

"Blackie, please look at me," she pleaded.

"I'm done looking at you, Lace," I said stabbing the tip of the needle into my arm before I glanced over my shoulder. "Get out!"

I let the heroin drain from the needle into my veins as the door closed. I pulled the empty syringe from my arm and flicked it onto the nightstand before untying the band and covered my face with my hands, waiting for the numbness to inebriate me.

Leather and Lace.

Opposites.

But the same torture lived inside.

The door opened again, and I lifted my head, prepared to drag her out by her hair if I had to but came face to face with Riggs.

"Get out," I seethed.

"You the reason Lacey just ran out of here crying?" The newly patched Knight questioned me.

"What's it to you?"

I rose to my feet, stumbling as the drugs swarmed my system, and crossed my arms against my chest as I struggled to glare at him.

He stepped closer, his eyes zeroed in on my arms before he lifted them to my face.

"You're using?"

I uncrossed my arms and reached into my back pocket where my gun was tightly secured and brought it around, aiming it at him.

"Get the fuck out of my room, Riggs," I shouted, unlatching the safety.

Bury me.

End me.

Chapter Three

BLACKIE

I prayed for death as I remained hunched over the toilet, ridding myself of the toxins that filled me but death never showed. I didn't miss this feeling, the hopelessness, the regret, the way my body felt as if it was being torn in two. The alcohol never did this maybe because drinking was as natural to me as breathing and I barely got drunk anymore. I pushed through the agony, ignoring the debilitating headache and stood up, flushing the toilet as I gripped the wall and made my way to the shower stall. I didn't bother turning on the hot water letting the ice cold water rain down on me.

I leaned my forehead against the tiles and closed my eyes as the pellets hit my back. Flashes of the needle sticking out of my arm haunted me first, quickly replaced with the prettiest face I ever laid eyes on. Even with the torment reflected in her eyes she still made me forget the shit I was and the man I felt I could be whenever I was with her.

I was addicted to the aura of Lacey as much as I was to any illegal substance. Drugs became a crutch in my life binding me to the demon I had become but one fix of her wiped that shit away. I was different in her presence, not the usual self-destructing asshole. But make no mistake about it, my addiction to Lacey was just as toxic as all the others because she gave me hope.

I didn't deserve hope so I didn't know what the fuck to do with it.

Her innocence was refreshing in a world so full of manipulation, crime and deceit. A world known as the Satan's Knights. The world I chose and the world I worshipped. The same world that destroyed any hope I had of being a better man. She became my light and that light's been shining down on me for years now, since Jack went away to Riker's and I would check in on her from time to time.

At first I did it out of duty but that smile of hers…it became my salvation. I still remember the first time she genuinely smiled at me, one I earned, not one manufactured by the innocent crush she had on me. Jack was doing time, and it was my job as his vice president and his friend to look out for his interests—first on that list was Lacey. I had taken her up to visit her father in Riker's and afterwards we stopped at the Vegas Diner in Brooklyn. She ordered disco fries with extra gravy on the side and when she finished her food she picked off my plate.

There were two old ladies fighting at the table next to us. One lady yelled at the other as she tried to shove everything from the table into her tote bag. I think the only thing she left behind was the menu. It was amusing to watch the klepto ignore the ranting and keep pocketing things until the table was clear. I tore my eyes off the two broads to watch Lacey cover her mouth and mask her laughter. I reached across the table and pulled her hand away from her mouth and stared at her as she smiled.

I wanted more of it.
I wanted to hear her laugh.
I leaned over, stretched my arm across the space that separated the two tables and tapped the klepto on the shoulder. The lady she was with continued to rant and rave about the cold coffee and the fact that the tables were too small.
I grabbed the bread basket off our table and tipped my chin towards her tote bag.
"Open it," I said, watching as she stared back at me with skeptical eyes.
I chucked the bread basket into her tote bag, followed by the ketchup bottle on our table. Lacey giggled, handing me the salt and pepper shakers next.
I turned to her.
"Give it a go," I told her.
Her smile spread wide across her face. The smile I earned and the one I became a fiend for.
She threw the sugar packets into the woman's tote bag.
"What are you doing?" The grumpy woman yelled. "Nina, for crying out loud you're taking their condiments!"
"Oh, Provie, shut up. They offered," the nice one argued.
Lacey leaned back in her chair and the smile that spread across her face became ingrained to my memory.

It was that moment, for purely selfish reasons, I vowed to keep her smiling and make her laugh more often. Because when she smiled at me, when she laughed with me, I felt like fighting instead of quitting, living instead of dying.
Lacey became my hope, and I gravitated to her like an electric current. She made me forget it was me who sold those innocent kids the drugs that ended their young lives. The same drugs Christine ingested when she killed herself. She pulled me into her light reminding me there was still good in the world, still things that were pure and untainted by filth.
Until last night.
I turned the water off, pushing my fingers through my hair and away from my face. The minute I drove my dick into that virgin pussy and tore her to shreds I tainted her. I ruined Lacey, selfishly taking something from her, something a piece of shit like me didn't deserve.
I didn't bother with a towel, and stepped out of the bathroom into the scene of the crime, staring at the desk where I fucked her.
Fucked her.
Her first time.
The fucking blood on my dick was the evidence.
Tainted by filth.
Branded by me.
The deeper I got inside of her, the deeper I drew my mark in her, branding her mine. Not just because I was the only one to have her but because the beast inside me threatened to never let her go.
I was fucked.

I had wanted her and more than wanting her, I wanted to ruin myself. I used Lacey mindlessly, to take away my pain, to secure a way out of this hell—to fuck the sweet little thing that's had my head up in knots for some time now.

I never banked on wanting her to make me feel. Instead of craving numbness, I yearned to feel and not the pain and suffering I was used to but the sweet agony of being inside her. It was ironic that she brought me pleasure, something foreign to me, and I brought her pain, something she came here last night looking to be freed from.

"Blackie, please look at me," she pleaded.

"I'm done looking at you, Lace."

As much as I was fixed on Lacey, I was nobody's hero. I wasn't some guy here to rescue her and take care of her. I was the kind of guy her father put a lot of effort into keeping her away from. I was the devil, and she was a goddamn angel.

I clipped her wings last night, and it was my job to fix that. I'd go talk to her, smooth shit over and tell her I was sorry for being a world class dick. The thought alone made me sick but severing the light she provided me with…that shit was vile.

I was fucked in so many ways and had no one to blame but myself…I wouldn't blame it on the drugs either because I wasn't a pussy like that.

Fucked beyond repair.

A dead man walking.

I grabbed my jeans, pulling them up my legs when my door opened and Wolf strode through.

"Put that shit away," he said, tipping his chin towards my junk.

"Don't you fucking knock?" I growled.

"You wouldn't have answered," he said pointedly, walking around my room and leaned against the desk. The fucking desk of all things, not the fucking dresser or the damn entertainment center…the goddamn desk.

"What do you want?" I said, pulling a T-shirt over my head.

"The Bulldog is AWOL, you know anything about that shit?"

"Yeah and so do you. Man's gone off the radar on the same day, every year, for the last thirteen years," I replied, crossing my arms against my chest.

"But he's always back before the sun comes up," he paused, his eyes pierced mine as he swallowed. "Tensions been rising around here. I'm not fucking blind, Black. I know you and the Prez got something brewing and the rest of us are here holding our dicks while you two figure out what that shit is," he ground out, pushing off the desk and advancing towards me. "I've been around long enough to know when shit gets heavy, he starts to lose his battle with his mind. Someone's gotta reel him back in and that someone's always been you," he added.

"He got himself a woman to do the reeling. In fact, lent her my truck yesterday so she could do just that," I retorted.

"Pussy can't shake the crazy, Black. Go get your fucking wheels back and while you're at it, bring back our leader," he demanded, leveling me with a stare.

I may rank higher than Wolf but he was the heart of our brotherhood, the glue that held us together when it started to wear. As fucking off the wall as he sometimes could be, he was also the guy who kept shit real around here.

The club didn't know about Jimmy, they had no fucking clue he killed Jack's brother or that we were playing the gangster. Jack had wanted to keep the club out of it, said this shit with Jimmy was personal and when the connection between the mobster and the G-Man came to light, I agreed with him. It was fucking personal as retribution and revenge usually are.

My self-destruction and my guilt over Lacey would have to take a backseat to the vow I made to my brotherhood. I was the vice president and it was my duty to be Jack's eyes and ears, his voice when his cracked and his mind when it failed him. Restoring my angel's wings and the light that radiated over her would have to wait.

The devil.

Here I am.

"I'm driving," I muttered.

"Fuck that, I want to live to see the next piece of ass I bang," he replied, twirling his keys around his finger. "You can ride bitch," he said with a grin.

Fucking Wolf.

For a man who cared so much about living to fuck, he drove like a man looking to die. I closed my eyes like a pussy as he blew lights and swerved in and out of traffic. The crazy motherfucker didn't drive a cage much but when he was behind the wheel his ass went fast and furious.

He pulled in front of Jack's house, nodding towards the Bulldog's bike that sat in the driveway and my truck parked behind it.

"At least Blondie kept your truck in one piece," he commented.

I grunted, reaching for the door handle.

"Good luck," he called as I climbed out of the car and slammed the door. I grabbed my balls and climbed the stoop, taking a deep breath as I pounded my knuckles against the door.

I closed my eyes, threw my game face on, because I was about to be the scumbag who looked my brother in the eye, the same friend who created my angel, and pretend like I didn't destroy her.

He pulled the door open and glared at me.

"Now's not a good time," he hissed.

"Too fucking bad, gave you twenty-four hours to wallow in your shit," I said, pushing past him and making my way into the house. The quicker I got a handle on him the quicker I could drag my ass to his ex-wife's house and apologize to Lacey.

My eyes fell on Reina as she tugged her shirt down and looked away.

"See you found your man. Thanks for keeping my car in one piece," I said, noticing the tears that streaked her face and turned to Jack. Looks like I wasn't the only one fucking up women these days. "What the fuck did you do?"

"Mind your fucking business," he barked.

"Oh, for fuck's sake, we don't have time for a lovers fucking quarrel, brother," I seethed. Fucking hearts, they were breaking everywhere.

"Take Reina home," he ordered, ignoring me as he stared at Reina.

"I don't need anyone to take me anywhere," she replied.

For fuck's sake.

"Either he drives you home or I do," he demanded.

"Fine," she hissed, turning toward me. "Give me a minute to grab my things."

I blew out a breath, glancing back and forth between the two of them before nodding curtly.

"Five minutes," I warned as I crossed my arms against my chest.

I watched on as she moved towards the stairs only for him to grab her arm and whisper some shit into her ear. She finally tugged her arm free and disappeared up the stairs leaving me alone with Jack. He stalked through the living room where the walls were long ago marked with holes from his fists punching through the Sheetrock in search of bugs he believed his brother planted when he became a Fed. He never plastered the walls, keeping the reminder of the menace, his mind was and what drove him to insanity the day his son passed away.

He grabbed a pack of Marlboros off the dining room table and walked back into the living room.

"Got a light?" he asked, pushing the cigarette between his lips as he walked past me to the front door.

Fresh air.

Good idea.

I took a seat next to him on the stoop and handed him a lighter in exchange for a cigarette. I studied his profile as he took a pull, searching for all the telltale signs of a breakdown but came up short. He appeared to be battling the war in his heart and not his head. Maybe pussy did shake crazy.

"You want to talk about that?" I questioned, looking over my shoulder.

"What's the point? You probably know more about my actions than I do," he muttered.

There was truth to that and the reason I was his vice president. I knew Jack and I knew his maker and for a long time I've been the one who merges them into one.

"Not talking about your breakdown, talking about your woman," I commented, taking a drag. "I was wrong about her, you know," I offered. I've never worked Jack down from old lady bullshit and was riding blind. Give me the manic shit. I'm all aces with that.

"How's that?"

"Guess you didn't listen to your messages yet," I grunted, remembering the calls I placed to him before the mayhem and after the needle. Funny how his daughter was my mayhem and not the gangster who shot me up. "Gold came by the clubhouse unannounced," I said, shaking my head, dismissing Lacey from my mind before turning and looking him in the eye.

Fucked up.

So fucked up.

"Gotta tell you man, you should probably wife that one," I said seriously, as I blew out a ring of smoke. I actually meant what I was saying to him. I think it would do him some good to have a genuine person in his corner, someone that accepted him as he was and didn't try to change him. Someone who loved him despite his mind. Someone who could learn to love even that part of him.

"She was there when Gold came by?" he asked, sounding irate. "Why the hell was she still there?"

Oh, that's right. This asshole wanted me to take his girlfriend car shopping while he took a trip to crazyville. And me? I fucking agreed to it. I also agreed to make things right with Lacey if she came by.

Fucking idiot.

"What part of *unannounced* didn't you comprehend?" I hissed. "It's fine, Jimmy thinks she's just a club whore."

It was probably best not to tell him I forced her on her knees and made her appear to be giving me head. Wow. Each memory was worse than the last.

"She didn't ask questions, just did as I told her—but she saw some shit," I added, looking out into the street and for the first time I tried to put myself in Jack's shoes. I wondered what ran through his head when he stared at the same street where his son laid as he took his last breath. It made me wonder why the fuck he didn't sell this house and move the fuck away.

But then the answer came to me.

He kept the house for the same reason he left the holes in the walls, to remind him of who he was before he got help and when he's tempted not to take his meds all he has to do is come here…it's all the push he needs to do the right thing.

"What kind of shit?" he asked, pulling me away from his thoughts.

"Gold didn't like I was the man delivering the product, said he didn't trust me. As an act of good faith, he forced me to sample the H," I admitted, running my fingers through my hair. "Wifey saw me with a needle in my arm and didn't run away, she just ran right to you."

I turned over my arm and flicked my skin and the bruise that marked it.

"No sweat, just once, didn't even leave much of a mark," I lied, leaving out the second hit I took after I sent his daughter away crying.

"I'm sorry. I shouldn't have let you deal with that prick by yourself," he responded. "I'm making a mess of things, letting everything with Jimmy get the best of me for months now."

"It'll all be over soon," I said.

"Even so, doesn't make it okay," he replied, cupping my shoulder. "You good?"

I had to look away from him, from the concern and guilt reflected in his eyes.

"I'm good," I replied, clearing my throat. "Be better when these motherfuckers are off the streets." I pulled down the sunglasses, masking my eyes as I turned back to him. "We will get them, right? We're going to make Gold and the G-Man pay aren't we?" I selfishly asked, needing his assurance, deserving nothing.

I needed to know we would end this nightmare. I needed to know G-Man could be stopped and finally pay for all the lives his drugs ruined and robbed. Mine. Christine's. Those kids and all the faceless strangers we fed throughout Cain's leadership.

"Yeah, brother, we are," he swore.

The front door opened and Reina stormed out.

"If you're taking me then let's go…now," she ordered.

Jack and I both stood at the sound of her voice. I started down the stairs as he climbed them and met her at the landing.

"Keys," I called, waiting as she dug into her purse and threw them at me. I gave them a minute to say their goodbyes or whatever the fuck they were doing before Jack turned to me.

"Meet you back at the clubhouse," he said, as I climbed into the truck and gave him a two-finger salute before closing my door. Reina slid into the passenger seat beside me, remaining silent as she stared at Jack through the windshield.

"Where to?" I asked, as I backed out of the driveway and turned onto the street.

"Take me to church," she whispered.

Fucking, hell.

Chapter Four

BLACKIE

I climbed out of my truck, slamming the door behind me as I stared back at the house, wishing I had something to numb me. I knew the minute my eyes locked with hers I'd be reminded of the piece of shit I was. There would be no light that greeted me, no pretty smile to warm me and make me wish for a better way. I turned out Lacey's light and put pain in the pretty eyes of my angel.

I ran my fingers roughly through my hair as I walked up the few steps, wondering what the fuck I would do or say that could make this better. As I made my way toward the door I could hear the muffled sound of music—I paused, trying to make out the song when I noticed the door was slightly ajar. Instantly, I reached behind me, pulling my gun from the waistband of my jeans and aimed it at the door as I toed it open with my boot.

"Lacey?" I called as I stepped into the foyer, the barrel of my gun pointed straight ahead as I kicked the door close behind me and followed the sound of music.

I turned the corner, stepping into the living room and spotted her on the couch. She lifted her eyes to mine, wiping them with the back of her hands.

I lowered my gun as my feet paused mid stride and I took in her face. Her usually flawless skin was blotchy and her eyes were swollen from all the tears she shed. Girl, must've been crying for a while. I can't remember ever seeing her cry and thank Christ for that because looking at her now was tearing me up inside.

I'm not the guy that dries tears and makes things okay. But right now? That's the guy I want to be. I can't fucking help myself when it comes to her. She makes me want to be all the things I'm not.

"I didn't hear the door," she mumbled, tipping her chin to the music playing from the surround sound.

"Door was open," I said, walking closer to her.

Her legs were bare, and she was wearing an over-sized T-shirt, her hair fell in waves around her face, the loose strands fell into her eyes but she didn't seem bothered, or even to notice.

I wish I never touched her.

I should've known once would never be enough.

I tucked my gun into the back of my pants, took a seat on the coffee table in front of her and lifted one of my hands to her face, brushing the hair away from her eyes before I cupped her chin and forced her to look at me.

"Don't cry," I said huskily.

She bit down on her lower lip and looked away so I wouldn't see the tears shining in her eyes.

"I'm fine, Blackie," she insisted. "I don't need a babysitter."

"That's not why I'm here," I rasped, bringing my other hand to her face and cupping her cheeks with my palms as I forced her to turn back to me.

She blinked at me but her eyes were blank.

I tore my gaze away from her as my eyes took another sweep around the room before finding hers again. I knew that look, seen it every time I went on a bender and looked at myself in the mirror afterwards. I shook my head, dismissing the thought. There was no way Lacey would do something like that.

My Lace was too pure for poison.

Not the manufactured kind.

Or the type standing before her, aching to touch her.

Something flickered in her eyes but she remained silent as she stared back at me. I swallowed, forcing the lump lodged in my throat down and pushed the dark thoughts that ran through my head away. I gently caressed her cheeks, noting the contrast in my skin compared to hers. My rough hands, covered in faded ink, slid over her soft, reddened cheeks. She reached up, wrapped her hands around my wrists and shoved my hands away from her.

"Go away," she hissed, inching away from me before she slowly stood up.

My eyes traveled the length of her, taking in the shirt that barely covered her ass and left her long legs exposed, reminding me how they wrapped tightly around me last night.

"You don't want that," I said, tearing my eyes away from her legs as she turned.

"You have no idea what I want," she retorted.

I shoved my hands into my pockets as I stared at her thoughtfully, trying to figure out what was going on inside her head and what the hell had become of my angel. Oh that's right... me.

I did this.

"Tell me what you want," I said, shrugging my shoulders even though I knew I was walking into a ring of fire. I'd give her anything.

Anything.

Just to see her smile.

"I want you to leave. I want you to turn around and walk out that door. I want you to forget about the reasons you came here and more than anything..." she paused, her eyes glanced around the room as she drew in a deep breath before finding their way back to mine.

"What?" I asked as I stood tall, taking a step closer to her. Then another.

Dangerous territory, man.

Fucking lethal.

"I want you to forget whatever you're about to say," she admitted, causing me to freeze mid stride. "Please," she added.

Her pleas from the night before replayed in my head.

Look at me.

Do you see me, Blackie?

I wanted to see her, to know what she was hiding behind the smile she gave the world, the smile she gave me, the one I lived for.

Give me your smile, girl.

She continued to look at me with a tortured expression on her face, eyes like her father's not just in color but in torment. I knew that look better than anyone, had seen it countless times but never in her. I've talked Jack off the edge, dragged him out of his head and silenced his maker but that was Jack.

This was Lace.

My angel.

And I was the reason she looked so conflicted. There was no maker to blame, just me.

Say it.

I see you.

"I see you, Lace," I whispered.

"A lot a good that does me," she said.

I shook my head.

"No good at all," I affirmed as I extended my hand, taking hers and pulling her against me. "You'd be better off if I never laid eyes on you," I added, squeezing her hand before I lifted my free one to her cheek. "Too late," I hissed. "Cause girl, I see you and now I can't fucking forget you," I admitted.

The song changed on her iPod and music filtered through the speakers. I watched recognition spark in her eyes as she turned her attention to the speaker.

"Did you ever hear this song?" she asked softly, her voice blending into the music.

"No," I said, taking a step toward her, bending my knees and bringing us to eye level. I leaned my forehead against hers, taking our joined hands and bringing them behind her to rest against the small of her back.

I didn't know what the fuck I was doing but I couldn't stop.

My lips grazed her temple as she pressed her body against mine, dropping our joined hands to wrap both her arms around my neck.

"Listen to the words," she demanded.

You're saying I'm fragile I try not to be

I search for something only I can't see

"Will you dance with me?" her voice pleaded as she whispered the question.

I learned then that even the toughest motherfuckers had weaknesses and mine was standing in front of me asking me to dance.

I didn't fucking dance.

But now I did.

My feet surrendered my soul, taking the steps to bring me closer to her and give her what she needed. I've been feeding off her light for so long, taking the sweetness of her greedily because I'm addicted to the hope she sparks in me.

Hope that there was a shred of decency buried beneath the leather.

Repay her.

Give her back her wings.

Make it better.

Looking at her now, the selfish reasons that brought me here faded away and were replaced by the need to put her first. To put her before me, to give her back her light and pull her from the sadness that had her crying in solitude.

Just this once I could do the healing and not the reaping.

My hands moved down her back, cupping her ass beneath the t-shirt that barely covered her and I rocked her against my body.

"Blackie," she breathed.

"Lacey," I groaned. "I didn't come here for this," I said, slipping my fingers beneath her lace panties.

"I know why you came here," she said, pulling back a fraction as her gaze dipped to my lips. "But I will do everything I can to change your mind," she promised.

It wouldn't take much.

"Do you remember the first time we started calling each other Leather and Lace?"

Honest to God, I wish I did. I wish I remembered every goddamn thing about me and her, then maybe I'd understand why she even gave me a second glance.

"No," I said.

"It was the first time you took me up to see my dad and the first time I got you to smile," she said as she continued to rest her head on my chest. "You had a chocolate shake waiting for me in the car and I forced you to take a sip," she continued.

I vaguely remembered stopping at Carvel on the way to pick her up. Jack rarely allowed Lacey to be around the clubhouse but the few visits she made he had one of the guys rent an ice cream truck. Wolf would pass out ice cream cones all day and chocolate was her favorite. I improvised with the shake, an attempt to remind her of good memories of her father and not the shit one she was about to make visiting him in jail.

"I was trying to persuade you to have a taste, and in your 'don't fuck with me' tone you called me Lace," she reminded me.

"I see how well my 'don't fuck with me' tone works on you," I muttered as I pinched her ass then squeezed both cheeks again. What I wouldn't give to bend her over and take that sweet cunt from behind.

She deserved better than that.

All the shit you see in the movies.

Things I'm not capable of doing.

"I'm not scared of you," she pulled back, cocking her head to the side as her eyes bore into mine.

For the life of me I couldn't figure out why.

"I never was nor will I ever be afraid of you, Leather," she said, threading her fingers through my hair. "I probably should be and not for the reasons everyone else fears you," she added, pausing a beat before she inched closer.

I need you to love me, I need you today.
Give to me your leather.
Take from me my lace.

"Foolish girl," I whispered.

"Shhh," she said. "Let me hang on just a little more."

But that time I saw you.
I knew with you to light my nights.
Somehow I'd get by.

I didn't say another word, and we both hung on, dancing to the song that seemed written just for us.

Leather.

Lace.

She pulled back slightly, brought her fingertips to my face before she leaned in and pressed her soft lips to mine. The instant her mouth was on mine I remembered the way she felt last night, how her inexperienced body eagerly arched into mine. I cupped her face with my hands, holding her still as my tongue swept across the seam of her lips, prying them apart. I felt her nails dig into the back of my neck as my tongue slid into her mouth tasting all she offered.

I came here to apologize for taking something I didn't deserve. I came here with every intention to make things right with Lacey—being here with her in my arms I realize now that last night wasn't going to disappear. It's always been easy to forget the consequences of my actions and give into temptation.

I broke the kiss to look at her because looking at her was almost as intoxicating as touching her. Her eyes fluttered open, her lips swollen and wet, pursed as she brought her hands from around my neck to rest on my chest.

"I can feel your heart beat," she said, lifting her eyes back to mine. "The only thing that makes me a foolish girl is wishing it'll beat for me one day," she murmured.

What the fuck was I supposed to say to that?

I bit the inside of my cheek and stopped myself from saying all the things she wanted to hear, knowing every promise that left my lips would be a lie.

It's a good dream.

To think this heart inside of me is alive and able to beat for someone else but a dream is all it is. I used to be that guy, the one who keeps a woman, loves her with everything he's got and everything he'll ever be. I had love, cherished it until I destroyed it. It don't matter how much I wish I can resurrect the man I used to be, or how much the girl before me deserves a man like that, that guy is dead and buried and won't rise again.

My phone rang inside my pocket, forcing me out of my head and into the present. I let her go, immediately feeling the loss of her in my arms, and reached into my pocket to pull out my phone.

I stared down at the screen and the name of the man who was calling.

And just like that the dream shattered.

"I've got to go," I hissed, silencing my phone before I shoved it back into my pocket.

She nodded, tucking her hair behind her ears as she took a step back.

"Hey," I said, placing my forefinger under her chin. "No more tears," I added.

She stared at me for a moment before nodding.

"No more tears," she repeated.

"Girl, ain't nobody worth your tears don't you forget that," I lectured. "Nobody," I reiterated.

I should've left it at that but I wrapped an arm around her waist and dragged her body against mine. I bent my head, claiming that mouth of hers one more time, knowing the taste of her would linger on my tongue and drive me crazy.

"Sure as hell not me," I rasped against her lips.

I finally pulled away, turning around and willed myself towards the door. I cursed myself for coming here, for touching her, for walking away from her…for everything.

"Blackie," she called out.

Fucking hell.

My hair fell over my eye as I turned my head and glanced over my shoulder at her.

"Thank you for not taking it back," she said hoarsely.

I narrowed my eyes in confusion, thought about asking her what she meant by that but left it alone, letting us both hang onto the dream of Leather and Lace for a little while longer.

I turned around, walked out the door, closing it behind me before I banged my head against it.

Give me a dire situation, a rival club looking to fuck with my brothers and I'll take every one of them out. Give me a motherfucking gangster and let me bring him to his knees. Give me an addiction, and I'll function. Give me a shitload of grief and I'll push through it. Give me a tombstone with my wife's name and I'll bring flowers every Saturday.

Fuck, give me Jack in the middle of a debilitating breakdown and I'll bring him back.

But don't give me this.

Don't give me Lacey.

Don't make me want to do right by her when all I know is wrong.

Don't give me Lacey when I'll never be able to keep her.

Lacey

Me: One.

My Maker: Too many to count.

Today I won the battle.

I was the one in control.

Not my mind.

Not Blackie.

Just me.

Just my heart.

Have you ever wanted something so badly? Have you ever been one of the lucky ones to get the one thing you want more than anything? It doesn't matter how it comes to you, how it finally becomes yours, all that matters is that it did. You don't get to bask in the glory because someone or something quickly tries to take it from you.

My maker has been taunting me since I left the Satan's Knight's clubhouse, filling my head with all the things Blackie probably came here to say.

He doesn't want you.
He used you to forget.
He doesn't really see you.

He told you what he thought would get him laid.
He didn't know you were an inexperienced virgin.
He'll never look at you the same.
He will say it was a mistake.
He's going to tell you it should've never happened.

But he didn't say any of that.
He danced with me.
He kissed me.
He held me in his arms and looked at me like I mattered.
Like I wasn't a mistake.
Like I was something he wasn't sure of.
Tomorrow it could all fade to dust but today…today I won.
I held on.
To Blackie.
To myself.

Chapter Five

BLACKIE

The bell chimed over the door as I entered the florist across the street from Green-Wood cemetery. The woman behind the counter was in her early seventies and she was taking a phone order. She lifted her head, peering at me over the rim of her glasses and smiled. The shop used to be her husbands but after he passed away their two sons took over but Roseann came in every weekend to help her boys out. She lifted a finger, signaling she'd be just a minute. I nodded, reaching into my pocket grabbing a few bills from the knot of cash I was carrying. I put the money on the counter and leaned my back against it, waiting for her to finish the order.

My phone vibrated inside of my pocket forcing me to pull it out and check the message. It was Jack; I had ignored his calls leaving him no choice but to text me. The message was short and to the point letting me know he was on his way back to the Dog Pound. The Bulldog would have to wait though. I've been coming here every Saturday for years now, since the first weekend after Christine's death and had never missed one. I wouldn't start now.

"Here you go, two dozen pink roses, extra baby's breath," Roseann said from behind me, holding the bouquet.

I turned around and took the flowers from her, leaning over the counter to kiss her cheek.

"Thanks, Ro," I said, pulling back.

She rolled her eyes as if to say there were no thanks required but then she cocked her head to the side and studied me for a moment.

"Wish I could've met her," she said.

"You wouldn't have met her if she was alive," I replied honestly. "Never bought her a flower while she was here, not a single rose."

Roseann remained silent as she frowned. I guess she pegged me as the doting husband and not the shit one I truly was. I slapped my hand against the counter.

"Keep the change," I said. "I'll see you next week."

"Take care, Blackie," she called after me as the bell chimed and I exited the florist. I jumped back into my truck and crossed Fort Hamilton parkway, driving into the tremendous gated cemetery. I parked across the road, turned on my hazards and started up the steep grassy hill. I spotted the prior week's bouquet, the roses had started to wilt and change color.

I reached the tombstone, laying the fresh bouquet at my feet before bending down to remove the cone with the partially dead flowers making her name visible against the stone. My stomach still twists each time I see *Christine Petra* carved into a tombstone. It's the reason I buy two dozen roses and not one. It's the reason Roseann adds extra white shit to the bouquet because the minute I stick the fresh flowers into the cone, her name becomes obscure. I changed the water, tossed the dead flowers into the trash can and replaced the cone with the new bouquet, blocking her name from my view.

"Hey babe," I said, rising to my feet, brushing the dirt from my knees. "I don't have much time today but I didn't want to miss a Saturday," I explained. "I never ask much of you, figure I've taken enough from you but I need a favor and I don't know who else to turn to."

I took a deep breath, pushing the hair out of my eyes as I stared at the roses. I don't even know if she liked pink roses. I should probably switch it up, maybe next week I'll get red... or purple, purple roses are different. They stand out, just like she always did.

"I fucked up," I said, mindlessly. "But that's no surprise especially not for you. It's different this time, this time I didn't just fuck with my life but with someone else's too. Someone I never wanted to hurt, someone who doesn't deserve the pain I inflict...someone as pure as you were when I met you. I don't know what the fuck it is with me. How a guy like me gravitates toward the innocent ones but I fucking find all of you," I hissed.

"I've never forgiven myself for taking something so perfect and destroying it, breaking it down until there was nothing left...I've never forgiven myself for what happened to you. It used to be your smile I was addicted too. It used to be your light that got me by. It used to be you."

I shook my head. "And now it's her. It's her smile that makes me forget what I did to you. It's her light that makes me want to crawl out of the darkness I binge on trying to torture myself until I pay for my sins. You and I both know how this ends though. I'll take and take until there is nothing left. I'll break her like I broke you. But as similar as the two of you are, you are different. She's young, hasn't experienced much and doesn't know how fucked the world really is. She'll break easier than you did. She'll hurt more than you did."

I paused, swiping my hands down my face as I ignored the vibration in my pocket signaling I had another text.

"The thing is, I went to her today to end things, to apologize for what I did, for what I took and to smooth things over. I don't want her out of my life but I need her to understand nothing can come from us because of what I am and who she is. I didn't get to do that and now I've got this fucking urge burning inside of me to be better for her. So, that favor? You've been leaving me, fading away from me, you hardly visit me anymore and I can't have that. I need you there, in my face, reminding me I'm not a man who can be fixed, that I'm a man who only knows destruction. I know I've got no right to ask a goddamn thing of you but please... please, find your way back if not for me, then for her. Do it for her. Don't let me destroy another woman," I pleaded with the slab of stone. "She's young babe. She's sweet as hell, not a bad bone in her body, a good girl with her whole life ahead of her," I continued to plead Lacey's case to my dead wife. "I need you back in my head. I need you in my dreams. I need you to remind me I can't have her. I need to save her from me."

I took a step closer and laid my left hand on top of the stone.

"I've got to head out but I'll keep coming for you, babe. Week after week, bouquet after bouquet, until I'm gone."

I wasn't naïve enough to say until we meet again because I'm sure wherever I wind up once I'm dead, Christine won't be there to greet me. No, we had our time and as short as it was, when it was good it was real good but, when it was bad it was fucking bad. She was at peace now, away from me, away from the bad shit. She was in a good place. Not somewhere I'd end up going.

I turned around, descended the hill and climbed into my truck. It didn't start right away, in fact, it didn't start up when I left Lacey either. Finally, it purred to life, the engine sounded a little louder than usual but whatever, I'd have Pipe have a look at it. Fucking cage. Give me my Harley and the road any day.

I hauled ass to the compound before Jack's panties got any more in a twist than they already were. He was worse than a woman, calling me off the hook...so fucking needy.

I turned into the compound, spotting Jack standing with Anthony Bianci and who I think is his mother-in-law and immediately rolled my eyes. Every time Bianci showed his face he delivered another blow. I couldn't wait to find out what fucking mess him or his retired gangster father-in-law got themselves into this time. Or maybe it had something to do with that motherfucker that forced me to sample the heroin. I couldn't wait to put that prick in the ground.

I parked my truck in its usual spot, happy to trade four wheels for two and climbed out, hitting the alarm as I started for the clubhouse. I kept my eyes trained on Jack as he brought his cellphone to his ear. I saw something flicker in his eyes as he turned to Bianci, confirming my suspicion that something was definitely up with the mob.

Bianci turned around, eyes frantically moving around the perimeter of the lot before setting them on me.

What the fuck?

Then it happened.

A deafening sound erupted from behind me, I turned to see what the fuck had just blown up and I was knocked flat on my back from the impact of the blast. I struggled to lift my head and spotted my truck hidden behind a cloud of black smoke and smothered in flames.

I sat there for a moment watching as my truck burned to ash before I got to my feet, turning around I stalked toward the clubhouse and the men that stood there, staring in shock. Riggs stepped forward, patting me on the back sympathetically as he shook his head.

"Well, fuck, that blows," he said. "Literally, like your car just blew the fuck up."

Fucking Riggs.

"Yeah, I caught that, thanks for pointing it out though," I growled, turning my cold stare toward Jack. "Get him the fuck away from me," I hissed, brushing the soot off my shoulders.

Jack turned to Bianci.

"Is this what I owe your visit to?"

Anthony bit the inside of his cheek before turning his attention to Grace Pastore who took that as her cue to step around, bringing her and the Bulldog face to face.

"The last time I visited with Victor he told me if there was any sort of danger, or I felt threatened that I should come here and see you. Now, I don't know what kind of deal you and my husband have but when I told him what I overheard today he told me to get my ass here as fast as possible," she said with a flustered sigh.

"I went to the café this morning like Victor instructed me to, he wanted me to bring Jimmy our financials, papers and what have you regarding our home. Jimmy didn't know I was there waiting for him, and I overheard him talking to one of his guys. He was going on and on about making you and your club pay for double crossing him. He said you would be his puppet, and he'd teach Vic a lesson once and for all, showing him who, and I quote 'is the fucking boss,'" she said, before nodding toward the front door of the clubhouse. "Seems like the puppet master is ready to make moves."

I grabbed Jack's cigarette out of his mouth and took a fucking drag because…my fucking truck just blew up and these assholes were making small talk about puppets and gangsters.

He looked at me before turning to Anthony.

"Any idea how he'd know what we had planned for him?"

"No fucking idea," he said, shaking his head. "We can't get in touch with Vic either. She's sent emails but no response. Might be in the hole."

Of course he was. Fucking gangsters.

"Fine time for him to get locked in solitary," Jack mumbled, turning to Grace. "Thanks for coming and clueing me in."

Oh, so we're going to have a heart to heart right now? My fucking truck was dust but let's make nice with Vic's old lady.

Fuck this.

I brushed past them, making my way inside the clubhouse and headed straight toward the bar, grabbing a bottle of whiskey from the shelf I guzzled that shit down. The door opened and Jack, Grace and Bianci filed through, going back and forth about Jimmy, Vic, summoning their inner Sherlock.

"And he hasn't knocked on your door?" Jack questioned.

Anthony shook his head, crossing his arms against his chest. "I don't think he knows shit, I think he surmises something and maybe he knew Grace was listening and wanted to see if she'd run here. That's why I took her, in case she was being followed," he explained.

I couldn't fucking listen to these idiots anymore.

"He blew up my fucking car, the bastard knows something is up," I shouted. "And it's not the drugs because that shit was pure," I added disgustedly.

I could vouch for the drugs. That was the purest heroin my veins ever fed off.

The door opened to the compound and Pipe and Wolf strode in.

"The fire is being contained. I called it into our friends over at the N.Y.P.D. and Jones is sending a blue and white over so it looks legit on paper," Pipe announced. He was good like that, providing a cover when things went south for the club. And it was a good thing too because on top of everything else we didn't need the fucking bomb squad sniffing around our shit.

"Your truck is toast, man," Wolf said, narrowing his eyes at me. "And you almost were too, so who's going to clue the rest of us in on what the fuck is going on here?" he asked as he pinned Jack with a scrutinizing stare.

Pipe glared at Bianci. "This got some shit to do with Pastore?"

I saw Jack's eyes darken and took it as a sign he was wallowing in his own shit. Now, wouldn't be the time to tell him told you so, but fuck, I warned him this shit would land on the Satan's Knights doorstep. Albeit I didn't bank on my truck being the first casualty. But he wanted to keep this shit on the low and now the club was staring at him like he was betraying them.

Jack turned to Pipe and Wolf, opened his mouth to explain but then he paused, spinning around and pierced me with a look.

"When you left my house this morning where did you go?" he asked with his jaw clenched and his fists tightly wound at his sides.

Was he fucking kidding me right now?

I took another swig from the bottle before stepping around the bar and crossing my arms against my chest and leveled him with a stare.

"I dropped your woman off at the church around the block from her house like a good little gopher," I growled.

"His woman?" Pipe asked, incredulously. "What the fuck is going on?"

"And after that?" Jack coaxed.

Lacey's face flashed in front of my eyes and for a split second I could still feel her in my arms, swaying as she leaned her head against my chest. I could still taste her and smell her shampoo as I pressed my nose into her hair.

"Where did you go?" he demanded, his voice growing louder, more impatient.

"Nowhere," I lied, watching as he tried to read me. Poor bastard probably thought I was high, drunk even. You see, I could read Jack, get inside his head before he even knew he was on the verge of a breakdown but that shit worked both ways.

Sometimes.

Jack could read me when I was high, when I was drunk, my eyes gave away my pain, they gave away the torment but no one knew what to make of me when I was straight because I rarely ever was. But now? I was straight as a pin, aside, from the hangover and the two shots of whiskey I just downed.

Go on and try Bulldog.

You won't get me this time.

I promise.

I turned my head, keeping the secret of where I was and who I was with to myself.

"I came here afterwards," I said, shoving my hands in my pockets before turning back to him. "What the fuck does that matter, anyway?"

"Because you had Reina in the fucking car with you and just like you could've been killed, she could've been too," he shouted. "Now one more time, did you go anywhere after you dropped her off?"

"You really want to go there? Because she took my fucking car and went to your house last night so who's to say your girl didn't plant the motherfucking bomb or set it up so whoever planted it had a chance to?" I hollered.

Deflect, man.

Turn the fucking tables.

"Whoa, hold up," Bianci intervened. "What if that was the plan?" he questioned, narrowing his eyes as he worked the scenario in his head before he diverted his gaze back to mine. "Reina took Blackie's car, went to your house?" Jack nodded in agreement. "Jimmy have any idea Reina exists in your life?"

Jack turned his attention back toward me.

"What happened when he came here yesterday?"

"I made her drop to her fucking knees and pretend to give me head," I seethed, shrugging my shoulders as if it was no big fucking deal.

"Mother of God," Grace exclaimed, closing her eyes in disgust.

Right lady, because your mob boss husband was a saint. He probably had three side pieces she didn't even know about.

I rolled my eyes and looked back at Jack. "Made it so Jimmy thought she was just a piece of pussy nobody cared about then I dismissed her."

"What if he wants you to think she's the one setting you up?" Bianci asked.

"We could sit here and play the guessing game all day long but until that motherfucker makes another move all we're doing is running in circles," I ground out.

A gunshot fired, smoke puffed from the barrel of the gun Wolf pointed it toward the ceiling. "About out of patience, Prez, so you might want to start fucking talking to the rest of us," he said, eerily calm.

The jig was up. The club wanted answers. I didn't blame them.

"I'll give you your answers," Jack bit out. "But right now I'm putting this club on lockdown," he declared, glancing around the room. "Go get your families, anyone you give a damn about and bring them here," he ordered, turning to Bianci. "That includes you, go get your wife and son," pointing toward Grace he continued, "And get her other daughter too," he instructed before turning back to us. "I repeat—anyone you give a damn about."

I watched as he grabbed his helmet off the bar and started for the door. "Church in an hour," he called over his shoulder.

"Where are you going?" I called as he opened the door and I followed him before he even uttered his answer.

"To get Reina and Lacey," he replied.

"You go get Reina, I'll get Lacey," I countered, falling into step beside him.

He raised an eyebrow, questioning me and I forced out a sigh in response.

"We going to sit here and argue about this or we going to get the women in your life to safety? Because I tell you brother, something happens to either of them on your watch, you ain't going to be able to deal with that. Trust me, that shit will be the death of you," I said.

And fuck, I wasn't going to sit back and let anything happen to Lace.

I slipped my arms into my cut, checked to see if my gun was loaded before shoving it into the back of my jeans. My eyes met Jack's, and I swallowed roughly.

"I got your girl," I assured him.

I got my Lace.

I didn't wait for him to agree or disagree. I would get her to safety, and no one would stand in my way.

Not Jimmy Gold.

Not even Jack Parrish.

"Thank you," he said as we straddled our bikes, revved our engines, and kicked our bikes into gear.

No thanks necessary.

I might not be able to save her from myself but I damn well could go on protecting her like I always did.

Like she was my Lace.

Chapter Six

Lacey

"Lacey! Blackie is here," my mother called as I finished applying my lipstick, giving myself a final once over in the mirror. My eyes were heavily lined with black liner and I had three coats of mascara on, making my dark eyes look bigger and almost black.

Very dramatic for a fifteen-year-old.

Just the look I was going for.

I stared back at the image reflected in the mirror, a smug smile formed across my mouth. Fifteen, my ass. With all this make-up I could easily pass for twenty, hell, I'd take eighteen, barely legal but still of age.

"Lacey!"

"I'm coming!"

I rolled my eyes, smacked my lips together before shrugging on the vintage leather jacket. My dad was serving time for a weapons charge. I didn't get to visit all that often, this would be my first visit. If it was up to my mom I wouldn't see him until he was released but where there is a will, there's a way. I found the jacket in the attic on a hunt to find our old family photo albums. It was hers, from a million years ago, well, not really a million, more like fifteen. It was one of the few things left from a time when Connie and Jack were a couple when my mother was Property of Parrish.

It worked for my mom.

She snatched the president.

I ran my fingers over the leather, turning around in the mirror to check how I looked, noting it fit like a glove, like it was made for me.

Like mother, like daughter.

Here's to hoping the jacket had the same effect for me and aided in nabbing the vice president of the Satan's Knights...Dominic "Blackie" Petra.

I've had a crush on Blackie since I was just a child. At ten years old I both fell in love for the first time and had my heart broken all by Blackie. He smiled at me and I knew love at first sight existed. Then he married his high school sweetheart and broke my heart.

I like to think I got over Blackie and grew up since then. I mean after all I'm fifteen years old now. I wasn't some kid with a crush and Blackie wasn't the same person I fell in love with at ten years old. He's sad all the time. He never smiles anymore. Not that I blame him. Blackie's wife Christine, overdosed and died. I'm not supposed to know that, but I overheard my mom and dad talking about it. He blames himself for her death and it's the reason he doesn't smile anymore.

Not for me or for anyone.

He used to have a killer smile. It was his smile that hooked me. Boys my age didn't smile the way Blackie did. He smiled confidently at me while boys my age smiled nervously, like they had no idea what to do around a girl.

Blackie knew.

I ran down the stairs and nearly collided with my mom. So much for trying to slip out of the house without her noticing the 'new' me.

"What are you wearing?"

"I found it in the attic and it fit," I said, shrugging my shoulders as I dropped a kiss on her cheek. "I've got to go, we're late."

"Lacey, wipe that shit off your face before you see your father," she warned.

"It's just make-up," I argued. "I'm fifteen years old, most girls my age have already dyed their hair six times by now." I left out that nearly all my friends dyed their hair and lost their virginity in the same week. "Love you," I called as I hurried out the front door as any typical teenager would do, leaving her mother in the dust behind her to chase after the guy of her dreams.

She was my age once.

She gets it.

Blackie was leaning against his truck smoking a cigarette when he lifted his head and his eyes met mine, causing me to stop in my tracks and stare at him. Dressed all in black, like always, black loose fitting jeans that hung low on his waist, a black t-shirt that stretched across his shoulders and chest and his leather jacket that hid all the tattoos that decorated his muscular arms. He hadn't shaved, scruff lined his jaw, making him look even more lethal than usual. He had hazel eyes, and they varied in color, sometimes they were brown and at others they were green. I couldn't help but wonder what caused the change, what made them one color one day and another the next. He had grown his hair out and wore it slicked back, the ends curling at the base of his neck.

For the first time I felt intimidated by him, like he was completely out of my reach, like I was just a fifteen-year-old girl with a crush on an older guy.

And like any teenage girl I wanted what I couldn't have.

"Get in, I got you your favorite," he said, pushing off the truck and walking around to the driver's seat.

"My favorite?" I asked as I climbed into the passenger seat, immediately spotting the large white Styrofoam cup sitting in the cup holder of the console.

"Chocolate milk shake," he declared, handing me a straw as he turned the key in the ignition. I was allowed at the Satan's Knights clubhouse a handful of times, special occasions, like bring your daughter to work day, that was fun, and Pipe's wedding to some foreigner that didn't even know how to say 'I do'. But each time my dad always had an ice cream truck parked on the lot and Wolf always handed me a chocolate milkshake or some days an ice cream cone.

Chocolate milkshakes.

One of the good memories of my childhood.

One of the few.

Still, to this day a chocolate milkshake will always make me smile.

I took a sip of the chocolaty goodness as Blackie started up the truck and peeled away from the curb. I glanced at him from the corner of my eye as my teeth clamped down on the straw and I smiled mischievously before pulling the straw from between my teeth and extending the cup toward him.

"Take a sip," I ordered.

"No," he replied, keeping his eyes straight ahead, but I didn't miss the slight arch of his eyebrow.

"No? Who says no to chocolate?" I asked incredulously, treating him to a dramatic roll of my eyes. "Take a sip," I demanded.

"Lace," he warned, taking a hand off the steering wheel to reach behind him and cup the back of his neck, the leather of his jacket stretching across his biceps, threatening to rip at the seams.

"Lace? Oh we're doing the nickname thing?" I cocked my head to the side as I continued to hold the milkshake out for him. "Fine. C'mon Leather, live dangerously," I coaxed.

"Leather?" he questioned, briefly turning to look at me.

"Leather and Lace. You and me," I smiled as I shrugged my shoulders before reaching out with my free hand and touching the leather that covered his arm. "Now, take a sip of the shake, you big brute and maybe, just maybe you'll crack a smile."

He rolled the truck to a stop and for a split second my smile faltered and I dropped the hand that was still touching his arm. I looked ahead to see the red traffic light in front of us, realizing that was why he stopped and sighed in relief, reclaiming my bravado.

"Used to be able buy you ice cream and you would shut up for a while," he grunted, taking the shake from my hand. "What happened to the little Lacey Parrish you could bribe with ice cream and candy?" he muttered as he brought the straw to his lips and took a gulp.

I grinned widely, watching his throat as he swallowed before he shoved the cup back at me.

"She grew up," I said, taking back the shake.

"Hardly," he commented, turning his eyes back to the road. I ignored that comment and relished in the slightest quirk of his lips.

Leather and Lace.

That was us.

I felt someone's hands on my shoulders, shaking me as a familiar voice called my name, interrupting my dream and disrupting my sleep. My eyes fluttered open and locked with the same hazel eyes that starred in my dream.

"Get up," he demanded, pulling my arms, forcing me to sit up.

"What?" I asked groggily, lifting my hands to my head that felt as if it was about to explode. "You came back..."

"Lace, get up and get dressed," he ordered. "Now!"

I stared up at him as bits and pieces of my memory flashed before me. I remembered wishing he wouldn't show up but knowing it was inevitable. I remembered battling with my maker for control. I remembered the thoughts that filled my head and most of all I remember Blackie. I remembered him holding me. He didn't turn me away and when I asked him to dance with me, he did. He left but I could tell he didn't want to, that, it pained him to walk away.

I was exhausted from the war within my head and succumbed to sleep easily, falling into a sweet dream of when things changed for us. Well, for me anyway. I like to think after that car ride to Riker's Blackie began to see me as more than just Jack's nuisance of a daughter. Still, it wasn't until last night when I felt he really saw me, the woman not the girl, the damaged soul and not the happy-go-lucky person I portray myself as to the world.

"Lace, I need you to listen. There's not a lot of time so you need to snap the fuck out of it and throw some clothes on," he ordered, glancing around the room, picking up a pair of my mother's sweats folded in the laundry basket at the foot of her bed. "Here, put these on," he ordered.

"What's going on?" I questioned as I threw my legs over the bed and studied the hard lines of his face and for the first time I noticed the gun he was holding. I stared at the gun for a moment before lifting my eyes to his.

"Did something happen? Blackie you need to tell me! Is it my father? Did he ever show up after yesterday?" I rambled, hurrying to my feet despite the headache I was experiencing. I still hadn't heard from my father, for all I know he succeeded in joining Jack Jr. on the other side. I felt the fresh tears sting my eyes, and I lurched for Blackie, grabbing his cut with my hands.

"Answer me goddamn it! Is he okay?" I heard my gasp immediately follow the question as he dropped his free hand to my hip, his fingers gripping me through the thin fabric of the t-shirt I was wearing. How was it that just a simple touch of his hand provoked feelings throughout my entire body? "Oh God," I said, glancing down at the gun he held in his other hand. "He found out. He knows about us. Is that it? That's why you came back," I reached up, covering my mouth with the palm of my hand as nausea washed over me.

"For fuck's sake," he growled, lifting his shirt and tucking the gun into his jeans, freeing his other hand. He took my face in his hands and bent down so our eyes were level.

"Get yourself together," he demanded.

"Blackie, I don't care— "

"He don't know shit," he seethed. "Club is on lockdown which means your sweet ass needs to get to the clubhouse. Now, pull yourself together Lace, and let me do my goddamn job," he hissed.

I stared at him quietly for a second.

"You with me, Angel?" he asked calmer, his voice more concerned than agitated.

I opened my mouth to answer, but the words became lost on my tongue when we heard a loud noise from somewhere downstairs.

"Shit," he said, dropping his hands from my face, reaching for his gun before his long legs swallowed up the floor space and he made his way to the window. I watched as he peered out of the mini-blinds.

Everything about his demeanor changed and I knew that was my cue to haul ass. I grabbed the sweats and shimmied them up my legs as he cocked his gun, pulling back the safety he crossed the room and listened at the door. I tip toed across the room to where he was standing and he turned around, piercing me with a look.

He closed the distance between us and bent his head so that his lips were just a breath away from mine.

"I want you to listen carefully, Lace. Can you do that for me?"

"Don't talk to me like a child," I whispered angrily.

"Quit acting like one then and pay attention," he snarled, grabbing my hand and dropping his gun into my palm. "Take my gun and hide in the closet. Do not come out until it's quiet," he instructed, his cold stare penetrated through me.

"What? No! What about you?" I fired at him.

"Lace, now!" He demanded, pushing my shoulders toward the closet. I shook him off, spinning around on my heel so we were face to face.

"Blackie— "

My words died as his mouth covered mine and his hands fell to my shoulders. My lips worked frantically to keep up with his pace as she expertly worked them until they parted. His tongue slid into my mouth as he walked me backwards until my back hit the wall. I moved to wrap my arms around his neck and deepen the kiss but his mouth abruptly left mine. He pushed me into the closet.

"If anyone fucks with you, shoot them. Don't fucking think just shoot," he demanded.

"I can't do that," I cried, my hands trembling as I gripped the gun and stared into his eyes. They were changing color as we spoke, turning a fascinating shade of green, I had never seen before.

"You can and you will," he said, crouching down before me. "You do whatever it is to save yourself because when this shit is over I'll be waiting to see that smile of yours," he whispered, reaching out to run his fingertips down my cheek. "Need that smile in my life, Lace… need it like air," he ground out.

I cried or maybe I whimpered, reaching for him but he was quick on his feet. He lifted his finger to his lips, silencing me before he treated me to a wink.

"Thanks for the kiss," he added, before he closed the closet door and left me in the darkness.

I covered my mouth with one hand and held the gun close to my chest with the other. I didn't know what was happening, but I knew the unfamiliar voices were enemies of my father, of Blackie's—everything my father tried to shield me from was right on the other side of the door.

"Where is she?" An unfamiliar voice shouted.

"Where is who?" Blackie responded calmly.

"The daughter!"

"How the fuck should I know. She wasn't here when I got here," he said.

"What are you doing here?"

"What the fuck is it to you?" Blackie growled.

"Don't play games with me Petra. I asked you a fucking question."

"You know I'm getting sick and tired of you all up in my business, Gold," Blackie sneered. "First you walk in on me getting head and now you charge in here when I'm looking for Connie," he added.

I knew in that instance why my father shielded me from his world. It was ugly and unapologetic.

"Connie. That's Jack's wife."

"Ex-wife," Blackie corrected.

"You have a thing going on with Jack's ex-wife?"

"What? You going to sit there and tell me you haven't thought about banging Grace Pastore from time to time? I saw Vic's old lady, man, she's quite the piece of ass, even at her age. Tell me, how many times have you tapped that shit?"

There was silence.
So very ugly.
So very unapologetic.
"Come on Gold, tell me. Oh, you poor bastard you never got a taste did you?" Blackie continued.
"Shut him, up!" The other voice roared.
"Come on, man…" Blackie started.
"You're going to understand something Blackie. You and your club aren't calling the shots anymore. It's time to teach Jack Parrish who the fuck the boss is, and it's time for you to become my puppet,"
"Not the needle. No more drugs, man,"
"But this is what you want. This is what you know. You said so yourself," the man taunted.
I heard Blackie groan and my heart shattered into a million tiny pieces. I closed my eyes and pictured his face, the pain that was always so evident in his features, and the tears escaped from the corners of my eyes.
"That's it, all done," the cryptic voice said.
Silence.
Then a thump.
My body shook as I envisioned the scene beyond the door.
"Grab him and let's go," the man ordered.
I heard Blackie moan one last time before I heard nothing at all.
I opened my mouth to scream but nothing came out.

He's gone.
You lost him before you ever had him.
He will finally go to the one he wants.
The one he loves.
The one he misses.
Christine.
You'll never have him.
Hang on to the smile.
Hold tight the kiss.
It's all you will get.

"Shut up," I begged, dropping the gun on the floor and lifting my hands to my ears. "Shut up," I repeated over and over again as my maker teased and tormented me.

He only came here because your father sent him.
He sacrificed himself because he wants to be reunited with her.
You're nothing to him.
He doesn't care.
Stupid, stupid girl.

I opened my eyes and glanced down at the gun as my mind continued to race, speaking all the cruel things *my maker* told it to.

He gave you his gun.
You should've helped him.
You should've opened the door and shot the man before he could hurt him.
But you didn't.
You did nothing.
Just like you did nothing to help Jack Jr.

I lifted the gun from the floor, my hand trembled as it wrapped around the trigger. Tears cascaded down my face as I cried for my brother, for Blackie and for the two people I sat back and didn't protect. I lifted the gun to my temple.

If anyone fucks with you, shoot them. Don't fucking think, just shoot them.

"Lacey!" Someone shouted in the distance.

I ignored my name being called, closed my eyes, and allowed the memory to drive my courage to pull the trigger.

"No, no, no," my dad cried. "Lacey, call 911!"
I remained perfectly still, watching as my dad held my brother's lifeless body in his arms. Blood poured from the back of his head, staining my father's jeans as he rocked him softly and screamed up at the sky for help.

"Lacey? Baby is that you? Where are you?" My father's frantic voice shouted, pulling me away from my memory, away from my demented head. He already watched one child die. This was my chance to do something for someone I loved. This was my chance to save him and spare him the mess of my death. I lowered the gun to my side and kicked the door over and over again until it flew open.

I wailed, charging out of the closet, tripping over my own feet as I tried my hardest to get to my father. He turned around as I ran from the master bedroom and into his arms.

I was out of control, out of my mind, hanging on by a thread.

"It's okay, daddy's here," he said, soothingly. "I won't let anything happen to you," he promised.

Blackie.

I pulled back, trying to gain control, sobbing hysterically as I rambled.

"They took him. He was here and I wouldn't listen to him...I told him to leave...that I didn't want to see him but then they broke into the house. They took him," I shouted, mixing the events from earlier when he came and with the visit that just transpired when he handed me the gun. The gun I was poking into my father's chest.

I glanced down at the gun, spreading my fingers wide and allowed it to drop from my hand.

My dad's eyes remained on me as he kneeled down and retrieved the gun.

"Slow down," he coaxed, lifting the gun. "Blackie gave you this?"

"Yes," I said through my sobs. "He gave me the gun and told me to go hide in the closet." I dropped my head into my hands, groaning as I relived the horrific sounds of Blackie signing over his life to some faceless monster. "I heard him tell them no, I heard him beg them not to put the needle in his arm and then I heard nothing." I dropped my hands from my face and stared at my father. I wanted him to tell me it was okay that Blackie would be okay and that he would make things right. But staring at him, seeing the look of defeat, the same look he had as he held my brother's body, I realized this was just another day in the life of Jack Parrish. He was used to the turmoil, the violence and, the death. This all came as naturally as breathing did.

    I stared back into my dad's eyes.
    Dark.
    Unapologetic.
    This was the life of the Satan's Knights.
    Welcome.

Chapter Seven

BLACKIE

"I Christine, take you, Dominic, to be my husband, to have and to hold from this day forward, for better, for worse, for richer, for poorer, in sickness and health, until death do us part," she vowed, her eyes shining back at me as she smiled.

I couldn't stop staring at her. She always looked beautiful whether she was wearing sweats or nothing but my cut, but put a wedding dress on her and she was the most gorgeous girl I ever laid eyes on. And me? I was the lucky bastard who got to marry her.

"I Dominic, take you, Christine, to be my wife, to have and to hold from this day forward, for better, for worse, for richer, for poorer, in sickness and health, until death do us part," I said, glancing at priest. "Can I kiss her now?"

The best day of my life.

A new beginning.

The beginning of the end.

You wanted me to visit you, but I've never really left you, have I? How could I when you won't let me...

I heard her voice but couldn't see her. I needed to see her. I needed to look into her eyes just one more time so I could memorize all the features fading from my memory. I heard muffled voices, a man and a woman bickering, then I felt the sting on my cheek. I knew that burning sensation— someone was fucking with me, laying their hands on me.

Christine's voice sounded in my head.

Open your eyes.

"Isn't that right? Tell her how you're a pussy who can't bring himself to take his own life," the man said. "Tell her," he shouted.

I matched the voice with the face and forced my eyes open. I could barely hold my head up as I tried to focus my eyes on him.

"I'll tell you whose life I'm going to take," I slurred.

Fight!

It was like we were sixteen year olds and I was fighting some punk ass kids in the school yard, while she stood behind the gate, shouting at me to fight.

I tried to grin but I couldn't feel my face. Still, I kept my eyes on Jimmy Gold as I promised to kill him.

"Yours," I promised.

And I would kill him. I'd fucking make it my life's mission to make this motherfucker suffer.

"Feeling bold are you? Maybe we should fix that," Jimmy crooned.

Fuck you.

I closed my eyes to stop the room from spinning and I heard Christine's voice calling out for me.

Blackie, I want you to listen. For once in your life please listen to me.
Where was she? Why couldn't I see her? I need to see her.
Just one more time.

Her voice faded, leaving me in silence until I heard Jimmy shout. I was torn in two, one half of me willing to succumb to the oblivion the drugs provided, the drugs he injected into me. The other half struggled against the poison, reminding me I had a duty to my club and to Jack. I needed to fight.

Fight.
No one fights harder than you.

For what? What am I fighting for if you aren't here?

Her. The girl you're trying so hard not to fight for. The girl you won't let in but the one that can make you better. Fight for her.

My eyes opened wide as Jimmy reared his hand back and slapped Reina across the face.
Stupid prick.
"YOU SPEAK TO ME WITH RESPECT," he yelled.
"He will kill you," I slurred, fighting with whatever strength I had left to keep my eyes trained on him. "Joke's on you, Jimmy," I managed.
That's it, stay in the game. Keep fighting.
"What're you talking about?" Jimmy laughed.
"She's not some whore we take chance a piece on," I said, licking my dry lips as I tried to form a grin. "You just laid a hand on the president's old lady."
"What's he saying?" he asked Reina. She turned her head toward me and I closed my eyes, working up the strength to give her a nod.
"He's saying you're fucked," she said. Then she called him a pussy and so help me God if I wasn't half dead I would've laughed.
"In case you haven't realized you're tied up at my mercy, the only one who is fucked is you," Jimmy sneered. I guess she insulted the motherfucker. "Well, maybe not quite yet but we can fix that," he continued, before snapping his fingers. "And I know just the person to give you one last fuck," he said, turning around and smiling as his eyes met mine. "It's brilliant!"
I lifted my head as he stalked towards me, kneeling in front of me before he cupped my chin and forced me to look him in the eye.
"You want to play me, try to fool me? I'm no one's fool. What was it you said? That you were just having a go at her before Jack came and finished her off? Yes, I believe that was it," he said proudly. "Going to make your lies become your truth," he warned. "And that's how we're going to deliver my demands to Mr. Parrish," he released my face and turned to his henchmen. "Let's go boys, need to set the mood!"
I drifted out, falling into the darkness that beckoned me. His voice loomed in the air. His threats and his promises echoed off the walls as I remained paralyzed by the drugs, unable to defend, to fight, to wage war against this motherfucker.
I became incoherent to whatever he said next as everything faded to black.

"Don't lay down and die," a voice whispered, but I was too far gone to decipher if it was Reina's voice or the ghost of my dead wife.

In the darkness I searched for her, desperate to see her one more time, hopeful that if I did it would erase the image of her lifeless body in my arms. I'd kiss her one more time and her lips wouldn't be cold like they were the last time they touched mine.

"Christine? Chris! We have to talk," I shouted as I stalked through our apartment, searching for her. I needed to fix this shit with her, needed to know how deep she had become with that douche bag Brantley. I prayed to God I wasn't too late that she didn't turn her back on me, that she didn't give me or my club up to the cops and more than that I prayed she didn't give up on us, on who we used to be before I became Satan's soldier.

Before I sold my soul to the devil.

I heard the water running in the bathroom and started down the hallway, glancing down at the water that saturated the floor. My boots sloshed through the water as I followed the stream to the bathroom and watched as it poured from the saddle of the doorway. I lifted my hand, tried to turn the doorknob, but it was locked.

"Chris!" I shouted, pounding my fist against the door.

Nothing.

I didn't hesitate as I took a step back before charging forward, driving my shoulder into the door, tearing it off the hinge with hardly any effort. I pushed the door out of my way as the water made its way past my boots. I turned my head and then I saw her.

My world stopped.

She was faced down in the tub, her arm dangling over the edge with a needle hanging out of it.

"No, no, no," I cried, pushing my legs through the water before bending down and lifting her body from the tub. I dropped to my knees, holding her as the water continued to run, overflowing the bathtub, drenching me. I turned her over so, her face was visible and noticed the shade of gray her skin had already turned.

"Oh, God," I whispered as my eyes filled. I blinked through the tears, clearing my vision so my eyes could do a sweep of her body, hoping to find a shred of life left. My eyes fell on the needle still sticking out of her arm, the rubber band tied tightly around her bicep.

A nightmare.

I was living a nightmare, the same one I inflicted on the parents of those young kids that overdosed on my product. Did they find their children with my needle still in their arm? The blood stopped flowing for those kids but the poison stuck. Their hearts stopped, but the needle stayed.

Just like the woman in my arms.

The one I vowed to love, honor, and care for all the days of my life.

Until death do we part.

Until now.

I bent my head, closing my mouth around the needle and pulled it from her arm with my teeth, spitting it onto the floor.

My needle.
My product.
I untied the band from her arm before leaning back against the wall of the tub and cried.
"I'm so sorry," I whispered to her, leaning forward to kiss her ice-cold lips.

I woke, thrashing violently as the nausea worked me over and I vomited.
"Blackie, look at me," Reina pleaded.
So this isn't hell.
I'm still fucking here.
"Look at me, damn it," she ordered.
There was nothing left, yet still I felt like I needed to get something up. I dry heaved over and over until my body calmed down and I could turn my cheek, wiping my mouth against the leather that covered my shoulder.
I lifted my beady eyes to Reina's.
"You're okay, you just need to remind yourself you're okay," she said, softly.
I closed my eyes.
I was okay.
But why?
Why me and not her?
I opened my eyes, blinking as I focused my attention on Reina.
"I'm not a junkie," I whispered.
People can change whether it's a choice or a result of circumstance... it's possible. Picking out a grave, figuring out the words to carve into my wife's headstone, deciding what she would wear when she was laid to rest, those were the things that forced me to change. I did the detox thing, suffered the withdrawals, thought, I was dying, prayed for it... but it never came. God didn't spare me and take her. He made me the survivor but he didn't grant me any favors. He knew the game he was playing when he took her and left me here. He spared *her* from *me*, granted her peace, leaving me behind to suffer without her.
Life.
It was his revenge on me.
Live.
Breathe.
A burden bestowed on me from the almighty maker of heaven and earth. Life wasn't some divine gift, it was my punishment.
"I know," she said. "Why is he doing this to you?"
"Because I deserve it," I admitted, turning back to her.
Jack will lose it if anything happens to her. He deserves some kind of good after all that shit he suffered. Losing your mind is one thing but losing your child is a whole different story. That man lived a lot of life, did a lot of penance and finally was granted his divine gift and I was staring at her. I wanted to do my job, to be able to protect the club, and protecting the club meant protecting its property and Reina? She was property of Parrish but reality set in and it settled fast. I didn't have the strength to save her in the state I was in right now. I didn't know much about her but I knew enough to know she was a fighter.
A survivor.

Her own hero.

"Listen, Reina, you need to keep your head because as long as he keeps feeding me that shit, I'm useless. Jack's on to him so it's only a matter of time before he and the club gets to you."

"To us," she amended. "He will not leave you behind, you're the closest thing he has to a brother. A *real* brother," she added.

Brothers.

"Right," I replied, closing my eyes. "Reina, do me a favor?"

"I'm kind of tied up right now," she said, forcing a laugh.

I smiled slightly before the wave of nausea washed over me again.

"Oh God," I moaned. "I need to throw up," I mumbled, hanging my head waiting for it to pass.

"Blackie, focus, if you let that shit control you, then the poison wins," Reina pleaded, pausing for a moment before she began again. "Tell me your real name. Blackie is your club name, right?"

"Road name," I corrected.

"Cut me some slack, I'm new to the old lady status," she said, her voice cracking. "Tell me your name," she repeated.

"Dominic," I whispered.

"Dominic," she started. "I like Blackie, better," she conceded.

"You're good people, Reina," I said.

Why was it the good always finished last?

"We will get the fuck out of here," I declared, clearing my throat. The way I figure it, God's not going to let me die here, under this dickbag Jimmy's thumb. He wants me breathing, he keeps me suffering so, Reina, has a fair shot of surviving this shit.

"Jimmy blew up my truck," I informed her.

Keep talking...Keep fighting.

"After I dropped you off I made a stop, must be when he planted the bomb," I added.

Lacey.

I hope they left her alone. I pray to whatever God willing to hear me that she listened when I told her to stay put.

"You don't think he planted it while I had the truck?" she questioned.

"Jack's house is covered with cameras, anyone watches him, and it's obvious Jimmy's been watching us, wouldn't be stupid enough to plant a bomb with the camera rolling," I explained.

"So where did you go?" she asked.

It almost slipped off my tongue.

Lace.

Her.

My angel.

My light.

"We being real with one another?" I asked.

"Yes."

"You about over the whole Jack being Danny's brother thing? I mean when you get the fuck out of here you're not going to hold some sort of grudge over the man's head are you?"

It was time for me to pass the torch to Reina. It was time for her to battle Jack's demons with him, it was her job to wear down his maker.

"I'm over it," Reina stated "I don't like being lied to, but..." she attempted to shrug her shoulders.

"I love him," she whispered.

Love.

It keeps us holding on.

Even when we don't know we've got it.

Even when we don't know we have a little left in us to give.

It's one of the divine gifts.

One of the few.

"Hold onto that, what you feel for him, it'll help," I said.

She stared at me silent for a moment before she spoke.

"What are you holding on to?" she asked hoarsely.

I looked away as Christine whispered all the words I never knew I needed to hear.

Let me go Blackie.

It's time.
It's not too late to change.
Change your life.
You did it once before.
You did it for me.
Change your life.
Do it for her.
But mostly, do it for you.
You.

"Which question do you want me to answer? Where I went after I dropped you off or what I'm holding on to?" I asked, finally.

"Something tells me both questions have the same answer," she said, softly.

"Yeah," I agreed, diverting my eyes to the floor.

A memory flashed before my eyes, the same memory I struggled to remember this morning when I held Lacey in my arms and she asked me if I remembered the first time she called me Leather.

I don't know why the memory came now, but it did and when I needed it the most.

"Lace? Oh we're doing the nickname thing?" she said mockingly, like a true smart ass. She was insisting I take a sip of her milkshake. "Fine. C'mon Leather, live dangerously," she teased.

"Leather?" I asked.

"Leather and Lace. You and me," she affirmed as she smiled at me.

That smile.

Man, I was gone.

She had the power to heal me, even if it was only temporary.

I lifted my eyes back to Reina's.

"Leather and Lace," I whispered.

Because the idea of me and her—it was all I had left.

The door opened, jarring the both of us and we turned our eyes to one of Jimmy's men. He carried a leather pouch tucked under his arm and knelt before me. He unzipped the bag and pulled a vile out, followed by a syringe.

Lace.

Her.

He roughly grabbed my outstretched arm and tied a band around it.

"Don't," Reina yelled. "Can't you see he's not a threat to you people? Why are you doing this to him?"

I turned my head to Reina, but all I saw was Lacey's face. My angel with the sweet smile and sad eyes.

"It's all good, Reina," I said, biting the inside of my cheek.

"Leather and lace," Reina whispered as the needle pricked my skin.

I closed my eyes and remembered dancing with her, holding her close as we blocked out the rest of the world.

A world where there was no maker.

A world where there were no drugs.

And Jimmy fucking Gold didn't exist.

The heroin took over.

Fight.

For her.

"Leather and lace," I slurred, fighting with every fiber of my being to get those words out.

Her.

Chapter Eight

BLACKIE

I used to think drugs took me to heaven, and if I'm being honest, when shit gets rough, I look for the easy way out. I'll hit the bottle and think I'm escaping hell. The truth is drugs are my *hell;* they numb the pain for a while but if I don't stay high all the time eventually I wake up, the numbness fades and the pain is only intensified. It's not just the mental pain that is worse but it's the physical pain which wasn't there before the drugs, but is present now. A pain so severe you forget about the original demons that haunt you and lead you to the drugs, a pain that tears through you and makes you wish were dead. It's a pain you wouldn't wish on your worst enemy.

Well, maybe that isn't entirely true.

I wish worse for Jimmy Gold.

A whole lot worse.

I'd like to cut his dick off and feed it to him as he bled out.

I hear his voice and decide that I'd rip the cocksucker's dick off with a pair of dirty pliers.

"Should we give him another hit?" One of his men asked.

Him? He's going to get his eyes ripped from their sockets with an ice cream scoop, or maybe a melon baller. Fuck that, I'll carve them out with my knife.

"Not yet," Jimmy murmured, crouching down before me as he took my face in his hands. "Time to give your president a message," he said, slapping my cheeks. "Take the cuffs off him," he ordered to the man standing behind him.

One of the first times Jack found me fucked up he smacked me across the face and told me to stand up. I remember thinking it was physically impossible and refused. You don't refuse Jack Parrish. Ever. He pulled me to my feet, holding me under my arms until I found my balance.

"You don't have to drown. You got legs that work, you stand the fuck up and keep moving. But if you don't get on your feet and you choose to drown in the poison, then you're a fucking pussy."

Jimmy rose to his feet, spinning on his heel, and pointed a finger at the other man. "Get the phone ready; make sure the lighting is clear so when we shoot the video there is no mistaking what Jack Parrish will be seeing."

The first douche bag un-cuffed me and pulled me up. On my feet, I stumbled, barely able to hold my head up.... but I wasn't a pussy.

And motherfucker, I'm not ready to drown.

"What are you doing?" I asked as he dragged me across the room to the slop sink. He turned the faucet on and I lost my fucking shit, at least I think I did. I struggled to fight, pushing back against his pull but let's be serious. I was no match for this son of a bitch, not with all the shit he injected into my bloodstream.

Still, I'm standing.

I won't drown.

Not now.

Not by this prick.

He grabbed a fist full of my hair and shoved my face into the basin of the sink. The ice cold water rained down over my head, awakening me and numbing me to everything other than the freezing temperature of the water.

Finally, he turned the faucet off and released his hold on me. I lifted my head, pushing the hair back and away from my face, turning around to face Reina. The man behind pushed me, forcing me to shuffle my feet across the cement until I was standing in front of her.

I watched as Jimmy's henchmen walked around me, making his way behind Reina and freed her hand. Jimmy knelt before her, cutting the zip ties from her ankles, before nodding to the man still standing behind Reina. He grabbed her hair, forcing her onto her feet and when her legs gave out he yanked harder on her hair.

"What the fuck man? C'mon leave her alone," I groaned as she shrieked in pain. "You're only making shit worse for yourself by fucking with her," I added.

"Shut up," Jimmy ordered, reaching down to his calf as he lifted his pants slightly, pulling the gun from his holster before lifting it to my head. "You don't speak unless I tell you to," he declared, glancing over his shoulder at the man pulling Reina's hair. "Give me the phone," he demanded, reaching over my shoulder to grab the iPhone. "Is it ready?"

I glanced at Reina, saw the fear in her and eyes and forced myself to ignore it and concentrate on focusing. I needed to get my head straight to figure out what this crazy son of bitch was planning.

"Yes," the lackey replied.

Out of the corner of my eye, Jimmy dropped the gun he had aimed at my head and fiddled with his phone. I turned my eyes back to Reina's.

"Stay with me," I mouthed, as Jimmy's second enforcer aimed his gun at me.

For fuck's sake.

The guy holding Reina by the hair, released her and cocked his gun.

"There is this old saying, maybe you've heard it," Jimmy began, as he circled us with his arm outstretched recording himself as he did. "Fool me once, shame on you. Fool me twice, shame on me," he arched his eyebrows and smiled at the camera. "I'm no one's fool," he declared, looking away from the camera he turned to face me. "You told me she was a whore. You said you take chance a piece on her sweet cunt, right?" he questioned. "Answer the question! Look into the camera when you do."

"Yes," I lied through my teeth.

"But you haven't sampled her have you?" he asked, turning around to Reina, trailing his fingertip along her collarbone. "But you're going to now and do you know why, pretty girl? Do you know why he will rape you?"

Rape?

Fuck no.

I'm a lot of things, a man who committed a lot of sins, but I was no rapist.

Let him pull the trigger.

Fuck it all.

I would not touch her.

"Because you're not a fool," Reina replied.

"I'm not touching her you sick fuck," I shouted over her. "Shoot me up, do what you got to do but I won't fucking touch her."

Jimmy laughed, ignoring me as he played back his video, scrutinizing it. Reina's eyes found mine, pleading with me to make it stop, to put an end to this torture.

I had nothing.

Fucking helpless.

At the mercy of drugs.

At the mercy of a mobster.

I was not my own man.

I was not worthy of my cut or my patch.

Satan's Knight?

No, I was Jimmy's bitch.

"It will be okay," I told her.

"Leather and Lace," she breathed. "When we get out of here will you tell me what it means?"

I stared at her silently.

No, I wouldn't.

Not for the obvious reasons, not because she was Jack's daughter but because in that moment, with death looming over me, Leather and Lace became sacred. It was a dream, something foreign to a man who is only granted nightmares, and I wanted to hang onto the dream a little longer. I wanted to hang on to the idea I could change, maybe be a better man, and as much of a stretch as it was I wanted to hang on to the idea I could be better for her. I wanted to believe I could be the guy she needed, to give her what she deserved and repay her for all the ways she heals me. Even if it's temporary.

"Yeah," I lied, because we weren't getting out of here and I could hang onto Leather and Lace until I drew my final breath.

"No, that was all wrong, let's try it again," Jimmy said.

"Trust me," I whispered faintly, resigning to my fate.

I drew in a deep breath, closing my eyes briefly, expecting to see Christine's face but it wasn't her haunting me, pulling me into the darkness. It was my angel; it was Lacey's beautiful face begging me to follow her light.

I'm sorry, Lace.

Here I come, Christine.

I opened my eyes as Reina closed hers and walked towards her.

"Thatta boy, make it good," Jimmy sang. "Her life depends on it," he said, reinforcing my decision to sacrifice my existence for hers.

I swayed as I took another step closer to my president's woman, reaching for her hand as I placed my other hand on her hip. Her eyes opened, and I turned my head, nuzzling her neck, avoiding her eyes.

"He loves you," I whispered against her ear, willing her to think of Jack.

"He's here with you not me," I whispered, kissing her neck as my fingers worked the buttons of her shirt. "Follow my lead," I demanded, against her throat.

"Cut to the chase," Jimmy ordered.

I tore my mouth from her neck.

Game time, motherfucker.

"Open your eyes, Reina," I said, squeezing her hand I still held in mine before dropping it and lifting both of my hands to her face. Her eyes fluttered opened and she stared back at me.

What I wouldn't give for one more glance into the dark eyes that owned me.

"Leather and Lace," I whispered. "Now close them and think of Jack," I said, as I closed my eyes and thought of Lacey.

And then it happened.

I kissed her.

To save her life.

I was about to tear my mouth from hers, to turn around and face the gun pointed at me but a hand reached around my shoulder and shoved a needle into my jugular. I lost feeling throughout my body, starting with my face. My mouth released Reina's and my hands dropped from her face.

"Blackie?" Reina shouted frantically.

Lace.

It was her face I saw when the life drained from me.

Her.

Lacey

After my father found me he brought me back to the Dog Pound where apparently everyone who mattered to the men of the Satan's Knights congregated. There were some new faces, who I learned belong to Victor Pastore. It didn't matter that my father was Jack Parrish, or that the people he kept in his circle were all the same, I still would've known the Pastore name. Victor's face had been on the front page of every newspaper a couple of months ago when he confessed to all his crimes. I'm not sure why his entire family has become my father's responsibility nor do I care. They all seem nice enough, bringing me into their circle, and doing what they've been trained to do. These woman, old and young, differed from me. While I've been at the sidelines of my father's lifestyle, these women played front and center. To them this lockdown was the norm, they didn't blink an eye when the men in leather scrambled around the clubhouse trying to form a plan of attack. They stood back, watched them do their thing, having faith they would return alive and in one piece, having done the job. The job being, bringing Blackie and Reina home safe and eliminating the enemy.

They were familiar with the enemy. He once sat at their table on holiday's, he was Victor's right hand, his newly appointed underboss. A title he claimed after he had a hand in the murder of his first one, Michael Valente, a man they called Val. Val's son was here too, strapping on a bullet-proof vest, ready to do whatever my father told him to, ready to get his revenge for his old man's death. It was so much to take in, so many faces to keep track of, so many lives that intertwined and I'm sure if the circumstances were different I would've been fascinated with all this.

I used to harbor resentment against my parents for keeping me away from the MC. It was a part of my father, so in turn it was part of me. These men that wore the reaper on their back have all for the most part, watched me grow up. Wolf and

Pipe were there for all my sacraments and they brought me flowers at my dance recitals. When I went on my first date, Wolf sat behind us at the movie theatre. Pipe taught me how to drive and when my father was in jail, it was Blackie who made sure I was okay. He made sure I maintained a relationship with my dad and when I needed a ride, he was the one who dropped everything to make sure I got to wherever it was I needed to go.

They may be men who ran on the wrong side of the law but these men where my family. I've heard my dad speak of his brotherhood, but seeing it firsthand, how they banded together, made it clear they were brothers in every way it counts. And though my head worked against me, filling my mind with doom, it was hard not to have faith they would bring Blackie back to them.

Back to me.

I don't think Blackie knows his worth. His worth to his club, to my father and to me. Does he know that these men are not whole without him? Does he even realize that my father doesn't function to the best of his ability unless Blackie is there to guide him? Blackie's presence is a strong aid to the lithium he takes, it's just as important to my father's treatment as any prescription drug.

Does he know that the thought of losing him scares the hell out of me? I'm not sure I could live without him in my life. And not because of the crush. Not because of the attraction or the one night we shared but because Blackie is my crutch too, not just my father's. He's the only one in this whole world who has the power to see me and accept me.

I'm damaged.

And no one knows.

He looks at me, sees the broken, the demons that come out and play whenever they want, his expression doesn't change.

He'll take me anyway I am.

Imperfections and all.

And maybe that's because he's full of imperfections himself.

Sometimes perfect can be found in imperfections, just like it's hidden in the word it's hidden beneath the flaws. It just takes one person to claim those imperfections and deem them perfect. Blackie is a drug addict, he's a drunk, a self-loathing man looking for a way out. He's the definition of imperfect. But you know what his perfect is? The hidden beauty of him? It's his heart.

His heart.

That's his perfect.

And I want to be the person who claims it.

I had escaped the Pastore women and found my way upstairs to Blackie's room. I laid on his bed and thought I'd take a nap but, the scent of his cologne on his pillow made it impossible for me to close my eyes and not think of him.

Everything in this room was a reminder of the one night we shared. The one never to be spoken of again. It wasn't how I thought I'd lose my virginity, not that I gave it much thought. After sixteen my v-card became more of a nuisance then some sacred thing I needed to hang on to. I'm not sure who is to blame if its society or my parents who sheltered me and made me think I was too good to give it up to just anyone. As a young girl I believed I needed to be in love with someone, that the person who took my virginity needed to be some perfect man I would spend the rest of my life with.

Then I became sixteen and found out I was the only fucking virgin left, or at least that's what it felt like. All my friends had done it, raved about how great it was and how many orgasms they had—then there was me, the president of the Satan's Knights daughter. I was crazy and still a virgin. It was unheard of.

Yet still I couldn't do it.

I couldn't just give it up to anyone.

My best friend, Noah knew my dilemma and even offered to rid me of my problem.

And as tempting as the offer was, I turned him down.

I think it was my subconscious guiding me, making me wait because the one who eventually took it was the only person to ever see me. It may not have been a fairytale, and it hurt like hell, but I wouldn't take it back.

None of it.

Not waiting until I found the perfect man.

Not waiting until I was nearly nineteen years old.

I didn't let anyone else take it because only one man deserved it.

He might regret it; he might be bothered by it but for me it was perfect. Perfect in an imperfect way. The hidden perfect in a shit load of flaws.

Just like the both of us.

Demons and addictions.

Leather and Lace.

Imperfect yet perfect.

My thoughts are interrupted by the commotion coming from the other side of the door. I heard Riggs shout at my father, then call for help. I quickly threw my legs over the edge of the bed and ran to the door. Pulling it open I peeked my head out as my father stalked towards the stairs. The look in his eye was ferocious and I knew even his medicine wouldn't help him. The maker has taken residence and the crazed look in his eye was the look of a man trying to balance reality and the poisonous fiction his mind was trying to make him believe.

I understand your pain dad.

I see it.

I live it.

"Stop him," Riggs hollered as he skidded to a halt at the stairs. "Pipe! Wolf!"

I stepped out of the room, tip-toeing the length of the hallway before leaning against the wall as Riggs ran down the stairs, stopping mid-way. I could see my dad trapped on the stairs, his brothers barricading him.

"Get out of my way," he ordered.

"Jimmy sent the video," Riggs explained in a huff, handing his phone over to Pipe. What video? I swallowed hard against the lump in my throat, pushing back the grim thoughts of what may be on the video.

Anthony Bianci, one of the mob guys, took Pipe's place blocking my dad from moving and Pipe hit play. I heard the unmistakable voice that belonged to Jimmy but being on top of the stairs, I could only make out every other word—by the way my father lurched for the phone I knew that motherfucker couldn't have been delivering good news.

"Jesus Christ," Pipe said, as Jimmy's voice sounded stating his demands and threats.

"I will kill him and I'm going to smile as I do it," my father hissed.

It was so weird to watch my hero of a father turn into a monster of a man. What I was witnessing was different from the manic episodes of the past. I think that's because this man my father was morphing into wasn't controlled by the crazy but instead, by the criminal.

"Chapel, now," Pipe ordered, sternly.

"There's no fucking time," my dad yelled.

I closed my eyes, sliding against the wall as the men continued to argue.

"Oh, so you have a plan? Because you're right we don't have a lot of fucking time and without a plan we're fucked. So pull your fucking shit together and grab your gavel," Pipe replied.

I glanced down at the watch on my wrist, watching as the second hand ticked away and felt fresh tears sting my eyes. For the first time the numbers on the clock weren't just numbers they were a lifeline.

I know now why people say time is precious, for when it runs out there is nothing and you're left wishing of all the things you could've done, could've said…if only you had just one more minute.

Tick.

Tock.

Tick.

Tock.

Chapter Nine
Lacey

My father stormed out of the clubhouse after they disappeared into the chapel and concocted a plan of attack. They looked like a pack of wild animals running out of here. The whole lot of them, the men in leather and the pretty boy mobsters with the tight t-shirts that promoted a gym called Xonerated on their backs.

I tried isolating myself, staying locked up in Blackie's room until the dreaded news came but, the door flew open and Nikki Pastore came barging into the room. She froze in her tracks once she spotted me on the bed, and smiled sheepishly—which was comical since it was obvious this girl didn't have a shy bone in her body.

"Shit, sorry, I didn't know anyone was up here," she cocked her head, glancing around the room. "Is this the Bulldog's room?" she questioned as she walked over to the dresser and started to search for something.

"No, it's not," I said, throwing my legs over the edge of the bed. "Is there something you need?"

I started towards her, as she shamelessly moved things around on Blackie's dresser, pausing to lift a picture frame. She turned around, holding up the frame as her eyes questioned me.

"Why is it all the hot guys are either married or gay?" she asked as I stared at the photo of Blackie and Christine on their wedding day.

"Where did you find that?"

"Right there," she tipped her chin at the dresser. "Under the mountain of black clothes," she replied, glancing down at the picture. "As my Aunt Gina would say, that's a fine piece of ass right there," she added.

"Blackie doesn't like people touching his shit," I informed her.

"Blackie?" she turned around and placed the frame on the dresser, standing it up so that the happy couple was rightfully displayed.

"The guy whose room you're ransacking," I explained, tearing my eyes from the photograph to meet hers.

"Does Blackie smoke?"

What?"

"Look, Lacey right? I'm having a nicotine fit," she stuck her arm out toward me, lifting up the sleeve to expose her nicotine patch. "This shit doesn't cut it, so again, does this Blackie character smoke?"

"Sometimes, but not usually," I crossed my arms. "There are no cigarettes in here."

She raised an eyebrow as she stared at me for a moment then walked over to the bed and dropped onto it.

"Bummer," she said. "I guess it's up to you then."

"Excuse me?"

"I need a distraction," she explained, rubbing her arm where the patch was.

"What? No. What're you doing?"

"Who's the hot guy with the bride?"

"Shouldn't you be downstairs helping your mother and that other lady turn this place into a trattoria or something?"

She smiled.

"A wise ass just like your dad," she mused.

"Did you just call me a wise ass?"

"I did," she affirmed.

"How do you know my dad?"

"He helped me and my boyfriend out one night. My ex-boyfriend shot up my father's nightclub and your dad took me and my Mikey to a safe house," she explained, leaning back on the bed. "Good times."

"Your ex-boyfriend shot up a night club?" I asked, wide-eyed as I sat next to her.

"Yeah, that prick bastard," she snarled. "Anyway, your pops... he came riding to the rescue, and drove me and Mikey to a cabin in the middle of nowhere. He slipped me a pack of Marlboro's and became one of my top-five favorite people."

That caused me to smile. There weren't too many people around my age that genuinely liked my father. Growing up me and my friends didn't spend much time around my dad, they barely knew him. They heard of him, knew his name, his club and made assumptions. Some of them feared the big bad motorcycle man—others thought it was cool to have a dad who was a biker but, they didn't get to interact with him. Nikki was the first person to tell me she was fond of my father and not because of the patch but because he was just a cool guy who helped her out of a jam and gave her a pack of cigarettes.

"So, who is Blackie and why are you here hiding out in his room?"

I was pulled from my thoughts, turned my eyes to her and shrugged my shoulders.

"He's the vice president of the club," I answered, looking away. "He came to get me, to take me here, when your father's pal showed up and took him," my words trailed.

"I didn't see the girl in the picture downstairs," she said, tipping her chin to the frame.

"Because she's dead," I lifted my eyes to the photograph, staring at the smile on Blackie's face and realized even the few times he smiled at me, his smile differed from the one in the photograph.

He was different back then.

He was happy.

"That's fucking awful," Nikki whispered, looking back at me.

"Yeah," I replied, lifting my eyes to her. "Nikki? You know Jimmy pretty well don't you? Do you think he can pull it off?" I paused, swallowing hard before I continued. "I guess what I'm asking you is—do you think he's going to kill Blackie?"

"Jimmy's a pussy," she answered. "No match for the men that walked out of here today," she paused, taking a deep breath before she continued. "You know not that long ago I was in your shoes, waiting for my father to come back and tell me everything would be okay. I did something foolish, something you shouldn't, I lost faith in my father and his capabilities,"

"My father is different than yours," I interrupted

"Not really. Different clothes maybe, mine preferred silk over leather. We're being real with one another, right? Both men are leaders, they are badass motherfuckers, that won't hesitate to lay it all on the line to protect the people that matter to them. My father used to don a fitted suit while yours wears a leather vest, but the values are the same. He will bring Blackie back," she assured me, laying her hand on my knee. "So, stop worrying about Mr. Drop Dead Gorgeous over there in the photograph and start worrying about how you will break it to your old man you've got it bad for his biker buddy," she warned, winking at me.

"What? No, you— "

"Don't worry, your secret's safe with me," she lifted a strand of my hair, twirling it around her finger. "We should do your hair. Maybe dye it…I think ombre would look amazing on you! But I'm going to need a cigarette before I mess with your hair," she pulled her hand back and smiled at me.

"And stop sitting up here by yourself. There's a bunch of crazy women downstairs pretending the men in their lives aren't criminals… it's like a goddamn support group down there," she winked and I couldn't help the laugh that escaped. She held out her hand, looking at me expectantly until I stood up, placed my hand in hers and followed her out of Blackie's room. We made our way downstairs and were immediately summoned by Grace and Maria to set the table, the table being a pool table with a checkered plastic tablecloth draped over it. These women weren't the support group, they needed the support group. My father was going to flip his shit when he came back, especially, when he saw his prospects who were supposed to be guarding us had become Maria Bianci's bitches and were slicing and dicing pepperoni behind the bar.

It was a real shit show.

But it was a good distraction from my heart that was breaking and my mind that was trying to shunt me.

I was beginning to set the table when the door to the compound opened and my father and Riggs stepped inside. I blinked my eyes, making sure they weren't playing the same tricks my mind was trying to, but he stood there looking around his clubhouse with the eyes of a remorseful man.

"Dad?" I screeched, dropping the plates on top of the pool table, making my way over to him. He turned his head, his eyes found mine, and he smiled half-heartedly.

"Have you heard anything?" I asked.

"No baby, I haven't. You ladies have been keeping busy," he muttered.

Nothing.

The clock is ticking.

He's running out of time.

He knows it and now it's time you do to.

I swallowed, closing my eyes briefly picturing Blackie's face, and it was enough to shut down the voice of my maker.

"It was Grace and Maria's idea," I tried to explain. "They said when you guys bring Reina and Blackie home, you deserve a meal. Well, that's what Grace said—Maria said you all should starve for being scoundrels. Though they both agreed, that Reina and Blackie would be hungry so they decided to do all this to welcome them home," I rambled nervously, stopping myself from begging him to promise me he was going to bring back Blackie.

He reached out, tucking a strand of hair behind my ear as Nikki walked up to us, pounding her fist playfully against his chest.

"Can I grub a cigarette, Bulldog?" she asked, flashing her killer smile and without hesitation my father reached into his cut and produced a pack of cigarettes.

"You're my hero," she exaggerated, pulling one from the pack. "If my mother looks for me tell her I'm slicing a salami or something," she whispered, before sneaking out the door.

"Nikki's going to dye my hair," I said looking after her. "I like her a lot and she might just be your biggest fan. She has faith in you so if she does, it'd be a shame that your own daughter doesn't," I paused as he continued to stare at me blankly. "I don't doubt that you'll save him…them," I corrected, before he pulled me against him, wrapping his arms tightly around me.

My eyes filled with tears as we held onto one another. All the things we never said to one another when I was a kid, was wrapped in that embrace. The fear of not being good enough resurrected. My insecurities of not being the child he wanted but was stuck with resurfaced. I couldn't shake the thought, the unexplainable fear he would do anything in his power to save Blackie and Reina, only for him to be reunited with Jack Jr.

It's hard to take your own life, but it's relatively easy to allow someone else the privilege.

"Dad," I said, pushing against his chest, lifting my eyes to his, and my fear became my reality. His eyes were his truth. There was nothing he wouldn't do to save Blackie and Reina, and if that meant his life or theirs, he'd most definitely choose theirs.

"I see that look in your eye and it scares me, scares me more than any man charging into my house, more so than Blackie telling me I need to hide in a closet because they're coming for me."

I took a breath, biting down on my lip as the memory of Blackie kissing me washed over me. I wonder if I will always think of that kiss when I think of Blackie instructing me to shoot anyone who messes with me.

I do that…associate things with poignant moments in my life.

"They say we associate things with our childhood; scents, songs, even toys. They're supposed to help us remember when our minds grow old with age and we are trying to hang onto our youth. I saw that look in your eyes my entire childhood and I'll never forget it. I hate that look because it's a reminder that for the last thirteen years, since Jack died, you didn't want to be here anymore. I remember looking into your eyes and wondering if that day was the day you wouldn't come back, to me, if you'd lose the struggle and end up with Jack."

I stopped for a moment, studying his features, wondering if anything I was saying would stick with him.

"You always came back," I smiled sadly, knowing he came back because he didn't find the will in him not too. "I told myself it was because you realized I was still here and I still needed you, that you knew how much I loved you and how it would break my heart if I lost you," I cried, wishing for it to be true.

"Lacey..." he interrupted but his sentence fell short, his mind was working him over taking him some place dark. Some place I was fighting not to go.

"Dad?" I said, trying to bring him back to me. "I know you miss Jack, but I'm still here," I whispered. "And I need my dad. I'll always need you so please promise me you'll come back to me."

Just bring him back with you.

"I love you, Lace," he whispered, pressing his lips to my forehead before bringing me back against him, his strong arms enveloping me. "And I promise you a pack of wild horses couldn't stop me from coming back to you. We'll make good memories, I swear it."

I closed my eyes, relished in his words and fought back the voice telling me they were a lie, choosing to hang on to his promise with everything inside of me...even my mind.

The door opened behind me and my club members walked inside.

"Bulldog," Pipe called, signaling it was time for them to leave again.

"Yeah—" my dad said, dropping a kiss on top of my head. "Dry those eyes, your old man will be back," he whispered.

Nikki stepped back into the clubhouse, spritzing herself with body spray to cover the scent of cigarettes and walked over to me. She ran her fingers over her hair as she looked knowingly at my dad.

"Come on, let's see about dying these locks," she offered.

I'm not sure if she befriended me out of gratitude towards my father or if she genuinely understood my fears. Maybe it was both.

"Thank you," he said hoarsely.

"Thanks for the stogie," she replied, grabbing my hands and leading me away. I glanced over my shoulder and watched as Riggs handed my father a bullet-proof vest. He strapped it on over his clothes before walking over to the reaper painted on the wall, laying one hand on the logo that signified the club before bowing his head.

Most people prayed to God but my father prayed to reaper on his back.

Jack Parrish.

My father.

The disciple of the devil.

BLACKIE

I'm dancing and I don't dance. I'm smiling and I don't smile. I am changed even though I've given up on change.

You in the moonlight with your sleepy eyes

Could you ever love a man like me
But that time I saw you I knew with you to light my nights
Somehow, I'd get by

Chapter Ten

Lacey

I knew he was there before I felt the dip in the mattress and his strong arms wrap around my body, tugging me against him. I could smell his cologne the minute he walked through the door but I remained on my side with my back facing him. I was too afraid to turn and meet his eyes, too scared he'd look right through me—like I didn't exist or worse send me away. He leaned into my ear pushing away my hair with the tip of his nose before his lips trailed down my neck and pressing his lips against my shoulder.

"I was so scared you wouldn't come back," I whispered into the darkness, covering his hands with my own. His hand was twice the size of mine and yet they looked as if they were made for one another.

"I'll always come back for you, Lace. Even when I shouldn't. Even when I know you're better off without me," he whispered huskily against my ear. I turned in his arms, fueled by the desire to look into his eyes and trust his words. His hair fell in front of his face as it usually did, forcing me to run my fingers through it and push the unruly locks from his expressive eyes. Blackie's eyes were hazel, changing colors like the tides, depending on his mood. They were the color of caramel as they stared back at me, a shade they only turned when he was at peace, a sign of contentment, a rare occurrence.

Peace.

I could give him that.

"Lacey, sweetheart wake up."

I heard my father's voice say, jolting me awake and away from my dreams. I felt his hand gently shake my shoulder, trying to wake me from my sleep. I buried my face in Blackie's pillow, breathing in the smell of cologne, wishing I could sleep forever...wishing I can dream forever.

"Lacey," my father said louder, forcing me to lift my head, roll onto my side and look up at him.

He looked exhausted, like he had been up for days, yet when our eyes met his lips curved upward. It was always a mystery to me when he took off on his bike. I thought he was just a man on a bike, a man who loved the open road. This whole ordeal has enlightened me to what it means to be a part of a motorcycle club. The patch on his cut labels him a one percenter, telling me ninety-nine percent of the shit he does is illegal and dangerous.

Which means, today he cheated death. Today he fought and today he won and I'd like to think a piece of him was fighting for me.

The look in his eyes before he left, that murderous look that told me his maker was in control—faded away and he was just my dad. Jack Parrish, the man and father not the president or the man controlled by his mind. I wrapped my arms around his neck and hugged him tightly as the scent of gasoline assaulted my senses.

"It's all over, Lacey...everything is going to be okay," he reassured me as he pulled back and studied my face. "You don't have to worry."

"What about Blackie? And Reina? Are they okay?"

He kept his eyes pinned to mine a moment before diverting them away.

"They will be," he said, voice full of conviction as he dropped his hands to his knees.

"Come on, get your stuff together. I'll take you home," he said, rising to his feet and started for the door, making it clear he would not give me much more information than that.

"That's it?" I scrambled off the bed. "They will be? That's your answer? That man was looking to take me and if it wasn't for Blackie he would've. What happened to him?"

He paused as he reached the door and turned around, glancing around at the room before his eyes found mine. He bit the inside of his cheek as he stared back at me. He wasn't an easy man to read, looking at his face rarely ever gave his thoughts away. It was that stone cold look that worried me though, the one that told me the wheels in his mind were turning and nothing good ever came from that. The more my father thought the worse things were—for everyone.

"We'll talk more in the car," he insisted, continuing to stare at me in deep thought. "Why Blackie's room?"

I shrugged my shoulders.

"It's closest to the stairs," I lied, shrugging on my leather jacket.

He didn't say another word, holding open the door for me and following me out of Blackie's room. I led him down the stairs, my stomach twisting in knots as I thought of all the possible things he would tell me.

The common room had emptied out for the most part. There were a few stragglers still here, like, Anthony Bianci who I overheard tell my father he was waiting on Riggs.

"Don't shoot the poor bastard," my dad told Anthony as he slapped him on the back. "Kid, might just surprise you. Who knows? Maybe he found his heart," he added, turning towards me. "Let's get out of here."

Bianci threw my father his keys, and we walked out of the Dog Pound. I have never been on the back of bike. Never. Well, that's a lie. I have a photo of my dad holding me on his bike. But take a ride on one? No, never.

I slid into the front seat as my father adjusted his mirrors and seat. He looked ridiculous sitting behind a steering wheel, almost comical and it doesn't matter how many times I tell him, or tease him he always insists that I'm being ridiculous. The man was born to straddle a Harley. It was like his god given right or something.

I waited for him to start the truck up and peel out of the lot before I spoke.

"Are you going to tell me what happened?"

"That doesn't concern you," he clipped.

"Technically, it does. You've never lied to me once are you going to start now? I'd like to know what would've happened if Blackie hadn't intervened. I'd like to know what he endured because of me."

He remained silent, his knuckles whitening as they clenched the steering wheel. I shouldn't have pressed but there was no stopping me.

"I'm not a little kid who will sit here and believe everything is okay. I learned a lot in the last couple of days. I get it, I get why you wanted to keep me away from your life. It's ugly. But guess what? Despite all your efforts I'm still a part of it. Jimmy proved that the minute he came looking for me. I'm property of the Satan's Knights…fair game. I deserve to know what happened because it affects me just as it does everyone else," I argued.

He swerved, pulling the car onto the shoulder of the Belt Parkway and shifted the gear into park before pinning me with a stare.

"You listen to me and listen good you are not property of the Satan's Knights. You are *no one's* property," he shouted, startling me, making it the first time my father has ever reprimanded me.

So much for not being treated like a child.

"He didn't endure anything because of you. That shit is all on me, Lacey," he growled. "Is that what this is about? You feel some sort of guilt over Blackie?"

"Are you telling me I shouldn't?" I asked incredulously. "There aren't too many people who will choose your life over their own," I added, angrily.

"It's his goddamn job to put you first!" He fumed.

That stung, and another lesson was learned…words are one powerful weapon. I'd have to be pickier with my own, make them count, make them hurt, just like my dad's did.

At least then I'd have a rebuttal.

Now, I just sat there like the young naïve girl he thought I was.

"He's in the hospital, hanging on but he suffered a heart attack," he said, finally.

My eyes snapped toward him and my mouth fell open as my heart lurched into my throat.

"A heart attack? What the hell happened to him?"

"Watch your tone Lacey, giving away a whole lot with the way you're talking," he warned.

"Giving away what? That I care about Blackie? Of course I do. You have yourself to thank for that because the moment you stepped foot onto that bus to Riker's he was there for me and he's never left," I trembled as my voice shot octaves higher with each word I spoke.

"Shit," he ground out. "Blackie's not some knight in shining armor Lacey. He traded places with you because that is his job. It's who he is. That man has a death wish and everyone knows it, including the man who took him. He loaded him up on drugs. Blackie should be dead right now but he's hanging on because his body is so immune to the poison he keeps filling it with. He's not a prince, Lace, he's the devil clothed in leather. He is the same as me and don't you forget that!"

"I know exactly who he is and I accept him as he is…the same way I accept you," I insisted.

I wasn't sure if he was trying to scare me away or warn me but either way it didn't matter. I knew Blackie had a drug problem I saw it with my own eyes that night. But, he was still a man, a broken man who lost his way. He could push me away, try to make me hate him, but I've known him nearly all my life…I know how good he can be.

"Best-case scenario, he makes it out of this and gets the help he needs," my dad added.

"And worse case?"

"He cheats death only to beckon for it to come again," he said as he pulled the truck back onto the Belt. "Can't make someone live when they don't want to. You can't keep them breathing when they want to suffocate."

I stared at him as he fixed his eyes back to mine

"Blackie's at the end of his rope, Lace."

I restrained from shaking my head and telling him to shut up that he was wrong. Blackie may be at the end of his rope, but I was going to give him another inch, I was going to be the one who pulled him back.

Just watch and see.

I fell back against the seat and stared out the window.

"I'm sorry you had to see everything you saw," my father whispered. "The world isn't always pretty but the one me and Blackie live in is downright ugly."

Duly noted.

Words.

They wound but they don't change the way a person feels.

Luckily, neither of us uttered another until he pulled up in front of my mother's house. She was on the stoop waiting for me, her arms crossed against her chest and a worried look adorned her pretty face. I climbed out of the truck just as my father slammed his door shut. He walked around the truck, meeting me at the curb.

"Lace..."

"Thanks for keeping your promise," I interrupted, reaching up and throwing my arms around his neck.

Daddy's little girl.

Until you're not anymore.

Until there is another man.

And sometimes he's just like the first man you ever loved.

Sometimes he's just like your dad.

Chapter Eleven

Lacey

I conned my mother into lending me her car, told her I needed a break from the last few days. The reality of my father's life was harsher than I could've imagined. She bought the act, handed over her keys and I made a beeline for the hospital.

To be honest, I don't think she bought my little act at all. I think my mother knows me better than she lets on. In fact, I sometimes think she's a witch and knows all my secrets. It wouldn't surprise me if she even surmised that I was going to see Blackie but for whatever her reasons were, she didn't try to stop me.

I should be more cautious, try to make more of an attempt to mask my emotions, make it harder for her to read me but it wouldn't work. My mother knows me but, more than that, she knows herself. She lived what I am living. I wouldn't be naïve to say she condones my feelings, but she gets them. She'd be a hypocrite to try to stop me.

It makes me wonder about my parents when they were young and in love, mainly my mother and what she was like when she was property of Parrish.

Property of Parrish.

I'm sure there are women who would cringe at being called someone's property. But there are a few things I know about the MC world and being a man's property doesn't mean he owns you but more that you own his heart.

You belong to his heart…to his soul, whatever is left of it.

Love, it's the only purity men like my father and Blackie have.

And to own that solitary piece of him…well, it's bigger than all the I love you's any man can say.

So, when I say I want to be Blackie's property don't look at me with pity.

Keep your pity.

Because being Blackie's property means I own the only piece of him that isn't *black*.

Being Property of Petra is owning his heart.

It's restoring his soul.

It's the unspoken I love you.

It's the unspoken vow to honor and cherish, protect and love one another.

It's belonging to the one person in this world created just for you.

At least that's what it means to me.

But what do I know? I'm just a girl who's been sheltered from the life she was born in to.

My stomach twisted in knots as I made my way into the hospital. I had no idea what floor he was on or what unit he was in but I quickly learned he was in intensive care. They allowed me to go upstairs to the unit but when I was buzzed in the nurse told me there was already a visitor and there was only one permitted at a time. I pleaded with her to make an exception but she wouldn't budge, closing the door to the unit and leaving me in the hallway.

Now what?

The elevator chimed behind me causing me to turn around as the doors opened and I came face to face with Riggs.

The universe isn't my friend.

It hates me.

"Ah, shit," he groaned, stepping off the elevator as he ran his fingers through his hair. "What the fuck?" he asked the ceiling before pinning me with a glare. "Your father know you're here?"

I rolled my eyes.

"I suppose you're going to run back and tell him," I accused.

"Fucking, Blackie…Man. Shit! Shit! Shit!" He rambled.

"How do you know I'm not here for another reason?" I said, placing my hands on my hips, cocking my head to the side as I challenged him. "Maybe I'm here picking up a prescription for birth control."

He narrowed his eyes.

"It was one time!"

"What are you talking about?"

"What do you mean what am I talking about? What are you talking about? You know what? I don't care. I have zero fucks left," he ranted.

"Are you okay?"

"No! I'm not okay. I have a pea. And a baby mama. And Bones in my ear telling me to own it…imagine? Me owning responsibility for something? It's fucking crazy. You should probably pick up that birth control or this could be you," he said, as he swiped his hand down the length of his body.

"Breathe, Riggs," I instructed, watching as the badass biker had a meltdown.

"I'm going to be a dad," he hissed.

"Congratulations," I smiled, earning me a glare in response. I guess impending fatherhood wasn't on the agenda.

"Not funny," he ground out, moving to walk around me. I quickly side-stepped him, blocking him by lifting my hand to his chest.

"Wait! Look, I'm sorry you're having a crisis and all but I need your help," I pleaded.

"Oh, hell no!" He shook his head. "I am not getting involved in this shit. Are you fucking crazy?"

"Riggs! I have to see him," I said, desperately.

"No, I don't know what the hell is going on with the two of you and shit, I don't want to know but I am not getting involved."

I raised an eyebrow when he stomped his foot to drive his point home.

Poor guy, he was falling apart.

"Riggs, please," I tried. "I want to see for myself that he's okay."

"Your father will kill you, him and me!"

"He doesn't have to know," I countered.

"Right," he said sarcastically, lifting his eyes to the glass door. "Fuck, I know I'm going to regret this. Wolf is coming this way, go fucking hide somewhere," he hissed.

"Where?"

"Behind the goddamn plant. I don't know just scram," he said, shooing me away.

I scrambled toward one of the chairs in the waiting room, lifting a magazine to my face as Wolf strutted out from the intensive care wing.

"Well it's about time you showed your pretty face," he seethed. "I'm fucking beat."

"Yeah, sorry. I was dealing with the end of my freedom," Riggs replied. "How's he doing?"

"No change," Wolf said, yawning. "I'm getting out of here. I'll be back in a couple of hours."

"Yeah, no worries, I've got it from here," Riggs assured him.

"You okay?" Wolf asked suspiciously.

"Peachy," he replied.

"Being a father isn't a bad thing," Wolf told him.

"No, of course not. This coming from a man with three sons. I wonder if you had a defiant little girl, what you would say?"

That last part was definitely a dig toward me.

Riggs was a shit head.

Wolf laughed as I peeked over the magazine and watched him get onto the elevator. Riggs waved goodbye to him and once the doors shut he turned his eyes back to mine.

"Come on little Miss Defiant," he called.

I knew it!

I dropped the magazine, rose to my feet and hurried the doors, ringing the buzzer before I turned back to him.

"Thank you," I said.

"You're not welcome," he grunted. "I never helped you."

"Of course you didn't," I winked, remembering the last time he caught me and Blackie.

"Hurry up, I have a refrigerator I need to pick up," he mumbled.

The nurse buzzed me in and I ran through the glass doors, leaving my accomplice to his pity party. I went over to the nurse's station and after I found out which room he was in, I started for him.

I was driven by my need to see him, to make sure he really was alive and that he didn't leave me. I wanted to hold his hand, lace my fingers with his, and thank him. Not just for switching places with me but for every single time he's been there for me, choosing my life over his.

I should've given his condition more thought, if I would've prepared myself maybe then my heart wouldn't have stopped for the split second it did when I laid eyes on him. He looked so different lying there, powerless and at the mercy of the machines keeping him alive, so fragile. He didn't look like the badass biker most men feared and woman tried to conquer, he wasn't the hero sent to rescue me, or the poor widow who didn't know how to grieve.

He was just a man.

A man who had been knocked off his chrome pedestal, a man flawed and fractured by the shitty hand dealt to him. He was Dominic Petra, not Blackie, not one of Satan's Knights, not even the man I call Leather but, simply Dominic.

We weren't Leather and Lace.

We were strangers.

It was that moment, with the steady hymn of his heart rate playing in the background, Dominic Petra and Lacey Parrish first met.

We were both stripped of everything we've come to know about each other.

We were the flawed characters of a story.

He was the addict who chose the wrong path.

And I was the mentally ill girl who loved him.

I've never admitted that to anyone.

That I think I'm ill.

Or that I love him.

I don't know when it happened, if it was something that grew over time or what but, it felt as if I had been doing it my whole life…like I was born to love both Dominic Petra and the fractured soul of Blackie.

I walked to the side of his bed as my eyes swept over in him, taking in every machine, wire and tube attached to him, the one that breathed for him, the one that monitored his heart rate and the other half a dozen—I had no idea what their purpose was. I leaned over, gently I brought my fingertips to his cheek.

"Leather," I whispered, as a tear escaped the corner of my eye.

As much as I wanted to know the man Blackie was before all the pain, the man in the photograph he kept in his room, I never wanted it to be like this.

Our timing has always been off.

An alarm sounded forcing me to drop my hand from his face and divert my frantic eyes to the machines as a nurse came into the room.

"What's happening?"

"The I.V. finished," she explained, disconnecting the empty bag from the pole and replacing it with a full one. My eyes followed the tube and saw it was plugged into a port in his bicep. She must've noticed I was staring at the port strangely because she explained.

"His veins were collapsing, so we had to put the port in his bicep," she said, glancing back at the machine. "Everything is good. I'll give you some privacy," she added.

I nodded, waiting for her to leave the room before I lifted his hand, turning his arm over and stared at the bruises that angrily marked his skin. I bent my head, trailing my lips over the track marks.

I lifted my eyes, peering up at his face from under the fringe of my lashes, wishing to God he could hear me.

"Everybody deserves a rewrite," I whispered. "Even you. Come back to me Blackie, let me help you this once, just like you've always helped me. We can rewrite our story together. I'll help you silence your addiction the way you silence my mind," I promised as I gently placed his hand back down beside him.

I brought my hand up to his head and touched the hair that hung shaggily around his face, brushing it back with my fingers.

"I remember the first time I saw you like it was yesterday. I thought you were the most handsome guy I ever laid eyes on," I smiled, blinking away the tears that temporarily blinded me. "All these years later and it's still true, no one else compares. You had me then Blackie, you had me at ten years old, you've always had me…and I want you—no, I need you to know you'll always have me. I want you to stop pushing me away. I want you to accept that I'm a part of your life. Stop thinking it's wrong because nothing that feels this right can ever be wrong. There is a lot of wrong in your life, change that, or don't but, leave what's right, what's good…leave us, let us be. I promise you we're worth it. Give me a chance to make you smile like you used to in that picture you have in your room. I'm not asking you to forget about her, or change your past. I'm asking for you to let me help you rewrite the rest of your life. It doesn't have to be like this. You don't need to keep punishing yourself."

You're wasting your breath.
Once an addict, always an addict.
You'll always be Jack's daughter and nothing more.

I shook my head, not willing to allow my maker take control of my mind. I was in control and I needed to hang onto it with everything in me because today Blackie needed me. I didn't have time to succumb to the lies my mind tried to make me believe.

I embraced the truth, the truth I've always known---Blackie needs me as much as I need him. He saw me long before that night I went to the clubhouse and asked him to look at me—the real me. He tries to deny it; he fights it but he feels it…the unexplainable connection between us.

They say everyone has a soulmate.

And his broken soul belongs to mine.

I leaned over his body and pressed my lips to his forehead.

"You're my hero," I whispered, pressing a kiss to his nose before pulling back and wiping my cheeks with the backs of my hands. "Wake up and I'll be yours."

Chapter Twelve

BLACKIE

You know you've committed too many sins, fucked too many people and ruined too many lives when the devil don't even want your ass. I should be dead but even Satan didn't want to save me from the nothing I had become. Nope, that prick bastard turned his back on me too.

That's when you know you're fucked and you start to wonder if you're fucking immortal. When I get the fuck out of here I'm going to Atlantic City, putting all my cash on Black because motherfucker I can't lose.

I beat the odds every-fucking-time.

Now, I was sitting in a hospital bed, hours after waking up from a coma. One I apparently had been in for nearly two weeks and trying to make sense of everything. When I first woke up I freaked the fuck out and judging by the frightened look of the nurse, held some sort of resemblance to the exorcist. I had a tube down my fucking throat and couldn't speak until they took it out. I tried to pull the damn thing out myself but the jerk off doctor stuck my hands in restraints and gave me a sedative because being out cold for two weeks wasn't enough.

Once the sedative wore off they returned to brief me on my condition. They think I'm a junkie and that I did this shit to myself. While there is truth to their conclusions they don't know that there was a woman who I got clean for and another that I wanted to stay clean for. They don't know that I intercepted Jimmy Gold from taking Lacey or that in the larger scheme of things I sacrificed my veins for the innocent kids growing up on the streets of New York.

A social worker was sent in to discuss treatment options and facilities. They started me on methadone since my heart was too weak to withstand the withdrawals and now I had a choice. I could continue with the methadone once I was released from the hospital or go to an in-patient drug rehab.

"I know you've been through a lot and we've dumped a lot of information on you, but for now we need to concentrate on strengthening your heart and getting you well enough to tackle the addiction," the social worker explained.

I turned my head.

"I tried calling her," she said after a moment and I snapped my eyes back to hers. "The girl that visits you," she explained. "But she's not on your contact list," she continued as she glanced down at the restraints binding my wrists. "There's been a brigade of people coming through these doors for you, a lot of people pulling for you, but her?" she shrugged her shoulders as she untied the restraint. "It's painfully obvious she needs you the most," she conceded, raising my free hand before placing it on the bed beside me. Her gaze met mine as she patted my hand. "Make it count, Mr. Petra." She paused. "Addiction affects not only the person using, but the people who love that person, well, they suffer too."

She patted my hand before turning around and walking out of the room.

I didn't need to question who the girl was.

I knew it with every fiber of my being.

Lace.

And the idea of her sitting vigil at my side, wishing for me to wake up and be the man that sees her, gutted me more so than waking up only to realize the devil chewed me up and spit me out.

I faintly heard a commotion come from somewhere outside my room and tried to focus on that instead of my insides that were churning. I turned my head just in time to watch the pack of men, wearing that unmistakable cut, bulldozing their way through the nurse's station.

"There he is," Wolf cheered as he was the first to enter my room. He was quickly pushed to the side by Jack. His eyes locked with mine as he started straight for me. His expression was unreadable or maybe I was in too much pain to decipher it, either way I didn't know what to expect. He pushed the machines out of his way, bent down, and took my head in his hands.

"My man," Jack said, kissing my head before he leaned back and pinned me with a stare. "Left side of the table's been empty, brother," he explained hoarsely.

Two weeks being out of commission, off my bike and away from my chair at the table was too long. I left my brothers in the middle of chaos and confusion, went back on my word when I said I'd demolish Jimmy, and ruined the deal with the Corrupt Bastards.

I shook my head slightly.

I should feel some remorse, guilt maybe for all the shit I put my club through over the last couple of weeks but I don't. I would do it again. I'd take the needle, let that bastard shoot me up with whatever the fuck he wanted. Give me another heart attack, do whatever the fuck you gotta do, but don't touch her.

Not Lace.

And not because she was Jack's daughter.

"I'm sorry," I said, lifting my eyes to Jack.

Sorry for taking your little girl and making her mine.

"You got nothing to be sorry for," Jack replied. "I owe you everything," he reiterated. "You saved Lacey, and you kept Reina sane," he continued. "You sacrificed yourself for the club and that shit deserves a whole lot more than a thank you. Need you well, Black, need you to reverse this shit Jimmy has you strung out on, knocking on death's door," he growled. "Whatever it takes, we've got you," he insisted.

I remember him pleading with me after Christine died to get myself clean. He promised me we'd change the direction of the club, kick the drugs to the curb and make her death count. And mostly he lived up to his promise but Jack never banked on this shit with Jimmy surfacing. Yet, here we are and now I'm hooked on methadone, compliments of the hospital. The last few years, staying clean, trying to honor my wife the only way I knew how… all went to shit.

"Ay!" Pipe agreed.

I went against my word the first time I sat in front of Jimmy, chose revenge over my vow to Christine when I stuck that needle in my arm but I thought I was doing the right thing. I thought it was a step I had to take to make my way to the G-Man. But Jimmy, that motherfucker, took two weeks of my fucking life and made me break another vow to my wife. Two fucking weeks meant two Saturday's I didn't bring flowers to Christine's grave.

"Did we get him? Gold is he…" My sentence trailed off as my jaw clenched with anger.

Two fucking weeks.

He better be dead.

"Oh, we fucking got him," Jack assured. "Lit that motherfucker up," he added.

"How?" I demanded.

I wanted to know everything, from the shock and horror in his eyes to the way his flesh smelled when the flames ate away at him. But before he divulged the sweetness of Jimmy's demise, Jack needed to explain how he pulled this shit off without me and the deal we made with the Corrupt Bastards.

Jack turned around and pointed his thumb over his shoulder toward Riggs.

"This son of a bitch right here, saved the day, your life and my sanity," he declared.

"And still no fucking pie," Riggs replied, shaking his head in disgust.

Riggs? He got the drugs for the deal? I know for a fact he didn't get that shit from the Corrupt Bastards because they wouldn't deal with a new face. I was the one that shook on our agreement. They were funny like that, or maybe smart, depending on how you look at it.

"What about the deal?" I questioned.

"We made a new deal," Jack answered.

I stared at him for a minute before narrowing my eyes in confusion.

"You got the drugs?" I asked, trying to sit up. It was a yes or no question so, I'm not sure why they're all tiptoeing around like a bunch of pussy's.

"C'mon man, don't worry 'bout that shit. You need to concentrate on getting off this shit and getting yourself good," Jack said, reaching over to help me sit up.

"I want to know," I insisted, glancing around the room before bringing my eyes back to Jack. I watched as he raked his hands through his hair, cupping the back of his neck as he bit the inside of his cheek and debated on what bullshit lie he would spew at me.

"We took the drugs from The Red Dragons," Riggs offered.

The room fell silent as I watched Bone's elbow Riggs in the gut.

They got the drugs from Sun Wu, the leader of the Red Dragons, the same club we went to war with when Cain controlled us. The Red Dragons were big time dealers back in the day but the G-Man shut their business down and used the Satan's Knights and Cain's addiction to aid in his cause. We shut down the Dragons, stole their business and left them high and dry. They were vulnerable at the time, their trade business wasn't off the ground yet and taking away the drugs was like cutting them off at the knees. Sun Wu supplied the cops with the location of the two bodies of those kids that overdosed and died. He was trailing me, I knew it then, but I ignored it because I was a greedy, cocky motherfucker who thought I was invincible. After the cops found the bodies, they built a case against me. Greg Brantley was new to the force and trying to make a name for himself, and the Red Dragons led his ass straight to me.

I proved to be invincible.

Christine not so much.

Brantley got his hooks in her.

"You got the drugs from Wu? Are you out of your fucking minds?" I barked, pulling the wires off my arm as I sat up.

"Blackie, it's good. We're good. Jones arrested Jimmy at Temptations with the drugs," Jack explained calmly. "Everything went like we planned."

Famous last words.

Nothing ever goes as planned.

Lesson fucking learned.

"We didn't plan to fuck the Chinese," I shouted furiously in between coughing.

"It's fine, brother. Wu and the Dragons have no idea it was us. We have a meet with them tomorrow for another shipment of guns. We're good man," Pipe offered. "We're fucking good man, relax!"

I was useless lying here in this bed, I needed to be out on the streets smoothing shit over with the Corrupt Bastards and keeping my eyes and ears open for when Wu discovered the truth.

"Tell him your news," Pipe ordered Riggs.

"What news?" I asked bewildered.

"Yeah, give it to him. He's going to love this shit," Wolf agreed.

I turned my attention to Riggs, watching as he snarled.

"Fine! I gave you mouth to mouth," he exasperated.

"Not that!" Jack said, shaking his head.

I rolled my eyes, looking back at Riggs expectantly.

"Shit," he sighed. "I'm having a kid," he continued.

"Give him the good stuff, tell him who's the baby mama," Pipe said, wiggling his eyebrows as he glanced at me. "Wait for it…"

"Fuck off," Riggs said, flipping the bird to Pipe.

"Riggs knocked up Bianci's sister," Wolf supplied.

"Come on guys," Bones started.

I stared at him blankly for a second. The only one possibly more fucked than me right now was Riggs. Not that having a kid was so fucking terrible, but having Bianci as an in-law? Fuck, if my heart didn't bleed for Riggs, even though he was a fucking pain in the ass. Even though he was responsible for the resurrection of Sun Wu.

"Glad I could amuse you fuckers," he grunted.

The glass doors opened causing me to turn my head and my eyes locked with Lacey's. She leaned against the door, taking a deep breath as she continued to stare at me.

Those eyes.

Man, I wasn't sure if I'd see them again.

It all came crashing down on me like a ton of bricks. The whole ordeal of being held captive by Jimmy and realizing the only reason I wanted to fight to live was to be able to look into those eyes one more time.

But with that, also came the truth—I was sitting here with a methadone drip and I'd never be what she needs. I already had the blood of one innocent woman on my hands, I'd fucking die a slow death before I covered my hands with Lacey's too. I did what I was supposed to do, I kept her safe and didn't let Jimmy get to her and that's where it had to end.

I remembered the pain in her eyes, the night she came to the clubhouse, and I fought to keep the memories of her wrapped around me at bay but staring into her eyes now, the pain was still there. Was I the only one who saw the demons reflected in those pretty eyes? I wondered if God put them there only for me to chase them away.

I shook my head, dismissing the thought, reminding myself I was poison, a man who couldn't even help himself let alone anyone else.

She's not my problem.

My club.

That's what I need to focus on…. getting the fuck out of this hospital so I can be the soldier I am. I had one goal and only one and that was to end the G-Man and all his connections, damn the consequences. Lacey didn't fit anywhere in my plans.

"You're okay?" she whispered, ignoring everyone as she stepped toward the side of my bed. "You're okay," she repeated, this time her words surer than the first time she uttered them. She reached out to touch me and I turned my head, my eyes meeting Jack's.

Wrong fucking place to look.

"I'm good, kid," I muttered, clearing my throat. "Going to want my gun back," I told Jack.

"Yeah," he agreed, his eyes wandering back and forth between Lacey and myself.

I felt her eyes on me and it took every fucking ounce of self-control I could muster up not to give in and look back at her, not to reach for her and pull her onto this bed with me.

"So a kid, huh?" I said hoarsely, turning to Riggs, pleading with him to save my sorry ass.

"Yeah, I'm going to be a dad," he confirmed as he stared back at me hiding his smirk.

"Congrats, man," I said, clenching the sheet with my fists as I ignored the hurt expression adorning Lacey's face.

"I'm glad you're okay," she whispered, turning on her heel before scrambling out of the hospital room.

Run baby, it ain't safe here for you.

"Lacey," Jack called.

Shit.

"Dude, speaking of Pea…" Bones started, glancing at the clock.

"Pea?" Jack asked distractedly, starring after his daughter.

"Don't ask," Riggs mumbled.

"Didn't Lauren have the doctor's appointment today?"

"Shit!" Riggs roared. "I've got to get out of here," he said hastily, starting for the door. "Glad you're awake, brother," he added before jetting out of the room. Bones rose to his feet.

"I better go make sure he doesn't fuck this shit up any more than he already has," he explained, giving me a two-finger salute before following Riggs out the door.

Jack turned to me.

"Time you and I had a talk," Jack said before glancing over his shoulder at Wolf and Pipe. "Do me a solid and go make sure my girl's okay," he barked.

"Isn't that his job?" Wolf pointed out as he tipped his chin towards me.

"Not anymore," Jack ground out, keeping his eyes steady on me.

Yeah.

We were about to have *that* talk.

Chapter Thirteen

Lacey

It's exhausting fighting with your own head and most of the time I believe it's worth the battle. In essence I'm the winner because I didn't feed from the lies my mind tried to fill me with. But what if they aren't lies? What if the thoughts that your mind creatively spins is the actual truth you were trying to ignore?

I have struggled to own my truth, the one that my heart tells me and not the one my mind does. I tell myself my mind plays tricks on me, that it wants me to believe one thing when I believe another. I argue that my truth is real because I feel it and don't think it. The heart is a thing of beauty, something that thrives on love and affection, not lies. So, when your heart calls to you, you listen to nothing but the beating vessel of truth.

But I don't know if those are the thoughts of a naïve girl desperate for someone to love her or if they are the thoughts of a strong woman who fought for control over her mind and found truth in the jaded eyes of the man she loves.

He barely looked at me. I visited him every day for two weeks, whether it was for five minutes or two hours, I didn't miss one day. I sat there, holding his hand and asked him all the questions I wished he'd answer, like why everyone calls him Blackie, and if the club chose him or he chose the club. I wanted to know everything about him, even the ugly, and then I wanted to be the one to show him that where there is ugly there is beauty.

I wanted him to wake up and realize that he was gifted a second chance at life, and as much as I wanted him to look at me and notice I was standing in front of him asking for a chance to love him—I wanted for him to look in the mirror and decide his life was worth something.

He woke up.

Thank God, for that.

But, he woke up and he looked right through me. It was like I didn't exist and every touch, every small gesture, and stolen glance—they were all figments of my imagination. A cruel trick my mind played on my heart.

The heart doesn't lie.

The mind does.

The heart is gullible.

The mind is vindictive.

I glanced around the empty hallway, taking deep breaths as hot tears streamed my face. I heard Riggs and Bones walk out of Blackie's room and I quickly spun around, wiping at my cheeks with the back of my hands and hurried down the hallway.

I needed to get out of here. I had already made a fool out of myself, charging into his room like his woman, earning suspicious eyes from the club….my father included. Everyone excerpt Blackie.

Get over it, you're nothing but Jack's daughter.

He doesn't want you.
He looks at you and still sees you as Little Lacey Parrish.
You're just a job.
You're nothing.

"Shut up," I hissed, through clenched teeth as I collided with another body. I lifted my head and stared at my father's girlfriend.

"Looking for these?" Reina asked, holding up my keys.

"How?"

"You dropped them on your way to see Blackie," she stated, reaching into her purse she pulled out a handful of tissues and handed them to me.

I forgot that I bumped into her. This morning we buried my uncle, my father's brother Danny, whom Jimmy Gold killed months ago. The feds had just released his body after closing their investigation and my father had Bones' set up a small burial at Green-Wood cemetery. After the service, when everyone was getting ready to leave, Pipe announced the hospital had called and Blackie had finally woken up. I went home with my mother, lied to her about meeting up with my friend Daniela and drove my ass straight here. I was in such a hurry I nearly knocked Reina on her ass.

"Dry your eyes," she insisted.

"It's not what it looks like," I tried to cover.

"Oh honey, it's exactly what it looks like," she laced her arm through mine as Wolf's voice sounded from down the hallway.

"Let's get out of here," she whispered, leading me to the bank of elevators. Once we were inside she pointed to the ceiling covered in silver paneling that acted like a mirror. I went to work wiping the mascara that painted my face.

The doors opened and we stepped off, making our way through the lobby and outside.

"How is he doing?"

I shrugged my shoulders, shoving my hands in my back pockets as we walked side by side with no direction. I glanced at her from the corner of my eye and she looked back at me.

"Leather and Lace," Reina said.

My feet stopped in their tracks.

"What do you know about that?" I asked, hastily.

She shook her head, reaching out she placed her fingers beneath my chin and turned my face to hers so our eyes locked.

"Just one thing," she whispered. "Those three words kept that man…," she glanced over her shoulder at the hospital. "…alive."

Butterflies.

Her words gave me butterflies and my dull heart, lured to sleep by mind, beat again.

Lies.
You know the truth.

"I doubt that very much," I whispered.

"Then how do I know about Leather and Lace?" she questioned, taking a deep breath before she ran her fingers through her long blonde hair. "I have no idea what goes on between the two of you and…I shouldn't even be saying this," she struggled, biting down on her lip. "Fuck it," she conceded. "I know you and I don't know each other long, or even well enough for you to trust me but hear me out okay?"

I nodded.

"When I first met your dad I was a woman who had given up on living a full life. I had been through hell and back and didn't know my place in the world or if I even had one. I had scars both visible and not and I let those scars dictate my future. I thought I wasn't worthy of sharing my life with someone and that I was destined to be alone. Then your dad came into my life and my past, the scars, it all sort of faded away. He took away my scars just by being the man willing to accept them as his own."

"Reina, I'm real happy for you and my dad but this— "

"I'm the person who lived that nightmare with Blackie. We thought we would die, Lacey, and when you're facing death there is one gift you're given and that is gift of truth. You can say anything you want out loud because no one else will know. You can admit the things you keep hidden, the words that have the power to heal the scars you're afraid to show the world because there aren't any consequences to your truth, it dies right along with the rest of you. Blackie told me to hang on for your dad. He reminded me of the one person I had in this world. He reminded me I had love waiting for me and I believe with everything in me that's what kept me sane and kept me fighting," she admitted as her eyes watered.

"I asked Blackie what he was hanging on for and he told me Leather and Lace," she whispered hoarsely. "You're Lace aren't you?"

I glanced down at the sidewalk.

I waited for my maker to appear and tell me Reina was lying but the taunting never came. My heart pounded in my ears, calling out loudly, demanding I listen. I slowly lifted my head as the tears rolled down my cheeks.

"I'm Lace," I confirmed.

"You're the reason he's breathing," she rasped.

"Why are you telling me this? My father---"

"I owe it to Blackie," she interrupted. "He may not agree, probably would deny every word, and if we're being honest that's why I haven't brought myself to see him yet. I can't look at him and not know how to thank him. He was in bad shape Lacey, real bad, and still he tried to help me. I don't know how to help him other than this…. admitting a truth, he is too damaged to admit himself. He's got scars, sweetie, and they run deep," she paused, reaching out to tuck a strand of hair behind my ear. "The man just needs someone to claim his scars."

"How do you claim a piece of someone when they aren't willing to give it to you?"

"We all want to be set free from our scars but some of us hold onto them a little longer than others. You can't force them from him but you shouldn't give up on him yet," she said.

I stared at Reina for a moment, digesting her words and trying to find the right ones to say back to her. Thank you didn't seem enough for the gift she gave me; the reminder of truth my heart already knew but my mind fought. The struggle would be rough, the battle between heart and mind, but I'd keep fighting it with everything in me because Blackie didn't give up. He fought for Leather and Lace, he fought for me....

I reached out, wrapping my arms around Reina, thankful she came into all of our lives and happy she found the strength to give herself freely to my dad.

There was hope to be found even in the most hopeless of situations.

BLACKIE

"Pretty bold move you made," I stated, staring at Jack as he leaned back, propping one foot against the wall and crossed his arms against his chest. I sat up further, pushing aside the wires connected to my arm and met his gaze head on.

Man to man.

Brother to brother.

He stared me down, choosing his words wisely as I grew increasingly pissed. I wasn't sure if I was pissed at him for questioning my loyalty or myself for giving him a fucking reason to.

"I didn't know I was doing such a shit job watching out for Lacey, that you decided to throw Wolf and Pipe on her ass," I accused.

"Did I say that?" he shook his head. "Did a fine job looking out for my daughter," he paused, kicking off the wall before taking two strides towards my bed. "Been putting her first for a while, without question, without concern, and I appreciate it Black," he continued. "You put me and my family, this club...everyone and anything before yourself."

"Yeah, so?"

"So, it's 'bout time you put yourself first," he countered. "Before this shit with Jimmy went south, you told me Reina and Lacey need me breathing, you remember that?"

I cleared my throat, turning my cheek.

I remembered.

I remembered thinking of how torn up Lacey would be if anything happened to her old man. How much I didn't want to be the man who had to deliver that news to her. I remembered picturing her pretty face and silently vowing to keep her old man safe, keep him coming back to her, because shit, I never wanted to see her fucking cry. Not if there was something I could do about it.

When did that shit change?

When did I go from being the man who prevented the tears to the one who caused them?

"You remember that?" he asked louder this time

"Yeah, Bulldog, I remember," I turned my eyes back to his. "That shit was no lie," I hissed. When Jack went away, I was running the club and protecting his interests. I could've put one of the guys on Lacey, make another man be the one to look out for her, but I was greedy for the sweet and innocent girl that reminded me of the good things life sometimes threw at men like us, men who were so undeserving of innocence.

"Neither were the words I said to you," he stressed, rolling his neck from side to side. "I need you breathing," he seethed. "I made a promise to you when I gave you that patch and made you my left at the table, told you we would clean up the mess Cain put the club in, we'd kick the drugs," he paused. "And after you laid Christine to rest, you made a promise to her, heard you crying with my own ears when you told her you would clean up, go get help and all that."

"I did," I shouted, gripping the sides of the bed angrily as I stared back at him. "I kept my word until Jimmy Gold landed on our doorstep…so did you."

Drinking didn't count. I didn't pick up that habit until I kicked all the others. I didn't promise anyone I wouldn't become a drunk. Fair game.

"So what? That's it? I should send Pipe to the corner with a fifty bag and you should shoot until your veins collapse? To hell with everything you, me, this fucking club worked for? We'll just let it all go to shit for some cock-sucking mobster? Turn his charred ass over to Vic and let him handle our business?"

"That was your fucking plan, not mine. You and Bianci came and told me we would feed Jimmy the drugs, set him up and get his ass sent to prison. We sat down with Vic and he gave his word, once we delivered Jimmy he'd end that miserable fuck's life and then make it his mission to get the G-Man. I didn't believe it but the man fucking swore on the bible, thought that shit counted for something," I sneered.

'That's still the plan," Jack said, calmly.

I narrowed my eyes at him, trying to decide if he was fucking with me or not. One minute he's talking about cleaning up the streets and ridding the world of scumbags like the G-Man and Jimmy ourselves and the next he's talking about handing them over to the mob on a silver platter.

"So what the fuck you busting my balls about then?" I grunted.

"You think Jimmy didn't have a crew in place, the motherfucker was working with the G-Man. You don't think that man will send someone to retaliate against the men who took his dealer off the streets?"

I watched as Jack cracked his knuckles.

"I'm not fucking worried about Sun Wu, Black, it's every goddamn pusher the G-Man has working from inside the prison he's rotting in, to outside these four walls. We don't have Vic anymore to aide in the clean-up this shit is all on us. His job is to eliminate the scumbags inside with him," he pinned me with a stare. "It's only a matter of time before these fucking streets becomes a war zone. I will say it once, and only once, you need to get your fucking act together and be the fucking man I know you are. If that means you taking time to go get clean, then that's what you do because when mayhem comes I need you," he rasped, raking his fingers through his hair.

"Appreciate the concern," I ground out. "I'll handle my shit. You don't have to worry about me becoming a liability to the club," I added.

"Oh fuck that," he growled. "You think that's why I'm here asking you to get well? Fuck liabilities. Everyone in this club thought I'd be a liability because of my mind, because I got some shit disorder that fucks with me, but you never gave me lip for it. Your confidence in my ability to run our club never shifted. I'm not here telling you to clean up because I'm worried you won't fucking do your job. I know you Black, been your brother for years, you function better on any goddamn poison than you do when your levelheaded. I'm telling you get your ass off the drugs because I don't want to put your ass in the dirt. Now, I just buried a brother, a real fucking brother, who never had my back the way you've had my back and that stung but digging a hole for you will fucking make me bleed."

I looked away as his words echoed in my ears.

His plea should've made me proud of my duty served as his vice president but his words fell flat for me. I didn't need his approval as the president of our club, I knew I had that, that I had earned his respect in that aspect. But hearing him beg me to turn my life around so I can do my job made me feel some kind of way, made me feel something I wasn't used to feeling.

Remorse and not for anyone other than myself.

I'm the man at his left, the self-destructing cowboy who will help him destroy any and all enemies. I'm his soldier, the man he relies on in our corrupt world of crime. He has faith in me when it comes to my job, when it comes to a promise I made my dead wife, but that's where it ends. Jack didn't think I could be a better man, he knew what I was, what I'd always be and that wasn't the kind of guy he'd ever want for Lacey. I could go on protecting her, doing my job as his second, but claiming her? Making her more than just a duty, turning my fucked up life around to be better for her? That shit could never be.

I'm Blackie, Satan's knight and that's all I'll ever be.

"I'm not going anywhere," I said, finally. "You might not be concerned about the Red Dragons but I am. They'll figure out we were responsible for the drugs, mark my words, and we're going to need to be ready. On top of that, we fell through on our deal with the Corrupt Bastards, they're not going to take what happened with Jimmy as an excuse for why they're sitting with a quarter million dollars' worth of drugs in their laps. I need to get the fuck out of here and smooth shit over with them before they think we were looking to fuck them all along. I will keep on with the methadone until things calm down for the club. The doctor mentioned a clinic, and when the time is right, when I know you don't need me front and center I'll kick the methadone on my own. No rehab. I did it once I can do it again," I assured him.

I diverted my eyes back to his as he nodded in agreement.

"Now, get your ass fucking strong because it's going to be a wild ride," he asserted, starting for the door. He paused, turning around and looking at me thoughtfully.

"My girl grew some kind of attachment to your ass," he muttered.

I sighed, dropping my head against the pillows.

"Well, we faced fucking death together," I ground out, staring up at the ceiling. "From what I remember, Reina held her own. That woman of yours gave Jimmy one hell of a fight," I informed him.

"Wasn't talking about Reina," he said, turning back and striding out the door without another word.

Yeah, I grew an attachment to her too.

Fuck me.

Chapter Fourteen

BLACKIE

The doctors hate me; the nurses do too. I'm their worst nightmare, the worse goddamn patient to enter this hospital. They keep breaking my balls, telling me I need to take it easy and all that shit. They lecture me by saying I have to condition my heart, do some kind of physical therapy to build up my strength. They think if they put me on a treadmill I'll jog my way to recovery.

Fucking bullshit.

These motherfuckers don't know I'm a bull.

I caused all sorts of havoc when I stepped off the treadmill, dropped to the floor and did push-ups.

Protocol.

They say I don't follow it.

I never followed rules and such, a little heart attack would not change that.

Once my stint in physical therapy was over, the nurse summoned for a transporter to escort my ass back to my room where my dose of methadone was waiting for me.

And a pissed off Bulldog.

"Look, Mr. Petra, you have a visitor," the cheerful transporter exclaimed.

"Joy," I said mockingly, sitting down on the edge of the bed and kicking back the dose of fake heroin as if it was a shot of the finest whiskey.

I pushed the empty paper cup onto the rolling cart before I lifted an eyebrow at the transporter.

"Something else you need?" I asked. The motherfucker was looking at me like I was supposed to tip him or something.

"Have a good day, Mr. Petra," he stuttered, scampering out the door, causing a grin to spread across my face.

I'm a dick.

"What did he do to you?" Jack asked, reminding me he was there. I turned around and glanced at him and shrugged my shoulders.

"They fuck with me, I fuck with them…it's a love-hate relationship," I said.

"I wouldn't want you as a patient," he replied, standing up from the chair and making his way over to me.

I wasn't expecting to see him, partially because I think he's onto the fact Lacey isn't just his daughter anymore, but the girl who has me twisted up in knots. The last couple of days, without the constant flow of my brothers visiting me, I sat here and thought of her.

"Lucky for you, you missed your calling in the medical field." I tipped my chin at him. "Looking at you, I'm almost afraid to ask, what the fuck happened now?"

He bit the inside of his cheek, sucked in a breath before he leaned against the wall and shook his head.

"You were right," he said.

"Going to have to be a little more specific," I replied, narrowing my eyes as I peered at him.

"Sun Wu knows it was us that took the drugs," he ground out.

"How do you know?"

"The motherfucker took Riggs. We didn't even know they had him, Bones was the only one who suspected anything. Well, him and Bianci but that's because Wu dropped his bike in front of Xonerated. They covered the bike and the front door of the gym in red paint," he paused, looking like he was debating on whether he should continue.

"Just fucking tell me," I said, clenching my jaw, making the decision easier for him.

"We were at Pop's getting the guns ready for the deal we made with the Dragons, waiting for them to pick the crates up and Bones voiced his concerns," he shrugged his shoulders, running his hand along the scruff that lined his jaw before he continued. "I figured Riggs had his head up his ass with all this shit going on with Bianci's sister and the baby and he went off the grid on his own—"

"Jack, I don't give two shits what you thought I want to know what actually happened," I interrupted angrily.

"The back doors of the van opened, they started shooting as they rolled his body out of the truck and sped off. Wolf and Pipe took a couple of shots at the van but they got away," he barked.

I blew out a breath, balling my hands into fists as I peered up at him.

"And Riggs?"

"They fucked him up, dropped him at our feet battered and bruised with a price tag on his head," he said, pushing off the wall he was leaning on and crossed the room. "Literally, the cock-sucking bastard shaved two, five, zero on Riggs's head," he muttered.

"Two hundred fifty thousand," I said.

"That's what you made the deal with Jimmy for, two hundred and fifty thousand dollars' worth of heroin but we didn't have time to get the drugs from the Corrupt Bastards like you planned, and on top of that we didn't have you," he argued. "We had to get the drugs from somewhere and it had to be the amount we agreed on. I wasn't risking your life or Reina's."

"I get it Bulldog, but we're going to have to pay that debt back to the Corrupt Bastards if we want peace. They aren't just going to take the fucking loss. So, now we have to come up with a half a mill or we will be at war with two fucking clubs," I seethed.

"You want to let me finish?" he growled.

"After we got Riggs patched up we paid Wu a visit, he demanded we give him the money or we would have three dead bodies on our hands," he continued.

"Why three?"

"Because when we took the drugs we killed three of his men and a dozen whores that were cutting and packaging the heroin," Jack ground out.

The story got better and better, the hole deeper, and the body count higher.

"You know Riggs did the security cameras at Sun Wu's property on Mott Street. Well turns out that's how he knew that Wu was keeping a stash house there.

He dipped into the feed and caught them cutting and packing the drugs. It was pretty cut and dry when we went in, didn't have time to work a plan. We shot our way through the front door, and put holes in anyone who got in our way. Somewhere along the way Wolf lost his cool and started shooting the whores and Riggs took his ski mask off," Jack explained, shaking his head before he sat down and dropped his head to his knees.

I clenched my fist, bringing it down on the rolling cart and sent all the contents to the floor.

"I gotta get out of here," I ground out.

Jack raised his head, fixing me with a glare.

"Riggs bought us some time. You need to get yourself fucking straight because I can't have you strung out on shit, wallowing in your misery because you know just as well as I do, giving that motherfucker his money was just the beginning," he fumed.

"Wait. Where did you get the money to give him?"

"Our boy Riggs is a rich boy living life as an outlaw," Jack said, shrugging shoulders. "Guess money doesn't make the world go round," he added. "The Bastards haven't contacted us for the drugs. If I had to guess that could go one of two ways…they can be pining for you to make this shit right or they could give a fuck less and looking for a way to end us."

"Well it shit as sure isn't the first one," I grunted, spreading my arms wide. "I'm stuck here, easy to find me, easy to get me, but only people strolling through that door are Knights," I said.

"I'm sending Pipe and Wolf into the field to sway some of the nomads into joining our charter. The only reason the club is standing is because we've had Bianci and the Valente kid watching our backs, pitching in with this whole Jimmy mess but they're not fucking Knight's. We can't put them on the back of a bike, put an AK-47 in their hands and a cut on their backs.

I crossed my arms against my chest and damned everything to hell.

"What about Lace?" I asked, instantly regretting the question as it left my lips. I watched as he cocked an eyebrow.

"What about her?"

"You put Wolf and Pipe on her ass and now you're sending them off on a goddam excursion," I pointed out.

He stepped closer, his eyes darkened making them almost as black as the shirt he was wearing. "What's going on Black?"

I forgot he was my friend.

I forgot he was the Bulldog, and that I answered to him.

He was just a man.

Just Jack.

And I was a man who had run out of fucks to give.

"Don't like her roaming around without protection when there are two fucking wars about to slam into our territory. I'm sure you don't either," I stated.

"Yeah, and I know why I don't…. not too sure why you don't," he questioned warily.

"It's real simple. She may be your daughter but you made her a part of all our lives," I ground out. "Can't order me to protect her one minute and not the next, can't give me her life, tell me it's precious then expect me not to put her high on my list of priorities. I'm not made that way and you of all people should know that, understand it, because it's the sole reason you asked me to look out for all those years ago…you knew I wouldn't be able to turn that shit on and off so, don't ask me too now," I chided. "So, if Wolf and Pipe are going out on the road, someone needs to keep an eye on her," I added.

He crossed his arms and silently assessed me, letting my words ferment in his head.

"Then I guess it's a good thing your ass will be out of here soon," he said finally before narrowing his eyes as he uncrossed his arms and stepped closer. "Let's pray I can hold my shit together, and keep my business away from her until her knight breaks free," he said, squaring his shoulders back before turning around. "Another reason for you to get your act together…apparently no one watches out for Lacey like you—not even me," he sneered, pulling open the door before pausing and looking back at me. "She's my daughter, Black, *mine*, my only surviving child. You remember that the next time you question my intentions," he paused. "Actually, do yourself a favor and don't question my intentions when it comes to my daughter."

He turned and strode out the door, closing it behind him.

What the fuck was wrong with me?

I ran my fingers through my hair, tugging at the ends as I stared at the door.

I was losing my fucking mind, spiraling out of control like an addict going through withdrawals and for the first time it wasn't drugs making me unravel.

It was her.

I meant it when I said there was no on and off switch with me. I wasn't the type of guy that was satisfied with a little, I wanted it all, pushed and pushed until I got it too.

I got my appetite wet with Lacey and now I'd never be sated.

It was that revelation that turned two impending wars into three and the third would be the bloodiest and most destructive.

Brother versus brother.

President versus Vice President.

Two men who only know one side now knew two.

His.

Mine.

I shook my head, releasing my hold on my hair and crossed the room as I pushed the thought away. I couldn't go to war with Jack…the idea was ridiculous.

Almost as ridiculous as thinking I'm capable of letting her go.

Chapter Fifteen

Lacey

I worked up enough nerve over the next week to face Blackie, allowing Reina's admission of Blackie's truth drive my courage to confront him. He might not be ready to hand me over his scars but I would let him know the way I felt. I had nothing to lose and everything to gain. He could either accept my feelings or he could push them away but either way I would not hide them.

Not from him.

Not from anyone.

Silly nicknames that started off as a joke, an attempt to get him to smile, became a lifeline for both of us. That had to count for something didn't it?

It means everything to me.

And now I know it means something to him too.

He was transferred to a private room and well enough not to be in intensive care anymore. I knocked before I stepped into his room, closing the door behind me as my stomach twisted in knots. I walked further inside and noticed he wasn't in bed, or even in the chair perched in the corner. I turned around and walked into the bathroom only to find it empty too. I stepped back into the room just as the door opened and when I lifted my head, my eyes locked with his.

I blinked, taking another look at the freshly shaved man in front of me and my eyes widened. He was dressed casually in a pair of black sweats and a plain white t-shirt that stretched across his broad shoulders. His hair that usually hung messily around his face was pushed back and tied in a short ponytail at the base of his neck. There was no scruff lining his jaw exposing all his perfectly hard features.

"Are you okay or do you need me to help you get back into the bed?" The nurse questioned from behind him.

"I've got it," he muttered, keeping his eyes on me.

The nurse glanced at me, smiled slightly before stepping out of the room and closing the door behind her.

"Hi," I choked. "I was starting to think you were discharged," I stammered, watching as he pursed his lips before his tongue took a swipe at his bottom lip.

"Not that lucky," he said, tipping his chin behind me. "Give me a minute?"

I glanced down at myself in confusion before looking over my shoulder and shaking my head, realizing he needed to use the bathroom.

"Oh, right…" I moved out of his way, lifted my eyes back to his and watched as they took a quick perusal of my body.

I had seen that look before, that night, and I remembered how it made me feel like the most desirable girl in the world.

A sound escaped his lips as he walked into the bathroom and closed the door. I swear that sounded like a moan or maybe a growl, whatever it was, it was fucking sexy. I lifted my hand to my throat, letting my fingers mimic the way his dug into my skin that night in his room, and dropped onto his bed.

I wonder if he remembered everything about that night the way I did. If he could still taste me the same way I could taste him.

The bathroom door closed jarring me away from my thoughts and forced me back to reality. I stared at him trying to remember the speech I recited in the car on the way here but the only word that came to mind was muscles.

Tight, sinewy, muscles covered in ink.

It was probably a mortal sin to look like that after having a heart attack.

"You're staring," he said as he crossed his arms and leaned against the wall in front of me.

I swallowed.

"So are you," I whispered.

He bit the inside of his cheek as he quietly assessed me before he nodded.

"I don't think I've ever seen you without jeans or facial hair," I shrugged my shoulders. "It's kind of a shock to the system," I continued, cocking my head to the side. "What's your excuse?" I asked, running my sweaty palms down my denim clad thighs. I watched him intently, waiting for his bullshit excuse and saw the faintest glimpse of a smile form on his lips.

God, I wish he smiled more.

He shook his head, the smile disappeared and for a split second I wondered if I imagined it.

"Make a man wish he didn't hit the bottle so hard," he muttered. "Then maybe I'd remember when you became so bold," he said, pushing off the wall as he turned and took a seat next to me on the bed.

Bold?

He thought I was bold.

He had no idea it was taking every bit of courage I had to be here, demanding he see the woman I am and not the girl I was. Maybe then he wouldn't feel so guilty.

I glanced down as his thigh brushed mine.

"Didn't think I'd see you until I got out of here," he started, fidgeting with his hands until he finally placed them on his knees and leaned forward. He looked over his shoulder at me. "Thought I scared you off the other day," he said, huskily.

"I told you once before I'm not afraid of you," I said, clearing my throat so it didn't sound so raspy.

He kept his eyes pinned to mine for a moment before letting them dip lower. I tried to follow their path but lost all train of thought when he placed his hand on my leg.

"I owe you an apology," he said, his massive hand wrapped around my thigh and gave it a slight squeeze before he lifted his eyes back to mine. "So, pretty…" he murmured.

His closed his eyes briefly before blowing out at a breath and standing up. I felt the loss of his touch instantly and automatically stood with him. He crossed the room, putting as much distance as possible between us before he fell back into the chair in the corner of the room and dropped his face into his hands.

"You don't owe me anything, Blackie," I blurted. "You saved me once again," I added.

"I'm not talking about that," he growled, lifting his head. "I'm talking about the night at the clubhouse," he clarified.

"No," I said, shaking my head, closing the distance between us until I was standing in front of him. I would not plead with him not to take back that night.

Not this time.

With Reina's words playing on repeat in my head I decided the only way for Blackie to accept this thing between us was to remind him of what it felt like to be with one another. Maybe if I reminded him of how it felt when the rest of the world faded and it was just us maybe then he'd think twice about his apology.

"No?" he questioned as he narrowed his eyes. "I took something from you, Lace, something you can't get back and something I won't forget. I fucked us both that night," he seethed.

"You didn't take anything I wasn't offering," I retorted. "I know you think I'm a little girl but I'm not and I haven't been for a while. You may be my first but you weren't the first man to touch me," I ground out. "I'm not some goody two shoes, too prim and proper to get down on her knees because her father is some big bad biker," I sneered.

"Shut up," he shouted.

"No! You said you saw me that night, but it was a lie wasn't it? Because if you did, you'd see I loved every fucking minute of having you. Open your eyes Blackie and take a look, take a good long look," I dared.

"I see you, Lace, been seeing you for a long time now," he said, reaching out and gripping my hips. "Don't tell me to fucking open my eyes because I'm trying so fucking hard to close them and not look at you. It's a real struggle to tame the beast inside me and not spread you wide and take you every which way a man can take a woman," he said through clenched teeth. "Trust me, I fucking see you, girl and you're all woman."

I licked my lips as I felt something down in the pit of my belly ignite. An animalistic sound escaped his lips, something feral, and oh so fucking hot.

Was the beast becoming unleashed?

Yes, please.

His fingers dug deeper into my hips and he pulled me between his legs.

"Sit," he commanded, pulling me down so that my ass sunk between his thighs. He brushed my hair aside, and I felt his hot breath against my ear as he leaned over my shoulder. "You feel that?"

I did.

His thick erection strained and twitched against my ass. A short breath escaped my lips as my back fell against his chest and his arms wrapped around me, pressing me tight against him.

"Answer me," he demanded.

"Yes," I whispered.

"Good, next time you doubt I want you, remember feeling my cock pressed against your sweet ass and know the truth was against you just as it was inside you," he affirmed, pressing his mouth against my neck. "It's time for you to open your eyes, angel, time for you to take a good long look at who you're playing with," he added as his teeth grazed the sensitive spot behind my ear.

I closed my eyes, pushing my ass against him as my hands gripped his hard thighs. My body fell into a trance, one induced by Blackie's words and for the first time in my adult life, sex wasn't something I needed to rush to do, a game I needed to play catch up on, it was something I craved. I wanted to explore, I wanted to learn, and I wanted to do it all with Blackie.

"I'm a greedy bastard Lacey, got marks on my arms," he paused, loosening his arms around me. "Open your eyes and look down," he ordered.

My eyes fluttered open, and I did as I was told, focusing on the track marks on his forearms that were slightly fading.

"Got marks down in my soul too, all proof just how greedy I am," he whispered, wrapping his arms around my waist again. The tip of his nose trailed down the side of my neck, pushing away the collar of my shirt and his lips fell over my shoulder.

"And this greedy bastard won't apologize for taking that sweet cunt of yours. This greedy bastard will forever hold onto that, take that shit proudly to my grave…"

His words trailed off as his teeth sank into my shoulder.

"My Lace…" he murmured against my skin.

I clawed his legs, desperate for more…more words…more of his mouth…just more. His lips glided over the flesh his teeth branded soothing the sting.

"I'm sorry, baby, sorry I didn't take my time with you. I'm sorry I didn't prime that pussy before I took it. I'm sorry I didn't watch you get off, that, I didn't make it good for you," he hissed.

"It was good," I replied quickly.

"Did you get off?" he questioned as his hands dropped from my waist to my thighs, slowly trailing down to my knees before forcing them apart.

I couldn't speak.

"You'd know if you got off, you'd be licking your lips and clenching your thighs because the memory alone would get you wet," he feathered my shoulder with kisses before pulling his head back. "Look at me Lace," he demanded.

He twisted me, lifting my hips, so I sat on his thigh, bringing us face to face, nose to nose.

"So sweet," he murmured as he took my face in his hands.

"Blackie," I whispered, my breath ragged as he turned me inside out.

"Goddamn Lace," he grunted, lifting his hips to push against me. "Like it when you say my name, angel," he said before he sucked my lower lip between his.

I wrapped my arms around his neck and for the first time in my life I felt like I belonged. I kissed him back, exploring his lips with mine, memorizing the feel, the fit, the way they meshed so perfectly.

Two imperfect people.

Perfectly suited for one another.

His fingers snaked into my hair, dragging them through the long waves until he fisted the ends, pulling my head back and breaking the kiss. I groaned in protest but his hot wet mouth closed over my throat and I forgot all about the loss of his mouth on mine.

"Please," I begged, as he continued to suck and graze my neck. I ran my fingers through his hair, dragging the rubber band at the base of his neck away and freed his hair from the restraint. It was my turn to tug on the ends until his head lifted and his hooded eyes met mine.

The room grew silent, the only sound was our breaths as we both stilled and continued to stare at one another.

"What?" I whispered.

He opened his mouth to speak when the door opened and Riggs strode in carrying a pizza box.

"Ah, fuck!" He groaned. "Why? Why am I the only one who walks in on this shit!?" he grunted, tossing the pizza box onto the bed before pointing to us. "You two got some sort of death wish!"

"Give us a minute, Riggs," Blackie ground out.

He rolled his eyes.

"Join an M.C. they said," he muttered, turning around. "It'll be fun they said," he continued as he slammed the door behind him.

I stared at the closed door for a moment, too afraid to turn around and look at Blackie, not ready to leave the perfect bubble we were secluded in.

"Lacey," he started.

"This is the part where you send me away," I said, swallowing against the lump in my throat before I found the courage to turn around and meet his gaze.

Yeah.

Here it comes.

"You're better off away," he stated. "You're too good for this life, girl," he said huskily.

"That's a poor attempt at softening the blow of rejection," I stammered, sliding off his lap.

"It's not rejection," he said.

"Feels like it," I spat.

"This is me saving you one last time because I'm worse than the man with the needle baby," he paused, standing up and closing the distance between us as he took my hand and laced our fingers together. "I'm the poison inside the needle," he said, lifting our joined hands to my cheek. "And you? You're everything good in this world. It's a good dream, Lace. You and me, it's a real good dream but dreams don't come true for men like me."

He dropped his hand from mine and took a retreating step back.

"They do when you want them enough," I replied.

He shoved his hands into the pockets of his sweats and focused his eyes on the floor. Without uttering a word Blackie made it clear our conversation was over and so was this stolen moment.

But there would be more.

I was sure of it.

Chapter Sixteen

BLACKIE

Four weeks.

Four Saturday's I missed.

On the fifth Saturday, I was discharged from the hospital and to my surprise, Jack was waiting for me. I hadn't seen him much since the pissing contest over Lacey and thank Christ for that; I didn't trust myself around him, her—basically anyone with the last name Parrish. Still, the fact that he brushed that shit aside and picked my sorry ass up from the hospital said something…in the larger scheme of things we were brothers.

I just wasn't sure how long we'd be able to hold onto that.

When it would stop being enough.

I cupped my hand, bringing it to my forehead to act as a visor and shield the sun that was temporarily blinding me.

"It's about time you got sprung," Jack quipped, reaching into his pocket and pulling out a pair of my sunglasses. "You're like a fucking vampire," he joked.

"Fuck off," I hissed, snatching the sunglasses out of his hand and fitting them to my face.

He laughed, slapping me on the back and tipped his chin toward the parking lot.

"Let's get the fuck out of here the boys are waiting at the clubhouse," he said as we headed to his truck. I folded my discharge papers and shoved them into the back pocket of my jeans.

"Church?" I questioned as he unlocked his truck and we climbed inside. I watched him nod as he started up the truck, leaning back in his seat before he pulled out of the parking spot.

"Been too long since the table was full," he said, glancing over at me. "Glad to have you back and not a moment too soon," he added before turning his eyes back to the road. "Reina's been cooking up a storm since six-fucking-thirty this morning," he fought back the smile itching to break free. "I don't know if she can cook, but the woman can sure as hell bake, so I think we're safe," he said. "Dinner's at seven."

"Dinner?"

"Dinner," he confirmed. "You beat the odds man. You and Reina made it out of that fucking ordeal, Jimmy got what he was due, sure, we got a boatload of grief to deal with but I'm taking that shit as a win, and we celebrate fucking wins," he resolved.

"I'm not complaining…it's just different," I said.

Celebrations at the Dog Pound usually involved a shit ton of booze, pussy and herb. I don't recall dinner…and none of us ever had someone cook it for us.

"Fuck, that's one way to put it," he grinned, peering at me from the corner of his eye. "Don't think Reina would appreciate it if I served up some ass with the lasagna she's cooking."

I laughed.

"Probably not," I agreed as my mind wandered and I stared out the window, wondering if Lacey would be at dinner.

I thought about her morning, noon and night, half the time I tried to sleep, hoping my mind would shut down and I wouldn't think of her but she fucking invaded my dreams too. It's the same dream over and over, that brings me back to that night when she showed up at the clubhouse and I fucked her. It's a rewrite, a second chance, and this time I take my time with her. I give her inexperienced body all of me, teach her how to let go and enjoy, how pain becomes pleasure. I give her everything and I take in return—the look in her eye when she comes, when her body succumbs to a pleasure she doesn't even know exists.

I take and take, lying to myself all the while, believing I'm giving her what she needs, what she craves. I thank the women who came before her and the experience they gave me, making me a capable man who can turn an awkward experience into one she won't forget. I work her over, gauging her body and the way it responds to mine. Every stroke, every bite, every goddamn flick of my tongue, I watch and I learn what she likes and what she dislikes. I give her more of what she likes, show her things she never imagined, and when she's primed, when I know I've made her as wet as possible I take her. I take that virgin pussy, make it mine and silently vow to be the only man who gets her.

Fucked up shit.

I clear my throat and take a second to rearrange my dick before climbing out of the truck and following Jack into the clubhouse.

"What took you two so long?" Pipe complained, rising from the bar stool he was sitting on.

"Leave 'em alone they were probably necking in the backseat of the Bulldog's truck," Wolf chimed in, a smile spreading across his face as he made his way over, reaching out and messing with my hair. "Glad to see you without the fucking wires and shit," he said.

"I hate you," I groaned, slapping his hand away.

"I only got love for you, brother," he teased.

"Get your ass's in the chapel," Jack growled, shaking his head as he threw his arm around Riggs. "Found your heart yet?"

"Working on it, Prez," he muttered, falling into stride beside him.

Heart.

Jack's been talking about having heart since he first took the gavel, thinks it's the only thing that will keep any of us from being reckless.

We didn't need heart.

We needed a prayer.

We needed God on our side.

Looking around the room, watching as Wolf dry humped the table and Pipe showed everyone pictures of his immigrant wife's new tits, it became obvious the heavenly father was skipping over this crew.

Jack whistled loudly calling attention of everyone at the table and got down to business. We discussed one disaster after another, tried to salvage what was left of our club but I'm not going to lie, we were fucked.

Financially, the club was hurting. All our money was tied up in the gun business and the deal with Wu was off the table, leaving us with no buyer. We all agreed that the Red Dragons were biding their time and wouldn't back down just because they got their money. Like, Sun Wu reminded us, we took three lives from him that were worth a damn. The broads didn't count, he'd likely dispose of them when they ran their course, anyway.

We needed to strengthen our club both in manpower and bankroll so, we set the plan in motion. Pipe would build up the garage, add an extension that gave him more room to work on larger jobs. Jack would go meet with Vic up in Otisville, iron out all the details for when Jimmy would finally be sent up there to rot, or be at Vic's mercy, however you wanted to word it Jimmy would meet the reaper. Jack also planned on working with Vic to protect whatever interests he had left now. Vic had juice with several unions, been greasing their palm for years, and Jack would try to get the club in on that. Someone had to take over that shit and before it went to a rival mob organization, Jack wanted dibs.

Wolf would hit the road, visiting charter after charter to recruit men. He had the roughest job of all because nomads were drifters, men who didn't stay in one place, men who got antsy and only loved the open road. He had to persuade these guys to come over and join the murder. Good luck with that, brother. I can't wait to see what he brings back...I predict a shit load of crazy because you'd have to be certifiable to voluntary choose this shit.

The rest of the club would be on high alert, keeping the clubhouse and our current interests protected.

That left me.

I was heading up north in a few days to meet with the Corrupt Bastards. It took some convincing, since everyone is more concerned about how I'm going to go out on the road when I have to be at the methadone clinic every morning at seven. But it's my face they want to see. It's me who struck the deal with them and me who needed to make shit right. I was going to offer them the guns we were going to sell to the Dragons. Bones was going to rig the van, pull up the floor and hide the weapons beneath it, fill the cage with automotive parts courtesy of Pipes garage, that way if I got pulled over on the highway I looked like a traveling salesman—the car parts type. Riggs is going to hack into my medical records and approve a weekend take home of the methadone and then I'll be on my way.

It was a lot to digest.

It all wouldn't happen overnight and as much as we wished there was a quick fix in the works for us we knew we needed to remain patient.

We needed to keep our heads and make sure we all stayed breathing.

But we had tonight, and we had Reina giving us a home cooked meal.

Tomorrow we would go to hell in a handbasket.

I told the guys I'd meet them at Jack's by seven and I could see the doubt in their eyes. They think I'm going on a mission, that, I'm going to walk out the door, call my dealer and get fucked up. It's tempting.

But not today.

Today I choose to be clean.

I left them to deal with their suspicions and straddled my bike. I didn't have much time before the sun set and the gates closed, so stopping off at Ro's wasn't in the cards. After missing four Saturday's there was no way I'd get out of there without that sweet woman giving me the third degree.

I stopped off at a bodega on a corner and bought three colorful bouquets of flowers, dropped them in my saddlebags and took off to Fort Hamilton. I dreaded seeing the dead flowers at Christine's grave and prepared myself for the guilt that would surface when I saw her name carved into the tombstone.

I parked my bike off to the side and killed the engine, grabbing the flowers as I climbed the hill.

Nothing could've prepared me for what I saw next.

Nothing.

I blinked to make sure I wasn't hallucinating but as I approached Christine's grave there was no denying the beauty kneeling before the tombstone was real.

Live and in the flesh.

My beautiful Lace knelt before my wife's grave, re-arranging a fresh bouquet.

My past met my present and for a second I wished for a future.

Beside her laid a wilted bouquet of flowers, one I hadn't brought there either.

"Hi, it's me again," Lacey said, as she leaned back tucking her haunches beneath her ass. "He'll be back soon," she promised before her voice trailed off and the only sound became the wind blowing through the trees. "I remember you," she said finally. "Not much, but I remember you. I was just a kid when you first came around with Blackie and well, I sort of hated you. No, that sounds horrible," she amended. "I was envious of you. That doesn't sound much better but it's true. I remember thinking you were pretty but then I saw him look at you and knew that wasn't the right word to describe you. In a world full of ugly you were his beautiful. You and Blackie, it's like you were the definition behind that saying beauty is in the eyes of the beholder because as pretty as everyone thought you were, they knew true beauty when they looked at him and watched him stare at you. You were the beautiful reflection in his eyes...the woman who made him smile. Even now that you're gone I still envy you but I'm not sure what it is I wish for more.... for him to look at me like he used to look at you or for me to be the one that brings back that smile."

I had no words.

None.

She was sitting here talking to my wife, confessing her feelings for me, and I stood there invading her privacy. I should've made my presence known, but I remained perfectly still as my heart broke for the woman I lost and began to mend because of the girl who brought her flowers.

She blew out a breath and slowly stood up, brushing dirt from her legs.

"Anyway, I'm going to get going but before I do, since this will be my last visit, I wanted to ask a favor. I'm not real religious and I know I'm probably just sitting here talking to a stone but just in case the afterlife really exists, can you look out for him? I mean I know you do already. Of course you do, you're his wife...but still, he needs an angel to watch over him," she whispered. "Who better than you?"

You.

She turned around, and I silently thanked God for the sunglasses that shielded my eyes as I stared at her. Her cheeks turned red as I extended my free hand and took hers.

"How long have you been standing there?" she asked, glancing down at our joined hands.

"Long enough," I said huskily, pulling her closer. "Lace."

I glanced down at the flowers she had brought and then lifted my eyes back to hers.

"You brought her flowers," I stated.

"I can explain," she started.

"Just today?"

"No, since you've been in the hospital," she explained. "I haven't missed a Saturday," she whispered.

I released her hand as I stared back at her for a moment then placed the flowers I was holding on top of the headstone. I ran my fingers through my hair as I paced the small area in front of Christine's grave.

"Blackie— "

I turned to her.

"How'd you know?"

"About a year ago, me and my dad came to visit my brother's grave, and we saw your bike. He told me you come here every Saturday and bring her flowers," she swallowed. "I just figured— " "Thank you," I cut her off, closing the distance between us and wrapping my arms around her, bringing her against my chest I bent my head, pressing my lips to her head. "Thank you," I repeated, murmuring the words into her hair.

"You're welcome," she said as she wrapped her arms around my waist.

I leaned back, tipped her chin upward with the pad of my thumb as she reached up and pushed my sunglasses up on top of my head.

"I get it, you know?" she whispered. "I know what it feels like to lose someone you love and how much it sucks being left behind."

She dropped her hands to my chest.

"I was five years old when I watched my brother die. I've been told my whole life, I was just a kid, and I didn't really know what was going on but it's not true. It's the one day of my life that has stuck with me and when I think about it I can't help blaming myself. Yeah, I was a kid, and kids are supposed to be carefree but that doesn't mean they shouldn't call for help when their little brother is running outside. I knew better, I knew that when I couldn't get through to my dad I should've went next door to the neighbor's house," she said as her eyes filled with unshed tears. "I'll live the rest of my life regretting I didn't do something to help him. And when I think how undeserving of life I am, I remember that my parents have already lost one child and I tell myself that life goes on and I have to push forward because I have people that need me."

I took her face in my hands, bending my knees to look into her eyes.

"This world needs you in it Lace, *you* make it beautiful," I rasped, leaning in and pressing my lips to hers gently. "You're the light that makes a man want to crawl out of the darkness he worships," I added, leaving out I was the man and she was my light.

Her lashes lowered before she peered through the fringe and back at me.

"I know you miss her. I know you blame yourself still and I also know if you could go back in time you'd trade places with her," she said, brushing the hair away from my face before laying her palm against my cheek. "But the world, my world, it would be *black* without you," she whispered. "I don't know how it happened, and I probably never will, but you're a big part of my life and my only wish is that you start living life again."

I watched as she cocked her head to the side, dropped her hand and smiled slightly.

"And that maybe you'd smile again," she added. "And if I was granted three wishes the third would be that I was the one to make you smile."

Then she winked at me and a single tear fell from the corner of her eye.

It was that image of her that would stick with me.

The one I remembered when I drew my final breath.

A plea from her to me.

To live.

To smile.

She made me want to.

"I'm going to go," she said, wiping away the tear with the back of her hand. "Give you some privacy but I'll see you at my dad's."

I nodded because speaking wasn't an option. If I opened my mouth, I wouldn't recognize my voice and the words I would say would bind me to a heaven I wasn't sure I deserved but one I wanted to live in.

I wrapped my arm around her waist and stepped toward her, bending my head to cover her mouth with mine. A gentle kiss that did what I thought only my words could do…a kiss that took me to heaven.

Chapter Seventeen

BLACKIE

Hope.

It wasn't the right word, but the only one that came to mind as I rang Jack's doorbell.

For the first time since Christine's death I felt something and allowed myself to keep on feeling. I didn't look for a quick hit to numb me. Instead, I embraced it and wondered if I could have more.

It was a foreign concept for me, to think there was a possibility of getting more out of life than what I planned.

To live and not merely exist.

I wondered if I was capable of looking forward to the future and if I could learn not to dread it.

I wondered if I could smile again.

And for no other reason than because Lacey asked me, and I didn't want to deny her.

I didn't want to deny her anything, least of all any of her wishes. I wanted to be the one that made them come true.

How crazy was that?

About as crazy as thinking I can.

The door opened and Jack greeted me, tucking a cigarette behind his ear.

"You're late," he observed with a smile, moving aside allowing me room to walk inside the house.

"Shut up and be happy I came," I mocked, brushing past him. "Where is everybody?"

"Dining room," he said, kicking the door close. "Reina said dinner would be done in a half hour, it's been a fucking hour," he quipped, following me into the dining room. I stopped at the entryway and spotted Wolf, pulling the elastic band of his pants and snapping them back into place.

"You look ridiculous," Pipe hissed.

"They're my eating pants," Wolf argued, diverting his eyes back to Jack who chuckled. Wolf pointed an accusing finger at him. "Laugh it up now, but when your jeans are digging into your gut, I'll be the one laughing," he said as he took a seat at the table and reached for the loaf of bread, tearing off a piece and handing it over to Pipe's wife, Oksana.

"You need carbs, girl, or a fucking cow or something," he quipped, shaking his head as he passed her the stick of butter. He turned to Pipe. "She's all tits, man. You need to put meat on those bones, man needs something to hang on to when he's motor boating those bad boys," he advised.

I turned to Jack.

"How long you think we have until Pipe flips the table and knocks Wolf on his ass?" I questioned.

Jack wrapped an arm around my shoulders, leading me into the dining room before tipping his chin to the chair next to the head of the table.

"My monies on Wolf," he said, sitting down at the head of the table.

I took the seat beside him, stretching my arm across the chair next to me and glanced around the table. Wolf, Pipe, and Oksana took the three seats across from me. Jack was at one end and I'm assuming Reina would sit at the other, leaving one seat free.

"Where is everyone else?" I asked.

"Riggs ditched us for quality time with the baby mama," Wolf informed.

"And now that Bones don't have a wingman anymore he's off looking for a wifey," Pipe added.

"You can help him with that, no?" Jack asked as he cocked his head and eyed Oksana. "Didn't you get her off a website?"

"Ukrainian Match.com," the red head confirmed.

"I didn't even know you knew how to use a computer," I commented, lifting my eyes as the kitchen door swung open and Lacey held the door open for Reina.

"Dinner is served," Reina exclaimed happily, carrying a huge tray in her hands. "I hope everyone's hungry."

Lacey turned around, clutching the salad bowl as our eyes locked.

I twisted uncomfortably in my seat but kept staring at her. I didn't care that we were surrounded by people or that her father was right next to me. I couldn't take my eyes off her and more than that, I wasn't sure I wanted to.

The last time we were together in front of everyone I acted like a dick.

That wasn't an option, but neither was pulling her onto my lap and wrapping my arms around her.

Reina came up beside me and bent down to kiss my cheek.

"Glad you came," she said before making her way to her seat.

"Thanks for this," I mumbled, turning back to where Lacey had been standing but she had moved, placing the salad on the table before moving to the right of me.

She glanced at my arm still draped across the back of the chair. I moved it so she could pull out her chair and take a seat.

"Black," Jack called, forcing me to look at him and take the tray of lasagna he offered.

I scooped some into my plate before turning to Lacey and holding the tray for her as she lifted the spatula and put a piece on her plate.

"Thank you," she said, taking the tray and passing it over to Reina.

"Put your fork down, Wolf, I'm going to say a toast," Jack commanded.

Wolf's fork paused mid-air as he pinned Jack with an incredulous look.

"You're fucking kidding me right?"

"Oh, I almost forgot!" Reina rose to her feet and disappeared into the kitchen a moment later she returned with a six pack of O'Toulle's non-alcoholic beer.

I raised an eyebrow at Jack who shrugged his shoulders and gritted his teeth.

"Drink the damn shit," he seethed.

Reina finished handing out the fake beer, and we all raised our bottles as Jack looked across the table at her.

"Got a lot to be thankful for— "

"Is he saying Grace?" Wolf whispered across Oksana to Pipe.

"Man, he doesn't know how to pray," Pipe mumbled.

"For fucks sake, really?" Jack ground out, raising his bottle again. "To Reina and Blackie," he said.

"Aye!" Pipe chimed in.

"To Reina and Blackie," Lace whispered beside me. I turned to her as her hand slid beneath the table and squeezed mine. I laced our fingers together as the pad of my thumb circled her palm.

"Cheers," Wolf added, taking a gulp of the beer. He sloshed it around in his mouth before spitting it out. "Fuck, what is this?"

Reina grabbed a napkin and wiped the beer from her arm.

"And this is why we don't have dinners," Jack commented, leaning back in the chair, guzzling his fake beer.

Oksana spit the beer out and smiled.

"Cheers in America!"

"Baby, no, no, no," Pipe cried, throwing his head into his hands.

"It's how you do cheers in America, no?" Oksana questioned, drawing her eyebrows together in confusion as she pointed her thumb over her shoulder at Wolf. "Mr. Wolf does it," she countered.

Lace snatched her hand away from mine, lifting it to cover her mouth as she laughed. The sound was intoxicating, and I was drawn to her like a moth to a flame. I felt my lips quirk slightly as she brought her free hand to her stomach and continued to laugh.

God, she was beautiful.

Really fucking beautiful.

I thought seeing her smile was the best but watching her laugh was even better. Her head turned and her eyes widened as she stared at me.

"Is that a smile?" she whispered.

I winked at her before biting the inside of my cheek to keep from grinning fully. I peeled my eyes away from her and concentrated on the food in front of me, catching Jack's suspicious stare from the corner of my eye.

"Oksana, what part of the Ukraine are you from?" Reina asked, clearing her throat as she stared across the table at Jack.

"The Ukraine is much big," Oksana offered.

"Got yourself a real bright bulb there, Pipe," Jack muttered.

"The food is delicious, Reina," I said, swallowing. "I stand by my statement when I told you, you should wife her," I told Jack.

"That's the plan," he said, looking back at her.

"Are you going to have a big wedding?" Lacey questioned.

"No, something simple," Reina stated. "Right?" she asked Jack.

"Just tell me when and where, Sunshine, I'll be there," he said, winking at her.

A chime sounded beside me and Lace lifted her hips to pull her phone from her pocket. Her fingers worked ferociously on the tiny screen and continued to chime. Her teeth sank into her lower lip as she placed her phone on the table and continued eating, picking the olives out of her salad and placing them onto a napkin.

I leaned over, snatched one of the olives from her napkin and popped it into my mouth before leaning against the back of my chair and stretching my arm over the back of hers. She glanced at me out of the corner of her eye, trying to hide her smile as she picked more olives and placing them into my dish.

"Riggs will be sorry he missed this, Prez. I vote we plan another one of these shindigs," Pipe said, looking at Jack who was glaring at my dish.

I met Jack's gaze.

"I expected Bianci to be here," I said, stabbing an olive with my fork and popping it into my mouth.

"Did you tell him what those crazy Italians did when we were off saving his ass?" Wolf asked with his mouthful.

Jack ran his hand over his face, holding back a chuckle as he shook his head.

"His mother and Pastore's wife turned the fucking clubhouse into a fucking trattoria," Pipe chimed in.

"Oh come on, I thought that was nice," Lacey argued as her phone went off three times in a row.

"You become a surgeon and forget to tell your old man?" Jack questioned, pointing his fork towards her phone. "What the hell is so urgent?"

Lacey lifted her eyes from the screen and met Jack's gaze.

"Very funny," she said sarcastically. "I have to go."

"Where are you going?" I questioned.

"Where do you think you're going?" Jack asked at the same time.

Lacey answered her father, turning her attention toward him.

"Noah is pledging a fraternity, and he asked me and Daniela to go to the party," she explained, looking over her shoulder at Reina. "I'm sorry but I promised him before I knew about the dinner."

"They'll be plenty more dinners," Reina promised.

"Daniela's outside, so I'm just going to run upstairs and change quick," she said, pushing back her chair and grabbing her plate. She moved behind me but stopped in her tracks, leaning over my shoulder and stretching her arm out as her breasts brushed against me and she snatched her phone off the table.

"Sorry," she whispered.

Little tease.

I watched as she stopped in front of Jack, bent down and kissed his cheek. I'm not going to lie…I was jealous as fuck and to prove it, a grunt escaped my lips.

"You're fucked," Pipe said, causing me to turn my attention towards him but lucky for me he was eyeing Jack.

"How so?"

"Are you serious?" Pipe scoffed.

"The idiot's right, you're fucked," Wolf put his two cents in. "Got a boy who pledged a frat two years ago…them little fuckers get down, make our patch parties look like choir practice with a bunch of nuns," he said pointedly.

I was losing my mind.

First, I was jealous of the peck Lace gave her father.

Then she mentioned this Noah character, add Wolf's little comments, and I was the one who was *fucked*…not Jack.

I had to rely on him to reign her in, tie her to a chair and tell her she couldn't fucking go to some frat house because if I said something, Jack would likely tie *me* to the fucking chair and stick a gun in my mouth.

Man, if he only knew what the fuck I was thinking.

I'd be dead.

"You have a son old enough to be in college?" Reina asked.

"Yeah, smart as a whip that boy is. It's no wonder because his mother is dumb as bag of rocks," he quipped, shoveling more lasagna onto his plate.

"So you going to let her go?" Pipe questioned, surprised.

"Why wouldn't I? In nineteen years she hasn't given me a problem," he shrugged his shoulders, diverting his gaze back to mine. "Be good for her to get out, be around people her own age. Especially, after this shit that went down, the girl needs a little fun in her life."

I don't know if he was looking at me, daring me to disagree with him or if he was doing it to torment me.

Either way, Jack was fucking with me and I didn't like it.

"I need to use the john," I said, rising from my seat and making my way through the house, as Lacey came down the stairs. She had changed into a black tank top and a pair of pants that looked like leather. I looked to the bathroom door in the hallway next to the stairs, pulled open it open, before checking to see if everyone was still at the table then I pushed her into the bathroom and closed the door.

"Nice outfit," I growled.

She bit her lip, as she leaned against the door, peering up at me from the fringe of her lashes.

"I think so," she murmured.

"Bet a lot of people will," I affirmed, pressing my palm against the door, above her head as I leaned into her. "Girl, you looking to be noticed?"

She didn't answer instead; her tongue took a swipe over her lip. I brought my free hand to her hip, pulling her hips against me and forced her to arch her back against the door. I leaned forward, nuzzled her ear as my fingers dug into her hip.

God, I wanted her.

I was thinking about taking her again.

And again.

Because the next time would be slow, making up for the first time but after that, after I gave her the good she deserved, I'd free the beast and fucking devour her.

"Remember who *saw* you first, Lace," I demanded, against her ear. "Remember who owns that part of you," I ground out, sinking my teeth into her ear lobe.

"Blackie," she rasped.

My hand traveled from her hip to the snap of her pants, skimming the waistband with my fingers before teasingly sliding them beneath the fabric.

"I want you to call me to pick you up," I instructed, removing my hand from the door and pulling the elastic of her pants so my other hand could slide further into her pants and tease her pussy.

"Yes," she panted, grinding against the palm of my hand.

"That's my girl," I growled, moving her panties to the side with one finger. "I can't wait to get my mouth on that sweet cunt," I said, running my finger up and down the seam of her pussy. "Make it real good for you, Lace…I promise."

She whimpered as I leaned back and removed my hand from her pants. I lifted my hand between us, wrapping my mouth around the finger that teased her pussy, sucking the taste of her off before pulling it out of my mouth with a pop.

"Make it quick. I'll be waiting," I ordered, pressing my lips to hers briefly before reaching behind her and opening the door.

I left her in the bathroom, closed the door behind me and leaned against it before I blew out a ragged breath.

Decision made.

I was going for the rewrite.

Chapter Eighteen

Lacey

I visited Christine's grave every Saturday for the last month as a way to repay Blackie for always doing right by me. I knew it meant something to him, that it gave him purpose in a world where he thought he didn't have any, and every week he missed a chance to bring her flowers was one week he thought less of himself.

The first time I brought the flowers I felt like I was doing something wrong, like I shouldn't have been there and didn't have the right. It's kind of fucked up, visiting the grave of a woman who was married to the man you love. It's not like they were divorced and fell out of love, they were a tragic love story, a modern day Romeo and Juliet, two people who loved one another but fell victim to corruption.

I know Blackie will always hold a certain love for her.

As he should.

That kind of love doesn't die, it stays with you, guides you into eternity.

I want that kind of love.

The second visit I felt the same way but as I stared at her name I forced myself to remember the faint images my memory carried of the woman who made Blackie smile. It was my eleventh birthday and my father threw a party for me at the clubhouse. It was awkward being the biker princess when there weren't any women in the clubhouse and the presents I got that year were just as strange. Wolf bought me a catcher's mitt and told me boys my age loved girls who played sports. Pipe, the poor bastard, he gave me a Barbie doll. Imagine? I decided I didn't really want presents after that, and I anxiously waited for Blackie to arrive.

He finally showed up, but he wasn't alone...Christine was with him and they looked so damn happy. I hated them both. Let me explain, I was an eleven-year-old girl, with a crush on a man, not a boy, and he was married to the prettiest girl I had ever seen. Prettier than my mom, prettier than my favorite actress. I realized then, even at that tender age when a girl notices boys, that Blackie only had eyes for her.

Of course they bought me the cool gift.

A caboodle full of lip gloss and nail polish.

Did I mention I hated them?

The third visit to Christine I talked to her. I told her the truth, confessed my feelings and then I apologized. I apologized for hating her when I was younger and for not getting to know her then. I told her I'd always regret not getting the chance to make a memory with her, something I could compare when Blackie took his trips down memory lane.

By the fourth visit, I knew he was being released and my time with Christine would come to a close. I asked her to watch over him and promised he'd return next week.

I never expected him to find me there.

If he went to the cemetery, found the flowers and wondered who brought them…I'd let him keep wondering.

But he not only saw me, he heard everything I said and for the first time I became his equal. Someone who could relate and understand. I took a chance, despite the doubt my maker tried to impart on me, hoping he wouldn't turn a deaf ear to me and pleaded with him.

He didn't argue or makes excuses.

He listened.

A spark of hope was ignited and even though I wanted to stay with him, never leave his side, I walked away and gave him his overdue visit with his smile keeper.

My dad and Reina were having everyone over for dinner, a celebration of sorts, thankful that that he survived. I was on pins and needles after I left the cemetery, worried about how he'd act in front of everyone and prayed he wouldn't act like a world class jerk. I didn't think my heart could take another blow, especially, not after sharing a tender moment and the softer side of the man clothed in leather.

He was relatively quiet as he sat beside me, eating the olives I picked out of my salad. He didn't ignore me or pretend like he wasn't feeling some kind of way about me. I'm not naïve enough to believe he had some sort of epiphany but I think he thought about the, what if and maybe, just maybe, he walked away from the cemetery carrying the same spark of hope I did.

My phone blew up, reminding me I had made plans with Daniela and Noah to attend this frat party. I hated college parties, especially the type that included sorority girls.

Fake.

Whiney.

Kappa Annoying.

I texted Blackie about twenty minutes ago the address I was at but he didn't answer me. I hope he didn't change his mind. He brought me into the bathroom, whispered sexy things into my ear as he slid his hand into my pants.

I glanced around the room at the guys doing keg stands and smiled.

There was no comparison.

Give me my guy over these any day.

"Come on," Daniela said, dragging me onto the makeshift dance floor. "Standing here in the corner won't help us nail one of the frat brothers," she insisted.

"That's fine with me," I mumbled, making the best of the situation and joined her. I suppose she needed a wingman. I felt a hand on my waist and spun around to meet Noah's handsome face.

My best friend was the poster boy for college jock but he wasn't a jerk like the rest of them. He was sweet, and I hoped pledging didn't change that about him.

"There's my girl," he exclaimed, hitting me with the scent of alcohol on his breath as he leaned in and kissed my cheek. "Thanks for coming."

"And miss your big night? Never," I teased.

"No, introduce me to your friend," the guy standing next to him said.

I lifted my head, smiled politely as I took him in. I had seen him around campus before. He might even be in one of my classes, maybe English, I don't remember…. nor did I remember his name.

"Lacey, Brandon. Brandon, Lacey," Noah introduced, turning around to glare at his friend. "This one's off limits, man."

"She yours?" Brandon questioned with a smile.

"She's mine," a voice said from behind me.

That voice.

Those two words.

It all gave me goosebumps.

He came.

BLACKIE

I wrapped my arm around her waist, pulled her against me and glared at the little fuck, watching as he stared back at me, surrendering his hands in the air.

"Didn't know they were letting parents chaperone," he laughed.

Kid had a death wish.

"Dude," the guy next to him warned. I had seen him with Lacey a handful of times. "Don't you know who he is? Man, read the fucking patch before you go saying something stupid."

Lacey twisted in my arms, lifting a hand to my face and forcing my eyes to hers.

"Let's just get out of here, okay?"

I nodded, diverting my gaze back to the little shit who rolled his eyes as Noah whispered in his ear.

She grabbed my hand and dragged me away.

"You look like you're going to snap his neck," she commented, over the loud music. Ignoring her, I stepped around her and pulled her through the sea of dicks fist-pumping away, hoping to get a blow job.

Wolf was right.

Lacey didn't belong here.

She belonged with me, on the back of my bike, in my bed…anywhere but surrounded by a bunch of little pricks who didn't know how to work their dicks.

I didn't stop moving until we were outside and standing in front of my bike. I unclipped the chin strap from my helmet, turned around and handed it to her.

"Time for your first ride," I said, urging her to take the helmet.

She cocked her head to the side, her dark eyes smiled at mine as she raised an eyebrow.

"You did that already," she teased, taking the helmet as she chewed on her lower lip. Hesitating for a beat before reaching up on her tip toes and pressing her lips to mine.

She pulled back, pulling the helmet over her head and moved to adjust the chin strap but I stopped her, pushing her hands out of the way and did it myself.

"That was nothing, girl," I promised.

She had no idea what she was in for and that thought alone got me rock hard. The idea of watching her face as she learned how to give and receive pleasure was enough to make me lose my mind.

I would have to muster up whatever self-control I could.

I wasn't fucked up, the methadone was keeping me straight. I'd remember every goddamn thing about her...the way she feels, the noises she makes, and the look in her eyes when she loses control.

I pulled away from her, patted the seat on my bike with one hand and adjusted my cock with the other. Poor thing was going to suffer for a while. I straddled my bike, revved the engine and waited for her to climb on behind me. After a quick glance to make sure she had her legs positioned right and her feet firmly planted on the pegs I tightened her arms around my middle.

"Where are we going?" she questioned against my ear.

"To heaven," I called over my shoulder, pulling away from the curb.

Strange words coming from a man who's been to hell more times than he could count.

But that's exactly where we were headed.

A heaven where she was mine and I was hers.

After she texted me the address where to pick her up, I excused myself from dinner, told the guys I needed to handle something and without leaving room for questions I took off. I debated for about ten seconds what I would do with Lacey once I had her...it wasn't like I could bring her to the clubhouse and after Christine died I gave up my apartment and moved my shit into my room at the Dog Pound.

I guess back then I didn't bank on claiming daddy's little girl.

So, with no other option, the decision was made I'd take her back to Staten Island and pray to God, it was the right move.

On the Verrazano Bridge she rested her head on my shoulder and I took one hand off the handlebars to touch her hand pressed against my shoulder.

"You okay?" I shouted into the dark night, against the wind and the sound of traffic, unsure if she even heard me.

She squeezed my hand, didn't even attempt to holler an answer until we were at the toll booth, then she leaned into my ear.

"I'm so much better than okay," she said.

I paid the toll and rode the expressway, getting off at the Todt Hill exit. As I veered off I questioned my plan and why I didn't just take her to a hotel. But I knew why...she deserved better than that. She deserved the best I could give and taking her here, opening this part of myself, this was the best I could come up with.

Five minutes later I turned onto a dead end and pulled into the driveway of the last house on the block before killing the engine. I dropped the kickstand and braced myself as I stared up at the house.

"Blackie?"

I turned my head, reaching down to take her hands in mine.

"Hmm?"

"Where are we?"

I glanced back at the house, taking in the appearance of it and how the weeds and bushes grew so out of control, nearly covering up the windows on the first floor.

"Home," I said hoarsely, clearing my throat before snapping out of the trance I was succumbing to. "Come on," I urged, giving her knee a squeeze.

She climbed off the bike and remained at my side as I watched her take off the helmet and uncover her hair that was a mess, trying to tame the unruly strands.

I looked at her and was granted the strength I never could find before. I dismounted my bike, took her hand and tucked her against my side as we continued the length of the walkway.

"Careful," I warned, tipping my chin toward the third step leading to the front door that was warped.

I could feel her eyes on me as I reached into my leather jacket and pulled out the keys, spinning the ring around my finger as I roughly threaded my fingers through my hair and cupped the back of my neck.

"I know you said this was home, but home should be a place you want to go to not somewhere you dread," she whispered.

I looked at her.

"I want to be here. I want to be here with you," I assured her. "I never expected to want to come back here or ever bring someone here…until you."

My eyes lingered on her face.

How could something so perfect be here with me?

How could she be the one who breaths life back into me?

I turned around, fitted the key into the lock and pushed open the stiff door. I watched her step inside and I felt a lump work its way into my throat. I bought this house at a time in my life when Lacey didn't exist in my world…sure, she was part of my life but she wasn't my everything.

Not then.

There were reasons I bought this house, and a woman I pictured greeting me at the door and it wasn't Lacey but looking at her now, as she tried to turn on the lights, it became clear that life worked in mysterious ways. You can plan your whole fucking life but it just takes one thing to change the course you're on…and sometimes you think it's the end but the end of something is the beginning of something else.

There was only one person who belonged here.

One person that could make me want to come home.

And that person was staring back at me with confusion written all over her pretty little face.

"You weren't even on my radar," I admitted huskily as I closed the distance between us and brushed her hand away from the light switch. I took her hand and walked her towards the back of the house, to the large empty room with floor to ceiling windows. The moonlight shone through along with the lights of the bridge that was off in the distance.

"Wow," she whispered, letting go of my hand to walk towards the windows. "What a beautiful view."

"You ain't kidding," I said as I leaned against the wall and watched her stare at the scenery.

Prettiest view a man like me ever got to see.

When did I become a lucky bastard?

She slowly turned around, the moonlight illuminating her face. I call her my angel and in that moment that's exactly what she looked like.

The angel sent to rescue me.

Mine.

There was that word again.

"Blackie, tell me," she started. "Is this your house? Why are we here?"

"Yeah, it is," I exhaled. "I thought a man's worth was measured in his possessions. Greed. It was all I knew and I kept reaching higher, making moves left and right, climbing the ladder and increasing my bankroll. I had no conscience, none at all. I would do a score, get paid, and instantly look for a bigger score, one with a higher payout and equally high consequences. I lost myself to the greed, and I began to lose Christine too. She didn't care about the money, the fancy things I'd come home with, all she wanted was the man she married in her life. I didn't see it then."

I paused, remembering the times she'd plead with me to stay with her, to be the man she fell in love with. I would lavish her with gifts and she'd smile but every piece of jewelry sat in a drawer.

"I thought I could fix things. I gave myself a year, twelve months of hustling hard and playing dirty. But Christine had a plan too and neither one of us thought to share it with the other," I sighed. "I bought this house nine months later, nine months too late because she was already working with the cops to bring me down," I confessed.

"She didn't go through with it though and never testified. She took her life and saved mine, robbing me of the chance to bring her here…to bring her home."

Lacey stepped toward me, wrapped her arms around my neck and held on for dear life.

"I'm sorry," she murmured against my ear. "I'm so sorry."

I pulled back, brushing away the hair that fell over her eye and tucked it behind her ear.

"Never wanted to come back here."

"So why now? Why are we here?"

"Because I found an ounce of hope in an angel," I said as I ran the pad of my thumb along her bottom lip. "You, Lace…you're my hope."

Ain't that some shit.

Chapter Nineteen

BLACKIE

"No more words, girl," I rasped, cupping her face as I leaned my forehead against her. "Just you and me, telling a story with our bodies from this point forward," I murmured against her mouth.

A slight moan escaped her lips before mine came down on hers, working her lips, sucking them between mine and prying that sweet mouth of hers open. My tongue slid home, taking a sweep of her mouth, tasting the sweetness that she possessed. One taste and I swore I tasted the next fifty years of my life. I used to think I wouldn't live passed thirty and here I am kissing Lace, wishing life went on forever.

She eagerly grabbed my jacket, desperate for more but I continued to kiss her slowly, bruising her lips as I sucked and grazed them with my teeth.

Baby girl needed to learn patience because she had a long night ahead of her, savoring her mouth was just the beginning, by the time my tongue got to her pussy she'd be so thoroughly worked up she wouldn't know her name.

I took another sweep of her mouth before pulling back and dropping my hands from her face, drawing in a deep breath as I stared back at her.

Just how I pictured her.

Lips swollen and parted, eyes dazed and confused.

I backed away, slipping my arms out of my jacket before throwing it onto the floor. I licked my lips as I circled her, taking her in from every angle, deciding what my next move would be.

"Take your clothes off," I commanded, crossing my arms against my chest as I leaned against the windows and stared back at her. "Slowly," I added.

Her eyes remained locked with mine as her hands trembled pulling her tank from the waistband of her pants.

"Are you nervous?" I questioned as she brought the shirt over her head, holding it awkwardly in her hand.

"It's different this time isn't it?" she asked, her voice shaking with each word.

"It is," I confirmed.

"You're going to see all of me," she whispered. "Remember every inch of me. There is nothing…no flaw I can hide," she rambled, finally throwing the shirt nervously onto the bare floor before she lifted her eyes back to mine. "I've never undressed in front of a man before."

I pushed off the glass of the window, standing straight as I cocked my head to the side and let my eyes travel the length of her.

"You don't have to be nervous. It's just you and me here, Lace," I assured her, extending one arm to unbutton her pants. "Leather and Lace," I added.

"Just my Blackie," she whispered.

"Just your Blackie," I confirmed, as her fingers gripped the waist band of her pants. She toed off her shoes before dragging the pants down her legs. I kneeled down, lifting one of her legs then the other and helped her remove her pants.

Still kneeling, I gripped her hips and brought her close, bringing my mouth to her stomach, allowing my lips to worship every inch of skin exposed from the wire under her bra to the lace that covered the part I ached for most. Her fingers curled into my shoulders for a moment before she lifted my chin with her index finger, forcing my gaze higher as her hands snaked around her back and her fingers unclasped her bra.

She brought one strap down her shoulder, then the other, crossing her arms briefly as she gathered the courage to bare herself to me.

"Just your Blackie," I reminded her.

"My Leather," she whispered, uncrossing her arms and letting the straps fall down, exposing the perfect tits I didn't pay much attention to the last time.

"My Lace," I growled, taking in her perfectly pink erect nipples begging me to take them between my teeth.

I rose to my feet, taking two steps to close the distance between us and bent my knees so my lips could trail down the nape of her neck. I licked her collarbone, sucked the sweet flesh of her shoulder into my mouth as my fingers danced down her arms. I laced my fingers with hers and brought her hands behind her back before pressing my palm against the small of her back and forcing her to shove her tits against me.

"Keep your hands behind you," I instructed as my lips made their way to the swell of one of her breasts. I heard the sharp intake of breath she took, my mouth stilled but remained on her breast as I glanced up at her. "Behind you," I repeated.

Once I was sure she wouldn't move I brought my hands back around and cupped her perky tits. I flicked my thumb over one nipple as my mouth closed over the other, sucking slightly before my teeth grazed the tip. I pinched the other one, rolling the bud between my fingers. I changed tactics allowing my mouth to suck on one as my fingers twisted the other.

Pleasure and pain.

You're going to learn how the two become one, girl.

The sounds that she made drove me wild and had all the blood rushing to my dick. A slow burn began to sizzle between us, her arousal igniting my own, forcing me to pull away from her and take a moment to nuzzle the valley between her breasts.

I had to remind myself that this was a rewrite, a chance to teach her sex was more than just eight inches of penetration. It's your mind surrendering and your body following suit.

Lose your mind, girl.
Lose yourself.
Let go.

She bent her knees, taking my face in her hands and tilted my head back before her lips descended upon mine. She kissed me, slowly, taking her time, discovering what she liked and what she wanted more of. Her teeth nipped my lips and then she paused, opening her eyes, looking at me for approval.

"Don't be afraid," I rasped. "Do what you want with me, use my body to learn what works for you, take what you need, Lace," I assured, wrapping my arms around her waist and dropping my hands to her ass. I grabbed her ass and lifted her up. She wrapped her legs around me, locking them at the ankles as I walked her towards the kitchen and positioned her on top of the counter. I hooked my thumbs in the flimsy lace of her panties and dragged them down her legs. I closed my fist around the lace, tucking them into the back pocket of my jeans.

"Aren't you going to take your clothes off," she asked, breathlessly as her legs dangled off the side of the counter.

I shook my head, stepping toward her, and placed my hands on her knees.

"Open for me," I coaxed, watching as she gripped the edge of the counter and bit down on her lip before she slowly parted her legs.

Heaven.

She leaned back, panting slightly as she peered at me curiously, waiting for my next move. I moved between her legs, tucking her hair behind her ears and took her face in my hands. She ground herself against me, inching her ass closer to the edge of the counter, desperate for friction.

I smiled at her eagerness, sucked her lower lip into my mouth and trailed my hands down her neck, over her breasts, squeezing them before gripping her hips and pulling her closer so her legs spread even wider and her cunt touched my stomach.

She whimpered, twisting her head from side to side as she ran her fingers roughly through my hair.

"Easy baby," I soothed, my lips sliding up and down her neck. "Got all night. You'll get there, girl…going to have you coming all over me—starting with my mouth."

I pulled away, ran my hands down her legs as I detangled myself from her and walked toward the corner of the room where there were two folding chairs propped against the wall. I opened one, carried it back towards her and positioned it in front of her. With one hand I reached behind me and pulled my shirt over my head, placing it on the counter next to her before I took a seat in between her legs and spread her out wide.

"Blackie," she murmured. "I want to touch you," she pleaded, taking the shirt and twisting it between her fingers. "Let me touch you."

"Not yet, baby," I said, wrapping my hands around her legs. "Lay back," I instructed as I pulled her closer so her ass hung over the edge then brought each extended leg to rest over my shoulders. I pressed my mouth to the inside of her thigh, closed my eyes as I was engulfed by the sweet scent of her arousal.

I've been through a lot of fucked up shit in my life. There have been more than a handful of times when I wasn't sure I'd live. Usually there's a gun aimed at my head or a lethal dose of drugs in my system, threatening to end me. Not this time. This time, I wasn't sure I'd survive taking Lacey.

She could make a man want to die a slow death.

One that involved her legs wrapped around you and your face buried in her pussy.

I continued to let my lips glide across the sensitive flesh, searing her, branding her with every swipe of my tongue before my mouth hovered over her pussy. I lifted a hand, pushing her lips apart with my index and middle fingers before my tongue took a swipe over the sweetness that was all Lace.

Her hips bucked, her knuckles whitened as she held onto the counter.

A groan escaped my mouth as she pressed her cunt against my tongue.

"Thatta' girl, give me that pussy," I ground out, nipping around her lips before I let my tongue delve into her, greedily lapping away, coating it in her arousal. I broke away, stared at her pink flesh, lifting her ass off the counter to change the angle and put my mouth back on her. I found her clit, grazed it, before devouring the bundle of nerves.

"Oh my God," she cried out, taking my shirt and covering her mouth with it, muffling the sounds her mouth made. I slid two fingers into her, felt her pussy clench around them as I tried to slide them in and out of her, all the while keeping my mouth on her.

I pulled my fingers from her, as she tried to sit up, our eyes locked and I lifted my fingers glistening with all of her and took them into my mouth.

"You taste like heaven," I said, pulling my fingers from my mouth and lifting my hand to her mouth. "Want you dripping, girl," I growled, bending down and went for another taste. She wrapped her hand around my wrist and her mouth closed over my fingers, sucking them, swirling her tongue around them, pulling them from her mouth and dropped her back against the counter.

I pushed my wet fingers into her pussy, a bit easier this time, as I worked her pulsing clit.

She started to fuck my face, arching her hips, grinding that pussy against my mouth as she called out my name. With my mouth firmly planted on her, soaking up everything she gave me I lifted my eyes and watched as her hands cupped her breasts and she writhed uncontrollably.

That's it girl.

Keep you coming.

I added a third finger as her pleasure consumed her, making her forget all about the pain of her pussy being stretched.

"I can't…I can't take it anymore," she begged.

"You can and you will," I assured her, pulling my fingers out of her and having my tongue mimic the act.

Her ankles locked around my neck and she grew perfectly still, screaming out my name over and over, almost chanting it.

Give me more, girl.

All you got.

I reached up, gripped her thighs, my fingers digging into her flesh as I nuzzled her cunt with the tip of my nose, turning my head from side to side, the light stubble on my face, teasing her sensitive cunt.

"This is mine, Lace, you understand?" I sucked her into my mouth, gave her a little of the rough before my tongue gave her the gentle. "Mine," I growled.

"Yours," she panted.

Good girl.

"You ready for my cock?"

I murmured against her pussy, still humming from her back-to-back orgasms and pulled back to look up at her. She laid sprawled out on the counter, her chest rising and falling violently as she tried to catch her breath. I unlatched her legs from around my neck, dropping them so they dangled weightlessly over the ledge before standing up to lean over her.

My beautiful Lace.

Covered in a sheen of sweat, her hair sticking to her face and her cheeks flushed.

Best fucking memory I'll ever have.

I pressed my mouth to hers, gently taking her hands and wrapping them around my neck.

She moaned against my mouth as I lifted her from the counter, my hands grabbed her by the ass and carried her to the middle of the room. I wished I would've thought this out better, but I wasn't about to stop. I laid her out on my leather jacket figuring it was better than nothing. Not much but still it was something.

Next time I'd give her a bed.

Fuck, I'd cover the goddamn thing in roses if I could.

She deserved that.

And so much more.

I went to remove her hands from my neck but she tightened her hold on me as her eyes bore into mine.

Forever.

Right there staring back at me.

"I..," she started, caressing my cheek with the back of her hand.

"Sshh," I whispered, covering my mouth with hers as I brought her down onto her back. I stood up, undid my belt before unzipping my jeans. Her eyes watched intently as I removed my boots, then my jeans. I wrapped my hand around my cock that throbbed to be inside of her, giving it a few strokes of my hand, forcing myself to keep my eyes open as I groaned.

Her eyes widened as the roamed my body before lifting to meet mine. She crooked her finger, beckoning me down to her, and like a man without will, I dropped to my knees, covering her body with my own. She spread her legs, welcoming me between them as she wrapped her arms around my neck and leaned up to kiss me.

"Is this is real?" she whispered against my mouth. "Tell me I'm not dreaming, that my mind isn't playing tricks on me," she pleaded softly, pulling back to gaze into my eyes.

"It's real," I rasped. "You and me, we're the real thing," I promised, kissing her temple. "You okay? You tell me if you need me to stop," I said, brushing my dick against her entrance.

She nodded quickly, and I pressed another kiss to her lips before pulling back and guiding my cock to her pussy. I inhaled sharply, lacing our fingers together and clamping them down against the floor over her head. Inch by inch I made my way inside of her, sweating as I painfully tried to force myself to go slow.

The sound of her short gasps as I worked my way inside of her aided in my restraint. I watched her face and when it began to contort with discomfort I dropped my mouth to her breast, taking her nipple between my teeth and taking her away from the pain of being stretched and filled with me.

I pulled out and charged back in, continuing to wreak havoc on her nipple, and brought my hand down between us, finding her clit with my fingers and began to massage the nub.

Her body began to respond, her back arched, and she slammed her feet onto the ground and used them for leverage as she pressed her pussy against me. She was tight, her cunt hugged my cock, squeezing it and making me lose my fucking mind.

She clawed my back with her nails as her body awakened, learning what it needed to do, how to move with mine and she began to work for her orgasm.

I started to lose control and my pace quickened. As I moved faster, I pressed hard against her clit and her pussy grew even wetter, making it easier for me to glide in and out.

"I'm going...it's...oh God, Blackie I can't stop," she rambled, lifting her head off the floor as her fingers dug into my shoulders.

I was fucked.... staring at her, watching her come, knowing I'm the only one who did that to her was enough to send me over the edge. I lost my shit, and the gentleness faded as I started to fuck her like I've been dreaming of.

I pounded that pussy like both our lives depended on it, mercilessly, until she threw her head back and screamed.

Pleasure.

Pain.

Now she knew.

I dipped my head and sucked on her neck, knowing it'd be the first of many marks I left on her. I didn't last much longer, slamming my dick into her three more times before tearing my mouth away from her neck and pulling my cock out.

Her body arched, her tits swollen and on display, calling for me. Our eyes caught for a brief second and it was like she could read my thoughts as her hands lifted to cup her breasts. She pushed them together, gave a slight nod of approval and I fucking went off, covering her with my release.

Mine.

She should've run away.

Never gave me a second glance.

Because now she'd never escape me.

Not after the dance our souls just took.

I swallowed hard, clearing my throat as I took a deep breath. She was a mess, we both were, but fuck me...I liked it. I liked staring at her, knowing I'm the one who made her like that. I reached out, shoving her hands out of the way and cupped her breasts, rubbing my release into her skin with the pads of my thumbs.

"I'm fucked," I admitted, continuing to circle my thumbs as I glanced up at her. "You got me twisted, Lace, so fucking twisted that I want to forget who I was before you," I rasped, leaning into her to steal another kiss from her sweet lips.

When I finally found the will to break away from her, I grabbed my shirt from the kitchen counter and went to work on cleaning her up. She grabbed the shirt from my hands, chucked it to the side pushing me down, forcing me on my back and crawling on top of me.

"I'm not going to break, Blackie," she whispered, her finger outlining the Satan's Knight's tattoo on my chest before she looked up at me. "I'm stronger than you think," she added. "I don't want you to hold back because you're afraid you'll hurt me."

I opened my mouth to speak, but she brought her finger to my lips and smiled.

"No, this time I get the last word," she demanded, laying her head against my chest. "Hold me, Blackie. I've waited a long time to be in your arms."

I reached over to the left of me, grabbed my jacket and draped it over her back wrapping my arms around her.

I didn't say a word.

Not one.

Chapter Twenty

Lacey

The moment Blackie pulled his bike up in front of my mother's house I immediately felt the loss of him. I never wanted the night to end, fearing I imagined it all…every kiss…every word…every time he grabbed my hair and told me I was his.

He killed the engine, turned off the lights and I knew our time had come to an end. I reluctantly climbed off the bike, wincing from the aches that would remind me tonight was real.

"I thought you said your mother wouldn't be home?" he asked, angling his head as he looked at her car parked in the driveway. I removed his helmet from my head and handed it to him.

"She isn't. They probably took a cab to the airport. My step-dad's company usually sends a car for them when they go away for business," I replied, watching as he straddled his bike and placed his feet firmly on the ground. Our eyes locked for a moment and he crooked his finger, beckoning me to close the distance between us.

"Why the sad eyes?"

I stepped toward him, welcoming the arm he wrapped around my waist and the fingers that brushed against my cheek, forcing a smile on my face.

"I'm just tired," I said, adding a wink for good measure, trying to mask my fear of our perfect bubble bursting.

"Sorry, not sorry," he smirked.

I reached up, swiping my thumb over his lips as a smiled blossomed across my face. "Ah, there it is…a hint of a smile," I paused, my eyes widening as an idea came to me. "I have the perfect plan," I enthused, grabbing onto his leather jacket.

"Oh, yeah?" he asked huskily, staring at my mouth as he spoke. "What's that?"

"Something fun, something you would never think of doing…I will get you to smile Blackie, and when I do, I'm going to keep you smiling," I promised. "So, here's what's going to happen—" He laughed, tightening his arms around my waist.

"I'm so fucked," he muttered, swiping a hand over his face.

"Shut it!" I demanded, pressing a quick kiss to his lips. "As I was saying, tomorrow you're going to pick me up and we're going to take a ride down to Coney Island," my plan died when something flickered in his eyes and the playfulness disappeared. "What? You have something against riding the Cyclone? Big Bad Biker doesn't get down with rollercoasters?" I teased.

"I'm not going to be around for a few days," he said, thoughtfully as he looked at me, threading his fingers through my hair.

"Where are you going?"

"North," he answered vaguely.

"Sounds like fun," I said quietly looking away.

"Not really. I won't even be riding my bike," he ground out. "Got club business to tend to that requires me to drive a fucking cage," he grunted, placing a finger under my chin and turning my eyes to his. "I'll be back, Lace and when I come back it's you I'm coming back for," he promised. "Take you on whatever ride you want," he added.

"I'll be waiting," I whispered, hiding my vulnerability as I prepared myself for the mental war that surely would take place once his bike peeled away from the curb.

"Good, now give me a kiss, angel," he demanded, tapping his finger against his cheek as he winked at me.

I leaned into him, pressing my lips briefly against his cheek before moving them to his lips. His moan was all the encouragement I needed, and I continued to kiss him, to love him, hoping wherever he was going, he'd bring the memory of me with him and when he came back it wouldn't all be a dream.

Blackie continued to kiss me, his hand traveling down my back to my ass where he grabbed one cheek as he pulled away.

"You better get going," he instructed, untangling his fingers from my hair.

"Yeah," I agreed, taking a retreating step back. "Be careful," I whispered as I bit down on my lip trying to keep the question from spilling from my lips but failing miserably.

"What happens now?" I blurted, watching as he narrowed his eyes in confusion. "Where do we go from here? I want to believe you when you say you'll be back and we'll pick up right where we left off. I need to believe that," I stressed, exhaling sharply as I shoved my hands in my back pockets and shrugged my shoulders. "I don't need you to sit there and promise me a happily ever after but I need to know there's hope for us. I know my father will be an issue, so will the club, but I also know that I'm willing to stand up for what we have between us. I'm just not sure you are," I whispered the final sentence.

"Hey," he started, lacing his fingers through the belt loops of my jeans and tugging me toward him. "Look at me… you trust me?"

I cocked my head to the side and looked at him incredulously.

"Answer me," he demanded.

"Of course I trust you," I replied.

"Then trust when I tell you I'm going to make things right for us. I told you your mine, Lace, and I fucking meant it. I'm a selfish bastard, I take what I want and I don't apologize for it. You and me, we're going to make heads turn baby, turn shit upside down but we'll come out of it standing. Just you and me. I promise you that," he ground out, his eyes darkening as he stared back at me with a conviction to match his words.

"I believe you," I confirmed, softly.

And I did.

My heart believed every word.

I smiled at him.

"Get your ass back to me," I winked at him, pressing a quick kiss to his lips as he released his hold on me. I turned around, struggling with each step I took that brought me further away from him.

"Lace," he called as I reached the driveway. "I'll call if I can," he offered as he started up his bike.

I glanced over my shoulder at him, our eyes locked and I tried to think of something to say.

I flashed him a smile and blew him a kiss, setting my mask in place, covering my features and the crazy that was already brewing inside of me.

Once I was inside, I turned around and looked at him one last time. He revved his engine, took one hand off the handlebars to give me a two-finger salute before he peeled away from the curb. I watched him drive off until he was out of sight— I stared at the spot in front of the house where he parked and wondered if he left a trail of skid marks on the asphalt. I wondered if they matched the ones he left inside of my head.

I stepped backwards into the house, closed the door and leaned my forehead against it. It was eerily quiet inside the house and my mind.

The calm before the storm.

I pushed off the door, turned around and started for the stairs, deciding that if I went to bed, maybe I could keep my maker silent for just a little while longer. My mind has allowed me peace for too long and was due to wreak havoc any moment, viciously tearing apart the best night of my life.

I have to remind myself I'm not the insecure type.

When I love, I love harder than anyone.

I whole heartedly believe I'm exactly what Blackie needs in his life.

I can make things better for him.

I can be the one who loves him unconditionally.

The one person who rescues him from the hell he thinks he belongs to.

Me.

I can do that.

But as strong as I can be, I am also weak.

Weak to my mind.

It's like my mind knows exactly when to strike. It's usually when I feel like I'm on top of the world then like any true villain my mind turns on me, the thoughts flood my head and I come crashing down.

Other girls are worried about their appearances. They think they aren't pretty enough or thin enough. Their hair is brown when it should be blonde or curly when it should be straight.

Not me.

I'm comfortable in my own skin and never wish to crawl away from it, to peel it off and replace it with something else.

In a perfect world I'd be exactly who I am, minus my head.

If I could escape my mind…I would.

It's the only thing about me I wish I could change.

I'm not sure which is worse.

Wishing for the perfect body or wishing for a different mind.

Sometimes I desperately want to tell my story, to share with the world what it's like to be mentally ill. However, that would mean accepting I am flawed and I can't bring myself to do that.

I can't say the words out loud.

I can't look in the mirror and admit my truth.
I'm crazy.
I hate that word. It's so harsh and ugly.
So I continue to sit alone and suffer.

I tell myself that even if I had the courage to confess I am a girl who struggles mentally there is no one in my life I would burden with my illness. Think about it, who should I tell? Who do I ask to help me with the nightmare I'm living? My father? The man who suffers from it himself?

Or my mother who blames my father's illness for the reason she doesn't have a son anymore?

Blackie isn't an option either. He's got his own struggles, his own torment and for the first time in a long time, he's trying to make that right for himself. He's got a long road ahead of him he sure as hell doesn't need my drama added to his full plate.

And then there is that other word that scares me to death.
Lithium.

It works for my father but there are thousands of people whom never adjust to the medication and are constantly having their dosages changed. There is also the possibility that Lithium wouldn't even work for me.

Another scary thought.

I'll continue living, struggling and envying those of sound mind. I'll enjoy the highs, embrace them, and push through the lows, hoping one day I'll find the strength to admit to myself, my family and the world that I'm ill.

I'll fight until there is no fight left.

I climbed into my bed, not bothering to change my clothes, and stared up at the ceiling.

He's going to realize the truth.
He's going to find out you're not some perfect angel sent to rescue him.
You're damaged.
You're a joke.
You think you can help him but you can't even help yourself.

I closed my eyes and felt the tears fall from the corners of my eyes as my demon emerged and brought me to hell.

BLACKIE

After I dropped Lacey off I took a ride, killed a little time before I had to drag my ass to the methadone clinic. I'll give Riggs credit, he's a mastermind when it comes to computers he hacked into the clinic's files and got the take home prescription approved. He even switched my case and provided me with a different counselor so my usual one wouldn't get suspicious.

I should've went back to the compound to get some sleep before hitting the road but every time I closed my eyes I saw Lacey's face and the fear she tried to hide from me when I dropped her off.

She doesn't realize I have spent a long time looking at her and that I know every emotion conveyed on her face.

That mask she tries to hide behind, it don't work with me.

I told myself I didn't have time to get into it with Lace, work through her anxiety but I promised to handle it. I'm a man of my word but, the thing was, I didn't have a goddamn answer for her. I didn't know how to make this shit work for me and her. I didn't know how I would turn to Jack and tell him I was about ready to claim his little girl. I didn't know how to choose Lacey and tell Jack to go fuck himself because any way you sliced it that's what I was ultimately doing.

I zipped the duffel bag, not even sure what the fuck I had thrown in there, slung it over my shoulder and started for the door. I nearly bumped into Jack as I shut the door and stepped into the hallway, flipping the glasses perched on top of my head onto my nose.

"Glad I caught you before you left," he started.

"Just about to head out," I said, as I locked my door. He tipped his chin towards the steps and we made our way downstairs into the common room.

"You sure you don't want to take Bones with you?" he asked, flipping one of the chairs backwards before he straddled it.

"Nah, no need. Besides, Boots, that crazy son of a bitch isn't going to want to see anyone's face but mine," I said, pulling out the chair across from him and sitting down. He passed me a cigarette and lit it for me.

"That shit needs to change. You mention that when you get face to face with the man," he stressed, taking a pull of his cigarette. "You tell him I'm the fucking president and all deals go through me from now on. He wants to break bread; he's going to break it at my table."

I cocked an eyebrow as I blew out a ring of smoke. It was obvious he was on edge, fighting for control of some sort. I studied him closely, deciphering if he was on the verge of a breakdown or just morphing into his "Bulldog" persona.

"What's got you twisted?" I questioned as he shrugged his shoulders and leaned over the chair.

"Got a lot of shit on my plate, Black. I think you know that," he flicked his ashes. "Do I really need a fucking reason to be twisted?"

"I guess not," I pushed back my chair. "Keep it cool Bulldog, ain't got time for the maker so you put that motherfucker down," I ordered as I rose to my full height. "I better head out before I lose my second wind," I muttered.

"You don't need to worry about me man," he paused. "Keep doing what you doing, concentrate on you. I'm seeing pieces of my old friend break through," he swallowed, gave me a quick nod. "Like it, Black, like it whole lot."

I ground out the cigarette into the ashtray and turned my eyes to his. I bit the inside of my cheek as he reached out and patted my shoulder.

"Keep climbing, brother," he encouraged.

As the words left his mouth I knew they'd sit with me for a long time, the same way they did when he told me to stand up and not drown. The only difference this time was the words he said gave me hope.

This hope thing was becoming my mantra. I was a man who coasted through life with nothing, let alone hope and now I had it in spades.

It amped me up to keep on the straight and narrow, to keep working on kicking the addictions, bettering myself so I could claim Lacey.

"I'll keep in touch," I said as he stood up.

"Keep yourself in one piece," he warned.

I nodded, grabbed my bag and headed for the door.

"Black," he called.

"Yeah?"

"I'm proud of you," he said, simply.

Hope.

Yeah, I had that shit in spades.

Chapter Twenty-one

BLACKIE

I wound up driving straight through, arriving in Boston just after being on the road for about five hours. My meeting with the Corrupt Bastards wasn't scheduled until that night so I crashed at a motel catching a couple of hours of sleep and a quick shower. I picked a fine fucking time to have a sit down with these fuckers. The Yankees were playing the Red Sox and since the Corrupt Bastards' clubhouse was on the outskirts of Boston I had to drive through the fucking chaos, hoping there weren't any checkpoints along the way and didn't blow this shit out of the water. The last thing I needed was to get pulled over by some Beantown pig looking to make an arrest on a vehicle with New York plates.

It was almost eight o'clock when I rolled past the gates of their compound and parked my van close to the clubhouse, manually locking the doors to make sure these bastards didn't fuck with my shit while I sweet-talked their leader into letting the two-hundred and fifty-thousand-dollar debt we had, slide.

I was familiar with the two guys hanging out in front of the clubhouse, no doubt awaiting my arrival. One of them was named Charlie and the only reason I knew that was because he had five tear drops tattooed to his cheek.

Five tear drops proudly declaring he took five lives.

That makes a face unforgettable.

"Look who the wind blew in," Charlie mocked, rolling a toothpick between his lips. "Nice of you to show your face," he added.

"Boots is expecting me," I ground out, holding myself in check as he assessed me.

"That he is," he affirmed, spitting out the toothpick and lifting his eyes to mine. A wicked grin spread across his mouth and had me reaching to check for my gun tucked into the back of my jeans.

A force of habit.

He turned to the guy next to him.

"Take him into the back. Boots been waiting long enough to see his face," he ordered.

I was itching to put Charlie in his place, throw him up against the brick wall, shove my gun in his mouth and vow to tattoo a tear drop onto my face when I took his life.

I might still do that.

But on the way out.

After, I unloaded the fucking guns and made peace with Boots.

Every peace treaty has a little blood on it.

I followed the Bastard into the clubhouse, taking note not much changes around here. They still have all the fucking Red Sox memorabilia covering the walls mixed with the mugshots of all the Bastards rotting away for the oath they took.

This charter of the Corrupt Bastards, MC was completely different from the Satan's Knights. While our club had certain limits, these guys had none. We were all up in arms over this drug shit we were neck deep in but these guys? Their primary source of income was drugs. Looking around the clubhouse, it was obvious they were swimming in product, feeding their whores as much as their bodies could stand. It was no wonder any of these sleazy broads could hold themselves up much less suck dick.

One would think that getting stuck with the product would be no sweat off their backs but any respective drug dealer who knows the game, knows every fucking gram counts. You stop looking at drugs as dust people snort, every rip is another dollar earned, the more money earned the more money spent on product and everyone knows the more product you have the more bills in your fold. It's a vicious cycle.

One I knew too well.

The guy leading me through the clubhouse stopped in front of a door and tipped his chin.

"Straight through there," he instructed.

I brushed past him, rapped my knuckles against the door before turning the knob and walking into the room. Boots was sitting behind the desk with one of the club whores spread eagle in front of him. His head was bent as he ripped a line off her tits.

"Fucking hell," I seethed, watching as he lifted his head his beady eyes met mine.

He slapped the whore's tits, nearly knocking her off the desk with the power behind his hand.

"Get out," he hollered.

"Boots, you promised me!" she whined, scrambling to her feet as she slid off the desk.

"Fuck you," he sneered. "Now get the fuck out of here."

She stared at him for a moment before turning around and looking at me. I swore for a moment her eyes pleaded with mine but I looked past her and directly into the eyes of the enemy.

"I patiently waited for this day," he started, sniffling.

The whore slammed the door behind her as I pulled the chair out in front of his desk and dropped into it. I leaned forward to pull out my gun and hold it up to him before nodding at him, awaiting the same gesture of respect. I removed the clip and placed it on top of the desk, cocking a brow and expected him to do the same.

"I don't owe you that," he commented, pulling back his vest and revealing the holster he wore beneath it. He pulled out the gun and mimicked the act, putting us on equal footing but reminding me it was a courtesy he granted me.

I didn't tuck the gun into the back of my jeans, placing it in the inside pocket of my leather jacket so I could access it easier. In under ten seconds I could pull the gun, load it and pop a bullet in this fuck.

"Let's cut through the bullshit and get down to it," I suggested, leaning back against the chair. "What do you want?"

"You got balls, Blackie, always did," he said, swiveling from side to side in his chair. "But a man in your position doesn't come into my house, talking down to me, and expecting a quick fix. It just don't work like that," he ground out.

"So tell me how it works. The way I see it you got every right to be pissed, but before you assume that my club was looking to sever ties with yours, listen to the facts. Fact number one, I came to you because I knew you could deliver what I needed. Fact number two, plans change, enemies strike and when it's do or die, motherfuckers like us…we do. Now, it was never mine, nor Jack's intention to stick you with the drugs man we were banking on, even after Jimmy Gold made his move the club still needed your product but there wasn't enough time to get to you. Then there is that little fucking issue you have, refusing to deal with Jack. I'm here to make things right with you but, also warn you that won't fly any more. Any deals going forward are conducted at the Satan's Knights table, with the Bulldog sitting front and center."

He laughed.

I continued to stare at him.

Motherfucker ain't nothing funny about what I just said.
Add that to your list of facts.

"You want facts Blackie? Here's one. Your fucking president is a goddamn nut job. You think I deal with you because of your past, your knowledge of drugs? I choose the junkie because I'm not about to deal with a psychotic fuck who swings a gavel."

I gritted my teeth, slammed my fist against his desk and leaned closer.

"This coming from a man I just watched snort coke off some worthless bitch's tits," I snapped. "You got a choice to make, Boots—I'm offering you a shitload of weapons in exchange for a truce. You can keep the guns for yourself or turn them for a profit on the streets, whatever the fuck you want. Lord knows you don't have a fucking conscience anyway, so take the deal. You'll make more off the guns than what we originally agreed on with the drugs."

"Or what?" he asked cockily.

"Take the fucking deal," I advised. "You don't want to declare war, Boots."

"*You* don't want to go war, Blackie," he scoffed. "Word gets around—the war you got going on with the Red Dragon's that shit is spreading like wild fire. Your club is hanging on by a thread as it, add another war to your agenda and the Satan's Knights are off the map," he claimed.

"It'd be a shame to watch a smart guy like you, a thriving businessman like yourself, lose everything in a power play. But, I guarantee you it'll happen. There have been few if any, that survived after they underestimated the strength of the Satan's Knights," I warned.

I wasn't walking away from here with a deal but I would not walk out of this fucking place without setting this fool straight. We may be hurting but that shit would turn around, men like us didn't exist to be defeated. Men like us beat the odds in the game of life…every fucking time.

You want to play motherfucker?

Come play.

But don't expect to win.

Never expect to win.

"You think I care about the Satan's Knights enough to go to war with them? I'll piss on your club, swallow you motherfuckers whole. It's not the club I got beef with, it's the man who shook my hand and pissed on my trust I have a problem with. It's you I want, Blackie, and no fucking deal you or your boys try to swindle out of me is going to work. You crossed me Blackie, there's no retribution for that. Be thankful if you leave here with a pulse and don't you ever fucking threaten me with the Satan's Knights. You have a debt to pay, your club has a debt to pay, I just haven't figured out what kind of payment I'm going to accept. So I'll bide my time, turn the hourglass and watch as the sand slips through to the other end and your days become numbered," he threatened, leaning back in his chair as a smile spread across his face. "And you know what the best part of that is? I won't even have to lift a finger because the Bulldog will snap when he finds out what you've been up to and that crazy cocksucker will cut your ass up," he enthused.

I froze as I pinned him with a glare, knowing the words he was about to say before they even left his lips.

"Been watching you, Black," he said as he rose from his chair and walked around the desk. He bent down, leaned into my shoulder and whispered into my ear.

"I know you're banging Jack's daughter."

I clenched my fists, turning my face just as he straightened up and our eyes met.

"What do you think will happen if his daughter became a casualty of war? If daddy found out his precious little girl died because she was the only way to make his vice president bleed?"

I shot up out of my chair, reached for my gun, forgetting the clip on the desk and pressed the barrel of the gun into Boots' temple.

"You stay the fuck away from her!" I pressed the gun harder against his temple. "Do you fucking understand?

YOU STAY THE FUCK AWAY FROM LACEY!"

"Next time you put a gun to my head, make sure it's loaded," he said as he gritted his teeth.

I slammed his head against the wall, lowered my gun as I stepped backwards and retrieved my clip from the desk.

"W-A-R," he hissed.

I should've shot him dead right there, splattered his walls with his brains and ended the mayhem before it started.

I'm sure I'll regret turning around and walking out of his office. I just prayed I didn't feel the regret as I lowered another innocent woman's body into the earth.

I didn't bother hiding my gun, walking back through the clubhouse like a crazed man, ready to shoot anyone who stood in my way. I ignored Charlie as he called out to me and stormed outside, heading straight for the fucking van. I banged my head against the driver door as his words played repetitiously in my head.

I knew that this meeting could go one of two ways, Boots could take the deal and keep peace or he would tell me to go fuck myself. I never prepared myself for the threat against Lacey.

She's not fair game.

She won't be put in the middle of this shit.

What do you think will happen if his daughter became a casualty of war? If daddy found out his precious little girl died because she was the only way to make his vice president bleed?

Boots' threat declared Lacey my property.

It wasn't a malicious attack on Jack. He wasn't promising to hurt his daughter to prove a point to him, to hit him where it hurts.

No, Boots words were aimed at me.

A vow to take what was mine, to cut me off at the knees and make me putty in his hands.

W-A-R.

He spelled out his declaration, mimicking the timeless card game and throwing Lacey into the middle of a fucking massacre.

I climbed into the van, threw my gun onto the passenger seat and turned the key in the ignition, pulling away from the Corrupt Bastards like a mad man trying to escape fate.

And then I realized I wasn't running away from fate but headed straight towards it.

I fought back the urge to turn the fucking van around and buy a vile of heroin shit, I'd settle for an eight ball of coke. I could've swiped some off the bar and no one would've even notice.

I lifted one hand off the steering wheel, pushed up the sleeve of my shirt and looked down at my forearms.

Clean.

I glanced up, stopped short as the traffic light turned red and spotted the tavern on the corner across the street.

Fate.

There she was.

I blew the light, making a sharp left and parked the van.

W-A-R.

It was coming.

But before we went to war with the Bastards I had a battle with the biggest bastard of all.

Johnny Walker.

Chapter Twenty-two

BLACKIE

"Last call, buddy," the bartender called from the other end of the bar. I stared at the amber liquid, swirled it around in the glass then knocked it back and turned it upside down lining it up next to the other empty shot glasses. I had quite the collection going on.

I pointed to the tower of empty shot glasses and peered back at the bartender.

"Two more," I ordered, slurring my words.

"You got a ride to wherever you're heading?" he questioned as he braced his hands on the edge of the bar and studied me.

"I got it covered," I tapped the empty glasses. "Let's go." I added another twenty to the stack in front of me and waited for him to move.

He sighed, reluctantly grabbing the bottle of whiskey from behind the bar, flipped over two shots and filled them to the rim—slamming his hand over the cash and stuffed it in his pocket.

So much for the concerned bartender act.

Anyone can be bought in this world.

Everyone had their price.

Sometimes a twenty got you what you needed, other times all the money in the world wouldn't suffice.

Sometimes the price was blood.

I emptied the second shot glass, numb to the burn of the liquor as it made its way down my throat. I pushed back my stool and stood for the first time in hours, stumbling and knocking over the bar stool.

"Easy," the bartender called. "Why don't you let me call you a cab?"

I waved him off as I found my footing and headed out of the bar. If I had any luck, I'd wrap the van around a pole before I did what I knew I had to do.

I unlocked the van, climbed into the driver seat and fumbled with the key, leaning my head against the steering wheel.

"But the world, my world, it would be black without you," she whispered. "I don't know how it happened, and I probably never will, but you're a big part of my life and my only wish is that you start living life again.

"I wanted to," I whispered, replying to the memory of her words. "You made me want to."

Then I was reminded of my own words.

It's a good dream, Lace. You and me, it's a real good dream but dreams don't come true for men like me.

I knew better.

I knew it would never work, that I wasn't good for her, that I had the capacity to ruin her.

It's me.

It's what I do.

I take the good in the world and make it ugly.

I take the innocent and feed them to the devil.

I can't change and the more I think I can the more I hurt the people who give a damn about me.

I hurt Lacey.

I hurt Jack.

I hurt my club.

I rubbed my face wearily, knowing the only way to make it right, to save her from being a pawn in a game of chess was to cut her free. She'd always be her father's daughter; no one could change that but she won't be my woman anymore.

I've never intentionally put her life at risk and I will not start now.

Even if it kills me.

Ironic isn't it? I've spent a good part of my life looking for a way out, looking to hurt myself and feel the pain I deserved. Who knew the answer was right in front of me? All I had to do was let myself have a bit of hope and an angel who loved me.

All I had to do was give in to the temptation and let myself have the one thing I wanted most in this world—even more than the pain I craved. I wanted the good girl who always had my back. The beauty with the sad eyes who just wanted the beast to see her, to worship her and to love her.

I had the story right from the beginning, from that first night I pushed Lacey away and sent her running scared.

I had to go for the fucking rewrite.

I had to give her the good.

I had to take more of her.

I had to watch her unravel and know it was me who did that to her.

I barely made it back to the hotel and parked the van in between two spots. Once inside I fell into the chair, not bothering with a light, accustomed to the darkness. I didn't care it was the middle of the night, I hoped she'd be sleeping and wouldn't answer the phone, giving me a few more hours to hold on to her.

A few hours to hang onto the dream of Leather and Lace.

I slipped my jacket off, turned it over and pulled out my gun first, then my phone. In that instant, I knew it'd be easier to pull the trigger than to press send on the call I was about to make. I lifted the phone to my ear, listened as it rang and said a silent prayer she wouldn't answer the phone.

"Hello?" she whispered groggily into the phone, forcing me to close my eyes and savor the sound of her voice.

I pictured her in bed, hair tousled, stretching her body along the mattress.

"Blackie?"

"Hey, babe," I rasped, clearing my throat before running my free hand over my hair, fisting it in agony.

"Is everything okay?" she murmured into the phone.

No nothing's okay.

It all fell to shit before we even had time to enjoy it.

"It's all good," I lied, trying to work up the nerve to harden my tone and break her heart. "Listen, Lace," I started.

"I miss you," she cut me off. "I wish you were here right now, or I was there. I miss the way your arms feel wrapped around me and your breath against my ear."

I dropped my hand, leaned my head against the back of the chair and closed my eyes, remembering the night I held her in my arms—on the floor of a house I never thought I'd step foot inside again.

A little slice of heaven.

Why give me heaven only to throw me back into hell?

"I do too," I admitted, huskily.

"When are you coming home?"

"Tomorrow," I said, opening my eyes and staring into the darkness. "I can't do it."

"What can't you do?"

I couldn't bring myself to break her heart and not for the selfish reasons I expected but because *I* didn't want to hurt.

I just didn't mean to say it out loud.

"I've got to go, Lace."

"Can I see you tomorrow?" she asked quickly before I disconnected the call.

"Yeah, angel," I whispered.

"Good night Blackie."

Tonight, I didn't hurt her with my words. I didn't scar her with my actions but I feared the inevitable.

Lacey would be hurt.

And it didn't matter if I was the one doing the damage or not, in the end it would still be my fault. But tonight, tonight, we held onto the dream for a little longer.

"Good night, Lace," I said, disconnecting the call and staring down at the screen.

I closed my eyes, pictured her smiling face as Boots' threat rang loudly in my ears. I felt the familiar pangs of self-loathing tear into me, ripping me a part, and I was transcended back in time. The last time I hated myself this much was when I held Christine's lifeless body in my arms. I was too late then, but I wasn't now. I didn't have to hold another cold body in my arms and wish for another way.

But as much as I have been able to protect her this far I knew the game Boots was playing—I knew it too well.

It's exactly what I would do if the roles were reverse.

I'd bide my time.

I'd let the motherfucker stew.

And as I sat there in the dark, watching the woman he loved, I'd smile to myself knowing I had the upper hand.

Drugs can be replaced.

Money can be earned again.

Buildings can burn only to be rebuilt.

A club can be divided and torn apart only to rise again.

But taking the life of the one that makes yours worth living?
That shit ends you.
It's the oldest play in the book and the most effective.

I reared my hand back and threw my phone across the room, watching as it bounced off the wall. I grabbed the arms of the chair and hoisted myself up, walking through the dark room to where the phone landed. The screen was shattered, mimicking the cracks covering my dead heart.

I'm going to miss her when the lights go out, when I'm alone in the dark remembering how it felt to be inside heaven.

I'll always think of her.

My Lace.

My lethal temptation.

I didn't sleep that night, my mind was racing like I did two eight balls of cocaine so, I checked out of the hotel and jumped into my van before the sun came up. I rode back to New York with a van full of guns, a broken phone and a goddamn hangover.

Only grief waited for me so why I was in a rush to run back to hell was a mystery. I couldn't sit in that room another second though because all I did was think of her and how I would have to break it off.

How the fuck was I going to do it looking at her, watching her eyes go dark as night as the torment of my words stabbed her? I couldn't do it on the phone and was a fool to think I'd be able to do it face to face.

By the time I pulled the van up to the Dog Pound I was exhausted, crashing from the booze and the mental anguish. I wanted to sleep for the next three days and if I was lucky when I finally awoke, the war would be over.

Fat chance.

I slammed the door of the van and damned the fucking thing to hell.

If I never had to drive a cage again it would be too soon.

The parking lot was relatively empty reminding me, Jack was due to go up to Otisville to visit Vic. Pipe was spending more time at the garage trying to expand and Wolf was searching the map for recruits, leaving Riggs and Bones in charge of the home front.

God help us all.

I entered the clubhouse, spotted Bones on the phone and tipped my chin in acknowledgement before heading towards the stairs. I reached the landing where Riggs was pacing back and forth in front of my door.

"What're you doing?" I asked, scratching the scruff that lined my jaw. He lifted his head and his eyes narrowed as he studied me.

I could only imagine what I looked like.

"Man," he hissed. "What the fuck happened?"

"Get out of my way," I ordered.

"You look like you fell off the wagon," he commented.

He should only know.

"What are you my sponsor now?" I dropped my duffel bag on the floor, shrugged my jacket off and viciously rolled up my sleeves, turning my forearms up. "Not a fucking mark. Now get the fuck out of my way Riggs," I growled.

"Black, I'm just concerned is all," he said, pulling off his baseball hat and scratching his head.

"Appreciate it but I'm not your fucking problem," I argued.

"Speaking of problems," he started.

"What?"

"You have a visitor," he said, glancing over his shoulder at the door. "Bones thinks she came by so I could help her fix her laptop."

"Yeah? And how'd she get in my room?"

"Pop-A-Lock?" he suggested.

I glared at him with my dry eyes that burned like a motherfucker. Did he expect me to believe she called a fucking locksmith, and he wasn't the one who let Lacey inside my room? This kid was a character, bitchin' about getting mixed up with me and Lacey but then he picks my fucking lock and covers for her.

Idiot.

"Thanks," I muttered as he stepped aside, allowing me room to open the door. He patted me on the back as I drew in a ragged breath and watched him walk down the hallway.

I opened the door and was greeted by the most beautiful sight I had ever seen.

I guess the devil wanted to fuck me a little harder, sharpen the blade before he twisted it deeper.

Lacey was sitting on my bed with her bare legs crossed, wearing nothing but one of my black t-shirts. She turned her head, brushed her long wavy hair away from her face as she smiled sheepishly at me.

"Welcome home," she started.

I didn't respond as I kicked the door closed and dropped my bag on the floor. I didn't bother to brush away my hair that fell wildly around my face, hiding my bloodshot eyes.

"Black— "

I cut her off, lifting my finger to my lips to silence her as I started for the bed.

For her.

I shut my mind off.

And motherfucked Boots all the way to his grave as my knees hit the edge of the bed and I watched her crawl toward me.

I wanted to do the right thing but everything in my being told me this…her and me, we were the right thing.

We were everything.

I reached for her, taking one hand and draped it around my neck before taking the other and doing the same. Then I let my hands travel down her sides, gripped her hips and tugged her body tightly against mine.

I hoped my actions conveyed my feelings because I couldn't bring myself to say the words. Not when I'd have to take them back.

I dipped my head, shaking my hair away from my face pressing my cheek against hers, taking in the intoxicating scent of her perfume. My mouth moved along her jaw, teasing her chin before finding her lips.

It started off slow, just lips touching lips, until we both realized that didn't even scratch the surface of what we needed from one another.

Bruised.

Swollen.

Her lips parted and invited me to taste everything I missed.

I slid my tongue inside of her mouth, my hands moved south, lifting the hem of the shirt and cupped her bare ass cheeks, digging my fingers into the mounds of flesh.

She fisted the hair at the nape of my neck and matched my rhythm, grinding against me as she angled her head and took what she wanted, using my mouth to quench her desire.

I dragged myself away from her mouth, torturing us both as we stared at one another.

I drew a breath, letting go of her and taking a step back.

"I need to take a shower," I stated, reaching behind me and pulling my shirt over my head. Lacey gnawed on her lower lip as she nodded, reaching for me and unbuckling my belt.

"You do that," she said finally.

"Don't move," I ordered, as she pulled my belt from my loops and twisted it around her wrist.

"Yes, sir," she murmured, her lips curved revealing her perfect smile.

Goddamn.

I unbuttoned my jeans, drawing down the zipper half way before I found the will to turn around and walk into the bathroom.

I turned the water on, glanced in the mirror and pushed the hair away from my face to stare at the beast looking back at me—the weak monster who didn't have the heart to break Lacey's after breaking so many before her.

It used to be so easy.

Until I cared.

Until I found the heart I wanted to claim more than the body that housed it.

"You're a motherfucker," I said back to my reflection.

I finished stripping and stepped into the shower, letting the water rain down.

I needed to shower with holy water. Maybe that would cleanse my soul and ease my conscience because I wasn't going to do it.

I wasn't giving her up.

I'd do whatever the fuck I had to do to keep her safe and keep her with me.

Let that cocksucker try to do something to my girl, I'd make that motherfucker squeal like a bitch.

W-A-R, motherfucker.

It's on.

Bring it.

I'll be ready.

I'll be waiting.

Because a long time ago I vowed I'd never let anyone take what was mine again.

You can say whatever you want about me, call me a junkie, tell me I'm worthless, but I've always been a man of my word.

When I made Lacey mine I took a silent oath to protect and honor her until my dying day.

As long as I have a pulse that girl will have someone who will cherish her life.

Some people need guardian angels.

And some need a knight cloaked in leather.

I was so wrapped up in my own head, and the revenge I was ready to seek I didn't hear the shower door open but somehow I knew my angel was behind me.

I glanced over my shoulder and watched as Lacey pressed her back against the shower tiles, splaying her palms flat on the wall as those eyes of hers, mischievously flirted with mine.

Her tongue sneaked out and ran along her lower lip.

She pushed off the wall, her hips sashayed as she took one step closer and pressed her hands against my chest. She rolled the barbell that pierced my nipple between her fingers.

There was no mistaking that look in her eyes...my good girl was rocking the sexy siren she discovered lived inside of her.

She lifted a finger to my lips.

"Not a word," she ordered.

Oh girl, I like that.

She grabbed my hips, a smirk teased her lips as she swiveled her hips and dropped to her knees.

Christ.

I fisted her hair, piling it on top of her head to get a clear view of her face and watched as her lips parted. Her hand closed around my cock, lifted it up as she angled her head and licked my balls.

Goddamn, girl.

She peered up at me, assessing my features for approval.

"Go, on girl," I encouraged.

She smiled.

"You don't listen very well do you? I thought I told you not to say a word," she said playfully, winking at me before she wrapped her lips around the head of my cock. She sucked the tip, slowly taking inch by inch into her mouth, working my dick like she owned it.

She did.

Lacey gagged, pulled her mouth away, composed herself and went back at it.

I lost my fucking mind and moved my hips as I fucked her mouth.

Sweet and innocent.

Sexy and curious.

All fucking mine.

W-A-R.

Come on, motherfucker, try to take this from me.

I dare you.

Chapter Twenty-three

Lacey

"Get dressed," Blackie said against my breast before he pushed himself up. After the shower that resulted with me being pressed up against the wall and Blackie on his knees, devouring me he carried my limp body to the bed. It didn't end there though, he then treated me to another orgasm with his hand, followed by another when he finally fucked me.

Three orgasms and I still wasn't satisfied.

"Do I have to?" I asked as I wrapped my arms around his neck and lifted my hips. "I mean there are so many things we can do that don't require clothes."

"Gonna make me work hard to keep up with you, Lace," he hissed, bending his head to take my nipple between his teeth.

I loved when he did that and when he twisted my nipples between his fingers because he always soothed the pain with his tongue.

Blackie's tongue was a God-given gift.

Either that or he was a talented man because I was sure there wasn't another man on this planet who could do the things he did.

"I think you can handle it," I murmured, locking my legs around his waist, trapping him between them.

"Oh, you do, huh?"

"Yeah, I do," I teased, lifting my hips and grinding my pussy against him.

"I've created a monster," he muttered, lifting a hand and grazed my cheek with the back of it. "Thought you were beautiful before, but seeing you like this Lace...smiling, face flushed and your pussy grinding on my cock, you're fucking gorgeous."

"I like the way you talk," I admitted. "I didn't think I would, but it turns me on."

"I see that," he grinned, as his fingers glided over me. "Your cunt gets nice and wet when I talk dirty to you."

His teeth nipped at my lower lip, tugging on it as he slipped two fingers inside of me.

"Mmm, what else gets you wet?" he questioned, thrusting his fingers in and out of me, stretching me.

Best reunion ever.

I had already had his mouth, his fingers and his cock and when he added the third finger it reminded me of the girth of his thick cock.

My hand couldn't close around it.

"Your mouth," I hissed. "Your beard when it rubs against me," I added.

"You like it when I fuck you with my mouth, Angel?"

He withdrew his fingers, reached behind him and unlocked my legs, planting my feet on the mattress as he spread me out.

"I like it when you fuck me. Period. End of story."

"Girl's feelin' loose," he asserted. "Keep talkin'," he grunted as he fisted his cock.

"Quit messing around, Blackie and give me what you and I both want," I ordered as I sat up and closed my hand over his. "Give me this."

He moaned encouraging me.

"Always," I whispered as I pried finger by finger off, replacing them with my own. "Say it. Promise me."

"Always," he vowed.

"Now fuck me and fuck me like you want to, without restraint. I promise you I can take it," I coaxed as my hand clenched around his cock and my other massaged his balls.

"Lace…" he struggled.

"Fuck me, Blackie," I said, bringing my hand to my lips before licking my fingers and bringing them back down to his balls.

"Do it!" I demanded.

He growled before he shoved my shoulders and my back fell against the mattress.

"Turn over," he ground out. "Now," he hissed.

Excitement erupted inside of me as I flipped onto my back. I didn't know what to expect and didn't even care. I trusted this man completely and was eager for all the things he'd show me, for every experience he'd give me.

"Put this under your stomach," he instructed, grabbing a pillow and smacking my ass.

I snatched the pillow from his hands and did as I was told, propping the pillow under me and lifting my hips.

"Give me that ass," he demanded as his big hands glided over my ass. "Goddamn," he muttered. "Clutch the pillow and stick that ass in the air," he instructed.

I hugged the pillow to my middle and spread my legs, my ass propped in the air and his hands found my hips, dragging me against him. He didn't ease in like the times before instead, he slammed his cock into me. I felt full, ready to burst as I pushed my ass against his pelvis and he continued to crash his hips against me.

"That what you want, Lace?" he ground out, letting go of my hips and cupping my breasts in his big palms forcing me to arch my back.

"God, yes," I croaked, glancing down at his tattooed hands that covered my pale flesh.

"Got the sweetest cunt. You want to come baby girl?" he questioned breathless before he pulled his cock out from me.

"Blackie," I protested, but before I could say another word he flipped me onto my back.

"Want to see your pretty face," he explained, maneuvering my legs so one rested on his shoulder and the other tucked against his side.

A fresh sheen of sweat glistened over his body, his hair still wet from the shower fell recklessly around his face and his eyes darkened as he pushed into me.

He was beautiful.

And he was mine.

No one would take that away from me.

No maker.

No one.

I knew he was close by the way his face contorted and his pace quickened. Yet, he was determined to get me off rotating my hips. Each swirl of my hips had my clit grinding against him, giving me the friction, I needed to fall off the edge. I tried to sit up and reach for him, finally succeeding as my hands took purchase of his hips. I hung on for dear life as I felt my orgasm take over my body.

"So fucking pretty when she comes," he groaned. "Shit!" He pulled away but my hands grabbed his ass and forced him back. He's pulled out every time since that first time, covering me in his release and while it's hot as hell and I get off on it I wanted to know what it felt like for him to be inside me when he came.

It was safe, but he didn't know that.

"I'm on the pill," I said, breathlessly as I lifted my eyes to his. "Don't stop, don't stop," I chanted, circling my hips as I tried to hang on to control. "Blackie!" I screamed as I dropped my head against his chest.

He cupped my chin, forcing my head back so our eyes met.

"Said, I want to see your face and fuck, girl, you're going to look at me when I come inside you," he declared. "Eyes up here," he insisted, pointing his index and middle finger at his eyes.

It was like an out-of-body experience—looking into the eyes of the man I never thought I'd have, sharing one of the most intimate moments between a man and a woman.

"Keep 'em open," he hissed, fighting to keep his eyes open too, pumping me one last time and filling me with his release.

I'm pretty sure I fell even harder for him, something I didn't think was possible.

He bent his head and took my mouth with his, kissing me tenderly.

I fell harder.

Even harder.

I was gone.

His hips slowed as he pulled away from my mouth and took a deep breath.

"See," I rasped in between breaths. "You can keep up," I tried to laugh, but it wound up becoming a lazy smile because I was too exhausted to even laugh.

But he did.

He actually chuckled before he kissed my cheek loudly as my leg dropped from his shoulder and he released the other. They dropped onto the mattress with a thud, everything ached and I loved every minute of it.

I whimpered as his cock left me, wondering if we could stay intertwined like that forever. He flipped onto his back and collapsed next to me, trying to catch his breath.

I reached for his hand, addicted to his touch and laced our fingers together as we laid in silence, listening to one another breathe.

"Can't let you go," he said so low I barely heard him.

I turned to him, nervously as he kept his eyes trained on the ceiling.

"What?" I questioned hoarsely.

He waited a beat before turning his cheek and staring back at me.

"You asked me before I left what will happen with us," he started.

Here it comes.
No.
"You're my girl, Lacey. Ain't nobody in this world I want other than you," he said.
"But?" I whispered.
"But Jack finding out isn't what I'm worried about," he revealed.
"It isn't?"
"No, baby it's not. The clubs involved in a lot of shit right now. I got a lot of things I need to make right on the outside before I can claim you to the world," he paused, lifting his hands to my cheek. "Don't look at me like that, I'm not ending this. We need to keep it on the down low until I'm sure you're safe with me," he explained.
"I'm always safe with you," I argued.
"Remind me of that when I doubt myself."
His words gave a glimpse to a vulnerable side of him I hadn't yet discovered until that moment. He wrapped his arm around my waist and pulled me down on top of him.
"I'll work it out," he promised. "And then we'll work on Jack," he added.
"And then?"
"Then, I'm taking you for a tattoo, get you some ink so you never forget who you belong to," he teased, squeezing me.
"Blackie! I'm serious, then what?"
"You tell me," he said, against my hair. "Tell me what you want and I'll move heaven and hell to give it to you," he swore.
"Heaven and earth you mean," I corrected, smiling as I closed my eyes.
"It's heaven and hell where I come from, baby," he affirmed.
"This," I said through a yawn. "This right here is everything I want."
And it was.
At nineteen years old I had it all.
Now, I had to convince my maker to let me keep it.

BLACKIE

I took her to Coney Island that night, rode the Cyclone three times and won her half a dozen stuffed animals—she gave one to every kid we passed that didn't have one. We were walking around Luna Park when out of the corner of my eye I saw a mother and her young son.

"But Mommy, please? One more try!"

"I already wasted twenty dollars trying to win you a prize that cost fifty cents," the mother argued with her son.

"Please mommy! I won't ask after this time," the kid pleaded.

"I don't have any more money to waste on games, Joshua," the mother hissed.

I let go of Lacey's hand, walked over to the trailer and laid a five-dollar bill on the counter. It was the game where you had to shoot water into the clown's mouth until you filled the balloon and it popped.

There are perks to owning a shooting range.

You can beat the clown all the time.

The bell chimed, signaling I won, and I dropped the water gun. I kneeled down, smiled at the mom and tapped the little boy on the shoulder.

"Hey, there kid," I started.

He looked at his mother for approval before he waved at me timidly.

"You see that girl over there," I said, pointing over at Lacey who smiled but looked back at me curiously.

"Yeah," the boy said.

"I'm trying to get her to go out with me and she told me she'd say yes if I win you a prize," I looked over my shoulder and tipped my chin to the water balloon that was declared a winner. "Think you can help me get the girl by taking the prize?"

He looked up at his mother, grinning from ear to ear.

"Can I?"

I lifted my eyes to hers, watched as she diverted her eyes back to her son.

"Sure, wouldn't want to leave the nice man hanging," she said as she turned back toward me. "Thank you."

I winked, slapping my hands against my knees and rose to my full height.

"Can I have the Spongebob?"

The clerk handed him the ugly yellow stuffed thing, and the boy smiled widely at me.

"Thank you! I hope you get the girl," he exclaimed.

I turned around, my eyes met Lacey's and the smile she wore became contagious.

"I hope so too," I told the boy.

I hope I get to *keep* her.

I said goodbye to the kid and his mom before making my way back to Lacey.

"You won that boy a prize," she commented, looping her arm through mine.

"Yeah, watching you put a smile on six kids faces when you gave them those prizes must've rubbed off on me," I said.

"Watch out Blackie, you're becoming more like a big teddy bear than a big bad biker," she joked.

I growled.

"Cut it out, Lace," I ordered, taking her hand and pulling her towards Nathan's Famous Hot Dogs. "Come on, I'm starving," I mumbled.

She was right. I was soft when it came to her. It wasn't a new development; there has always been a place inside me carved out just for her, but every minute I spent with her I fell deeper.

And she fell too.

Deeper in trouble.

Deeper in danger.

And the both of us threatened to fall deeper in love with the story we were writing.

For her it was an original piece.

For me it was a rewrite.

A story about an Angel and the Devil.

We needed a miracle.

Or just each other.

Maybe we were the miracle.

Ah, fuck. I *was* soft.

Tomorrow I was going to shoot something.

Anything.

Chapter Twenty-four

BLACKIE

I haven't touched a drink in two months, sixty-one days to be exact, since that night in Boston. Sixty-one days sober and sixty-one days Lacey remained safe and out of the arms of the enemy.

The club had enemies lurking all over the place and we were living life waiting for the world to be pulled out from under us.

When Jack returned from his visit with Victor, I clued him in on what had gone down with the Corrupt Bastards, leaving out Boots threats against Lacey. That shit was mine to deal with, not his and not the clubs. The club needed to worry about the dynamics of war and be prepared for when the Corrupt Bastards made their demands clear.

And then we still had the motherfucking Chinese to worry about.

Every which way we turned, there was someone waiting to fuck with us.

The thing that worried both me and Jack most was that both rival clubs were quiet. They let time pass, life moved forward and the weak ones thought everything would blow over.

But Jack and I knew better.

On his last visit to see the caged mobster, we found out that Jimmy was being sent to Otisville any day now. He needed clearance from one more doctor, there was no more surgeries lined up, that motherfucker was fucked. He was a scary looking dude before, but now he had burns covering ninety percent of his body—that motherfucker was vile.

Life's a bitch.

Then you die.

Or some biker sets your ass on fire.

That wasn't the only news Jack brought home with him. Pastore signed over his union contracts to the club, giving us partial control over the docks and partnered us with Rocco Spinelli, the mobster taking over Vic's territory now that his organization had been dissolved. He was also interested in buying out the gun contracts we had in place with Wu.

Things were coming along, we had protection from Spinelli, should we need extra hands and Bianci was always willing to strap on bullet-proof vest to help the cause. I gave Jack a lot of grief over his ties with Pastore, mainly with Bianci—in the end I respected both men for their loyalty to our club.

Wolf was back...empty-handed but swore he had it handled and that we needed to hang tight.

The new blood was coming.

Pipe had expanded the garage, put the club in the red but vouched for the loss if the business didn't prosper. Pipe was a cheap bastard, guy didn't waste a penny so if he offered to put up his own cash, you knew that fuck had something up his sleeve.

All in all, we were keeping busy, working our shit out and getting the club back to where it needed to be. And the best part about that shit? We weren't using drugs to do it.

We didn't sell them.

We didn't orchestrate deals with them.

And I didn't do them.

I was still on the methadone, but that shit would change soon too. I didn't want to be a man who checked into a clinic every morning for a fix. I wanted to be the guy I was on the weekends.

The guy that sanded floors in a house he had neglected for years. A man who allowed Lacey to pick the paint for each room even though her choice of colors drove him insane. The kitchen was aqua blue.

When she wasn't driving me mad with paint samples she was driving me mad with her smile. I wonder if she knows the power she has over me with that thing.

I shouldn't limit her control to just her smile.

It was everything she did.

There were so many layers to her I never knew existed but I was discovering all of them and there wasn't one I didn't love.

I didn't see much of her during the week between my obligations to the club, her school schedule and keeping things from Jack, we were lucky if we found a night to be together. She didn't bitch about it, or bust my balls which I appreciated, especially since I needed to keep reminding myself that Boots had eyes on her.

A week after I returned from my meeting I gave up trying to convince myself that I should let her go. I pulled Bones to the side and lied through my fucking teeth. I told him with everything going on with the Dragons and the Bastards, it was best if we kept an eye on Lacey. Then I told him he needed to keep this shit between us, using Jack's illness as my excuse for keeping him in the dark about putting one of our brothers on his daughter for protection. I only had him tail her when she was at campus that way he didn't catch on to what was going on between us.

Jack spent most nights with Reina but he blocked out every Sunday to have dinner with Lacey.

Every Sunday after dinner, she came back to Staten Island—back to me.

Aside from my blue kitchen, I had a bed, one we put to use often.

My girl, was learning she liked to take charge in the bedroom. Her favorite position was when she was on top, riding me as I whispered filthy things into her ear. But the dirty talk didn't stop there, Lacey got in on that, using her words and her body to tell me exactly what she wanted.

I want your mouth on my cunt, now.

Goddamn, I was lucky.

Fuck me, Blackie.

Yeah, baby.

And my favorite...

I want to try something different.

She nearly killed me when she sucked an ice cube into her mouth and dropped to her knees, giving me the best fucking blow-job I ever had.

Yeah, I was a lucky bastard.

My phone rang inside my jacket, pulling me away from my thoughts as I took the call.

"Talk to me," I answered.

"Get your ass to the range," Jack ordered.

"For what?"

"Wu made his move," he growled before disconnecting the call. I put two fingers into my mouth and whistled as I rose from my chair. I grabbed my gun from the table, checked if it was loaded before tucking it into my jacket pocket.

"Yo, let's go!" I hollered.

Wolf and Pipe turned to me as Bones came bounding down the stairs. Nobody asked questions, they knew…we were waiting for this moment and it was finally here. They strapped their vests on, loaded their guns and straddled their bikes.

Jack and Riggs had gone to some shindig over at Bianci's house and arrived before us. I wasn't expecting to see the place swarming with blue and whites and took that as a sign things were worse than we expected. If Pops placed a call to 9-1-1 instead of the cops we had on payroll someone was hurt. Pops was Cain's old man and allowed us to keep the gun range in his name for legal purposes. The man was never patched, nor did he want to be, and a part of him blamed the reaper on our backs for taking his son's life.

I assessed the damage as I dismounted, noting the front of the building was riddled with bullets.

"Jesus Christ," Pipe hissed behind me. "How's this place still standing?"

I glanced over my shoulder at him then turned around and scoped the property for Jack and Riggs. They were standing in front of the cops and Jack was going head to head with the man I despised most in this world, more than Boots, more than Wu…he was mouthing off to Craig Brantley. The biggest dick to make his way into the N.Y.P.D.

"Shit," I growled, as we killed the engines of our bikes and assessed the damage at Pop's shooting range. I stared at the front of the building, riddled with bullets, then took casual strides toward the dozens of cops swarming the joint.

"Easy," Wolf warned, placing a hand on my shoulder trying to reign me in. "Keep your head, Black."

"He's right. We got a lot of eyes on us right now," Pipe added.

I gave them both a quick nod before we started for Jack and Riggs. I kept my eyes on Brantley watching the motherfucker grin and gloat before I came up behind Jack and he lifted his head.

"Well, look who it is," he taunted, stepping around Jack and closer to me. Jack glanced over his shoulder at me, wedging himself between me and the douche bag who held just as much blame as I did that Christine was dead.

"Relax Bulldog, no need to get possessive over a junkie," Brantley mocked, flexing his jaw. "Scum like that's not worth the effort," he added.

"You would know right, Craig?" I clipped, as Jack placed his hand on my chest, holding him back. "I'm good," I told Jack, shoving his hand off my chest as I glared at Brantley.

I might not deserve to be here but neither did this motherfucker.

The both of us had Christine's blood on our hands and this son of a bitch wanted to point fingers.

"Instead of taunting my brothers why don't you assholes do your job and find out who shot up Pop's business," Jack suggested.

"We intend to," Craig promised. "Who'd you piss off this time, Bulldog?"

"Don't bust my balls. Do your job or get the fuck out of here, put all those hard earned tax dollars to use," Jack hissed, turning around to face the rest of us and nodded toward Pops.

"You people probably never paid taxes a day in your life," he sneered.

I rolled my eyes, deciding this jerk off didn't deserve anymore of my time and followed Jack toward Pops.

"Hey, Blackie, I'd watch my back if I were you. It'd be a shame if you suffered the same fate as Christine," he crooned.

I froze in my tracks.

He didn't get to say her name.

He didn't get to use her death against me.

"Fuck," I heard Jack hiss as I spun around and charged for the douche bag who wouldn't let my wife rest in peace.

"Keep her name off your fucking tongue or so help me God I'll slice that thing right out of your fucking mouth," I roared.

Jack grabbed the back of my jacket and pulled me back before my hands closed around Brantley's throat.

"Sounds like you just threatened a police officer," he tormented.

I blew out a ragged breath, shrugged Jack off me and took a dangerous step closer to Brantley, piercing him with a deadly glare.

"You got a hard on for me, motherfucker?" I whispered, extending my arms outward and crossing one wrist over the other. "Go on, lock me up," I coaxed.

His eyes dipped to my wrists before turning his head side to side and glancing at the brothers in blue.

"Pussy," I hissed.

Just as I thought.

Man wanted to play the good cop in front of his precinct but he was as dirty as the sole of my boots.

"You okay?" Jack questioned.

"I'm fine," I confirmed, tipping his head toward the ambulance rolling into the parking lot.

We walked away from "Dirty Harry" and made our way to Pops. He was crouched down on the ground over the young worker's body. The kid had taken a shot to the leg and would be fine but Pops was obviously shaken up. Wu had shot the joint up and taken our guns, desecrating any future deal we were trying to make with Spinelli.

"We're sure it was Wu?" Riggs asked.

Good question.

I pinned Jack with a look, questioning him with my eyes, knowing we had two clubs gunning for us when everyone else only was worried about one.

"Yeah, they didn't even try to hide their identity, sending their message loud and clear," Wolf said as he lit up a cigarette. "Those fucking Dragons, man," he took a puff and turned toward Jack. "Give me the green light, make them watch as I fuck all their mothers," he offered.

"Christ, Wolf," Bones snarled. "What the fuck did their mothers do to you?"

"Them bitches brought those fucks into the world," he insisted.

Fact.

Jack patted my shoulder, assuring me it was Wu, and proceeded to Pops, giving him his undivided attention. I turned around and stared at the damage, knowing it would take a lot to bounce back from this.

I overheard Jack promise Pops he would make things right.

"Yeah, you will," Pops announced as the paramedics pushed him aside to work on the kid. "Don't feel like revisiting history son, did my time, buried enough innocent lives to last a lifetime." He rose to his feet, brushing the dirt from his pants and stepped closer to Jack. "You need to get a handle on these bastards before they draw more blood," he demanded.

Another fact.

The paramedics pushed us aside and worked on the kid, applying pressure to the wound as the other opened the ambulance doors. They lifted the stretcher into the back of the ambulance and Pops climbed up, taking a seat on the bench beside the kid. The paramedic closed the door before running around to the driver's side. The sirens sounded and brought me back to the day I sat on the floor holding Christine and waited for help.

I shook my head, refusing to go back to that hell, knowing I didn't have time for that trip. I walked back over to Riggs and Jack, back in beast mode, ready to make someone pay for every hole in the building in front of me, not to mention the one made in that innocent kid's leg.

"What are we going to do here?" I questioned, rolling a toothpick between my teeth before I glanced back at Brantley.

I wanted to spit in that motherfuckers face.

I wanted it more than my next breath.

"You know they're going to be riding our asses now," I informed Jack as I stared at the posse of assholes standing around doing nothing.

"Fuck 'em," Jack hissed, blowing out a heavy sigh.

"Gladly," I ground out, spitting the toothpick onto the ground before lifting my eyes back to Jack's. "We putting this club on lockdown?"

"No, not yet," Jack said, surprisingly. "For now round up the prospects, put them on Reina, Lacey, and Lauren," he ordered, turning his eyes to Riggs. "That going to be a problem?"

I realized the club needed all hands on deck and I would have to pull Bones off Lacey and saddle her with a prospect. That didn't rest with me, knowing no one would ever value her life more than me. I reminded myself we had eager prospects, young guys that would do nearly anything to earn their colors.

But would any of them stand in front of a gun aimed at her?

They better or I'd be the one pointing the gun at them.

I diverted my eyes to Riggs and watched as he fought for control over his emotions, his eyes conveying all the fear a man has after he's found the life that's worth more than his.

Riggs was scared of losing his heart.

I felt every ounce of his pain.

"It's a precaution, Riggs," Jack assured. "We need to bide our time and keep our heads. We can't keep our heads if we're worried about our women. You feel me?"

A third fact.

I paid close attention to the pep talk Jack was giving Riggs, pretending I was the one on the receiving end of it.

"Then trust me when I say we will get these motherfuckers," he declared. "We always win, even when it looks like it's impossible. You know why? Because I've lost too much to let anyone else ever take a goddamn thing from me and mine."

He was talking about his son.

And I was picturing his daughter.

"Get that look out of your eyes, Riggs," he ordered. "Looks like you found your heart, kid. Now, you have to hang on to it."

A final fact we all needed to keep in mind.

Heart.

It wasn't only the thing that kept you from being reckless it was what gave men like us purpose in this world.

I walked toward my bike, glanced back at Brantley just as my phone chimed, signaling I had a text message.

I tore my eyes away from the bastard, pulled out my sunglasses and covered my eyes before I straddled my bike. I reached into my jacket and looked down at my phone. The screen showed a message from a foreign number. I swiped my thumb across the screen, opened the message and a photo of Lacey appeared on the screen. She was carrying books, making it clear the photo was taken while she was at school. Another text came through from the same number, containing a message.

I haven't forgotten about her.

Heart.

The one thing we're all afraid to lose.

Chapter Twenty-five

BLACKIE

I left Pops and headed straight for the Dog Pound, my phone burning a hole in my pocket, the picture of Lacey plastered to my mind. I opened the door, found the prospects playing a game of pool and stalked toward the table, grabbing the white ball from the felt top and threw it against the wall.

"Games over," I sneered. "Time for the three of you to stop playing with your dicks and earn your fucking patches."

I pointed to Toke, the youngest of the three, and the one who has been sitting around the longest. "You get on your bike and ride to Dee's Diner. From this point forward, you are Reina's shadow. She needs to take a piss you hold the fucking stall closed. Do not let her out of your sight," I ground out.

"Yeah, you got it," Toke said, grabbing his leather vest off the back of a chair.

"Go," I bellowed, turning my eyes on Bosco. "Get your ass to Riggs' apartment and keep his woman and that baby she's got on the way breathing. I don't give a fuck if she pulls a bat out on you and takes a swing or if her mother shows up wielding a frying pan—you do whatever the fuck it takes to make sure no one touches her or that kid she's about to bring into this world. You hear me?"

"Loud and clear," he assured, dropping his pool stick and moving quickly toward the door.

"That leaves you," I said, cracking my knuckles as I stepped closer to Mack. He stared back at me with hungry eyes, clenching his fists as he rolled his neck.

Yeah, he's the one.

"Kingsborough College," I stated. "You find Lacey and you stick to her like glue."

I took a step closer, reached behind him and cupped the back of his neck.

"Anyone so much as blinks at her wrong you take them fucking down. Don't think, just do. Do you understand?" I questioned digging my nails into the nape of his neck as I clenched my jaw. "One fucking hair on her head gets harmed, I'll cut you and bury you deep in the earth."

"I got you," he said.

"No, you got *her*. You got *her* life in your fucking hands," I corrected. "A life that means more than yours, remember that," I hissed, releasing his neck. "Now get on," I ordered.

I watched him straighten his jacket before he walked out the door and off to guard my girl. My phone rang again inside my pocket, dread filled my body as I reached for it and saw it was Lacey calling.

My fingers hovered over the screen, itching to answer and hear her sweet voice one more time. I pictured her pretty face, that smile, those eyes that bore into my soul and knew there was only one choice.

My love or her life.

Her life.

I declined the call, turned the ringer off and went to shove the phone back into my pocket but stopped myself. I pulled up my contact list and debated on whether to make the call.

One phone call and a twenty-minute drive to the projects is all it would take to forget.

And I wanted to forget so badly.

I wanted to forget how she made me feel and how she made me want to be better.

But I didn't want to forget *her*.

That alone was enough to stop me from making the call.

I took off on my Harley in search of a place where Lacey was still mine and wound up home, standing in the middle of my aqua kitchen.

Every wall, every new fixture, even the doorbell she had me install reminded me of her. I'd never be able to step into this house after tonight. I lifted the folding chair in the kitchen and, swung it against the freshly painted walls.

Jack kept the holes in his walls to remember a time when he was too proud to get help. If he ever doubted his choice to get well and do the right thing all he had to do was remove one of the many pictures and stare at the offensive reminder.

I dropped the chair, letting the metal clang against the wooden floor before I kicked it across the room and stalked through the house. I stepped outside, slamming the door to a life I wasn't meant to have.

A dream that was never mine.

I needed to remind myself of my destiny and reiterate why I was about to give away the only thing worth a damn in my life.

It was time for a wake-up call, something to bring me down from the high of being happy and drag me back to the reality I deserved.

Back then, I thought it was ironic the house I bought was only mere minutes from the home of one of the families I destroyed.

Then I thought it was the devil fucking with me.

Now, I know it was fate.

I turned down the street I used to sit on for hours and stared at the two-story home with black shutters. I parked my bike across the street from the house and killed my engine. I could still see the newspaper headlines so vividly as if they were in front of me for the first time. I remember seeing the photos of the two boys that overdosed in the obituaries.

Both boys were waked at Scarpaci Funeral Home on Hylan Boulevard, on the same night and buried in Resurrection Cemetery on the same day.

I never told a soul, but I went to each of those boys wakes.

I sat in the back of the chapel and watched their mothers cry over their bodies as a priest ask God to forgive them and welcome both children into the gates of heaven.

Heavenly Father, please protect Alex Rossi.

Dear God, watch over Peter Corona.

I'll never forget the names of the boys whose lives I robbed.

I'll never forget their mothers.

And when I start to, I come here and wait for Mrs. Rossi to come home from work. I look at her, years later, and see how she never healed from the loss of her son.

Then, I drive to Resurrection Cemetery and pay my respects to Peter Corona, and the grave next to his where his mother was laid to rest a week after she buried her boy.

She committed suicide, left a note behind saying, she needed to be with her son.

I reached into my pocket and pulled out my phone as I glanced into the side-view mirror of my bike and saw Mrs. Rossi's car turn onto the street.

I'm sorry.

So, fucking sorry.

I made the call.

A half hour later I was driving away from the projects.

I turned into a real pussy, shocking the hell out of my dealer when I passed up the heroin and opted for the eight ball of coke.

But as much as I wanted to bring myself to hell.

I couldn't bring myself to forget *her.*

And if shooting up risked that, risked robbing me of the memory of her pretty face I wouldn't mark my arms.

Only to save the memory of Lace.

Look at that, even in the end she wound up being the one who saved *me.*

When I got back to the clubhouse I went straight for the bathroom, lined up two lines of coke and snorted them with a rolled up twenty-dollar bill.

I lifted my head as I braced my hands on the counter and peered at the devil in the mirror.

My name is Blackie and I am an addict.

That was my destiny.

I felt the burn of the powder in my nostrils and sniffled until it passed before I wiped the counter clean. I knotted the tip of the bag and shoved the remaining coke into my pocket before leaving the bathroom and headed straight for the bar.

I pulled the half-empty bottle of Johnny Walker off the shelf and took a seat at the bar.

It was the wrong move because the minute I sat down the door opened and for a minute I imagined Lacey walking through it, just as she did that first night.

I knocked back a shot, blinked and saw Riggs.

I turned around, hoping he wouldn't cut me any slack, but he didn't even seem to notice I was clutching the bottle like it was my salvation and poured myself a refill.

He was too wrapped up in his own hell to notice I was reliving mine.

"Tell me I did the right thing," Riggs demanded, as he filled his glass again.

"I don't even know what you did," I muttered, watching as he placed the bottle down and stared at his glass.

"It don't matter, just tell me what I need to hear," he said, downing another shot.

"You did the right thing," I muttered, not giving two fucks about this kid's problems—drowning in a sea of my own.

Still, he's been the only man in my corner with this shit with Lacey. He's had my back and hers when no one else would've given me that respect.

I owed him the same.

Not to mention it wasn't that long ago that he saved my life by shooting me with the Naloxone trying to reverse everything Jimmy Gold did to me.

He saved my life.

He gave me a chance to be with Lace.

Yeah, Riggs deserved my respect.

"You looking to forget? That shit won't do it," I told him, swapping the bottle of tequila he was nursing with the bottle of Black.

"I'm sorry," he grunted as I took a swig of his tequila.

"You have a fight with your ol' lady?" I questioned.

"I don't have one of those," he replied.

I let him believe the lie because every now and then we needed to escape reality.

"Right, the baby mama then," I corrected.

Riggs liked herb, and I had just swiped some when I grabbed the coke. I pulled it from my pocket and broke up the pot on top of the bar.

I leaned over the bar and grabbed the rolling papers from behind it before I sat back down and rolled a perfectly tight joint.

"What was that shit with the cops earlier?" he asked.

If Riggs needed a distraction, talking about what a scumbag Brantley was, would be the way to go.

"Ah, me and officer Brantley go way back," I slurred, bringing the end of the paper to my lips to lick and seal it. "I don't know who gave that piece of shit more of a hard-on me or Christine," I added, passing him the joint as I met his curious eyes.

He paused for a minute, composing himself and lit the joint.

"Never heard you talk much about your wife," he said, inhaling sharply.

Yeah, I kept that shit under lock and key. Only the people who were around for it truly knew the whole story.

"So, this rat, the cop, he's been itching to put you away for a while? And Christine? He wanted to arrest her too?"

I laughed.

"Nah he didn't want to arrest her," I said before taking a toke. "Christine wasn't some low-life junkie, Riggs," I explained, angrily.

People often had the misconception that Christine was using but she never took a drug in her life. I often think that she didn't mean to kill herself and like me she was simply trying to forget the mess our life together had become.

She didn't know she was shooting enough heroin to put down a horse.

She didn't know.

"I didn't say she was," he said solemnly, pouring us both a shot.

To hell with sobriety.

"It's what you think because it's all anyone in this fucking place ever talks about. You've got this image of Christine, a woman you never met, lying face down in a bathtub with a fucking needle in her arm but that's not the woman I married. Everyone in this club assumes I drink because I feel guilty she overdosed with the shit we were selling, but they're wrong, so fucking wrong."

"So why do you do it?"

"Sure, it's got something to do with it. If I wasn't dealing heroin she wouldn't have been able to get her hands on it. But, Christine would've found some other way to end the nightmare she was living," I told him the truth and not the fairytale I liked to believe.

"I was a shitty husband," I admitted. "I put this club before her. I put the drugs, the money, the goddamn patch before the sweet girl I fell in love with when I was fifteen years old. See, she knew me before the club, before the corruption and the mayhem and she had to watch me morph into a Knight. It was all good when I was just a prospect, still had time for my girl and the crazy shit we used to do."

I smiled faintly, thinking back to all the things we used to do like the time we got caught skinny dipping in her parent's pool.

"I don't know Lauren all that well, ran into her a few times since you two started up, but she seems spunky. Christine used to be spunky. She used to love life, and more than life, she loved me. She loved me hard, felt that shit down in my bones."

And when her parents caught us she defended me to them.

She chose me over them.

She chose us.

I cleared my throat and continued.

"After I patched in, Cain pushed me to the front lines. I was eager to earn, eager to prove I would do anything for the club," I angled my head to the side and studied his profile.

"Sort of like you," I pointed out. "In our time of need you stepped up and became a front runner. That isn't lost to the club, Riggs, and you don't have to keep proving your worthy of your patch," I added.

"I'm not," he argued. "I'm just doing my job."

"I thought the same thing and kept doing my job. I ran drugs, guns, women…whatever made the most profit and never looked back. I forgot about the love I had at home and what it felt like to go home to a warm body. I pushed the thoughts of how fucking good it felt to crawl into bed and have the sweetest woman wrap her legs around me. She didn't know what I did, and if she did, she didn't care. I could've killed a man, sometimes did, and she still welcomed me home, into our bed, night after night."

"So how did it all change?"

"I started pushing her away. Cain made a deal with the G-Man and we moved more drugs, became the biggest operation on the east coast."

"The G-Man is the guy Jimmy Gold was working with to push Pastore out, right?"

"Yeah," I confirmed, taking another shot. "Anyway, there is only so much bad shit you can do before it catches up to you and changes who you are. It didn't bother me at first, I had shoeboxes full of money and in my head, I was doing it for a good reason. I would buy Christine her dream house, make sure my woman had everything she wanted, the best of everything. I told myself I was doing it for her, making up for the douche bag I was on a daily basis. I didn't have a conscience

I only had a goal, but I didn't plan on being the reason two seventeen-year-old kids died," I confessed.

A house I was just starting to make a home.
Rest in peace Alex Rossi and Peter Corona.
Rest in peace my love, Christine.

"It changes you," I repeated, hoarsely. "Knowing that two kids, who had their whole lives ahead of them died, so you could make a quick buck—it fucking wrecks you, man. That was the beginning of the end for me and Christine. I stopped going home, started staying here every night. I couldn't look at her; I couldn't let myself have something as good as her when all I ever did was take the good from other people."

I sighed, pushing back the bottle.

"She thought I was cheating on her and that's when Brantley came around. He was a rookie then, looking to make a name for himself and thought he'd start by taking down the Satan's Knights. He's smart, I'll give the son of a bitch that. He looked for the weakest link, found it was me, and used my wife as bait."

Here I was all these years later, still the weakest link only there was a different innocent woman being used as bait.

"He gave Christine all the attention I wasn't giving her anymore, made her feel things I gave up on making her feel, and promised her all the things I couldn't. He used her, played on her broken emotions and convinced her I would wind up dead because of the club. I found out they were having an affair, put two and two together and confronted her but she had already made a deal with him. She would get the drugs from me and prove I was dealing the shit that killed those two kids," he said, solemnly. "Instead of giving me up she gave up her life."

As similar as the stories were they were different.
As similar as Lacey and Christine were…they too were different.
I was Lacey's one and only.
I was supposed to be Christine's one and only too.
Christine gave her life for mine.
And I'd give mine for Lacey's.

I covered my face with my hands and felt Riggs pat me on the back. A groan escaped my lips as I dropped my hands from my face and pinned Riggs with a stare.

Don't be me, man.
Hang on to that woman of yours.
Hold that baby of yours and fucking enjoy life.
You only get one.

"Jack's been trying for a long time to get this club on the right track, to give us some peace. He thinks he can turn us into a legit club and make us proud to call ourselves the Satan's Knights—but he's in over his head. We're in too deep, and every time we think we are pulling ourselves out of the hole, some other fucking threat comes along. Whether it's a man in a fur coat or a fucking Chinese emperor, there will always be a fucking cancer that will drag us down."

Truth.

I glanced down at my hands, turning them over and displayed my palms.

"See these hands? They have a lot of blood on them and that's all I see when I look at them, all the blood and all the faces of the people who bled from these hands."

They didn't have Lacey's though.

I could still close my eyes and see her pretty face and not her blood on my hands.

"Blackie…" he started.

I shook my head and interrupted him.

Let the devil teach you something.

"You got something good with Bianci's sister, stop trying to prove yourself, man, you paid your dues. Now, take a step back and don't let that girl doubt she has you because when *you* don't have her anymore you're going to feel it," I promised as the words got stuck in my throat.

And when you feel it you're going to wish you were dead.

Chapter Twenty-six

Lacey

Something was wrong.
This time I didn't have to wait for the sadistic voice to poison me with foolish thoughts.
This time I felt it with every fiber of my being.
With every crack of my heart.

The inbox you are trying to reach is full.

I disconnected the call and shoved the phone into my pocketbook before I ran my fingers through my hair and stared up at the gray sky willing myself not to cry. I blew out a breath and tried to tell myself that I was overreacting that I was used to bad things happening and didn't know how to enjoy the good.
But I couldn't shake the feeling my world was crumbling, and I didn't even receive an invitation to the end.
I grabbed my mother's keys from my purse and started for the campus parking lot when I heard someone call my name.
"Lacey, wait up!" I turned on my heel and saw Brandon running across the grass with a smile on his face.
"Shit," I muttered. Why won't this guy get the hint?
"You in a hurry?"
"Actually, I am," I said, forcing a smile.
"I was going to ask you if you wanted to go grab a quick bite," he said, shoving his hands in his pockets as he flashed a smile. He had such perfectly straight teeth and a smile so white he looked like a poster boy for Colgate.
"That would be nice Brandon but I'm…I'm seeing someone."
"The old biker guy? Come on, Lace, you're not serious are you?"
"Lacey," I corrected through gritted teeth.
Only the people who loved me called me Lace.
"Yes, the biker and as for his age…," I shrugged my shoulders. "Well, let's just say I skipped past the two decades a guy feels he needs to be an adolescent. Blackie's a man, not a boy trying to become one." I smiled sweetly.
Brandon's eyebrows drew together in confusion.
Exhibit A.
Poor bastard didn't even know when he was being schooled.
He had about another decade of the stupidity left.
"Thanks for the offer. I'm sure you'll find another date," I added, turning around and leaving the dumb-fucked boy in the grass.
I made my way to the parking lot, found my mom's car and was about to climb into the car when I spotted the Harley parked two rows over. My eyes moved from the chrome to the man straddling it, taking in the unmistakable reaper sewn

into the back of his leather vest. I slammed the door to my car and stalked across the two rows, watching the prospect turn around and meet my gaze.

I had seen him a few times when Blackie was still in the hospital and my father was keeping a watchful eye out, making sure Blackie was protected. I didn't remember his name though, causing me to glance at the patch that declared his road name.

Mack.

Where the fuck was Blackie?

I lifted my eyes to his and crossed my arms under my breasts as I studied him.

"Who sent you?" I asked, hanging on to whatever strength I could muster up before I had no choice but to surrender.

He remained perfectly still and silent.

"Was it my father? Was it Blackie? Where are they?" I demanded.

Nothing.

I uncrossed my arms and shoved my palms against his chest.

"Answer me goddamn it! Are they okay?" I screeched, holding back the emotion threatening to surface.

"They're fine," he finally said.

I should've felt some sense of relief but I didn't. All I felt was another crack shatter my heart.

"But that's all you'll tell me isn't it?" I dropped my hands from his chest and stared into his crystal blue eyes that were blank.

I took a retreating step, glanced at his bike before diverting my eyes back to his.

"Better straddle that bike we're going for a ride *Mack*," I sneered, turning on my heel as I power walked back to my car.

My hand trembled as I opened the door and quickly slid inside the car. I gripped the steering wheel as the hot tears fell from my eyes.

Told you he didn't really want you.
Told you it would all end.
Told you he'd chew you up and spit you out.
But you didn't listen.
Now you'll suffer the truth.

I dropped my head against the steering wheel and wondered if I could shake the crazy. I pushed back, started the car and forced myself to concentrate and block out the doubt that threatened to ruin me.

Blackie had told me himself that the club was in a bad place, danger lurked around every corner and we needed to keep things quiet between us until it was all straightened out.

He said that.

I didn't imagine it.

If there was a threat he would be the one protecting me. He wouldn't send some prospect to guard me for a multitude of reasons but mainly because no one watched out for me like Blackie did.

Because no one cared for me like he did.

He told me he couldn't give me up.

It wasn't a lie.

Every moment we spent together was not something I conjured up in my head. Those moments were pure, and they were beautiful.

They were real.

Every kiss.

Every unspoken I love you.

Every time he held me in his arms and squeezed me to make sure I was real.

I didn't imagine any of that.

And I sure as hell didn't imagine the way he smiled.

I couldn't have.

I didn't imagine the rhythm of his heartbeat that played for me when I laid my head against his chest or the way he looked at me like I was his savior.

Like I was an angel.

You're no angel.

Maybe not.

But for a moment in time, I was his angel.

I don't know what made me think back to that first night, but I remembered pulling up to the clubhouse and seeing Blackie's bike knowing with every ounce of life in me he'd make it okay.

He'd take away my pain.

I chose to think my maker was granting me a gift by allowing me to recall the memory. I held onto it and I chased that memory all the way back to the clubhouse, hoping for a repeat.

It could happen.

Tell me it could.

Please?

I pulled into the compound, didn't even bother parking the car and pulled it right in front of the Dog Pound. I climbed out of the car, slammed the door and spotted Riggs sitting on top of a picnic table in front of the clubhouse. He lifted his head and my eyes zeroed in on the bottle he was holding onto for dear life. His eye was swollen and a fresh bruise grazed his cheek.

"I should tell you not to go in there," he mumbled.

"Are you okay?" I questioned, taking a step closer to him as he doubled over in pain clutching his ribs.

"Run," he ground out.

I disregarded his injury and lifted my eyes to his.

"What?"

"Turn around and get the hell out of here Lacey. It's a fucking war zone here—hearts are breaking all over the place," he slurred, raising his hand from his abdomen to his chest rubbing the spot between his pecs.

"Heart," he whispered. "What a joke."

Listen to him.

I shook my head, swallowed the lump in my throat and forced myself to believe my heart and not my mind. I left Riggs to wallow in whatever misery he was succumbing to and walked into the clubhouse.

One day I will look back on tonight and wish I had listened to Riggs because the moment I stepped inside the Dog Pound I became a casualty of war.

I lost the war with my mind.

I lost the war with Blackie.

I lost everything.

Blackie lost too.

He didn't even turn around to see who had walked in, too engrossed in snorting the line of cocaine off the bar to notice me.

Too busy fucking losing his battle with drugs.

"So, is this why you're not answering my calls?" I questioned as I stalked across the room to the bar, slapping my keys on the table as I grabbed a hold of his hair with my free hand and lifted his head.

I turned his cheek and forced his bloodshot eyes to meet mine.

"Why?" I whispered.

He stared at me quietly, licking his lips before he brought his hand to his nose and sniffled.

"Why what?" he asked, turning back around using a credit card to push the left-over coke into a line.

No, God...I had to stop him.

I had to do something.

I thought my purpose was to show him a new way, to show him there is more to life than grief but it was clear my purpose in Blackie's life was to save him from himself. I stepped around the bar and bent my head, blowing the coke across the wooden bar with a big burst of air from my lungs.

I never feared Blackie until that moment.

Until he looked at me and I swore I saw the devil in his eyes.

And then I realized I wasn't looking at Blackie anymore but I was now face to face with Satan's knight, the Devil's soldier.

"Don't like it, girl? Don't like what you see?" he asked as he pushed back his chair and stumbled onto his feet, gripping the back of the stool to steady himself.

"What's the matter?" he taunted. "Got no love for the drug addict? No love for the man I truly am? This...," he gritted, pounding his chest with his fist. "This is me, Lace, this is Dominic Petra the man you hold on a fucking pedestal."

I shook my head and bit down on my lip to stop the tears from spilling because this wasn't about me, this was about him. This was his war.

I was just an innocent victim of it.

"No it's not," I insisted. "The man I hold in such a high regard is the man who wants to better himself, the man who has been dealt a shit hand in life but plays his cards until the bitter end, hoping the dealer will throw him a *queen*."

"That man is a myth, something you dreamt up inside that pretty little head of yours," he hissed, lifting his hand to his head. "He don't exist." He pointed to me and then himself. "Neither do we anymore," he ground out. "Go dream a different dream, girl."

He knows I exist.
You can't hide me anymore.

I was standing in front of Blackie, watching *his* lips move, listening to *his* voice but I couldn't understand why *my* maker was controlling *him*. Every word that came from his mouth was something my mind would say to drag me down.

These weren't Blackie's words.

They were the words of my maker.

I dropped my head into my hands and fought for control.

For clarity.

For Peace.

And then it occurred to me I struggle every day to tame something I have no control over. Being an addict, that's a choice, something you can control. I have watched him for two months choose himself over drugs but today he chose to be an addict. Today he chose to lose.

I dropped my hands and lifted my head to stare at him with vengeance.

Vengeance for not believing in himself, for not seeing what I saw, for not loving himself enough to love me.

"People have problems they can't control, real issues that inebriate them and then there's you who every single problem you have has been self-created. When are you going to stop doing this to yourself?" I shook my head. "Why won't you let yourself be happy?"

"Who says I'm not happy?"

"It won't work. You can't lie to me. I've seen you happy now. I've seen you smile and I've seen you laugh," I paused, brushing away the tears that fell from my eyes.

"I saw *you*, the man behind the mask and the layers of leather you use as armor. I fell in love with that man. I saw the real Blackie; I saw Dominic Petra."

"Dominic Petra died a long time ago," he sneered, grabbing the bottle off the bar and taking a swig. He didn't even flinch as he chugged the poison. "And the man you think you know is nothing more than a guy who got his kicks off banging a young girl, someone who wasn't touched, someone he could take advantage of. Your father sheltered you too much. He should've brought you around here more, then maybe you wouldn't dream so much. But you're young, there's still time for you to learn…"

"Don't do that. Don't cheapen what we are because you're fucking high."

He placed the bottle back on the bar and leaned in close pinning me with a cold hard stare.

His eyes were dead.

Just like his soul.

Another crack in my heart.

"What we are is nothing," he hissed. "You are nothing to me but Jack's daughter and a virgin pussy I got to play with."

I didn't even realize my actions until I felt the sting on the palm of my hand and saw the red handprint on his cheek.

It's over.

"Again," he ordered.

"No," I shouted.

"Again!" he demanded, crooking his finger beckoning me to inflict more pain on him.

I backed away from the bar, shaking my head as tears rolled down my face. He dropped his hands and took a step back himself.

"Get out," he rasped. "Get out and forget you ever saw *me*."

It was all a lie.
I told you so.

I grabbed my keys from the bar before walking out from behind it and started for the door. I had nothing left to give, no fight left inside of me and so I surrendered.

I stopped in front of the door and slowly turned around to meet his gaze.

"I could've been your queen. All you had to do was let me," I whispered through my sobs, before turning back around and walking out the door.

There are two sides in a war and only one winner.

So how come we both lost?

Chapter Twenty-seven
BLACKIE

After my wife died I relived her death for six months straight. I'd wake up drenched in a cold sweat from the nightmare of looking into her lifeless eyes and being the one who forced them closed.

Whoever says history doesn't repeat itself never walked a day in my shoes.

For the last month, since the night I ended things with Lacey, her face has haunted me. I relive the moment I looked into her eyes and told her she was nothing but her father's daughter and a piece of pussy. It's the look reflected in her eyes as she rears her hand back and slaps me that consumes me, night after night—the look of pure defeat and unexplainable heartbreak.

She loved me.

Heard that shit with my own ears.

And she'll never know how much I love her.

I lived life without fear until I fell for Lacey and, Boots threatened to use her against me. Not once in all my years on this earth, have I been afraid of anything. But after that message came through on my phone, that picture of her at school—I knew fear.

I hurt her.

I bruised her ego and broke her heart.

I wounded her with my words.

I saved her from me.

I saved her life.

I can live with the guilt of my actions as long as she's breathing.

As long as she's safe.

If you can even call this shit living.

No, this shit isn't living.

I know what living is and for a short while I lived and I lived hard.

Living is holding her in my arms.

Living is watching her face light up when I walk into a room.

Living is Lacey's smile.

Her laugh.

The way she blushes when I tell her she's beautiful.

Her kiss.

And her touch.

Living is watching the woman you love take what she needs from your body and as she's doing it, she looks into your eyes and you can see forever.

Living is loving Lace.

This is death.

The death of a man wo was never good enough to live and share a memory with someone as pure as her.

I could've done it another way but even now, after time has passed, I can't think of another way where it would've worked. Lacey saw through me, she saw past the demons and the self-destruction. She saw the remnants of my soul and a glimpse of who I wanted to be.

I had to make her hate me.

Take that beautiful love she had for me and turn it into ugly.

I'll never forgive myself for what I did to her, no matter how much I try to tell myself I had no choice, my angel didn't deserve to believe she was worthless in my eyes.

She wished for me to live.

She wished for me to smile.

And she wished to be the one who made me smile.

She got her three wishes.

My only wish for her is to know she is everything good left in the world.

She's beauty, and she's hope.

She's strength, and she's passion.

She's the light you look for when you're stuck in the darkness.

She's just...she's an angel.

She was my angel.

And now she's free.

I bent my head, pressed my finger against my left nostril and sucked up the line of coke through the right one.

"Fuck, I didn't know anyone was in here," I heard the new guy Stryker mumble. I had been too consumed by my thoughts to hear the door open He stared at the residue on the counter as I straightened up and glanced at him through the mirror.

"I'll be out in a minute," I growled, glaring at him through the glass.

Wolf had done his job, found four lost souls willing to join the mayhem, and Stryker was one of them. He was twenty-eight years old, drifting from one charter to the next, looking for his place within the club and thought he'd find it here in Brooklyn. We had just voted these guys in—watched as they cut through the stitching of the patch declaring them each a nomad, replacing it with one that declared them a brother of Brooklyn.

Now, it was time to introduce them to the fucked up shit they signed up for. It was time to introduce them to Sun Wu and the Red Dragons to give them a taste of blood. Rocco Spinelli gave us the heads up on a shipment Wu was receiving down at the docks. Jack was ready to strike—it was time to send a message back to the Chinese motherfucker who shot up Pops.

Saddle up, boys because we're going to intercept their shipment.

"All right, but man, I gotta take a piss and we need to get our asses in gear," Stryker argued, crossing his arms as he diverted his eyes from the coke back to my face.

"I don't share," I ground out.

"Not my thing," he retorted. "Didn't know it was yours," he added as I bent down to rip another line but with his eyes drilling a hole into my back I couldn't fucking do it. I grabbed the towel and put it under the water before I soaked up the remaining coke and turned back to him.

"There's a lot you don't know kid," I said, twisting the towel in my hands as I stared at him. "You stick around long enough, you'll uncover all our secrets and collect a few of your own."

"We all got secrets man," he replied. "Some of us hide them better than others, but every one of the Satan's Knights has a tale to tell or we wouldn't be brothers," he added before he glanced down at my bare chest. "Nice tattoo," he commented.

I looked down at the new ink that covered the left side of my chest.

"You play?" he questioned.

"Play?"

"The notes, man, you play an instrument?"

"No," I answered, shaking my head as my hand covered the music notes that marked my chest. "Bathroom's all yours," I ground out before stepping around him and leaving him behind.

I grabbed the first black shirt I could find and was about to pull it over my head when I glanced at the mirror, at the tattoo I got three days after I broke Lacey's heart.

I've learned as life goes on that the things we hold close to us, the memories we cherish of the people we love, they fade from our minds. We forget the moments that change us and give us purpose.

I didn't want to forget.

I wanted to hang onto that slice of heaven I had and even when the drugs drag me down and force me to black out, I want to stare at the reminder.

A reminder of a dance I shared when I thought I'd never dance.

I wanted to remember Leather and Lace.

Take the story and the dance with me when I died.

Music notes.

To a song that reminded me of a girl who changed me.

A girl I didn't see coming.

A girl I loved and always would.

I pulled the shirt over my head, secured the vest and slid my arms through my leather jacket, tucking my gun into my waist band and grabbing an extra magazine. My club was waiting for me outside ready to move, thirsty for blood, eager to reclaim the name our predecessors gave us.

Revenge took over our souls as we rode silently, full of determination, leaving whatever shred of decency any of us had at the clubhouse and unleashed the animals we truly were.

The Satan's Knights were back.

We were stronger.

Harder.

We had been fucked with for too long and now it was time to brush the dirt off our shoulders, remember the criminals we were, and destiny that awaited us. Jack led us to the pier and killed his engine first. The rest of us followed suit, pulling our weapons and crouching down as we ran up the pier where the vessel was docked. Sun Wu and the Dragons were nowhere in sight, not scheduled to unload their shipment for another hour. Jack paused at the container and passed an envelope to Rienzi, Rocco Spinelli's foreman, before he snapped the plastic seal off the doors giving us access to Wu's merchandise.

There were wooden crates stacked from the floor to the ceiling, filling the entire container. The clock was ticking, forcing us to hustle and get the fucking job done before Wu showed up and made this shit messier than we planned.

Stryker and Deuce, another fool who decided Brooklyn was the place he wanted to call home, charged in first, tucking their guns away. I kept my eyes trained on Stryker, curious about the man who claimed we all had secrets and watched him get down. The guy looked like he had trained for this shit as he got down on one knee, placing one palm over the other while Deuce put his boot clad foot onto Stryker's hands hoisting him up. Deuce pulled a crate from the top and dropped it onto the floor beside us. Neither of the nomads stopped what they were doing to the see what the fuck Wu was selling, they demolished the first row of crates, proving their worth to the club.

The last crate they dropped opened and Wolf sifted through it with the tip of his gun.

"Well, well, looks like Wu wanted to get fucked after all," he mocked, as he held up a pink dildo.

Riggs strolled curiously over to the crate, pushing around the contents, and pulled out a bunch of sex toys.

"I bet this one is labeled butt plugs," Pipe said, prying open the top of another crate.

"Dump it," Jack ordered.

Pipe raised an eyebrow, questioning Jack.

"You sure about that, boss? Bet we can turn this shit for a pretty penny," he countered.

We weren't about to start pushing dildos on the street. This move was to show these motherfuckers we would not sit back and take it in the ass anymore. It wasn't about taking their shit and turning a profit but more about sending a message—you don't fuck with us.

"Dump the fucking shit," Jack barked, as he lifted a crate over his head and threw it into the water.

I grabbed the next crate and hoisted it into the river. As Stryker and Deuce unloaded the container, one by one we silently dropped the merchandise into the Hudson. Looking around at my brothers, I could see the aggression painted on their faces.

Stryker was right.

We all have secrets.

We all have nightmares that haunt us.

And being the devil's soldiers provided us with an outlet for the torment we all suffered.

We emptied the container, dropping the last of the sex toys into the river, creating quite a sight.

"Pack it up," Jack demanded, as he reached into his back pocket and produced a can of spray paint and nodded toward Rienzi. He closed the container, locking it up with a new plastic seal before taking a step back and letting Jack do his thing. He pulled the cap off the bottle, throwing it into the water before putting his finger on the aerosol can and writing a message to Wu.

Fuck you.

In bright red letters across the door.

Jack took a step back, admiring his handy work then dumping the can of paint into the water and turning around to face us.

"Clear enough?"

"Still think we should've fucked him with one of his toys," Wolf clipped.

"Message is clear," Pipe confirmed, smacking Wolf upside the head.

Jack and I stepped toward Stryker, Deuce, Cobra and Linc, offering them a pat on the back, impressed with their efficiency. I extended my hand to Stryker as I met his gaze.

"Welcome home," I muttered.

"Thanks, man, nice to finally have one," he said, cracking his knuckles as he stared back at me.

We all got secrets man. Some of us hide them better than others, but every one of the Satan's Knights has a tale to tell or we wouldn't be brothers.

We were half way down the dock when Jack fell into step beside me.

"I've had my head wrapped around this shit with Wu for weeks—working with Spinelli to find the right time to make our move," he started, stopping in his tracks and turning to me. "You're using again," he accused, running his fingers through his hair. "I turn my back for a second, thinking you finally got your shit together and when I turn around you're more fucked then before. What's your deal Black? What demon caught you this time?"

"Not your problem," I ground out, turning to face him. "If I want your two cents I'll ask for it, but until then do us both a favor and worry about yourself and your own demons—let me handle mine," I sneered, turning around and stalking down the pier.

I paused when I heard the roar of the engines, glanced at our parked bikes and knew shit was about to go down.

"Shit, we've got company," I shouted over my shoulder as I pulled out my gun.

Everything moved in slow motion as the Red Dragons started shooting at us. Without hesitation, we ran down the rickety peer toward the enemy, our guns drawn lighting the shipping yard a blaze as we fired back.

It's not the story behind us that makes us the Satan's Knights it's this. Taking the lives of people and doing it without remorse. It's the blood that decorates us as our bullets pierce their heads and their brains splatter back at us.

I swiped the back of my hand over my eye and pulled back my hand staring at the crimson that painted my skin.

Blood.

That's what it's all about.

Lacey

Life is comprised of moments, joyful ones and tragic ones. We all have two faces, but the lucky ones can merge both expressions, they can take the good with the bad and understand that life is sometimes not what you expect.

Sometimes life is more and sometimes it's less.

Not everyone can be happy all the time.

And so we learn to hang on to the happiness and use it as a crutch to get us through the sadness that envelopes us and let it guide us back to the joy.

If you're one of the lucky ones.

I stared at the two masks hanging from the mirror above my dresser. One mask featured a smile while the other displayed a frown. My freshman year of college I took a drama course, and the professor gave us these masks to use as a tool to summon the emotions of the characters we were portraying.

I dropped the class but kept the masks because for me they were so much more than a tool. Those masks are who I am.

The smile conveys how I feel when my maker is silenced.

The frown reminds me it will all come crashing down, and I was only smiling during a brief pause from my truth. My maker will return and bring me down from whatever manic state of happiness I was now experiencing.

I'm not one of the lucky ones.

Over the last month I have slept more than anything else because when I sleep…I dream and in my dreams, I see him.

I dream of our story.

I dream of the smiles.

And then I wake, try to hang onto the happiness of the dream, pray it guides me out of the depression I am in…but it doesn't.

I want one more chance to smile.

One more chance to be a girl in love.

One more chance to be normal.

It doesn't come.

It never comes.

And so I close my eyes again.

Maybe next time.

Chapter Twenty-eight

Lacey

I awoke to the sound of a knock on my bedroom door but didn't bother turning around. I knew it was my mother and I knew the look on her face would break my heart—what was left of it. I kept my back towards her, laid on my side
as she stepped into my room and closed the door softly behind her.

"Lacey, it's almost noon," she whispered.

I didn't answer.

A moment later I felt the dip in the mattress as she laid beside me and wrapped an arm around my waist.

"My sweet girl," she murmured, smoothing down my hair. "My beautiful, sweet girl. Please talk to me," she pleaded.

"I'm fine," I said numbly.

"You're not fine and I've ignored it too long," she whispered. "I know what's going on Lacey," she revealed.

Slowly, I turned around, brave enough to face her, wanting her to take away my pain.

Desperate for the love only a mother could give.

Maybe just maybe she could be the one to help me through this. Not that long ago I felt like I was walking in my mother's shoes, falling in love with an outlaw, trying to see the good in him. She did it.

And when it failed when she was no longer his...she survived.

Maybe this wasn't about the maker.

Maybe it was just about my heart.

I didn't know anymore.

"You loved daddy didn't you?"

"Of course I did."

"And it hurt when it was over didn't it?"

"Yes," she whispered.

"But you're still standing. The world kept moving for you," I murmured.

"And it will for you too," she assured me. "You just have to let it. You have to realize you have nothing to be ashamed— ""I'm not ashamed," I interrupted. "I fell in love and for two months of my life I had it all...everything I ever wanted. He may not have been perfect in your eyes or someone you or daddy would've picked for me but what we had was perfect."

I watched as she blinked and tried to mask the confusion in her eyes.

"Two months?"

"Yes, for two months I was Blackie's girl," I admitted. "No one knew and now I'm wondering if I imagined it all."

"Lacey," she started.

"Please, don't. Don't tell me it was wrong because it was the only thing right in my life," I argued.

She closed her mouth and remained silent.

"I don't want to talk about it anymore," I said.

"Talking about it might help," she replied. "Lacey, I can't sit here and watch you suffer like this anymore. I can't sit here and go through this again."

"What are you talking about?"

"It's like watching it happen all over again, only this time it's my child I'm losing and I've already lost one," she gasped, lifting her hand to cover her mouth as she shook her head.

She knows.
She knows she's stuck with the damaged kid.
Look at what you're doing to her.
Look at her cry.

"What I'm trying to say is— ""What you're trying to say is you think I'm crazy," I rasped as I climbed out of the bed and stared back at her.

"No, Lacey, I'm not saying that at all," she argued, getting out of the bed to quickly walk around it, grabbing a hold of my hands as her eyes pleaded with mine.

"I love you," she whispered.

"I'm not crazy," I insisted.

"No you're not," she agreed, through her tears.

"I'm going to be okay. I'm going to be fine," I struggled. "I'm not like him. I'm just sad."

"You're just sad," she repeated.

"I've been cooped up in this house too long and it's getting to me," I pulled my hands back and turned around, walked to my dresser and lifted my phone. "I need to be around other people. I need to live a little and I need to forget."

"Lacey," my mother tried.

"I'm fine mom," I demanded, stepping back when she extended her hand to take mine. "Leave me be," I warned.

She stared at me helplessly.

I remembered that look in her eyes.

It was there the day my brother died.

I closed my eyes, remembering my mother run down the street, seeing my father hold their lifeless son in his arms. She collapsed onto the ground and my father placed Jack's body into her arms, allowing her to hold her baby one final time. I could still hear the cops trying to convince my parents to let him go and the shrill cry that escaped her mouth when they tried to take him from her. It was my father who wound up taking him from her arms and it was he who laid him on the gurney. They didn't cover him like they do in the movies, they let his parents, our parents, see him one final time just as he looked when he slept instead of bringing a sheet up to cover his angelic face.

I opened my eyes as the tears streamed my cheeks.

I was the reason that day existed in our hearts.

I was the reason my mother lost her son.

I closed the distance between us and wrapped my arms tightly around her small frame.

"I'm okay, mom," I cried. "I'm sorry I scared you."
She needed for me to get it together.
She needed me to put my mask on.
She squeezed me tightly, and I heard her whimper against my shoulder.
"You're okay," she whispered. "You are stronger than you know."
I pulled away, lifted my hands to her face and wiped away her tears and forced the smile she needed to see.
"I am strong," I assured.
She searched my eyes and for the first time I wished I had her eyes and not my dad's maybe then I'd be more convincing. Finally, she nodded, leaned forward and kissed my forehead.
It took a while for her to leave my room, afraid I'd switch masks, but I kept it together long enough to convince her I just needed a break. I called Daniela in front of her, even put the call on speaker, so she could listen and be at ease, knowing I was trying to put one foot in front of the other. When she finally left me alone I showered, threw something on and twisted my hair into a top knot. I could still see the concern etched across her features when I went downstairs to say goodbye.
If she thought she'd succeed she probably would've tied me to the chair and not let me leave.
I met Daniela at the Dunkin Donuts on 86th street, ordered an iced coffee and pretended to listen as she rambled on about her birthday. Her birthday was Monday, but she wanted to celebrate tonight since it was Saturday night. One of the guys in Noah's fraternity had a hook with Kettle Black in Bay Ridge and promised to get us in without I.D.'s.
"You're going to come aren't you?"
I didn't want to.
I wanted to go back to bed but, that wasn't an option with my mother suspiciously watching me—looking for signs I was more my father's daughter then hers. So, I decided to keep my mask on and be the happy-go-lucky girl everyone thinks I have the ability to be.
"Yes, I'll be there," I promised, taking a sip of my coffee as I turned my head toward the window.
My eyes zeroed in on the Harley across the street and for a moment I assumed it was Mack's. That guy was a permanent fixture in my life and has been camped out at my mother's house for the last month. My mom brings him coffee in the morning before she goes to work.
Yeah, she does.
He even changed my stepfather's tire the other day.
One big happy family.
"It's going to be so much fun," Daniela beamed. "Now, I have to figure out what to wear."
My fake smile diminished as I continued to stare out the window and spotted Blackie walking out of the liquor store across the street. He straddled his bike and then his head turned and our eyes locked.
I saw him.
He saw me.

Another stolen moment to add to the story.

He flipped his sunglasses down and I knew even with the tinted glass over his eyes he was still watching me but then he turned his head and pretended like he never saw me.

Like I never existed.

I watched him peel out of the spot and speed away.

"What do you think?"

I think I lost my fucking mind.

I glanced back at Daniela.

"I've got to go," I said, standing up. "You're going to pick me up at nine right?"

"Yes," she replied, confused.

"Okay, I'll be ready." I promised, before I grabbed my empty coffee cup and chucked it into the garbage. I gave my friend one last fake smile before leaving the coffee shop. I heard Mack's engine before I even reached my car. I hope he's ready to drive around in circles because I had no idea where I was headed but I was on a mission to find peace.

Or my mind.

Whichever.

I wasn't picky.

An hour later, I pulled into Green-Wood cemetery. I wonder if I'm the only one who gravitates to this place hoping to find answers. I don't know what it is, but when I'm here I'm almost as much at peace as the souls that call this place home.

I climbed the hill and glanced over my shoulder to see Mack bowing his head. He didn't get off his bike, allowing me privacy for which I was grateful. I stared at the tombstone, ran my fingers over my brother's name as I dropped to my knees.

"Hi, Jack," I whispered as I glanced down at the Yankee cap resting in front of the stone. "I guess dad paid you a visit," I murmured, tracing the N and the Y on the cap before I broke down in a fit of tears. I don't remember ever crying as much as I did right then and there. It was as if all the tears I should've been crying over the last thirteen years emerged at that moment.

"I'm so sorry," I sobbed. "It's all my fault you're here and not…doing what every other teenage boy is doing. This hat should be on top of your head, not resting on your grave. You should be here but you're not because I didn't do anything to help you. I stood there and watched you run into the street. Me! I did that! I'm the reason you wound up underneath a car and I'm the reason Mommy and Daddy don't have their son. I'm the reason, Jack," I cried.

"Lacey," my father's voice croaked.

I lifted my head and saw my father standing behind me. His hands were balled into fists and he kept them at his sides as he stared at me with an unspeakable amount of grief pouring from the depths of his dark, soulful eyes.

"I'm sorry," I shrieked. "I'm so sorry, Daddy." I dropped my head into my hands as my body writhed with sobs. I felt him drop onto the grass behind me before he wrapped his arms around me and pulled me against him, rocking me in his arms as he laid his chin on top of my head.

"Shh," he whispered against my hair. "You have nothing to be sorry for," he murmured.

"Not a damn thing," he assured, his voice cracking as he spoke.

"It's my fault. I should've called for help and I didn't,"

"You were five years old Lacey," he gritted, pulling back and turning my head so I could see his face. "You were just a baby yourself. It was my job..." he paused, his lower lip quivered as he fought to control his emotions. "...it was my job to protect your brother and watch after him," he ground out. "Mine and only mine."

He lifted his hand to his head.

"I wasn't thinking straight," he admitted.

"You couldn't think straight," I whispered.

"My maker...," he started.

"...was speaking, and you had no choice but to listen," I finished.

He stared at me speechless and I watched the man most people feared, the man who I thought was larger than life—I watched as a tear slid down his cheek.

"You had no control over what your head was forcing you to believe. The voice was so vivid, so real, you believed every word. It didn't matter that your heart knew better, you weren't the one in control anymore. You were a victim of a brutal attack of words that ripped apart your world and fed you straight to the devil. Maybe you tried to fight, wear your maker down, but you can only fight for so long, until you're exhausted and you have no choice but to surrender."

I stared at my father as he swiped his hands over his face and looked back at me with remorse. His apology for what his voice couldn't bring himself to say.

He knew.

And I was the one to tell him.

I was the one to break the silence.

My voice.

And not the voice of my maker.

"Lacey," he croaked, reaching for me as I pushed off the grass and rose to my feet.

"I'm sorry you lost a son. I'm sorry you were left with me and I'm sorry I fell in love with your friend but like I can't control my mind...I can't control my heart."

His face changed instantly. His eyes hardened and his jaw clenched.

"You what?"

"I fell in love with Blackie but you don't have to get all bent out of shape about it because he doesn't feel the same way. I should've listened to my maker, but I didn't. She knew his loyalty was with you and not me. She knew he could never care for me the way I cared for him. She knew everything, but I tried to fight." I paused, watching my father's face contort with mixed emotions. "I surrender," I whispered. "I'm ready to admit I'm crazy,"

He was on his feet in a flash, forcing me to blink and stare at him in shock as he grabbed my shoulders and leveled me with a stare.

"Don't you dare," he hissed. "You are not crazy," he ordered. "You hear me? You are not crazy and don't ever...," he paused, shook my shoulders to drive his point home. "*Don't you ever* let anyone tell you otherwise!"

He released his grip on me and took a step backward, pacing the small area in front of Jack's grave.

"It's not your fault," I called out to him. "You didn't do this to me."

He turned around, and I peered into the eyes of the mentally ill man who tried so hard to escape his maker. I saw determination and anger fight to break through the sorrow and grief reflected in his eyes.

"Sure I did," he rasped.

Freedom has a price.

The price of my freedom became my father's torment.

I'm sorry, daddy.

I'm so very sorry.

Chapter Twenty-nine

JACK "BULLDOG" PARRISH

I've lost one child.
Held him in my arms as his body turned cold.
Watched his Mama kiss him one final time.
Kissed his lips before they closed the coffin.
Had my brother's hold me down so I wouldn't follow his casket into the earth.
Burying your child, knowing your life goes on and his doesn't is hell in its purest form.
I wake up each day and it's the first thing on my mind.
Another day I'm here and he isn't.
The day ends and I close my eyes only to see his face.
Since Jack Jr.'s death I have told myself there is no greater pain, nothing worse than knowing my illness and my pride is what took my son's life.
But there is a pain that might not be greater but just as harsh and just as annihilating.
I didn't see it coming, or maybe I chose not to see it. Who wants to believe that their child is sick? My ex-wife voiced her concerns months ago when I dropped Lacey off after that shit went down with Blackie but I ignored it.
I told Connie she was *crazy*.
Lacey was just feeling some girl shit for my vice president.
She was a typical girl with a crush.
What the fuck did I know about any of that?
Nothing.
I knew nothing.
But I know what it is to be manic-depressive. I know the villain that lives inside my head, someone I call my maker.
And I know that motherfucker well.
So does Connie, she's the one who pleaded with me for years to get help. I ignored her then just as I ignored her now when she told me she was concerned Lacey may be manic. I blew her off, told her she couldn't blame my illness on everything wrong with the world.
I didn't want to believe that I could be the reason my daughter lives in eternal darkness, the lights were already turned down for one kid and as fucked up as it sounds, at least he was at peace.
Lacey doesn't know peace.
And I know what that's like.
Hearing her say the words, watching the pain in her eyes as she introduced me to her maker made it real and broke every chamber of my heart.
As a parent we want what is best for our children. We want to give them a shot at life, one we weren't granted...at least that's the kind of parent I tried to be to Lacey. I wanted to protect her from the evil. I tried so hard to keep her away from

my club. I thought that shit was evil and destructive but, all the while she had evil and destruction living inside her head.

Lacey lives and suffers with a mind that feeds her uncontrollable temptations, forcing her to swallow what she knows and believe the doubt that her maker inflicts. She can be happy for a little while but then her mind takes over and shatters her happiness by making her think it wasn't real or she didn't deserve it.

She crashes and when she does all there is darkness.

And a bottle of lithium.

Or in her case nothing.

Connie had called me earlier in hysterics and after listening to her plead her case I went downstairs and stared at the photos that covered my walls. I slowly removed one of the frames and stared at the gaping hole in the wall, a reminder—I'm a manic depressive and I waited too long to get help. A hole that mimics the one left behind when my son left this world.

Jack I'm telling you, she's not right. I know the signs I lived them—with you. You need to talk to her. Please. You're the only one who can help her.

I called Mack, and he told me Lacey was at the cemetery. I knew then that Connie was right. I don't know why, but in my heart I knew there was something wrong with our girl. I wasn't prepared to find her sobbing, blaming herself for Jack's death. I wasn't expecting to hear her tell me she was in love with Blackie.

But the thing that killed me was when she finished my sentences.

She confirmed my nightmare.

Then my precious girl told me it wasn't my fault.

But it is.

If I didn't have this shitty illness, she wouldn't either.

I gave it to her.

And now I had to make it better.

I had to help her find her sunshine and pull her back from the darkness.

I had to protect her from her maker.

Because being her father meant being her protector, the one person who was never supposed to hurt her.

I'd make it right.

I walked over to her car, opened the door for her and took her hand as she climbed out. Connie opened the front door, instantly grabbed Lacey and enveloped her into her arms.

"I'm okay," Lacey assured her mother as I followed them into the house, closing the door behind them. Connie's husband, Rob, rose from the couch and extended his hand.

"I'll give you guys a minute," Rob offered.

Rob's been good to my daughter, treated her like his own and he earned my respect. I shook his hand, gripping it hard.

"You're as much a part of this as the rest of us," I told him. "Stay."

I felt Connie's eyes on me and turned my head so our eyes locked.

"Lace, give us a minute," I requested.

"So you can talk about me and make decisions for me? I'm an adult you can't do that. I have as much— "

"So I can apologize to your mother," I interrupted.

"Jack, you don't have to apologize," Connie whispered, wrapping her arm around Lacey's shoulders as she stared back at me.

I held up my hand and shook my head, stopping any further words from spilling out her mouth.

"I should've listened to you then and now," I asserted. "Maybe things would be different."

"Or maybe they wouldn't," she said. "No one knows better than you and I, sometimes you don't get a choice, sometimes there's a bigger plan."

I stared into her eyes, bloodshot and full of unshed tears and swore to myself to take the pain away from her eyes. I put that pain there, all those years ago, when the lines on her face weren't yet visible and before we leave this earth and are reunited with our boy, I will take that pain away.

"Got a chance this time to make it right though," I rasped, reaching out and taking Lacey's hands, pulling her out of her mother's arms. I bent my knees, stared into her eyes and hoped she'd find the will reflected in my eyes. "Say your peace and say it loud, give your truth to your mother and let us help you."

Lacey stared back at me, her lip trembling as she breathed through her mouth.

"It's okay," I whispered. "You're going to be okay but to get better you have to accept it. You need to say it out loud and not be scared or ashamed."

She nodded as she took my hand and turned around to face Connie.

"I need help," she admitted, hesitantly. "Because there are times, more often than not when I can't control my thoughts, when everything I think I know is ripped from me and I can't make sense of it all anymore. I have tried to; I swear I've tried…but I'm so tired of fighting with myself. I just want to be normal but I'm scared," her voice trailed off as she cried along with her mother.

She diverted her eyes to mine.

"I'm scared the medicine won't work and that I'm stuck like this. I've known for a long time there was something wrong with my head but I never said it out loud. If I go get help and it doesn't work there is no hope so, I fight and I hold off because I'm not ready to live the rest of my life knowing I'll never be happy…truly happy. I'm silent because in silence there is hope."

"Look at me," I said, grabbing her shoulders. "I'm your hope, okay? When you doubt yourself and your ability, you look at your old man and know there's a hope. A bastard like me doesn't deserve peace, but I got it, and I'm hanging onto it. You, Lacey, you're sweet and you are loving, you're a good girl with a great big future and if I got it, then you better believe you'll have it too because I can't believe that God would give me good and not you."

She brushed away her tears and choked back a sob before a smile slightly formed on her face.

"You're happy," she whispered.

"I am," I admitted. "I found happiness, baby, and you will too," I whispered. "I promise you. We will get you the best help there is and do whatever we got to do to make sure that bitch of a maker shuts the fuck up," I said hoarsely as I winked at her.

She let out a giggle and glanced over her shoulder at her mother.

"I might not have said it that way but your father's right," she smiled reassuringly.

"That's because you never agree with me," I teased, blowing out a breath as I brought Lacey into my arms.

"What happens now?" she asked against my shoulder.

"I'll call my doctor in the morning and set up an appointment," I looked at Connie, who nodded in agreement.

"Until then, why don't you get some rest? Tomorrow's another day," Connie added.

"We'll order dinner, or I can go to that take-out place you like and pick it up," Rob offered.

Lacey pulled out of my arms, pushed her hair back before looking between all of us.

"What?" I asked, knowing she was debating on whether to tell us something.

"It's Daniela's birthday tonight, and I promised her I'd go out," she said, bringing her bottom lip between her teeth.

"Don't you think you had a long day?" Connie questioned.

"I think I feel like a weight has been lifted from my shoulders and for just one night I want to be a nineteen-year-old girl who isn't mentally ill. I want to be Lacey. Tomorrow I'll be the girl who goes on lithium," she said, turning her eyes back to mine.

Sometimes I think God gave me a daughter just to soften me.

"Have fun," I muttered, as Connie stared daggers at me and Lacey smiled at me.

"Thanks Dad."

"But Mack goes with you," I added. "And if you start to feel a certain kind of way you call me."

"I'll be fine," she assured.

"Yeah, you will," I agreed.

She leaned in and kissed my cheek, then her mother's and lastly Rob's.

"Thank you guys," she murmured hopefully. "I'm going to go get ready."

I watched her hurry up the stairs and waited until she was out of sight to turn to Connie and Rob.

"You really think going out is a good idea?" Connie questioned as she crossed her arms against her chest.

"I think she's been cooped up dealing with this on her own for a long time and having one night to be carefree is good for her," I argued.

"He's got a point," Rob chimed in.

"Fine," Connie said reluctantly. "So you'll call the doctor in the morning?"

"Yes, get her an appointment as soon as possible," I affirmed.

"There's one more thing," she started, glancing at the stairs again before lowering her voice and continuing. "Blackie."

"What about him?" I asked as I narrowed my eyes at her, wondering where she was going with this.

"You should call him and tell him what's going on with Lacey. She cares a lot about him, Jack and whether it's a crush or not I don't know but I do know she can't afford to be confused by her feelings for him."

"A crush or not? Of course it's a crush, you going to tell me otherwise?"

"I'm telling you to talk to Blackie and let him know what's going on. Until we have this under control it's in her best interest if he stays away from her. She can't handle having her heart broken when she's trying to mend her head."

I remained silent for a moment, processing that my daughter might have genuine feelings for Blackie and wondering what his part in all this was.

"I'll talk to him," I ground out before turning toward the door. "Call me if she needs anything," I added before I walked out the door.

As I started for my bike I grabbed my phone about to dial Blackie when my maker decided to menace me.

I told you but you didn't want to listen.

You stupid prick, you're too blind to see what's been in front of you.

He looks at her differently.

He notices things about her you don't.

He's protects her better than you ever have.

He becomes alive when she walks into a room.

How's it feel motherfucker?

To know I'm right and you're wrong.

"Everything okay, Prez?" Mack asked, pulling me away from the war inside my head and back to the present.

"Where's Blackie?" I questioned, the voice of doubt fresh in my mind.

"Not sure. Want me to call him?"

"Can't order me to protect her one minute and not the next, can't give me her life, tell me it's precious then expect me not to put her high on my list of priorities. I'm not made that way and you of all people should know that, understand it, because it's the sole reason you asked me to look out for her all those years ago…you knew I wouldn't be able to turn that shit on and off so, don't ask me to now."

What the fuck did I do?

I lifted my eyes to Mack's.

"Nah, I've got this," I hissed.

There's only one way to shut the motherfucking voice down and that's hearing the truth. I needed Blackie to tell me my maker was fucking with me. I needed him to confirm he was nothing more to Lacey than Blackie, her protector.

Nothing more.

Because heaven help everyone if my maker was right.

Chapter Thirty

BLACKIE

I stared at my house and took another hit of the joint I was smoking. After I saw Lacey across the street from the liquor store I rode my bike for hours, fighting against the need to pick up the phone and call her.

I wanted to hear her voice.

Hear her say my name.

I reached for my phone and saw three missed calls from Jack. I couldn't bring myself to call him back because the truth was I was resenting the man. How fucked up is that? I was hating on my chosen brother because I fell for his daughter because I broke a code and I couldn't take responsibility for it.

I already hated myself for my past and needed someone else to hate for my present and my future.

I hated Jack because I wasn't good enough for his daughter.

I hated Jack because he'd never let me have Lacey.

I hated Jack because he kept her safe.

I hated Jack because I had to give her up.

I flicked the end of the joint into the street, started my bike up preparing to get the fuck out of there and away from that goddamn house, when my phone rang.

Mack.

Something twisted inside me.

First three calls from Jack and now the prospect I had on Lacey was calling me. I quickly accepted the call and dreaded the news on the other end.

"Talk to me," I demanded.

"Black, I really hate to do this shit but I got a call from my sister and my mother's being rushed to the hospital," he blurted. "Lacey's at Kettle Black on 3rd Avenue with one of her girlfriends. Should I call Jack or one of the other guys?"

"No," I said, ripping my engine. "I'm on my way."

I disconnected the call, shoved my phone into my pocket and peeled away from the haunted house of memories.

I should've sent someone else, but I was a greedy motherfucker who needed to see her.

I wouldn't touch her.

I wouldn't even look at her long enough to notice me.

Yeah, right.

Lacey

Today was a win for me, finally freed from my secret and granted a sliver of hope by the two people who brought me into this world. It wasn't as bad as I thought it would be and my parents are much stronger than I give them credit for. I thought finding out I was sick would break them but it didn't. I should've known better. I should've realized my father is Jack Parrish and nothing brings him down, not his mind, not his grief and not an illness he can't control.

And my mother?

She was married to my father, endured a lot of shit being his wife, she's a strong breed too.

I am their daughter which means their strength lives within me and I need to reach deep inside and pull it to the surface.

I need to make this illness my bitch.

Tomorrow.

Tomorrow I am Lacey Parrish the girl who kicks her maker's ass.

Tonight I'm just a normal girl celebrating her best friend's birthday, trying to forget she has a broken heart, and a broken mind. I grabbed the beer in front of me and laughed on cue when one of Daniela's friends made an attempt at a joke. It didn't feel natural--laughing, or even smiling and that was probably because I knew what made me smile and what it felt like to genuinely laugh at something.

I knew happiness.

I'd felt it.

And all this is just a cheap imitation of the real thing.

I miss him.

I miss him so much and when I freed myself from my silence I wished he was there. He should've been there. He's my person. The other half of me that was put on this earth to make me whole.

"Oh my God," Daniela cried, elbowing me as I brought the beer to my lips, causing me to nearly spill it down my shirt.

"What?" I asked, shoving her hand away and taking a sip.

"Are all the men in your father's motorcycle club fucking hot as fuck?"

She couldn't have been talking about Mack, I don't care how turned on girls are by the bad boy...that man was downright scary. I turned my head in the direction she was staring and saw Riggs walk into the bar, flocked by four men I had never seen before—all of them wore the Satan's Knights patch on their leathers.

Riggs' eyes found mine, and he started for our table.

"Oh my God, they're coming this way! How's my hair?" Daniela rambled as she played with her hair, pushing it over one shoulder.

"Well look who it is," Riggs crooned.

"Riggs," I acknowledged, bringing the bottle back to my lips.

"Does your father know you're here?"

"Who's her father?" The man wearing camouflage pants asked. He wore a leather a gray t-shirt underneath his leather jacket and a pair of dog tags dangled from his neck. His caramel colored eyes were pinned to mine, and he flashed me a smile full of mischief.

"Why don't you call him and tell him," I challenged Riggs.

"Stryker, this is Lacey…," Riggs introduced. "…the Bulldog's daughter."

"And I'm Daniela, no relation to the Bulldog," she chimed in from beside me.

"Shit, she's Jack's daughter?" Stryker asked, tearing his eyes off me.

"I'm not Jack's daughter," Daniela offered.

"She's not just Jack's daughter," Riggs muttered, looking back at me. "Does *he* know you're here?"

"*He* don't care where I am or if I'm even breathing," I sneered.

"I'm Deuce, this is Linc and the guy with the tattoo of a snake crawling up his arm is Cobra," Deuce told Daniela as he took a seat next to her.

Ladies and Gentleman we have a charmer on our hands.

I rolled my eyes and looked back at Riggs.

"Look, Mack is outside and I don't need another babysitter," I said hastily.

"Is that why they call you Cobra? Because of the snake tattoo?" Daniela asked.

"No," he muttered.

"Tell her why everyone calls you Cobra," Stryker taunted as he threw an arm around his shoulders, swiped the baseball hat off his head and messed his hair.

"Dude, you're stomping all over my game," Deuce argued, eyeing Daniela.

"How'bout a drink darlin'?" his voice had a twang to it, making it clear he wasn't a Brooklyn native.

"Mack's not outside, Lacey," Riggs informed me, pulling me away from the distraction Stryker, Deuce, and Cobra provided.

"Guess it's a good thing you're here then," I replied as I pushed back my chair and stood up. "I'm going to get a refill."

I wasn't in the mood for Riggs, or any of them for that matter. They all reminded me of Blackie. I made my way to the bar and ordered myself another beer before digging into my pocket for some money.

"I've got it," the person behind me said, stretching his arm around me and slapped a twenty on top of the bar. I glanced over my shoulder and saw it was Brandon. "Consider it my attempt at a truce," he smiled.

"A truce," I repeated.

"I shouldn't have insulted your boyfriend," he clarified, stepping around me and taking the beer from bartender and handed it to me, clinking his bottle to mine. "I was jealous and out of line."

I studied his features for a moment and decided he looked sincere enough. I tipped the neck of the bottle to his.

"Thank you," I said, taking a sip of the beer.

"Friends?" he asked. "I mean I don't want him to show up and beat the fuck out of me for buying his girl a drink," he explained.

"We broke up," I replied, wondering if we were even officially together. "You're safe," I mumbled, watching as Daniela walked away from our table with Deuce and the rest of the guys to play pool. Minus Riggs. He probably went to call my father.

"I'm sorry to hear that," Brandon said, taking a swig of his beer.

I looked over at him and raised an eyebrow.

"No you're not," I accused.

He brought the bottle down and smiled at me.

He had a nice smile.

Not nearly as nice as Blackie's.

"Maybe not," he admitted. "I'm starving, why don't we order some wings and you can tell me all about it."

"How about we stick to wings and beer and leave the rest out?"

"Deal," he said, pressing his hand against the small of my back and guiding me back to the table me and Daniela had been sharing.

By the time we finished the food and Brandon ordered another round of beers the bar was packed and I was actually having a half-way decent time. Brandon was funny and had me laughing which was a breath of fresh air after all the crying I had been doing over the last month, especially the last twenty-four hours.

I turned my head slightly, still laughing when I spotted Blackie standing by the door staring at me. The laughter died as I closed my eyes and prayed my mind wasn't playing with me.

Not tonight.

Please not tonight.

I slowly opened my eyes, blinking rapidly as I continued to stare at him.

He looked ragged, like he was wearing himself thin and had the weight of the world on his shoulders as he leaned against the wall and continued to stare at me. I couldn't take my eyes off him. My ears fell deaf to whatever it was Brandon was saying and I struggled to stop myself from standing up and running to him.

I was pathetic.

I saw his chest rise and fall as he took a deep breath before he finally turned his head and walked straight toward the bar, ignoring me as he passed our table.

"Are you okay?" Brandon asked, jarring me from my thoughts and away from Blackie who turned his back to me as he took a seat at the bar.

"Fine," I croaked, turning to look at him. "I wasn't expecting to see him is all," I explained as I reached for my beer bottle and pushed it aside because it was empty. I snatched Brandon's and tipped my head back, guzzling the ale hoping I'd forget Blackie ever walked into the bar or into my life.

"Easy," Brandon murmured against my ear. "Don't let him get to you," he whispered, wrapping an arm around my shoulders as he continued to speak against my ear.

Riggs walked up next to Blackie, and I watched as they downed a couple of shots. Riggs turned around, waved at me and I returned the gesture with a glare.

I bet he called him when he realized Mack wasn't here.

For someone who is always bitching about me and Blackie and whatever the hell you call this thing between us, he's always throwing himself in the middle.

Blackie glanced over his shoulder at me or maybe at Brandon but quickly turned back around and shook his head.

"Hey," Brandon said, placing his index finger under my chin and forced my eyes to his. "Let's dance," he suggested.

Dance.

I remember the first time I heard Stevie Nick's song Leather and Lace and how certain I was that the song was written for me and Blackie. At the time I never thought him and I would ever dance to it but I'd listen to it every now and then and hoped one day we would.

And then that day came.

"Listen to the words."
You're saying I'm fragile I try not to be.
I search for something only I can't see.
"Will you dance with me?"

He wrapped his arms around me without question and danced with me, to my favorite song. A love song about a girl who is fragile yet tries not to be and a man who never thought he was good enough.

Go on and tell me that song wasn't written for us.

Lovers forever, face to face.
Stay with me, stay.
I need you to love me.
Give me to your leather.
Take from me my lace.

You can't, can you?"

I looked back to the bar and watched him push back the stool and make his way through the bar towards the restrooms. I diverted my eyes back to Brandon.

"How about a raincheck on the dance? I have to use the ladies room," I said as I stood up.

I didn't wait for him to answer me and took off in the same direction as Blackie. The door to men's room was closed, so I leaned against the wall across from it and waited for him to come out.

Face to face, me and him, leather and lace.

When he didn't emerge right away I started for the door, prepared to open it and walk right inside to pull him away from whatever self-destruction he was no doubt engaging in. Why after everything, after the way he hurt me, did I still want to be the one who healed him?

I know why.

I love him.

And I still believe he loves me.

The door opened as I reached for the knob and we walked right into one another. I lifted my head and met his gaze, recognizing the warmth in his eyes before they quickly turned cold and uninviting.

"How long are you going to pretend I don't exist?"

My voice was so low I wasn't even sure he heard the question until he stepped closer, the scent of his cologne assaulted my senses, weakening me and making me copy his footsteps until we were a breath a part.

Hold me.

Tell me it was all a lie.

Tell me you love me as much as I love you.

Let me be your queen because you'll always be my king.

"Until you disappear once and for all," he seethed, glaring at me, shattering the hope reborn in my heart.

Then he was gone.

Like a phantom.

All he left behind was tears in my eyes and the scent of his cologne.

What's it going to take for you to realize he doesn't want you?

I get it.

I finally get it.

I wanted to go home, climb into bed and wait for tomorrow. I stepped out from the darkened hallway and scanned the bar for Daniela but she was nowhere in sight. I made my way back to Brandon who was exactly where I left him and playing on his phone.

He lifted his head and smiled at me when I reached for his hand.

"Can we get out of here?" I pleaded.

"Sure," he said instantly, reaching into his pocket for some cash. He glanced at the check, threw a few bills on the table and continued to hold my hand as he led me to the bar. He stood behind Blackie and called over his shoulder to the bartender.

"The bill is on the table," Brandon said.

I saw Blackie twist in his stool and quickly I turned my back to him, unable to withstand another blow to my heart.

Goodbye Blackie.

I let Brandon escort me out of the bar into the parking lot and toward his car. He opened the car door for me, held it while I climbed in and then bent down so he was level with me. He lifted his hand to my cheek.

"Anyone who lets you go is a fool," he said, softly.

I stared at him for a beat and then I was consumed by the need to feel something, anything other than pain and confusion. I wanted to erase Blackie from my mind and my heart and had no idea how to do that. But here was Brandon, and he wasn't looking at me like I was nothing, like he wished I'd disappear.

I reached for him, wrapping one arm around his neck as I leaned and pressed my lips against his. The instant our mouths touched and his tongue pried my lips apart I felt like I was having an out of body experience.

He broke the kiss, closed my door and jogged around the car. Once he was inside he locked the doors and leaned over me again. I didn't have a chance to ask him why or even object because his mouth crashed over mine.

I became lost in my mind, comparing the way Brandon sloppily kissed me to the way Blackie expertly did. This wasn't making anything better, just making me miss him more and feel cheap and worse than that, made me feel like I was going against my heart.

I heard him drag the zipper of his jeans down and I quickly pushed my palms against his chest but he pressed himself against me and shoved his tongue deeper inside my mouth.

I pushed again and this time his hands found my hips and pushed me back against the fabric of the seat. I felt the hardness of his dick against my leg and knew I was in trouble. I turned my head, pulling my mouth away from his.

"Brandon, stop! I don't want to do this," I protested.

"Yes you do," he insisted as he ripped my shirt open. "I'll make you forget that old fuck ever existed," he growled as he dipped his head and his mouth closed over the lace that covered my nipple.

I closed my eyes, forced myself not to cry and reached for the unlock button on the door.

His hands moved to my jeans just as I opened the door and screamed.

"Help!"

"What the fuck do you think you're doing?" Brandon growled, grabbing my legs as I tried to scramble out the door.

"Get off of me! Please! Someone help!" I shouted as he dragged me back.

"Fucking bitch. Get the fuck back here!"

Tears streamed down my face as panic and fear set in.

"Please!" I screamed into the dark parking lot.

I let out a shrill cry as Brandon grabbed a fistful of my hair and yanked me backward. Then he released my hair, and I fell face down and half way out of the car.

"What the fuck?" he sneered.

"Motherfucker, you know what *no* means? Huh?" Blackie shouted.

Blackie.

My knight.

The man that always rides to my rescue.

I crawled out of the car, stumbling onto my feet and turned around as tears clouded my eyes and I watched as Blackie reared his fists back and attacked Brandon.

"No, stop!" Brandon cried, his pants around his ankles as Blackie bloodied his face with one shot after another. "Shit, I'm sorry! Help!"

I watched in horror as Blackie grabbed Brandon by his ears and threw him onto the ground, wedging a boot between his legs. Brandon wailed as blood poured from every crevice of his face.

"Blackie!" I shouted.

He was going to kill him.

"C'mon motherfucker, cry for me. Cry like the bitch you are," Blackie demanded as he pounded the back of Brandon's skull against the asphalt.

"CRY!" He shouted, lifting him by the ears and slamming his head against the ground again.

"WEEP MOTHERFUCKER!"

There was blood everywhere.

So much blood.

"Open your fucking eyes. Look at me!" Blackie ordered, as a siren sounded from somewhere close by. I glanced around the parking lot and saw people running from the bar towards us.

"Blackie, the cops are coming! Please stop!" I shrieked.

Stryker and two of the other guys ran up beside him and tried to pull him off Brandon but Blackie wasn't having it. There was nothing and no one that could stop him.

"Blackie man, you need to get the fuck out of here. Let's go," Stryker called, turning his eyes onto me.

"LOOK AT ME!" Blackie shouted.

This is all your fault.
Look what you did.

I closed my eyes and let out a scream that vibrated through my ears.

Make it stop.

"You see this face? Remember it. I'm the one who fucking did this to you," Blackie snarled, just as I opened my eyes and watched him slam the back of Brandon's head against the ground.

The moment Blackie released his hold on Brandon the world stopped for us.

Two lost souls died.

Two broken hearts stopped beating.

And the higher power writing our story typed the two words you dread.

The End.

One of the cops grabbed Blackie's arms and forced them behind his back as he lifted his eyes from Brandon's body and stared at me, baring his soul to me.

I love you.

It was reflected in his sorrowful eyes.

Along with every word scribed of the story of us.

I felt the scream throughout my body but couldn't hear it all I could hear was the officer read him his rights and confirm it was all over.

Lovers forever.
Blackie and Lacey.

Chapter Thirty-one

BLACKIE

I can still hear her pleas for help and the image of her crawling out of the car only for that motherfucker to drag her back in—it consumes my mind. I close my eyes and I can see the tortured expression on her face as Brantley slapped cuffs on my wrists and read me my rights.

I've experienced a lot of shit in my life, felt all sorts of fucked up things I wasn't used to feeling…like sorrow, like remorse, but what I felt when I beat the fuck out of that kid was something entirely different. I wasn't a man fighting for his club, or an outlaw looking to be a menace. I was a man fighting for his woman and in that instant I was capable of anything.

There was no remorse for my actions.

I'd do it all over again.

And again.

I swore I'd never touch her again, told myself I was no good for her, and she wasn't safe because of me.

I thought giving her up was the answer.

But watching her with another man, seeing another motherfucker try to take what was mine, made me realize I was wrong.

I might be a degenerate, a dangerous son of a bitch with a shitload of problems but I love Lacey and there's not a thing on Earth I won't do for her.

Not a fucking thing.

As long as she keeps needing me I'll keep showing up.

Shove me in a cell, handcuff me to a bench and throw away the key but I promise you, as long as I'm breathing…if she needs me I'll find a way out. I'll always find a way back to her.

Always.

And right now it's killing me I'm locked up when I should be holding her, reassuring her she's okay and this nightmare will go away.

She needs me.

And I'm not there.

I tried to pull my arm free, felt the metal of the handcuffs dig into my wrist as I screamed out in frustration.

She needs me and there is no end in sight.

No way out.

No looking into her eyes and making it right.

There's nothing.

JACK "BULLDOG" PARRISH

I don't know how many fucking times I called Blackie, but that fuck hasn't answered not one goddamn call. I don't need this shit, honest to God, I don't. I've got a daughter on the brink of a mental breakdown, a war with the Chinese and a goddamn head that won't be silenced.

I don't need to worry my vice president is off the grid on a mission to kill himself and I don't need the suspicions my mind is feeding me about him and Lacey either. That shit needs to be put to bed.

I needed to concentrate on Lacey, on getting her the help she needs and rallying the people in her life to become a support system because being mentally ill isn't something that gets fixed instantly with a little pill. It's a process to even be diagnosed and then when a doctor labels you bipolar they fuck with different medicines until they find one that helps control the chemical imbalance the brain is feeding off.

My little girl has a long fucking road ahead of her and as her father and the man responsible for this shit that's become her life, so did I, which means Blackie needs to step the fuck up and handle the club.

"Jack?" Reina called, pulling me away from the mess inside my mind and forcing me to focus on the beauty sprawled across my chest.

She lifted her head and my hands instantly went for her hair, threading it through the sea of gold.

"Hmm?"

"You all good?" she questioned, running her hands over my chest as she straddled me.

"I'm good, Sunshine. You make it all better," I assured as my hands gripped her hips. Reina shut my maker down better than any medication ever could. She took me away from the darkness and reminded me I had life to live and no time to fall into a trap that was created on hypotheticals.

She talked me through the war inside my head and when all else failed, my Sunshine would sing, soothing my soul with her voice and quieting the demon possessing me.

Life was good with Reina in it.

"She will be okay," Reina whispered, as she caressed my cheek. I reached up, cradled her face in my hands and brought her mouth down to mine. I'm a fucking lucky man.

"When you going to marry me?" I growled against her mouth.

Her lips curved, and she pulled back slightly to look into my eyes.

"Anxious to make me Property of Parrish?" she teased, pressing another kiss to my lips.

Sunshine was my second chance.

A man like me gets a second chance he hangs onto it with everything he's got.

"You've been Property of Parrish, since I first fucking laid eyes on you," I reminded her. "Time the whole world knows it."

She laughed, dropping the sheet she had tucked under her arms and granted me the sweetest view. I was about to flip her onto her back and take her another time when I heard the doorbell ring.

I glanced over at the clock on the nightstand.

"That can't be good," Reina murmured, sliding off me. We both threw the covers off us and climbed out of bed. I pulled on my jeans, she threw on a t-shirt and we moved towards the stairs, following the sounds of a fist beating down my fucking door.

"It's probably Blackie all fucked up," I seethed, hurrying down the stairs.

"I thought he was getting clean?" Reina said behind me.

"Yeah, me too," I grunted as I reached the front door and pulled it open. Stryker turned around, his expression grim as he rubbed his hands over his short hair.

"We got a big problem," he said, stepping to the side and revealing my daughter.

"Oh my God," Reina gasped from behind me, pushing me aside to grab a hold of Lacey. My disheveled little girl stared back at me blankly as black make-up streaked her beautiful face and she clutched Stryker's leather jacket around her trembling body.

"What the fuck happened?" I roared, grabbing a hold of Stryker's shirt and pushed him up against the wall. "Why is she with you?"

"Jack!" Reina shouted, wrapping her arm around Lacey's shoulders and bringing her against her. "Get it under control," she ordered, eyeballing the broken girl in her arms and ushered her into the house.

I released my grip on Stryker.

"Start fucking talking," I demanded.

"Look, I don't know all the details but she left a bar with some guy, the next minute someone comes into the bar screaming there's a fight in the parking lot. By the time me and the guys got outside, Blackie was beating the fuck out of the guy Lacey was with," he recounted.

I narrowed my eyes at Stryker, trying to comprehend everything he was saying as he continued to talk.

"Bulldog, it's bad…real fucking bad. Blackie went fucking nuts and rightfully so the little fuck was going to rape her."

Everything stopped.

I stepped backward and pinned Stryker with a glare.

"What did you just say?"

"He didn't get a chance too, man," Stryker proceeded, cocking his head to the side as he peered back at me. "Did you hear me? Blackie got to him before he could hurt her. Jack, he saved her," he insisted.

I fell in love with Blackie but you don't have to get all bent out of shape about it because he doesn't feel the same way.

"Where is he?" I demanded.

"The cops came and arrested him," he said as I brushed past him and into the house, looking for Lacey.

"Lace?" I called, following the sounds of her sobs and found her in the living room, pacing back and forth in front of Reina.

"It's all my fault! He's going to go to jail because of me!"

Can't order me to protect her one minute and not the next, can't give me her life, tell me it's precious then expect me not to put her high on my list of priorities.

"Lacey," I shouted. "Baby, look at me," I demanded, as I watched helplessly as she unraveled, and we swapped roles. I was the person on the receiving end of a manic breakdown and she was the one with no control.

"Dad?" she questioned, turning around abruptly to stare at me. "Oh, thank God! You have to take me to the police station!" She ordered, grabbing my shoulders as I stood there unsure how to help her.

"Why aren't you getting dressed? Did you hear me? You have to take me to the cops, I have to tell them what happened so they can release him."

"Lacey," I croaked, my heart breaking as I watched her lose her battle with her maker.

"No! You're not listening! He saved me," she cried. "He saved me, again!" Tears streamed down her cheeks. "Brandon would've raped me, Dad. Do you understand? Rape! Blackie stopped him and now we have to help him. I have to help him!"

I closed the distance between us and wrapped my arms around her, looking over her shoulder at Reina.

"Call your doctor," I ground out, knowing Reina might have better luck reaching her doctor than I would have reaching mine at this hour.

She nodded, starting for the stairs to retrieve her phone.

"Grab my clothes," I called after her, pulling back from Lacey, I brushed the hair away from her face with the back of my hand and wiped the mascara that ran down her cheek. "Dry your eyes," I said, blowing out a breath. "Blackie wouldn't want you crying."

I never thought I'd be pleading Blackie's case to my daughter.

Never.

"I'm going to go down to the station and get it all straightened out," I promised, already working out what I needed to do in my head. I looked over at Stryker. "Get Pipe on the phone, he needs to meet me at the station," I told him, in case a judge took pity on our vice president and granted him bail Pipe would need to get our finances in order.

"Okay, well let's go," Lacey said, pulling out of my arms.

"You're not coming," I told her as Reina bounded down the stairs with my boots, jacket and shirt in her hand.

"The hell I'm not!" She protested walking towards the door. Stryker was quick to block her exit as I pulled my shirt over my head. "The cops need to hear my side I was the one attacked, I'm the one who can make it better," she cried, digging her index finger into her chest. "Me! I have to make it better."

"Listen to me! You need to let me get down there and handle this my way. If there comes a time when I need you to talk to the police then I'll have one of the guys bring you down to the station but for the love of God, Lacey I need you to stay put!"

"Lacey, come on, let your father do his thing," Reina comforted, taking Lacey's hands. "He wants Blackie out just as much as you do,"

"No he doesn't," she argued, staring back at her. "He couldn't, possibly."

I bit the inside of my cheek to keep myself in check and watched on as Reina brought Lacey back into the living room.

"She's showing signs of PTSD you might want to take her to the hospital," Stryker suggested, forcing me to turn to him.

"What do you know about that?"

"A fuck of a lot, I was discharged from the Army two years ago," he replied. "She should talk to somebody."

"We got it under control," I ground out. "Now, get your ass over to the compound and rally up the boys. I want Bones here first thing watching out for them. Do we know what precinct arrested him?"

He froze for a second, shrugging his shoulders and twisted his neck from side to side before he answered me.

"The one, two, two," he replied, pulling open the door.

I shoved my boots on, not bothering with the laces and charged out the door with Stryker on my back. I had the boys meet me down at the police station. Pipe had the bail bondsman on speed dial and Wolf…that crazy fuck, went and pulled the clubs lawyer from his house and dragged him to the station in his pajamas. Riggs wasn't answering his phone so, I had Bones go over to my house and watch over my girls.

The police love fucking with us, stringing us along and with Brantley heading the case we got nowhere real fast. They were keeping Blackie locked up in a holding cell until he was arraigned but since it was the weekend that wouldn't be until Monday.

The lawyer was able to get inside and talk to him but when he came back out of the interrogation room he shook his head and added another three grand to the bill. Blackie wasn't talking, not to him, not to the cops…no one.

He'd talk to me.

I wouldn't give him a choice.

I needed answers.

There are two things in this world you don't fuck with when it comes to me and that's my family and my fucking respect.

Someone fucked with my daughter tonight.

Someone hurt her real bad, violated her and disrespected her.

And someone saved her.

Blackie, the man I trusted with my daughter's life but never thought to trust him with her heart.

Or her mind.

Chapter Thirty-two

Lacey

Reina called her shrink and asked for an emergency house call—all I kept thinking was my father told me I wasn't crazy and I shouldn't let anyone make me think I was.

What a joke.

It doesn't get crazier than a house call and a tranquilizer.

I suppose I should be thankful for the reprieve because without the sedative I would still be reeling—picturing Blackie's face as he was arrested, recalling the blood on his hands.

Or fighting with my father to do something, anything, just make it right. Blackie didn't deserve to rot in a jail cell over me but for some reason my father is dismissing me and insisting on taking care of it his way

It's my word that will free Blackie.

I'm the one who was attacked so why am I sitting here with Dr. Spiegel going over my moods, behaviors and introducing her to my fucking maker.

"You seem distracted," she commented.

"I'm sorry I was nearly raped less than twenty-four hours ago and watched the man I love get arrested. Oh, and let's not forget I'm crazy," I said sarcastically.

"You're not crazy, Lacey," she said softly.

"Right, says you," I crossed my arms and peered at her. "What else do you need to know? I think I laid it all out there for you, no? My father was diagnosed when I was five with bipolar disorder. I watched my little brother get killed and was never the same after that. I have the ability to be happy until my mind casts a shadow of doubt and I come crashing down. I feel like I'm fighting a losing battle and I'm exhausted all the time. Sometimes I've gotten so deep in my mind that I have even contemplated killing myself because I can't bear it any longer. I'm ashamed that I'm not normal and I don't want to disappoint my parents because I'm all they have left. So doc, tell me, are you sure I'm not crazy? Not even a little?"

"Bipolar disorder can be treated, ignoring it is the problem, and you'd be surprised by how many people are just like you," she affirmed. "We will make it manageable Lacey but you've had an emotional few days. Tomorrow, I want you to come into the office and we will do a full work up so we can start treatment. I'd like to talk about what goes on when your 'maker' calls to you," she continued, using her fingers as quotes when she mentioned my maker.

I heard the front door slam shut, and I glanced over her shoulder, trying to get a look at who had walked in but I couldn't see shit. I turned my eyes back to Dr. Spiegel.

"Are we done for today?"

"That depends on you," she replied, cocking her head to the side to study me like I was a science experiment or something.

"I'm all talked out, Doc," I said as I continued to divert my eyes towards the hallway and struggle to listen to the voices talking in hushed tones.

"And you'll meet me at my office tomorrow?" she stressed.

Damn, how did my father do this?

He has no patience.

Like none.

It was almost comical imagining him sitting in a chair, in front of a shrink firing questions at him. I bet he motherfucked a lot during his sessions.

"I'll be there," I promised, rising from my chair. "I appreciate you coming to see me," I added.

I don't know if I should be grateful that my family had shrinks on call like this or absolutely terrified that we were all fucked in the head. I'm going to go with grateful since I didn't feel like I was ripping apart at the seams anymore. I was relatively calm, albeit a medicated calm, but whatever works right?

I left Dr. Spiegel in the living room and followed my father's voice towards the kitchen. I stole a peek and spotted my father hunched over, his hands braced against the edge of the counter as he spoke.

"Just lay it on me," he demanded.

I looked to Riggs, watching as he pulled off his hat and ran his hands over his hair roughly.

"I went to the hospital like you told me to and checked on the fucking kid," Riggs hissed.

"Please, tell me the little shit's alive," my father interrupted.

"Barely, he's on life support," Riggs muttered. "You might want to sit down for this one," he suggested.

"Just tell me!"

"All right but I warned you," Riggs grunted. "As I was leaving, I saw the kid's father arguing with someone in the hallway. The name Boots ring a bell?"

"Boots? That's the president of the Corrupt Bastards," my father said, a vein bulging from the side of his neck. "He was at the hospital visiting the little cocksucker who tried to rape Lacey?"

"No, he was threatening the father," Riggs clarified. "Apparently, they had some deal going on and the father was angry because the deal didn't include his son winding up in a coma."

"What deal? Riggs! Get to the point!"

"I don't know all the details but after the father went on a rant about his son dying because of some debt he owed the Bastards'—Boots told him, his son was never supposed to rape Blackie's girl and whatever deal they had with him was now off the table," Riggs words trailed off.

"Blackie's girl," my dad drawled as if he was testing the two words out to see how they sounded coming from his mouth.

I swallowed hard, watching as he swiped a hand across the counter and sent everything crashing onto the floor

"Jack," Riggs tried.

"Blackie's girl," he repeated.

"Jack!"

"You telling me my daughter nearly got raped last night because of some shit with a rival club or are you telling me she was attacked because Blackie's got a claim on my daughter?"

"I think it's both," Riggs admitted.

It was hard for me to wrap my head around Riggs' words. Brandon was just some frat guy who thought his dick was holier than thou. But he wasn't. His father had connections to another motorcycle club, and he was using me as a pawn to stir up trouble only Brandon couldn't follow the fucking plan.

If I wasn't sure I was mentally ill before I'd start to wonder.

As for my father? I hope he took his meds today.

Add the truth of me and Blackie being dumped on my dad and I'd say he was ten seconds away from blowing his top.

"I've seen them together," Riggs blurted.

Goddamn Riggs.

Riggs held up his hands in protest as my father's head snapped and his eyes narrowed at him.

"Before you kill me, hear me out," he protested, and I watched as my dad remained perfectly still.

Man if looks could kill, poor Riggs would be six feet under.

"He loves her," Riggs continued.

I didn't care about my father's reaction, too wrapped up in the three words Riggs blurted.

Blackie loves me.

It was a bittersweet moment for me, knowing that his friends saw the love he had for me, and that I wasn't alone in witnessing it. Riggs gifted me the medicine no doctor could. He gave me peace of mind, he shut down the skepticism of my maker by affirming what I knew in my heart.

I wasn't wrong about him, about us and last night when I looked into his eyes and saw them full of love, I hadn't imagined it.

It was all real.

The story.

The moments.

The love.

It really happened and those three words were all I needed to hang on. I'd savor them, rely on them when the doubt surfaced and I would use them to bring me back to life.

"The poor bastard don't even know it but that girl of his, or yours...whoever she belongs to...Lacey healed Blackie," Riggs continued. "He's falling apart, dropped off his program and turned his life to shit again because he doesn't think he deserves her. He's afraid like hell he will fuck it up and lose her or worse, he's terrified he will cause her harm."

"Blackie told you this?"

"No. I've got eyes man, and I got a woman I pushed away because I'm feeling all those things. It's easy for me to spot what I'm going through in someone else."

"You don't know what the fuck you're talking about. Blackie wouldn't do that. He wouldn't get involved with my daughter. He's my goddamn vice president, the man I chose to sit at my left, he's my fucking *brother*," he roared.

"Heart," Riggs said.

"Ain't got shit to do with what you're talking about!"

"It's got everything to do with what I'm talking about. You told me months ago Blackie's heart beats for a woman he lost a long time ago and he's just waiting for the day he is reunited with her. You and I both know that man has had plenty of opportunities to end the nightmare he's living, but he doesn't," he shouted, advancing toward my dad. "He keeps on pushing through because he's got *heart*, something that keeps him here and not in Green-Wood cemetery. If he's your brother, you'll ease that man of the burden of his conscience. Now, if you're going to kill me, do it now and make it fast and painless. Or you could let me slide because I've got a kid on the way and I'd like to get the chance to love my kid as much as you love yours."

Riggs reached into his pocket and pulled out a folded piece of paper before sliding it across the counter at my father. He didn't lift his head as he placed his palm over the paper.

"The Corrupt Bastards run an online gambling site. The kid's father owed them a hundred grand. That's his account profile," Riggs said before turning around.

I stepped into the kitchen, blocking him from leaving as I stared back at him.

"Thank you," I whispered, wiping the tears that had fallen from my eyes.

"You're not welcome," he hissed, glancing over his shoulder at my dad. "Got your work cut out for you Little Miss Defiant, going to take a whole lot of glue to patch him up," he grunted before stepping around me and leaving me alone in the kitchen with my father.

"Dad," I whispered.

He kept his head lowered as he peered back up at me.

"Not now Lacey. Not now," he warned.

I felt like I should apologize to him but I wasn't sure what I was apologizing for. For breaking his heart? If it wasn't Blackie who I fell in love with would he still be this upset? Is it because I'm his daughter or because Blackie is his brother?

I saw him break, his knuckles whiten as he gripped the counter and I feared what was running through his head right now.

Silence.

Please.

"Dad, please look at me," I pleaded.

He waited a beat before releasing his hold on the counter and crossed his arms against his chest as he finally looked at me.

"Make this right," I demanded, quietly, taking a few more steps closer to him. "You have to help him get out because if you don't I will. I'm not leaving him in there to rot after what he did for me and you shouldn't want to either."

"Don't tell me how to handle my business Lacey," he ground out. "Time for you to take a step back and concentrate on your own issues and leave Blackie to me," he said, clenching his jaw as he spoke.

He unraveled his arms, continued to stare at me for a moment before he shook his head.

"Fucking, hell," he muttered, brushing past me before leaving me alone in the kitchen.

I closed my eyes when I heard the front door slam.

Daddy's little girl just broke her daddy's, heart.
Actually, Riggs did.

Chapter Thirty-three

BLACKIE

I scrambled off my cot, taking three steps towards the metal toilet and dropped to my knees. I've been here nearly a week, one fucking week with no junk to shoot, snort, or swallow. I was denied bail and charged with attempted manslaughter but if the fuck dies the D.A. will change it to murder.

I was wishing for death.

That's why I'm not cooperating with the club's lawyer too much. After, sitting down with him when I was held at the police station he told me he was going to use Lace to testify. I decided to just let it all be. Whatever happens, happens. I'm not putting this shit on her, she didn't ask that fuck to touch her…just let it be. Let it be over for her.

Brantley thinks he won, that I'm threatened by the charge *murder in the first degree.*

Bring it, cocksucker.

I've got nothing on the outside.

These walls and these bars are it for me. That's okay because when I'm not violently throwing up from not having my drugs, I relive the memories of my life.

The good.

The bad.

The ugly.

Then I think of her.

And I momentarily wish for the kid to live, for a way out of here or a goddamn miracle. Then reality sets in and I'm stuck in the memories because it's all I've got and all I'll ever have.

I'm not just Satan's Knight, I'm his fucking predecessor, here on earth.

And this is my hell.

I started going through withdrawals the morning of my arraignment. I hadn't snorted or taken anything since the bar and I was feeling it. After I broke things off with Lacey for good, I stopped going to the clinic and getting my dose of methadone. I replaced the fake heroin with the pills, crushing and snorting them to get my fix but, after I was shipped here they started me on the program again.

The C.O.'s bring me to the medical building every morning, I get my dose; they check my vitals, and send me back to my fucking cell to rot in hell.

It's not enough.

Never enough.

But as long as I have a pulse, they don't give a fuck because their job is to keep me alive so I can pay for my sins. Every inmate sent here, the government pays for, actually the taxpayers pay for. So, you over there with the fat check and nine-to-five job, you're the one paying for the methadone in my bloodstream right now and the ham and cheese sandwich I'll eat for dinner but won't manage to keep down.

I'm close to caving and finding a way to get the drugs I need. People think a man gets locked up, and he's at the mercy of the state, you become their property...what a fucking joke. You may lose your name and get a number when you get locked up but you can score whatever the fuck you need in jail. The correction officers here are more corrupt than the streets they pulled me from. As long as you give them a cut, you can sell, trade, or steal whatever the fuck you want.

And right now I want a fucking needle and the shittiest heroin I could get my hands on. While I may be able to score drugs, it ain't the pure shit like I've been used to. It's the bottom of the barrel shit, that's been cut down to basically nothing but beggars can't be fucking choosey.

"Petra, on your feet!" The C.O. patrolling my cell block shouted as he rattled his keys, trying to find the one to unlock the bars that confine me. I leaned back on my haunches, swipe my mouth clean with the sleeve of my shirt before standing on my wobbly legs.

"It fucking stinks in here," he commented as he stepped inside my cell.

I wish I didn't throw everything up into the toilet, I'd love to fucking bless this prick and his smug face.

"What the fuck do you want?"

"You've got a visitor," he said, twirling his key ring around his finger.

I peered at him, running my fingers through my hair, pushing it out of my eyes and away from my face.

"Let's go," he said, leading me out of my cell and down the cell block.

Jack and Wolf showed up at my arraignment but I didn't pay my brother's any mind. I wasn't ready to talk to Jack about business or more importantly what had happened that landed my ass in this mess. I didn't trust myself with him.

The last couple months I've been lying through my fucking teeth to him.

And to myself.

I walked into the visitor's room and spotted Jack instantly, the patch we worshipped stitched proudly into the back of his cut. I should've turned around and denied the visit but I'm a glutton for punishment and man, did I deserve my punishment.

I walked to the table, dropping into the chair in front of my president and slowly lifted my eyes to his.

Get your game face on Blackie.

"Christ, you look like shit," he growled as his eyes raked me over.

"Good to see you too," I retorted, dropping my head into my hands because it felt like it weighed more than my neck could hold.

"Are they fucking with you in here?" he asked as he glanced over his shoulders at the correction officers guarding the room.

I spread my fingers across my face and pierced him with my dark eyes.

"Why are you here?" I questioned, wanting the visit to be over before it even began.

"I'm here because you're my fucking brother. You saved my daughter from getting raped," he hissed, meeting my gaze as I dropped my hands and leaned back in the chair. "If you hadn't been there…well, I don't think I have to tell you, we both know what would have happened."

Fuck.

Don't thank me. Don't fucking thank me.

I didn't do it for you.

I did it for me.

"She okay?" I asked, tearing my eyes away from him.

It's been driving me crazy that I left her to deal with the repercussions of that night by herself. She's all I think about and I'm going mad thinking that prick hurt her before I managed to get to her.

"She's a fucking mess," he hissed. "She blames herself for you being in here."

"That's fucking ridiculous," I snapped, turning my eyes back to him. "Make her cut that shit out," I demanded. "She didn't ask for that cocksucker to take advantage of her."

He stared at me for a moment and I held his gaze, watching as the wheels in his head turned round and round.

"Anyone would've done it. She was crying, begging for help, anyone with a fucking conscience would've done what I did," I ground out.

Lies.

The truth was, no one would've went to the extreme I did, another man, would've made sure she was safe and left well enough alone. Maybe he would've roughed the son of a bitch up but he wouldn't have crushed his skull against the ground. Only one other man would've done the same as me and I was looking at him.

She was his before she was mine.

"Something came to light," Jack said finally, scratching the scruff lining his jaw.

I knew the facial expression he was sporting, and I knew it well. He was contemplating his words, choosing wisely and feeding off my expression to see which way he goes.

Don't let the mental shit fool you.

Jack Parrish knows how to play you.

He's smart and calculates his every move, backing you into a corner when he's got something over you.

"Yeah, what's that?"

Let's play.

I've got nothing left to lose.

"The lawyer says if he lives the sentence will be five years max with your record but with Lacey's testimony he can probably get you three. So, I sent Riggs down to the hospital to check on the status of the prick," he stared, rolling his neck from side to side.

"Lacey's testimony? Get the fuck out of here, leave her alone," I clipped.

He narrowed his eyes as he cupped the back of his neck and peered at me.

"I need to get you the fuck out of here. I got my hands full and don't need you sitting here on a fucking vacation. Wu is going to make a move any day now.

She's got no fucking problem testifying and if it helps your case then what the fuck is the problem?" he sneered.

"I don't know, Jack, she's your daughter. You want her reliving that night? I don't," I growled.

Careful, man, you look like you give a fuck.

"Look, I don't want her involved in this shit or anyone else for that matter. Let it be, man,' I ordered. "Whatever I get, I get, whatever happens…I'm good," I added.

"Sounds like you're giving up," he said, his jaw clenching with every word he spoke.

"Maybe I am," I said. "Maybe it's fucking time. How long am I going to do this shit for? I can't keep cheating my fate," I admitted. The truth was I didn't care about doing the time. It put space between me and Lace, gave her a chance to go on and live her life the way she was meant to. By the time I was finished with my sentence she'd move on, maybe get married, or even start a family. If I'm out that's not going to happen.

I won't let it.

"Your fate?" he slammed his palm against the table, earning the attention and wary eyes of the correction officers. Jack raised his hand to the C.O., an attempt at an apology as well as a silent vow that he would control himself.

Control and Jack didn't go hand in hand.

He was *uncontrollable*.

He leaned over the table, glaring at me as he spoke through clenched teeth.

"I'll tell you what your motherfucking fate is…it's riding alongside me. It's sitting at the left side of my table and being the fucking soldier you signed up to be. That is your fucking fate, Blackie. Your fate is your place in your club, it's the patch sewn into your cut, not this shit," he growled as he glanced around the visitor's room.

"The club needs you on the outside," he seethed as he leaned back in his chair and stared back at me.

"And you?" I challenged. "Where do you need me?"

"That depends on how you answer the next question," he replied, propping his elbows on the table and leaned forward. "Riggs spotted the father of the kid arguing with someone you know pretty fucking well," he said pointedly, pausing to chew on his lip before slapping his palms against the table. "Boots."

"Boots was with the father of the kid that tried to rape Lace?"

Everything inside me went numb as I stared at Jack waiting for him to answer.

"Apparently, they had a plan. The Corrupt Bastards have an online gaming site and the father owed the club a nice chunk of change. Boots was going to squash the debt if his kid got close to Lacey— "

"Listen to me, you got to shut Boots down," I cut him off, leaning over the table. "You hear me? You need to put that motherfucker down before he gets to her," I demanded, pushing back my hair and zeroing my eyes onto his.

"Tell me why," he ordered. "Tell me why Boots is going after my daughter, Black," he whisper shouted, leaning his body further over the table. "Say it!" he growled, through clenched teeth.

Game over.

I leaned forward, met his gaze head on and gave him the truth that's been suffocating me.

"Because she's mine," I seethed, waiting for his reaction but he kept his face like stone as he stared at me. "Boots knows, he's been watching us for months."

"Months."

"He's been watching me since I was in the hospital," I confessed. "I was going to tell you but then I went up to meet with him and he knew. So, I broke things off with her. I made it ugly so she'd hate me and stay away from me, hoping that Boots got the message she didn't matter," I paused. "He saw me love her, and I needed to reverse that shit."

"Love her," he hissed.

"Love her," I confirmed. "Now you got what you wanted from me, time for you to get out of here and take care of him. You do what you got to do to keep her save," I demanded. "Or you get me the fuck out of here so I can do it... your choice."

Jack lifted his head, his dark eyes pierced mine and watched him morph into the Bulldog as he lunged for me, pulling me by my prison garb over the table.

"You motherfucker!" He roared as the C.O.'s moved quickly through the visitor's room and pulled the alarm. "You put a claim on my daughter behind my back and then you fucking toyed with her head!"

"Only reason I fucked with her head was to save her goddamn life. Trust me man, never wanted to let her go. Never!"

The correction officer's pulled him back, forcing him to release his hold on me.

"You have no idea what you did," he hissed, fighting against the guards. "Had a fucking doctor come to my house and diagnose my daughter a manic depressive and you go and fuck with her head," he growled. "This is over! You! You're done. I'll be waiting for you on the other side Black... me, the motherfucking Bulldog."

He always had the last word.

This time his parting words had the ability to wreck me.

Manic depressive.

My Lace.

"I came here, hoping someone, anyone, would see me."
"I see you."
"You see what I allow you to. No one sees the real me,"
No.

Why didn't I pay closer to attention?

I threaded my fingers through my hair, tugging viciously on the ends before slamming my head against the metal table as they buzzed Jack out of the visitor's room.

I came clean and gave him the truth... my truth, I loved Lace.

And in turn he gave me her truth.

My Lace was battling a disease she had no control over, and all the while she was trying to better me she was suffering in silence. I should've been the one helping her, giving her whatever she needed, supporting her the way she tried to support me.

I was always looking to save her.

I never thought she needed to be saved from herself.

I never wanted to inflict that type of pain on her. I wanted to hurt her, yes, make her hate me because hating me kept her away and kept her safe. I never would've done it if I knew what my words could do to her.

I've seen Jack go over the edge time and time again, sometimes it's a great big event that pushes him other times it's nothing. When the maker comes out and play there's no rhyme or reason.

"Petra, let's go," one of the C.O.'s demanded, grabbing my arm and pulling me onto my feet.

She needs me and I'm not there.

She needs me to right everything wrong I put in her head. She needs to know she's more than what I let her think she was… she was fucking everything. She was my heart.

"Let's go!" he pulled my arm again, but I kept my feet firmly planted on the ground.

"I want my phone call," I demanded.

And one more chance.

Chapter Thirty-four

BLACKIE

I took three strides, swallowing up the floor space and braced my hands against the cement wall, breathing heavily as I tried not to scream in frustration. The cell door slammed shut behind me, echoing off the bare walls confining me to my memories. I cursed the day my demoralized self, had noticed Lacey as a woman. A goddamn woman with a tiny waist and hips meant to hold onto as I bent her over and appreciated the sweetest ass I ever laid eyes on. Not to mention tits that could make any man lose his mind.

It was so fucking easy to lose my mind and forget my morals.

Morals I still wasn't sure I had in the first place.

I curse the day she stopped being Jack's daughter and became the object of my desire and my affection because it was all over from that point forward.

I was too wrapped up in consuming her and feeding off her light to notice she was crying out for help. That night she came to the Dog Pound she wasn't a girl looking for a man to pay her attention and take her virginity. No, Lacey was looking for someone to help her, someone to share her pain with.

I waited for the C.O.'s to change shifts and then asked to use the phone. Things were different than they used to be, now you used your commissary money to make a call instead of calling collect and hoping it was accepted.

The officer who brought me down to the call room was all right. He wasn't a ball buster and didn't give two fucks about anything but punching a clock and bringing home a paycheck. He wasn't on a power trip, just a guy who worked as a correction officer because the city finally called his ass and offered him a job.

"Take your time," he said, turning his back and giving me some privacy.

"Thanks, bro," I called, picking up the phone and leaning my head against the wall trying to debate on what the fuck I would say. I wasn't even sure I should call her after everything I said and everything I did. Being so close to Jack all these years I knew firsthand how delicate someone's mind was when they were mentally ill. After a while I learned Jack's trigger points and could avoid them. Lacey was different, for all I knew I was the trigger point, the thing that set her maker off. I wasn't sure if calling her would cause her more harm than good.

Then I picked up the phone and dialed the number of one person who could help guide me and wouldn't turn her back on me. All I had to do was remind her of three words and a promise I made when we were dying.

I waited, listened patiently as the phone rang and then her voice reached me. It was strange how a familiar voice could make you feel the repercussions of your actions and remind you of life on the outside, life beyond the prison cell.

"Hello?"

"You made me promise if we lived I'd tell you what Leather and Lace meant," I rasped, clearing my throat to mask the emotion in my voice.

"I'm still waiting," Reina said softly. "Whenever you're ready."

"I'm ready," I swallowed. "It's me and Lacey. It's Lacey, she's my Lace. She's the face I pictured when we thought we would die. It's her face I hung onto and wished to see again," I admitted, letting out a ragged breath.

"I know," she confessed. "I've known since the hospital she was your reason, your why and your purpose," she added.

"Jack was here," I started. "I told him the truth, Reina. You might want to prepare yourself for that ride," I warned.

"Blackie, you didn't call me to warn me about Jack," she coaxed.

"No, I called you because I didn't know who else to call. I'm stuck here when I should be there, with her, helping her through this shit. I'm calling you because I need to know she's okay. I'm calling you because I need you to remind her I'm here and I'm begging her to hang on to those three words. I'm begging *you* to help me remind her of them."

"I'm sure she'd want to hear them from you and not me," Reina said.

"I don't want to upset her," I rasped.

"Blackie, you want a reminder? Here's a reminder. You told me to hang on because Jack needed me. You told me he loved me and I was the one who fixed him, made me believe I had to get back to him because I was what he needed most in this world," she recalled. "Now do yourself a favor and make the call because the one thing Lacey needs most right now is hearing your voice remind her of everything she knows in heart but is too weak minded to hang on to."

I remained quiet as I soaked up her advice.

"Are you there? Did you hear me? She needs you," Reina called. "And in case you need another reminder, something to force you out of your own hell and bring you back to her, let me give you what you need to hear too…Leather and Lace. Make the call Blackie, and make it right, make it count," she challenged.

"I hear you," I assured. "Thanks, Reina," I added huskily.

"Just returning the favor, my friend," she replied.

Make it right.

Make it count.

I could do that.

Lacey

Today was a big day for me. It's my first day back at school and the first day I took the Lithium the doctor prescribed. Now, it's a waiting game to see if it works or if we will have to adjust the dosage or possibly try a different medication. I'm confident that I'm going to kick my maker's ass.

Surviving the rest of this semester? That I'm not so sure about.

"Everyone's staring at me," I whispered to Daniela as we walked to the campus store. I know my treatment with Dr. Spiegel is helping because I would be having an anxiety attack right about now, wondering what everyone was saying behind my back.

I knew they were talking.

I just didn't care.

Let them talk.

"They're not staring at you," Daniela insisted. "And even if they are it's not because of anything you did but because Brandon fooled everyone," she added.

I don't know how true that is either. I overheard some girls talking in the bathroom. They think I'm the bitch who had her daddy's motorcycle gang beat the fuck out of Brandon because I didn't want to go down on him.

People talk.

They always do.

Even when they don't know what the fuck they're talking about.

After I overheard Riggs tell my father what he heard at the hospital I confided in Daniela, because sometimes you just want to talk to your girlfriends and not a shrink. She admitted that when she was making plans for that night, Brandon asked her if I would be there. Of course that led to a crying session with Daniela, where she blamed what happened to me on herself for a good two hours.

The truth is, it would've happened anyway, even if she didn't invite him or tell him I was going.

He's still in the coma and every day he doesn't wake up things become worse for Blackie. I wish I could see him or speak to him especially after what Riggs told my father. I wanted to thank him for what he did. I wanted to tell him how much I loved him and I wanted to tell him about everything that was going on with me.

I didn't even care if he told me how he felt.

If he didn't say a word.

Just knowing he was listening was enough.

Daniela and I grabbed a coffee and went to our next class. I pretended to be paying attention but my mind was elsewhere, busy dreaming of what could've been. It doesn't look like we will get another chance at making our story work. If Brandon dies, Blackie's sentence changes and he's looking at murder.

I'm waiting for my father to give the green light and have the lawyer escort me into the station so I can make a formal statement but talking to my father these days is a struggle. He won't even look at me and has made it very clear that talking about Blackie is out of the question.

A part of me wishes we never hid from him, maybe if he had gotten a chance to see us for himself he'd know it wasn't something to frown upon. Sometimes the heart rules and if you're lucky it lasts. I think if my father would've seen us follow our hearts straight into each other's arms he might be a little more lenient. If he saw the ease of our relationship, the stolen moments that sparked a fire in our hearts, or if he would've seen us smiling whenever we were together than maybe Jack Parrish would understand Leather and Lace.

No man will ever be good enough for me in his eyes but no man cared more about me than Blackie, even before we were anything, when we both thought we were nothing…even then we were still something.

The other part of me is happy we kept our time to ourselves. For a short while we were on top of the world. All the sorrows and regrets of his past faded away and the trials and tribulations of my mind disappeared.

I fell harder than I thought was possible and as I fell Blackie swooped in, claiming my heart. He gave me the broken pieces of his heart and with every kiss and every smile he asked me to put him back together.

So what went wrong? He loved me. I know he did, hell even Riggs saw it. So why did he wound me with his words and break my heart? Was it because he didn't have enough faith in himself? He should know by now I have enough faith in him for the both of us. He should know that he didn't have to prove his worth to me. I believe when you love someone as hard and as fierce as I love Blackie, there is no reason to prove anything other than your commitment to that person. I believe, God creates a second half of your soul and puts it into someone else, if you're lucky you cross paths with that person and get to be one half of a great love story. You become complete and a full heart and a mended soul is all the proof you need. You begin to write an epic love story, one you never saw coming but will always be thankful for.

The words come freely.

The actions speak for themselves.

The love evolves without trying.

It's a rare form of beauty.

Only the lucky ones get to experience.

I was lucky for a little while.

Then my luck ran out.

But I had the story scribed into my heart and that would never run from me.

My phone vibrated on top of my desk, pulling me away from the heartbreak and into the present creating a ruckus and all eyes turned around to see. I stared at the screen and saw it was an unknown caller.

"Miss Parrish, do you need to take that?" My professor chastised.

"Nope," I smiled sheepishly, turning my phone on silent before I flipped it over and laid the screen against the desk. "I'm sorry."

I rolled my eyes at my classmates that continued to stare at me before I glanced down and pretended to take notes.

I had no fucking clue what was going on but hey, I faked the good student like nobody's business and continued to doodle until the professor called class.

I grabbed my books, shoved them in my bag and followed everyone else out of the room. I turned the ringer back on as I walked down the hall and noticed the alert that I had a voicemail. I walked with Daniela into the parking lot, she went her way and I went mine. When I was inside the car, I pulled out the phone and stared at the screen, my thumb hovered over it before I played back the voicemail.

"Lace, it's me," Blackie's voice filled my car and my heart. I heard the gasp escape my lips as he paused, forcing me to check and see if that was the end of the message.

"I'm…I don't know where to start. I guess I'm calling because I want to hear your voice. I want to hear with my own ears you're okay. All right, well I'll try reaching you again later if they let me use the phone."

Another pause.

"I miss you, Angel. I miss you like crazy and I keep picturing your pretty little face. So fucking pretty," his voice trailed off and then I heard him clear his throat. "Hang in there, girl. I'll try and call again, hopefully I'll catch you," he said before ending the voicemail.

Chapter Thirty-five

BLACKIE

There comes a time in life when you've tried all you can and have no choice but to look up to a higher power to guide you. It's usually when you've made a couple of wrong turns and you've lost your way. You have no idea where the fuck you are and don't know where to go from here and instead of winging it you look for signs.

I didn't have to look too hard for my sign. It came right after I made the phone call to Lacey and she didn't pick up. Her sweet voice filled my ears, my soul and the emptiness inside of me since I pushed her away. I contemplated hanging up and not leaving a message at all but I couldn't do it. I physically couldn't do it anymore.

I folded.

The dealer had one card left, and it wasn't a queen.

I had already passed that one up.

I left the message and now I'm left regretting I didn't put it all out there for her. I told her I missed her and that I wanted her to hang in there but I should've told her I loved her. I should've told her I made a mistake and I'll spend every day regretting the one day when I pushed her away. It was foolish, so fucking foolish. I have never doubted my ability to protect her, not once, not since I vowed to Jack I'd do whatever it takes to make sure she was always okay. I gave my brother, peace of mind when they closed the cell doors on his ass, I gave him my word I'd always put her before me.

When my truck blew up, and we had to put the club on lockdown I volunteered to grab Lacey because I trusted myself with her life more than I trusted Jack.

That's a fact.

It's funny what you realize when all you have is three walls and prison bars to stare at all day…your mind is constantly working.

I could've taken care of Boots. I could've put that motherfucker to sleep and avoided all this shit but, I didn't think. I was too wrapped up in the consequences, worried about the club and all the drama we already had brewing with the Chinese.

For the first time in my life I had something I was scared of losing. Never felt that way before. Not even with Christine. It fucked me up, and I lost my way.

I fucked up the rewrite.

"Let's go Petra," the C.O. called, jingling his keys against the metal bars.

I lifted my head off my cot and looked over at him as he unlocked my cell.

"Let's go where?"

"Visitor," he muttered. "Well come on, I don't have all day," he hissed. I threw my legs over the side of the bed and rose to my feet. No one's come up to see me since Jack visited two weeks ago. I at least expected a visit from Pipe or Wolf if not to keep me in the loop with the club than to rip me a new asshole for my affair with Lacey. I'm sure Jack's spreading that shit like wild fire, as he plots my demise.

I don't want to believe that he'll leave me here to rot. I want to think that despite everything he remembers we're brothers by choice, and I've always had his back and always will. I didn't plan on falling in love with his daughter. I didn't plan ahead and he of all people knew that. He's the one who has pleaded with me frequently to find my heart and live again.

Careful what you wish for Bulldog.

Shouldn't have given me her life.

He made her mine without even realizing it.

He put her in front of me and asked me to live again.

I listened to him, opened my eyes and there she was.

An angel tempting the devil.

I was buzzed into the visitor's room and scanned the perimeter searching for the reaper and whoever was wearing it. I glanced over my shoulder at the C.O.

"I see no one I know," I told him, turning around. He placed hand on my chest and tipped his chin over my shoulder.

"Look again," he ordered.

I turned around and this time when I searched the room I didn't look for leather and mayhem, I searched until I found my queen.

Eyes dark as the night met mine.

All the noise faded.

And the people crowding the room seemed to disappear.

It was just her.

My angel.

I started for her as she pushed back her chair and slowly rose to her feet.

Face to face.

Here we were again.

Leather and Lace.

Just when you think you're done. That you've lost everything and you have nothing left, nowhere else to go, that higher ground shakes things around and gives you a new path.

I was staring my path in the eyes and the future never looked so bright.

I was a man behind bars, with no release date, not even sentenced yet but, still a man who had a future.

That pretty face was my future.

"What're you doing here?" I asked, finding my voice as we stood across from one another with the table between us. Her eyes scanned me, zeroing in on my inmate number before finding mine again.

"I'm visiting my favorite Knight," she whispered, offering me a smile as she cocked her head to the side. "What do you think I'm doing here? I miss you."

I closed my eyes as her words punched me in the gut.

She had no fucking idea how much I missed her.

No fucking clue.

"I miss you too," I rasped, opening my eyes.

"They told me I wasn't allowed to touch you," she murmured, eyeing the guards positioned around the perimeter of the room.

I followed her gaze before turning back to her and shrugged my shoulders.

"Yeah, you might slip me something," I explained as I let my eyes travel down her body and back up to her face. I could stare at that face for the rest of my life and never want another.

"You look good, Lace," I said. "Real good," I tipped my chin toward the chair beside her.

"Thanks," she said, pulling out the chair. She took a seat and raised an eyebrow waiting for me to do the same. I felt a muscle twitch and my lips curve slightly as I took the seat in front of her.

I placed my palms flat against the table and kept my head down as my eyes bore into hers.

Come on girl.

Follow my lead.

She kept her eyes trained on mine and mimicked my stance, placing both hands flat against the table.

That's my girl.

"I told you father something but I should've told you first," I said, straightening up but kept my hands firmly where they were. "I should've told you a long time ago, should've told you when you came to the Dog Pound but instead I was cruel to you. Time you got the truth, girl."

"Then give it to me," she coaxed.

"Every word I said that night was a lie. You stopped being Jack's daughter a long time ago. At first I didn't want to see it, I didn't want to see you but it was inevitable. You were created for me and only me. I told you were nothing more than...," I stopped, shook my head unable to repeat the harsh lie and blew out a breath before I looked back at her. "You're everything," I whispered.

I caught the sheen of fresh tears in her eyes before I diverted mine down to her hands and saw her curl her fingers. She fought to keep the stance we were both holding, itching to move them and lift them to her face.

"Keep your hands flat," I whispered.

She blinked, and the tears slipped from the corners of her eyes.

"You okay?"

She nodded.

"It's coming," I teased, winking at her.

My sweet Lace, full of life and so much strength left behind those dark eyes.

"I love you Lacey," I whispered the words and gave her my smile, inching my hands closer to hers.

"I'm sorry you're hearing it like this and not some grand way. I'm sorry I let you think for one second I didn't give a damn."

"Stop," she croaked.

I furrowed my brows and stilled my hands.

"Say it again."

My lips quirked.

"I love you, girl. Only you. Forever you," I swore.

She smiled at me, making me forget she would walk away and I would go back to my cell.

"I love you too," she said through her tears. "I knew you loved me," she whispered. "In my heart I knew I had your love and when my mind told me it was a lie I fought against it."

"You keep fighting," I interjected. "You hear me? You walk out of here today and you keep fighting that shit, never let that maker win," I stressed.

"I'm guessing my dad told you?"

I nodded.

"He was vague. You want to clue me in?"

I watched her look down, spread her fingers a part and slowly slide them closer to the middle of the table before she let them be.

"I've known for a long time," she admitted. "Every breakdown my father has had made it easy for me to diagnose myself."

"Why didn't you tell me?"

"You've got your own demons, Blackie. You don't need mine," she murmured.

"Yeah, babe, we both got demons we can't stand, but you took mine and when I get out of here you're going to give me yours," I told her. "I don't know when that will be so you've got to promise me you're going to stay strong and do what you got to do to keep it quiet up there," I said, motioning to her head with my chin.

"I'm in therapy," she informed me. "And…," she paused and took a deep breath, working through her confession. "I'm on lithium."

"That's good, Lace. Hey, look at me," I said, waiting for eyes to reach mine. "It's a good thing."

"It is?" she laughed.

"Yeah, it means you're not ignoring it and you're not waiting for it to consume you. It takes a strong person to admit there's something wrong and an even stronger person to follow through with treatment," I said. "I'm proud of you, real proud, Lace."

"So you don't think I'm crazy?"

"Not that crazy but yeah, you got to have a little crazy in you to fall for a guy like me," I said. I bit the inside of my cheek and watched the smirk play on her mouth.

I missed her mouth.

"What about you?"

"I'm fucking certifiable," I admitted with a laugh.

"That's not what I meant," she insisted. "What about the drugs? Are you getting help?" she glanced around the room. "Is that even an option here?"

"I'm working it out," I said, glancing over my shoulder to take in the positions of the guards. I kept my eyes on them as they were engrossed in a conversation and moved my hands across the table and covered hers.

The simplest touch was all I needed to remind me of how she felt in my arms.

I tore my eyes from the guards and stared at her as she looked at our hands, intertwining our fingers together.

"Did you ever think something as simple as holding hands would mean so much?" she lifted her eyes to mine. "When did that happen?"

"The day you forced me to drink a milkshake and reminded me I could still smile," I answered. "Promise me something?"

She nodded her head.

"Don't miss me too much," I whispered, as my thumb stroked hers. "Keep on with your therapy, take your medicine, and finish school."

Her hand closed over mine, squeezing it as she held on for dear life.

"Another stolen moment," she murmured. "Is that all we will ever have?"

"Can't promise you the world, no matter how much I want to, not while I'm in here."

"And when you're out? What happens then?"

"Hey, Petra, no touching!" The guard shouted from across the room. "You got two minutes to wrap it up."

I gave her hand a squeeze before pulling mine back.

"Then, I claim my queen," I said, pushing back my chair and drawing in a deep breath before I stood. "I love you, don't forget that okay?"

"Never," she promised as the tears fell from her eyes again. "I hate this," she admitted.

"Me too," I said as I took three steps backward, not ready to turn around and walk away from her.

"Blackie, wait," she said, standing on her feet. "I didn't get to thank you."

"Thank me for what?"

"That night, for what you did. You saved me again."

"Just returning the favor, Lace."

"What?"

"You saved me first," I said, turning my back before I couldn't. Every second I stared at her face made it harder and harder to walk away. I took another two steps but stopped because I didn't know when I would get to see her again. I turned around and looked at her one more time.

Let them throw me in the hole.

Take away my phone call privileges.

Ban my visitors.

It would be worth it.

I never played by the rules and today wouldn't be the day that changed.

I closed the distance between us with every officer's pair of eyes burning a hole into my back I walked straight up to my girl.

"C'mere, girl," I whispered, reaching for face and cupped her cheeks with my palms before I pressed my lips to her forehead.

"Petra!"

"No more maker," I told her. "Just you and me... Leather and Lace," I said against her skin.

My hands fell from her face as the C.O. grabbed me from behind and pulled me back.

So fucking worth it.

Chapter Thirty-six

BLACKIE

Another month passed, thirty days without word from Jack or any of my brothers' other than a deposit into my commissary account. After Lacey's visits they suspended my phone privileges and banned any visitors' other than my lawyer for sixty days. They could've sent word through the suit but all I've been granted is radio silence. It's one thing to leave me here because Jack's thinks I stabbed him in the back, but that doesn't change my place within the club. I didn't dishonor my brothers or my patch and as the fucking vice president of the Satan's Knights I deserve the respect of knowing where my club stands.

I went away with two wars beating the fence, one with the Chinese and the other with the Corrupt Bastards. I can't sit here and think that shit is just staying idle while I'm locked up. Boots made a move, pinning that kid on Lacey, he's decided what it is he wants and he'll make his demands if he hasn't already. Then there's Sun Wu, that motherfucker's vendetta didn't die and after we fucked with his shipment he's probably out for blood. No holds barred.

Tomorrow I'm scheduled to meet with my lawyer so he can tell me all about the deal he's been trying to iron out with the district attorney. According to him, there is no way around doing time, and I should take the deal since the kid still hasn't woken up and the doctors are trying to convince his parents to pull the plug.

I got nothing.

No remorse whatsoever.

Which makes me wonder about the type of person I am. When I found out those two kids died I felt something. I felt a shit ton of grief and regret. I sat in the back of the funeral home and wished I could give each one of those mother's back their sons.

This was different, there was foul play, and it was on Lacey.

Kid deserved what he got.

If it makes me a heartless motherfucker so be it.

And the father's just as much of a dick because he threw his son into the line of fire trying to save his own ass.

Don't have kids if you aren't willing to lay it all on the line. Don't bring another life into the world if you're not willing to trade yours for theirs. I'm no one's father, so what do I know? But give me a kid, give me a precious life, one I helped create, and tell me to protect that kid—you better believe I'm giving that kid everything I am and everything I ever wanted to be.

I think that's the biggest rewrite a person gets in life.

Making a new life and making good on all the wrongs you did in life by giving your kid all the chances you never got.

Kids.

Never thought much about them, been too wrapped up in wanting nothing to dream about having everything.

But having a little girl call me daddy, who looked like Lacey and maybe a little bit like me, was one of the things that made me hope Brandon woke up from the coma I put him in.

The dream was ripped from me when I heard the cell door squeak open and the C.O. step inside.

"Got yourself a cell mate Petra," he crooned, crossing his arms against his chest as he looked over his shoulder. "Try to play nice, will you?" he added, before stepping outside the cell and allowing the man about to invade my small space step inside.

My eyes narrowed as Stryker walked into the cell, holding his linens under his arm.

"Good luck," muttered the C.O. before he slammed the bars close and strut his ass down the cell block. I stood from my cot, walked over to the bars and looked out to see where the guards were before turning around and narrowing my eyes at him.

"What the hell are you doing here?"

Stryker threw his linens on the top bunk before turning around and facing me.

"I heard the bologna was top notch," he said sarcastically before glancing around the cell. "This blows, huh?" he shook his head and diverted his eyes back to mine. "Do you snore?"

"Stryker," I seethed, clenching my fists as I took one step, making us almost nose to nose. "What are you doing here?"

"Drug charge, nothing crazy just possession," he stated.

"And it's a coincidence that you're my cellmate?" I questioned.

"Nope, not a coincidence at all. I come bearing news and instructions," he said, pointedly. "But I should warn you, none of it is good."

"Christ," I hissed, running my fingers roughly through my hair before I lifted my eyes to his. "Lacey?"

"She's fine," he paused, cocking his head to the side as he peered at me. "You fucked the Bulldog with that one."

"Yeah, well, he needs to get over it. It's not like I don't have good intentions when it comes to her but, he wouldn't know that because he's too busy being a bitch."

"He's too busy fighting a war to even consider what kind of man you'll be to his daughter," he argued. "But he's decided that your life matters, whether it's to him or her, I don't know but that's one reason I'm here," he paused, ran his hand over his head before continuing. "The Dragons came after us," he informed me.

"How bad?"

He blew out a breath, rolling up his sleeves and glanced down at the ink that covered his arms before he lifted his eyes back to mine.

"Stryker, how fucking bad?"

"We lost Bones," he muttered.

I stared at him in shock as I dropped onto my cot and processed his words. It's been a long time since we've had a fallen brother. You start to think your club is invincible and nothing will ever get you down. Then something like this happens, you lose one of your own, and you realize everybody bleeds. We all die and none of us are ever safe.

"They attacked us at the compound, got us good, Pipe was expecting a shipment of automotive parts and when the truck pulled into the gates we thought it was the delivery. They opened fire, Riggs's baby mama was there…"

"Oh God," I groaned.

"She was hit and would've been again but Bones stepped in front of the second shooter and took the bullet for her," Stryker continued. "Bones didn't make it out of surgery, they delivered the baby, kid was born three pounds and was put a respirator."

"And Lauren?"

"Took her awhile to come back to the land of the living but she finally got to meet her boy," he said, taking a seat on the john across from the bunk.

"Jesus," I muttered. "How did Riggs not lose his fucking mind?"

"Man, I don't know but, shit, he stepped up. He didn't leave that hospital for a second, if he wasn't sitting with his woman then he was holding his baby—telling him stories about the mom he didn't meet yet and the uncle he never would."

I brought my hands up to cover my face, processing what he said and thought about Bones and Riggs' friendship. We all talk about brotherhood, call one another brothers by choice but those two, they were tight, they were a younger version of the old Jack and the old me.

"Tell me we got them. Tell me we made that motherfucker pay," I growled, dropping my hands back to my sides.

"It's taken care of," he confirmed.

"How?"

"We waited because Jack wanted to give Riggs the respect—Sun Wu nearly took out his whole family, it seemed only fair he's the one who put Wu in his grave. We hit his club as planned but Riggs had a different plan, one he concocted with Bianci. They took out Wu personally."

"Shit," I ground out.

"Yeah, it's been fun."

"What about the Corrupt Bastards?"

"Riggs went up to see them, that guy Boots met with him and for a hot minute we thought he struck a deal with them but then all this happened and Boots never reached out which leads Jack to believe he was never going to take the offer to begin with," he said, shrugging his shoulders. "So that's still a live wire we have to kill."

Boots wouldn't take a deal. I offered him a sweet one. If he agreed to something with Riggs it was only because the prick knew he made a mistake using Lacey as a pawn in his game. That motherfucker is trying to back pedal his way out of the shit he put himself in. He probably heard the news about what went down with the Chinese and thinks Jack is too preoccupied to make a move on him, and with me doing a bid that fuck thinks he's safe.

Wrong.

"Going to ask you one more time and this time you better answer me. What are you doing here?"

"Got a message for you," he revealed.

"Yeah, I bet you do. Give it to me," I ordered, watching as he walked towards the bar and checked to see if the coast was clear before turning back to me.

"You need to get yourself transferred to Otisville. As long as that kid you fucked up is half dead there isn't anything Jack can do. Lacey gave her testimony to the cops but that douche bag Brantley squashed it. There's only one way out but in order for that to happen, you need to be in Otisville with Vic Pastore, that's where the connections are."

"The lawyer is coming here tomorrow to meet with me and discuss a deal from the district attorney," I commented.

"There is no deal, and the lawyer isn't coming because tomorrow your ass is being carted to Otisville. You trust Jack or what?"

I used to trust the man with my life but I don't know if he wants me out. I mean put yourself in his shoes. He knows me better than anyone, knows the shit past I have and that at the end of the day no matter how much I try to get help I'll always be an addict. He knows what I'm capable of, he's seen me kill for crying out loud. How can he not want me to rot here? Every day I waste away here is a day his daughter lives a life without me. That's got to be a win for him.

But take the title of father away from Jack, leave him as the president of the Satan's Knights and my brother...now ask me if I trust him.

Yes.

With everything I am.

He's got my back.

I looked back at Stryker.

"How does he expect me to get transferred?"

"You're going to kick my ass," he seethed. "With the charges you got pending, they'll move you because they think you're a fucking liability or a goddamn nut job. Either way when the bus comes you're going to meet the Don," he wiggled his eyebrows. "Heard he's a real winner too," he exaggerated as he climbed on top the top bunk. "Now, I'm all talked out and tomorrow I've got to get my pretty face fucked up by your sorry ass so I'm turning in," he paused, glancing down at me. "Try not to put me in a coma too."

"I can't make any promises," I muttered.

"Glad we had this talk," he said, shifting around on the bed. "You got to be a midget to fit in this fucking thing," he complained.

"Stryker," I called.

"What?"

"Why us? Why in God's name did you hang your hat here?"

"I fucking ask myself the same question every day," he replied, letting out a long yawn. He didn't elaborate or divulge anything new and I didn't really expect him to either. He doesn't have roots, and doesn't make ties, he's not going to give me any of his truth. Stryker was just like any other nomad I've met...a mystery.

The next morning, they brought us into the yard and I beat the fuck out of Stryker, broke his nose and got my ass shipped to Otisville where the don himself, Victor Pastore was waiting for me.

Chapter Thirty-seven
JACK "BULLDOG" PARRISH

"Bulldog, we gotta roll," Pipe called as he walked towards his bike. "The kids alive."

"Praise Jesus," Wolf ground out, spitting out his toothpick and clasping his hands together before he rubbed them in anticipation. "You get the kid to drop the fucking charges and then I'll cover his face with a pillow. Time to make the little shit sorry his father's sperm ever found the egg."

I stared at him as I fitted my gloves and straddled my Harley.

"You're a sick fuck," I said as I shook my head. "But I'm the one with the fucking crazy pills."

"I'm not playing Bulldog, I don't give a fuck if the kid can't talk, you grab a fucking pad and paper and fucking write his confession. If you're too much of a pussy, I'll sign the goddamn thing."

"You're pushing, Wolf," I seethed. "I'm ten seconds away from making *you* sorry your old man's swimmers ever set sail."

"Someone's got it lay out there for you," Wolf interjected. "We need Blackie out and this shit between the two of you needs to get resolved. This club can't afford anymore fucking problems, we're swimming in them or drowning depending on the fucking day."

"Wolf's right," Pipe chimed in, tightening his chin strap. "It's fucked up thinking any man's got your girl's heart let alone one of us but it could be worse," he pointed out. "Blackie's got a big heart and the fact it's been dead for so long, means it's well rested and ready to work overtime. Let's get him out of the can, give him a chance to prove himself and I swear to you, he fucks with your little girl, Wolf will kill him," he vowed.

"Why me and not you?"

"You're much more creative," Pipe shouted over his engine.

I shook my head and revved my engine leaving those two clowns behind me and peeled out of the compound. I needed no one giving me advice when it came to my daughter. I also didn't need anyone reminding me my brother was in jail or why he was there.

It was never a question of whether I'd do whatever I could to get Blackie released. I'm not a fool, I know Blackie's worth to this club. The man is loyal to the core, something you don't find much of anymore.

I can't get on board with him having a thing for my daughter. After my son died I sat in my room at the clubhouse with a gun in my hand. I pleaded with my predecessor Cain to give me the junk I needed to be reunited with my boy. Cain shot me down, reminded me I still had Lacey and one day she'd grow up and be a looker. She'd need her daddy to filter through the shit and protect her heart or she'd end up with someone like us.

For a long time after that conversation, I'd look at my little girl and hear Cain's voice in my head. I didn't think she'd grow up as fast as she did. I wish I didn't spend so much time worrying about the older years and paid more attention to the younger ones.

The years when she was still only mine.

Now I had to share her.

I never learned how to share.

I didn't want my first lesson to be sharing my daughter with Blackie.

But like everything else in my life, some things were just out of my control.

There was one thing no one would take from me, one part of me I'd always have power over and that's my ability to get down. First, I'd start with the kid's father, because that son-of-a-bitch should've taught his boy manners and how to use his fucking dick. He thinks he's been sparred a debt, that motherfucker is in over his head and he's in with me.

The motherfucking *bulldog*.

We parked in front of the hospital, dismounted and started for the door. I glanced over each shoulder making sure Wolf and Pipe were ready to get down with me and saw the devilish look in both maniac's eyes. We'd get the job done.

Free Blackie.

These two assholes behind me were about to have shirts made if I didn't get him out. I'm not going to lie, I want him out. This last month I could've used my V.P. with everything we've had going on. As much as I want him out, I don't know how I'm going to handle watching my daughter run into his arms.

She thinks he's her knight in shining armor.

I used to be.

Maybe that's what it is. Maybe it's not about giving her to Blackie and trusting he's going to do right by her. Maybe it's losing her and wondering where I'll fit in her life.

We made our way to Brandon's room and Pipe tapped my shoulder.

"Go ahead, I got this," he affirmed, brushing off his shoulders.

Wolf pulled open his jacket and grabbed a pen from inside his pocket before he shoved it in my face.

"Get it signed and sealed and I'll deliver the fucking sentence," he grunted. I grabbed the pen and pushed open the door to the kid's room. Lacey sat beside Brandon's bed with his mother on one side of her and the father across from her.

She lifted her head and pinned me with a stare before turning to Brandon's mother. "Thank you for helping him write this," Lacey said, tapping her pen to the pad of paper and then she turned to Brandon. "Thank you for doing the right thing," she offered.

"We're sorry what happened," the kid's mother said. "And I know Brandon is too, isn't that right?"

"What the hell is going on?" I hissed.

"Brandon is dropping the charges against Blackie," she said, lifting the pad as my eyes zeroed in on the signature on the page.

"The cops will be here any minute to take his statement. I thought it would be best if we had this just in case someone should change their mind," she said, diverting her eyes to the kid's father.

"No one is changing their mind," I said, walking up behind the man who used his son as payment plan. "Time for you and me to take a walk, buddy."

"Dad," Lacey started, but I shot her down with a glare.

"Go outside and wait with Wolf and Pipe," I ordered. "Now." Then I looked over at the Brandon's mother. "You too lady, out."

"Sir, my son---" "Is lucky I need him alive," I interrupted. "Now, I'd like a word with the guy who tried to rape my daughter and the man who put him in the position. If you want to stick around and watch that's fine with me but I can guarantee you, you won't like what you'll hear," I paused. "And not what you see either."

I could feel Lacey's eyes stare me down and under other circumstances I would've thought twice about talking like this in front of her. I've tried real hard not to unleash the bulldog in front of her but now I didn't give a damn. Now, I knew she didn't scare easily and wasn't afraid of the life I tried to shield her from. Now, she chose it.

Both women turned around and made their way out of the room. I walked over to the door, peeked through the blinds and locked the door.

"Mr. Parrish," the elder man started.

"Shut your fucking mouth!" I cut him off, walking around the edge of the bed to the run my hand over the buttons of the machine pumping air into Brandon's lungs.

"The only one talking right now is me. Do you understand?" I asked.

"Yes, sir," the father choked out.

I looked down at Brandon and watched as he stared back at me blankly.

"You fucked with the wrong girl," I seethed. "Thank whatever God you pray to that Blackie was there to stop you. If you would've succeeded I would've cut your little dick off and fed it to that sweet woman who's been sitting vigil over you."

The father flinched at my crass words causing me to divert my eyes toward him.

"You got something you want to say old man? Because I've got a plan for you too."

"The doctors say he's permanently deaf," he hoarsely informed me.

"How's that feel?" I asked, pushing off the respirator and standing tall as I stared him down, confusion masking his features.

"How's it feel to know you put your son in the middle of a situation only to save your own ass? Does your wife know you're gambling degenerate that asked his son to step in when he couldn't pay?"

"It wasn't like that," he argued. "I didn't have a choice! I wouldn't have done it if I knew Brandon would be hurt, or even if I knew he'd hurt your daughter. Boots told me he wanted him to get close to her, get a little information about that Blackie guy. He'd let the debt go but if I didn't send Brandon in, he'd kill him." He glanced down at his son. "I never wanted any of this. And now Boots is saying because Brandon did what he did—" "What's the matter you can't say it?" I ground out. "You can't bring yourself to say the word can you? Say the fucking word! Be a man and say what you're fucking son did to my daughter."

He stared at me silently.

"SAY IT!" I demanded as I outstretched my hand, my fingers hovered over the plug.

"Rape," he blurted. "He said because Brandon tried raping your girl that the deal was off the table and he owned me."

I arched an eyebrow.

"I used to work for the club. I was their mechanic for a long time, seen a lot of stuff go down. I don't want to be under his thumb. I won't survive being in debt to him, neither will anyone in my family. I got a daughter man, just like you do, and I've already compromised one child."

I walked around the bed, pushing down the sting of his words and focusing on what I was there to do.

"That man preys on girls," he rambled. "Brandon's going to drop the charges on the guy and then we're out of here. I'm taking my family and getting the fuck out of here before another kid becomes a victim."

"Let's get something straight, Boots doesn't own you.... I do. And you're not going anywhere until I say so, until I'm sure Blackie's out and then I'll decide what you can and cannot do, where you can and cannot go," I growled.

"He's already threatened my daughter twice," he cried as I started for the door.

"Don't like it do you? It's not a good feeling when someone takes advantage of your girl is it?" I turned around and point my finger between his eyes. "Stay put or I'll deliver your daughter to him myself."

I glanced over at Brandon debating whether to acknowledge the poor slob in the bed, deaf and barely able to function. I decided to let it go---his mother would wipe his ass for a long while. Blackie took care of him and took care of him good.

I should probably thank him.

After I kick him in the balls.

I pulled the door open, and the mother lifted her head, wiped her tears and brushed past me as she ran into the room.

"Relax lady, they're still breathing," I called over my shoulder before turning to Wolf who followed her. I placed my hand against his chest. "Where do you think you're going?"

He looked at Lacey.

"We got the confession now it's time to deliver the sentence," he explained, staring back at me like I was half tanked. "Don't sweat it, Bulldog, I'll be quiet."

"No need. Blackie gave the kid his sentence already," I muttered, turning around to stare at my daughter leaning against the wall, holding her man's ticket to freedom in her hand.

"Are you going to call the lawyer or should I?"

I walked over to her, took the pad from her hand and shoved it under my arm.

"I'll handle it," I insisted.

"Make sure," she said, rising on her tiptoes to press a kiss to my cheek. She used to do that a lot when she was little. She also used to stand on my shoes and beg me to dance with her.

Yeah, I should've paid more attention to the younger years.

I wrapped my arms around her and gave her a slight squeeze before she pulled out of my arms and started down the hallway.

The older years sucked.

I watched her walk away and cleared my throat, pushing down the lump in my throat.

She's not your little girl anymore, my maker taunted.

She'll always be my little girl.

Chapter Thirty-eight

BLACKIE

I followed the guard through the cell block and immediately noticed the differences between here and Rikers. First, this place was fucking huge and housed twice as many inmates and double the amount of correction officers. The inmates here didn't give two fucks about anything, most of them knew they'd die here and the few that weren't doing life sentences, would probably die before they busted out. They were rowdy and taunted the officers as they walked me to my cell. The guard behind me stopped at one of the cells on the way, slipped the inmate a book and took one back in return. I glanced over my shoulder and watched as he opened the book, dipped his eyes to the page he opened it to and smiled before closing it again.

No wonder they carted my ass here.

This place was fucked.

The guards were on the take and the one's inmates didn't have in their pockets were the ones who were fucked. I had no doubt that Victor ran this place, both the inmates and the fucking men who were supposedly guarding them. He probably makes a pot of sauce in his fucking cell on a Sunday.

The officer in front of me stopped and turned to his left as he reached for his keys.

"Delivery," he commented as he unlocked the cell, stepping aside as I turned to the man behind the bars. My eyes zeroed in on the perfectly white canvas sneakers before they traveled the length of the blue jumpsuit and landed on the aging face of Victor Pastore.

His hair had grayed since the last time the newspapers snapped a picture of him but it was immaculately styled, not a silver stain out of place and slicked back with a half a ton of hair gel. He was thinner than when he went in and his normally tan complexion was still olive in skin tone but much paler, even paler than when I insisted Jack bring me to meet the man all those months ago when we first went head to head with Jimmy Gold.

Victor stood, shoving one hand in his pocket, mimicking the way he used to unbutton his designer suit and hide one hand in his pants pocket as he walked. He had that walk, the media used to love to catch him leaving the court house because his stance alone sold papers and made ratings. He was cocky, arrogant and a goddamn legend people worshipped.

It didn't matter he was a gangster and his record spoke for his crimes, he was a good guy to the people he loved and his neighborhood. He didn't let the power go completely to his head, sometimes he managed to keep it humble, which these days was unheard of.

His reputation made it hard for people to believe the man in a thousand-dollar suit, playing stick ball in the street with the neighborhood kids, spent the night before robbing a truck and killing the driver, leaving is body on the side of the road. The stories were endless and my personal favorites were the ones told about the Vic from years ago when Michael Valente Senior was his underboss—those two were a force to be reckoned with. Yeah, those were my favorite, when the mob was still the mob and Vic and Val ran New York with old school values.

After, Val died, Victor wasn't the same man he became harder as his quest for revenge consumed him. Jimmy was elected his underboss. I'm not really sure how that works, if it's something Vic chose himself or if his organization sat down and took a vote. I'm going to say there isn't democracy in the Pastore Organization. There is Vic and then there's everyone else under him enforcing his final rule.

I looked over my shoulder at the guard who slipped him a paper brown bag, wondering for a moment what determined if you got a book or a bag full of goodies from Santa Claus over here. Yeah, Vic ran shit, even behind bars he had the correction officers enforcing his command.

"Thank you," Victor said, opening the bag and peering inside before nodding in satisfaction and turning his eyes back to mine. "I've been expecting you," he smirked, glancing over my shoulder at the two guards. "I'll take it from here boys," he said, dismissing them.

"You got it, Vic, be back in an hour to bring you to church," the first officer promised as I stepped inside and he closed the cell door.

I dropped the few belongings they gave me onto the bottom bunk and turned around, raising an eyebrow at Victor.

"Church?"

"Man needs God when he's locked away for the rest of his life," he explained. "He repents his sins and hope that changes where he ends up after he takes his final breath," he continued.

"I bet he does," I murmured, knowing those words would stick with me for the rest of my life. They were the words of a man who spent his whole life defeating the odds and now staring at him, his luck finally had run out.

A man up until a few weeks ago I was destined to become.

"Jack came up about a week ago to catch me up to speed with our situation," he said, as he bent down and stripped his thin mattress of its sheet.

"Glad, he found time for a visit," I gritted. "Look, Vic I'm not really sure what the plan is or if there even is one—

He turned around, his gray eyes pinned me with a hard stare.

"There's always a plan," he interrupted. "We'll have you out of here by the end of the week as long as you play by my rules," he paused, cocked his head the side and started again. "Heard there's a certain someone on the outside waiting for you."

I drew my eyebrows together as I crossed his arms and deciphered his words, wondering which enemy he was referring too, not surprised that he would have intel on that sort of thing.

He smiled, revealing perfectly straight teeth as he winked at me knowingly.

"Your choice woman has my friend up in arms," he teased.

"I bet he had a mouthful to say," I mumbled.

"He voiced his concerns," he said as he tied one end of the sheet around one of the metal bars. "Take it from me, it's hard on a man when he looks at his daughter and realizes she's all grown up and you're not the only man in her life anymore."

He walked to the other end of the bars and tied the other corner of the sheet around a bar, covering the bars, before he turned back around and wiped his hands clean.

"You've met my daughters, haven't you?"

"Yes," I confirmed, watching as he walked over to the small sink and grabbed a photo taped above it of his two daughters, Nikki and Adrianna. "And your wife," I added. "You're a lucky man."

"Yes, I used to be," he agreed and brought his index finger to his lips before pressing the kiss to the photograph. "And then my luck ran out."

He placed the photograph back in its rightful spot but continued to stare at it.

"I was about your age, married with two little girls and the biggest empire in New York. I was on top of the world, untouchable, and unstoppable, making more money than anyone could've imagined. My wife was dripping in diamonds and my kids didn't want for a thing. I'd go out all night, hustle hard and come home in the morning just as Grace was getting the girls ready for school. I'd give them a quick kiss, promise there would be a surprise waiting for them when they came home and handed my wife a knot of cash. I thought that's what made a man successful."

I used to hate Jack's alliance with Victor, I thought it was bad for the club to mix our organization with his. I didn't like breaking bread with the mob and thought we ran in different circles. But I learned our club and his organization had many similarities, we were both outlaws and mostly we wanted the same things as far as our town. We wanted to keep the concrete jungle under our thumb, run shit our way, with no interference from others. We wanted to make money, and when we started to…well, we wanted to make more because stacks of hundreds under your mattress wasn't enough. You wanted the shoeboxes in your closet full too.

"I used to think that too," I admitted. "I was married, lost her though and when I did it didn't matter how much I gave her it didn't keep her in my life."

"I know," he said. "But you, you got a second chance," he pointed out. "You'll get out of here and there'll be a life waiting for you. It's an opportunity to live hard and fast but for the right reasons, for the reasons that make life worth living."

He coughed heavily as if he was choking. I jumped to my feet, ready to pat him on the back but he held up a hand in protest and continued to cough up a lung.

Pride.

He still had it.

"That's better," he said, taking a deep breath.

"You okay?"

He stepped to me and placed his palm to my cheek and I felt like I was in the Godfather with Marlon Brando and not in a jail cell with Vic.

"Do yourself a favor…when you get out, make changes, make your life count, kid, because it's too fucking short. Don't fall back into old ways and don't let breaking the law come before the one who keeps you warm at night. Don't become me because it'll hurt, worse than any bullet ever could—knowing your wife cries herself to sleep every night and you have two daughters you never got to walk down the aisle or dance with."

He paused, dropped his hand and looked away before continuing.

"I've got a granddaughter due to be born any day now I won't ever get to meet and a grandson who will soon forget his Pop if he hasn't already. So ask me now, was it all worth it?"

"Don't beat yourself up about it Vic. It takes a good man to get a woman like you got, and even more special man to raise two daughters as great as yours. You must've done something right," I told the man.

"Remember that when you're breathing fresh air, kid. Remember when life gets hard there's always another way, hang onto your woman and let her show you the way. And if you're lucky you'll have a couple kids…," he smiled, fighting back another coughing fit. "And they'll be girls. You'll look at them and wonder how you ever pulled a trigger or dug a hole."

The coughing won, and it took a few minutes for him regain his composure.

"Do you need a glass of water or something?"

"Water won't cure what I have," he muttered.

"Are you sick?"

He took a seat on the bottom bunk and glanced up at me.

"I've been diagnosed with lung cancer, not sure what stage yet, but I'm guessing it's pretty far off," he took a deep breath. "It is what it is," he brushed an invisible piece of lint from his jumpsuit.

"Christ, I'm sorry Vic," I muttered, running my fingers through my hair. "Does your family know?"

"No, no point in telling them," he answered. "My girls are finally happy, genuinely happy and they're safe. They miss their dad but they're moving on with life, as they should. Adrianna is about to give birth and is finally living her happily ever after with Anthony. And my Nikki, well, Michael paid me a visit and told me he was going to ask her to marry him. He's a good kid, Val would be proud. Then there's my Gracie, and I won't tell her because she's still hanging onto the years when we were young."

He lifted his pillow, removed the pillow case and pulled a razor blade out.

"When it's your time, it's your time," he said kneeled down on the floor and sharpened the edge of the razor against the concrete.

"What are you doing with that?" I whispered.

He lifted his eyes to mine and smiled widely.

"It's Jimmy's time," he revealed.

"He's here?"

"It seems like just yesterday you and Jack paid me a visit and we first concocted this plan," he smiled nostalgically. "I always liked playing God, now I get to play it with that no good prick's life."

He viciously scratched the razor against the cement, obviously angered just thinking about Jimmy Gold.

I got his pain.

That motherfucker ruined my life too.

The only difference is I have one to get back to and Vic didn't. I felt sorry for him and I knew if I told him that I'd kill what was left of his soul. He didn't want anyone's pity.

"They'll be coming to bring me to the chapel. Do me a favor?"

"Yes," I said.

"Continue to sharpen this when I'm gone, but make sure you put the sheet up. You don't have to worry about the guards but the scum we're locked up with, they're all rat bastards," he said, taking my hand and opening my palm before dropping the blade into it and closing it.

"Nice and sharp, like the tip of a needle," he instructed.

I glanced down at the weapon in the palm of my hand as Vic walked behind me and untied the sheet from the bars. I shoved the razor under my mattress and watched as Vic grabbed his bible. Two minutes later a correction officer took him to church.

Two minutes later I was devising a plan of my own.

Chapter Thirty-nine

BLACKIE

Nice and sharp, like the tip of a needle.

His words repeated over and over inside my head as I mimicked the way he tied the sheet over the bars. I grabbed the blade from under the mattress and took a seat on the cold floor, letting the razor slide between my fingers.

So smooth.

I pictured Jimmy's face as he sat across from me that day he showed up at the Dog Pound, provoking me to resurrect the devil I tried so hard to bury.

Victor tells me you're familiar with the business, that, you used to be one of the biggest players in the game.

Even the mighty players fall.
Just look at Vic.
But I didn't just fall, Jimmy Gold knocked me off my horse and dragged me to hell.

I'd like to think a man like you knows his product, enjoys it even, won't you have a taste for me?

I scratched the razor against the concrete subconsciously as I relived the nightmare that nearly killed me. I recalled drawing my sleeve up my arm and tying the rubber band around my bicep. I could almost feel the needle prick my skin and when I closed my eyes I watched as my thumb pressed down on the top of the syringe.

There you go.
Just a little more.
All done.

I've been at war with myself for a long time and if I would yield Victor's advice I needed to put my addictions to rest. I needed to go religiously to meetings when I got out and more than that I needed to hang on to the picture he painted for me. The woman home waiting for me and the dream of a family that could be mine.

But before all that, to give myself to Lacey completely I had to free myself from the demons that threatened to pull me away from her. I wasn't like Victor; I learned the hard way money and power aren't everything, not when you're pulling your dead wife out of a bathtub. I had my own issues though and as much as I was addicted to drugs I was addicted to pain. I let people get to me through my heart and I'd have to end that by ending all the people who threatened to take my heart away from me.

Starting with Jimmy.

Ending with Boots.

I didn't even give a fuck about the G-Man anymore. If that man never got what was coming and lived to a ripe old age only to rot away in a cage, that, was good enough for me. Vic gave me a glimpse of the future, providing me with a wake-up call and a new dream.

I wanted the picture he had taped to the wall, but I wanted that photograph tucked safely into a frame on the nightstand next to my wife.

I touched the edge of the blade, continued to sharpen it before glancing around the cell, searching for an answer to a question I wasn't going to divulge.

You want to know what happens?

Watch and see motherfucker.

I promise to give you a good show.

I narrowed my eyes as I stared at the metal toilet bowl screwed into the wall and the floor. I crawled across the floor and placed my hands on the bowl, remembering the morning after that first prick of the needle in five years and how I remained hunched over the bowl. I inspected the toilet bowl and found what I was looking for. I used the sharpened edge of the razor as a flat head screwdriver and twisted the bolt attaching the metal thrown to the wall.

Then my voice rang in my ears after Gold tried forcing me on Reina.

I'm not touching her you sick fuck.
Shoot me up, do what you got to do but I won't fucking touch her.

I twisted and twisted until I pulled back my hand, revealing the three inch bolt and ran my finger across the flat tip.

Nice and sharp, like the tip of a needle.

I moved away from the toilet, placed the sharpened razor back into Vic's pillowcase before I went to work on the screw.

Lacey's face worked its way into my brain as my hand quickened the pace, stripping the ridges that swirled around the metal, smoothing them down as I created a point.

I couldn't wait to see that face again.

I couldn't wait to kiss that mouth of hers again.

Or hold that soft body in my arms.

I couldn't fucking wait to be inside her and watch her eyes as she became mine over and over again.

Yeah, I had a fucking future, and it was so goddamn beautiful.

"Nice and sharp," I repeated.

"Just like the tip of a needle," I whispered.

I heard the keys dangle before the officer fitted them into the bars and I quickly hid the weapon I was making. Vic pulled back the sheet and stepped into our cell.

"How was church?" I muttered.

"God is good," he replied, placing his bible under his pillow. "He forgives us all."

"Yeah? You think?" I asked, wiping the sweat from my brow and pushing my hair away from my eyes.

"I know," he assured as he climbed into the bottom bunk. "Tomorrow is a big day," he said, yawning. "Tomorrow I become God."

No you don't.

I do.

I climbed onto the top bunk and once I was sure Victor was sleeping, I continued to sharpen the screw against the wall.

God was good.

But I was the devil.

Chapter Forty

BLACKIE

I watched Victor take the comb resting on the sink and run it through his silver hair, meticulously combing it back. He slipped on his sparkling white sneakers and brushed down the front of his jumpsuit before he turned around and smiled at me.

"My sources tell me by tomorrow you'll be a free man," he assured me.

I didn't ask questions, relying on his word and the hope that Jack pulled off whatever the fuck he and Victor planned.

"Give Jack some time to come around," he advised. "A father needs to see the proof that when he leaves this earth his daughter will be well looked after. We don't always deserve the peace of mind but some of us need it, anyway. Give it to him. Make her happy."

"I plan on it," I said huskily, barely recognizing my own voice.

He crossed the small floor space of the cell and reached under his pillow for the bible, opening it to the middle where a ribbon acted as a bookmark and laid the open book on the bed.

My legs dangled over the edge of the top bunk and I leaned forward, watching intently as he emptied the pillowcase and lifted the razor, inspecting the sharpness of it with his finger before he lifted his eyes to mine and smiled.

"You do good work," he complimented.

"Always aim to please," I said as he placed the razor onto open page of the Holy Scripture before he covered it with the ribbon and closed the book.

"Let's go Pastore," the guard called from behind the sheet.

I jumped down from the bunk and shoved my hands into my pockets, fingering the weapon rubbing against my thigh. Victor untied the sheet at one end and let it hang from the other as he tucked his bible under his arm and waited for the guard to open the cell.

"Wait," I called.

Victor looked over his shoulder at me.

"Think God could find forgiveness in me too?"

He studied me for a moment, remaining completely silent and I thought he would deny me. I knew what he was going to do, he never tried to hide it from me and now I was asking him to allow me to bear witness. His lips quirked, and he granted me the faintest hint of a smile.

"Come, my brother, you want to see God work in mysterious ways? Let me show you his divine powers," he said, his voice almost sounding like a hymn.

The C.O. raised an eyebrow at Vic but the mob boss paid him no mind, leading me out of the cell. As we walked the cell block I felt the inmates eyes on us and wondered if they knew what was about to go down. I diverted my eyes to Vic and watched as he held his head high and moved his lips. I leaned closer trying to listen to him and I heard every other word but it was clear the man was praying.

It takes a certain breed to do the things we do and each of us has our own way of getting in the zone. Whether it's reliving the pain you suffered in life or listening to a particular song there's something that gets you pumped and ready to take blood, a ritual one partakes in before he sanctions the beast within and takes a life.

I'm not sure if Vic prays to God or if he really thinks he becomes him, but it's almost fascinating to watch him evolve into a holier than thou persona.

We stepped into the chapel which the only thing that showed God's presence was the small wooden cross hanging on one wall, high enough that no one could reach it and use it as a weapon. A man in a cloak stood in the front of the room and Victor made the sign of the cross as he passed him, taking a seat in one of the folding chairs in the front of him.

I glanced around the otherwise empty room before I took a seat beside Victor and watched him lay his bible on his lap. The officer that escorted us stood in the back of the room, leaning against the wall as the priest recited mass to us.

I kept looking towards the door, rubbing my hand over my pants over the screw resting in my pocket, anticipating the moment when I came face to face with Jimmy Gold.

The moment never came.

Church continued.

Vic received Holy Communion.

I sat back and watched.

Then the priest walked over to Vic, he dipped his thumb into Holy Water and drew the sign of the cross on his forehead with his finger.

"God forgives you, son," he said.

"Amen," Victor whispered as he closed his eyes and became one with God.

The priest dropped his hand, looked to me and side stepped until he stood before me and dipped his finger back in the Holy Water. My eyes widened as he lifted his hand and I felt the cool water touch my forehead, surprising me I didn't go up in flames when his finger touched my skin.

"God forgives you, son," he repeated.

I stared back at him, forgetting the response I was supposed to say and watched as he dropped his hand before closing his bible.

A moment later he was gone.

The officer followed him out the door and left Vic and I sitting in the first makeshift pew of the prison's chapel. I wondered if every inmate finds God or just the fucked up ones.

The door opened, forcing me to tear my eyes away from the wooden crucifix and stare in horror at the man who walked into the room. He was ugly, scary looking as all hell, he was the devil. A man who used to be covered in some of the finest ink had skin that was so worn and badly burned that it was almost translucent and the parts that weren't were sutured with pink puckered flesh.

The left side of his face resembled the villain Two Face from the Batman comics.

I had to look away because staring at him for too long made me feel sick.

Jimmy was so badly scarred the only thing that made him recognizable to the people who knew him was the gold tooth he flashed when he opened his mouth to gasp. His eyes moved back and forth between me and Vic, finally deciding to stay glued to the man he once called his boss.

I forced myself to keep my eyes on him, ingraining his appearance to my memory, then I remembered what my brother's said Jack did to his finger and I looked down.

The Bulldog took a saw to his pinky finger and sliced through the bone just as Jimmy had done to his blood brother Jack.

Five fingers on one hand.

Nine on the other.

I realized why Jack didn't kill him that day.

Suffering is worse than dying.

And this motherfucker suffered.

Now it was time for him to die.

It was time to put him down like the fucking dog he was.

"We meet again, Jimmy," Victor crooned, as he ran his fingers over the leather cover of his bible.

"Guard!" Jimmy shouted.

"They won't save you," Victor said, calmly as he took a step toward Jimmy. "No one can."

Jimmy opened his mouth to speak but really, what could he say? He was sorry? Cry for help? There was no one there to hear his pleas. And God was before him, ready to bring him into the land of eternal temptations.

But before God had the chance to take him I was going to. I slid my hand into my pocket as Victor circled Jimmy.

"I've been waiting a long time for this reunion, to see your face, to look you in the eye and tell you who the boss is," he seethed. "Always wanted the title didn't you? You didn't give a damn what you did or who you killed to get to the top. That was your first mistake…wanting what was never yours. The second was killing Val, that man was my brother, someone you never could hold a candle to. The third was fucking with my children, bringing that guy around Nikki, using her to get me out of your way. I won't even start about the heartache your hand caused Adrianna. If you hadn't killed Val, I never would've sent Anthony to prison. But I'll take the blame for that one," he paused, as he opened the bible.

It's now or never.

I closed my hand over the screw and took three steps closer to Jimmy.

"You kept going, leaving a path of destruction behind you. You've drawn blood and left scars, you've killed and you've stolen…now it's time for you to ask God for forgiveness," he said.

I closed my eyes, and I was back in that basement, standing in front of Reina, pleading for her to hang on to Jack as she reminded me of the girl with the sad eyes waiting for me.

Leather and lace.

"Forgive me, father for I have sinned," Jimmy cried.

"Yes, you have," I heard my own voice say as I wrapped my arm around his neck and pinned him against me with my forearm as I reared the hand that held the weapon and drew it down, aiming for the same spot he stabbed my neck with the needle.

My hand never came down as Victor grabbed my hand from behind and twisted it behind my back before he pressed his knee into my back and forced me down onto the floor. Jimmy stumbled out of my arms and fell onto the floor.

"What're you doing?" I hollered as Victor stepped over me, dropping the bible onto the floor beside me.

He never answered my question as he kneeled over Jimmy.

"Father forgive me," he hissed as he took the blade to Jimmy's throat and sliced him from ear to ear, blood poured out, leaving Jimmy in a sea of crimson.

Vic dropped the blade, turning his palms over to stare at Jimmy's blood that covered his hands before he wiped down the front of his prison blues.

Victor Pastore was a man of his word.

Deal done.

He glanced over his shoulder at me.

"Tell my wife I love her and tell my girls their dad will always watch over them," he said hoarsely before he stood on his feet, carefully stepping over the body, making sure he didn't get another speck of blood on his fresh white kicks. He walked over to the door and pounded his fist against it until the guard opened the door.

"Take him to the morgue," Vic muttered, looking at me one final time. "And take *him* back to his cell."

I turned back to Jimmy's body.

"Tomorrow when you get yourself released, remember you've got a little life left and make it count," Vic said before walked out the door.

I didn't see Vic after that.

He was never brought back to our cell.

And the next morning I was released.

Just as he promised.

Victor Pastore was a man of his word.

Chapter Forty-one

BLACKIE

I strode pass the barbed wire fences; the sun beating down on the worn leather jacket on my back and I spotted Riggs leaning against his truck. He pulled his sunglasses off and smirked at me, spreading his jacket wide and revealing a t-shirt that read *Free Blackie*.

"How fucking great is that? Wolf had them made," he said, pushing off the car and taking a step toward me.

I glanced down at the writing on his shirt and then back at his face.

"They sent the pretty boy to pick me up?" I said, reaching for him to pat him on the back and do the manly hug thing.

"Yeah, it's your lucky fucking day," he quipped, pulling back to take a better look at me.

"Heard through the grapevine you got yourself a little boy," I smiled as his whole face lit up at my mention of his son.

Wow, that was a change.

He whipped out his phone and pulled up a photograph when I spotted the ink that covered the knuckles on his right hand spelling out the two words…*Own it*. He turned the screen around, displaying a photo of a baby boy with a Harley Davidson onesie and a sideways Yankee cap on his tiny head.

"That's my Eric," he beamed, proudly. "Pretty fucking awesome, huh?"

"Amazing," I said, taking the phone out of his hand to get a better look at the kid.

Truly amazing…God takes but God gives.

"So what do you say? You ready to blow this popsicle stand or what?" he asked as I handed him back his phone.

"Yeah," I said, grabbing a hold of his forearm before he turned around. "Hey…I'm sorry about Bones."

"Yeah, me too," he rasped, drawing in a deep breath. "But he'll always be with me," he added as he made a fist and brought it against his chest. Like the other hand each knuckle had a letter only this hand was dedicated to his best friend, our brother…*Bones*.

He dropped his hand and his eyes darkened before he placed his sunglasses back on his face. "I took care of that cocksucker," he growled. "Made sure that motherfucker never gets to hurt another person I care about."

He tipped his chin toward the car signaling for me to get inside as he walked around and climbed into the driver's seat.

"What about you?" he asked as he started up the truck.

"What about me?"

He shrugged his shoulders, placed one had on the steering wheel and with his other hand he opened the console. I leaned over and saw my gun sitting pretty inside.

"Thought you might want to take care of business before you go off and get the girl," he said, closing the console with his elbow.

"Who said I'm going to get the girl?"

"You better go get the girl after how many times I put my ass on the line," he warned.

I smiled.

I couldn't wait to go get the girl.

But Riggs was right.

First things first.

I reached over, opened the console and took my piece out. I checked to see if it was loaded before dropping the safety on it and opening my jacket to tuck it back where it belonged.

"My man! Now, that's what I'm talking about," Riggs enthused, grinning. "Blackie's back…back again," he rapped, mocking the Eminem song, Back Again.

Yeah, I'm fucking back.

One more chance to get it right.

"Take me to my bike."

Throughout the drive Riggs brought me up to speed on everything I had missed while in lock up. It seemed like everyone was getting hitched and the club that used to be about drugs and corruption was turning over a new leaf. Pipe was doing big things with the garage, expanding it was definitely a good move because Jack took over the union contracts Vic had with the Atlantic Express buses. Riggs was trying to get the club on board with opening a security company, and I told him he had my vote at the table. I think it's good we start making legit money. That doesn't mean we're a bunch of pussy's though. Jack put up his house, took the equity out and handed over a lump sum to Pops to repair all the damage done to the shooting range. We have a new buyer for our guns too, Rocco Spinelli, the mobster moving in on Vic's territory.

And then there was the new blood—I had already gotten to know Stryker a little better and would make it my business to learn what made the rest of them tick.

I knew Riggs had his hands full while I was away so I didn't think to ask him about Lacey and how she was doing but he offered. He told me about the talk he had with Jack and how he confessed knowing there was something going on between us. He also mentioned that when Jack went to get the confession and make the kid drop the charges Lacey was already there doing his dirty work.

My girl wants her man back.

I'm coming, angel.

Gonna' take real good care of you.

Once we finally pulled up the Dog Pound Riggs parked the truck, and I made my way over to my bike. Someone had my baby detailed, all her chrome was freshly polished and my helmet was hanging off the handlebars.

The boys knew I had a score to settle, and they had everything ready for me to do what I needed to do.

I straddled my bike, revved the engine and let my baby purr to life.

Sweetest fucking sound.

I glanced over at my side view mirrors and saw Wolf and Pipe walk out of the clubhouse. Wolf gave me the finger as he grinned while, Pipe gave me a two-finger salute. Riggs crossed his arms and mouthed the words two words he lived by...*own it.*

I glanced around the lot, looking for Jack but neither he nor his bike were anywhere in sight, reminding me there was one war still raging and it was the one between him and I.

I took Vic's words to heart and tried to put myself in Jack's shoes.

I'd make him see I was the right man fit to take his daughter.

He'd cross over to the other side.

All he had to do was see her smile and God, I would make her smile.

I lifted one hand in the air, saluting the men who had my back and took off on the open road. I had a long ride ahead of me but I kept myself focused by picturing Lacey's face. The quicker I took care of business the quicker I could get my girl.

I hope she didn't have plans because she wouldn't be leaving my bed for at least a week.

Probably longer.

It was a little less than five hours when I neared my destination, turning onto the narrow road and slowed at the motorcycle blocking the road. I was about to reach into my jacket and pull out my gun when I noticed the patch on the back of the man straddling it.

He turned around, lighting a cigarette before his eyes met mine.

Jack.

He held the cigarette between his lips, lifted his feet and turned his bike around as I pulled up beside him.

I knew then I never had doubt his loyalty to me. We might not see eye to eye, and he might hate me right now, but he always would have my back as long as I kept doing the right thing.

He gave me a quick jerk of his head before he throttled his bike and waved me off in front of him.

Jack didn't give me words he gave me his actions and by letting my bike ride in front of him was his way of showing me respect. He knew what I was about to do, and I didn't even have to tell him. He was there, waiting for me and it was as much personal for him as it was for me.

It was *our* girl we were making safe.

It was *our* revenge for what happened to her.

It was *our* move.

We pulled up to the Corrupt Bastards' clubhouse and there was two men standing outside by the door. I looked over at Jack about to ask how we should handle it but before I could get the words out, he drew his gun, closing one eye as he lined up his shot and pulled the trigger. The second Bastard, pulled his gun on Jack but the Bulldog was too quick, turning his gun without even aiming and shot him between the eyes.

We dismounted quickly before the rest of the men inside had a chance to ambush us. Jack reached behind him and pulled another gun from the waist band of his pants as I grabbed mine.

"Heads up," he called, throwing the gun to me. Then he reached into his jacket and grabbed another.

Jesus.

I shook it off and kept at it, kicking open the door to the clubhouse, with a gun in each hand and the Bulldog behind me pointing his guns over my shoulders at anyone who dared to take a shot at me.

"Go," he growled.

"What the fuck?"

"Incoming," shouted another.

"Too much talking, not enough shooting," Jack hissed, taking a shot over my shoulder at the first asshole to question our presence, before he took out the other one who thought it was smart to announce we arrived.

Another Bastard emerged from behind the bar holding up a rifle.

I turned slightly, Jack's arms stretched over my shoulders and we fired at him unison, watched his body arch as our bullets pierced him.

"Where the fuck is he?" Jack bellowed at the girl who ran out from the back of the bar, her bare tits bouncing as she tried to take cover.

Two more men came out from who knows where firing their guns at us, we spun around, chest to chest, each one of us acting as a suit of armor for the other. We returned fire, shooting over one another's shoulders until we put them down.

"Keep it moving," Jack ordered, and I led us toward the back where Boots was most likely hiding like the pussy he was.

"Looking for me?"

All right, so maybe he grew a pair of balls.

I spun around and there was Boots smiling back at me with a gun pointed straight at me.

"Look at you two, making nice and all. Tell me, did you two mend your differences just to pay me a visit? I'm touched. Or did you decide to let him have your daughter's pussy after all?"

"Black you going to shoot this motherfucker or am I?" Jack growled

"He's mine," I hissed, pulling the trigger on both guns at the same time Boots pulled his. Jack lurched for me, knocking me down before he threw himself down on the floor, rolled over and took another shot at Boots.

Two bullets from me and one from Jack.

Boots fell backwards as his hands moved to contain the blood pouring out of his chest.

I was quick on my feet, stepping over Jack to make my way to Boots.

Boots stared up at me, his lips quivering and eyes wide with shock.

"Told you to stay the fuck away from her didn't I?" I seethed, adrenaline coursing through every vein in my body. "I warned you not to fuck with mine," I shouted. "Now you fucking pay the price," I hissed bending down over his body and pushed the barrel of my gun between his lips. "How's your gag reflex motherfucker?" I asked before I pulled the trigger, fragments of his head splattered everywhere.

"Shit," Jack muttered, pushing off the floor. "Hate to be the one who's gotta clean this mess," he commented staring down at what was left of Boots.

I lifted my hand to my cheek, brought it back down and stared at the blood that covered my hands.

This one's for Lace.

"C'mon let's get the fuck out of here, before we're the two assholes cleaning this shit up," I said, shoving my gun into the waistband of my jeans and handing him over the other gun.

"Keep it," he said, stepping over Boots and following me out of the clubhouse. Once we were outside, he leaned against his bike and pulled out his pack of Marlboros.

"That was fun," he said with a smirk, shoving the cigarette between his lips and reaching for his lighter. "But fuck, I'm getting too old for the Cowboys and Indians shit." He lit his cigarette, and I grabbed a rag from my saddlebags and wiped the blood from my face.

Silence fell over us as I wiped my hands on the rag and pinned him with a stare.

"Let's get it over with," I started, watching as he arched one eyebrow and took a drag of cigarette. "You get one shot, right here, right now," I said, taking two strides towards him. "Make it good because it's all you're going to get."

"You think taking a swing at you will make things right between us?" he questioned, blowing out a ring of smoke before laughing in my face and shaking his head.

"So what do you want from me? You want me to apologize to you? I can't and more importantly I won't do that because apologizing would mean I regret it and I don't."

He growled or grunted, I couldn't be sure but some animalistic sound escaped his mouth as he glared at me.

"Why her?"

"Why not?"

"Really?" he questioned before he fell silent for a moment. "She's my daughter," he seethed.

"I know that," I said. "And I love her."

"Ah, fucking hell," he muttered, turning his cheek to me. I reached out and flicked the cigarette out of his mouth.

That got his attention.

"Quit that shit," I hissed. "You want to walk your girl down the aisle don't you? Stick around and see your grandchildren, no?"

"Grandchildren," he repeated, shaking his head. "I shouldn't knock you out I should shoot your ass."

"You could do that," I said, shoving my hands into my pockets as I shrugged my shoulders. "But then you'd have to tell Lacey you shot the man she loves."

"Come on, enough with that word!"

I bit the side of my cheek and tried not to smile.

He crossed his arms against his chest and kept his eyes trained on his boots for a moment.

"She's not like us, you know, she's fragile."

"She's stronger than you know," I assured him

"You really love her don't you?"

"I do."

He nodded then straddled his bike and gripped the handlebars tightly.

"You better treat her good," he said hoarsely.

"I will," I paused, before extending my hand, still speckled with Boots blood. "You have my word."

He looked at my hand before gripping it and his eyes met mine.

"Your word is gold, Black."

And just like that Jack Parrish handed me the thing he cherished most in this world…he gave me his daughter's life and told me to take care of it as my own.

It was time to tell Lacey who she belonged to.

Girl, I'm coming for you.

Chapter Forty-two

Lacey

I yawned for what seemed like the twentieth time in five minutes and glanced across the living room at Reina, who was sprawled out on the couch eating saltine crackers and sipping on ginger ale.

"Are you sure you're okay?" I questioned as I placed my hands on my knees and stood up.

"Fine, it'll pass," she insisted.

"Well, if you're sure, then I will head out. I'm exhausted," I declared, rising to my feet.

She shot up like a jack-in-the-box, nearly spilling the ginger ale all over herself as she scrambled to her feet and made a beeline for the bathroom.

So much for calling it an early night.

I followed her into the bathroom and watched as she dropped to her knees and hurled into the toilet. I bent over her, scooping up her hair and held it back as she continued to empty the contents of her stomach.

"Damn, Reina, what the hell did you eat? Maybe we should take you to the hospital, you might have food poisoning," I rambled, turning my head I felt nauseous just watching her.

"It's not food poisoning," she muttered, leaning back and taking a deep breath before she reached over and flushed the toilet. I helped her to her feet and stood behind her as she turned the faucet on and brushed her teeth.

"If it's not food poisoning what—oh my god!" I stared at her wide-eyed through the mirror.

"Yeah," she confirmed, with a mouthful of toothpaste.

I grinned as she spit into the sink and wiped her mouth.

"I'm pregnant," she confirmed, before a smile spread across her pale face. "That's the first time I said it out loud."

"Dad doesn't know yet?"

"I found out yesterday and he's been on the road," she explained, running her fingers through her long blonde hair before she turned around and looked at me. "What're you thinking?"

"I'm thinking how fucking awesome it will be having a little Parrish running around here," I grinned, pulling her into my arms. "You're going to make my dad so happy," I whispered.

"I hope so," she said as we broke apart.

"I know so," I winked at her. "Now, go lay on the couch I'll get you more ginger-ale. Did he say when he would be coming home?"

"He should've been back already," she surmised as we walked out of the bathroom. "Okay, then he should be here any minute."

I nodded toward the television.

"There's still another twenty seasons of Grey's Anatomy we can watch on Netflix until he gets home."

She laughed, and I made my way into the kitchen to grab another can of ginger ale for her.

A baby.

Wow.

That was great news, and I was genuinely happy for my father and Reina. The both of them deserved happiness and nothing brought happiness like a new life. Still, I couldn't help the ache in my heart and was ashamed to admit I was a little envious of them. Not, of the baby but of the happily ever after.

I've been sitting here, waiting and waiting and every night I went to bed alone. My dad promised me he'd have Blackie out but every night he wasn't here with me felt like an eternity. I sound selfish and I hate that because as miserable as I am, Blackie must be ten times more.

It hurts my heart knowing he's there all alone, with no one to talk to. He can't even call me or anyone for that matter since my visit when he broke the rules and touched me.

I miss his touch.

I miss the way it feels to lay my head on his chest and listen to his heart beat inside of his chest.

I miss his arms wrapped around my waist.

I miss his lips on mine

I miss his lips everywhere.

But most of all I miss the way he looks at me and smiles.

I heard the engine of a bike, glanced out the window and saw the headlights in the driveway turn off.

Dad was home.

I closed the refrigerator door, took the can and a straw out of one of the drawers when I heard my father's voice.

"Lace!"

I grabbed my jacket off the chair and draped it over my forearm, deciding it was time for me to get out of their hair and let Reina tell my dad he would get a chance at a new beginning.

I stepped out of the kitchen and spotted my father by the front door. He remained perfectly still as he stared at me for a moment with a blank expression on his face. I nervously turned to Reina who was sitting on the couch smiling.

Did she tell him already?

Then I heard the distinct sound of footsteps creeping up the front stoop. I turned my head just in time to watch as my father step to the side.

"There's my girl," Blackie rasped as he made his way inside the house.

The can of soda slipped from my fingers and rolled onto the floor as I brought my hands to my face and stared back at him in complete and utter shock.

Was he really there? In front of me?

He was.

Oh God, he was here, crooking his finger as he smiled widely at me.

A grin spread across my face as I dropped my hands and ran to him. He spread his arms wide, bent his knees as I charged at him, wrapping my arms around his neck just as he lifted me off the floor and squeezed me tight.

"Easy," he laughed.

I squealed in delight, pulling back to take his face in my hands and pepper him with kisses. I finally stopped, threaded my fingers through his hair brushing it away from his face.

"You're really here," I whispered, unable to stop smiling.

"Yeah, I am," he said huskily, leaning his forehead against mine. "God, I missed your face." He pressed his lips to my nose, leaned back and touched them to my forehead before finally letting them brush over mine.

He slowly planted me back on my feet, taking both my hands in his and stared back at me.

"Time for you and me to go home, girl."

My face was going to hurt from smiling so much. Then I remembered we had an audience, and I looked over my shoulder at my father. He stared back at me, watching intently as Blackie wrapped our joined hands around my waist and pulled my back against his chest.

"Go give the poor guy a hug because he ain't going to see you for a while," he said against my ear, dropping his voice even lower when he spoke again. "You're going to be busy for about a month," he ground out, as he let go of my hands and dropped his mouth to my shoulder kissing me softly then stepped back.

I hurried over to my dad, wrapped my arms around him and kissed his cheek.

"Thank you," I told him, pulling back to meet his gaze. "Thank you so much."

"Take good care of each other," he muttered.

I gave him another peck on the cheek before turning to Reina and hugging her tightly.

I spun around and Blackie was holding out his hand for me to take.

"You ready?"

"For what?"

"The rest of your life," he said simply, pulling me against his side as he slung his arm over my shoulders and escorted me to the door. Blackie took me away from my father's house and brought me back to the pages of our story because we still had a lot of story to write.

An entire lifetime.

BLACKIE

I got my queen.

She was on the back of my bike, her arms wrapped tightly around me as we rode in silence to the house *she* made a home.

She was safe.

And we were both free of the demons that held us captive.

Free to be the people we were meant to be.

Leather.

Lace.

Me.

Her.

A love story no one saw coming but one that was perfect.

I pulled my bike into our driveway, killed the engine and glanced over my shoulder at the beauty who was already scrambling to get off the bike. She pulled my arms, walking backwards as she dragged me to the front door.

I'd never get tired of looking at that face or seeing that smile.

That smile and those dark eyes that was all I needed.

No drugs.

No alcohol.

I never wanted to be numb again because feeling everything she provoked in me was the sweet temptations that made life worth living.

Give me all you got girl.

And I'll give you all of me.

Her arms snaked around my waist as I tried to find the key, causing me to stop what I was doing and glance down at her dainty fingers that splayed against me stomach. I laid my hand over hers and turned the key, taking her hand I pulled her around me and lifted her into my arms. I kicked the door open and carried her into the house.

I thought I had it all figured out.

I figured I had the good, lost it and never would have it again.

But I had nothing until I had everything.

Until I had her.

I didn't bother turning on the lights as I kicked the door close and started straight for the stairs, to the bedroom that was now ours because there was no way in hell I was letting her leave me now. She'd move in with, paint every room in this house a crazy color, but this was her home now.

I was her home.

And she was mine.

I sat her down on the foot of the bed and took a step backwards.

"We'll talk," I started, shrugging my leather jacket off. "We'll talk until there is nothing left to say but not now."

She unzipped her jacket and drew the sleeves down her arms.

"Not now," she agreed.

"I need a quick shower," I groaned, staring at her mouth as she wet her lips with her tongue.

"Go," she ordered. "You have five minutes."

I let out a laugh as she pulled out the rubber band that was holding her hair back, letting her hair fall in waves around her face.

"Blackie, you keep staring at me like that and I'll take your five minutes away. The only reason I'm even agreeing to it is because I know you're probably dying to take a shower in your own house."

"Lots of things I'm dying to do, girl," I hissed, reaching behind me and pulling my shirt over my head. "Got a lot of time to make up for."

"Shower. Now." She demanded, pointing her finger toward the bathroom, then her eyes zeroed in on my chest and her hand dropped. "When did you get that?" she asked, stood from the bed and walked over to me.

I glanced down at my chest and ran my fingers over the music notes that covered my left pec.

"Before I went away," I revealed, dropping my hands to my jeans and continued to undress, drawing the zipper down.

She stepped closer, brushing away my hands and forcing them to my sides.

"Why music notes?" she asked as traced the ink on my chest.

"To remind me of a dance I had with the girl I love…," I dipped my eyes to the tattoo. "…to a song I never knew existed until she asked me to dance with her."

"Leather and lace," she whispered, lifting her eyes to mine.

"Love you, Lace," I murmured, bending my head to cover her mouth with mine.

It took all the self-control I could muster up inside of me to pull away from her, knowing when I let myself take her there would be no end in sight.

She moaned as my teeth grazed her lower lip.

"Blackie."

"Five minutes," I promised, releasing her lip before I turned around and walked straight into the bathroom.

"Three!" She shouted from behind the door.

I laughed as I turned on the water and took the quickest shower of my life. Tomorrow I'd take one for an hour and enjoy the little things like showering in the comfort of my own house and not a fucking federal prison.

Tonight, I'd enjoy the bigger things, like fucking my girl, making up for every night I couldn't.

I opened the door and walked into the bedroom, stopping dead in my tracks when I spotted Lacey in the middle of the bed wearing nothing but a sheet tucked under her arms.

"You were longer than five minutes," she pointed out, cocking her head to the side as her hair fell over one shoulder.

"We got all night, girl," I said, walking toward the bed. "All night, every night, forever."

She smiled as she raised herself up on her knees, hugging the sheet over her breasts.

"Lose the towel," she ordered.

"Lose the sheet," I demanded as I brought my hand to the knot hanging low on my waist.

I watched as she drew her lip between her teeth and diverted her eyes to my waist, walking on her knees to the edge of the bed as she clutched the sheet to her chest. I took another step, my knees hit the edge of the mattress and just as I reached for the sheet she reached for my towel.

She threw her head back and laughed, swinging the towel in the air, claiming victory.

But the victory was all mine because the sheet fell from her body, exposing the body I have been dreaming about, night after night. Her laughter died when I reached out and grabbed her hips.

"God, you're perfect," I muttered, bending my head to press my mouth against her shoulder blade. "So, fucking perfect," I growled against her skin.

Her hands snaked around my neck as my mouth crossed her collar bone and kissed her other shoulder. I worked my hands up her sides until they found the sides of her tits. I bent my knees, bringing myself eye-level with them, taking one erect nipple between my teeth.

Lacey's nails dug into my neck as I tugged on her nipple before flicking my tongue over the sensitive flesh.

"I like that," she gasped. "Give me more," she demanded.

I moved to her other breast, rolled the puckered nipple between my fingers, tugging on it before I dropped my head and sucked it into my mouth.

"That's it," she murmured. "So good."

I released her nipple, straightening up and let out a groan as my cock brushed against her stomach.

"Lay back," I growled. "And spread your legs."

She did as she was told, playing with her tits as she laid her back against the mattress and spread her legs as wide as she could. I wormed my way between her legs, spreading her pussy, coating my fingers with her wetness.

I had gone straight to hell, got myself kicked out and came home to the sweetest heaven known to man.

"Missed this," I growled, as my fingers pressed against her clit and sent her squirming beneath me. Her hips arched, her body begging for more as a moan escaped her lips. I removed my fingers and peered up at her as I trailed the same two fingers up the center of her body, to her mouth.

Her lips parted, and she took my fingers into her mouth, sucking what was left of her off them.

Fucking lucky.

So, fucking lucky.

I pulled my fingers back and charged them into her tight cunt.

"That's a girl," I rasped as she clenched around my fingers making me work to slide them in and out of her.

That tight cunt was all mine.

Only man to get inside that heaven.

Her hips lifted off the mattress and rotated against my hand.

"Get it, girl, work for it baby," I said, letting her pussy take my hand and work it to her advantage. I fisted my cock with my free hand, stroking the beast as she quickened the pace of her hips, riding my hand until she came.

"Give it to me, girl, work that pussy," I commanded.

"Keep talking, dirty," she pleaded, as she brought both hands up and threaded her fingers through her hair. Her tits bounced up and down with every thrust of her hips, driving me fucking crazy. I hadn't fucked in months and if she kept at it, this shit would end real fast.

"Let me pull my fingers out of your cunt and give you my mouth."

"More," she yelled, shaking her head from side to side, detangling her fingers from her hair to grab her tits.

What a fucking sight.

No dream compared.

I ripped my fingers from her pulsing cunt and bent my head to her bare pussy glistening with her arousal and licked her up and down before flicking my tongue over her clit.

"Goddamn it yes, Blackie, give it to me," she pleaded. "Give me all of you."

Always, girl.

Until the day I die.

My teeth grazed the bundle of nerves and her hips bucked as she began to slowly ride my mouth, quickly finding a rhythm that suited her. Her hands found the back of my head and pressed my face against her cunt.

"That's my girl, take it," I hissed against her heat before diving back into her.

And I'll keep giving it.

"I'm going to come again," she panted. "Oh God."

Cover me girl.

I was going to lose my fucking mind if I didn't get some kind of relief. My dick felt like a piece of steel between my legs that was going to explode any minute.

Patience.

Take what she's giving.

My tongue lapped at her as she came down from the orgasm, her legs spread wider and her back dropped back down onto the mattress.

"Oh that was so good," she exclaimed breathless. I pushed back on my knees and took a deep breath as I watched her chest rise and fall. I grabbed my cock, wiped the pre-come on the head of my cock before lifting my eyes to hers.

"If I don't fuck you now I'm going to explode," I huffed, groaning as I watched her move onto her knees.

"I want to be on top," she expressed.

I fucking loved that she wasn't shy in the bedroom, demanding what she wanted of me and taking it. I rolled over onto my back and slapped my hands against my thighs.

"Get on," I urged.

She smiled as she straddled me, teasing my cock by rubbing her pussy against it.

"I'm not going to last that long if you keep doing that, girl," I grunted.

She leaned forward, her lips hovering over mine as her eyes found mine.

"Kiss me," she whispered. "I dreamt of your kisses every night I didn't have you with me," she revealed.

I reached for her face, cupping her cheeks and brought her mouth down to mine. She moaned into my mouth as I pried her lips apart and slid my tongue inside her.

Taste good, girl?

That's all you.

I got drunk on that taste.

I got high on that taste.

Now it's your turn.

She reached down, wrapped her hand around my cock and guided it to her cunt before she lifted herself only to lower herself onto my cock, taking inch by inch until she was stretched and full.

God, girl.

She tore her mouth from mine, splayed her palms flat against my chest and worked her hips, riding my cock like she was a fucking jockey.

Christ, what the fuck happened to little miss innocent.

Me.

Let's ride, girl.

I grabbed her ass and pushed off the mattress, charging my cock into her repeatedly before she slammed my back onto the mattress and shook her head.

"This is all me," she purred. "You just lay back and let me welcome you home babe," she whispered, lifting off me. "Look down, watch me take your cock and know I'm going to be taking it for the rest of our lives."

Dead.

I was fucking dead.

"Look!" She shouted as she lowered herself onto me, forcing me to watch my cock disappear inside of her.

She took my hands and placed them on her tits.

"Watch me fuck you, Blackie," she hissed, as she rotated her hips and leaned forward, finding friction as she rubbed her clit against my pelvic bone. I reached up and took her nipple into my mouth before she pushed me down again and quickened her pace. I wrapped my arms around her and grabbed a hold of her ass while she worked me over.

Her hair stuck to her face and her breath came out in short pants as her tits bounced in my face. I lost my fucking mind and felt my release threaten to explode.

I gritted my teeth and tried to hang onto it a little longer.

"Fuck me, girl. You're so goddamn pretty when you're riding my cock," I growled. "Shit, I'm going to lose it, Lace," I warned.

"Give it to me," she hissed. "Fucking give it to me, Blackie…I can't hold it anymore," she cried.

I grunted, as her pussy constricted around my cock and grabbed her hips and pulled her off me before slamming her down on me once…twice…three times.

She screamed out as I let go of her hips and came inside of her. Her sweet cunt took every drop I gave before she collapsed on top of me.

"Welcome home, babe," she breathed, dropping her head against my chest. I was half dead but wrapped one arm around her, squeezed her tightly, and pressed a kiss to the top of her head.

"Thank you," I whispered against her hair. "Look at me," I commanded. She lifted her head off my chest and stared back at me.

So pretty.

I reached out and tucked her hair behind her ears before cupping her face with my palms.

"Thank you…," I repeated hoarsely. "…for showing me how to smile again. I'm not grateful for much in this world, but I'll thank God every day, for the rest of my life, you came into the clubhouse that day and forced me to look at you, to see you, my angel, the same girl who has been right in front of me for years. You stuck with me, girl, saw me through the ugly and gave me the good I thought I'd never see."

She smiled at me.

And I knew that smile was my saving grace.

She opened her mouth to speak but I quickly placed my index finger to her lips.

"Not done yet," I told her, removed my finger and leaned forward to press my lips to hers because I couldn't stare at that mouth and not claim it every single time.

"Thank you, for loving me and helping me rewrite my life," I rasped.

"Your story," she corrected, swallowing hard before she reached for my face and leaned her forehead against mine. "Our story," she decided. "And there are so many blank pages left for us to scribe."

"Our story," I agreed, closing my eyes momentarily before opening them and staring into the dark eyes that owned my soul. "You want a preview of what those blank pages will say?"

"Oh, you know think you know the way it ends?"

"Never ends, girl," I whispered. "Even after the ink is dry and all the pages are full, they'll still be a place where our story is told. I'm not much for the afterlife but I know without a shadow of a doubt this thing you and I are writing doesn't end because the pages run out or time for that matter…it keeps going. The story goes on long after we've said our final goodbyes, it lives on in the eyes of the kids we'll make together."

"Kids?" she croaked.

"A house full," I confirmed with a quirk of my lips. "I got big plans for us," I added, winking at her as her smile spread even wider.

Those pages are going to be full of her smile. They'll tell the story of a man and woman who stuck by each other's side. A woman who breathed life into a man and a man who kept her safe. I'd be the man that kept my angels halo shining.

"I love you," she whispered. "I love you so much, Dominic Petra."

"I love you too, with everything I am and everything I'm capable of being now."

"I'm so glad you're home," she exclaimed as she laid her head back on my chest and wrapped her arms around me tightly.

Thank you for giving me the best fucking homecoming ever.

But you're home now too.

This is your home girl.

Me.

You.

Home.

The End

Epilogue

BLACKIE

I pulled the car into the driveway, turned it off and left the keys in the ignition. I reached over and grabbed the two bouquets of flowers, tucking them under my arm before reaching for the iced coffee and the bag I picked up from the drugstore. I got out of the car and walked over to my bike, placed one of the bouquets in my saddlebag before I climbed the steps to my house and opened the front door.

"Lace," I called as I kicked the door shut and started for the kitchen. I glanced around the aqua blue kitchen, dropped the flowers and coffee onto the counter and teared open the tiny white bag. I pulled out Lacey's prescription bottle and replaced it with the empty bottle next to the coffee pot.

I'm so proud of my girl.

There aren't too many people who get diagnosed with a debilitating illness and find the strength to conquer it. Day after day, Lacey wakes up, turns on the coffeepot and takes her meds and starts her day. She had lived thirteen years in silence, afraid of the judgements and what would happen if she admitted she was sick.

She's not silent anymore.

But her maker was.

That's not saying there aren't days when she needs a little extra reassurance, when I tell her I love her more than usual. It's those days I hold her close and talk about the future with her. I give her the good, make her dream, and promise to make them come true and then I'll dance with her. The few times her mind tried to torment her, she'd look at me with those sad eyes and I'd know she was struggling. I'd ask her to dance with me and be reminded of the first time we danced. I didn't know it then, but she was battling her maker that day too.

I try my best, but in the end it's Lacey who defeats that bitch of a maker. Girl's stronger than she knows, stronger than all of us put together. She makes broken look beautiful and strong look invincible.

I heard her hurry down the stairs and braced my hands on the counter, waiting for her burst into the room like a tornado. She was always late…and usually it's my fault but, today that shit was all on her.

"I'm so late," she groaned, skidding to a halt when she spotted the coffee and flowers on the counter and lifted her eyes to me. "What's this?"

I laughed, stepping around the counter to stand in front of her. "I knew you wouldn't have time to stop," I said, tipping my chin to the coffee.

"And the flowers?" she smiled, reached for the bouquet and brought the flowers to her nose.

"I wanted to," I replied, closing my hand over hers and dragged the flowers down so I could bend my head and take her mouth.

I wrapped one arm around her waist and pressed against the small of her back until her body was flush against mine and she moaned.

"You're going to make me even later aren't you," she murmured against my lips.

Normally, I'd sway her, throw her over my shoulder or onto the counter and make her forget all about being late but not today.

She had to go to work.

I had to take care of business and start writing the next chapter of our story.

"No," I said, pulling back and pressing a kiss to the tip of her nose. "We'll pick this up later tonight, when I don't have to rush and can give you everything you want and you can give me that scream you make— "

Her hand covered my mouth but didn't hide the humor reflected in her eyes. I wrapped my hand around her wrist and kissed it before bringing it back to her side.

"I've got to go to the clubhouse but after your meeting I'll meet you and we'll go for dinner," I told her, pushing her hair over her shoulder. "And then we'll come home and you can scream all you want," I promised, winking at her.

"Sounds like a great night," she grinned, taking another kiss for the road before she turned around and grabbed her coffee. "Love you," she called over her shoulder.

"Love you too, girl," I replied and followed her out the door. She got into her car as I straddled my bike, both engines came to life and we went our separate ways.

Lacey went to work saving souls, and I went to visit one.

I pulled into the cemetery, grabbed the flowers from my saddlebag and headed up the hill to the grave I visited weekly because I was a man of my word and promised Christine I'd keep bringing her flowers as long as I kept breathing.

I don't bring two bouquets anymore, and I don't ask for extra baby's breath either. I removed the old flowers and replaced them with the new bunch. Her name was visible, and that's okay because it allows the world to know Christine Petra was a part of it, that she was here just for a short time but enough time to leave a mark.

She left a mark on me and will always have a spot in my heart.

"Hey babe," I started, crouching down in front of the headstone and traced my thumb over her name. "So it's not Saturday, but I thought we'd switch it up a bit," I explained. "I've got something kind of big going down tonight and I couldn't help but think about the first time I did what I'm about to do."

I grinned, recalling the memory I used to hate revisiting.

"I was so goddamn nervous with you," I confessed. "Maybe because we were so young and I had no fucking idea what I was doing, what I was asking of you and what I was promising to be myself. I had no clue what it took to make it work or how hard it sometimes could be, I thought it was the next step for us and so it seemed right. I'm glad I did. I'm glad you said yes and let me put that ring on your finger. It was good, Chris, we were good for a while and when I think of you, I think of the good. No more bad memories, not anymore. Now, when I think of you I don't think about the last time I saw you but of all the times before, when you were full of life…the times when you smiled. Your smile was the mark you left on this world and that's how you should be remembered. So, that's what I'm going to remember…your smile."

I stood tall, pressed my finger tips to my lips and touched the top of her stone.

"Check in from time to time, stay with me, I'll make you proud and maybe I'll even make you smile from time to time."

I dropped my hand and shoved both of them into my pockets as I stared down at her name one final time.

"Rest easy, girl." I whispered before turning around and heading back to my bike.

One more stop.

And then it was game time.

Time to go all in and throw out the wild card.

I made my way to the Dog Pound and spotted Jack leaning against his Harley smoking a cigarette. I pulled up next to him and killed my engine before I turned and met his stare.

"You're late," he grunted.

"No, I'm not," I argued, throwing my leg over my bike.

"Well, what the hell is the big emergency?" he growled, flicking his cigarette into the street.

"And here I thought you'd be happy to see my face," I quipped.

I reached into my pocket, pulled out a box and dropped it from one hand into another, repeating the move over and over as I tried to figure out what the fuck to say to the man who was my brother.

I'm not going to lie and tell you things aren't different between me and Jack. I'm no long his friend, his vice president and his partner. I'm the man he trusts with his daughter, not just her safety, not just her life, but her heart.

It took some getting used to.

There were lines drawn in the sand.

But in the end, Jack knew I loved Lacey more than anything.

He respected that.

And he took a step back.

Now it was my turn to show him the respect.

"Whatcha got there, Black?" he questioned, blowing out a deep breath as he stared at the tiny box in my hand.

I lifted my eyes to his as I extended my hand and offered him the box.

"Shit," he muttered, taking the box from my hands and lifted his eyes back to mine. "Is this what I think it is?"

I nodded as I crossed my arms against my chest.

"Open it," I urged.

He glanced down at the box in his hands and hesitated a moment before he snapped it open and drew in a deep breath.

"I love her, Jack but you already know that. I want to marry her. I want to give her my name but I won't do that without your blessing."

I watched as he closed the box and looked back at me.

"There isn't a goddamn thing on this earth I wouldn't do for her. I'll take good care of her. I'll give her whatever she wants and I'll make sure she— "

"Shut up," he interrupted, handing me back the box. "You don't have to plead your case to me, Black."

He ran his hand over his head.

"At least you'll make an honest woman out of her," he grunted, reminding me how much it burned his ass that Lacey moved in with me as soon as I got released from prison.

He sighed, reached out and grabbed my shoulder.

"Real happy for you, Black. It took me a while to get over that it's Lacey that makes you happy," he admitted. "You'll understand one day, when you have kids of your own. They get under you man, they make your heart so big and so full you don't know how you ever lived without them." He swallowed, took a second and then continued.

"You got my blessing."

"I was going to do it with or without it," I joked.

"I hope you have ten daughters," he spat.

"I hope so too," I said, grinning as I pocketed the ring and stared back at him.

"See you on the other side, *brother*," he rasped, leaning back against his bike. "Go on, go get your girl."

I nodded as I straddled my bike and gripped the handlebars.

Time to draw that final card.

Time to start write chapter.

Girl, I'm coming for you.

Bonus Epilogue

Lacey

I graduated college one year to the date with a degree in social work. When I first started college, I was like every other ordinary freshman, having no idea what I wanted to do and no major. College was just one big party and the thing you did to make your parents proud.

Then life happened.

Blackie happened.

Someone who had been in my life for so many years became my life. Our perfectly imperfect love started with two people chasing away the demons that dragged the other down.

For me it was my mind.

For him it was his addictions and his grief.

I was just a girl with a crush who fell in love with the bad boy and waited for him to open his eyes and see me standing before him.

He was just a man who had given up on himself, a man who resolved never to smile and enjoy life, a man who didn't think he was worthy.

He opened his eyes and looked right through me, down to the depths of my soul. I don't know who realized first, if it was him or me, that discovered we each held the other half of one another's soul.

We're not perfect.

Far from it.

And our struggles didn't just disappear because we fell in love. I'll always be bi-polar and he'll always be a recovering addict. Our battles are different yet the same both result in extreme highs and desperate lows but we're stronger than the things that try to bring us down.

Together, my maker and his addictions don't stand a chance.

I see him smile and I can face the world, my mind is just another hurdle I can conquer and the best part of that is knowing I do the same for him. That smile is all the inspiration I need to be a survivor of mental illness and mine is all he needs to be a survivor of substance abuse.

I glanced around the room of people and smiled at them, hoping they found the smile in the world that saved them.

"Who wants to begin today?" I asked the group.

"I'd like to," said a familiar voice, startling me and forcing me to turn my head to the door and the man standing there smiling at me.

My savior.

My Leather.

I am a social worker and I work for the Woman's Health Center as well as Addiction Angel, a local Staten Island organization that helps addicts get into a rehabilitation program suited for them. I also volunteer one night a week at the Y.M.C.A. and run the Narcotics Anonymous group.

Blackie has attended my meetings and has spoken about his struggles as an addict, inspiring the people I work with on a daily basis.

However, I wasn't expecting him tonight. In fact, when I left the house he kissed me goodbye and told me he was going to the clubhouse.

He walked toward the circle of people, pulled out an empty chair but didn't sit down as he kept his eyes pinned to me.

"My name is Dominic Petra, or Blackie to some," he said, winking at me. "And I'm a recovering addict." He glanced around the room, looking at all the faces and recognizing the torment reflected in their eyes. "I have been sober and clean for thirty-eight months."

A round of applause erupted from the circle as he turned his attention back to me.

"Thank you," he said, as he pointed to me. "But I wouldn't have been able to kick my habits and stay clean if it wasn't for this woman right here."

I smiled at him.

"That, right there," he whispered, shaking his head slightly as he continued to stare at me but speak to the room of people looking at him, wishing for a sliver of hope.

"That smile," he continued. "It's my why, my purpose and my hope. It's that smile that reminds me I've got a whole lot of life left inside of me. I don't need drugs to numb me I've got something that makes me feel the good stuff I forgot existed, like love, like joy and instead of dreading the future I learned to reach for it."

He took another step closer.

Then another.

He stood before me.

"Why would I ever want to be numb again when I've got someone who makes me feel like I'm on top of the world?"

I swallowed against the lump in my throat as fresh tears filled my eyes.

"Why would I send myself to hell when I have an angel who brings me to heaven?" he whispered.

Then I watched in shock as he dropped onto one knee in the middle of the circle, his lips quirked as he reached into his leather jacket.

"Why would I ever want anything other than her?"

He pulled out a tiny black velvet box and flipped the lid open.

"I wouldn't," he answered his own question. "I don't want anything other than you, girl. You brought me back to life, gave me a second chance, one I didn't think I deserved, but you insisted I did. Thank you for that. Thank you for being the angel who rescued me and showed me how to smile again. You've given me so much but there's one more thing I'm going to ask of you…marry me, Lace, give me forever, let me be the one who shows you the good and the beautiful… let me give you my leather and take from you your lace."

When you find yourself at the end of your story and you think there is nothing left, I hope you'll think of me and Blackie and realize there's always a chance for a rewrite.

Remember to smile.

Remember society doesn't get to label you.

Remember life is good even when it's bad.
Remember you are stronger than you know.
Remember me.
Remember him.
Remember Leather and Lace.

And know that what doesn't kill you makes you stronger and your temptations are only lethal if you let them be.

"Of course I'll marry you," I whispered. "There isn't a single thing in this world I've ever wanted more than to be your queen."

Remember to play your cards until the end.

ETERNAL TEMPTATIONS

JANINE INFANTE BOSCO

Chapter One

Grace

Everyone loved him.
The way he walked.
The way he talked.
The clothes he wore.
The smile he adorned when he was victoriously acquitted time after time—crime after crime. In the public eye he was cocky, arrogant, a man confident in his ability to beat the odds. To me he was just the man I fell in love with when I was sixteen years old.

Victor Pastore was more than what society thought he was. He was more than a criminal, not just a notorious gangster conquering the streets of New York, he was my first love.

And my last.

I lost my love somewhere along the journey. He became the kingpin and the Vic I knew, the man with a big heart and bigger values, that man died. If I had to put a time stamp on when it happened, I'd say it was right after Michael Valente was murdered. Michael was my husband's underboss and he and his wife, Maryann, were our best friends. Michael, or Val to most, stepped into the line of fire when a rival organization tried to take down Victor. Val sacrificed his life for Vic's and my husband could never make peace with that. His mission in life no longer was to keep rising but to seek revenge for the blood of his brother.

Everything else faded including me and our two girls. He severed his relationship with our eldest daughter, Adrianna, by sending her boyfriend, Anthony, who was also his enforcer, to jail. He planned to have Anthony avenge Val's death in prison but the man he thought was responsible, someone they called the G-Man, was transferred. At the time Vic's connections didn't run that deep. Anthony spent three years in jail for a crime he didn't commit and never got the chance to commit the one Vic sent him to do.

He barely paid any mind to our youngest, Nicole, and I started to think of that as a blessing in disguise. Nikki pushed forward with no validation from her father, made a life for herself without Victor hovering over her. I reasoned that since he didn't have a hand in her happiness then he couldn't rip it away like he did with her sister.

I tried to make sense of Victor's actions, especially after we found out that Adrianna was pregnant but there was no talking to him. That's when I mourned the man I loved and realized I was married to a stranger.

Adrianna and Anthony lost that baby and each other.
Victor lost his daughter.
And me? I watched the foundation of our marriage crumble.

It's grueling to watch your child suffer, knowing your husband ultimately caused every bit of her pain. Adrianna not only suffered a miscarriage but the heartbreak of losing Anthony. She wound up meeting someone, and though her heart was elsewhere she found solace in the attention Vinny provided. A part of me thinks if Victor would've stepped up, Adrianna wouldn't have been looking for someone to pay her attention and lick her wounds. But then I wouldn't have my beautiful grandson Luca, I'm a firm believer that life works in mysterious ways.

For a brief pause after Luca's birth my Victor came back to us. He took one look at that little boy and his heart grew ten times in size. Luca became Victor's chance at redemption and I even started to think he'd be able to repair his relationship with Adrianna. A baby is one of life's most beautiful blessings and Luca's birth was just what our family needed to mend.

I'll never forget finding Victor in the corridor of the hospital, staring at Anthony as he watched Luca through the window of the nursery. I looked into my husband's eyes and saw regret, something he never expressed in all our years together.

Anthony was there when Adrianna went into labor and he never left her side. He watched that boy take his first breath and when we arrived at the hospital we found him in the hallway looking at the boy, wishing he was his. He may not have been Luca's biological father but God made him his dad.

Things started to look up for our family; Victor was around more, spending quality time with the girls and Luca. He was still on the rise, his empire grew both financially and in power making him the ultimate mob boss and his organization trumped all others.

I foolishly believed he put his quest for revenge behind him.

Like everyone else I believed he was invincible, his empire indestructible. Victor Pastore would reign over the streets he loved forever and I'd be the woman standing in his shadow, perfectly content with him having his glory, knowing he wasn't the type of man you held back. I watched Victor soar to the top and knew my place was to be the one who grounded him when he needed the reminder that beneath the Teflon he was a husband, a father and now a grandfather.

Then the call came that Val's wife had tragically died in a car accident, leaving their son, Michael, the sole survivor of their family. Vic harbored guilt that he didn't step up and take care of Mike and Maryann after Val died and so he thought he could make up for that by bringing Val's son into the fold.

Victor was opening a new night club called Temptations and his plan was to give Mike a legit opportunity to make something of himself. He wanted to bring him back home, have Michael manage Temptations and hoped to fix another broken relationship. I commended him for trying to do the right thing, even if it took him a while to figure out what that was.

My husband was repairing the relationships he severed bringing hope back to our family.

Life was good.

But it usually is before it turns bad.

The night Temptations opened began the descent of a mob boss. We learned the hard way that even the most powerful men sometimes get knocked off their throne.

I don't know if I was too naïve or simply immune to the life we dangerously lived but I never saw the disaster that was heading straight for us—the end of Victor Pastore.

The destruction of an empire.

The death of a man.

The ruination of a family.

The end of Victor and Grace.

The buzzer rang, dragging me away from my thoughts and forcing me back to the reality of what we had become. I spot him immediately, sitting in the far left corner of the packed visitor's room in the federal penitentiary.

This is our life now.

We're doing a life sentence.

He's paying for his crimes behind bars and I'm paying for them in an empty bed.

His head is bowed as he stares down at his hands that are neatly folded on the table. I freeze in my tracks, taking a moment to stare at the man I so deeply love despite his flaws. A sad smile spreads across my lips as I take in his appearance, noticing his hair has grayed even more so than the last time I saw him. He aged well, his features the same as they were when we first met, only now there are faint lines on his face that tell his life story. He's still the most handsome man I ever laid eyes on.

I was transfixed back to that night when our world crumbled, staring adoringly at my husband, unbeknownst to him, I studied him through the eyes of the rest of the world.

It was opening night and Temptations' capacity seemed to be at its limit. Everywhere you turned people were smiling, laughing or dancing.

The music blaring from the impressive sound system faded away and was replaced by Vic's laughter. It was easy to see why people were drawn toward his larger-than-life personality. He owned the room. The people surrounding us hung onto his every word but when he turned around and stared into my eyes as he wrapped his arm around me, he was just Vic, the man beneath the designer suit.

Success.

It was the number one word in Victor's vocabulary. He did nothing half-assed, always gave one hundred percent, and this club was no exception. From the marble floors to the over-the-top sound system, my husband didn't skimp on one tiny detail. The extreme flashiness was what people had come to expect from Victor.

He boisterously laughed at a joke Jimmy was telling, turned to me and the laughter died in his eyes, replaced with something foreign yet familiar...love and affection. He bent his head, pressing his lips to mine; I closed my eyes feeling nostalgic as one kiss reminded me of the thirty-five years of kisses we shared.

"I love you, Gracie," he murmured, pulling back from my lips staring into my eyes as the back of his hand caressed my cheek.

I wish I had of taken a photograph of him, of us, and the last time we were together when everything was just as it was when we were young.

Before the mob.

Before the suit.

Before I lost Victor to a life full of crime.

He lifts his head, turning it slightly and our eyes lock.

Nostalgic.

"Behind every great man is an even greater woman who made him this way. You're my greatness, Grace, and I want you by my side forever…say you'll marry me."

Tragic.

"It's time, Gracie. I'm turning myself in."

Bittersweet.

"It doesn't matter that I'm here and you're there…you'll always be my love, Gracie."

I walk toward him watching as he rises to greet me, stepping around the table to pull my chair out. While most inmates aren't allowed to touch their visitors, Victor seems to be the exception to the rule. Openly wrapping his arms around me he squeezes me tight like I'm his salvation. I relish in his touch.

Several moments pass before he breaks our embrace and motions for me to take a seat, pushing my chair under the table once I do.

Always a gentleman.

His fingertips graze my shoulder before he walks back to his seat and stares back at me.

"My Gracie," he whispers, smiling faintly as he reaches for my hand.

It doesn't get easier.

Every visit is another knife to my heart.

And when I leave here I know I'll feel empty inside and wish I never came because seeing him like this, knowing all we have is an hour surrounded by strangers and a few stolen touches, is my damnation.

But then I tell myself if I don't have these moments, I have none, and I need to cherish them just as I cherished every moment we shared in our life together.

"How are you?" he rasps. "How are my girls?"

I reach into my pocket and pull out the few photos I was allowed to bring him and place them on the table between us. Releasing my hand, he lifts the photos, handling them with such care, like they are a fine piece of china.

"Oh God," he breathes. "Is this…" His voice trails off as he turns the photo around to face me.

I smile warmly, knowing very well how much he needs my smile at this moment.

"That's your granddaughter, Victoria Grace," I reveal, introducing him to Adrianna and Anthony's daughter. The little girl I held in my arms minutes after she was born. The same girl Vic will never come face to face with.

"She's beautiful," he says, turning the picture back and staring at it in awe.

"She is," I agree. "She weighed seven pounds, three ounces, just like Adrianna did when she was born," I continue. "Both Anthony and I were in the room when she gave birth. I swear, Victor, I have never seen anything more beautiful, and I don't mean the birth but all the love surrounding it. It happened so quickly, well not really, she was in labor for nearly twenty hours, but when that little girl was ready to make her grand entrance it was beautiful chaos. Adrianna was crying, the poor thing was exhausted, but Anthony grabbed her hands, held them tight and forced her to look at him…" I pause, taking a minute to recall the moment myself before lifting my eyes back to Vic's and noting that he is hanging on my every word.

These were the moments we should have been sharing together. Instead, I have to create them with words and Vic has to experience the birth of our granddaughter through my eyes.

"Adrianna focused on Anthony, kept her eyes locked with his as she pushed and not a minute later their baby girl's cries filled the room," I whisper. "It was precious."

"I bet it was," he breathes, placing the photo of Victoria on the table before lifting the next one. "Luca is getting so big," he marvels, laughing at the photo of our grandson with a backward Yankee cap, pointing to his shirt that read *'Don't even think about dating my sister'*. "Anthony's training him young," he jokes, showing me the photograph.

"You're not kidding," I confirm.

"He's a good father," he says huskily, taking a deep breath. "A real good father."

He placed Luca's photo next to his sister's and lifted the next.

"Look at her smile," he whispers as he studied our daughter, Nikki's, picture. I had taken it right after Michael proposed to her. I'm not sure she had even said yes before the flash went off.

Victor lifted his gaze to mine.

"Was she surprised?"

"She was shocked. I believe her first words were 'get the fuck out of here' and then she said yes," I wink at him, sharing a knowing look that our daughter was a spitfire. "And then she cried."

"Why?"

"Because Michael told…" I pause, blinking away the tears that suddenly fill my eyes as I recall my daughter breaking down after Michael revealed he had visited with Victor. "…he told her they had your blessing and he had asked you for her hand in marriage."

He smiled widely as he wiped at his own eyes.

"You'll walk her down the aisle won't you?"

"Yes," I promise.

He nodded.

"Get her whatever dress she wants. I don't care what it costs, you make sure she has everything she wants. If you need extra money you go to Jack Parrish, he'll give you whatever you need."

"Okay, Vic," I reply softly, watching as he looks away for a minute.

"You know I'm happy," he whispers. "I am," he assures me, turning around so I can look him in the eye. "I'm happy because I know that my two daughters will be taken care of, that they have men in their lives that will truly do anything to keep them happy and will love them like they deserve to be loved."

"Yes, we're very fortunate that our daughters have found happiness."

"There is one girl I'm worried about though," he confesses. "You."

"I'm fine, Victor," I admonish.

"No you're not and it's my fault. I promised to take care of you and love you all the days of my life. I vowed to share a life with you and left you to live it alone. I love you, Gracie, and I'll never go back on that promise I made when I said I'd love you until death do us part."

"I love you too, Victor," I say quietly, reaching across the table to take hold of both his hands. "And our life may not have gone as we planned but I don't regret a single thing."

"I regret not being home as much as I should have been. I regret not enjoying the little things I took for granted, like tripping over your slippers on the way out the door or when I'd walk in and find you sleeping on the couch with a book tucked under your nose. I miss the little things, Gracie. I miss watching you sing on Sunday mornings while you made me meatballs. I really miss your meatballs," he quips, winking at me before reaching across the table to wipe away my tears with his fingers.

"Life is too short for regrets, Vic, and while we may only have these visits now, we'll have eternity together," I vow.

"Grace," he starts, dropping his hand from my face as he draws in a harsh breath.

"I mean it, Victor, I believe that with my whole heart. You have to believe it too because these visits aren't the last of us," I exaggerate.

"Gracie, they're moving me again," he says regretfully.

"What?" I swallow. "Where?"

"Down south," he answers. "The lawyer will fill you in on all the details," he adds as his eyes do a quick sweep of the room. "It's the last leg of the plan."

"Oh for heaven's sake," I hiss. "To hell with the plan!"

"Lower your voice," he pleads.

"No, Victor, I will not. Look at you, this is it, do you realize that? You keep digging your hole and for what? Some sick vendetta?"

"I gave my word."

"You gave your word to me thirty years ago."

"Gracie, you're right this *is* it…look at me. You see where I am? There is nothing left. I love you, as God as my witness I love you with my whole heart but I'm being transferred, and it's for the best."

"How can you say that? How can you tell me you love me and choose this life over that love time and time again?"

"It's not like that."

"Sure it is," I hiss.

"Gracie…I'm dying."

Have you ever heard someone speak but felt like you were dreaming and the words were a nightmare? You wish to wake up, you beg for it, but it doesn't happen. You think it's your subconscious forcing you to live through the pain and anguish of the words but it's not and then you realize you're living not dreaming.

The knife twists.
The hope diminishes.
And the life sentence becomes shorter.

Chapter Two

MICHAEL

I left New York after the murder of my father, never believing I'd drag my ass back to the concrete jungle—I never wanted to. Then my mother was in a bad car accident and Victor Pastore showed up just in time to hold my hand as I pulled the plug on the life support. At the time I detested the man, blamed him for my father's death and even my mother's. If my old man didn't die protecting Victor, we never would've moved away and she wouldn't have been on that highway when a truck crashed into her car.

He brought me back to the streets I grew up on, the same streets he and my father ran together for nearly two decades. I never planned on sticking around and only came back to bury my mother beside my father. After the dirt settled over my parents, Victor propositioned me, trying to ease his conscience and offered me a legit job running one of his new nightclubs, Temptations.

I knew jack shit about running a night club. I was a carpenter, a man who worked with his hands and wore construction boots. I wasn't cut from the same cloth as my father or Vic. Designer suits weren't my thing and ties were just a noose around my neck. But then I laid eyes on Nikki, Vic's youngest daughter, the girl who had called me Mikey ever since she was an awkward teenager with braces and frizzy hair. Actually, she called me Mikey before that, when she was just a kid following me and her sister around like a shadow.

There was nothing fucking awkward about the chain-smoking sexpot with perfectly straight teeth and lips that teased a man even when her mouth was closed. She no longer wore pigtails and fancy dresses that her mother forced upon her. She wore clothes that hugged her body, showing off her narrow waist, an ass you wanted to sink your teeth into and breasts you wanted to lay your head on. Her legs, let's not talk about her legs and how every time I stared at them I wanted to wrap them around my waist. Fuck that, I wanted them around my neck. She had traded her ballet shoes for stilettos. I swear every pair of shoes she owns scream 'come fuck me'.

I'm cool with that.

Since I'm the one fucking her and those sexy shoes are digging into my back night after night she wraps her legs around me.

Yeah, you guessed it, I took Vic up on his offer for the sole purpose of getting to know the girl I left behind and the woman she had become. She had a boyfriend at the time, some douchebag named Rico, who at first glance I knew he was a no good motherfucker. I had no proof though, and Nikki needed to learn that shit for herself. She needed to be the one to realize the scum that Rico was. So I did my thing, flirted with the girl I wanted, got under her skin and made her realize I wasn't going anywhere.

The whole time I was making moves on Victor's daughter, he and his goons were training me to be America's Next Gangster. Well, not really, I mean they weren't training me to whack someone. Anthony took me to some shooting range owned by a bunch of bikers and taught me how to fire a gun. The thing was I didn't need anyone to teach me, I had my father's blood running through my veins and that shit came as natural as breathing. I was a sure shot, just like my old man. I bet he'd be proud.

Victor wanted me to protect myself, so the piece I started carrying was just a precaution, a weapon I'd only fire if someone tried to fuck with me now that I was working for him.

Along with the loaded gun, they fitted me for the custom designer suits he and my father donned back in the day. I was a reflection of both Victor and *Val*, and my Timberland boots would not make the cut.

As the transformation continued, Nikki's relationship crumbled and our friendship changed. She became my girl without becoming my girl if that makes any sense. She didn't know it at the time, but after the night she and I hit the club scene, I realized who she belonged to.

It was the grand opening of Temptations, Nikki's twenty-first birthday and my first night as the disco dancing gangster when everything changed.

What's a grand celebration without a fucking shootout?

Not a Pastore function that's for sure.

It came to light that Rico was working Nikki the whole time, a ploy to get close to Victor and avenge some fucking shit. It was time to put my training to use and protect Nikki, shooting at anything that got in my way from getting her the fuck out of the war zone my new job had become.

When I got us out of the club, the president of the motorcycle club that owned the gun range was waiting for us. Jack Parrish and Victor Pastore worked together on several occasions, creating an alliance that benefited the streets they both loved.

Victor eventually showed up at the safe house, informing us that his organization was at war and no one was safe. He sent us to Florida, handed me Nikki's life and told me to keep her safe. He didn't mention he was sending me to the fucking *Golden Girls*. I discovered that shit when I pulled into the fucking retirement community and Vic's sister greeted me wearing a goddamn negligee and his mother tried to shoot me with a rifle.

Even now, well over a year later, I'm standing on top of my roof, nailing down the shingles and I'm still haunted by those lunatics. Lifting my shirt up to wipe the sweat from my forehead, their voices ring in my ears.

"I swear to God, Bert, you drive like a snail on a Percocet. Get me the hell out of this car," Gina's voice taunts.

"I floored it on the Belt Parkway," Bert, Gina's seventy-year-old boy-toy argues.

"Forty miles per hour is not flooring it," Gina shouts.

I must've been in the sun for too long because I hear a car door slam shut, like they weren't miles away in the sunshine state.

"Ma, we're here. Ma! Oh for Christ's sake, plug in your hearing aid."

"Grab my gun," Red shouts. Big Red, Gina and Vic's four foot eleven mother with fire engine red hair.

"You let her take her gun? What does she need a gun for?" Bert asks incredulously.

"You're on our soil, boy," Red argues. "You need to be prepared for a drive-by. Grab the gun! Shit, we forgot the cannoli's."

"The house looks different," Gina comments. "Oh, hot damn! Look who it is!"

No.

No fucking way.

Come on!

I lean over the edge of the roof and I'm pretty sure my eyes fucking explode in their sockets as they land on the fucking circus parked in my driveway.

Gina's beehive hairdo was extra fucking high, teased two feet in the air as she bats her fake eyelashes and waves up at me. I guess I should be grateful the fucking lady wasn't wearing a bra and bloomers like the last time I saw her. Red was waving too—waving a gun.

Bert, that poor bastard was unloading the fucking car. Unloading the fucking car!

This must be what having a stroke feels like.

"Nikki," I shout, pulling at my hair. I move to back away from the edge, desperate to erase the image of 'Sophia and Dorothy Petrillo' from my brain but my jeans catch on one of the nails I hadn't yet hammered down. I tug my leg free, lose my balance and nearly falling off the fucking roof. In a last ditch effort to save my ass, I grab onto the gutter.

"Oh my God! We have a jumper," Gina shrieks. "Mikey, baby, please! Gina's here, we'll get through it."

"I'm not jumping off the roof you whack job! I saw you and I fucking slipped," I call down to her.

"That is the sweetest thing I ever heard," she says, elbowing Bert in the gut. "How come you never did that?"

"Hang off a roof?" Bert asks confused.

"Nikki," I shout again. Where the hell is she?

"Jump, boy! Big Red's got you," Red yells, dropping her straw bag and tucking her gun into whatever cleavage she has left. She spreads her arms wide as if she is going to catch me before Gina pushes her aside and copies her stance.

"I've got him!"

"What the hell is going on?" Nikki questions.

I peek down at her, watching as she freezes in her tracks and takes in the fucking festivities.

"Aunt Gina. Nana. What…what are you doing here?"

"We're here for the party," Gina exclaims, looking over her shoulder before bringing her eyes back to me. "Mikey, did your ass get tighter since the last time I saw you?"

"What party?" Nikki asks.

"Hey, Princess, think you can help me get down from the roof before we ask the crazies anymore questions?" I holler, banging my forehead against the gutter in frustration.

"Sorry, babe! I'll go get the ladder."

"Boy don't need a ladder. I've got my arms wide open ready to catch him," Red insists.

The mother and daughter duo continue to bicker over who would be my savior as Nikki comes back, dragging the ladder behind her. She and Bert prop up the ladder along the side of the house and I worked my way over to it.

"Easy, baby," Nikki calls as she holds the ladder in place and I start my descent. I did contemplate staying up on the roof thinking that a sun burn was safer than the fate that awaited me down below.

Stepping off the ladder, I turn to Nikki.

"What are they doing here?"

"I have no idea," she hisses, plastering a smile on her face turning back to her relatives. "What a nice surprise."

Bullshit.

"Even though my heart is broken I had to come," Gina explains, reaching for Nikki's left hand and inspecting the ring I put on her finger. "You did good, Mikey," she approves, turning Nikki's hand every which way to look at the diamond from every angle. "That's some rock. Ma, come look at the rock," she orders.

Wiping my hands over my face as Red scurries over, I blow out a ragged breath and watch the old lady snatch Nikki's hand.

"Did you get it appraised? I know a guy who can do an insurance job. You give me the ring we'll say the house was robbed and you can collect."

I drop my hands from my face and stare at the little old lady.

Now I know where Vic got his ways from.

"Thanks, Nana, but I'm going to hang onto it for a little while," Nikki says, turning to Bert and eyeing the suitcases. I saw the horror flash in her eyes and I chuckle to myself. At least she wasn't three stories up on the roof when she realized these clowns were planning on a long visit, one that involved five suitcases.

"Um…so…you guys planning on a long visit?" Nikki croaks.

"Long enough to stay for the wedding," Gina reveals.

"We haven't set a date," I blurt out.

"Better get on that, boy," Red says, patting my back. "We didn't drive all the way here just for the engagement party."

"What engagement party? What are you people talking about?"

"You can't get engaged and not have a party," Gina answers. "Bert, bring the bags inside the house."

"Bert, drop the bags or so help me God, I'll drop you!" I point to him, giving him a deadly glare to emphasize my words.

Nikki threads her arm through mine and smiles at our unexpected guests.

"Can you guys give us a minute?" she asks, pulling me toward the stoop and dragging me up the stairs.

"They're not staying here, princess. It's them or me! I swear," I growl as she pulls me inside the house.

"Calm down," she asserts as she laces her fingers around the belt loops of my jeans, tugging me closer to her. "It's kind of cute they came all this way because we're getting married, don't you think?"

"No, nothing they do is cute. They're fucking bat-shit crazy. Even Bert has started acting like them," I argue, narrowing my eyes as she moves her hands to the hem of my t-shirt and starts to work it up over my stomach.

"Yes, they're crazy but they're family, Mikey," she says, lifting my arms up and pulling my shirt over my head. She reaches around me and locks the door before she takes a step back and starts to unbutton her shirt.

"What're you doing?"

"Trying to make you forget that my aunt has the hots for you and my grandma is itching to shoot someone?"

"You forgot Bert."

"Poor Bert, he's innocent in all this," she adds, dropping her shirt to the floor before reaching behind her and unsnapping her bra.

"They can't stay here, Nikki. I'm not strong enough to go another round with your aunt. I still have nightmares about her teddies.

A giggle escapes her mouth as her bra falls to the floor.

"I'll call my mother, tell her to come pick them up but, first things first," she coos, crooking her finger as she mischievously winks at me.

"You want something, Princess?" I grunt, reaching for the zipper on my jeans. I watch her turn around and shimmy out of her shorts, revealing her perfectly round ass, inch by glorious inch. She steps out of the shorts and snaps the elastic of her thong against her hip as she peers over her shoulder at me.

"I think you know what I want, Mikey," she teases, walking over to the couch. Bending over, she shoves her ass in the air and braces her arms against the back of the cushions.

"Goddamn, Princess," I ground out, moving behind her, smacking her ass with the back of my hand. My hands travel up her curves and around to squeeze her tits.

"The question is, are you going to give me what I want?" she taunts, wiggling her ass against my crotch. I release her breasts and push my pants down my thighs freeing my cock.

"Say it, Nikki, give me the words and I'll give you what you want," I hiss, stroking my cock with one hand and slipping my finger beneath the elastic of her thong with my other hand, pulling the fabric away from her.

"Fuck me, Mikey," she demands, spreading her legs wide and lifting her ass higher.

My princess didn't have to ask me twice.

I grab her hips and bury my cock into her pussy, stretching her wide as I slam my dick deep inside of her.

"That's what I like," she cries out, pressing her ass against me as I reach around her and grab her tits, rolling her nipples between my fingers. My hips crash against her ass, as my cock works her wet cunt.

The doorbell rings followed by the persistent knocking on the door.

"Ignore it," she orders, reaching behind her to grab my ass, digging her nails into my cheeks as I continue to fuck her mindlessly. I run my hand down the front of her body stopping at her pussy to circle her clit with my thumb.

"Fuck!" Nikki screams.

"Nikki? Are you okay? Open the door!" Gina demands.

"I'm coming!"

"Well it's about time! It's hot as hell out here!" Red hollers.

Chuckling, I bow my head and kiss Nikki's shoulder. Her pussy clenched around my dick as she went off like a firecracker.

That's it baby.

Come for me.

Slamming into her one final time, my teeth graze her shoulder and I let go of my release, grunting as I thrust my hips and come inside of her.

"Watch out I'm going to shoot down the door," I hear Red shout.

Nikki bursts into a fit of laughter as I collapse over her.

"Laugh it up, Princess," I mutter against her shoulder.

"I love you, Mikey," she whispers, glancing at me over her shoulder.

"Love you too," I murmur, pressing a kiss to her cheek before I slowly pull out of her. "Go let them in and I'll fire up the grill."

"Really?"

"Yeah, we'll feed them and send them to your mother." I wink, bending down to pick up my pants. "Just make sure your aunt keeps her clothes on until she leaves and we're all good."

She grins at me, wrapping her arms around my neck and squeezing me tightly.

"I can't wait to marry you, Mikey."

I can't wait either, Princess.

Chapter Three

ANTHONY

My eyes flutter open at the sound of my sweet, baby girl's cries. Turning over, Adrianna groans beside me, I feel around the nightstand for the baby monitor. Sitting up, I lean over my wife, extending my arm over her shoulder to turn the video monitor to face both of us. Crying at the top of her little lungs, Victoria kicks her legs in the crib. I bend my head and kiss Adrianna's bare shoulder.

"Go back to bed," I murmur. "I've got her."

Her head falls back on the pillow with a thump as she closes her eyes.

"Are you sure?" she asks, already half asleep.

"Sleep, Reese's," I whisper. Throwing my legs over the side of the bed I pick up my sweatpants from the floor and pull them on.

I pad through our bedroom, across the hall to our daughter's room, and head straight for my princess.

"Hey, hey, hey, what's all this noise about?" I chastise, trying my hardest to perfect that gentle, baby voice that everyone seems to use when they talk to babies. I'm sure I sound like a fucking idiot, but I don't give two fucks.

There isn't a damn thing I wouldn't do for my kids.

I used to think the mob was everything, that being a gangster meant I was someone, but I was nobody, just a regular street thug—until my son Luca called me daddy.

Being a dad—that's everything.

And now there are two little lives I am responsible for.

Leaning over the side of the crib, I lift my crying girl and cradle her against my bare chest, right over my heart where her and her brother's names are tattooed. I would have added Reese's to the growing list of names, but she already occupies my back. It seemed only fitting that the girl who has had my back since the day I met her was inked over that part of me and the two blessings she gave me placed right over my heart.

Adrianna loves the tattoo on my back and sometimes when we're lying in bed, she outlines the entire piece with her finger. She traces the year on top, the year that symbolizes when our life first began. Then she bypasses the A, which takes up most of my back and runs her finger along the year we supposedly ended, the year I went to jail. She finally acknowledges her first initial by pressing a kiss to the center of my back.

We weren't supposed to get this happy ending we're living, but we defeated the odds. I tried to stay away from her. I came home from jail after spending three years doing time for a crime I didn't commit. I Did everything in my power to push her away. I made her doubt everything we were, all the love we had for one another and forced her into the arms of another man.

I can't say I regret my actions because then we wouldn't have Luca. I'm only going to say this once so you have a better understanding of who Adrianna and I are. I'm not Luca's biological father but that doesn't make him any less my son than Victoria is my daughter. I was there when he came into the world, and the minute I held him in my arms, was the minute he became mine. It amazed me how much I could feel for someone. At first, I rationalized my feelings as Luca being an extension of the woman I loved but it was so much more than that.

It was the way he looked at me.

The way he squeezed my finger with his tiny hand.

The way he ran to me whenever he saw me.

It was the way he said my name and asked me to lift him onto my shoulders.

I love Luca for the little boy he is and not for his DNA.

After the shootout at Temptations, when Adrianna shot and killed Rico—the gunman who was about to whack me—we decided life was too short and we weren't going to waste any more time not loving one another. Victor released me of my obligations to the mob and encouraged me to give his daughter a good life.

It was Victor who originally tried everything in his power to keep us apart, it made me uneasy at first as I didn't know what to make of that. He took the rap for killing Rico, gave me his blessing and told me to enjoy the family I deserved. In essence, the man who stole my happiness was the one responsible for giving it back to me.

"Tell daddy what's bothering you, princess. Are you wet? Let's change your diaper and then we'll get you a fresh bottle," I whisper as her cries begin to ease and walk her over to the changing table. I tickle her belly, and that smile that Adrianna keeps telling me is gas, appears, melting my heart.

A heart I used to think was black.

I change her, reposition her onesie before lifting her back to my chest and carry her down the stairs. I fix her a bottle before heading back upstairs. I settled myself in the rocking chair I bought Adrianna after she told me she was pregnant. Rocking to a steady rhythm I stare at the perfect life I had a hand in creating. Victoria looks just like her mother but she has my blue eyes, something we weren't sure would stick.

"How about a bedtime story?" I ask, nuzzling her cheek, drinking in that addicting smell of a baby.

I may not know a single fairy tale, but I know a great love story, the one I created with her mother.

"Once upon a time there was this guy who thought he had everything figured out. He thought running on the wrong side of the tracks made him a man. He wanted respect on the streets and didn't care what he had to do to get it. It wasn't until a princess came along and turned his whole world upside down. It was then he realized no one respected him. They feared him and that was something completely different. So, this guy, he tried not to fall for the princess, but she made it real hard. She was a spitfire, a girl who knew what she wanted and wasn't afraid to go after it. I was the lucky bastard. Shit, I mean, I was the lucky guy she wanted."

I'm still getting used to keeping things PG around the kids but I try to make a conscience effort. Even started setting my alarm a half hour before everyone wakes up so Luca doesn't realize me and his mother never wear clothes to bed.

"It was hard not to fall in love with everything about her, including the way she ate her popcorn, mixing in Reese's Pieces into the bucket whenever I took her to the movies." I smile thinking back to the first date she conned out of me. I was supposed to escort her and Mike Valente to the movies but the two of them set me up. Mike took off to chase a piece of ass and Adrianna reeled me in—hook, line and sinker.

I was a goner.

"We were young, real young, and foolishly we thought we'd be together forever, that nothing could ever stand between us," I continue, staring down at Victoria. I feel the lump form in my throat thinking about the first time Adrianna told me she was pregnant with the child we lost. Closing my eyes, I recall the words I spoke as I broke Adrianna's heart, telling her the baby didn't survive. A part of both of us died that day, and even now, after the healing, there's still an empty spot in our hearts for the baby we never met.

"Things happen, baby girl, and as hard as you try, sometimes you can't stop them from taking over. They pull you away from the things you want most and make them so far out of reach you give up, but I know you are going to learn, and you will learn from your mommy that you keep fighting for what you believe in. Let no one stop you from going after what makes you happy."

If I had one wish for my daughter, it would be that she grows up to be a strong woman like her mother. Someone who won't back down from a challenge. Someone loyal to both herself and those she loves. A woman who knows her worth, knows what she wants, and is the only one in control of her heart.

"I promise you I'll never be the dad that takes away your smile because I'm too scared to watch you walk away. That doesn't mean I'm not going to screen your dates and follow you around with a baseball bat, but when the time comes, and you find someone who loves you more than they love the air they breathe, I won't be the dad that takes that from you."

I won't do to her what Victor did to us.

I've forgiven him.

We both have.

Our daughter is named after him for crying out loud.

Instead of harboring resentment we took what happened to us as a lesson in parenting. For me, I know now I have eighteen years or so to prepare myself for the day my daughter tells me she's in love. I look at Victoria and as much as I don't want to understand why Victor did the things he did, I understand his fear. Looking down at the baby I created, knowing these days and nights are the shortest part of her life, they'll go by in a flash and she'll grow up before I know it. That's fucking scary. She'll bring home a guy and with my luck, he'll be like me, and I'll feel like I'm losing a limb as she walks out the door holding his hand.

I glance down and watch her wrap her hand around my pinky.

I won't stand in her way though.

I'll think back to these moments, hang onto them with all I am, and remember that she was once the little girl who wrapped her hand around my pinky but also the girl who wrapped her whole self around my heart.

We give our kids roots and then we give them wings and watch them soar.

That's the kind of dad I want to be.

"Well aren't you going to tell her the best part of the story?" my wife asks, pulling me away from my thoughts. I lift my head and watch her lean against the frame of the door, tightly tying the satin belt of her robe around her waist.

The beauty of life is some things are just meant to be, nothing and no one can stop them from happening.

Me and Reese's.

Meant to be.

She pads into the room, making her way over to me and our baby. Wrapping her arms around my shoulders she leans over and smiles down at our daughter.

"They proved everyone wrong and lived happily ever after," she whispers, pressing her lips to my cheek.

"Yeah, they did," I agree, as she drops her arms from around me and steps in front of me. "I thought you were sleeping."

"The monitor was on," she explains with a smile placed firmly on her plump lips. "You're such a great dad," she whispers, eyes shining bright. "I thought I couldn't possibly love you any more than I did when I was fifteen but then we had kids and…well…my heart is so full," she rasps.

Patting my knee with my free hand I adjust our daughter with the other and reach for Adrianna, pulling her onto my lap.

"Love you so fucking much, Reese's," I murmur against her ear.

"This is the good life, babe, the one we never thought we'd see, isn't it?"

"Yeah, this is the good life," I confirm, and even as I say the words they don't seem to adequately describe what we were living.

"She looks wide awake," she says, running the back of her hand over Victoria's cheek.

"She's a wild one," I agree, glancing over at our smiling baby.

"Wonder where she gets it from," Adrianna teases, crinkling her nose as she leans her back against my chest.

"Mommy? Daddy?" Luca groggily calls from the door.

"Hey, buddy," I reply, watching as he wipes the sleep from his eyes and stares at us.

"Is it morning?"

"No, baby, it's not. Your sister woke up for a bottle," Adrianna explains, holding out her arms. "Get over here."

Luca runs over to us, jumping into his mommy's arms and lets her pull him onto her lap.

"Tori, you need to sleep," Luca tells his sister, leaning closer to her. "It's okay though. I don't like to sleep either. You can't play when you're sleeping," he says while yawning.

Cherishing the moment, despite the pins and needles shooting down my leg, I wrap my free arm tightly around my wife and son as I continue to cradle my baby girl with my other arm. It was one moment ingrained into my heart and soul—a moment I'd remember when my kids were all grown up and their mother was still sitting on my lap.

The good life.

Right here in my arms.

Chapter Four

JACK

It never becomes easier—visiting my boy in a cemetery, staring at his name perfectly etched into a tombstone. Each visit is a reminder of how fucked the world truly is, a testament that no one is ever safe, and even the good die young.

I'll never completely forgive myself. Every birthday my son doesn't celebrate I feel the guilt of his death. I'm an outlaw, a choice I made and one I live day after day, washing the blood off my hands without blinking an eye. There are days I get off on it, when the smell of flesh burning excites me. The adrenaline rush of my bullet as it races against the one fired by my enemy ignites my pulse. Those are the days when the 'Bulldog' is in control and Jack Parrish fades to black.

Yet, my crimes are not what stole my son's life.

Go figure that one.

My mind, my ignorance—ultimately my illness—took Jack Jr.'s life. You people think God is your maker, that he is the one who created you and who controls your destiny.

Good for you.

But he isn't mine.

My maker is my mind, it's who I answer to, it's my maker who controls me. I'm a manic-depressive and there was a time when I was too proud to admit that. Silence. It's golden until it's not. Until you're picking out the tiniest coffin in the funeral parlor and your wife is crying buckets of tears as she searches the house for your son's favorite teddy bear so he can take it with him into eternity.

Then you find your voice.

And you say the words you've denied for so long. You speak your truth and confess that you are ill and you are weak minded. *"I'm bipolar and I need help."*

Lithium becomes your savior and sometimes it's not enough but you know you're nothing without it. You clutch that orange prescription bottle, hang onto it with everything you have left, because you have another child on this earth that needs you.

There have been times, too many to count, when I've struggled with my conscience and my desperation to end my life and be reunited with my son. But in the end it's my daughter, Lacey, that keeps me here. That pretty girl, with eyes that are so like mine, not just in color but also in anguish.

I never understood how I picked living over dying. Choosing between my children, how did I make that decision? How or why I chose to stay behind for Lacey and not dive into eternity with Jack? I called myself a pussy, too much of a coward to take my own life but now I know why I subconsciously chose to keep breathing. My little girl needed me, and not just to be her dad but to be her inspiration.

Lacey was diagnosed as being bipolar a couple of months ago after carrying the burden of silence for as long as she could remember. I've lost one child due to mental illness and I'll be damned if I will lose another. My Lacey, my sweet, innocent, little girl with a smile so big and bright she has the power to lighten even the darkest of hearts.

Fucked.

The world was so fucked, and those who survive it are the strongest of souls.

Bending my knees, I crouch down in front of my son's tombstone and run my fingers over his name.

"Hi, son," I whisper. "I'm sorry it's been so long since my last visit." I express my remorse as I recall the last time I sat in this exact spot. I had cradled my daughter in my arms as she cried and professed her truth, introducing me to the demon living inside her head.

"Things are better," I start, dropping my hand from his name as I draw in a deep breath. "Your sister is on medication and knock wood, it seems to be working. She's got Blackie watching out for her and I know he will lay down and die before he lets her fall into the dark abyss again."

Silence, my heart heavy as I try to find the words I came here to say. Instead of finding my voice I relive the memory of walking into my house and handing over my daughter's heart to my vice president. I remember feeling like I had lost a piece of my heart as I watched her walk out the door and climb on the back of Blackie's bike. I stared out that window for a long fucking time before my woman steered me back in. I knew better than anyone what two little words could mean to a person, but the two words she uttered were two words I never expected to hear.

"I'm pregnant."
Two words and I was back in the game. I turned around abruptly and pinned her with a look.
One look.
Some men wore their hearts on their sleeves.
Mine was reflected in my dark eyes.
"I know it's a shock, and I should've waited for a better time—"
I closed the distance between us and lifted my finger to her lips silencing her.
"You're pregnant?"
She nodded.
Sunshine.
Always pulling me out of my self-created darkness.
Always saving me from myself.
I dropped my hand, reached for her with my other, threading my fingers through her hair as my mouth crashed onto hers.
Two words that promised a future and gave me heart, something to keep me from being reckless.

The wind blew picking up the stray leaves that had fallen over Jack's grave as I bit the inside of my cheek

"Boy, I don't know how to tell you this," I admit, scratching at the scruff that lined my jaw. "Your old man is going to be a dad again." I laugh half-heartedly. "The way I see it the man upstairs thinks one of two things; either he's giving me one more shot to nail this dad thing or he's giving me another life because I deserve it. Maybe I didn't fail at being a father as much as I think I did. As much as I'd like it to be the latter—I highly doubt it. I've got sins, boy, sins that don't disappear, that can't be forgiven with a bow of the head and a Hail Mary."

Pausing for a second, I reach into my cut and pull out a pack of cigarettes. I stare at them before tucking them back into my pocket. I need to quit this shit if I'm going to run after a toddler.

"As much as I feel undeserving, I can't help but stay awake at night and watch Reina sleep. I stare at her belly and try to picture what your brother or sister will look like. I wonder if he's a boy if he'll look like you and then I wonder how I will feel, looking at him and seeing traces of the boy I lost. Then I think of all the things you and I never had the chance to do together. I'll be able to do those things with him and that makes me feel so fucking guilty. I guess I came here today to relieve myself of that guilt and make a promise to you. I came here to remind you how I wished every day since you left this earth for one chance to fulfill one memory with you. I want you to know that if this baby is a boy, he can never take your place in my heart. Every time I get a chance to do something with him that I never did with you, I'll think of you, Jack. You'll be right there with us, every pitch of the baseball, every goddamn time I take him to a game and every single birthday he blows out his candles…. you will be with me, right where you've always been, in the center of your old man's heart."

I run my hands over my head, angling it so I can stare at the clouds. It is times like this a man wishes he had found God instead of the reaper.

"And if it's not too much to ask, pull some strings for your little brother or sister—talk to the man upstairs—the man that's been looking out for you since you left me, and ask him to spare the baby of the illness your sister got from me. Ask him to spare one Parrish child the demons of his father."

I force down the lump in my throat as I bow my head and reach for the cigarettes again. Fuck this shit, I'll quit tomorrow. Shoving the cigarette between my lips a hand falls to my shoulder as I pat my pockets searching for a lighter.

"I thought I'd find you here," my Sunshine's voice whispers from behind me, forcing me to glance over my shoulder and look at the woman who has healed me in more ways than one. She bends down and takes the cigarette from my mouth, snapping it in half. "What happened to quitting?"

"How long have you been standing there?"

She didn't answer, brushing her hands over the denim that hugged her thighs before taking a seat on the grass next to me. She kissed her fingertips and brought them to Jack's tombstone before making the sign of the cross.

at least one of us has God in their corner.

Maybe our kid has a shot after all.

"Why didn't you tell me?" she asks softly as she stares at my son's headstone.

"Reina," I start, sighing heavily.

"Don't do that, Jack," she insists, turning her eyes to mine. "You and I are in this together and if having this baby—"

"Having this baby means everything to me," I interrupt. "Don't you doubt that for one second, Sunshine. You want to talk fears, then let's talk…tell me why you keep dancing around marrying me," I argue. "I put that ring on your finger a while ago and you keep giving me the run around."

"I don't know what you're talking about," she mutters.

"Oh no? If you don't want to marry me than tell me. Right here. Right now."

"If I didn't want to marry you, I wouldn't have said yes when you asked me. How could you even ask me that?"

Her eyes peer into mine as they fill with tears.

"Of course I want to marry you."

"Then what's stopping you?" I ask, reaching out to tuck her golden hair behind her ear. "You're carrying my baby in your belly, Sunshine. You should carry my name too."

"I'm afraid of having everything because when you have everything you have everything to lose," she confesses.

"Already have everything," I rasp, dropping my hands to her belly that has already swelled slightly with the proof of all we had. "Marry me, Sunshine. We can go to city hall tomorrow and sign our names to our hearts, but for the love of all things holy, marry me."

She drops her hands over mine and looks up at me.

"Is this another Property of Parrish thing?" she teases, giving me a glimpse of her smile.

I divert my eyes to our hands then back to hers.

"It's clear who you belong to, Sunshine. I put a baby in you and branded you mine forever. I want to marry you because I'm ready to live by my vows. I'll give you all I am and promise to for the rest of my life," I tell her, lifting one hand to cup her chin drawing her closer. Dipping my head, I cover her mouth with mine and kiss her with whatever gentleness I can muster.

"Marry me," I say against her mouth.

"Yes," she whispers, leaning forward for more of my mouth. "But nothing big. I want it to be about family," she demands, wrapping her arms around my neck.

"Small, got it," I agree, hiding my smile as I pull her onto my lap and kiss her some more.

"Lacey will be my maid of honor and of course you'll have Blackie as your best man, won't you?" she questions in-between my attack on her lips.

"Yeah, yeah," I mumble, threading my fingers through her hair, angling her head so I can kiss her neck.

"Maybe we can have the priest come to the compound."

Right, maybe he'll bless the table we congregate at too. Father whoever could not only marry us but cleanse the Satan's Knights of their corrupt souls.

Oh, Reina.

Crazy never could fix crazy.

But fuck if that matters.

We might be two completely different breeds of crazy but we are suited for one another. She silences my maker with her soft voice and I tear down her insecurities, making those scars that mark her body, Property of Parrish—just like every other inch of her.

"We'll have to invite the Biancis and the Pastores, but other than that we'll keep it to just your brothers," she rambles as my teeth graze her neck. "Oh, and we'll have to make sure we have some of that non-alcoholic beer for Blackie."

"Whatever you want, Sunshine. I'll have Wolf and Pipe blow up balloons, bring in a goddamn support group for Blackie, whatever it takes as long as it puts a smile on your face," I growl against her skin.

A sexy, low rumble of laughter works its way up her throat and escapes her lips, spreading joy throughout the open space meant for tears and prayers.

Sunshine.

"Do you think Riggs could be our videographer?"

I lift my head, arch an eyebrow, questioning her as she continues to ramble on. She was turning my club into a circus.

Wrapping her arms around my neck she winks at me as a smile spreads across her face.

"We're getting married," she whispers.

"Yeah, we are," I rasp, sliding my hands down her hips as I glance over her shoulder at my boy's headstone. "You hear that, Jack, your old man is getting hitched."

Reina's arms pull me into her embrace.

"You were right when you said he'll be with you always but you left one part out…you forgot to tell him he'll always have a place in our family. This baby has a guardian angel protecting him or her, and that angel is his brother," she murmurs, clearing her throat before she pulls back and takes my face in her hands, forcing my eyes to lock with hers. "You feeling some kind of way, you tell me, Jack. Me."

"You," I say hoarsely.

"Me," she agrees.

Two words that meant nothing to anyone else in the world but two words that meant the world to us. They are the words that became a vow and when the day comes for Reina to take my name and for us to pledge our love and commitment, it's those words we'll say to one another, the only ones that mean anything.

You.

Me.

The words Reina and I live and love by.

Chapter Five
RIGGS

Join an MC they said.

It'll be fun they said.

They left out I'd be summoned to kidnap a crazy Italian woman and her grandkid, or that she'd hit me in the face with a frying pan. It's probably a good thing I had no idea the Bianci twister was headed straight for me, otherwise I wouldn't have met my Kitten.

The feistiest pussy in all the land.

Ha!

I crack myself up.

All jokes aside, the day my president, Jack Parrish, ordered me to grab 'Carmela Soprano' and the boy, was the day my whole world changed. It was the detour I never expected but the one that led me straight to the girl of my dreams. Dreams I never knew I had until I had her.

When I first met Lauren Bianci, the mob guy's little sister, she was dancing in a bar—a bar called the Pink Pussycat. See, my job was to bring Bianci's mother upstate so she could stay with her daughter while the mob folk shot the fuck out of one another. If you ask me, they should've let mama Bianci stay behind—give that woman a kitchen appliance and send her after your toughest enemy. Anyway, I took the Italian nutcase to her daughter's apartment only to find out little Miss Innocent was lying to mommy dearest and her big brother. Her roommate sent me to the Pink Pussycat, that's when I came face to face with my Kitten for the first time. One look in her big, blue eyes, framed by black glasses, and I was gone. The Riggs everyone knew and loved was gone and the Tiger was born.

You heard me right.

Kitten and Tiger.

That's us.

As much as I didn't bank on her coming into my life, Lauren never saw me coming. I was just as much her detour as she was mine and together we would take each other on one hell of a ride.

At first I thought I was just chasing tail, going after something I couldn't have—a guy just having fun. But the more time I spent with her, the deeper I fell into her, and as much as we flirted, as much I wanted to bang her brains out, she became my friend. I didn't have any friends that were girls but I couldn't stay away from her. I looked forward to the text messages we'd send one another and the few times she'd visit her brother—I even drove up to bumble-fuck New York again to see her face.

I was out of my mind and to prove so, I even invited her to my patch party. Yeah, I invited Kitten to my pussy party. Who the fuck does that? This guy right here. And you know what? Best fucking decision of my life. I can say that now, almost two years later.

Most brothers in my MC look back at the night they got their colors as a turning point in their life because they finally became one of the Satan's Knights. I look back at that night and I forget all about the patch I received because that was the night I first took Kitten. I took her up against the wall of the Satan's Knight compound and put Pea inside of her. Not intentionally of course, but yep, you heard me right—I knocked up Kitten.

I didn't find out right away and if I'm being honest, I was a dick, both before and after I found out about the baby. I stopped talking to Kitten after the night at the clubhouse, and thinking back now, I have no idea why. The best I can come up with is I was scared. Yeah, scared, because I was feeling all sorts of shit I wasn't used to and I was starting to think about Kitten, morning, noon and night.

I think I had a nervous breakdown after I found out we were having a kid and that she had already named it Pea. I was scared shitless to become a father, to be responsible for a little human—for eighteen plus years. But I wasn't about to let Lauren do it by herself. I wasn't going to be a deadbeat dad, nah, not me. I would own that shit.

Own it.

These are the two words my brother and my best friend, Bones, said to me after I told him I was having a kid. These are the two words I live by, and the two words I want scribed on my tombstone when I drop dead.

Kitten moved in with me and we played house for a while. I bought a refrigerator and she covered it with our baby's sonogram photos. Life was good. I had my Kitten, and we were having a Pea.

The motherfucking Chinese had to go ruin my shit. Fucking Sun Wu and the Red Dragons, those motherfuckers threatened to take everything I loved from me—my Kitten and my Pea.

They would've succeeded too if it wasn't for Bones. My best friend stepped into the line of fire when Sun Wu's men shot at Kitten. He jumped in front of her saving her life. That bullet would've killed my Kitten and probably my kid.

It killed Bones.

He saved them and I didn't even get a chance to thank him. There isn't a day that goes by that I don't look at my son or Lauren and think of the brother God didn't give me but the one I chose. We named our son, Eric after Bones, and both Kitten and I tell him stories about the uncle he never got to meet.

Join an MC they said.

Take the detour.

Find your heart and own that shit.

I pause, pushing the carriage past the park gates and pull off my sunglasses to check out our surroundings. There are a couple of kids playing in the sandbox but the little kid with the fisherman's hat looks like he has that shit on lock down, claiming the three babies with dresses all for himself.

His parents need to teach him how to share and spread the wealth.

I turn my attention to the sprinklers, ready to introduce my son to the love of bikinis but the bigger kids run that part of the playground.

"All right, Eric, time for you to learn how to woo the women," I say, eyeing the empty swings before looking down at my son who's rockin' a pair of sunglasses just like mine. "Don't look at me like that, I know they're empty but give it a few minutes and they'll be lining up to swing with us," I promise. "Just follow my lead and I'll have you ten play dates by the time your mom's finished getting her nails done."

He leans forward grabbing a fistful of Gerber Puffs and throws them at me.

All right, he's not a believer—but he will be.

I push the carriage to where the swings are and unlatch Fort Knox. I swear you need to be a brain surgeon to take a kid out of a carriage. Forget about opening this fucking thing—I had to watch a YouTube video just to unfold it. Thank God, Kitten is meeting us here, otherwise I would strap this fucking thing to the roof of my truck.

I place Eric in the swing, tighten the seat belt, see now, this one isn't so bad, one click and my boy is set. Watching as he curiously looks around the playground I push him. After a few pushes a smile makes its way across his face.

That shit never gets old.

Watching your child's eyes widen in wonder, smile in joy as he decides he likes the new experience—it's fucking incredible. Something I almost didn't get the chance to experience.

"You like that, don't you?" I grin as he giggles. That sound is contagious, causing me to laugh as I watch him cheer with every high the swing takes and clap his hands with the lows.

A mother walks up next to us and places her daughter in the swing next to ours.

"Showtime," I whisper into Eric's ear. "Now, the trick isn't getting the girl…it's keeping her once you've got her. You need to keep it fresh, excite her when she least expects it and always make her know how much she means to you. I'm not saying you have to marry the first girl you nab, but if she's the one you love, always make sure you tell her. Never let her wonder—that reminds me," I say, pulling back the swing for a second to whip out my cell phone. I swipe my thumb across the screen and compose a new text message.

Me: Roar.

I grin watching as the little gray cloud appears and two seconds later my phone chimes.

Kitten: Meow. XOXO

It chimes again when I'm about to put my phone away.

Kitten: I just finished drying my nails. Where are you guys?

Me: By the swings.

Kitten: Did Eric get any dates?

Me: Still working on it.

Kitten: LOL. See you in a few.

I pocket my phone and lean close to Eric.

"Mommy's on her way," I say, giving him another push and watch him eye the girl on the swing next to him. "That's my boy! Get her Tiger!"

The girl squeals and Eric doesn't take his eyes off her. Her mom pushes her higher, and she turns to Eric and sticks her tongue out at him.

"Oh, the little vixen is playing hard to get," I hiss, pushing Eric a drop higher.

"How old is he?" the mother asked.

"He'll be one next month," I reply, biting back the cringe as I ask her how old her daughter is, preparing myself for the math equation. "How old is she?"

"Seventeen months and three days," she replies proudly.

See, math equation. Why couldn't she say the kid was one?

"Nice," I reply, leaning into Eric's ear. "She's a cougar."

"There are my boys!"

I turn around at the sound of Lauren's voice and smirk as she completely brushes past me and goes straight for our son.

"There's my little guy," she coos, reaching for him.

Knowing the drill, I pull my baseball hat off my head and run my fingers through my hair. It'll take Kitten a good ten seconds of lovin' on our boy before she even realizes I'm here. She takes him out of the swing and brings him against her chest, showering him with kisses—totally ruining his game.

Her blue eyes zero in on me and her grin widens as she leans forward, covering my mouth with hers. I wrap my arm around her waist, slide my hand into the back pocket of her jeans and press her against me, sandwiching Eric between us as I kiss her until he wails.

"Hi baby, how was your afternoon?" she asks me, setting Eric down on his wobbly feet and taking hold of his hand. He just started walking and takes more falls than he does steps but he's determined.

Determination is something our kid has in spades.

He was a fighter from the day he took his first breath.

"It was good. We went for lunch, had some pizza, a few beers and now here we are."

I grab the carriage, follow her out of the swing area as she and Eric lead the way. My eyes dip down to her ass, which has gotten slightly rounder since Eric was born, her breasts are bigger too—not that I'm complaining. I'm an ass and tits kind of guy, well, not really, I'm just a Kitten kind of guy. Anything she's selling, I'm buying.

"I saw a pretzel stand over there. Why don't we go feed the ducks?" she asks over her shoulder, running after Eric as he found his groove and has taken off toward the pond.

"I'll grab the pretzel," I offer, pushing the empty carriage along to the pretzel guy. I order a pretzel and two hotdogs, one I scoff down before even making my way back to Lauren and the baby. I hand her the hotdog, but she shakes her head, taking a bite of the pretzel instead. Breaking off a piece of pretzel, she crouches down next to our son and hands it to him, showing him how to feed it to the ducks waddling around them.

Watching Lauren with Eric was like watching a dream come true. We talked a lot about dreams, it was Lauren's thing, and I might sound like a pussy but it was becoming my thing too. I loved the nights we lay in bed after screwing each other senseless where Lauren would tell me all her dreams. Her dreams became my dreams, and I vowed to make our dreams come true. Every last one of them, and after all her dreams come true, I'll make her dream some more.

"Let's have another," I blurt.

"Another what?" she asks as she breaks off another piece of the pretzel. "There is plenty here," she adds, naively holding up half of the pretzel.

"Let's make another baby," I clarify, pulling off my sunglasses and turning my hat around so when she lifts her head and stares into my eyes she'll see I'm serious.

Eric tugged on her hand, wanting to go closer to the ducks and she lost her footing for a second. She lifts Eric into her arms as she rises to her feet and pins me with her wide baby blues.

"Are you serious?" she questions, Eric on her hip, trying to lean down and feed the ducks some more. I swear my heart fucking threatened to explode.

I nod, clearing my throat before flashing her a grin and wiggling my eyebrows in suggestion.

"Come on, Kitten, let's make another Pea," I coax, stepping closer to her and taking her hand, pulling her against me. "Think of all the fun we'll have trying."

"We didn't have to try too hard for Eric," she reminds me. "What if we get pregnant right away?"

"Even better," I say, bending my head to kiss her neck. "I love it when you're pregnant, you're fucking insatiable."

She swats my shoulder.

"Watch it," she warns.

"Right, I forgot. You're ducking insatiable," I correct, appeasing her of no cursing in front of the baby rule. We duck a lot around here.

She laughs.

Best ducking sound ever.

What do you say, Kitten?" I ask, pulling back and bending my knees so we're eye level. Her teeth sink into her bottom lip as she stares back at me silently for a few moments.

"I hope you got enough sleep last night, Tiger," she teases, her lips spreading into a smile. "It's going to be a long night."

Cupping her chin with my hand, I bring her mouth to mine, smiling against her lips as I kiss her.

"Bet your ass it is."

Yeah, there was going to be a whole lot of ducking going on for Kitten and Tiger.

Chapter Six

BLAKIE

I pull my bike into my driveway, cutting the engine as I stare up at the house I never thought I'd live in, never wanted to live in, until Lace. She's got me doing a whole lot of things I never thought I'd do again; laughing, smiling, girl even has me dancing out on the back deck at night. She strung lights along the fence and some nights I find her dancing beneath those twinkling lights. I stare at her for a few moments, basking in my angel's glow and then her eyes find mine and her smile widens, lighting up my whole fucking world.

She drags me out of the house and forces me to wrap my arms around her and dance. Sometimes we dance to our song, 'Leather and Lace', other times she chooses a different song. It depends on her mood and where her head is at. If it's our song that's playing, I know she's struggling and I give her all I've got. I try to take her out of the darkness that inebriates her, like she's pulled me from mine, time and time again.

I am a recovering addict, someone who used to think the only thing he had left in this world was poison. I used drugs and alcohol as a crutch to get me through, to numb me from the pain and bring me to the state of oblivion I craved. Lacey stormed into the Satan's Knight's clubhouse one night, trying to escape her own demons, and the girl I had protected since she was fifteen, became my sole purpose for breathing.

One night.

That's all it took for her to get underneath my skin.

She reminded me of the man I was before my first wife, Christine, died. The man before the corruption, the man before the bottle of Johnny Walker, and a syringe full of heroin. She showed me I could still be the man I used to be, that he was still alive buried beneath the leather. It was because of Lacey I realized how badly I wanted to be that guy again and how much I didn't want to quit life.

As much as I'd like to say Lacey is the reason I stay clean—she's not. Sure, having her in my life, being the man she loves, it's all part of the equation but it's not everything. It shouldn't be either. I stay clean for myself because I want to be the man who keeps her. I want to be the man who gets to write her story with her. I want to be better because I am more than a needle and a bottle of booze. I stay clean because I want to live.

I'm an addict but I've found a new addiction, one that will bring me to my knees and one that will keep me breathing—I'm addicted to Lacey's smile.

That smile is the only addiction worth having.

Her happiness is the only high I crave.

I climb the front stoop, hoping when I open the door it's that smile that greets me. I fit my key into the door and pause as I hear the music blasting through the house, a grin plays across my face.

I've gotten used to smiling.

Something I hadn't done in years.

It's the little things we take for granted. The little things that we forget make life worth living.

I open the door, kick it closed with the heel of my boot and follow the sound of the music. It's not our song that she's playing, which means Lacey's maker is silent today.

Her maker is her mind.

Some people believe God is their maker; that He controls Heaven and Earth, but for my Lace, her maker is her mind. Lacey is bipolar and her mind controls her. While I have a sponsor who talks me off the ledge, Lace has a bottle of Lithium.

I know what you're thinking—*they're fucked.*

But we're not.

Each day we wake to a blank page, we pick up the pieces of our shattered souls and write our story. A story that portrays hope and the struggles of life.

I freeze in my tracks as I reach the kitchen and spot her dancing to the beat of the music, singing along to a tempo of her own. Girl can't sing for shit but she can move.

Goddamn can she move.

Prancing around in nothing but one of my black t-shirts—fanning, she was fanning the charred something or other on top of the stove—she's the most beautiful sight a man like me ever saw.

The girl can't cook either but that doesn't stop her from trying. I think that's what I love most about her. *No* and *can't* are two words that are not part of her vocabulary. It's the resilience rooted deep in her veins that makes her who she is.

Lacey doesn't need a hero.

She's her own goddamn hero.

And if there is something she wants to conquer, step the fuck out of her way because she will leave her footprints on your back as she walks right over you to get what she wants.

It's fucking incredible to watch.

Sneaking up behind her, I wrap my arms around her waist and drag her body against mine, causing her to squeal happily.

"You're home," she says, turning in my arms as she wraps them around my neck.

"I'm home," I murmur, bending my head to take her mouth. My lips skim hers back and forth before taking her lower lip between mine. Slowly, I coax her mouth open, slide my tongue over hers, getting high off her taste.

"Goddamn, girl, you make me never want to leave," I growl against her mouth, pulling back slightly to cup her face with my hands.

I only let you leave because you promised you'd always come back," she whispers, reminding me of the vow I made to her when I was released from prison.

I'll always come back for you, girl.

I press another kiss to her lips before glancing over her shoulder, at what I assume is supposed to be dinner.

"You cooked." I clear my throat, raising an eyebrow. "New recipe?"

"Yeah, but it's the last time I use that website for anything. I swear I followed the directions perfectly." She turns, frowning at the blackened meal.

What's it supposed to be?"

She laughs before sinking her teeth into her lower lip and lifting her eyes.

"If I said blackened chicken would you believe me?"

Slapping her ass playfully, I smirk, unable to stop myself from squeezing he lace covered cheek.

"Babe, you know I love the way you look in my shirts but I'm running out of clothes," I say, fingering the hem of my shirt before fisting the back of it. I pull her against my chest and grab a hold of her hips, pressing that sweet ass of hers against my strained cock.

"You love it," she accuses.

I do," I admit, brushing her hair over her shoulder and pressing my mouth to her neck. "But I can't take you to dinner dressed in my shirt," I add, reluctantly releasing her with a groan. "Go get dressed. I'll take you to that Asian place in the mall you like."

"But what about the blackened chicken?" she teases, throwing me a wink.

"Can't even feed that shit to the hungry, Lace," I say. "Go get dressed while I clean the latest disaster to strike the aqua kitchen."

"One day I will make something that knocks your socks off and you will beg me to cook," she says pointedly as she struts out of the kitchen.

I didn't doubt it.

I know better than to underestimate her.

It took me a good half hour to clean the kitchen. I chucked the bird into the pail and squirted half a bottle of dish soap in the charred pan and let it soak. Lacey bounded down the stairs fifteen minutes later, dressed in clothes that hugged the body I worshipped and we took to my bike. She wrapped her arms around my waist and pressed her body against my back as we hit the road.

She might be Jack Parrish's daughter but the girl never took a ride on a bike until she took a gamble on me. She loves the road, almost as much as I do, and jumps at any chance to go for a ride.

When we arrive at the restaurant, we are quickly seated and don't bother looking at the menu, ordering our usual. We share our day with one another. I tell her about the NA meeting I attended and she hangs onto my every word, finding it fascinating as any student majoring in social work would. She's got a year or so left before she graduates college and that's when I plan on putting a ring on her finger.

After dinner, I take her into the mall and we walk in circles because I didn't want to let her in on where I planned on taking her. I can count on one hand how many times I've actually shopped in the mall so I had no fucking idea where Victoria's Secret was located. After we walked the entire mall, I finally found the fucking place and dragged her inside.

"What're we doing here?"

"What do you think we're doing here, girl," I reply, wrapping one arm around her, sliding my hand into the back pocket of her jeans as we walk side by side into the store.

"Is that your plan for tonight? A live Victoria's Secret fashion show?" she asks, lifting up a black lace thong and twirling it around her finger.

I lean into her, breathe in the scent I've come to love—vanilla and honeysuckle.

"Who said I'm waiting for tonight?" I whisper huskily against her ear.

On top of everything else that Lacey has given me she's given me something I hold sacred—her body. I'm the only man who's been inside her, the man that helps her explore her sexuality. I've introduced her to pleasure and pain, showed her how the two become one. She's discovered what she likes, what gets her off, and is very inquisitive to try new things in-between the sheets. Every new experience for her is a rewrite for me—it's the fucking icing on the cake.

She turns her head, brushing her lips against mine before she whispers.

"I like where you're going with this."

She turns around, eyes on mine as she walks backward and lifts her hand holding the thong, crushing it in her fist, crooking her finger with her other hand, beckoning me to follow her.

Damn, girl.

Ignoring the eyes of the associates following us around the store, Lacey picks things out, filling my arms with lingerie as she sifts through the tables finding her sizes.

Told you we'd turn heads, girl.

"Can I start you off in a fitting room?"

I raise an eyebrow at the woman questioning me, forcing a blush out of her.

"I mean—"

"That would be great," Lacey interrupts, smiling wide at her as she shuffles the lingerie from my arms to the associate's.

"Are you looking for something specific?"

Lacey turns, her eyes gleaming mischievously, as she gives me a smile.

"I'm looking to bring this big brute to his knees," she says, turning back to the associate. "You got something that might do the trick?"

I bite the inside of my cheek as my eyes burn into her.

You want me on my knees, girl, you got it.

"I think we can find something," said the associate responds, her face redder than a fucking apple.

"I don't know, he's a tough nut to crack," Lacey teases.

Brazen, girl.

"Let's get you into a fitting room and take your measurements. I think I have something perfect for you," the associate suggests.

"Go on girl, give it your best shot," I encourage, tipping my chin for Lacey to follow the associate.

Lacey spins around on her heel, sashaying her hips as she makes her way toward the dressing room, glancing over her shoulder to make sure she has my attention.

You got me, girl.

I wink at her, crossing my arms against my chest, the worn leather of my jacket straining against my biceps. She disappears into the dressing room with the sales lady as I walk around the store picking out things I want to see on Lacey. The sales person emerges, walking over to a rack and grabbing a few more things for my girl. I glance down at the clothes in my hand and decide it's time for the sales lady to step out of the dressing room and for me to step in.

"Excuse me," I call, lifting my full arms. "Can you find her sizes in these too?"

"Sure just let me get this to her and I'll grab those from you," she says, hurrying back to the fitting room. I sigh, glancing around at the people staring at me.

Yeah, I was a sight.

Cloaked in leather, covered in tattoos, with an arm full of lace.

Story of my life.

The sales lady returns a moment later.

"Let me take that from you." She holds out her arms and takes the Lace from mine. "You want *all* of this?"

"Everything," I confirm. "And whatever else you think she might like," I add, striding toward the dressing room. She stares after me, her mouth agape causing me to chuckle as I rap my knuckles against the fitting room door.

"I don't think this fits," Lacey says, not knowing that it was me she was talking to and not her lingerie fairy godmother.

"Open the door, Lace," I demand, bracing my arms over the frame. "C'mon girl," I probe.

She was quiet for a moment before she replied.

"It's unlocked."

Dropping my hand to the door knob, I glance over my shoulder. Fuck it, I turn the knob and push my way inside. I kick closed the door and twist the lock before I turn around and lay eyes on the sexiest woman I've ever had.

Legs for days.

Wearing a white, lace thong, paired with a garter belt clipped to sheer thigh-high stockings, with matching lace trim, she was a fucking dream. The bra she wore lifted her already perky tits and pushed them over the sheer material so they appeared to be spilling from the cups. I was a lucky man.

"Girl," I hiss, my eyes meeting hers in the mirror.

"So, you think it's time I trade in your t-shirts and parade around the house in this kind of get-up?" She laughs, obviously nervous as she bites her lip.

I didn't answer her with words.

Gave her my eyes and let them answer for me.

Yes.

Fuck yes.

"Turn around," I order, taking a step closer, swallowing up the space between us.

"Blackie," she whispers, turning around and locking her eyes with mine.

"You wanted me on my knees, girl," I growl, dropping on one knee. I press my palms against her thighs, forcing them apart before dropping my other knee down on the floor. "Got me right where you want, right where I belong."

I brush my hair away from my face before palming her pussy over the lace and inching my index finger beneath the material.

"What if she comes back?"

"Then she'll know she did her job properly," I tell her, shoving the lace away from her pussy and reaching behind her with my free hand. Squeezing her ass, I bring her sweet cunt to my mouth and run my tongue down her center.

"My Lace, so fucking good, so fucking pretty," I mutter in-between slow laps of my tongue. She grabs onto my shoulders, fisting the leather in her hands as I peel back her lace and take my fix.

Leather and Lace.

A temptation so sweet—a man drops to his knees just to survive.

Chapter Seven

Grace

Juggling the groceries in one hand, I open the door and disarm the alarm, turning around to face the quiet house.

"Gina? Bert? Ma?" I call out into the silence.

I drop my keys on the console table in the hallway and make my way into the kitchen, setting the brown paper bag, full of groceries, on the counter. Robotically I unpack the bag, waiting for the boisterous voices of my in-laws.

After I returned from my visit with Vic, I found Michael and Nikki on my doorstep with my in-laws in tow. Vic's sister, her 'companion' Bert, and my ninety-four-year-old mother-in-law were staying with me for the time being. They drove up from Florida after finding out Michael had proposed to Nikki. I think they're disappointed we're not throwing the happy couple an engagement party. Nikki is having a hard enough time planning a wedding without her father to even think about planning an engagement party.

I grab the colander and toss the fresh string beans into it before running the water over the vegetables. I break the ends of the string beans, discarding the tips into a bowl as I go.

"Whatcha got there Gracie?"

Victor's arms circled my waist as I leaned over the sink and cleaned vegetables—fresh from the garden I planted in our yard.

"String beans," I said as he leaned over me and turned off the faucet, spinning me around in his arms. "What are you up to Mr. Pastore?"

"Does a man have to have an agenda to want a moment with his wife?"

"Victor..." I admonished.

"Fine," he relented, smiling sheepishly at me. "I have a surprise for you," he admitted, leaning down to press his lips to mine. "C'mon, we're going for a ride, Gracie."

I stop cleaning the string beans as the memories work their way to the surface. Since my visit with Vic I haven't had a moment alone. I'm not sure if that's a good thing or not. I've been begging God for a moment of quiet, just a sliver of silence, which is ironic, since my husband turned himself in all I have left is silence. It drives me mad, sitting here, day after day, alone in this big house with nothing but the memories of the life we shared, the life we made that was cut short.

I felt the car stop rolling and Victor's hands on my shoulders.

"Can I take the blindfold off now?"

"Not yet," he replied and even with my eyes shielded I knew my husband was smiling at me. I felt it in my bones, I heard it in his voice. Vic's smile, his

happiness, it was just as contagious as everything else about him. I grinned as he opened my door and helped me out of the car.

"Just a few more steps, Gracie," he crooned, placing his hands on my shoulders. "Right there. Stop. Are you ready, sweetheart?"

"I'm ready, Victor," I whispered nervously. I never knew what to expect with Victor and usually I rolled with the punches. After all, I was the wife of the most notorious mobster in New York. What other choice did I have?

He lifted the blindfold and slowly I opened my eyes blinking against the sunlight as I stared at the brick mansion that took up more than half of a block. It was a corner property, a house we had passed a bunch of times, one I always stopped to look at.

"Welcome home, love," Victor whispered against my ear.

Victor thought I used to stare at this house with envy but the truth was I'd look at it and wonder what kind of people lived in a house like this. I assumed the previous owners had a big family to need a house of this size to call home. And then the monstrosity became ours and I had the answer to my question.

The little, semi-detached, two family we were living in since we first got married wasn't big enough, no, it wasn't grand enough for Victor Pastore and his family. Victor had risen to the top, and every king needed a castle. Our house wasn't a home but a statement to the rest of the world.

I want to scream; I want to cry. I want to wake up from the nightmare. I swipe my hand across the counter, sending the fancy canisters lining the granite counter top shattering against the floor. Flour and sugar splatter everywhere, and I don't give a damn.

It feels good.

Next to go flying across the kitchen is a ceramic bowl full of fruit and after that I pull the pots and pans off the rack hanging above the island. Tears stream down my cheeks as I wreck my kitchen and grieve for the man I loved and lost, the life we made and the future we no longer have.

Grabbing things out of the drawers, I fling them over my shoulder with no regard until I hear my name.

"Grace!"

I freeze, dropping the wooden spoons to the floor as I slowly turn around and stare back at my sister-in-law. My cheeks flushed with embarrassment as my body quivers. I open my mouth to speak but can't find the words.

"What the hell are you doing?" she asks calmly, stepping over the debris as she walks further into the kitchen.

"I'm sorry," I sob, shaking my head as I take in the destruction. "I don't know what came over me."

Shamefully, I peel my eyes from her and bend down to pick up the pieces of the shattered canisters and ceramic bowl. Gina closes her hand over my wrist and cups my chin with her other hand, forcing my eyes back to hers.

"Grace," she soothes.

"Where is your mother?"

"Bert took her upstairs when we heard the commotion," she replies.

"Good, I don't want her to see this," I mutter, taking a deep breath as I lean back on my haunches.

"We went to see Victor," she reveals.

"Oh," I say, turning away from her.

"He told me, Grace," she whispers.

I drag my eyes back to hers, seeing they're full of unshed tears. I had thirty years of training under my belt and before I volunteered any information, I knew to ask first.

"He told you what?"

"I'm not a fed or some lawyer looking for you to give up Victor's secrets, I'm your sister-in-law, and I'm telling you I know the truth, but if you want me to say it, fine."

It was force of habit, not admitting the truth about anything, never being the one to start a conversation for fear of giving up too much information. But it wasn't the habit that stopped me from speaking my truth, it was fear. Since my last visit with Vic I haven't uttered the one word that would truly end us.

I used to think it was prison.

Then he said the word.

"Cancer," the same word Gina just uttered.

One word was all it took to destroy a lifetime. One word that opened the flood gates to my tears.

It was one thing to accept that he was in jail, that for the rest of our lives he would be behind bars and I would be behind the brick walls of our home. I accepted we'd never share a bed again, or wake up to the dawn of a new day together. I accepted that every milestone we should have experienced together in our golden years, I'd experience by myself. I'd walk our daughter down the aisle and when the priest asked who gave this woman's hand in marriage, I will dutifully reply—her father and I do. I would sign all our cards love Victor and Grace, and tell our grandchildren, 'grandpa sends his love' or 'grandpa picked out your present' ensuring Vic remained part of our lives.

However, now God was testing me again and my husband was dying.

I can't accept that.

I can't accept that he refuses treatment.

I can't accept I won't be by his side as he draws his final breath.

I can't accept that I'll get a phone call from the warden telling me my husband died surrounded by bars instead of the family we created.

I can't.

"Grace," Gina coaxes. "He's worried about you, and quite frankly so am I."

"He's worried about me?" shaking my head, I wipe my cheeks with the back of my hands. "Always worried about me when he should be worried about himself. I'm fine. I'm not the one who is rotting away in a jail cell."

"You might not be in jail, sweetie, but you're wasting away just like your husband."

"I'm fine! I'm not the one who is sick. I'm not the one who is dying," I cry.

"Don't kid yourself, Grace. Vic is dying but so are you. You're dying inside and you can smile and try to pretend like it's okay but he sees it. Every time you visit him he looks into your eyes and sees that the light has gone out. Even if the man didn't have cancer, he'd wish for it because watching your spirit die is too much for him to take."

"What am I supposed to do, Gina? How am I supposed to act? Tell me! Tell me how I'm supposed to feel?"

"Stop hiding how you feel. Stop fucking smiling when you want to cry. Stop pretending," she orders. "Let it out, Grace, because keeping it bottled up is killing you too."

"My girls..." I whisper.

"Need their mother," she replies.

"Don't you think I know that?" I seethe. "Don't you think I know this will break their hearts? Why do you think I haven't told them yet? I don't even know where to begin, I'm so angry. I'm so mad at him. I feel guilty for being angry because he didn't ask to be sick but like everything else, I'm the one left here to deal with it. I'm the one who has to tell our daughters their father has a few months to live. I'm the one who has to tell them he's being transferred to a prison down south so he can follow through with some sick vendetta. I'm so angry that he's being transferred, robbing us of the visits we can have before he dies."

"He's doing it on purpose, Grace. It's not only about the promise he made that biker and his club but it's because he doesn't want you and his girls to see him deteriorate. He wants you to remember him the way he's always been."

"What about what I want? What about what the girls want? We never had a say in much but we're the ones who will suffer when he leaves this world. —We should have a say! I vowed to love him through sickness and health and I thought when the time came that one of us became sick we would be there for one another. I've been robbed of my vows. I should be there taking care of him. I should be holding his hand when he takes his final breath! I should be able to say goodbye..."

I take a deep breath, trying to compose myself as I stand, bracing my hands on the counter and bow my head.

"How am I going to live without him?" I sob.

"You already are," Gina replies.

"It's not the same," I argue. "How am I going to live the rest of my life, never being able to hear him call me Gracie, never being able to look him in the eye and see our whole life reflected in those eyes?" I shake my head before glancing over my shoulder and staring at Gina.

"How am I going to tell our girls their father is dying? How am I going to be strong enough for them?"

"I'll help you, Bert will help too and so will Ma. You're not alone, Grace. We're crazy and maybe a little eccentric but we're family and we all love Adrianna and Nikki..." she pauses, "We love you too, Grace."

I spin around, dropping my hands to my sides and lean my back against the counter.

"I have to tell the girls," I say finally.

As a parent we try our best to shelter our children, even when they become adults, we can't help ourselves and still we try to protect them. I can't protect, I can't shield my daughters from losing their father but I will be their rock, their strength when they're too weak with grief.

And when their hearts start to mend, then and only then will I grieve. Alone I will mourn my love, my life. My Victor.

Chapter Eight

VICTOR

Dragging the comb through my gray hair, I make sure not a strand is out of place. Smoothing down the front of my jumpsuit, I flash back to a time in my life when I used to fit the most expensive cufflinks to my silk shirt. Some might call me vain, even eccentric, but in my world, appearances are everything. It's that first moment when you meet someone, when they size you up with their eyes and decide your importance to them. You are either someone they want to know or someone they'll forget.

I was nineteen years old when I sat at a table with the five most lethal men in the mafia. Each of them ruled one of the five most prominent crime families in New York City. I was just a kid, another street thug looking for the easy way out. I wasn't the first young guy looking to take the oath they were selling and I wouldn't be the last. But I walked into that warehouse with confidence and a demeanor like they only saw when they stared in the mirror. I was the youth who had an old soul and enough swagger to demand they notice me.

I wasn't someone you forgot.

I was Victor fucking Pastore, and I would be the man ruling their streets long after they took their final breath.

Me.

I would be the boss.

The man in a designer suit that men feared and civilians gravitated to.

Victor Pastore the mobster—the fucking legend.

And for most of my life that is who I was. I was the man you wanted to know, the guy you wanted in your corner and it didn't matter that I was a criminal. I lied, robbed, and killed to get to the top, but to the public I could do no wrong—I was a fucking god.

Even here, locked up, I'm somebody. I'm the guy with juice, the man you come to in the yard when someone is trying to shake you down for your commissary.

I went from running New York to ruling a federal prison. Everyone is in my pocket, from the COs to the warden, they all answer to me. The feds want to think they took me off the streets, cleaned up the city and freed it from the mob, but that isn't so.

There was no elaborate case against me that took years to build. I was a man on a mission to save what I had destroyed—my family. Not the one I ruled but the one I created with my wife, Grace. I was too busy building an empire to realize I was losing the people that mattered most to me. The flashy lifestyle they were accustomed to became more of a burden than something glorified, and as everything spiraled out of control, my daughters both threatened to fall victims to the mob, each of their lives compromised.

I had a choice to make.

My empire or their lives.

I confessed to every crime I committed, every hit I ordered, and gave my family one final gift—sparing them the life I brought them all into as a judge sentenced me to spend the rest of my existence in a cell.

They are free of my sins, my crimes and my organization.

Free from me.

My eyes wander to the photograph of my daughters taped to the wall of my cell. Their smiling faces stare back at me—those faces are the legacy of Victor Pastore—the husband and father.

"Vic, you have a visitor," the guard calls, forcing me to tear my eyes from the photograph and glance over my shoulder at him. I watch as he unlocks my cell, sliding it open and stepping aside.

"Thank you," I say, stepping out of my confinements and pat him on the shoulder. The inmates stare at me as he escorts me down the cell block. They call out to me, "You the man, Vic. You the man."

Those words used to make me feel something but they're lackluster now, just words. A man is nothing without his woman or his family. Without them a man becomes lost in the bitterness.

They buzz me into the visitor's room, my eyes immediately dart around, searching for one of the men I summoned here. The clock is ticking for me and it's time to put all the final touches on the plans I've worked hard to create. In a few short weeks I'll be transferred down south where the ultimate enemy is, the G-Man, the man I vowed to bring to his death.

One last hit.

And it can go either way.

My life or his.

There are ends I need to tie and people to say goodbye to.

The end is near, the curtain will close and all that will be left is the name that made headlines and the legacy he left behind.

I spot the suit, threads of silk, colored in a deep charcoal and tailored to fit the man.

I taught him well.

He lifts his head, leans back in the metal chair as he takes in his surroundings. His green eyes finally pausing when they met mine. He pushes back his chair and rises to his full height to greet me. I noticed he wasn't wearing a tie and the top button of his dress shirt was unbuttoned, his collar was popped, we'd have to talk about that.

"Uncle Vic," he greets, stepping around the table to extend his hand to me. The guard stares at my nephew's hand before turning his back and allowing the gesture. I slide my hand into his and pat his cheek with my free hand.

"Rocco," I say, shaking his hand. "Thank you for coming."

I tip my chin toward the chair as I drop my hand from his.

"Sit," I order, watching him do as he was told.

Rocco was Grace's sister, Anna's son, her eldest child and the one who struggled most of his youth between right and wrong. His father, Rocco Spinelli Sr., was a drug trafficker and when his kids were young, he was deported back to Italy. Anna took Rocco and Gina, her daughter, to Italy afterwards to live, wound up returning five years later after her husband was murdered in a drug deal gone south.

Anna died seven years ago after a long battle with breast cancer and her son came to me, looking for a job. He despised what his father stood for, hated the fact drugs and greed were associated with his name, deciding he wanted to change the way people perceived Rocco Spinelli Junior.

I gave him a job within the organization and he worked his way up to becoming the soldier in charge of the trade business. Rocco was in charge of the docks, controlling the Longshoremen's Association and the local union contracts I had in my pocket. He reminded me a lot of myself, thirsty for power and eager to make a name for himself.

I schooled him on the values and code that the Pastore family abided by. We weren't about drugs, and no innocent children would overdose on our watch. We kept the streets as clean as possible, shutting down any dealers that threatened to sell their product on our territory. After he mastered that I sent him down to Miami Florida and put him in charge of my interests there. I owned three night clubs down there and business was thriving. Miami was flooded with drugs but they didn't touch my clubs and that was all Rocco's doing. He kept things clean and profitable.

"Anthony should be here any minute," I began, folding my hands neatly on top of the table. "How did everything go with the men?"

"Everyone thought the Pastore family was dead. They were just about ready to disburse your territory amongst the five families when I walked in and introduced myself," he informs me. "The boss of the Pastore crime family."

Smiling, I imagine the stunned faces of every mob boss rivaling against my organization, looking to take over my territory. I made it clear a long time ago, I wasn't someone to be underestimated.

I stare back at Rocco—the future of my empire.

We'd never die.

Never end.

Rocco Spinelli would carry the legacy of Victor Pastore—the gangster. My empire would continue to reign even after I was buried.

"Did you square away everything in Miami?"

"Joaquin DeLeo will take my place, controlling the clubs and small business ventures I have down there. As for New York, I'm pulling Rienzi off the docks like we discussed, and I will appoint him as my underboss. We'll be small for a while as soldiers and enforcers climb the ranks but I'm not worried. You're sure Parrish and his club will have my back until I can strengthen the organization?"

"Son, you know better than to question me," I chastise, turning my head as my son-in-law appears in the room. Anthony stood out amongst everyone in the room and although his appearance differed from Rocco's, wearing a pair of sweatpants and fitted t-shirt that stretched across every muscle he worked hard at strengthening, there was no denying he was a force to be reckoned with. He used to be the most lethal man in my organization, the one who did most of my dirty work, allowing my hands to remain clean and his covered in blood.

He traded in his title as my enforcer to be my daughter's husband, and though the mob runs in his veins, something he won't ever truly escape, he wakes every day and attempts to be everything I never was. He is a husband that comes home night after night and a father who tucks his children into bed and reads them a bedtime story.

Anthony narrows his eyes and pins them onto Rocco as he makes his way toward us.

"Anthony, so glad you could join us," I greet, waving my hand to the empty seat beside Rocco. "Have a seat."

"What the fuck is this, Vic?"

"Relax," I soothe. "That's why you're here, for me to explain."

"Bianci, always a pleasure," Rocco sneers, his gaze never wavering under Anthony's scrutiny.

He's perfect.

Anthony pulls out the chair and sinks into it, crossing his arms against his chest, covering the Xonerated logo branded to his shirt.

"You said I was here because you had a message for Jack," he started, tipping his chin toward Rocco. "He have anything to do with that?"

"He is the message you will bring to Jack Parrish's doorstep," I explain, cocking my head to the side as I stare back at him.

"What?"

I opened my mouth but Rocco leaned forward, tapping his hand against the edge of the table, beckoning Anthony's attention.

"Let me clarify for you. You will bring me to the Satan's Knights compound and introduce me to my new ally as I am now the boss of the Pastore family."

Anthony's eyes divert back to me.

"You're shitting me, right?"

"Problem?" Rocco challenges.

"Yeah, motherfucker, there's a problem," Anthony hisses. "What the fuck is going on, Vic? I thought this was done, I thought the organization was null and void."

"You thought wrong," Rocco declares.

"I'm not talking to you, motherfucker," Anthony barks, slamming his fist against the table.

"You better control yourself, Bianci," Rocco warns.

"Enough," I interrupt. "Anthony, Rocco has already sat down with the five families. It's done. He will control all aspects of the organization. You really didn't think I would sit back and watch people pick apart my empire; just let them have at it, did you? I thought you knew me better than that," I accuse.

"I'm not understanding, Vic," Anthony says, gritting his teeth as he runs his fingers through his slicked back hair. "After you went away, Jimmy became the acting boss," he started, pointing a finger at Rocco, "Where was he?"

"I knew before everyone, before I even turned myself in that Jimmy had gone against me, that he was working with the G-Man even before Val's death. After the shoot-out at Temptations, when Adrianna pulled that trigger, I had to make changes. My family couldn't go on suffering for my crimes. Then Nikki was kidnapped by Deke Rogers and Mikey was shot and nearly killed. I went to Rocco and told him I was turning myself in. I told him what Jimmy had done, that he had a hand in killing my underboss and that I had to still get the G-Man." I pause, taking in the shocked expression on his face. Ah, you got to love the element of surprise.

"It was all part of the plan, Anthony. I went to Rocco before they cuffed me in Florida and after he took his oath I turned myself in. I let Jimmy dig his hole deeper and deeper, bided my time and Rocco's, giving him an opportunity to know my organization like the back of his hand. It's time for him to reign now, especially with me being transferred to the G-Man."

Anthony remained silent.

"You're going to take Rocco to Jack, make sure the alliance we have with the club carries over with Rocco as the boss. Rocco will run the family with the same values and earn Jack's respect just like I did. Now, I've given Jack and the club control over some of my interests but other than that, Rocco will run things from now on. Jack knows Rocco is in the business but he doesn't know he's taking over my organization and that he is now the boss of the Pastore family. The Pastore family isn't going under like everyone assumed it would."

"This is bullshit," Anthony seethes.

"Why don't you say it, man? You're only grief with Vic's decision is that he chose me instead of you," Rocco accuses.

Anthony snaps his head and glares at Rocco.

"Know what the fuck you're talking about before you speak. It was my choice to leave this life, mine and mine alone."

"Right, and you got the out that nobody gets. You got to walk away and claim a life for yourself. You got a fucking family, man, a beautiful family…you don't need to be in my shoes," Rocco says. "I don't have what you do. I've got no one that stands a chance at getting hurt by the choices I make. The only life I'm responsible for is my own."

Anthony balls his fists as he digests Rocco's words for a moment before turning his gaze back to me.

"You're slick, Vic. Always have been and always will be I suppose," he mutters.

"And don't you forget it," I tell him, leaning back in my chair. "Which leads me to the next order of business, I didn't forget about you or Michael for that matter. —You'll always need protection and the Satan's Knights can only do so much. The club has their own enemies they have to worry about and can't always be relied upon to take care of what's mine. Rocco will provide protection to both of you as well as your families for a legit place within the organization," I reveal.

"Adrianna will kill me if I go back, Vic. I can't do that to her, I won't do that to her and I won't do that to my kids—"

"I'm not offering you your old place back. I'd never do that," I interrupt. "Someone will have to run the contracts for the docks and I want that someone to be you. I've set Michael up to be the foreman in the local union, Rocco will make sure the union is covered and all jobs they bid on they'll get."

"So, we'll still be in the fold and earn the respect and benefits of being made men without having to kill anyone?" he asks incredulously, anger dripping off of each word.

"So you'll be protected," I correct, leaning forward and pinning him with a stare. "I'm making sure my family is taken care of because when I die I won't be here to protect any of you."

Anthony narrows his eyes, staring back at me skeptically.

"What aren't you telling me?"

"I've told you all you need to know. Now, Jack's waiting for you to introduce him to his new ally…you know better than to keep the Bulldog waiting," I reprimand.

I push back my chair, standing before signaling for the guard to take me back to my cell.

"Give my daughter a kiss and tell those two babies of yours their grandpa loves them," I rasp before looking to my nephew. "Button your collar and buy yourself a tie goddamn it. Appearances are everything."

My legacy will live on in the lives of the two men staring at my back as I walk away from them. One will carry my family and the other my empire.

I'll die but my name will always live on.

Chapter Nine

JACK

Inspecting it for any rough edges, I run my hand over the freshly sanded table making sure Bosco had taken my order seriously when I demanded him to sand and prime this damn thing. This table was as much a part of our club as I was. It had been through hell and back just like everyone who ever sat around it. My predecessor, Cain, and his old man, Pops, built this table with their own hands and it has held up through war, death and the exchange of power. As long as I hold this gavel this fucking table will stand tall, and should the day come when I retire from this life, Blackie better be prepared to have his sanding papers ready.

I pull out the chair at the head of the table, taking my rightful seat, and lean my back against the worn chair as I reach for my pack of cigarettes.

I have to quit.

I bring the cigarette to my lips and fish through my pockets for a light.

Tomorrow I'll quit or the day after that.

I light the Marlboro and take a nice, long drag.

I'll quit smoking before the kid is born for sure. I better or Reina will have my balls.

I scowl at the clock on the wall, noting these fucks are five minutes late for church. The door slams open in that moment and the circus comes barreling through.

"What part of 'church in five minutes' did you bitches not comprehend?" I growl, blowing out a ring of smoke.

I watch my men take their seats, Blackie sits at my left and next to him is Riggs—the next seat stands empty as we keep it in place for our fallen brother, Bones. Wolf and Pipe park their asses across from my vice president and the self-proclaimed Tiger. The club's new blood fill the seats at the other end of the table.

Our club has grown, adding Linc, Deuce and Cobra into the mix—thank fuck for that because we need all the men we can get. And let me not forget about Stryker, that poor bastard is doing a bid in Riker's for a possession charge. He got the shit end of the stick, finally decided to trade in his nomad patch and take a seat at my table, only to get his ass thrown in the can. After Blackie got locked up, I had to send someone inside to keep him safe and deliver my right hand his orders. I'll make it up to him somehow.

Our brotherhood didn't stop there though, we've recruited some new prospects, and they stood in the back of the room, leaning against the wall.

I'm not getting a bigger fucking table, let those fuckers stand.

"Sorry boss, but I had to take a piss and Pipe wanted to watch, been a while since he found his dick, he needed a reminder of what a real cock looks like," Wolf explains.

"Fuck you, Wolf," Pipe replies. "My dick is just fine."

"If you can find it," Wolf chuckles.

"I'm going to kill him," Pipe vows, staring at me. "With or without your consent."

"Enough ladies, let's get down to business," I begin, biting the side of my cheek so I don't laugh as Wolf holds up his pinky finger, mocking the length of Pipe's dick.

I glance over at Riggs, watching as he messes with his phone. I grin, tipping my head toward Blackie who leans back and peers at the screen of Riggs' phone.

"You naughty Kitten just wait until I get home," Blackie reads from Riggs' phone out loud, disguising his voice to mock the Tiger.

"Hey, man! That shit is personal," Riggs snarls. "That's foul, especially after I kept your shit with Lacey under lock and key."

"Calm down, Tiger. You know I've got nothing but love for you and your kitten," Blackie teases.

"I bet if I pulled out your phone and did a read-a-long, Jackie boy wouldn't be laughing," Riggs fires back, narrowing his eyes in my direction.

"Point for Riggs," I mutter, not needing a reminder that Blackie's sleeping with my damn daughter.

Wolf throws his head into his hands and groans before pinning his eyes toward the other end of the table where the nomads stare at us like we are a bunch of assholes.

"Do us all a favor and don't become pussy whipped like the rest of these assholes," he begs. "You fuckers are all I have left to keep me from looking for a fourth wife."

"Shouldn't the fact you have three exes be enough to stop you from seeking a fourth?" Linc questions grinning at Wolf. "We'll leave the ball and chains on that side of the table."

"I wouldn't mind a ball and chain," Deuce drawls, flashing his smile full of southern charm.

"Been a while since you found your dick too, huh?" Wolf questions Satan's cowboy.

"Nothing wrong with the man looking for a good woman to keep him warm at night, especially after coming back from the dark side," I argue, glancing back at Deuce. "Boy's looking for his heart—"

"Here we go again," Riggs mumbles.

"Found yours didn't you?" I fire back.

"What about you, Cobra? You're awfully quiet," Blackie interjects, leaning back in his chair and crossing his arms against his chest.

It took a moment but Cobra finally lifted his head acknowledging that Blackie had asked him a question.

"I may have taken a chair at this table but I'm loner at heart," he replies hoarsely.

I peer down the length of the table at the man covered in ink from his neck down to his toes and stare into his dull eyes.

Demons.

Each one of us sitting here has them. Some of us hide them better than others, then there's Cobra who wears them on his skin. Each intricate piece of art tells his story, portraying his demons and giving us insight to the man of mystery.

"I'm almost afraid to ask, but fuck, someone has to grab their balls, why are we here, Bulldog?" Wolf asks, forcing me to peel my eyes off Cobra's arms and the face tattooed on his forearm.

"Two reasons, but since Bianci thinks he can waste my time just like the rest of you, I'll give you the good news first," I grunt, knowing any kind of news coming down the pipe from Victor is bound to give me a fucking headache. "I'm getting hitched."

"Yeah, we know, got that woman of yours wearing a rock as big as Pipe's dick," Wolf taunts.

"She finally give you the green light?" Blackie asks.

"Yeah," I grin. "One month from today Reina will officially become Property of Parrish."

"Praise Jesus," Pipe mocks, clasping his hands together as he stares up at the ceiling.

"So does that mean more of them family dinners you two like to put on?" Wolf probes.

"That means you idiots get to whip this shithole into shape because we're having the wedding here."

"Here?" Pipe asks incredulously.

"Where else would the Bulldog get married?" I reply.

"Clearly, this won't be a black-tie affair," Linc chimes in.

"Reina wants to keep it simple and I want to do whatever the fuck makes her happy," I tell them. "Any of you have a problem with that?"

My eyes roam the table, daring one of them to speak before I settle my gaze on Blackie.

"And you, you'll be at my side just as you are now," I ground out.

"You asking me to be your best man?" Blackie queries, biting back a grin.

"It's only fitting since Reina's asking Lacey to be her maid of honor," I mumble.

Blackie leans over, places his arm on my back and gives me a firm pat.

"I've got you, brother," he says sincerely.

"I object, I mean I get it, he's your VP and all that, but best man? Just tell me…was I even in the running?" Riggs questions.

The door opens and Bianci strolls through, leaving it open behind him.

"Well if it isn't my favorite brother-in-law," Riggs cheers, turning his attention to Anthony. I think the little fucker has ADD or some shit.

"Don't recall you marrying my sister," Bianci growls.

"Made her my Kitten, Bianci, that shit is worth more than my given name," Riggs shoots back.

"You're late," I accuse, glancing over his shoulder at the open door. "Any particular reason?"

Bianci turns around as a suit comes through the door, not just any suit but Rocco Spinelli, the newest gangster wannabe to hit the streets.

For fuck's sake, these mob folk are fucked, as Riggs would say.

And they always fucking wind up on my doorstep.

"What's he doing here?"

"Parrish," Rocco greets before diverting his eyes to my brothers. "Gentlemen," he adds.

"That's a first," Wolf grunts. "Don't recall the last time anyone called any of us a gentleman."

"Your mother called me one last night when I bent her over," Pipe retorts.

"My mother's been dead ten years."

"I'm not above it, man," Pipe says matter-of-factly.

"Oh fuck, that's wrong," Deuce declares.

"Enough!" I shout, slamming my hand against the table, fixing Bianci with a hard stare. "Start talking," I order.

Bianci shakes his head, blowing out a ragged breath as he runs his fingers through his hair roughly before turning back to Rocco.

"What's the matter, Bianci? Cat got your tongue?" Blackie queries from beside me. His voice thick with agitation and suspicion.

"Apparently," Rocco mutters, standing tall as his gaze falls onto me. "From this point forward I am the boss of the Pastore organization. I will handle all prior and future endeavors that carry my uncle's name."

"Your uncle?"

"Victor is my uncle," He clarifies.

"What the fuck kind of bullshit is this?" I roar, rising from my chair. "And why am I finding this shit out now? Start fucking explaining, Bianci."

"I knew he was his nephew. I didn't know shit about him taking Victor's place," he sneers, glaring at Rocco. "That shit is as much of a new development to me as it is to you."

"So, Vic pulled the wool over your eyes?" Blackie questions.

"Vic did what he had to do," Rocco argues. "Now, you've worked with me in the past. I don't think I need to remind you people of the massacre you left behind on my pier after I gave you the tip on Sun Wu's shipment." He raises an eyebrow as he unbuttons his fancy suit jacket and slides one hand into his pocket.

This fucking guy was Victor's clone—just a younger version of the dapper don himself.

Wolf leans across Pipe, snaps his fingers at me to get my attention, and with his face set in stone he finally speaks.

"You want me to pop a cap in this fools ass?"

I couldn't even ask God to help me. That son of a bitch turned his back on me a long time ago. No, this circus was all me, these monkeys were mine. Fuck my life.

"The way I see it, nothing has to change where your club and our organization is concerned. We all want the same thing—to be the only people who run these streets and keep them clean. I'm here to ensure that remains intact and give you my word I will raise hell and bury any motherfucker who pollutes my city with shit."

"Your city," I repeat.

"My city," he confirms. "It could be ours, Parrish. We could take this fucking town and turn it into something no one expects, have people bowing and praying at our feet but you've got to give me the same respect you gave Victor."

Victor earned my respect.

This guy strode into my chapel and demanded it.

"Not looking to step on your toes man, looking for a partnership. I'm starting out small, it's going to take a lot to get my name out there, for people to know this face but I'm determined. I want your partnership but I won't be at your mercy," he vows, reaching into his pocket to produce a business card. He places it on top of the table and moves it in front of me with his index finger. His green eyes examine me as he shoves his hands back into his pockets and shrugs his shoulders.

"Your call, Parrish. You can either sit back and watch me rise to the top or the Satan's Knights can ride beside me. It's what you people do right, ride to the death?" he turns on his heel, his gaze lingering on Bianci for a moment before he walks out the door like he didn't just turn shit upside down.

"What the fuck was that, Bianci?" Blackie accuses.

"That," he points his thumb toward the door, "Isn't going away and apparently neither is the Pastore name."

"That guy is Vic's looney toon sister's kid?" Riggs asks.

"No," he says. "Look, I'll give you whatever fucking information you want but the truth is, Vic has trained him for this since before Temptations went up in smoke. He knew Jimmy was a fucking rat bastard before any of us did. He never planned on letting that sick fuck take over anything."

"You're telling me that Vic knew before he turned himself in that he would have this guy running his shit?" I ask him, shaking my head as I take it all in.

"That's exactly what I'm saying. You got questions for Vic then you better drag your ass up to visit him because he's being transferred to the G-Man within a couple of weeks."

Blackie's head shot up at that. We all wanted the G-Man to pay for every fucked up thing he did but nobody wanted his blood more than Blackie.

"It's almost over," Bianci adds. "Time's running out."

He runs his fingers through his hair and stares at the floor.

"I've gotta get out of here. I need to get to the gym," he mutters, lifting his head and starting for the door.

"Bianci," I call.

"No, Jack, I'm out of here," he grounds out, taking off before I could get in another word.

"I'd hate to be the heavy bag he's about to hit," Wolf comments.

"He misses the life," Riggs states.

"Ain't that a fact," Blackie mumbles.

Lifting the card Rocco left behind, the voices surrounding me fade and I stare at his name. Fucking Vic, man, always one step ahead of everyone. Just when you're ready to count him out he stands tall and demands the show go on.

"Clear out boys," Blackie orders, reaching for the gavel and slamming it against the table, knowing I had checked out and was wrapped up in my head.

Once the room empties, Blackie is the only one left. I sink back into my seat and flick the business card at him.

"What're you thinking, Bulldog?"

"I'm thinking Victor Pastore is someone the world won't ever forget. That motherfucker won't let anyone forget him." I pull out a cigarette, hastily bring it to my mouth and shake my head in wonder. "Just when you think you're out they pull you back in," I mutter, the cigarette dangling between my lips.

"You reciting mob movies now?" he pulls the cigarette from my mouth and takes a drag. "Shit, we're fucked." He takes another pull before handing me back the cigarette.

We went from passing blunts to passing Marlboros.

Times are changing.

Thank fuck for that.

"Okay, look, the way I see it, and you know I've given you all sorts of shit for getting in bed with Vic from the start," he reminds me, "The way I see it," he repeats, "Vic's never steered us wrong. He's been as loyal to our club as anyone who has ever worn our patch." He shrugs his shoulders, placing the business card flat on the table. "He's a man of his word and if he sent Rocco to us, then he did so with good intentions. I say we give the guy a shot."

I stare back at him, noticing for the first time his hair wasn't hanging in his face. The son of a bitch even trimmed the scruff on his face. Leaning forward, I inspect my brother, seeing the whites of his eyes. Gone were the beady, bloodshot eyes of an addict. The pain he hung onto for dear life was gone too. And I know if he sheds his jacket I won't find a track mark either.

Blackie was reborn.

Maybe he was right.

Maybe everyone deserved a shot.

At least one.

"I'll make arrangements to visit Vic and give Rocco a call," I say finally.

"Good."

"What's good is seeing you like this," I reply. "Been a long time since I saw you happy."

"Yeah, well, without mentioning her name, she's the one responsible for the man I am."

"You can mention her name," I grunt.

Blackie laughs.

Fuck.

He laughed.

My little girl is the woman responsible for bringing that laugh back to the world.

"I'm heading home," he declares, rising from his seat. "Lacey's waiting for me."

Yeah, that shit is going to take some getting used to.

A whole motherfucking lifetime.

Chapter Ten

Adrianna

I was fifteen years old when I realized I was born to love Anthony Bianci. He was twenty years old and at the crossroads of his life—stuck between the streets and the man he was at heart. He didn't have a father figure growing up and thought that to be a man he had to follow in the footsteps of the men in the neighborhood—men like my father. Anthony knew the consequences of the mob; knew he'd break his mother's heart when he dropped out of school to become my father's lackey—fulfilling what he thought was his destiny. It didn't matter how pure his heart was, he was jaded by the empty promises my father bestowed upon him. A young man desperate for the mob boss' approval.

Back in the day, Anthony's quest for the mob was the only thing that mattered to him. Power, money and respect were the things he craved most in the world. They were his forbidden temptation—until I came along and our love then became the forbidden temptation.

I knew our love was everything before it was something.

He did too.

That's why he fought against it for as long as he did. Realizing there was no use fighting—when loving was worth more than any order sent down the chain of the mob—Anthony gave in to love. He gave me his love, took mine in return and promised me the world. He promised me the good life.

Our love was bigger than the mob—it would withstand the most trying circumstances and prevail each time someone tried to destroy us. Most of the time it was us doing the damage, but when it wasn't us ripping one another's hearts out, it was my father trying to destroy us.

I never made Anthony chose me over the mob, it was something he did of his own accord. He chose our family over the only life he's ever known, and as much as I love him for it, I also understand the struggle behind his decision.

Men like my father, like my husband, are often pulled from the streets but those streets, the lifestyle, it will always be one with the man. My husband wakes up every morning and goes to work like every other blue-collar guy. He owns a gym and when he's not training himself he's taking the time to teach underprivileged kids how to box, hoping they'll never be one with the streets.

Because Anthony knows firsthand that once you're a street guy—that doesn't end. It doesn't matter how good life is, or how much he loves his family, the streets will always be ingrained in his soul.

As much as Anthony wants to think he's out of the mob, a part of him always will be stuck. It's the reason he is the first to help Jack Parrish and his club. It's the reason he goes to visit my dad without me.

Like today.

Today he went up to visit my father, only he never came home afterward. He didn't call like he usually does when he's on his way back, and when I tried calling him he didn't answer. Knowing something must have transpired, I asked my sister and Mike to watch my kids and took off for the gym.

The gym was locked, most of the lights were off but peering through the glass door I spot him. I stare at him momentarily, watch as he pummels the heavy bag in the dimly lit corner of the gym. Boxing was something he picked up in prison and mastered, making it look like an art form. He's light on his feet, moving them expertly as he dances around the bag. Grabbing my keys, I unlock the gym and continue to stare at him. I watch the cords of every sinewy muscle in his back flex as he throws jab after jab. It ignites a fire within me. I try to focus on the reason I came here but my body is out of control, like a frayed live wire.

I grab the pads from behind the counter and fit them snuggly to my hands before making my way toward him. Anthony is a man who always makes sure he's aware of his surroundings, a force of habit for someone who has spent most of his life looking over his shoulder. Yet, he didn't know I was there watching him, completely in the zone which confirmed he was off.

Stepping around the bag, I make my presence known as he goes for a right cross. His blue eyes peer up at me and his face glistens with a fresh sheen of sweat as he reaches for the chain used to suspend the bag and stops it from swinging toward me.

"Let's go, Bianci," I urge, holding my hands up as I step to the side.

He takes a deep breath, pinning his eyes to mine as he contemplates my offer, giving a slight shake of the head.

The leather makes a slapping noise as I smack the pads together, holding them up to him again.

"I said, let's go, Bianci. Now, let's go. Give me your best shot," I taunt.

His eyes narrow into tiny slits as he taps my pads lightly with his gloves.

"You call that a jab?" I hiss, rolling my eyes.

"Adrianna," he grits.

"And here I thought you knew how to work a pair of gloves," I bait, holding my hands higher as the jab finally comes.

Right cross, uppercut, hook.

He releases a series of short breaths as he works those jabs against the pads before switching the combo.

Uppercut, cross, jab.

"That's it, give me your aggression, babe," I demand, moving my hands just as he taught me.

"Goddamn it, A," he hisses, before holding his stance and stilling his hands.

Lifting one hand to his mouth, I watch him bow his head and tear the glove from his hand with his teeth. He takes a deep breath before removing the other one, using his free hand this time. I drop my hands to my sides and follow him to the bench. He unravels the tape from his hands as he straddles the bench.

"What're you doing here?" he says.

"Looking for you," I admit. I started to remove the pads from my hands but he stops me, grabbing my hands he pries them off himself.

"I'm sorry I didn't call," he rasps.

"Yeah, you want to tell me what's got you twisted?" I ask, cocking my head to the side as he examines my hands. "Did something happen with my father?"

"It's nothing," he insists, bringing one of my hands to his lips then the other.

"Bullshit, Bianci." I call, pulling my hands back. I lift them to his face, forcing his eyes to mine as I straddle the bench and inch closer to him.

"When I went to visit your old man, I figured he was just giving me another message to deliver to Jack, but he had another visitor, your cousin, Rocco," he explains.

I squint in confusion. Rocco and Gina are my first cousins on my mother's side, and to be honest we don't have much of a relationship with them. We did when we were younger but then their father was deported and they moved back to Italy. Gina is off killing it as some big shot investment banker and the last I heard, Rocco was living in Florida.

"Apparently, your father's been grooming him for a long time to take his place within the organization," Anthony mutters.

"What? Wait a minute, you're telling me Rocco is going to be taking my father's place?" I shake my head in confusion, I drop my hands from his face and place them over my knees, processing what my husband was telling me. I lift my head and look at him as I piece it together.

"Yeah," he confirms.

"And that bothers you," I state, sliding back an inch to better assess him. "Because a part of you wishes it was you taking over, am I right?"

He reaches behind me, grabbing a towel and wiping his face.

"I don't know," he admits, wrapping the towel around his shoulders. "I spent most of my life doing all sorts of fucked up shit, thinking one day I'd be the one Victor handed his empire over to. I sold my fucking soul to the devil and have to live every day with the sins I've committed. This guy comes out of nowhere, spends a year or so under Vic's thumb and suddenly he's in charge."

He twists the ends of the towel in his hands as he stares back at me.

"You want the truth? I'll give you the truth, Reese's. I should be the one in charge, not your cousin," he confesses.

My eyes widen as I stare back at him.

"What are you saying?" I question, taken aback by his confession, trying to understand him and control my own feelings at the same time. Was he telling me he regrets our life? Did he regret choosing me and Luca over the lifestyle he grew accustomed to?

"Don't look at me like that, Reese's," he says, reaching for me and pulling me between his legs. "This is why I didn't come home, I needed to make sense of what I was feeling so I could better explain myself."

"I never asked you to choose," I blurt. "I accepted you for who you were. You were the one who insisted you couldn't be with me, you insisted Luca shouldn't grow up the same way I did, and while I agreed, it was never me who made you choose."

"You want to let me explain?" he argues calmly, brushing away the strands of hair that had fallen from my ponytail.

"It was my choice, and it was the best decision I ever made in my life. If given the chance, I'd always choose you and our kids over that life. But, that life was a part of me for so long, A. It's all I knew, all I know. Until now, since your father turned himself in, there has been one situation after another pulling me back in—

keeping me in the game even if it's just sitting on the sidelines waiting for Jack to call me and tell me he needs information or for me to rough someone up for him. I thought your father's organization was being phased out, I didn't know the whole time he was preparing Rocco to take the reins. There is no place for me in that world anymore and it got me thinking about how I don't know life without the mob. I've always had my hand in something and now there isn't anything left."

He pauses, letting his hands travel down my arms, lacing our fingers together as he continues to stare at me.

"Even Jack's been reminding me I don't have a place within that life anymore. The only reason I made a move when the Red Dragons attacked the MC was because that shit was personal. They shot my sister and forced my nephew to be born before his time, if it wasn't for Riggs coming to me, well, I wouldn't have been involved in taking them down either."

Lifting my fingers to my temple, my head pounds from all he has laid out for me and I begin to knead my fingers against my skin.

"Are you telling me you want a patch now? That you're going to buy a Harley? Because I'm telling you right now I will not be called an old woman. I am not okay with that," I insist, dropping my fingers from my head. "That's Lauren's gig, not mine."

He grins at me.

That wicked grin of his that makes my insides melt every single time. All these years later, I'm still a sucker for that cocky grin and those eyes. Man, those eyes, so cold and uninviting to everyone else, but to me they were home.

"I'm pretty sure they call them old ladies," he corrects, taking hold of my hands again. "And no, I'm not buying a Harley although I wouldn't mind seeing you on one." he Winks, smiling faintly before his face grows serious. "I guess what I'm saying is, I don't know life outside the mob."

He leans his head against mine.

"You married a criminal, baby, that shit don't fade," he whispers, pressing his lips to mine fleetingly. "And while I'm not proud of it, I'm not sure I know how to be an upstanding citizen." He lets out a breathy laugh before glancing around the gym. "I mean is this it?"

Cocking my head to the side, I wrap my arms around his neck and absorb his words. I understood that. The uncertainty of who you are. I feel it all the time and never voice it.

"I feel like a fucking pussy for even saying this," he admits, before leveling me with a stare. "I love you. I love our kids and the life we made and I don't want you to ever doubt that. You are everything I ever wanted and I have no regrets. Not a single one."

"I get it," I whisper, reaching up to thread my fingers through his black hair. "And I think what you're feeling is as natural as breathing. You're happy with your life but if you're not a husband and father, who are you? I ask myself that every day, I just never thought enough to tell you. I ask myself, who am I, if I'm not Victor Pasture's daughter, Anthony Bianci's wife and Luca and Victoria's mom. I mean, I don't even have a job. I'm Adrianna Bianci, wife and mother, but then what?"

"And that's not enough?"

"It is now, but will it always be?" I question.

I thought saying those words made me selfish. There are people who wish for my life, who want nothing more than to find their one true love, marry that person and raise a family. And here I am hoping the happy ending I wanted so badly will be enough for me. But the more I think about it, and think about what Anthony is saying, the more I realize I'm not being selfish, I'm being human.

"Who would've thought once we had it all we wouldn't know what to do with ourselves?" he asks, chuckling slightly as he pulls my head against his bare chest. "You know what?"

"Hmm?" I murmur against his skin, tracing our children's names with my index finger.

"We have all the time in the world to figure out what we both want out of this life. We'll figure it out and we'll do it together," he promises. "You and me, Reese's, we'll get it. We always do."

"I know that," I whisper, pulling back a little. "I want you to promise me you won't shut me out. I want you to remember I know this life just as well as you and that I've lived it too. I might not miss it the same way you do but I will always understand it. Remember we both chose our life over that one, and when you're missing the soldier in you, then you come to me and I'll remind you why that soldier surrendered."

"Yeah?" he rasps, running his hands down my back. "How you going to remind me?"

His fingers toy with the hem of my tank top, inching it up my body as I voluntarily lifted my arms over my head, inviting him to remove my shirt.

"Leave that to me, Bianci." I wink at him. "I promise to always keep it fresh," I add, as he stands and pulls the shirt over my head. His eyes dip to my full chest that threatens to burst out of the sports bra I'm wearing.

"Promise me," I whisper as his eyes find mine.

"I promise you, Reese's," he hisses, bending down as he slides his palms under my ass and lifts me off the bench. "Now, give me that mouth of yours," he demands as I wrap my legs around his waist. "And let me at you."

Chapter Eleven

Nikki

"Uncle Mikey, again!" Luca shouts in between giggles.

"Guys, keep it down," I whisper-shout, as I stare down at my niece. I didn't realize how much a baby could cry. Jesus, I don't remember Luca being this much work, but then again I was nineteen when he was born. Ah, nineteen—when all that mattered was what outfit I'd wear to the next hot club.

Mikey comes barreling into the living room with Luca on his shoulders. My nephew's arms spread wide and his little lips were trying to make airplane noises.

"It's a bird. No, it's a plane. Wait a minute…it's Luca Bianci!" Mikey says as the pair zoom around the couch.

"What time did they say they were coming to get their kids? Never mind, call your sister and tell her if they're not here within the hour we're charging them."

"Uncle Mikey," Luca sings. "Fly!"

"Call. Her. Now."

"My hands are kind of full," I say, staring down at Victoria who is sprawled across my chest. She looks so angelic when she sleeps but she has her mother's horns when she's awake. I can't wait until she grows up—oh the fun.

The doorbell rings and Mikey looks to the ceiling.

"You do exist." He averts his eyes back to mine. "He does exist!"

"Careful, baby it might be Aunt Gina," I tease, throwing him a wink before he flips me the finger and answers the front door.

"There's my boy!" Adrianna cheers.

"Yes, here he is," Mikey says as he crouches down to remove Luca from his shoulders.

"But I don't want to leave! Mommy I want to live with Aunt Nikki and Uncle Mikey," Luca exclaims.

"What? No! We have monsters under the beds," Mikey blurts, lifting Luca into his arms. "But you can visit whenever you want," he continues, ruffling the top of his hair before handing him to Anthony. "As long as Daddy picks you up after an hour. Seriously, what happened to watch the kids for an hour I have to go to the gym," he chastises, turning his attention to my sister.

"We had a little one on one sparing match," Adrianna hints, wrapping her arms around Anthony's waist.

"Oh, that's just dirty," Mikey groans.

"You two look like you had things under control," Anthony says, lifting Luca onto his shoulders.

"Come and get your daughter," I whisper to my sister. "She just fell asleep."

We all walk into the living room together, my sister and Anthony pause in their tracks and stare at me like I had grown a second head or something. Mikey plops down on the sofa across from me and wipes the sweat from his brow.

"Look at you guys playing house," Anthony teases, raising an eyebrow at Mikey.

"Maybe it's time Luca and Tori had a cousin," Adrianna chimes in, taking a seat next to Mike and draping her arm around his back. "I can see you two running after a little Valente."

"If you two have the baby itch then by all means keep breeding but leave us the hell out of it," Mikey responds.

"Daddy, I'm tired," Luca yawns.

"Yeah, it's getting late. C'mon, Reese's grab the baby," he says before turning his gaze to Mikey. "Ain't nothing like having a kid, man."

My sister walks up to me, bends down to carefully transfer the sleeping beauty from one pair of arms to another.

"He's right you know," she whispers, cradling her daughter as she stares back at me. "You'll be a great mom."

I fake a smile, big and bright, and pretend like everything is right with the world. It's not that I don't want kids, actually, I'm not sure what I want. I never gave kids much thought. When Luca was born I decided to be the fun aunt and then Victoria came along and still I was content with being Aunt Nikki. I'll be the one these kids come to when they're too afraid to go to their mom and dad. I'll be their ride when they get themselves into a jam and I'll be the one who smooths things over when Anthony decides to kill Tori's first boyfriend.

Aunt Nikki, the fun aunt.

I glance across the room at Mikey and watch him stand and press a kiss to Tori's sleeping head before giving Luca a high five.

He jokes around a lot, complains even more, but, Mikey loves Luca and Tori. He'd be an awesome dad and if I close my eyes and let myself picture it, I can see us with a kid or two. But that's an image my mind has to work for, one that doesn't come naturally.

Since we were kids, my sister always talked about getting married and having babies. I swear she came out of the womb with a copy of *Modern Bride* tucked under her arm. I was the opposite. I never liked to play house and would rather hang out with the boys in the school yard than play with dolls.

Does it mean I'd be a crappy mom? I'm not entirely sure.

I stand as Mikey escorts Anthony and Adrianna to the door. I watch as he leans against the closed door and peers back at me.

"Thank God," he cries. "I'm fucking beat."

He locks the door behind him and pushes off it, reaching for me. "You coming to bed?"

"I'll be right up," I say, pressing my lips to his. "I need a fucking cigarette after all that."

"Okay," he murmurs against my mouth. "Don't be too long."

"I won't." I smile, lifting my hands to his cheeks. Mikey was my dream come true. Not too many people can say that they nabbed the guy they've always wanted—but me? I totally can. I often ask myself why me, why did I get the happily ever after? And sometimes I'm afraid to question it at all. Sometimes I just sit back and wait for the other shoe to drop because nothing is ever easy in life.

I watch Mikey climb the stairs before grabbing my cigarettes off the table and heading out to the back porch.

I knew it would happen eventually, I knew the other shoe would drop. I just assumed it would be something we could control, something we could work through. Something less threatening, less agonizing. I never expected the thing to rip apart my happiness to be an illness neither of us could control.

Taking a long pull of my cigarette, I try to ease my nerves and shake my head, hoping the thoughts will disappear. I'm overreacting which is so out of character for me. I'm not the girl that worries, or drives herself mad with maybes. I'm the girl that rolls with the punches and when life gives me lemons I make spiked lemonade—a shot or two of vodka and that shit is delicious.

So why am I sitting out here crying?

I angrily wipe my tears only for them to be replaced with fresh ones. Staring at the cigarette in my hand, watching as it burns, I realize I don't even want it. I was hoping it would relieve my anxiety but all it does is remind me how bad smoking is for me. I flick it over the porch and jump when I hear the sliding door close behind me.

I turn my back to Mike and try to blow into my eyes to stop the tears.

"I'll be right in," I say quickly, willing my watering eyes not to betray me as he steps closer. His fingers knead my shoulders as he leans close.

"Princess," he whispers.

I close my eyes as he slowly spins me around in his arms.

"Look at me," he demands softly.

I can't.

I want to disappear.

"Nikki, look at me," he insists.

Clouded by unshed tears, I blink my brown eyes and peer into his that are full of concern and confusion.

"Shit," he growls, wiping my cheeks with his thumbs. "Why are you crying?" I imagine Mike feels panicked watching me unravel. I can count on one hand how many times he's seen me cry and three of them were over the last few weeks. He gets frazzled when I'm emotional, like I'm a freak of nature he doesn't know how to handle.

I don't blame him.

I hate emotional Nikki too.

"Is this about your dad again?"

Right. My dad. The reason everyone thinks I'm distraught. I suppose my dad being in prison is partially the reason I'm sad, but it's not everything—it's not the main reason I've been bursting into tears at the drop of a hat.

After Mikey proposed I was upset, and I cried whenever I thought about our wedding and how my dad wouldn't be there. It's not so much him not walking me down the aisle but knowing I won't dance with him. I'm not even talking about the sappy dance a bride and her dad usually share, I'm talking about real dancing, where you break a sweat and have everyone on their feet watching you. Dancing was kind of our thing, we'd tear up the floor at every family function and on the most important day of my life, he won't be there. Not to give me to Mikey or to dance with me.

It sucks.

It hurts.

"It's not my father," I snap, pushing him away and taking a step back to put even more space between us. "Not everything is about our wedding and my father spending the rest of his miserable life behind bars."

I hated the words I spoke as they left my mouth. I hated the tone they carried and the sharpness of them, but more importantly I hated the look they caused in Mikey's eyes.

"I'm not a mind reader, Princess. You're going to need to elaborate and I'm not allowing you to brush me off so you better choose your words," he grounds out, crossing his arms against his bare chest as he waits for me to explain my attitude and the tears we both weren't sure how to handle.

"Two months ago my period was late, like two weeks late," I start, assessing Mikey's features, waiting for him to show some sign of a freak out but his face remains neutral. His eyes are blank as he gives me his undivided attention.

"I took a test, and it came back negative," I caution, taking a step closer. The sigh of relief I expected never came. "I wound up missing my period that month altogether but the following month I got it and it was worse than ever before. The bleeding was so bad and the cramps felt as if my body was splitting in two. I was scared and didn't know what to make of it. I started to think the test was wrong, maybe I took it too soon and I really was pregnant and the bleeding, the cramping—well, I thought I was having a miscarriage."

Finally, Mikey shows some reaction biting the inside of his cheek as he uncrosses his arms and runs his fingers through his hair.

"Why didn't you tell me?"

"I wanted to be sure. I didn't want to tell you something like that without knowing for sure," I pause, tearing my eyes away from him to stare at my bare feet. "The test was negative, Mikey. It was just me over thinking or maybe it was a sign telling me I needed to go to the doctor."

"Did you?" he asks. His voice thick with emotion and rough like gravel all at the same time.

"Yes." I look up at him through the fringe of my lashes. "Turns out I wasn't miscarrying, there was most definitely no baby but he also didn't know what the cause of the problem was and sent me for a whole lot of tests. It could be a number of things."

"Like?"

"Mike—"

"Like?" he repeats, clenching his teeth as he speaks.

"Like a cyst on my ovary that has burst or endometriosis. And then there is my personal favorite…uterine cancer," I hoarsely finish, bringing another cigarette between my lips. My hand shakes as I fumble with the lighter but still manage to light the end.

He reaches out, takes the cigarette from my lips and breaks it in two before he grabs my hands.

"It's not that," he insists. "I don't know what any of the other things are but it's one of those. I'm sure of it."

"How?"

"How do I know? That's easy, Princess," he says, bringing one hand to his lips then the other. "I came back to New York because of you and I'm not done with you. I gave you that ring because I fully intend to grow old with you. You should know by now when I have something in my head it doesn't disappear. It will happen, Nikki, me and you growing old and relying on Viagra."

I laugh as he wraps my arms around his neck.

"You should've told me," he whispers.

"I'm sorry for keeping you in the dark."

"That isn't why you should've told me. You're not alone Nikki, you've got me and I'm in it for the long haul. There isn't anything in this life you're ever going to face alone as long as I'm breathing."

"I have an appointment next week, the doctor said he should have my results by then."

"I'm there," he declares, wrapping his arms around my waist and dragging my body against his. "And whatever it is, I swear to you we'll get through it."

I underestimated Mikey, it wasn't about the wedding but the partnership. The vow to stand beside one another in even the bleakest of times. Naively we think the happily ever after is the rainbows and roses crap you read in fairy tales but it's not. The happily ever after is having the right person to hold your hand and weather any storm. It's an unbreakable bond between two people. That's the happily ever after.

I know one thing for sure, even if those test results are bad I still have my happily ever after. I still have my Mikey and nothing can change that.

Chapter Twelve

Lacey

I stare at my face reflected in the mirror hanging above my dresser and bring my fingertips to the corners of my mouth. I press the pads of my index fingers into my skin and slide them upward, watching as the edges of my lips blossom into a forced smile.

Fake.

Manufactured.

Dropping my fingers, instantly the fake smile falls too and my natural frown appears. Just like the drama masks I keep inside the top drawer of my dresser.

I tear my eyes from the mirror and pull open the drawer, pushing around my lingerie until I find the masks I keep buried at the bottom.

For the longest time those masks depicted the person I was, the person I was before I admitted my truth. I am bipolar and those masks are the two sides of Lacey Parrish. The smile is for the girl I am when I'm not fighting for control over my mind and the frown is when my maker reigns over me. Some people call God their maker, believing he controls everything—Heaven and Earth, but for me the only thing that controls me is my mind. My mind is my maker and for most of my life I have been a victim of the vicious villain that lives inside my head.

I freed myself from the silence and used the only weapon I had against my mental illness—my voice. I sought help and was diagnosed and now I start my day with a daily dose of Lithium. It took some time adjusting to my medication but mostly my maker has been shut down. One would think I'd find relief in that, or it would make my life easier but instead I feel lost—like I don't know who I am without that voice doubting everything I know and feel.

I guess I've become so used to the struggle I don't know how to live life normally. My therapist tells me it's natural but what does she know. To her I'm a textbook, just a case study, she has never lived with my mind, she doesn't know how I became one with my maker.

It sounds sadistic, even to my own ears, but I sort of miss that voice. At least I had an excuse for the devilish thoughts that filled my head with doubt. Now, those thoughts are mine, they are pure and they are real.

I close the drawer, taking the masks and bring them to my chest. I step out of my bedroom and stare at the empty room across from the bedroom I share with Blackie.

I should be on top of the world.

I should be smiling.

I've got everything I ever wanted, everything I never thought I'd have, everything my maker tried to keep from me.

And yet today I'm miserable.

There is no voice telling me my happy life will be ripped from me. No voice feeding me lies, telling me I've conjured the whole thing up.

The facts that are driving me into a depression.

Cold hard facts that are dragging me down.

I've avoided reality for so long I have no fucking clue how to deal with it. I don't know how to make sense of everything I'm feeling because I'm still learning how to differentiate real life from my illness.

I think people automatically think once someone undergoes treatment they're healed with a snap of their fingers, but it's a process, erasing everything and starting fresh. Learning how to exist normally is just as much a struggle as living in torment.

Add adjusting to living on your own with a man to the mix, and the fact that your father has been avoiding you because you fell in love with his best friend, well, I'm fucked and that's putting it mildly.

My stepmother is pregnant and while I'm genuinely happy for Reina and my father, for this new life we're all going to love to pieces, I can't help feeling some kind of way.

What if this new child is born like me? And if I'm asking myself that question, I wonder if my father is too. Is he worried that another innocent child will fall victim to the illness that is generated in his DNA. I become angry because I know how it is to live impaired by my mind and wouldn't want that for anyone let alone an innocent child. I can't help thinking that it would be negligent to bring a child into this world, knowing there is an illness he or she may inherit.

Since I've been diagnosed I try to put myself in my father's shoes. He's survived mental illness and somehow he doesn't let it dictate his life. I try to understand his logic and ask myself if I could live like him. I've always wanted children, and now that I am with Blackie, I want nothing more than to give him everything he's ever hoped for but never thought he'd have. I know he wants kids, maybe not now but eventually he wants to fill this house and the blank pages of our story with children.

I close my eyes and I can see it all so vividly, the life we dreamed of having—the little girl with her daddy's eyes and her mommy's sweetness. She'd have a smile so big and so bright that it will melt her daddy's heart. In my dreams we always have a girl, and she's the apple of Blackie's eyes. She'd be his true angel, and I'd be the one who gave her to him.

I want it so bad.

For that dream to become our reality but how selfish would that be? Or would it? Am I letting my own fears, my own demons dictate Blackie's future? On one hand I think it would be cruel of me to have a baby, knowing I could pass down the illness that runs in my family to my child and watch my baby suffer like I have. Then on the other hand it would be cruel to take that dream from Blackie especially when the man just started dreaming again.

It's times like this, when I want to talk to my dad, when I wish things were different for us. If there was anyone who might understand my thoughts it would be my father, but he's not ready for me to discuss babies with him. He barely can handle me living with Blackie.

Funny how even when I'm not silent—I am.

I walk into the empty room and lean against the wall furthest from the door, looking around the space. It would be the perfect room for a baby. I slide down the wall, bring my knees to my chest and rest the masks on top of them.

Happiness.

Sadness.

Would I ever find the middle ground?

I close my eyes and drop my head to my knees, deciding I was done with the torment for the day. All I want is to forget reality just for a little while.

I was too engrossed in my thoughts to hear the front door close, or the sound of Blackie's boots pounding against the wooden steps, but the moment I hear him call for me I lift my head and stare up at my *Leather*.

"Lace," he whispers, threading his fingers through his hair, pushing it away from his face as his eyes dart around the room before they gaze into mine. "What're you doin'?"

I shrug my shoulders.

"Nothing," I say. Advancing toward me, he crouches down in front of me and continues to stare at me, concern etched across his beautiful face.

"Everything okay?"

I glance down at the smiling mask and force myself to mimic the gesture. He diverts his eyes to the masks on my knees, gently reaching out to take them from me. I wanted to snatch them back, hang onto them like a child clutches a blanket for security but refrain from it.

He stares down at them for a moment before lifting his eyes back to mine. He places the masks on the floor beside him before reaching out and caressing my cheek with the back of his hand.

"Talk to me, girl," he coaxes. "Did you forget to take your medicine today?

His question feels like a slap to the face and causes me to flinch. It wasn't an accusation but a question of concern, yet it angered me he would even ask.

"Of course I took my medicine," I snap. "They're not magic pills, Blackie. I still have the ability to feel, just like every other human being."

"Then tell me what your feeling because I'm not a mind reader, girl," he replies, keeping his voice calm.

"I'm just sad is all," I mutter. Frustration chomps at the words, making them sound edgier, meaner and more aggressive than I mean for them to be. If I don't have a smile plastered to my face at any given time everyone automatically assumes I skipped my meds and unleashed the crazy.

"I'm allowed to be sad," I argue.

"Of course you are but if you're sad then you need to tell me why," he demands. "Let me make it better for you," he adds, softly.

I shake my head, wishing it was as easy as he made it.

"You can't fix every part of me that's broken no matter how much you want to," I rasp, pushing off to stand. I go to walk away, meaning to put space between us until I gather control over myself because Blackie didn't deserve my demons—not when he had his own threatening to avenge.

But he had a different plan. Closing his hand around my ankle he stops me in my tracks.

"Lace," he rasps, demanding my attention. He rises, his hand traveling up my leg as he stands to his full height. "Don't underestimate me," he says gravely. "Give me your broken pieces and let me glue them back together."

"You can't," I insist, my voice barely audible. "It's not fair to you."

He brings his hands to my face, bending his knees to make his eyes level with mine.

"I love you, Lace," he says simply. "And all the broken pieces of you are the missing pieces of me."

I understood those words better than anything because I owned the broken parts of him too, claimed them a long time ago when he gave me his fractured soul.

His gaze burns into me before giving me a slight nod as he lifts me into his arms. I surrender my pieces to him as I wrap my arms loosely around his neck and let him carry me out of the room of broken dreams.

He carries me into the bathroom, sets me down on top of the vanity before taking my face in his hands and pressing his lips gently against mine.

"Hold tight," he murmurs against my mouth. Shedding his leather jacket and hanging it on the door knob he rolls up his sleeves and crouches down alongside the bath tub. He runs the water, sticks out his hand to test the temperature before he turns back to me.

"Get undressed," he says softly, crossing his arms against his chest as he waits for me to follow his instructions. I grabbed the hem of my shirt, work it over my head and drop it to the counter, sliding off to stand up and shimmy my shorts down my legs.

He turns around once the tub is full and closes the faucet. I strip down to nothing by the time he turns back to me, his eyes firmly planted on my face as he extends his hand.

"Come on, girl," he urges as I take a step closer to him, dropping my hand into his. He holds me as I lift one leg over the wall of the bath tub and sink into the warm water. Lifting my eyes to his, I see the concern reflected in them. He gently pushed my shoulders back so I lean against the back of the tub. Running one hand over his face, he stares at the water for a moment, drawing a deep breath and reaches for the washcloth.

"Blackie," I whisper, wrapping my hand around his wrist and forcing his eyes back to mine. "I'm okay," I assure, feeling guilty for not rising up and masking my depression.

"I know you are," he insists, leaning over the wall of the tub and pressing his mouth against mine.

His lips are soft as they work mine, slowly easing them open sliding his tongue over mine. I lift my wet hands to his face, dragging my fingers through his hair as I kiss him back, hoping my kiss calms the worry in his eyes.

"Lean back," he murmurs against my mouth before easing back from me. He squirts some body wash into the cloth and lifts it to my neck, slowly soaping me up. Intimately, with the gentleness he buried beneath his steel exterior, he takes care of me, calming my thoughts and forcing me to relax.

I close my eyes as the merry-go-round ride of emotions I was on comes to a halt. He works the lukewarm washcloth over every inch of my body in silence, the only sounds heard are those of our breathing and the water lapping around my body.

After a while he stops washing me and my body feels the loss of his touch, forcing me to open my eyes and watch as he squeezes out the washcloth and drape it over the mouth of the faucet. He turns his eyes back to mine and tips his chin toward my hair.

"Do you want me to wash your hair?" he asks huskily.

I shake my head as he pulls the stopper from the tub and lets the water drain before he rises to his full height and grabs a towel from the rack on the wall. He spreads it wide as I stand up and step out of the tub and into his arms. He wraps the towel around me. I feel his large palms circle my body, through the thin cotton of the towel as he pats me down. I glance down, secure the towel to my body, tucking the edge just above my breasts while I watch him take a step back and hold out his hands.

Blackie leads me into our bedroom, drops my hands as we reach the edge of the bed and he pulls down the comforter. He glances over his shoulder at me and extends one hand to my breast, unraveling the towel from my body, before looking back toward our bed.

I climb in and he draws the blanket over my body, bending his head to kiss my forehead.

"You're okay," he whispers, and for a moment I wasn't sure if he was telling me so or trying to convince himself.

"Lay down with me," I plead, watching his Adam's apple as he swallows. He hesitated for a moment, pulling back from me as he took a deep breath. "Please?"

He nods, taking a seat on the edge of the bed and bends down to undo his boots. I lift my head from the pillow and rest on my elbows, watching as he strips down to nothing but his boxer briefs. He palms his cock, pressing down on it as he tears his eyes away from me and walks around the bed. His body is a work of art—tattoos decorating every corded muscle on display. I watch him pull back the sheet and climb in beside me, turning on his side to face me before lifting his hand to trace a finger down my cheek.

"So damn pretty," he rasps, reaching for me with his other hand, tucking me against him as he rolls onto his back. I lay my head against his chest. I peer at the tattoo covering his left pec, the music notes to our song dance across his skin, reminding me of that first dance he gave me and all the ones that followed when my mind betrayed me.

No matter how broken down I feel, or how tired I am from the war I battle internally, I rise up because this man gives me the confidence I need to beat my demons. Laying here, wrapped up in his arms, I'm reminded of the hope we've brought into one another's lives and despite all the heartache we've endured, it's our love that prevails. We're stronger than our demons and we've survived the most lethal of temptations. We'll rise because we have each other and nothing can stop us—we won't let it.

"I've had a bad day," I confess, tracing my finger over the music notes.

"You want to tell me about it?" he asked softly, threading his fingers through my hair.

"I went by my dad's today and Reina was glowing, talking about the baby and how she and my dad are already trying to decide on a name," I pause, lifting my head from his chest to stare into his eyes. "She's happy, so is he, and I look at them and I wonder how they're not scared. I sound like a hypocrite because I don't blame my father for my illness but the facts are there, Blackie. I'm bipolar because it runs in my family, because I inherited this from my father. I know he didn't want this for me and that it kills him knowing I share his pain but then I think about the baby and wonder if it's even crossed his mind that the child he's about to have can be diagnosed too."

I quietly watch as he absorbs my words and doesn't respond.

"I'm not trying to dampen their happiness but I want to understand how they're able to push away the fear and embrace the beauty of it…because I can't. I tried putting myself in their shoes and thought about us having a baby and I don't know if I could do that, if I could risk an innocent child the burden of my illness."

He lifts his hand, brushing away the tears that slide down my cheek.

"I want kids," I whisper. "I want to give you a whole house full of babies, but how selfish would that be of me?"

"Lace, you think for one second your father isn't tormenting himself, asking himself those same questions? I don't doubt he's not consumed by that same fear but he's got Reina there, hanging on to hope that their kid will be perfectly healthy. And if he's not, then they'll deal with it like every other parent deals with a child's illness. Think about it, baby, there is no controlling what we're handed. People who are healthy, who have no traces of illness in their genes have babies that are born with birth defects and sickness they never even heard of. It doesn't make them bad parents, if anything it strengthens them, because it takes a special person to care for a sick kid, no matter what the illness."

"So, if we had a baby, and she was like me—"

"We'd love her like we would if she wasn't like you. We'd give her all we could because we're those people…the ones that can't be beat no matter how deep they're dragged down. If our kid had any illness, bipolar or fuck, I don't know, if she was born with a heart defect, that kid would have the best life we could ever give her because we didn't give up on each other and there is no way in hell we'd give up on our baby."

He cradles my face in his hands.

"Our baby could be perfect and grow up just fine, only to turn out like his dad…and then what? We let him rot? Or we drive his ass to rehab until he gets straight? We don't get a choice in what we get…we grab it and hang on with all we have."

"How do you do that?" I marvel, shaking my head as I stare back at him. "How do you always make it better for me? You're always saving me, Blackie, and most of the time it's from myself."

"Yeah, well, it's our thing. We're both our own worst enemy but that's why we got each other. I'll keep slaying your demons, keep you smiling because that smile of yours, destroys all the ugly inside of me."

"It'll be okay," I say.

"It'll be okay," he assures.

"We've got a lot of love to give a baby when the time comes."

"A shit ton," he agrees, smiling at me.

"And it might be fine."

"Either way it'll be fine, I promise."

"Can we name our son Leather?" I tease, feeling the weight fade from my shoulders.

"No," he laughs, wrapping his arms around my waist, flipping me onto my back as he leans back and stares down at me. "You're going to be a great mom someday." He smiles, bending down to kiss me. "And when the time comes, we'll work through it, girl."

Yeah, we will.

We'll keep rising.

Because we're Leather and Lace.

And we're stronger than we know.

Chapter Thirteen

Reina

Stepping out of the shower, I lean over the vanity and wipe my hand across the steam fogging the mirror and stare at my reflection. I didn't look so translucent anymore, the color returning to my complexion. The first trimester of my pregnancy was trying on me, and the first eight weeks of the second as well, spending most days hunched over the toilet, releasing anything I put into my mouth. The morning sickness has faded and I'm starting to look like my old self, still pale compared to Jack's olive skin but I don't look like I am knocking on death's door. I'm still waiting to recognize that glow everyone seems to think I have. It's probably a myth but I'm still hoping to see it.

My eyes travel downward as I turn to my side and drop my hand to my tiny belly. I narrow my eyes, hoping to find the slightest change from yesterday, or the day before that, desperate for more evidence of the life Jack and I created. The doctor has assured us that he or she is growing just fine and any day now my pants won't fit me. Who is excited to buy maternity clothes? This girl right here.

"Come on lil' Parrish. Mommy wants to be able to show you off."

I bet he gets his hard head from his daddy.

He.

I don't know why but I have this feeling we're going to have a son, another little boy for Jack to love, a second chance for the man who lost his first son so tragically. Our son won't take the place of Jack Jr., he'll be his own person, with his own spot carved in our hearts and Jack Jr. will always have his place too. He'll be a part of this new journey even if only in spirit and memory.

I lift my arm and stare at the puckered flesh that travels down my body, a reminder I survived a tragedy too. The rawness of my skin isn't an angry shade of red anymore, slightly fading to pink, but always visible. Reaching for the scarring cream, I slowly work it over the keloids that mark my flesh. I used to hide from my scars, believed my life was over because of the ordeal I had gone through and then I met Jack. He claimed my scars as his own and as they slowly fade in color, they also fade from my mind. I don't let them dictate who I am and I don't hang onto them anymore. They're a part of me but I am not defined by them any longer.

The door behind me opens and the cold air from the bedroom creeps into the steam-filled bathroom, setting a chill through the air. I feel goosebumps rise across my marred flesh and lift my eyes to Jack's.

Silently, he struts up behind me and my hand freezes against my scarred skin as he wraps his fingers around my wrist and brushes my hand away from my scars. He reaches around me and takes the tube off the counter top and squeezes some into the palm of his hand before tracing the scars with his own hand, working the ointment into my skin.

Jack bends his head and presses his open mouth to my shoulder as his fingers glide over the scars he has memorized. He knows every ridge, every curve—all the damage left behind from the fire.

"Mine," he growls against my skin. His teeth graze my shoulder before lifting his eyes to mine. "All fucking mine," he hisses. His hands are greasy from the lotion but continue to slide down my sides until they take hold of my hips and pull me against his naked frame.

I feel the thickness of his erection press against my ass and I press into it, earning a deep, guttural groan from him in response.

"Goddamn," he grunts, spinning me around with a twist of my hips so we are face to face. I clench my thighs as I stare into the dark pools of his eyes and before I can process the ache vibrating throughout my body, Jack grabs my ass, hoisting me onto the counter and spreads my legs wide to fit between them.

I grip the edge of the vanity as he arches my back and leans my head against the mirror. "Been too long since I had my fill of you, Sunshine," he growls, tugging me closer so my ass hangs over the edge of the vanity.

"You had me last night," I remind him breathlessly.

"Never enough," he mutters, running the heel of his hand between my breasts, down my stomach, pausing just over my navel. Bending his head, he presses his lips to my belly before finally resting his hand over my pussy. Arching against his hand, I am desperate for him to give me more, to spread me apart and shove his fingers inside of me.

A wicked grin works his lips as he brushes my wet hair from my face and grabs a fistful tugging my head back so my neck was all his for the taking. His tongue runs along the nape of my neck, picking a spot to suck between his lips and mark as his own.

I cry out, lifting my hips and gyrate against his hand just as he runs two fingers between the lips of my pussy, rubbing my wetness against my clit. I was hypersensitive, something new since the pregnancy, and with every stroke my body threatened to cave. His fingers left my clit and pushed deep inside my folds, filling me as his lips closed around one my nipples.

To say we were both enjoying the effects of my pregnancy would be an understatement. Jack couldn't get enough of my body and I was never satisfied. His fingers thrust in and out of my heat, working me up to my first orgasm of the day, knowing without a doubt I'd have at least two more before the days end.

"This pussy's always so wet for me," he grits, removing his fingers and bringing them to his mouth, sucking my essence from them before peering at me devilishly. "Sweeter than pie," he growls, winking at me as he drops his hands to my knees and spreads me out.

"You're killing me, Parrish," I pant, lifting one hand from the edge of the vanity to grab my breast, I roll my thumb over my sensitive nipple. I drop my head against the mirror, banging it slightly as I lift my hips and beckon him to claim me.

"Love it when you say my name," he rasps, fisting his cock and lining it up with my slick heat. He slams into me grabbing my hand from my breast and laces our fingers together, raising our joined hands over my head and against the mirror. He takes hold of my leg with his free hand, pressing it against his hip as he thrusts mercilessly inside me, giving me all the roughness I've come to crave from him. My body screams, drenched in sweat from both the steam of the shower and the steam we were creating with our bodies. I slide along the granite as he pushes himself deeper giving me everything he has. Reaching for his shoulder, my nails dig into his skin. He slams our joined hands against the mirror again as he rotates his hips and quickens his pace.

"Jack," I yell, feeling my body dive over the edge as my orgasm slams into me. Clenching around his cock, every thrust of his hips becomes a struggle as I breathe through the pleasure.

"Love the way you feel, love watching your face when you come all over my cock," he grunts, working through the vice my pussy has over him.

"Give it to me," I demand, arching once more before he lets out a slew of curses and grabs his dick, pulling out of me. I brace my hands against the vanity, watching through hooded eyes as he paints my stomach with his release, branding me and the baby inside me Property of Parrish.

All his.

He lets go of his cock, grabs my hips and inches his thumbs across my stomach, the pads of his fingers working his come into my skin, mimicking the way he rubbed the cream across my scars. He takes ownership of my scars and my body. I was branded by the Bulldog and freed from my past with the promise of a future full of sunshine.

"You," I whisper.

"Me," he pants, drawing in a deep breath as I reach for him, lifting his head as I take in the few gray strands of hair at his temple. I press my lips to his temple and lean my forehead against his.

"I have to take another shower," I murmur.

"Better make it a quick one," he replies, pulling back to kiss me gently. "Don't want to be late to see that baby inside you."

I smile, my eyes filling at his words and the sweet way my rugged knight looks at me. He didn't know it but the darkness that shadowed him was fading and he was living in the light.

He helped me down from the vanity, turned around and started the shower. As I stepped into the stall, he playfully slaps my ass and grins at me.

"Fifteen minutes, Reina, ain't got time for another round with you," he teases, tipping his chin toward the shower. "Go on, Sunshine. I'll be waiting for you."

I take a quick shower and dress, taking advantage of my jeans that still fit me and pair it with a Satan's Knight tank top. When I finally make my way downstairs Jack is sitting on the front stoop, twirling the keys to his truck in his hand and about to light a cigarette.

"Jesus, Jack, I thought you were trying to quit," I scold, reaching down and plucking the cigarette from his lips. I drop it onto the cement, crushing it with my heel before pulling out a pack of gum from my purse. "Chew on this," I demand. "You know they say it's an oral thing that you're so used to having."

"Reina," he growls, popping the piece of gum into his mouth. "Leave it be, unless you want to tag along everywhere I go and give me something to fixate on every time I get the itch," he grounds out, grabbing my hand and leading me to his truck.

I'm not sure that's a bad idea or that I'd mind.

He shakes his head, mumbling something under his breath as he opens the passenger door for me.

"Get in," he orders.

"Why aren't we taking the bike?" I question, pulling my head out of my ass and the thoughts of being Jack's oral fixation. "I figured we'd still ride until I became too big to lift my leg over the bike," I add.

"Not taking any chances," he grumbles, slamming the door closed before opening it again. "Put your seat belt on," he barks, slamming the door shut again and walking around the front of the car.

I shake my head, laughing quietly to myself. Jack was always ordering me to lock the door, wear a helmet and scolding me about my seat belt. If one didn't know which side of the tracks his bike's tires skidded across they might confuse him for a law-abiding citizen.

He rarely drove his truck but the few times he did he was cautious of the speed limits. I questioned him once, it was when we first dated and I took a ride with him to drive his daughter home. He told me speed limits were enforced for a reason and he wasn't risking *his* precious cargo.

Say what you want about men like mine but there is no denying the heart that drives Jack Parrish. It's bigger than his name, bigger than his patch and even bigger than his club. It's an honor being his, because being his means I'm loved and cherished.

We pulled up to the doctor's office and he drops me off in front so I can sign in as he parks the car—and sneak a cigarette. When he meets me inside the waiting room, he smells similar to the little tree air freshener hanging from the rear-view mirror. I bet if I reached into his leather jacket I'd find the 'new car' scented tree in his pocket.

He takes my hand and places our joined hands on his knee as he glances around the room, taking in his surroundings, focusing mainly on the poster of a baby.

"Nervous?" I ask, watching as he scratches at the scruff lining his jaw.

"No," he insists looking back at me. "Anxious," he corrects.

"Reina DeCarlo?" the nurse calls out and Jack stands first, pulling me to my feet and leading me toward the nurse.

She leads us into an exam room, takes my blood pressure and weight before instructing me to remove all clothing from the waist down and hands me a paper gown to change into. I quickly change, folding my clothes and handing them to Jack who sits on the chair beside me and watches me climb onto the exam table.

"This guy's got some fucking job," he grunts, motioning to the stirrups.

I chuckle nervously knowing any minute the doctor will enter the room and introduce me to the second great love of my life.

Jack's hand closes over my knee as he looks up at me.

"If I forget to tell you…thank you, Sunshine," he says hoarsely as his eyes bore into mine.

"For what?"

"Everything," he states simply, moving his hand up to my stomach. "All this."

The door opens and the doctor walks in, lifting his eyes from my chart to greet us.

"Good afternoon, how are we doing?" he asks, extending his hand to Jack. He lifts his hand from my stomach and shakes the doctor's hand. The doctor takes a seat on the stool in front of me and signals for the nurse to hand him a new pair of gloves.

"Good, the morning sickness finally eased up," I tell the doctor, watching as he fits his hands into the gloves and turns on the sonogram machine.

"Very good, the urine sample you gave showed everything else is fine." He grabs the tube of gel and the sonogram wand. "How about we take a look at this baby and hear that heartbeat?"

"Yes, please," I say, my voice catching as Jack grabs a hold of my hand and leans forward. I stare at his face and watch his eyes become glued to the screen as the doctor squirts the blue gel over my stomach and presses the wand against my skin.

Kaboom, kaboom, kaboom.

"Is that the heartbeat?" Jack rasps.

"It sure is," the doctor confirms. He pauses to measure the beats before a smile spreads across his face. "Nice and strong."

Kaboom, kaboom, kaboom.

I divert my eyes from Jack's face to the screen as he squeezes my hand and the image of our baby fills the screen.

"Well, I'll be damned," Jack mutters.

"That's the head," the doctor points out, moving the wand around my belly and laughing. "Well now, look at that."

"What?" I ask, wiping the tears from my cheek.

"Do you want to know what it is?"

I turn to Jack, his eyes widen as he peels them from the screen and lifts them to mine.

"Do you?" he whispers.

A part of me did but the bigger part of me wanted to be surprised. I don't know if he read my answer from my eyes or if he felt the same. He turned to the doctor and replied.

"Let's keep it under wraps, doc," he states, lifting my hand to his lips.

"Nothing wrong with a surprise," the doctor says. "Everything checks out. The baby is right on target," he announces removing the wand from my belly and wiping away the gel. "The nurse will print you out some of the photos and I'll see you next month."

"Thanks, doc," Jack says, handing me my clothes and helping me sit up. The doctor exits the room, and I dress as the nurse prints the photos and hands them to Jack before she leaves us alone.

I am putting on my shoes when I lift my head and see Jack staring down at the photograph in awe. He reaches into his jacket and pulls out his pack of cigarettes. I open my mouth to object but before I can he turns around and steps down on the trash can, opening it and throwing the pack inside. He shoves the photos into his jacket pocket and holds out his hand for mine.

"I quit," he states.

"Just like that?" I ask, raising an eyebrow.

He lays his hand over his chest, over the pocket where the pictures are safely tucked inside of and shakes his head.

"Don't want to miss a goddamn thing, Sunshine. So, yeah, just like that," he says, pulling me to my feet and wrapping his arms around my shoulders, he bends at the knees and claims my mouth.

He kisses me thoroughly as the sound of our baby's heartbeat echoes inside my head and I silently thank God for the first time since the tragic fire.

I thank him for letting me survive.

Because surviving wasn't so bad.

Especially when I had so much to live for.

No, surviving was a blessing, the first of the many I have been granted.

Chapter Fourteen

Lauren

I dare someone to tell me that being a mom is an easy job. While it is the most rewarding job I've ever had, it is also the most exhausting. I'm fucking tired as hell and if I'm being honest, I have no idea how my mother did it. I mean she was by herself with two kids and always seemed to hold it together. Me? I have a gallon jug of Carlo Rossi Sangria in the fridge at all times.

Eric is perfect.

The best little boy in the whole world—when he's sleeping. The first few months was easy, he ate, slept and pooped. Then he turned eleven months and found his legs. Eric took his first steps and life as we knew it changed forever. He's constantly running around, getting into things he shouldn't be—hence the wine.

Between the work out I get from running after a toddler and the one Riggs gives me every night, I've officially lost all my baby weight. Don't get me wrong there is no denying my body has changed from my pregnancy. I still have that bitch of a pouch above the scar from my cesarean and the stretch marks over my stomach never really faded much either. I'm okay with the changes though and that's mainly because of Riggs. He calls my stretch marks my colors and tells me to own them. He tells me the scar hidden under my panty line is my patch, branding me Eric's mom. He takes the MC thing a little too far but with him it's go big or go home. It's all part of his larger-than-life personality.

"Eric, no!" I groan as he grabs a handful of SpaghettiOs and flings them at me. He giggles mischievously. Yeah, there's no denying Eric's got his daddy's personality.

Heaven help us all.

"That's a bad boy," I scold, wiping the spaghetti sauce from my cheek, sure I missed some as I dig the spoon back into the dish and try to feed him some more.

I try to make those silly airplane sounds and bring the spoon to his mouth only for him to smack it away with his chubby hand and shake his head.

Yeah, I was acing this motherhood gig.

I shove the spoon into my mouth and take a bite. Don't judge me, at least it's not one of those puff things that melt in your mouth. Usually, Eric and I share a tub of those for lunch.

"Okay, you're done," I declare as he smashes the few SpaghettiOs that fell onto the table into his shirt. I unclasp the harness from his body and lift him out of the chair, placing him down on his feet and watch as he waddles off into the unknown.

I take a minute to throw the bowl and spoon into the sink, figuring that's how long I had until he made another mess out of something. Riggs baby-proofed the apartment, well, sort of. He bought those foam noodles you buy for the pool, cut them in half and duck taped them to every straight edge and sharp corner. I tried explaining to him they sold all sorts of gadgets, and he didn't have to make his own but there wasn't any way to convince him. The other day when Eric started opening the cabinets, I went to Babies R Us and bought the baby proof locks before Riggs engineered some sort of device to keep them closed.

The thing about baby proof locks is sometimes they work so well the adults can't open them either. The locks went out the window when Riggs wound up pulling the cabinet off the hinge. Now, if you look at our kitchen, there are chain links tied around the knobs, and every cabinet is secured with a padlock. I don't even remember the code to open the fucking things and gave up trying to figure them out.

I turn around just in time to watch Eric rip his diaper off and run around the coffee table naked.

Please don't poop.

Please don't pee.

The doorbell rings as I chase Eric around the table, attempting to put a new diaper on before I had a bigger mess. I've learned how to put his diaper on while he stands. I'm like a damn magician when it comes to those things, that *Brady Bunch* lady ain't got nothing on me.

I grab Eric, lift him in the air as the bell rings again and yank the door open just as my sweet baby boy pees all over me.

"Oh dear Lord," my guest screeches in horror, forcing my eyes away from my wet t-shirt to the couple standing at my door. The woman is immaculately dressed in linen pants and a deep navy, cowl neck, short sleeve shirt that matches her leather pumps. Her blonde hair perfectly drawn away from her face, fixed in a stylish braid, her face had minimal make-up. She didn't need make-up, a natural beauty that didn't have a wrinkle on her flawless skin. If I had to guess she was in her early fifties and that's only judging by the man with graying hair that stood beside her, dressed in a three-piece suit.

I was used to the suit thing, my brother had spent most of his life hanging around mobsters dressed just like the man before me, but it was clear this guy wasn't from that life. No these two people weren't part of the get rich or die trying lifestyle, they were born wealthy; it was in their DNA.

What I didn't get was why the hell they were here, looking at me and my son as if we were aliens.

"Can I help you?"

Mrs. Fancy Pants opened her mouth but Mr. Three-Piece Suit was the one who actually spoke.

"We're looking for Robert Montgomery," he declares, clearing his throat as he raises an eyebrow at Eric who is picking food out of my hair and flicking it at them.

"Riggs isn't home," I reply, swatting Eric's hand from my hair as I narrow my eyes at the couple. What the hell did he get himself into now?

"Riggs? What is a Riggs?" the woman questions.

The man inches closer to the woman's ear.

"That's his alias," he informs her.

"I'm sorry, who are you people?" I ask gritting my teeth as my son pulls on my hair.

"We're Robert's parents and you must be the girl he impregnated. Is this the child?"

I didn't even have a chance to dwell on the whole impregnated thing as my eyes bulged and threatened to fall from their sockets. Oh my God! These people were Riggs' parents. Here I was with pee on my shirt, spaghetti in my hair and a naked baby on my hip.

Yeah, their son really struck gold with me.

I was the pick of the litter.

"Oh my God! I'm sorry, please come in," I say, moving aside and glancing over my shoulder at the apartment. For fuck's sake it looked like a tornado hit the place. Then I remembered what I looked like, talk about a twister.

They carefully step foot inside the apartment, stepping over toys and whatever else was lying on the floor. I watch as Riggs' dad stares down at his shoes and my bra that lay beside his fancy loafer.

I shake my head, bending down to snatch the bra and sheepishly smile at my—in laws?

What a nightmare.

I try to balance Eric in my arms as he tries to wiggle free from them, reaching out to his grandparents.

"I'm Lauren," I say hopelessly, forcing a smile as I glance at Eric and my hope becomes restored. These people came here to meet their grandson, they don't care about what the house looks like or what I look like for that matter. I smile genuinely as I turn to Riggs' parents.

"And this little guy is Eric," I introduce. "Eric, say hi to grandma and grandpa."

Riggs' dad coughs or maybe he was choking. I couldn't be sure but his mother looked as if she was having a stroke. Her whole face turned red like a tomato, and the drop out nurse within surfaced, knowing that was a sure sign of high blood pressure.

"Mr. Montgomery, can I get you a glass of water?"

The man continues to hack up a lung, and I extend my son into his grandmother's arms.

"Hold him a second while I get him a glass of water," I insist, placing Eric into her arms and watch as she holds him at arm's length. "He doesn't bite," I add before taking off for the kitchen.

Well, except for that one time when he bit my leg and drew blood. I grab the first cup I see, a Mickey Mouse sippy cup and fill it with water. I didn't bother screwing on the cap with the crazy straw, something tells me these people are the type who use the fancy crystal my mother only breaks out on holidays.

At that moment, Riggs comes barreling through the front door as I turn around.

"Kitten, I'm home!" He calls, kicking the door closed as he continues to look at something on his phone. "And I'm fucking horny as—" I cringe as the words fly from his mouth and thrust the cup toward Mr. Montgomery, spilling it all over the front of his suit.

"What the ever-living fuck is this?" Riggs stammers.

"Riggs! Language," I scold, eying our son.

Mrs. Montgomery gasps as she peers over Eric's shoulder and looks at her son for what I assume is the first time in years.

"What the hell did you do to yourself?" she shrieks.

Riggs pulls his sunglasses off and closes the distance between him and his mother, taking Eric from her before turning toward me.

"Are you off your rocker? Why did you let them in here?"

"You're covered in tattoos!" His mother declares.

"They're your parents what was I supposed to do? Slam the door in their face?"

"Yes, absolutely!" He hisses, shifting Eric into his other arm. "Are you okay? They didn't try to sell you to the highest bidder did they?" he asks our son, examining him thoroughly before looking back and forth between his mother and father.

"Robert," Mr. Montgomery starts, clearing his throat as he wrings out his suit jacket.

"Riggs, my name is Riggs," he corrects, gritting his teeth.

"Fine, fine," the father says, holding up his hands in defeat. "Lenore, stop gawking at his tattoos for heaven's sake, you are only making matters worse."

"It gets worse than a Satan tattooed on his arm?" she asks outraged. "Is that why you have an alias, are you part of some devil worshipping cult?"

Riggs turns to me. "I'm sorry, Kitten, but I can't duck my way out of this one. No, this one deserves a good old fashioned fuck," he grunts, whipping around to face his mother. "Are you fucking shitting me, lady?"

"Robert, Riggs, whatever the hell you're calling yourself these days, we didn't come here to cause any trouble," Mr. Montgomery explains.

Riggs raises his eyebrows as he stares at his father incredulously before narrowing his eyes and pointing an accusing finger at his father, then his mother, the finger moving back and forth between both parents causing me to become dizzy as I try to follow it.

"Wait a minute," Riggs says. "Wait just one damn minute. What the hell are you two doing together in the first place?" he turns to his mother. "Shouldn't you be chasing after, what is it you're up to husband number five?" he asks before diverting his eyes to his father. "And you, how come you're not off striking oil somewhere in the Gulf or wherever it is you dig holes."

"Fernando and I didn't work out and your father doesn't dig holes. If you paid any kind of mind to his business, maybe you wouldn't be living like this," She says, spreading her arms wide as she gestures to our apartment.

Well now, that was just mean. Sure, the apartment looked like it had been ransacked by a pack of ninjas but we had a rambunctious toddler running the show. Didn't she remember what it was like when Riggs was a baby?

"It's really not as bad as it looks," I argue.

"Don't do that, shit, Lauren," Riggs interrupts, pinning me with a glare, shaking his head. My eyes widen at the use of my name and not the nickname he was so fond of.

The Tiger meant business.

"We don't owe these people shit, least of all an explanation as to how we live," he chastises before turning his glare onto his parents. "Now, you don't get to show up on my doorstep and ridicule me and my family."

"Robert if you would just let us speak—"

"Ain't nothing you say I want to hear," Riggs seethes as he caresses Eric's back mindlessly. Eric leans his head against his dad's chest and starts to calm.

"We don't even know who you are anymore," Lenore comments, shaking her head as she shoves a hand at him, letting her eyes travel the length of him. "You look like a street thug, not a Montgomery."

"Lenore, that's enough," Mr. Montgomery shouts.

"You've got ten seconds to get the fuck out of my house before this street thug drags your ass down to the gutter," Riggs threatens.

"I told you we should've called," Mr. Montgomery hisses, grabbing Lenore's elbow before piercing his son with a look. "We'll go for now, but we'll be back. We came here for a reason, son." He diverts his eyes to mine. "It was nice to meet you, Lisa."

"Her name is Lauren," Riggs hisses, grabbing my arm and pulling me to his side. "Get out," he demands. "And do yourself a favor, forget the reason you came here. Neither of you are welcome in my house or around my son," he grounds out.

I stare at Riggs' parents, albeit they were rude and thought the sun shined out of their asses, but they were still his parents, still Eric's grandparents. I kept my mouth shut and watched Mr. Montgomery's face fall and Lenore's remain perfectly frozen in place. She had a hard face, nothing inviting and loving about it and made me thank God for my mother. Maria Bianci was crazy as hell but she would give you the shirt off her back and was always there for me and Anthony. Lenore Montgomery, or whatever her last name was these days, was not the mother you rushed to in your time of need.

I glanced back at Riggs as he kept his eyes trained on the door.

"Out," he hollers, startling Eric who was falling asleep in his arms.

Mr. Montgomery reaches into his pocket and extends his hand, offering me his business card.

"Lenore and I would like to get to know our grandson," he explains as I take the card from him. "It was nice to meet you, Lisa," he adds.

"Lauren, her fucking name is Lauren," Riggs mutters, taking the card from my hand, before he walks toward the front door and pulls it open.

His parents hesitate a moment before starting for the door. Mr. Montgomery pauses in front of Riggs, lifting his hand to Eric's head but deciding against it at the last minute.

"He looks just like you," Mr. Montgomery says before walking out. Riggs slams the door behind them.

I stare intently at Riggs, watching as he takes deep breaths through his nose and releases them through his mouth, mindlessly running his hand gently down Eric's back.

"Riggs," I start, not really knowing what to say. We never spoke much about his parents but I knew enough to know they were estranged. Riggs washed his hands of them long ago and never looked back. He took his own detour away from the lifestyle of the rich and famous and found what made him happy. He found the Satan's Knights and then he found me. Still, watching him interact with the people who brought him into this world, the resentment he harbored toward them so evident, it made me want to peel back the multi-faceted layers of him and discover who he was before the MC, before the name Riggs, when he was simply Robert Montgomery.

"I'm going to put Eric down for his nap," he says, snapping out of his trance as he walks off toward the baby's room.

I stare after him a moment before turning around and groaning as my eyes scan the mess. I'm pretty sure I failed at making a good first impression on Riggs' parents, I suppose we're even now. After all, he did gag my mother the first time he met her.

Yeah, we were awesome at meeting the parents.

Chapter Fifteen

RIGGS

Staring down at my son, I brace my hands on the edge of the crib and watch him sleep peacefully, knowing he's the only cure to the anger flooding my veins. It's pretty much a mind fuck to think the one thing that calms me and brings me back to focus is my son. I was so scared to be a father and not just because I was the pimp daddy of the MC world but because I had no fucking idea what being a dad entailed. I don't have memories with my father, and my mother's a nagging witch who still tries to use me to keep up with appearances. They hired a fleet of nannies to raise me and when I was old enough to break free from them I fled like a nun running away from a whore house. If it wasn't for my best friend Bones and his mother, who was our housekeeper, I wouldn't know how to be a man.

"Don't worry little guy, those vultures won't get a chance to sink their claws in you," I promise as I grit my teeth.

Fuck that.

I press a kiss to my son's head before turning to leave him to his nap and face Kitten. Running my fingers through my hair, I let out a groan knowing I'm about to be interrogated by my favorite feline. I was in no mood to rehash my shitty childhood but I knew Lauren wouldn't let that shit die. She's a woman, asking questions came with the chromosome. I blame this shit on my dick, if I wasn't horny, I wouldn't have come home early, I would still be at the clubhouse. I never would've laid eyes on the two people I never wanted to see again as long as I lived.

Kitten is waiting for me in the living room nervously biting her lip and staring into space. She lifts her head when she hears me walk into the room and pushes her glasses further onto the bridge of her nose.

"Riggs—"

"Why would you let those people in here?" I interrupt.

She blinks, her big blue eyes narrow as she stares at me with confusion.

"They're your parents," she says incredulously.

"No, they're not," I insist, waving my hand between me and her. "You and me? We're parents. Those two assholes don't know the first thing about being parents. For fuck's sake, you were there, you saw how that woman held our son. She held Eric like he carried the Ebola virus."

"So maybe they're different—"

"Different? God, Kitten, open your eyes," I growl, losing my patience and my sanity, and losing it with the person who didn't deserve this side of me. Still, I couldn't help myself and unleashed the fury building inside my gut since the moment I stepped foot inside this apartment and saw my parents with *my* family.

"Baby," she starts, closing the distance between us as she runs her hands down my arms, lacing our hands together. "My eyes were open and yes, your mother needs some work but your dad? I don't know," she shrugs. "He looked sincere. He looked at you and he looked at Eric…he cared."

"Don't you think for one moment those people came here with good intentions. They found out they have a grandkid, not too sure how the fuck that happened but whatever. Eric carries the Montgomery name, and that shit means a lot in my parents' world. They look at me and then our kid and they don't want him to turn out like me, they need someone to rule their fucking empire after they croak."

I pull my hands away from Lauren's and run them over my face in frustration.

"They figure they can mold him to be the perfect heir," I continue, tearing my hands away from my face and pinning Lauren with a hard stare. "I don't want them near Eric."

"Riggs—" she starts.

"Lauren, it's not up for discussion. I don't want them near him or you for that matter."

"So if they show up here again, then what? Slam the door in their face?"

"Yes, and if you have a problem doing it then call me and I'll come home and take care of them."

"Riggs, people change. Why don't you take a few days to think about it, maybe even give your dad a call and hear him out? Give them the benefit of the doubt. Who knows, maybe finding out they have a grandson is a second chance for them—maybe they can right all the wrongs they did with you."

I fell in love with Lauren for many reasons but mainly because of her heart. She's good people, loves big and fights hard for what she believes in. She's everything I've ever wanted in a woman but right now I wish her heart was a little bit smaller, her will to fight for what she believes in not so strong. I wish she'd realize not everyone is worthy of a second chance.

She closes the distance between us, wrapping her arms around my neck and peering up at me from the rim of her glasses.

"I'm not doubting you have your reasons for feeling how you do but I always wished my dad would've walked back into my life, that he'd realize what he walked away from and want to be a part of my life, especially after Eric was born. My dad isn't coming back, Riggs, and while your parents didn't walk away from you they came looking for you. Your father is the only chance Eric has of having a grandpa."

Picking a piece of spaghetti out of her hair, I bend my knees, bringing me level with her mouth before pressing my lips against hers.

I take it back.

I wouldn't change a fucking thing about her.

But that didn't mean I wouldn't change *everything* about my parents. If they had a sincere bone in their body, maybe I'd consider giving them the benefit of the doubt but my mother didn't want to be a grandmother, she wanted to show Eric off like he was a prize filly. Then there was my old man, standing alongside 'Mommy Dearest' with the same useless expression his face carried when I was five and asked him to play catch with me. If he isn't turning millions into billions, he has no fucking clue what to do with himself.

They'll try to throw their money around, offer to put Eric in a fancy school and probably enroll him in fucking fencing classes. I know the consequences of being a Montgomery heir and I don't want that for my son. I want him to be his own person, someone who creates his own destiny. If he grows up and tells me he wants to join the fucking circus, guess what, Kitten and I will be at every show cheering him on with big red noses.

My mother looked like she was about to have a stroke when she looked at me. It didn't matter she hadn't seen or spoken to me in years. She was disgusted by the ink that covered my skin and in the back of her twisted head she was probably scheduling an appointment with her plastic surgeon to see if they could be removed.

The tattoos on my skin tell my life story one she never took an interest in.

And if she knew the life I chose over the one she wanted for me she'd be appalled. If she knew Lauren was shot, or that Bones died because of some beef my club had she'd fucking lose her shit.

This is who I am.

And as Lauren takes me as I am, loves me for who I am, that's all I need. The only man I need to be is the man that owns her heart.

I'm not a Montgomery.

Though, the trust fund they set me up with helped when I fucked that shit with the Chinese. Thank God for that fucking thing.

I slide my tongue between Lauren's parted lips and take my frustrations out on her mouth. Cradling her face in my hands, my thumbs caress her cheeks as she tightens her hold on my neck and presses her body against mine.

That body.

My hands drop away from her face and slide down her curves, finding the hem of her t-shirt. I start to work the cotton up her body, breaking away from her mouth to pull the shirt over her head.

"Are you trying to shut me up?" Kitten asks as she reaches for the button on her denim shorts. Her breasts are heavy, full, and her nipples, those perky things were begging for Riggsy boy to play with them.

"Maybe," I admit, bending my head to take one nipple between my teeth. I tug on the bud before drawing it into my mouth and running my tongue over it. "Is it working?"

"Promise me you'll give it some thought."

"I promise you I'm not thinking about my parents while I have your nipple in my mouth. Now take your shorts off, Kitten," I order as my hand slips into the waistband of her shorts and my fingers graze the lace covering her pussy.

"At least you're honest," she groans as she shimmies out of her shorts. I drop to my knees, lifting one foot at a time and rid her of the shorts that pool around her ankles. Next, I cup the cheeks of her ass with my palms and bring her closer and brush my mouth against the scar from her cesarean.

Her fingers work my hair as my teeth latch onto the elastic of her panties and drag them down her body.

"I'm going to be real honest with you," I murmur as she steps out of her panties, pulling her glasses off her face and shaking out her hair. She gives me the come fuck me eyes and puts her sexy face on. I should to tell her she didn't need to do all that because I always want her. I wanted her from the minute I came home, dressed in a wet t-shirt, with SpaghettiOs in her hair. Lauren is the sexiest woman I have ever laid eyes on. "Honesty is me telling you you're beautiful. Honesty is my word that you're all I need to get by in this world. Honesty is you and me becoming one and forgetting there even is a world outside this apartment. You, Kitten, you're everything and that's the fucking truth. It doesn't get any more honest than that."

Her breath hitches as I grab a hold of her thighs and push them a part, all the while keeping my eyes locked with hers.

Love those eyes.

She braces her hands on my shoulders and I shift so I am sitting on the floor, staring up at her.

"Come here, Kitten, give me my honesty…give me you," I rasp, reaching behind her to cup her ass and bring her down to me. She wraps her arms around my neck as she takes a seat on my lap.

"This what you want?" she asks breathlessly as she rocks against my erection straining to break through my worn jeans.

"No," I admit, lowering my back until it was flat against the carpet. "Up here, Kitten," I say, pointing to my mouth before taking one of her hands and guiding her up my body until she was positioned right where I wanted her, hovering over my face. She looked down at me, her hair wild around her face as her tongue traced her bottom lip.

"Give me *you*," I plead.

She closes her eyes and lowers herself onto my waiting mouth. A moan escapes her as my tongue parts her lips and delves inside. Honesty was knowing I'd never get tired of this. I grip her hips as she arches against my mouth, my tongue teasing her, lavishly licking my way until I find her clit. She cries my name as I suck it into my mouth.

Honesty is knowing my name was never truly mine until I heard her say it.

Scream it.

Cry it.

Whisper it.

I pull my mouth back, glide my fingers over the path my tongue took before pushing two of them inside her and slamming my mouth back over her clit. She fists my hair and quickens her pace, riding me, taking what she needs from me.

Honesty.

Woven within every move she made.

Pushing my fingers deeper, I flick my tongue over her clit, once, twice and find it. Her pussy squeezes my fingers, quaking against my mouth as the rest of her tries to remain still and soak up the aftershocks of her orgasm. I feel the change in her, her body going lax over her mine, her grip loosening on my hair and the hold she had on my fingers easing allowing me to guide them out of her. I let my tongue take another swipe before leaning back, watching as she rolled off me and onto her back.

"Honesty is admitting the Tiger gives great head," she pants.

Grinning, I kick off my boots and work my jeans down my legs before reaching behind me and pulling my shirt over my head.

"Are you going to fuck me now?"

"God, I love it when you talk like that. Keep talking," I demand, positioning myself between her legs. The head of my cock teases her glistening pussy.

"Just before you were trying to shut me up and now you want me to talk," she teases, bending her knees and closing them around me. "What do you want to hear me say, Riggs? You want me to tell you how badly I want your cock? How I was disappointed you left this morning before wrapping my mouth around you?"

"Fuck yes, more of that," I grunt, bending my head to graze her nipple.

"Or maybe I should tell you I fingered myself in the shower this morning wishing it was your cock fucking me."

"That's it, Kitten," I hiss, taking her hands and slamming them over her head as my dick pummels into her drenched pussy. "Take my cock," I demand, sliding in inch by inch, filling her until she screams.

Fuck the world. Fuck the people who brought me into it. Everything could go up in smoke and I wouldn't give two fucks. This right here, this moment, wrapped up in Lauren, this was everything. To hell with everything and everyone else.

I pull out, push back in, branding her mouth with kisses as I give her all of me, all the honest parts of my soul. I lose control, pounding into her mercilessly but Kitten takes me as always, matching my tempo. Jerking my hips, I groan coming and coming like a fucking champ. After I've emptied my balls, and sure I'm paralyzed, I collapse over Lauren.

She wraps her arms and legs around me, holding me close to her as her hands travel the length of my back.

"I love you, Riggs," she whispers against my ear.

I remain tangled in her, joined to her as I roll us over and lie on my back, draping her body over mine like a blanket.

"Love you too, Kitten," I say pressing a kiss to the top of her head. "Call your mother, see if she'll watch Eric tonight."

She lifts her head from my chest and frowns.

"She's watching Tori and Luca today there is no way she will watch Eric tonight too," she says, trailing her finger down my cheek. "Grace called Anthony and Adrianna over to discuss Victor's transfer."

"These mob folks are so greedy. Jack is off the grid too because Victor summoned him up to the can," I inform her, shaking my head. "Fucking Victor, always messing with me."

Lauren giggles before she bends her head and kisses my lips quickly. I trail my hands down her sides and hold onto her hips.

"See...now if you were talking to your parents we could've asked them to watch Eric," she says.

I raise an eyebrow at her.

"You sure about that? You'd let those clowns watch Eric?"

She bit her lip, wincing as she shook her head.

"Maybe not. I mean not for a while and maybe the first time we'd supervise. Oh, fine. I don't think I'd let them watch Eric either."

"Now look who's being honest." I wink at her.

She smacks my shoulder playfully.

"Still think you should consider calling your dad."

"I think it's time to shut you up again, Kitten."

"What did you have in mind?" she asks with a hint of mischief playing in those blue eyes.

Honesty was knowing my Kitten was down to play. Honesty was finding all sorts of ways to keep her quiet, well maybe not completely quiet. I like hearing her scream my name.

Chapter Sixteen

Grace

The first time Victor was shot the girls were young. Nikki was still in diapers and Adrianna was in pre-school. In those days, Vic worked nights, he'd leave right after the girls were tucked in for the night and return in the morning just in time for breakfast. It was a Tuesday; I had overslept and was frazzled, trying to get the girls dressed so Adrianna wouldn't be late for school. I was used to doing things for the kids on my own and instead of wondering why Vic hadn't returned I went about my day feeding and dressing both girls. I didn't bother dressing myself and hurried out the door with mismatched pajamas only to find Val's car blocking mine in the driveway. He and Maryann got out of the car and started for me.

He didn't need to say the words, I knew something was wrong the minute my eyes met Val's. Maryann took Nikki from my arms and bent down to talk to Adrianna

"Come on, sweetheart, Mikey is in the car. Aunt Maryann will take you guys to school," she said before peering up at me. *"Give your mommy a kiss,"* she added.

I snapped out of my trance, smiled when I felt like dying because I was a mother and my job was to shield my daughters from the world Victor and I brought them into. I kissed Adrianna's head and watched Maryann lead her away.

"How bad is it?" I questioned, keeping my eyes trained on Maryann as she peeled out of the driveway with our kids.

"He's okay. He took a shot to the stomach, but he's going to be fine," Val said as he placed a hand on my shoulder.

"This time," I muttered numbly as I finally lifted my eyes to his. *"Until one day you knock on my door and tell me it's not okay."*

"Not on my watch, Grace. You won't hear those words from me," he promised.

It would've been easy to believe his words, after all, they were exactly what I wanted to hear but I knew better. Even then I knew one day this would all catch up to us. Val was true to his word, he never delivered the words he promised he wouldn't. I wish Victor made the same promise to me but he was too busy making other promises he wouldn't keep.

That was the first time Victor cheated his fate. He's been shot a total of six times, arrested over twenty-three times and has beaten sixteen cases. Each time I got a visit or a phone call from one of his guys and each time I wondered if that would be the time I had to sit my girls down and tell them their daddy wasn't coming home.

Now the time has finally come and all the preparing I've done throughout the years is lost. I have no idea how to do this. They're going to have questions, ones

I don't have the answers to. I wonder if I knew thirty years ago this was how it was going to end, if I would've married him and vowed to stand by him until death do we part.

"Ma, how many times do we have to tell you to lock the door?"

Adrianna's voice startles me and I jump before spinning around to face her and Anthony.

"She's right, Grace," my son-in-law adds before bending down to kiss my cheek.

"I could've sworn I did," I mumble, forcing a smile as I wrap my arms around my daughter. "Thank you both for coming. I hope Maria didn't mind watching the kids?" I turn to Anthony and question him with my eyes.

"Watching the kids keeps her out of trouble," Anthony replies with a shake of the head. "Or at least it stops her from breaking Riggs' balls."

That made me smile genuinely as the back door swings open and my youngest storms in like the tornado she was, my smile widening ever so slightly.

"I'm fucking late and I suck but I'm here and I brought Dunkin," She exclaims waving a Box of Joe enticingly.

"Where's Mikey?" Adrianna asks, grabbing the mugs from the cabinet.

"He'll be here, he had to see a customer about an estimate," Nikki explains as she hugs me. "I miss you," she whispers against my hair before she pulls back a fraction and smiles. "Where are the crazies?"

"They took Nana to bingo at the church," I explain, laughing at her reference to my in-laws.

"When are they going back home?"

"That depends on when you're getting married," I tell her. I'm not pressuring her to get married but a part of me is worried she's stalling because of Victor. I want to reassure her it's okay for her to move forward and her father will be there in spirit.

Spirit.

That word makes it sound like he has already passed.

We pull apart as I clear my throat and tip my chin toward the living room. "Why don't we all have a seat?"

"Ma, I'm not going to lie, you're freaking me out," Nikki says warily.

"Yeah, what's going on? Why the family meeting? Did something happen with dad?"

I avert my eyes between my two girls before turning to Anthony. It hadn't dawned on me until now that he may already know about Victor's condition. Staring at him he looks just as anxious as the girls and it became clear that Victor faded Anthony out of the limelight of the organization just as he a promised. I guess there were some things he kept his word about.

"I went to visit your father," I pause, offering Nikki a smile. "I showed him the photograph of your engagement and told him all about it. He was so happy for you and Michael. He made me promise to tell you to pick out the wedding dress of your dreams."

I take a moment to keep myself in check, to keep the tears at bay and the emotion buried, reminding myself this isn't about me. It's not about my feelings but rather my girls, our girls. Nikki glances down, toying with her engagement ring before looking back at me.

"It fucking sucks he won't be at my wedding," she admits, turning to her sister. "It was fitting your son gave you away to Anthony, the three of you were becoming a family." She violently wipes away a tear.

"And you'll have me to walk you down the aisle," I interject. "He asked me to do that you know, to walk you down the aisle, to give your hand to Michael with his blessing."

"I still feel guilty," Nikki whispers. "I still blame myself for him being in there."

"The only one who should be blamed is me," Adrianna argues. "I'm the one who pulled the trigger. I'm the one who did the crime he confessed to committing. If anyone is to blame for daddy not being at your wedding, it's me, and I'm so sorry. I'm so sorry I took that from you," she cries.

"Stop it! Both of you stop it," I insist, inching forward to take their hands in mine. "Your father is in jail because he deserves to be, because for the last thirty years your father has done a lot of bad things. I never wanted to admit that, especially not to you girls but what's the use in hiding it when both of you have witnessed him in action, both of you have suffered at the hands of his organization. That was too much for your father to handle, his conscience too heavy with guilt to continue as he was. It was his choice to turn himself in and his alone. Does that mean you should blame him? No, it means he finally earned the respect he always craved. You can be hurt, you're entitled to be, but you should always have respect for the man who gave his freedom for us to live a life free of his sins. Your father loves you both so much," I assure, turning to Adrianna and then to Anthony before I continue.

"He is so proud of you two and those babies you created," I smile, cocking my head as my gaze settles on my son-in-law. "He's grateful for you."

Anthony takes a deep breath before giving me a slight nod of his head, showing his appreciation for my words. Anthony wasn't a man who needed gratification from anyone but having Victor's appreciation was closure for him. He never wanted to hate Victor, he looked up to him, but my husband was threatened by Anthony's hold over our daughter's heart.

"Did you show him Victoria's picture?" Adrianna asks.

"I did," I say, looking back at her. "Just as beautiful as her mama."

"You didn't call us here to recap your visit," Nikki whispers. "You're stalling, ma," she accuses.

"Your father's being transferred to a federal prison in North Carolina two weeks from Friday," I reveal, pausing to gage their reactions.

"I knew that," Anthony confesses, turning to Adrianna. "That means we need to get you two up to see him at least once before he gets on that bus," he tells them, knowing all about the last hit Victor was going to commit. Maybe he didn't fade as much as we all thought he did.

The last hit.

Another promise he'd keep but to the men in leather this time.

"What's the urgency?" Nikki asks. "I mean I get it, North Carolina isn't a hop, skip and a jump away but you're making it like once he gets on that bus we won't be able to visit him anymore," she continues.

"He's being transferred but his visitation will be revoked shortly after he's gotten his new number," Anthony explains.

"Why would they do that? Has he done something to get his privileges taken away?" she asks as she looks back and forth between us.

"Your father's connections will not hold any merit down south," he answers vaguely.

"Anthony's right, you need to go visit your father," I whisper, clearing my throat in hope to find my voice. "I don't know how the transfer will work but I'm sure you know what you're talking about," I say to him, before drawing in a breath. "However, that's not the reason you *need* to go."

I don't know why my eyes drift to our wedding photo hanging on the wall over the fireplace but they did and I continue to stare at it wishing I could hear his voice, wishing for him to hold my hand and be with me as I say the words that seal our fate.

A woman could wish all she wants, doesn't mean those wishes will come true. I've had my share come true and now it's time to turn the lamp to someone else. I hope they have better luck than I did. I hope their wishes never turn to burdens.

This was my burden to carry alone.

The burden of truth.

"Visit your father as much as you can over the next two weeks, let him know how much he means to you and reassure him that you forgive him. Promise you'll never forget him and will always keep him in your hearts. Remind him that you're happy and swear you'll take care of each other. Say goodbye to your dad and remember you'll always be daddy's little girls," I whisper, finally peeling my eyes away from the photo on the wall and finding the courage to face Adrianna and Nikki. "Tell him it's okay and that he can be at peace," I cry, blinking away the tears I tried so hard to hang on to but the words I was asking my daughters to tell their father were also the words I'd have to say myself.

I'm not ready for goodbye.

I'm not ready for the end.

"Victor's sick," I sob.

"What do you mean sick?" Adrianna yelps. "Sick as in he's dying?"

"Dying? What? No," Nikki whimpers.

"I'm sorry," I mutter, pulling one of Victor's silk handkerchiefs from my pocket and wiping my eyes.

"What does he have?" Anthony asks.

"Lung cancer and from the medical records the lawyer showed me it's really bad. They gave him a year, two years ago."

"Two years ago? You've known he's been sick for two years and you kept it from us?" Adrianna accuses, rising to her feet as she glares down at me through her sobs.

"He didn't tell me either, Adrianna. I found out the same day I found out about the transfer," I argue.

"What about chemotherapy or radiation?" Nikki questions.

"It's too late its stage four and your father has refused any treatment. I spoke to the family doctor and at this stage the best any doctor would recommend is making the patient comfortable. However, Victor isn't just any patient, he's an inmate and they don't care if he's in pain or if he's losing oxygen."

"I can't fucking believe this!" Adrianna shouts, wiping her face angrily as she paces.

"Reese's calm down," Anthony soothes, rubbing her shoulders only for her to shove his hands away.

"Don't tell me to calm down! He's refused treatment for two years! How am I not supposed to be angry about that? For two years he's been making plans for Rocco, playing fucking 'chess' so his goddamn organization remains intact instead of taking care of his health. For two years he made sure he had all his ducks lined in a row when it came to the mob but what about us? What happens to us after he's gone? We're the ones who will mourn him long after he's buried and the suits that come to pay their respects will forget Victor Pastore ever existed!"

"A, that's enough!" Anthony shouts as he stares at me.

"You mentioned Rocco," I begin, wondering why she was talking about my nephew. What did my deceased sister's son have to do with Victor's organization? "Adrianna, what does Rocco have to do with your father's business?"

Adrianna crosses her arms under her chest and turns to her husband.

"Go on and tell her," she demands. "Stop protecting him and tell her."

He steps closer to her and pins her with a glare.

"I quit protecting your old man a long time ago," he hisses.

Twisting the handkerchief in my hand, I stand from the sofa and step between them.

"Both of you stop right now," I order.

"Your dear nephew is now the boss of the Pastore organization," Adrianna chides. "Daddy wouldn't give it up, he couldn't let it go so he groomed Rocco to be the boss. He couldn't give up the mob but he gave up his life without hesitation."

I spin around to face Anthony.

"Is it true? Victor gave the business to Rocco?"

"Yes," he confesses, taking my hand. "Listen to me Grace, everyone's emotions are all over the place but there's more to it than just handing over his business to someone." He glances over my shoulder at Adrianna. "Every mob boss from here to California will now take a page from the book Vic wrote because even in death he protected his family. Don't think for one minute he wasn't thinking of everyone standing in this room. He won't be here to protect the people he loves, but he made sure someone else always would by keeping the business within the family. Handing it over to his nephew, he is keeping his enemies away. If he didn't name a successor, then we are vulnerable and a free for all to take whatever kind of action they see fit."

"You were singing a different tune the other day," Adrianna accuses, her tone more subdued, the fight in her diminishing.

"I didn't know he was dying, Reese's. That changes everything, I understand why he made the choice he made. Think about it, since the day they locked your father up he's always had his hand in something, think back to the visits in the jail and the respect he gets from the COs. Look what he did for Jack, how he helped to get Blackie released, he's always had some sort of control. The only way he'd ever lose control is if he lost his life."

My head was spinning trying to make sense of everything Anthony was saying but as much as I wanted to see the silver lining in Victor's decision I harbored too much resentment. Anthony knew Vic's business like the back of his hand, he understood the life and its consequences and even knowing that what he was saying was probably true I didn't want to hear it.

I was so sick of the mob and everything it stood for.

I was always second to the mob, decisions that should've been between me and him never were, they were decided between him and his associates, him and his underboss, him and his lawyer.

Just once in thirty years I would like to be asked my opinion.

Just once I would like to come first.

I turn around and spot Nikki sitting on the couch crying staring off into space. Walking over to her, I wrap my arms around her and cradle her to my chest, consoling her as she breaks down and cries.

The front door opens and Michael walks in stopping in his tracks as he glances around the room at us. His eyes zeroing in on Nikki as she pulls out of my embrace and stares back at him.

"You told them?" he asks, stepping toward her but again he freezes causing me to curiously study Nikki's face.

"Told us what?" I ask, my eyes darting back and forth between the two of them.

"Shit," Michael hisses.

"Nikki?" I coax, swallowing the lump in my throat.

"I got bad news from my doctor."

I instantly felt the air leave my lungs as the words left her mouth and I asked myself, how much can one family possibly endure?

Chapter Seventeen

JACK

I swipe my hand along my face, scratching at the scruff that lines my jaw as I try to think of what to say to the man sitting across from me. I came here with every intention of ripping Victor a new asshole for springing the whole Rocco thing on me and pulling the wool over my eyes. But before I could give him the lashing he deserved the son of a bitch told me he had lung cancer.

"How long have you known?"

He folds his hands neatly on top of the table as he holds my gaze.

"A while," he admits vaguely.

My eyes work him over, trying to find the signs I likely ignored but aside from the occasional coughing fit and the few pounds he'd shed, I had nothing. He still looked as dapper as ever. Even in his white canvas sneakers and prison jumpsuit.

Fucker.

"I can't imagine they send the doctors from Sloan Kettering to this joint," I seethe, shaking my head as I lean back in my chair.

He smiles faintly.

"It wouldn't matter if they did. I've refused all treatment," he reveals. I open my mouth to criticize his decision, but I stop myself. I don't know that I wouldn't have made the same decision given the circumstances.

"When I found out it was already stage four. There is no use in putting myself through that, putting my family through that, only to prolong the inevitable," he says as he shrugs his shoulders. "I'm behind bars, Jack, it's not like I'd have more time to spend with Grace and the girls. They gave me a year tops, it's been two," he grins cockily, a trademark just like the suits he used to wear. "It's like God knows I have a plan I need to see through."

"Or the devil knows," I mutter.

All the same," he agrees.

"Your family know?"

The smile disappears from his face at the mention of his loved ones and he averts his eyes to the other inmates visiting with their families and not their biker buddies.

"I told Gracie her last visit up," he says, turning back to me. "The woman I thought would love me until my death is starting to hate me."

"Brother, I've been in that woman's presence quite a few times, even after they locked your ass up, she's got nothing but love for you. The kind that doesn't die when you do but finds you long after your ass is buried. That woman will be loving you even as the flames climb your limbs and drag you to hell."

His face remains still as stone as he digests my words, giving them, some thought before he finally speaks.

"You'd know first-hand how easily those flames can climb," he quipped.

That I do.

There are still times I close my eyes and zone out to the memory of Jimmy Gold's body helplessly hanging as the flames danced up his body. The image is so vivid and so real I can almost smell the flesh burning, and fuck me, it excites me.

"My lawyer came here yesterday; the transfer is set for the Friday after next."

"Two weeks," I reply, blowing out a ragged breath. They were transferring him to a maximum-security prison down south where our number one enemy was caged. Victor would make that motherfucker meet his maker. The G-Man was going down and Victor Pastore was the one making it happen. One last hit for the mobster everyone knew and loved.

"You'll get word once the job is done," he assured. "Retribution will finally be served."

Retribution for the sins my club committed under our previous president's reign. Retribution for those kids that died on Blackie's product, for the stash his wife ingested when she killed herself. Retribution for my brother, Danny's death, and the scars on Reina's body. Retribution for Vic's underboss, Val.

But retribution came with a price and that price was Vic's life. Sure, he was living on borrowed time but once he ripped the life from our enemy he'd be thrown in solitary, spending the rest of his days by himself with nothing but the past to haunt him and the devil waiting to greet him.

My eyes lock with his as I realize this is goodbye, the last time Vic and I will be face to face. What started off as an alliance between outlaws to keep New York clean of drugs became a brotherhood of sorts. We were different and yet the same, both of us ruled different aspects of our city and our partnership allowed us to maintain control over our interests. When I first met Vic, I knew nothing about the man other than what the newspapers printed but then he shook my hand and from that very first handshake I knew he'd have my back and my club's.

"I came here looking to raise hell on your ass for springing this shit with Rocco on me," I start.

"He'll do for you and your club what I no longer can," he interrupts. "He's young and he'll probably make a ton of mistakes, just like you and I did when we were first starting out but he'll always back your club."

I shake my head as I continue to stare at him.

"You don't know defeat do you, brother?"

"Defeat is for the weak," he announces, bowing his head for a moment before lifting his eyes to mine again. "Rocco wasn't my plan, Anthony always was, he was the man who I wanted to take control over my business. He was my plan, but he was also my daughter's plan. I had to choose between Anthony being the man who ruled my empire or the man who guarded my daughter from that same empire. Plans change, Jack, you know that better than anyone."

"Ain't that a fact," I sigh, leaning forward on my elbows as I pin him with a hard stare. The man could read people and I knew when he looked back at me he saw the sincerity in my eyes.

"I got you, Vic, and I got your girls as long as I'm breathing I'll always make sure they are. Business will always be business but family is family. I can't make any guarantees on the streets but you have my word your girls will always have a place in the Satan's Knights family."

I extend my hand across the table, watching as his eyes divert from mine to my hand and back. He slides his hand into mine, his grip just as firm as all those years ago.

The first handshake when he had my back.

And now the last handshake when I promise to always have his.

Dead or alive.

Heaven or Hell.

"You're good people, Parrish," Victor says.

"You're not so bad yourself you guinea bastard," I joke, giving him one final firm shake before dropping our hands. Victor chuckles, tipping his chin toward me as I brace my hands on the edge of the table and push out my chair to leave.

"See you on the other side, brother," I rasp, standing on my feet.

"I'll have the scotch waiting for you, Parrish."

I could see it—me and him knocking back a couple of shots before we tangoed with the devil and paid for our sins in the afterlife.

Until then, brother.

I turned, starting for the correction officer guarding the metal detectors when I heard Vic cough. I don't stop, I just keep walking, reaching the guard before I turn around and peer back at him. He was hunched over the table, coughing into his hand. One of the C.O.'s was behind him, helping him to his feet but he brushed him off.

I turned and strode out of the visitor's room before he lifted his head and found me staring at him, leaving his pride intact—for it was all he had left.

I walked away from the prison and made my way to my bike, feeling as though Vic was already gone. I fitted my helmet to my head, about to straddle my bike when I heard my phone go off. Reaching into my jacket, I pulled out my phone and glance at the screen to see Cobra was calling me.

"Yeah," I answered.

"Prez, we got trouble," he replied.

Of course we do.

"What kind of trouble?"

"The kind that requires a lawyer and your ass at the seventy-ninth precinct."

"Going to be awhile before I get my ass anywhere. I'm leaving Otisville now. Where the fuck is Blackie?"

"Don't know. I called him too but he ain't answering," he replied.

"What about Wolf and Pipe?"

"Yeah, they're being cuffed as we speak."

"Fucking hell," I seethe before ending the call and thumbing through my contacts to get Blackie on the horn. Motherfucker knows better than to ignore my calls.

He picked up on the fourth ring proving my point.

"Yo," he answered.

"Don't fucking 'yo' me. Where the fuck are you and be careful how you answer me. I ain't in the mood to hear some shit about you and Lace."

"I just left my N.A. meeting," he explained.

I couldn't get mad at the fucker for not answering his phone—not when he was off bettering himself and making a life for him and my girl.

"Cobra called—some shit with the cops is going down. Wolf and Pipe were arrested. I don't know if anyone else was too but their bringing them down to the seventy-ninth precinct. I'm leaving the prison now but it will be awhile before I get back."

"It's been too fucking quiet," he growled into the phone. "I'm on my way."

"I'll meet you there," I say before disconnecting the call and shove my phone inside my pocket, revving my engine before peeling away from the prison.

Blackie was right—it's been too quiet.

Only Satan knows what's coming.

Chapter Eighteen

BLACKIE

Cracking mu knuckles, I step away from my bike and climb the steps of the precinct, throwing on my game face as I reach the top step. These fucking pigs want to play with us then bitch we're going to play. I roll my neck, working out the stiffness as I prepare myself to face officer douchebag, Greg Brantley—the motherfucker who has a hard on for me since the day he first laid eyes on my first wife, Christine.

I push open the doors and stride into the police department, waiting for the bells and whistles to go off signaling my arrival but that shit doesn't happen. I ignore the cop pushing paper at the front desk as my eyes scan the room searching out Brantley, knowing for sure he's the one behind this bullshit.

"Can I help you?"

"Where's Brantley?" I clip, pulling my shades down as my eyes drill holes into the female officer in front of me. She licked licks her lips as she stares at me for a moment, *girl my people and your people don't play nice together*.

"I've got this, Bailey," dickface croons as he makes his way toward me. "What's the matter? Parrish having a mental breakdown so he sent you to bail his boys out?"

I flash him a smirk as I glance around the room.

"Everyone with a badge has a pair of balls," I say, turning to Officer Bailey. "I'm sure even she has a set hidden somewhere," I accuse before pinning my eyes back to Brantley. "Why don't you bend over and show her where you tuck yours away."

The grin on my face widens as a gasp escapes Bailey's mouth and Brantley grounds his teeth.

"What's the matter, Officer Bailey, you didn't know Brantley over here is a pussy dressed in blue?"

"Keep talking, Petra and I'll throw your ass in a cell too," Brantley threatens.

"On the same fabricated charges you cuffed my brothers on?"

"We have a witness placing five men wearing the Satan's Knights patch robbing J & G liquor store, nothing fabricated."

I narrow my eyes, taking a step closer to him as I grind my teeth.

"You came charging into the Dog Pound and arrested five of my guys on petty larceny?"

I was two seconds away from snapping this motherfucker's neck in front of the whole fucking precinct. Brantley smiled at me as he reached into his pocket and grabbed his phone. I debate popping a cap in the back of his head as he turns around and takes the call.

"Petra," I hear Jones call and peel my eyes away from Brantley's head and the vision of his brains splattered on the floor. I shake my head as I close the distance between me and Jones and I grab the front of his uniform.

"What the fuck, Jones?"

He glances over my shoulder and I followed his gaze toward Brantley, watching as he hurries out the front door of the precinct. I look back at Jones and shove him back, releasing my hold on him.

"I don't give a fuck about that cunt. Now, I'm going to repeat the question one more fucking time," I tell him, dropping my voice down to a whisper. "Club pays your ass a lot of money for things like this not to happen, so again…what the fuck, Jones?"

"I was on a domestic call when it came over the radio. I couldn't fucking leave the call I was on to go to the clubhouse they'd fucking know I was in your pocket. I came here as soon as I could. He brought them in on bullshit charges, he keeps saying he's got a witness but I've searched every fucking interrogation room and haven't found anyone. I don't know what he's up to, but he's up to something," he mutters, taking another sweep of the busy room before tipping his chin toward the hallway. "Follow me and I'll take you down to the holding cell before he gets back."

I follow him down the narrow hallway, down three flights of stairs to the rat infested basement where the holding cells are. Before we even round the corner I hear them; Pipe, Wolf, Riggs, Bosco and another voice I couldn't place.

"This is a bunch of bullshit, when I get out of here I'm suing the city," Pipe hollers.

"Brantley you fuck, tell your mother to get the lube ready because I'm going to fuck her six ways to Sunday when I get out of here," Wolf adds.

"Let me out! I'm not part of the cult. I don't even have a tattoo. I've never owned a leather jacket in my life," the unfamiliar voice whines.

"Keep talking. I'm going to tie this bitch up," Riggs grunts.

"Ignore him," Bosco mutters.

"Man, I'm itching to hit something so be careful who's side you choose," Riggs warns.

We round the corner, and I clear my throat, making my presence known to my men as my eyes zero in on the only one of the five that didn't belong to me.

"What the fuck is he doing here?"

"He came to pay us a visit, crying he had information for us before the police showed up," Riggs says, using his fingers to mimic a gun pointed at Ronan Summers, and pulls the imaginary trigger.

Summers was the father of the little shit that tried to rape my girl. He's a gambling junkie that hooked up with the Corrupt Bastards MC and some online gambling site they had. When he couldn't pay he offered up his son, Brandon, the Bastards sent Brandon in to get close to Lacey. The cocksucker decided he would take things a little further and tried getting inside *my* Lace.

Depending on who you ask, Brandon is lucky to be living, some might argue he's better off dead being as he's permanently deaf and fucked mentally from the brain injury. I would've preferred him dead and buried but then Lacey wouldn't have been able to get him to drop the charges.

Yeah, like I said, lucky to be living.

Skeptically, I stare at Ronan watching as Riggs grabs him from behind and wedges him into a headlock.

"If I find out this shit has anything to do with you," Riggs seethes.

"Let him go," I order, earning a glare from Riggs.

This isn't the first time Ronan has showed his face around the clubhouse spewing nonsense about having information we might be interested in. We never pay him any mind though, send the fucker on his way figuring he's looking for a handout. Usually he cries that Brandon's medical bills are choking him but he's a degenerate gambler and a fucking liar too. I like my money in my pocket just as every one of my brothers.

However, this shit with Brantley came out of nowhere and maybe it's time someone listened to what this fuck has to say.

Ronan's eyes were wide with fear as they settled on me.

"Why," he stammers as his eyes move nervously around the cell choosing Wolf to hide behind. "Don't hurt me man!"

"For crying out loud," Wolf bellows, grabbing Ronan from behind him. "Would someone hear this little jerk-off out so he stops showing up at the clubhouse? I'd rather be locked in a cell with officer dick bag than this guy."

"I offered to shoot him," Riggs says.

"Why were you at the clubhouse?" I demand calmly.

"Like I've told you before I have information I think you might want," he says, ducking behind Wolf again. "Maybe if you listened to me before we wouldn't be in here."

"Start talking," I say, crossing my arms against my chest. I tip my chin toward Riggs and watch him grab Ronan by the back of his neck and push him forcefully against the bars.

Ronan looks over his shoulder at Riggs who shows his teeth like a feral animal, clearly Riggs was out of patience and missing his kitten.

"Well, why don't we talk figures first?" Ronan suggested.

Riggs kicks him behind the knees and he drops to the floor.

"How about I leave your ass in jail?" I question through my teeth as I bend down to level with him.

"Times up," Jones announces, grabbing the back of my cut and pulling me back from the bars. Standing straight, I turn my head as I hear the distinct sound of footsteps bounding down the metal stairs.

Brantley walks over to us jingling a set of keys.

"Turns out the witness said the five men he saw weren't wearing a patch after all," he sneers. "You're free to go but I'd watch my back if I were any of you thugs," Brantley warns as he unlocks the cell.

"Thanks for the advice," Pipe replies, flipping him the bird.

"I think I'll just stay," Ronan offers.

Riggs kicks him in the ass.

"Move it," he shouts behind him.

Wolf was the last to exit the cell, turning around to smile at Brantley.

"Payback's a bitch officer and her twins name is karma. I always loved twins how 'bout you?" Wolf laughs as he thrust his hips and humped the air. "Can't wait for them to fuck you."

I shove my hands inside my pockets and shrug my shoulders as I lock eyes with my enemy.

"Always a pleasure, Brantley," I taunt before following my men.

"I'd sleep with one eye open if I were you, Petra," Brantley calls out.

"I already do," I reply, not bothering to turn around. I reach into my jeans and grab my phone, dial Cobra and order him to bring the cage around to the front of the station. My eyes fixate on the back of Ronan's head as I wonder what this little shit knows, if anything at all.

Wolf grabs two handfuls of paperwork off one of the detective's desks and throws it up in the air like confetti before we step outside.

"Did you have to?" I grunt.

"Yes, of course," he insists. "Now let's get the fuck out of here—" His words cut off as he collides with Riggs.

"Fucking shit! Why'd you stop walking?" Riggs questions Ronan, but the fucker was paralyzed, looking like he saw a ghost. I step around Wolf and Riggs to study Ronan's face and follow his eyes across the parking lot to where Jack was pulling off his helmet.

Jack strode across the gravel toward the biker I was sure we'd never see again. Charlie Teardrops was one of the few surviving members of the Corrupt Bastards. After I was released from prison, Jack and I found retribution on the fucking club that sent Brandon after Lacey. We slaughtered those fucks, including their president, Boots. Charlie wore the teardrops tattooed to his face as proudly as he wore his cut. Those teardrops symbolized the murders he committed for the patch he wore on his back.

Charlie averted his eyes to me before he looked over my shoulder, causing me to turn and watch as Ronan tried to make a run for it. Quickly, I grab him by the back of his neck and whisper against his ear as I lean over his shoulder.

"You wanted to talk, spook, we're going to talk," I promise.

Cobra pulls the van up in front of us and Pipe opens the back doors. I eye Riggs, wait for his nod before he grabs Ronan's arms and pulls it back igniting a shriek from the man before he throws him into the back of the van.

"You're mine fuck-face," Riggs declares, climbing in behind him. Once the boys were in the back of the van, I shut the doors and smack the side of the van giving Cobra the okay to get out of here. The van peels away as my boots pound the gravel and I make my way next to Jack catching the tail end of their conversation.

"You miscalculated, Parrish, by assuming my club was dead in the water. The Corrupt Bastards are very much alive, stronger than before and deadlier than ever. I hope your boys enjoyed their time with the NYPD."

"Watch who you're threatening, Charlie," Jack seethed. "Remember what happened the last time the Corrupt Bastards threatened the Satan's Knights."

"Not a threat," he said, lighting up a smoke. "I'm just giving you fair warning I want control over the docks and will stop at nothing to get it. Now that Pastore is up the river, the way I see it you can either relinquish your control or I can take it from you."

"Why in the Devil's names would I do that?"

Charlie took a drag of his cigarette before flashing a cocky grin toward Jack.

"I have resources bigger than you and your mob friend, Parrish," he says pointedly.

Jack steps closer to him, takes the cigarette out of his hand and glides the glowing tip to Charlie's face, stopping just before the cigarette meets his cheek.

"I always admired the ink on your face, maybe when I pull the breath from your lungs I'll mark my face just as you did."

Charlie shakes his head unfazed by Jack's words as he stares back at me.

"Your days as the 'Bulldog' are numbered, going to turn your ass into dog meat."

"You and what army?" Jack sneers, flicking the ashes onto Charlie's lap before letting the butt fall to the ground. He crushes it with his boot before turning around to face me as he dismisses Charlie. "We all good?" he questioned me.

I nod my head before watching Charlie tip his chin to someone standing behind me. I didn't give into him, knowing well enough he was provoking me and focused on my president.

"Always, brother," I answer.

Jack nods before turning back to walk to his bike and I take that as my cue to do the same. I catch a glimpse of Brantley standing on top of the steps of the station staring back at us. Charlie revs his engine and speeds out of the parking lot, saluting Brantley as he drives past him.

"Didn't see that one coming," Jack comments as he fits his fingerless gloves to his hands.

Yeah.

Me either.

But then again we never usually see the mayhem; that shit creeps up on us time after time and bites us in the ass.

Chapter Nineteen

JACK

Gritting my teeth, I walk into the Dog Pound and take in the mess. Tables have been flipped, chairs broken and the mug shots that hung proudly on the walls have been thrown across the floor. Mack was busy sweeping up shards of broken glass while Linc and Deuce worked on turning the couch back to its rightful place. The rest of the guys had parked their asses at the bar as Bosco grabs a bottle of whiskey and the few glasses that Brantley and his crew hadn't fucking broken. He fills their glasses, offering me one, but I brush him off, ignoring all of them as they stare at me, not ready to delve into this shit storm just yet.

Not without the help of a bottle of scotch.

I pour that shit straight down my throat.

The fiery liquid harshly warms my belly, but it's not enough. I throw my head back and swallow more, waiting for the liquor to take the edge off. Placing the bottle down on top of the bar, I zero in on the man sitting in the center of my brothers, tied to a bar stool with a gag in his mouth and Riggs' gun pointed to his temple. He stares back at me, his eyes wide with fear, just the way I like them.

"Someone going to tell me why this fuck is here?"

"Says he's got information we want," Blackie offers as he walks up behind Ronan and grabs his shoulders. "Isn't that right?"

Riggs slams his shot glass down on the bar as Ronan starts to mumble. He grabs a fistful of his hair and smashes his face into the bar.

"Motherfucker just nod your fucking head," Riggs growls.

My eyes sweep around the room at my disgruntled club and the decision becomes clear. I need to grab the reigns on this shit.

"Church, now and bring him," I say tipping my chin toward Ronan as I grab my scotch and head into the chapel. Their stools scrape against the floor behind me as they rise and follow suit.

"Where is Cobra?" Blackie asks, taking a head count of everyone.

"He had some personal shit come up," Deuce announces. "He'll be back by sunrise."

That didn't work for me. He wasn't a nomad anymore and his place was at this fucking table. I point a finger at Riggs and motion to Ronan.

"Remove the gag," I order.

Leaning close, Blackie whispers so only I can hear his words.

"Got real spooked when he saw Charlie outside the precinct," he informs me.

"Ouch!" Ronan cries.

"Oh, you're such a pussy," Riggs hisses, balling up the gag and throwing it into the center of the table.

"You got our attention Ronan, time for you to talk and before you even ask I'll clue you in on some shit. I don't give a fuck if you're broke, if you and your family are living off white rice. Don't give me some shit that your son's medical bills are hammering you; this is the face of a man who doesn't give a fuck. I don't want your sob story I want your motherfucking truth and if you think you will walk out of here without giving it to me, then you're more fucked than I thought because my man Riggs is itching to pull the trigger on your ass."

"Just waiting for the nod of your head boss," Riggs adds, pulling his gun from his leathers and placing it in front of him on the table. "Bang! Bang! Motherfucker."

"Kill me because I'm as good as dead anyway," Ronan cries. "And not because I owe Charlie sixty grand but because he saw me with you guys."

"Ronan, start at the beginning," Blackie demands.

"I'm not saying shit until I have your word you will protect me," he replies crossing his arms against his chest.

Riggs lifts his gun and aims it at him, pulling back the safety.

"Shit," Ronan whimpers. "Fine, Charlie's been building a new club with whatever Bastards are left, you know the ones you didn't kill?"

"Smartass," Blackie mutters.

"Keep talking!" I shout.

Ronan swallows hard as he stares back at me. I wasn't sure what he was looking for—remorse? I've got none. Was he trying to size me up and call my bluff? That shit wouldn't happen. I mastered the art of staring a person down and if this motherfucker was waiting for me to blink he'd be waiting a long time. A person's whole world can change in the blink of an eye and with the number of enemies I have chomping at the bit I know better than to close these fucking eyes—not even for a half a second.

"About a month ago Charlie showed up at my house, he had copies of Brandon's medical bills and swore he'd help me get rid of them. He told me that the Corrupt Bastards were very much alive and under his thumb, he was rebuilding the club with the help of some guys in pretty high places. He gave me a business card and on the back was a website to a brand new gambling site he created. He offered me a credit of fifty grand," he explains.

"They don't have that kind of cash flow," Pipe interrupts. "Charlie has to be working with someone who has serious dough, someone who doesn't have a paper trail and easy access if he can rebuild and offer a credit of fifty grand on the strength of a couple of months."

"Brantley got a call when I was there, before Jones brought me down to the holding cell and he walked outside. Ten minutes later he comes downstairs and releases everyone, we go outside and find you talking to Charlie," Blackie says, lifting his eyes to mine as he works out the scenario.

"What you getting at Black?"

"Brantley was stalling until Charlie showed up so we would see him and know he was the fuck behind this whole thing," Blackie explains.

"He was waiting at the station when I pulled up," I comment, scratching at the scruff lining my jaw.

"It's bigger than Brantley, maybe he's got Officer Dickhead in his pocket but he's got someone giving him cash to rebuild and it ain't no cop," Pipe adds.

"Um, guys…" Ronan starts.

"I'm getting too old for this shit and I think we all agree this club has seen enough surprises to last a lifetime. We need to find out who the fuck he's working with and we need to find out quick," I order, reaching into my pocket to grab the pack of gum—fucking gum.

I let out a growl, shaking my head as I pop six Chiclets into my mouth.

"Fucking hell," I sneer. "Riggs get a tap on Charlie's lines. Pipe, you look into his books and one of you start tailing Brantley," I boom, pointing between Linc and Deuce, deciding which one I was going to pick. I focus my eyes in on Linc. "You. You stick to the cocksucker like a fly to shit," I order. "He so much as blows a light I want to know."

"What if he takes a shit?"

"You tell Blackie," I reply.

"Hello?" Ronan whines, raising a hand.

"Did anyone tell you to fucking talk?" Riggs barks back at Ronan.

"That motherfucker is too cocky. Whoever he's working with is a big fucking name," Blackie says, still mulling it over.

"We're going to need someone on the inside," Wolf adds. "Gotta put life inside that clubhouse."

"Hello! Guys! You're forgetting something." Ronan exclaims.

"What's that?" I huff as I pin him with a glare.

"I need protection from your club," he demands.

"Now why the fuck would we do that?" Blackie asks, finally leaving his thoughts on the table and joining the land of the living.

"Charlie saw me with you guys which makes me dead meat. I owe him money and he's going to think I went to you looking to settle my debt," he rambles.

"Isn't that what you did?" Blackie asks.

"You're missing the point! Did you hear me at all? He will kill me!"

"Thank fucking Christ someone will end your miserable existence," Riggs says, glancing around the table. "Is it wrong to wish I was a Bastard?"

I lean back in my chair, chewing my gum as I size up Ronan. He wants protection, protection he shall get. But, I'm not a generous motherfucker and that shit comes with a price.

"Come here, Ronan," I coax, crooking my finger as I eye the watch on his wrist. He pushes back his chair and stumbles to his feet, shuffling toward me. "Take off your watch," I instruct, feeling the eyes of all my men.

He fumbles with the clasp, removing the cheap stainless steel watch from his wrist before he hands it to me. I lift the watch, turn it over and examine it thoroughly before turning my eyes back to Riggs.

"Heads up," I warn, tossing the watch across the table into his waiting hand. One glance into my fucking eyes and Riggs sees deep into my twisted mind. Knowingly, he turns the watch every which way before shoving it into his pocket.

"I'm on it," Riggs assures.

"Hey!" Ronan starts.

"You'll get it back, Riggs is just going to polish it up for you," I lie. "You want protection from my club, I'll give that to you but there's a price."

"I don't have any money," he cries.

"I don't want your money," I say calmly as I lean forward and grab a hold of his shirt, dragging his body down so we are at eye level. "You're going to be my eyes inside the Corrupt Bastards' clubhouse. You're going to go back and tell them we beat the fuck out of you, turn this shit around so Charlie doesn't suspect your lips were loose. You'll hang around and beg him to give you more time to pay your debt, even offer to get in with us. You're going to show up bloody and you're going to tell that motherfucker you want revenge on the Satan's Knights."

"But none of that happened. You didn't beat me up," he argues as I released my hold on him and smile.

Riggs walks up beside me and rears his fist back.

"Yes we did," he says as his fist collides with Ronan's jaw.

"Pack it up boys," I adjourn, slamming the gavel down as everyone rises from their seats and Ronan drops to his knees as Riggs pounds his face. "Riggs has a job to do," I chuckle, striding toward the door.

"He's going to fucking kill him," Linc states.

Glancing over my shoulder, I can't contain my grin as I watch Riggs throw Ronan a beating.

"Break it up after twenty minutes," I tell Linc before walking out the door.

I stop in my tracks when I spot Reina sweeping up the glass in the common room. She lifts her head when she hears us barrel through the door and locks eyes with me.

"Sunshine," I greet.

"You boys were busy I see," she says sarcastically, lifting the dustpan full of glass. She was wearing a Harley Davidson tank top that fit snugly across her breasts and her belly. The evidence of my baby growing in her belly was staring me in my face. I fucking loved it. I thought Reina was fucking beautiful the moment I first laid eyes on her but seeing her pregnant with my kid, beautiful didn't do her justice. She was happy. Fuck that was gorgeous.

It's fucking true what they say—a happy wife, a happy life.

"Jack," Blackie starts, placing one hand on my shoulder.

"Later," I grunt, walking away from him and straight for my woman.

She winks at me, continuing the task of dragging the broom across the floor, taking care of my clubhouse just as she would my home, knowing they were one. I grab the broom from her hand and toss it across the room before wrapping my arms around her waist and pulling her against me.

"What do I owe the pleasure?" I murmur as I run my mouth along her jaw.

"I thought you were visiting Vic," she whispers, her fingers toying with the ends of my hair. "I picked up my dress and didn't want you to see it in the house so I thought I'd leave it in your room upstairs."

I brush my lips across hers.

"Hmm," I hum, taking her bottom lip between my teeth.

"Jack," she breathes.

"Yes, Sunshine?"

"We have an audience," she whispers.

"I don't give a damn," I hiss, sliding my hands down to cup her ass.

She cups my face with her hands and pulls back an inch to study me.

"I love you, Parrish, and I like lovin' on you in private," she scolds, a smirk playing along her full mouth.

A groan escapes my lips as I think of all the ways I love on her—starting with that mouth. Yeah, I was going to fuck her mouth first then I'd spread her out and feed off her pussy before I slam my cock home deep inside her. I'd give her lovin', all the lovin' she needed.

"Upstairs. Now," I order, smacking her ass.

She laughs as she unravels her arms from my neck and turns to the room full of watchful eyes.

"Oh! I came here for another reason," she announces.

"Sunshine…" I groan. She swings around to pinch my forearm before turning back to my brothers.

"I left everyone's wedding invitation on the bar," she says. "They're all addressed, so just find which is yours."

She pauses, scrunching up her face as she glances from face to face.

"Where's Riggs?"

"Busy," I mutter.

"Help!" Ronan cries.

"Ain't no one gonna help you," Riggs shouts from the chapel.

I roll my eyes and take her hand, leading her away from the chaos and toward the stairs.

"I wanted to make sure he got his invitation," Reina says, looking over her shoulder.

"Don't worry, Reina, we'll make sure we give it to him," Blackie says, closing the door to the chapel.

"Don't get any blood on the floor," she calls as I lift her into my arms. "I'm done cleaning up after you guys."

Reina got my blood flowing on a regular day but seeing her step up, owning the role as my ol' lady, well, that undid me. It made me feral, turned me into a fucking savage. Poor Sunshine, she was going to get a dose of Parrish like never before.

Chapter Twenty

VICTOR

I open my eyes. God has granted me another day. It didn't matter that when I woke I felt as though a cinder block was resting heavily on my chest. My lungs working overtime for each breath they push out. I was still alive.

Every night, before I lay my head on my cot, I count down the days until my transfer and before I close my eyes, I pray to my Heavenly Father to keep me alive until then. Last night it was thirteen days, today it will be twelve. Almost there.

It's not about the last hit and that's probably the only reason he's keeping me alive. Every day I wake is another day I get to reminisce about my family. I've got three visits left and today my phone privileges are reinstated. I'm entitled to one phone call per month, and it turns out that since it's the end of the month, I'll get this month's and one more before the transfer.

Today I don't have to stare at a picture and relive the last thirty years of memories. Today I get to hear my bride's voice. Grace used to speak with a tenderness to her tone, she used to look at me like I was her everything, her whole damn world. Now the tenderness is gone from her voice and when she looks at me she tries to hide the anger boiling inside of her. My sweet Gracie is full of resentment and the beautiful love we created is dying right along with me.

This isn't how we're supposed to end—a love like ours isn't supposed to turn ugly. I remember in the beginning I felt like I was on top of the world and it wasn't the rush of the mob or the greed of power, it was Grace's love that made me soar to the top. She made me feel invincible every time I looked into her eyes and knew I had the love of a good woman. We had old school love, the type that makes a man wonder how he ever got so lucky in his life. We had the type of love people write songs about, and I'm not talking about that crap you hear on the radio these days, I'm talking Frankie Valli, 'My Eyes Adored You' or Elvis' 'The Wonder of You'.

I've got twelve days left.

Twelve days to get my Gracie to fall back in love with me.

Twelve days to restore that lovin' feeling in her eyes and remind her why she fell in love with me in the first place.

Twelve days to give us the ending we deserve and if I get it right, maybe one day someone will write a love song about the beautiful love we lost and found one more time.

I close my hand over my mouth and cough, my throat raw from the endless coughing fits and my chest heavy from the attack on my lungs. Hunched over the sink, I turn the faucet on and dip my mouth under the stream of water, hoping to relieve the ache. I'm deteriorating much quicker than I expected. I guess I got cocky after surviving way passed the time the doctors initially gave me. After I refused treatment, they warned me it would happen just as it is. A snap of my fingers and everything would just go downhill, my body would shut down from the strain I was putting on it. Cancer was like a collision you knew was coming but couldn't slam on the breaks quick enough.

After five minutes of coughing and gasping for air, I try to straighten my shoulders and tap on the bars for the guard.

My voice is barely recognizable, considerably hoarse as I speak.

"I want my phone call," I struggle, gripping the bars to steady me. My gray hair falls over my eye and for the first time I don't bother to fix it. I peer at the correction officer and watch him shake his head.

"Come on, Vic," he mutters, fitting the key into my cell door and opening it. He offers me his hand but I brushed it away, squaring back my shoulders and hanging onto what is left of my pride as I stride down the cell block.

When I first arrived here, the inmates used to stand behind the bars and cheer me—I was a fucking legend in here. Now, they look at me with remorse, even they don't want the legend to die. It used to make me feel good, it used to be the thing that got me by, and then I realized it all means nothing. They're hanging on to the Vic they know from the headlines, the man who beat case after case. They don't want that man to die. They don't give a fuck that leaving my family behind is killing me more than the fucking cancer is.

They think I'm the man.

I'm no man without my woman.

The guard escorts me to the phones and I grab the first receiver I see, not bothering to stand in the line with the other inmates. Leaning against the wall, I dial our house number first. I wait for her to answer, sending up a silent prayer that she's home.

Please answer, Gracie.

"Hello?"

A faint smile appears at the sound of her voice but quickly disappears when I hear her sniffle.

"Gracie, love, it's me," I rasp.

"Oh, Victor," she whispers, clearing her throat before she speaks again. "Wait a minute I thought you couldn't call."

"They reinstated my phone privileges," I explain, pausing for a moment. "It's so good to hear your voice. How's my beautiful girl?"

She laughs through her tears. It's a laugh full of sarcasm rather than one of joy but still manages to warm me deep down, all the way to my bones.

"You wouldn't be calling me beautiful if you could see what I look like right now," she accuses.

"Nonsense," I admonish. "You've always been beautiful in my eyes." I swallow the lump in my throat and smile. "Always will be too," I whisper.

"Always the sweet talker," she says sadly.

True.

In the beginning I dazzled Grace with my fancy words and grand gestures until I learned she didn't need all that—having me was all she needed. Even after realizing that I still sweet-talked her and surprised her any chance I could get.

"What're you wearing?"

"Victor!"

Trying not to succumb to another coughing fit and ruin one of our final moments I try to keep my laugh at bay.

"Paint me a picture, Gracie," I plead. "Please?"

The sound of her soft breath sings against my ear as she remains silent.

"Where are you?" I coax.

"In our bedroom," she responds hesitantly.

Closing my eyes, I picture her sitting on the foot of our bed with the phone to her ear.

Go stand in front of the mirror, Grace," I instruct, keeping my eyes closed as I envision her slowly rise from the bed and pad across the worn carpet of our bedroom to the floor to ceiling mirror we keep perched against the wall in the corner.

"Are you looking at yourself?"

"Yes," she whispers.

"Tell me what you see. Start from your head and work your way down to your toes."

"My hair is up in a bun…"

"Let it down, Grace. Please."

"Okay," she murmurs, the phone shuffling around before her sweet voice fills my ears again. "It's down."

"Good girl," I whisper. "Do you have your glasses on?"

"No, today isn't the day for this, I'm not wearing any make-up and the dark circles beneath my eyes are on display. I've got more wrinkles than I care to admit and the lines that pinch the corners of my eyes seem to have doubled overnight."

Her hair was dark brown when I first met her but after she turned forty, she started dying it hoping to restore her youth, and now my Grace had blonde highlights. I picture her blondish hair flowing around her face, a perfect contrast to her olive skin freckled from the sun. Her brown eyes are no doubt tired and dull from the stress she's been under but I try my hardest to see the eyes of the young girl I fell in love with and not the woman I broke. The lines she describes match the ones I have on my face, they are the lines that tell the story of our life together. For all the thousands of smiles there are faint lines on each of our faces. For every hundred tears is another bunch and the rest are made up from the ups and downs of life, the seasons of change and the lessons we learn, both beautiful and trying at times.

"My lips are pale pink and there is a beauty mark on my lower lip that just won't go away," she continues.

I smile as I think of all the times I kissed that beauty mark and all the others she keeps hidden beneath her clothes. Like the one on the back of her upper thigh or the several that pepper the swell of her breasts.

"I'm wearing my favorite nightgown, the blue silk one you bought me three Christmases ago. Do you remember it?"

"How could I forget it?" It was October when I bought the silk nightgown and matching robe and for two months I pictured her wearing it. When I finally gave it to her on Christmas morning, I made her run upstairs and put it on. It wound up on the floor twenty minutes later.

"I've lost weight, so it's gotten big on me but I can't part with it," she admits, growing silent for a moment. "When I'm lonely or missing you I put it on and I feel close to you."

I lift my hand to my face and brush away the tear that betrays me and slides down my cheek.

"I miss you too, Grace," I whisper before clearing my throat. "Keep looking at yourself in the mirror and let me tell you what I see, okay?"

"Okay."

"I see my bride, my wife, the mother of my children and the woman I share grandchildren with all wrapped up in the beauty staring back at you. I remember when I first met you, I thought there wasn't a more beautiful woman in the whole world but you proved me wrong with every passing year becoming even more exquisite. When you look in the mirror, I want you to remember this conversation, remember my voice telling you how beautiful you are, and with every passing year remember you only become more beautiful. When you stare at the lines upon your face, embrace them, for they are the story of us etched into your skin."

Her sobs make me pause giving us both a chance to collect ourselves.

"Every year you age I want you to remember how beautiful you are," I persist, choking on my words as I bow my head and lean my forehead against the wall. "I won't be there to remind you but when you look in the mirror, I want you to recall this conversation and know wherever I am I'm whispering in your ear, telling you you're still the most beautiful woman in the world," I finish hoarsely.

"Victor, I can't do this. I'm not ready for goodbye," she whispers.

"This isn't goodbye," I insist. "This is me reminding you of the man you fell in love with, reminding you why you ever took this crazy journey with a man like me in the first place. This is me giving you the attention you deserve, Grace. I know I'm late but better late than never," I say as my throat tightens.

"I don't need a reminder as to why I took the journey, my heart reminds me with every beat it takes," she whispers.

"You got good at the sweet talk too," I joke, fighting the cough but failing. The next few moments are quiet on her end as she listens to my lungs fail me and the cancer rear its ugly head. I drop the receiver attempting to shield her from my fate. Once I finally have it under control, I lift the receiver back to my ear.

"Victor?"

I'm here," I rasp.

"I filed a request with Bureau of Prisons for permission to have you treated by a private doctor," she reveals.

"Grace—"

"I've stood by your side through everything, Victor, every single thing and most of the time I didn't even blink an eye. But now it's your turn to remember something. I need for you to remember the vows we took and how I promised before God to love you in sickness and in health. I'm sorry but I can't sit back idly this time."

I could argue with her but what's the point, they won't grant her the request, and by the time she gets her answer I'll probably have already passed. There was no crime in letting her hang onto hope while I restore what's left of us.

"Okay, Gracie," I pacify. "We'll play it your way, sweetheart."

"Wow," she whispers. "I didn't think I'd ever hear those words."

"First time for everything," I tease. "I am running out of time and the COs already tapped his watch ten times, but tell me, how are our girls?"

"I told them the truth," she admits. "They're heartbroken to say the least but they will come and visit this week."

"I'll fix it," I promise. "I'll make it okay for them to let me go," I assure her.

"That's not up to you," she argues. "They're entitled to feel however they want. You're their father for crying out loud. You can't fix death, you can't repair the hole it leaves in one's heart," she says heatedly. "I'm sorry I don't mean to yell."

"It's okay." I draw in a deep breath, rubbing my chest as I fill my black lungs with air.

"There's something...I have to...I have to tell you," she hesitates. "I wasn't going to say anything, but I never liked being kept in the dark and you have a right to know."

"Tell me," I urge.

"Nikki is having some medical issues. They took all kinds of tests and tomorrow she will get the results."

"What kind of medical issues?" I ask. My bravado disappearing as the question leaves my lips.

"She went to the gynecologist because she was having irregular bleeding and severe cramping so the doctor sent her for a full checkup."

"Well, what are they testing her for?"

"A bunch of things," she says vaguely.

"Gracie don't beat around the bush," I demand hoarsely.

"It could be anything, a cyst breaking down or maybe it's endometriosis but they want to rule out uterine or ovarian cancer as well."

Tears well in my eyes as I imagine my youngest daughter. Her smile always so big and bright just like the biggest star. A light that can never be dimmed, no matter how hard she was pushed.

Please, keep shining.

"I'm going to the doctor with her and Michael tomorrow when they get the results," she continues. "She's going to be fine," she assures me.

"Of course she is," I rasp, blinking away the tears. "You need to believe that too," I remind her knowing she was probably driving herself mad with worry. The urge to scream fills me as I realize I am forcing Grace to endure something alone. Again. I should be there holding her hand as she forgets about herself and becomes Nikki's strength.

"God wouldn't do that to me," she utters. "He wouldn't take you and our girl from me. He isn't that cruel."

"Listen to me, Gracie, she's going to be fine. God's just testing her. He's going to teach her a lesson by showing her how strong she truly is."

"Pastore, it's time," the guard calls.

"I've got to hang up now, Gracie," I say regretfully. "I love you, beautiful," I whisper.

"I love you too, Victor," she cries.

I couldn't bring myself to say goodbye and knew she couldn't either. I hang the receiver up gently before releasing an anguished scream and lifting the receiver into my hand again, slamming it down over and over before dropping it and turning around to the CO.

"Take me back to my cell," I ground out.

Once the cell closes, and I am alone in my cage, I close my eyes and there she is—my Gracie.

Only this time she wasn't alone. This time she was with Nikki.

Twelve days.

Three visits.

One more phone call.

Chapter Twenty-One

Nikki

There is nothing worse than waiting, and it seems like that's all I do lately. I waited for my test results, I'm waiting for the fucking nurse to call my name and then I'm sure I'll wait some more once they stick me in a room and tell me the doctor will be right with me.

I'm hanging onto my sanity by a thread. Between my health scare and learning my father's dying, I don't know what to do with myself. One minute I want to lock myself away and cry, the next, I want to scream and hit something. In the end my tears win and I cry for my father, for my mother, and for me and my sister.

Growing up a mobster's daughter was never easy, me and my sister lived life differently than our friends. We followed a different set of rules than them and were overcompensated for the things we couldn't do because our father was a dangerous man. Friends never slept over at our house because their parents wouldn't allow them to, too freaked out by the bullet proof windows and the bodyguards lurking around the front door.

Dating was no picnic either. The few guys brave enough to date us went through the ringer. Look at Anthony for instance, my father fucked him harder than anyone. Then there was the other type of guy that went after the mobster's daughter, the one who hoped one day to be part of the Pastore organization. Let's not forget the guys like Rico who used and abused me to get close to my father. That ended in bloodshed.

However, all of those things weren't as bad as waiting for the dreaded day the inevitable happened and we got the call that daddy's not coming home. I always thought my father would die just as Mikey's dad did, caught off guard, shot in the broad day light, his lifeless body lying in a pool of his own blood. If you ask Adrianna, she'd tell you our dad would go down guns blazing until he couldn't physically pull the trigger anymore.

If someone really wanted to kill daddy, they'd have to blow his trigger finger off.

Those were her exact words.

Surprisingly, we were both wrong and I don't know if I should be grateful for that. Is suffering from cancer better than dying from a gunshot wound? Which is the lesser of the two evils?

I was just accepting the fact he'd be in prison for the rest of his life, thinking he'd live to a ripe old age and I'd still be able to see him, still be able to speak to him on the phone and even write to him. Bottom line is he'd still be in my life one way or another.

Now I have to get used to the fact my dad is dying and by the time I do he will already be dead and I'll have to live with the fact I no longer have my father in my life.

It's a vicious cycle.

I think we all sometimes think about losing our parents; we wonder how we will feel, how our lives will go on and imagine how empty life will be, not just on holidays such as Mother's Day or Father's Day but the ordinary days, the days when you get a speeding ticket and you want to vent to your dad. For so long your parents are by your side, guiding you, cheering you on and making sense of the things you don't understand. Even as an adult they never cut the cord, they simply take a step back, never too far, always there for you as you face the things that scare the shit out of you.

There was a time in my life when I felt bitter, when I resented my dad for his lifestyle, a time when I blamed him for everything wrong in our family. My dad made a lot of mistakes in his life but he's still my daddy, my first hero, my first love, the first man who ever loved me unconditionally and the man who brought back the love of my life. He gave me my eternal love; he gave me Mikey.

I only hope that he knows how grateful I am.

I turn to Mikey and watch as he flips through a parenting magazine, shaking his head in amazement at the article he pretends to read. I lean close to him, placing my hand on his knee and wait for him to turn his gaze to me.

"Remind me to thank my dad when we go see him," I whisper.

"Thank him for what?" he questions, closing the magazine and taking my hand in his.

"Everything good in my life," I reply, glancing across the room at my mother sitting in her chair reading her prayer book.

I smile at her, she took that little green book everywhere. She's had it since I was a kid, starting every morning with a cup of coffee and a prayer to Saint Anthony. Some people pray to Saint Anthony when they lose something or when they really need something good to happen, my mom prays to Saint Anthony because her father's name was Anthony and praying to his patron saint makes her feel close to him. She prays for our health, for our happiness and for my father. She always prays for my father.

For his sins and for his redemption.

After all, he's her eternal love, and she's praying they end up in the same place.

"Your phone is ringing," Mikey whispers, brushing my hair over my shoulder, pulling me away from my thoughts. I grab my purse off the floor and sift through all the useless shit I stuff in there before pulling out my phone.

I don't recognize the number, but it's not the familiar numbers of creditors that are usually looking to get me. I accept the call.

"Hello?"

"Nikki, it's daddy."

My fingers tighten around the phone as tears cloud my vision. His voice is different; the baritone voice I remember is now hoarse and raspy—breathless.

"Nicole, are you there?"

"Yes," I cry. "I'm here Dad."

My mother lifts her head and her eyes peer into mine as I nod.

It's really him.

Watching me intently, Mikey closes his hand over my knee.

"How's my girl?"

It was a question I had heard him ask me countless times. A question I usually gave a half-assed answer to, but now it was a question that had tears uncontrollably rolling down my cheeks.

I'm not good.

I'm brokenhearted.

I'm scared of what the doctor's going to say.

I'm scared I'm sick.

I'm scared to visit you because I know it'll be the last time I see you.

I'm scared of losing you.

I'm scared of living without you.

I'm not good, Dad.

"I'm okay," I lie, swallowing the lump clogging my throat and all the things I truly want to say.

"Your nose is growing," he says, clearing his throat. "I spoke to your mom yesterday and she told me what's been going on."

Mikey stands and walks over to the nurse, returning with a box of tissues as he kneels before me and dries my eyes. As quickly as he wipes my tears they are replaced with new ones.

"I'm a little nervous," I admit.

"I know you are, sweetheart, but you're going to be fine," he says adamantly. "You know how I know that?"

"How?" I ask, glancing across the room at my mother who was staring up above with tears running down her face.

Saint Anthony answered her prayer.

He doesn't answer right away. I strain my ears to listen to the muffled sound of his cough and moments later his raspy voice returns.

"You've got a fire burning inside of you that nothing, and no one, will ever tame. You're the most resilient girl I've ever known and you don't know defeat, nothing will ever knock you down. You're a fighter and only you determine when you're done fighting. You're the one in charge of that clock, sweetheart, and no one is going to count down the seconds and call you out."

I bite my lip, listening as he draws in a deep breath. I close my eyes, envisioning him standing before me and speaking face to face instead of over the phone.

"Tell me something, Nikki, are you going to let anyone or anything call the shots in your life? Are you a fighter? Are you ready to back down?"

"No. I am a fighter and I don't back down for anyone or anything..." I wipe my eyes with the back of my hand. "Because my dad taught me to control my destiny. You taught me how to fight for what I want."

"And what do you want most?"

Right now more than anything I want to hug you.

"To live out my dreams," I whisper.

"Then what are you going to do?"

"Live out my dreams," I answer.

"That's my girl. Don't you forget that. No matter what, don't you forget that," he insists.

"I won't," I promise.

"I love you, Nicole," he whispers.

"I love you too, Dad," I sob. "I'll see you the day after next."

"I'm looking forward to it, sweetheart," he says. For the first time in a long time I hear my father's voice crack, and I know he is crying right along with me.

"Nicole Pastore?" the nurse calls.

Not ready to hang up, I feel my heart shatter even more as I lift my head and stare at the nurse.

"The doctor's ready to see me," I say regretfully.

"Remember who's in charge," he says.

"Me," I affirm.

"That's right."

I don't want to hang up," I admit.

"Go, I will see you in a few days," he soothes. "It's going to be okay, Nikki. I promise you it will be okay."

I nod as if he is standing before me, clutching the phone as though it's my salvation.

"I've got to go, sweetheart," he says. "Keep shining," he adds before ending the call.

You see what I mean? Your parents are never too far, always stepping in right when you need them. My dad called me to remind me of who I am, instilling all the values he taught me throughout the years. I'm a fighter and I always have the last word when it comes to the course of my life. Then, when I couldn't bring myself to hang up, he did, knowing I *needed* that too.

I'm going to miss that.

Mikey takes my hands as I pocket my phone and pulls me to my feet.

"We've got this, Princess," he assures me, pressing a kiss to my lips.

"Yeah we do," I agree, squeezing his hands before glancing at my mother. "Will you come in with us? We could always use the extra pair of ears in case we miss something or forget to ask an important question."

"Of course," she whispers.

Three of us physically walk into the doctor's office but four spirits were present. My father was with me, his words fresh in my mind as I sat down and listened as the doctor read me my results. I knew then that my dad will always be with me. Even after he passes, his voice will always float around in my head, reminding me of all the things I sometimes forget, reassuring me I am Victor Pastore's daughter and I am a fighter. Like my dad, I don't know the meaning of defeat.

Endometriosis.

I didn't have cancer.

And while I probably should've been devastated that my case was so severe and that the doctor suggested surgery, I was too relieved that I didn't have cancer to give my illness much thought.

My mom closes her eyes and silently thanks Saint Anthony, and I close my eyes and thank my dad.

Mikey squeezes my hand tightly as he breathes a sigh of relief.

Today I was going to bask in the glory that I was okay, just like my dad promised.

Tomorrow I'd worry about the possibility of not having a child.
I'll probably cry.
I'll probably wish things were different.
I'll ask myself *why me*.
What did I do to deserve this?
I'll worry about what it means for my relationship.
But then I'll remember my father's words, and I'll fight.
Because I determine the course of my life.
My dad taught me well.

Chapter Twenty-Two

MICHAEL

Nikki rarely woke up before me. Our mornings consist of her hitting the snooze on the alarm six times before I have to drag her cute little ass out of bed. So when I opened my eyes and stared at her empty side of the bed, I knew something was wrong.

I throw my legs over the edge of the bed and pull on my basketball shorts that were haphazardly hanging off the lampshade beside our bed and went in search of my princess. Her first stop is usually the kitchen. Nikki can't function without half a pot of coffee in her system, but I walked into an empty kitchen. She hadn't even turned the coffee pot on yet. I flipped the switch, rubbing the sleep from my eyes as I notice the back door slightly ajar.

I push the blinds aside, spot her lying on one of the lounge chairs smoking a cigarette and make my way onto the porch. She lifts her eyes to mine and quickly crushes her cigarette in the ashtray sitting between her legs. As I walk closer to her and take a seat on the foot of the lounge chair, I see the traces of tears that stain her flawless face.

I feel like a useless fool every time she cries, but the truth is I have no idea what to do with her tears. I don't know how to make them stop, hell, half the time I don't even know why she's crying. There is so much negativity circling her, pulling her in different directions and instead of making it better for her I wind up with whiplash. As soon as I think I know how to help her feel better, something else comes along and shakes everything up. Mine and Nikki's relationship is easy, we come and go as we please, answer to no one and live life according to our own standards. There is no drama, no constant flow of issues we have to deal with, it's been smooth sailing until now.

I lift her legs and stretch them across my lap before bending my head to place my lips against one of her knees.

"What's going on in that head of yours, Princess?" I question, running my hands along her calves as I stare into her sad eyes.

"Nothing," she insists, shaking her head before she forces a smile. "Everything's peachy."

"I might not be the brightest crayon in the box but I know when something isn't right with you, Nikki," I reply, holding her gaze. "Don't shut me out because once we start pretending what affects one of us doesn't affect the other, that's when this thing we're building falls apart," I pause, reaching out to run my finger along the bridge of her nose. "We're better than that," I insist.

She covers her face with her hands and remains perfectly still for a moment before threading her fingers through her hair and gripping the ends in frustration. I narrow my eyes in confusion as she lifts her head and stares back at me.

"What do you want, Mikey?" she asks softly.

"What do you mean?" I question, trying to figure out how this became about me.

"Do you want kids?" she huffs. "We're getting married, but we never discussed what happens after we say I do. Did you plan on having children? Did you want to travel the world? What do you want to do for the next sixty years?"

She's right, we didn't discuss the future much, but I didn't think there was anything wrong with that. When two people are compatible like we are, who needs plans? They always change anyway. You can plan your whole life, every last detail, up to the prayer card given to the people who attend your wake, but it only takes one gust of wind to blow your plan to shit.

Nikki and I don't need plans, we only need each other. For the first time in my life I'm sure of something and I'm sure I want to marry her. I want to spend the next sixty years riding the tides with her and wherever we wind up is exactly where we're meant to be.

"I'll start," she offers. "I never pictured myself with a fleet of kids."

"A fleet as in more than one?"

She smiles but her eyes still hold traces of doubt.

"Do you want a baby, Mikey?"

I think about the question, cupping the back of my neck as I try to picture me and Nikki with a little squirt of our own. One baby I could probably handle but when you use words like fleet, well, shit, I start to twitch. But if you have one then I think you have to have another, being an only child gets lonely. I didn't realize it when I was younger but after my father was murdered, I kept thinking if my mom wasn't here, his death would be my responsibility. I'd be the one to identify his body, plan his funeral and decide what was on the back of his prayer card.

Everything I had to do alone when my mom died.

So, if kids were in the cards for me and Nikki there would have to be two of them. But if they weren't, if she didn't want to have children, then I'd be fine with that too. As long as I've got her I'll be happy being a part of whatever she desires because she's ALL I want. Everything else that comes along with her will be the icing on the cake.

I guess I have my answer.

"I love Luca and Victoria and when I'm around them, my heart melts but when I'm around other children, I don't feel any sort of way. I don't get the warm, fuzzy feelings everyone with baby fever seems to talk about," she rambles, releasing a breath and blowing the hair out of her face.

"Baby fever?" I ask, tucking the strands behind her ear.

She chews on her bottom lip before blurting out her next thought.

"My biological clock doesn't tick I'm not even sure it has batteries. The only thing I'm sure I want is you, everything else I'm uncertain of. I'm twenty-three years old, I'm not supposed to have life figured out," she huffs exasperatedly.

"So what are you worried about? We'll figure it out together as it comes."

"Mikey, you were there, you heard the doctor when he explained how severe my case was. He specifically warned us that not only would I probably have to have the surgery more than once but having a child would be extremely difficult."

He didn't say impossible.

"I may not have put much thought into having children but before yesterday I had the choice and now it's been taken from me," she whispers, taking my hands into hers and squeezing them. "But that doesn't mean it has to be taken from you."

She's lost her mind.

The stress of waiting for the test results, her father dying, throw in her bat-shit crazy relatives visiting, it's made her lose her ever-loving mind. I pull my hands out of hers and grip her hips tugging her onto my lap before reaching up and cupping her face. Her eyes widen, and I loosen my hold on her cheeks but continue to keep my eyes on her.

"We're only ever going to have this conversation once so listen real good, Nikki," I order. "I asked you to marry me, put a ring on your finger for the whole world to know you're mine. I didn't do that without seriously thinking it through. It's not that I wasn't sure you were the only girl I'd ever marry, but I wanted to be sure I could be everything you needed in a husband.

Before you, I never thought about settling down, I didn't want to be tied to another person. I told myself I was content living alone, but in reality I didn't want to let myself get close to anyone because every person I've ever loved has been taken from me. After my mother died I never planned on sticking around here but I couldn't walk away from you. We were nothing, barely reacquainted with one another when your smart mouth dared me to stay here, I knew I couldn't go back to Pennsylvania. It was the best decision of my life and I thank my mother every day for sending me you."

"Mikey—" she starts, but I silence her, placing my finger to her lips.

"Not done saying my peace, Princess," I say, calmly. "I know life without you, I know the man I am without you by my side and that guy doesn't hold a candle to the man you make me. I stayed in New York for you, hoping you'd give me a shot to be the guy you spend the rest of your life with. You…you're my why, always and forever baby—" My words are cut off by her mouth as it crashes over mine. Wrapping her arms around my neck, she pulls me closer to her, sliding her tongue between my lips.

I gave in as I always did because giving in meant I won too.

Winning is being her guy.

Winning is having her in my life.

Winning is finding the one person I'm meant to travel through this crazy thing called life with.

Winning is Nikki becoming my wife.

Winning is us.

And if it's just us in the end, well, that's winning too.

Breaking the kiss, I watch as her eyelids flutter open and look into those brown eyes I'm going to stare into for the rest of my life. Those eyes look back at me.

"Ask me again what I want," I demand huskily.

"What do you want, Mikey?"

"If you decide you want to have a baby then we'll do whatever we have to do to get you pregnant," I waggle my eyebrows suggestively, teasing her with the possibilities. "If you decide you want to get a dog instead, I'm cool with Beethoven. You want twelve cats, a parrot and goldfish, I'll turn this house into a zoo. If you want all that and then decide you want the kid, then we'll move the zoo into the yard and baby proof the house. Whatever you want, I'm game, as long as I get to be your guy. That's all I want."

"Twelve cats?" she queries with a smile.

"I'd get you a goddamn lion if it made you smile."

"You love me," she declares.

"More than anything," I agree.

"I love you too, Mikey," she whispers, leaning her forehead against mine. "And every day I thank your mom for sending you to me too."

Cradling her in my arms, I turn her around. Lifting her, she wraps her arms around my neck as I stand and carry her toward the house. I press my lips gently to hers.

Winning.

Thanks Mom.

Chapter Twenty-Three

ANTHONY

One of the shittiest jobs that came with the title of Victor's enforcer was sitting on a mark. Sitting in a car, sometimes with a pair of binoculars, waiting for someone to make a move was boring as fuck. Most times, when the order came down the pipe I cursed Vic to the high heavens. I wanted a piece of the action and following a schmuck around the streets of Brooklyn wasn't my idea of action.

I'd follow whatever asshole played Victor dirty like a shadow, learn his routine—down to the time he took his final shit of the day. In the early days I'd report my findings to Vic and he'd dismiss me of my duty, sending in the big guns to take care of whatever beef he had. As the years went on, Victor loosened his hold on the leash he had on me and after I gave him my intel he would send me back to take out the garbage.

It's been a long fucking time since I sat in my car with a lukewarm cup of coffee, staring at a dark building waiting for signs of life. The last time I was in this position was when Vic gave me the order to check up on Maryann Valente and Mike. The night I followed him after he got the call she was in the hospital and we found out she had passed.

I thought my days of doing this shit were done but I'm the asshole who took it upon myself to sit here. There was no order, no mobster demanding I sit here with my thumb up my ass. No, this shit was all my fucking idea.

The people in my life are hurtin' and I don't know how to make it better for them. There is no one to blame, no kneecaps to break, no fucking cocksucker to whack. In the Pastore crime family we're all about an eye for eye. The need to place blame heavy in our black hearts.

I can't take Vic's cancer away, can't add more time to his existence and I can't break the son of a bitch out of jail so his final days are with the people who love him, the same people I love.

But sitting around and waiting for him to die isn't an option either. I can't sit back and watch my wife cry trying to prepare herself for her final visit with her father. I woke up this morning and found her sitting at the kitchen table feeding the kids and writing a list of things she wants to say to her dad. She's worried she'll forget something and knows there is no second chance, not in death.

Victor and I have had our ups and downs, our fair share of bad blood and resentment, but the truth of the matter is I'll always be thankful for the gift he gave me when he gave me his blessing to finally make a life for myself and his daughter.

The Pastores are just as much a part of my family as my mother and sister. I hold Nikki in the same regard as I hold Lauren. Then there is Grace, they don't make them like her anymore. That woman doesn't have a bad bone in her body, been through hell and back and still she smiles.

Her smile is fading, and it's a fucking shame to watch.

I'm sure people will talk, they'll call me an asshole, say I can't let go of the life. But this is my life, this is all I know and when I'm at the end of my rope, running out of options it will always be this life that leads the way.

My connections in the mob may have diminished and my pride keeps me from reaching out to Rocco, but when there's a will, there is a motherfucking way. Luckily my sister fell in love with a fucking genius. Riggs is a goddamn asset. I wish we had his expertise back in the day, maybe he could've gotten my ass released from jail sooner. One click of the mouse and he erases life and creates new. It's fucking sick, especially for me, I barely know how to operate an iPhone.

Anyway, with a couple of strokes of the keys Riggs can get the information it would take me weeks to get if I did it the old fashioned way—following someone, collecting their secrets and using it against them. Maybe I snatch the person on the way to work, or there is always a good old fashioned beat down, either way they're gums get loose and they spill.

"I'm fucking starving, where is this douche?" Riggs complains, digging into the console of my truck and pulling out a bag of Reese's Pieces. "Jackpot," he cheers, tearing open the corner of the package and pouring the candy into his mouth.

I keep my eyes trained on the headlights approaching the barbed wire fence as Riggs grabs his phone and pulls up the license plate we're waiting on.

"Showtime Bianci," he confirms as the black sedan crosses the gates and turns onto the gravel road.

Shifting the car into drive, I wait a beat before peeling out of the spot and following the Buick.

Riggs lifts his ass, pulling out a clip from his back pocket and loads his gun before nonchalantly going back to chowing down obnoxiously on the candy. I hadn't asked him to tag along on my mission, all I asked was for him to get me the information I needed, but his stubborn ass insisted he come along.

It's been a while since you pulled a trigger, bro, your finger might be rusty.

He had no fucking idea.

Not a clue.

I could hit my mark with my eyes closed, but I wasn't planning on filling anyone with lead tonight.

"Tell me again his routine," I order, keeping one hand on the steering wheel as I lift the ice cold cup of coffee to my lips. Shit was putrid.

"You don't give a fuck about his routine, you want the dirt on him, you're going to use that shit against this slob and if he doesn't agree to the terms then we'll blow his dirty little secret wide open. Fuck that, we'll grab both the wife and the whore, introduce them to one another before making the dickhead choose which one gets to live," he growls.

"What the fuck is wrong with you?" I ask, raising an eyebrow.

"Ah, pent up aggression," he says with a shrug of the shoulders.

"I don't want to hear some shit about my sister not giving you…"

"Are you kidding me? Kitten would never survive without my cock, she's the real tiger in the bedroom," he says smugly.

Maybe I would pump someone full of lead tonight.

The fucking Tiger himself.

Then he'd know for sure there ain't nothing rusty with me.

"Shit, I forget you're her brother sometimes," he grins. "You should see your face man, P-R-I-C-E-L-E-S-S."

"Try harder to remember," I say through clenched teeth.

"It's my folks that have me all out of whack, itching to shoot someone. I thought beating the fuck out of that weasel, Sommers, would satisfy me, but nope I may have an anger problem."

"Clearly," I mutter, turning right behind the sedan I was following. "What's got you riled up?"

"Lauren didn't tell you about my folks?" he crumbles up the empty bag of Reese's and flings it out the window. "I suppose that's a good thing," he contemplates. "Maybe she forgot."

"Talk."

"My parents showed up on our doorstep, insulted your sister and ripped into me for my life choices," he sneers.

"I thought you had nothing to do with your parents," I say.

"I didn't. They dropped from the fucking sky like a bunch of vultures."

"Well what do they want?"

"I didn't ask. I kicked their asses to the curb when they gawked at me and my family. Fuck that shit, fuck them, fuck their millions, fuck it all."

"Yeah, you might want to look into that anger problem," I advise.

"Oh, give it up man. If your pops showed up on your door step what would you do?"

"We're not talking about me," I evade.

"Yeah, you'd fucking whack that prick," he surmises.

Probably.

"My father left my mother high and dry, turned his back on his kids and never gave us a second thought. You turned your back on your family and they show up on your doorstep anyway," I counter. "Don't know your folks but that shit has to count for something."

"It counts for nothing. They heard they got a grandkid and are looking for him to rule their oil empire."

"Not a bad gig," I argue. "It could be worse. Eric could wind up sitting in a truck with Luca both of them locked and loaded looking to wreak havoc on the warden of a federal prison."

"Shit, imagine that," he laughs.

"Let's not, let's hope those two boys are more like their mamas than us," I say. "Call your old man, Riggs. Look at what we're doing, think about why we're tailing this fuck home. Life's too short for regrets, man."

"You left the mob and became a philosopher. I can't wait to see the A&E documentary they do on your ass," he quips, tipping his chin to the car in front of us as it rolls to a stop at a red light. "Let's get this motherfucker," he adds, reaching for the door handle.

I nod watching as he pulls a ski mask over his face and jumps out of the car. Riggs runs around the front of my truck and right up to the driver of the sedan, pulling the door open as he cocks his gun straight at the warden of Otisville. He pushes him into the passenger seat and climbs into the front seat, speeding through the red light with me right behind him.

My phone rings inside my pocket and I drive with one hand to retrieve it.

"Mike, now's really not a good time," I growl, trying to keep up with Riggs as he swerves in and out of traffic with his gun aimed at the warden. "Jesus," I hiss. I got saddled with two pains in the ass brothers-in-law.

"Forget the dance," he says quickly. "Get me a priest."

I told Mike about my plan this morning and asked him if there was anything I should add to my list of demands. He only had one request; that his girl gets to dance with her dad one last time.

"Priest," I mutter as Riggs pulls the sedan down a deserted ally. "Got it. Need to hang up now, Mike," I rushed, ending the call and grabbing my piece from the glove box. I pull the safety back and get out of the truck. I leave the engine running so we can make a clean break.

For a split second I wonder why Mike gave a fuck if Vic was read his last rights, but as quickly as the thought crossed my mind it disappears. Riggs pulls the warden out of the car, dragging him by his feet onto the asphalt.

"Do you have any idea how much fucking trouble you're going to be in?" the warden spits at Riggs.

"Do you have any idea how much trouble *you're* going to be in when I grab the piece of ass you've been hiding and bring her straight to your unsuspecting wife?" Riggs fires back. "Now shut the fuck up before I put a bullet in your ass."

"What do you want? I'll give you whatever cash I have. Take my watch, it's a presidential Rolex," the warden cries.

Riggs lifts the warden's wrist and inspects the expensive arm candy he was sporting.

"Pretty nice watch for a man on the state's payroll," Riggs comments, dropping his hand before slamming his boot against the man's chest, keeping his gun aimed at the warden. "I bet I know how you can afford that sweet watch and how you pay the mortgage on the fancy house you keep your wife in or the dope apartment you stash your whore in on the Upper East Side."

I step into the warden's view, kneeling beside him so he can get a better look at my face, my blue eyes pierce him like daggers.

"Warden, you remember me don't you?"

His eyes flicker before narrowing as he swallows hard.

"Bianci, inmate number two-six-eight-three-five-nine," he recites.

The motherfucker had the memory of an elephant, reciting my inmate number without error. That's right, me and warden Valez go way back. Back to the days when I was incarcerated.

Back in the day, Vic couldn't afford to send someone inside with me, with Val murdered and his organization vulnerable he needed all his manpower on the streets alongside him. He may have thrown my ass in jail without regard for the life I was leaving behind but he kept me alive. He greased Valez's palm to ensure my safety while I was locked up, a fact I didn't discover until recently. I was untouchable while I was in jail and no rival organization stood a shot of getting close to me.

If he really wanted me out of his daughter's life all he had to do was squash his deal with Valez and the G-Man's men could've taken me down. Yet here I am, free and married to his daughter.

Vic did that for me.

Now this one was for him.

"That's right," I said. "Now, I want you to listen carefully. My man over here he's got a slippery finger and some daddy issues he's looking to unleash."

"What the fuck man?" Riggs says, smacking me upside the head with the heel of his gun.

"See? He's a loose fucking canon. It'd be a shame if he shot you before you had a chance to do as I say."

"Look, I've done my best for Pastore while he's been in my prison."

"I know and the family appreciates all you've done this far but we have a few more requests we need you to make happen."

"I can't do shit about his transfer, the Bureau of Prisons controls where he goes and because he's ill, they are carting him to a medical facility."

I knew all about that. What Valez didn't know was we took care of that too. The Bureau had changed the location of Vic's transfer, dragging his ass further away from New York and not to the prison that the G-Man was in. Good ol' Riggs came through again, tampering with G-Man's medical records and diagnosing the motherfucker with testicular cancer, placing him in the same prison as the Vic.

"It's not about the transfer," I explain. "Vic will be in Otisville until the end of the week and we intend to get our money's worth out of you."

"Do as he says motherfucker. I've got a man sitting on your whore's doorstep and another one hiding in the bushes of your home, spying on your wife as she showers," Riggs threatens.

"What do you want?" Valez growls.

"For starters, you're going to reinstate Vic's phone privileges. He'll be allowed to call his wife as much as he wants until he gets on that bus," I begin.

"Fine," he hisses.

"I'm not finished," I sneer as Riggs bends down, inching the tip of his gun against Valez's mouth.

"No more interruptions, asshole," Riggs reprimands.

"As I was saying, his daughters will visit him, the last time they see their father won't be in a crowded visitor's room with every Tom, Dick and Harry doing time watching them say goodbye. You'll provide a private room for their final visits. You can keep a CO in the room with them but they'll be allowed to touch their father, hold his goddamn hand if they want to. Same goes for his wife, when Mrs. Pastore comes up to say goodbye to her husband she'll get the same respect," I instruct.

"Anything else?"

"A priest."

"He'll be given his final rights when he's transferred," Valez says.

"Get the man a priest or so help me God…," Riggs grunts.

"We want the priest present when the daughters come to visit," I say, not really sure where the fuck I was going with this since it was Mike's idea. I can't imagine any kind of good coming from the girls being there when Vic is read his last rights.

"Fine," he agrees.

Reaching into Valez's jacket, I pat him down, searching for his phone. I pull it out of his jacket pocket and hand it to him.

"Call the prison, Valez," I order, pausing for a moment. "Now." He stares at the phone in my hand momentarily.

"Well, he didn't fucking stutter," Riggs growls. I watch intently as Valez reaches for the phone.

'Thatta boy.

I've still got it.

Chapter Twenty-Four

Nikki

Adrianna and Anthony went through the metal detectors first. My sister was a pro, all the visits she paid Anthony had taught her well, she didn't even flinch when the female correction officer patted her down. This morning she called me and reminded me to wear a sports bra, anything with an underwire would set the detectors off and I'd either be forced to remove my bra or denied my final visit with my dad.

Still, even with the helpful tips from my sister and the few visits I had under my belt I felt like a fish out of water. I was ashamed to say I wouldn't miss this and only because no more visits meant not seeing my dad anymore.

I lift my hands, spread them wide to match the way my legs are parted and stare at my sister as the officer pats me down, checking for any weapons or contraband. I roll my eyes, chewing on my bottom lip as the bitch pats down my ass.

"These people don't know Daddy, huh?" I question my sister, averting my eyes to the guard with lingering hands. *Bitch, I don't roll that way.* "Newsflash, Officer Feel Me Up, if I was going to sneak anything to my dad it would be a Soppressata and you wouldn't be able to find it unless you had an x-ray machine handy," I sneer, dropping my hands before I smugly walk through the metal detector.

"Be sure to tell your dad that," Anthony says, tugging my ponytail. "He'll get a kick out of that," he teases, winking his crystal blue eyes.

I grab my sister's hand as Mikey makes his way through the metal detector, snatching his father's watch they made him remove from the basket and fastening it back on his wrist.

Adrianna squeezes my hand reassuringly as we are ushered through a series of fire safe doors, handed off to one guard after another before a big burly man dressed in a suit that was clearly three sizes too small in the waist, greets us at the end of long narrow hallway.

"Where the fuck are they taking us?" I whisper to my sister as I stare at the man who is locking eyes with Anthony.

"Bianci," he mutters.

"Warden," Anthony replies, holding his gaze. The two men stare off for what seems like forever before the warden glances over his shoulder at the metal door. He turns around, rapping his knuckles three times against the small pane of glass. Another correction officer opens the door and steps to the side allowing us room to walk inside.

My stomach rolls as Mikey presses his hand against the small of my back and together we follow Anthony and Adrianna inside the private room. I breathe a sigh of relief when I glance around the empty room, not ready for the moment I'll see my dad. There's a table centered in the room and six chairs, two on one side of the table and four on the other. I don't question the other chair, figuring it was for a guard or something.

"Why didn't they bring us to the visitor's room?" Adrianna asks, turning around to face Anthony with worried eyes. "Did something happen?"

"Relax, Reese's," Anthony soothes, placing his hands on her shoulders as he bends his knees, making himself eye level with her. "It's all good, baby."

The door opens as I spin around to face Mikey and my eyes glance over his shoulder to the guard stepping out of the way for my father. I watch with trepidation as my father strides through the door. His head is down, shielding his face from my view but I notice his hair is grayer than the last time, even thinner but still immaculate, not a strand out of place.

"Enjoy your visit, Pastore," the guard says before closing the door behind him.

Slowly, like a scene in a movie, my dad lifts his head and whatever response he was about to give the guard becomes lost on his tongue as his eyes find mine and my sister's.

"Well, I'll be damned," he whispers hoarsely.

Tears blur my vision as I smile widely and run to him, wrapping my arms tightly around him. He's thin and another man may have been knocked down by the gusto behind my embrace but not my dad. Standing his ground, he wraps his brittle arms around me and hugs me back with everything he has left inside his worn body.

"My, girl," he whispers against my hair. His voice is different, gone was the deep lethal voice that only warmed around his family and all that cancer has left behind is a raspy voice full of strangled breaths.

I was being selfish, holding on for dear life not willing to give my sister a chance at embracing our father but I couldn't bring myself to unlock my arms from around him. He smelt like Old Spice cologne, the generic crap they let inmates buy with their commissary not the Yves St. Laurent he usually wore.

His aging face comes into my view as he slowly pulls back. His complexion is awful, his olive skin was now gray and the whiskers he had along his jaw blended into his skin. Aside from the dark circles shadowing them, his eyes are the only feature that still resembles traces of him. Eyes that are full of pride, love and smile at me just as his mouth does.

"You're beautiful," he rasps, taking my hand in both of his and bringing it to his pale lips. "How'd the doctor's visit go?"

"I'll be okay," I choke out.

"I want all the details," he demands in between breaths, releasing my hands and looking across the room at my sister. Reluctantly, I step out of the way and grant my sister her time with our dad.

I wasn't sure what to expect from Adrianna, she always had a bumpy relationship with our dad. I knew she loved him as much as I did but this wasn't only goodbye for her, this was the last chance she had at forgiving our father for all the mistakes he made.

"There's my other beauty," Dad says, shuffling his feet closer to Adrianna.

She didn't try to meet him half way instead, she bowed her head and her body writhed with sobs. Anthony wrapped an arm around her waist and bent his head to whisper something only she could hear.

Dad's pace quickened as he continued toward Adrianna. Her husband continued to whisper words into her ear and she nodded in understanding. She lifted her head just as our dad reached her and Anthony took a step back, giving him room to take his daughter into his arms and comfort her just as he used to when we were kids.

"Dry your eyes," he whispers, swaying slightly with his arms tightly wound around her tiny frame. "You've cried enough over me," he adds.

Big fat tears ran down my father's cheeks causing my heart to break a little more with each one released.

Adrianna pulls back, taking his face into her hands and smiles, giving him the brightest smile, she had. When we were kids, she used to look up at him as she is now, like he was her favorite person in the entire world. Like he was her hero.

He smiled sadly as she stared at him, memorizing every feature of his face.

"I love you," she whispers. "I'm sorry if I sometimes didn't show it, so sorry I ever made you doubt it."

He shakes his head, wiping away the tears cascading down her cheeks with his thumbs as he cocks his head to the side.

"I've made a lot of mistakes in my life but my biggest regret will always be failing you," he confesses.

"You didn't fail me, Daddy," she cries. "I know that now," she whispers.

"I couldn't let you go," he explains. "I didn't know how to, I couldn't accept you weren't my little girl anymore."

He tucks her hair behind her ear and grants her a bittersweet smile.

"But that isn't so now, is it? You'll always be my little girl, won't you?"

"Always," she assures.

He pulls back and glances over his shoulder toward me, extending his hand and willing me with his gaze to join them. I close the distance between us as Adrianna drops her hands from his face and my dad grabs a hold of my hand and pulls me into the crook of his arm. With both me and my sister stuck to him like glue, he showered the top of our heads with kisses before choking out the words I'll always remember.

"You're both Daddy's little girls and always will be even in eternity," he utters. His thin arms squeezing us tightly against his sides. "I love you both with my whole heart and all I ask is that you never forget that."

Anthony and Mikey move to the back of the room as Dad guides us to the table, pulling out our chairs and tucking our legs beneath the table before he walks around and takes a seat on the opposite end. He reaches across and takes one hand from each of us and holds onto our hands for dear life.

He insists we have all done enough crying and wants us to make the most of our time together. He starts with me, giving me his undivided attention as he sets his intent gaze on me and makes me recall every detail of my doctor's visit. I tell him about my diagnosis and my plan of action. I explain the surgery to him and tell him I will most likely have difficulty having children.

I see the unmistakable forlorn look in his eyes and I smile back at him.

"I'm okay, Dad. Mikey and I discussed it and we're not even sure we want kids but if we decide we do, well, he'd move Heaven and Earth to give me whatever I want. I'm going to have a great life." I promise him, my voice cracking as I say the words.

"That you are," he agrees, leaning back in his chair as he glances over our shoulders at the two men who claimed our hearts. "I don't think I could've picked two better men for the two of you," he says thoughtfully, returning his warm eyes back to us. "I remember your First Holy Communion," he recalls, speaking to my sister. "Val and I joked that you and Michael would one day end up married," he laughs, turning his gaze to me. "Yet you're the one who will become a Valente."

"Pastore-Valente," I correct.

"That makes me proud and I'm sure wherever Val and Maryann are they're smiling down too," he says with a wink.

He turns back to Adrianna.

"Anymore grandbabies in the future?"

"Probably one more," she says. "If it's a girl her name will be Frankie and if it's a boy Anthony Jr.," she informs him so grandpa knows the names of any future Bianci children.

"Paint me a picture, girls," he requests. It was one of his favorite sayings, a staple in our childhood memories. He closes his eyes, as he did so many times throughout the years, and asks us to show him the future, one he won't be a part of.

We tell him our dreams, our hopes for what may come. We vow to always take care of our mom and keep the traditions they instilled in us alive. There was no shortage of tears and the love between a father and his daughters was very much alive and always would be.

With life comes death. Sometimes you don't see it coming, sometimes you have time to prepare for it but either way it leaves you raw and wondering how your life will go on without those who made your life have meaning. It will be hard, they'll be days I'll cry, days I'll sit at the cemetery and talk to a stone, days I'll look up to the heavens and wish for a sign. But, life will go on for me and my sister and sometimes we'll feel guilty or wish he was here. The world will still turn with our father's love forever alive in our hearts.

"Use the Long Island house," Dad says in-between coughing and struggling for breath. "Create memories just like we used to when you were kids."

"We will, Dad," Adrianna promises. Reaching into her pocket she pulls out several folded pieces of paper. She unfolds them, splays them on the table and mentally checks off the things listed on the pages. The last page remains folded, and she places her hand over it, pushing it toward dad.

"You wrote me a letter on my wedding day," she says, pausing as Dad covers her hand with his. "I can't say goodbye to you," she lifts her eyes to his. "I can tell you I forgive you. I can tell you I love you and I always will. I can promise you I will live a good life and teach my children all the valuable lessons you've taught us. I can give you all those things and my solemn word you may leave this world but you'll never ever leave my heart...I can't say goodbye."

She turns his palm over and places the letter against it before closing his hand and bending her head to kiss it.

"All the words I can't bring myself to say are in that letter," she whispers, dropping his hand to stand and walk around the table. She bends down and wraps her arms around him. "I love you, Dad," she cries.

Anthony and Michael walked over to the table, Mikey stands behind me, his hands bracing on the back of my chair as he keeps looking toward the door.

Adrianna and my dad embrace for several minutes before she pulls back and Anthony extends his hand to my dad. Dad slides his hand into Anthony's and stands up, shaking his hand and bringing him into his arms.

"I'm sorry," my father says. "You're a good man and I'm proud to call you my son-in-law."

"I'll always take care of your daughter, Vic," Anthony declares. "I'll give her all the love a man can give a woman."

"I know you will, been watching you do it since you first laid eyes on her."

My vision blurs as the clock ticks down and time closes in on us. The door opens and the guard steps inside holding the door open for my mother. She freezes in her tracks as she takes in the scene before her.

"Gracie," my father rasps.

A priest steps into the room and lays a hand on my mother's shoulder, startling her and forcing her to enter the room. The guard closes the door and leaves us all alone with the priest as Mikey walks around the chair, bends his knees and brings his eyes to mine. He takes my hands in his and I stare at him blankly.

"Nikki," he says, clearing his throat before he squeezes my hands in his and smiles. "Marry me," he whispers.

"What?" I ask confused. We already had done this. I glance at the ring on my finger, yep, see, we're engaged.

"Marry me right now, right here, in front of your dad."

I feel my throat close and tears flood my eyes as I glance around the room and then back at the man I love on his knees. I had to be dreaming, this wasn't happening right now. I mean it couldn't be.

"We don't have a marriage certificate," I blurt.

"We'll get one," he promises. "You can still do the whole dress thing and we'll have a big party for your crazy aunt and grandmother, we'll do it all. But we can do it now too, in front of God, with the man you want to give you away."

Tears spill from my eyes as I glance at the priest.

"Can we?"

"I can marry you in the eyes of God," he affirms.

I looked over at my dad, my mother has now moved to his side, her arm tightly wound around his, leaning her head against his shoulder as they stare back at me.

"Will you give me away, Daddy?"

He nods as he cries.

"It would be my honor," he replies huskily.

I smiled before averting my eyes to Mikey.

"Let's get married," I say, leaning my forehead to his.

The next few minutes feel like a whirlwind as the priest takes his position in the center of the room; Mikey stands to his left and Anthony right beside him. Across from them my sister stands. All eyes were on me as I looped one arm through my father's and the other through my mother's as I take six steps toward my groom.

My mother reaches up and kisses my cheek, whispering in my ear how much she loves me before taking two steps back and allowing me this unforgettable moment with my father. He unravels my arm from his and cups my face with his hands. Cocking his head to the side, he stares at me silently for several moments.

"Remember I love you," he whispers before placing a kiss to my forehead. He drops his hands from my face and takes my hand in both of his as he turns to Mikey.

Then the one thing I gave up on ever hearing was said.

"Who gives this woman's hand in marriage?"

"I do," my father croaks, taking Mike's hand and placing my hand inside of it.

"Thanks, Vic," Mikey replies, dropping a kiss to my hand before releasing it and shaking my father's hand. "Thanks for giving me my life back."

It may not have been the wedding little girls dream of, but it was perfect. I became Mrs. Michael Valente Jr. in Otisville prison, in the eyes of God and in front of the people I loved most in the world.

And my dad gave my hand to the man he trusted to take care of me for the rest of my life.

He got his peace of mind.

And I got my dream come true.

That was our final goodbye.

A day I'll remember for all of eternity.

Chapter Twenty-Five

Nikki

I was emotionally exhausted, leaving a piece of my heart behind the barbed wire fence of Otisville Penitentiary when I kissed my father's cheek one final time and headed out of the prison with my new husband.

I never saw that one coming.

On the car ride home, Mikey explained how he had Anthony pull a few strings to make sure a priest was present at our visit. I didn't ask questions, too grateful to care the lengths my brother-in-law went to help Mikey out.

I was Mrs. Michael Valente.

So what if it wasn't legal, Mikey and I were husband and wife. It was etched in our hearts and with God as our witness and my father's blessing. It didn't get any more official than that for me.

Mikey pulled our car into the driveway and I stared out the window at our house. Maybe we'd raise a family, maybe we'd get a dog, who knows? But I knew for sure, that contained within the walls of our home would be tons of love.

"You ready to go home, Mrs. Valente?" Mike asks, smiling as he turns off the car and stares at me.

I avert my eyes away from the house he grew up in, the house he worked so hard to make ours since we first moved in. I wasn't there for him when his mom passed, I tried to be there for him when his dad was murdered but we were young. I hope we never know loss for the next fifty years but if we should I will be there for him just the way he has been there for me. I will be the pillar he holds onto when the storm rages on and when it finally passes when the clouds part and the sun breaks through, I will be the reason he smiles.

I don't know what I did to deserve him, I'll never understand it but I'll always thank those who gave us life and left us behind, sure they had a hand in the magic that was me and Mikey.

I grinned widely at him, tired of crying and wanting so desperately to give him back the pieces of me I lost through the storm that's been raging around me.

"Mrs. Valente," I squeal, grabbing his hand over the console. "You're my husband! How fucking crazy is that?"

He chuckles, running his free hand through his hair as he leans against the seat and smiles lazily at me.

You're stuck with me now, Princess," he says, his eyes searing me as he draws out a heavy sigh and waves his hand down the length of him. "All this is yours."

My teeth pierce my lower lip as I try to hide my mischievous grin and let my eyes travel the length of him.

"Never forget who you belong to, Mikey," I joke as he lifts my left hand to his lips and brushes them softly across my knuckles. The pad of his thumb twirls my engagement ring around my finger as he averts his eyes back to mine.

"We need to get wedding bands," he declares. "And a marriage certificate."

"Yes, but for no other reason than I will need it to change my name legally," I agree, pausing for a moment. "I'm your wife, Mikey," I say, taking our joined hands and resting them over my chest. "We're married in here, where it counts most."

"That means tonight is our wedding night," he says suggestively, waggling his eyebrows.

"It does, and it also means today's date will be our anniversary, you know for the future," I wink.

He laughs as he leans over the console, reaching for me with his free hand and guiding my lips to his.

"What do you say we make this union official, Princess?"

He murmurs the question as his lips glided glide over mine teasingly.

"The last first time we have sex as a married couple will be the first of many last first times," I say thoughtfully.

"What're we waiting for?"

"For you to carry me over the threshold," I say pointedly.

His mouth instantly leaves mine and in a flash he is out of the car, opening my door and pulling me out. He takes my hand and leads me up the front stoop, climbing two stairs at a time until he stands in front of the door.

Mikey crooks his finger, beckoning me to him to close the few steps separating us, capturing me in his arms by the second step.

"Shit, my keys are in my pocket," he mutters.

I snake my hand around his frame and pull the key ring from the back pocket of his jeans.

Look at that.

We already aced the teamwork shit.

He walks us closer to the door and bends his knees so I can fit the key into the lock and unlock the door. His massive boot kicks the door open and we both glance inside our home before our eyes find one another's.

"Ready to make this the last first time you're carried over the threshold?"

"So ready," I say, tightening my arms around his neck.

He grins, taking one large step over the threshold before gruffly whispering into my ear.

"Welcome home, Mrs. Valente," he croons.

The last first time Mikey *welcomed* me home as his *wife*.

He kicks the door closed, sets me down on my feet and we stare at one another for a few moments. This was it, the beginning of the rest of our lives, and as scary as that was it was also exciting. It was as if the life I knew before today was tucked away safely in a box full of memories and our home was our blank canvas. My father's voice rang in my ears.

Paint me a picture.

Mikey and I were going to paint him one hell of a picture.

I look at my husband wondering if he was as excited and as nervous as I was. Would we fuck up? Probably. Would we fix it? Always.

Simultaneously our lips spread into grins as we find our footing and I turn around and run up the stairs.

He follows me.

He'd always follow me just as I had followed him in the past.
I'd always let him catch me.
After all, he let me catch him.
His arms snake around my waist as he reaches our bedroom. His fingertips curl into my sides, tickling me and sending me into a fit of giggles.
Laughing felt almost foreign after all the crying I had been doing but it felt good to let go of my grief and live in the moment.
Mikey's hands slide underneath the hem of my shirt, his fingers draw circles on my skin as he presses my back against his front and leans his chin on my shoulder. My laughter tapers off as I twist in his arms and wrap my arms around his neck. Staring into Mikey's eyes, every uncertainty I carried fades away from me and all that is left is the promise of forever.
Making one another happy, *forever*.
Living in the moment, *forever*.
Experiencing life together, *forever*.
Loving one another, *forever*.
Forever him and me.
I reach for the hem of my shirt and pull it over my head tossing it on the floor before raising an eyebrow, daring him to mimic me.
The last first time I *dared* him as *husband* and *wife*.
With one hand he reaches behind him and lifts his t-shirt over his head, dropping it onto the floor beside mine. I extend my hand and close my fist over the rosary beads that dangle from his neck—his mother's.
Thanks Maryann, for creating the perfect man for me to spend forever with.
I lean down and kiss the crucifix before releasing the beads. I run my fingers down his arms, his muscles flexing beneath my fingertips until they take purchase on his hips. Mikey trails one hand down my stomach and pops the button of my jean shorts with his fingers. He reaches out with his other hand and draws the zipper down before crossing both arms against his chest and taking a step back.
Take off your clothes, Princess, his eyes dared.
Dare accepted.
I slide my thumbs through the belt loops of my shorts and tug the denim down my thighs, bending over suggestively as I work them all the way down. I step out of them, turn my back to him and reach behind me to unclasp my bra, letting the straps fall down my arms. Braless, I spin around and face him, watching as his hooded eyes dip to my breasts. My nipples hardened under his intense gaze as I drag my thong down my hips.
Mikey pushes my hands out of the way and takes over, looping his fingers under the lace and inching it down my hips, baring my most intimate secrets to him. He drops to his knees, his lips gliding over every inch he has uncovered, continuing down my legs and stopping at my knees. He lifts one foot from the ground and draws the lace down. I go to kick off the thong that dangled from my other ankle when he drapes the leg he is holding over his shoulder. My fingers tangled in his hair, grasping it for leverage as he repeats the motion and lifts me onto his shoulders, depositing me on the bed.

I watch with lustful eyes as he pushes my knees apart, waiting for him to slide between them but he doesn't. Instead, he stands there for a moment drinking me in.

The last first time he *stared* at his *wife, naked and waiting for him*.

He unbuttons his jeans with one hand as he cocks his head to the side. I watch his Adam's apple as he swallows hard and lifts his eyes to mine.

"You'll always be the leading lady of my dreams," he vows hoarsely.

I park my lips to tell him he was the dream, the only one worth having, the only one that ever came true but he presses his finger to my lips silencing me.

Not another word was spoken between us as he finishes undressing and finds his place between my legs. His lips trail down my neck, sucking, grazing and licking all the sweet spots his mouth owned. I squirm against the comforter as his mouth travels lower, finding one breast, squeezing the other, taking my pert nipple between his teeth and tugging on it before his tongue soothes the sting his teeth leaves behind.

His mouth moves across the valley of skin between my breasts, his tongue tickling the flesh until he sucks my other nipple into his mouth. Mikey's hands grab a hold of my hips and force my back to arch as he presses my pelvis against his, teasing us both by grinding his cock against my pussy, letting me know how badly he wants me. I wrap my legs around his waist and press myself against him, my nails digging into his shoulders as I urge him to give us what we both needed.

He shakes his head, releasing my nipple and unraveling my legs from his waist before placing a trail of wet kisses down my belly. My whole body quivers in anticipation as he hovers over my pussy, pushing my legs as wide as they can go. With a feral gaze he stares at me, sighing in appreciation as his fingers ran down the seam of my pussy.

Mikey came back into my life unexpectedly, broke down the walls I had built without me even noticing and then he rebuilt the walls, adding windows to let me shine through the panes. He showed me what true love is without realizing true love existed in his touch.

His gentle caress against my skin ignites a fire inside of me and I fist the sheets as I press myself against his hand, riding the two fingers he slides inside of me. Mikey keeps his eyes on mine as he expertly works me, soaking his fingers and priming me for him. His thumb finds the tight bundle of nerves and strokes it slowly, both pleasuring and torturing me equally.

"Mikey," I gasp, swirling my hips and moving to the rhythm he creates. He quickens his pace, curls his fingers inside me and presses down on my clit.

My vision slips away from me, my voice dead, and my hearing faded leaving me vulnerable to the orgasm that takes over my body and forces me to feel.

The last first time I orgasmed as his wife.

My body dips into the mattress as I came down from the natural high his fingers grant me, and before I can catch my breath, Mikey withdraws his hand from between my legs and guides the head of his cock to my entrance. His hand wraps tightly around his dick as he runs the tip up and down my pussy, lubricating himself with all of me.

The last first time he pushed himself into me *without* protection.

The last first time I felt him deep inside of me with *nothing* between us.

The last first time my *husband* made love to me.

We had a lifetime of firsts still to come and each one of them would be the last first we ever had.

Chapter Twenty-Six

Grace

It was the early eighties; Maryann and I were barely legal but that didn't stop us from painting the town red. I had a part-time job at Rosalie's bakery, making just enough money to spend my paycheck—that's a lie. I never received a paycheck, those days we were paid in cash, sixty dollars stuffed in a white envelope that Rosalie scribbled my name on. It was enough cash for me to buy a brand-new outfit every Friday. I would take my envelope, cross three avenues and make my way to Something Else boutique on 86th Street.

I teased my hair six inches to the sky, applied enough blue eyeshadow to my eyelids, you had no choice but to notice my almond shaped eyes. Lastly, I ripped the tags and put on my silk turquoise jumpsuit. Maryann stole her father's car out of the garage and picked me up at exactly ten o'clock. Studio 54 was packed, the line to get inside the club wrapped around the block but Maryann grabbed my hand and walked us straight to the front of the line.

"I'm a friend of Val's," she told the bouncer guarding the door.

At the time, I only knew Val as one of the neighborhood guys. He, like most of the guys our age living in Bensonhurst, hung around with the old-timers, the made-men, goodfellas—you know the type of men I'm talking about. Gangsters.

I didn't know if Val was in fact a made man or part of a family, I just knew one day he would be and I understood why Maryann had taken a liking toward him. Who didn't find that type of man sexy? There was nothing more attractive than the unattainable bad boy who exuded charisma.

The bouncer lifted the red velvet rope and escorted us into the pulsating night club. I remember the song playing as I stepped foot onto the colorful dance floor that lit up as the patrons danced the night away, 'How Deep Is Your Love' by the Bee Gees. It was one of my favorites and I wanted to dance so badly but Maryann had other plans, taking my hand as she dragged me across the dance floor to the bar where Val stood. He was surrounded by a bunch of guys, some I knew and others were a mystery. A delicious mystery.

"Order us a couple of Long Island Iced Teas and I'll be right back," she shouted over the music.

I sat down at the bar and ordered the drinks, glancing across the bar as she worked her way into the circle and straight to Val. The bartender placed the two drinks in front of me and I waited five minutes before I pulled the little paper umbrella from the glass and lifted the straw to my lips.

I averted my eyes back to the other end of the bar and noticed Maryann and Val had disappeared from the crowd.

"Those things are lethal," a voice said from behind me, forcing me to spin around on the bar stool and stare at the most handsome man I ever laid eyes on.

The first thing I noticed was his clothes. He wasn't dressed like the other men. His charcoal gray suit looked as if it was tailor made for him. He opted to wear a black turtleneck under the suit, no button down, collar popping shirt for the handsome stranger before me. He did however engage in the fad of gold chains. My eyes zeroed in on the crucifix dangling from the thick, gold rope chain hanging around his neck. I lifted my eyes to his face and was greeted by a smile I'd never forget.

His eyes drifted toward the two drinks that sat in front of me to the empty stool beside me.

"May I?"

"Sure," I said, twirling back around to face the bar as he slipped onto the stool and signaled for the bartender.

He ordered a Martini, dry with extra olives as I toyed with the paper umbrella and brought my drink to my lips for another sip. The song changed, Tavares filtered the nightclub with their hit, 'More Than a Woman'.

"What's your name, beautiful?" he asked, casually draping an arm over the back of my stool.

"Grace," I said, mesmerized by the way he stared so intently at me.

"Grace," he repeated, testing the name on his tongue, grinning once he decided he liked the way it sounded.

"And who are you?" I stammered, taking another sip, hoping to calm my nerves. This man had the power to undo me with a simple glance.

"Me? I'm the man who's going to marry you one day," he said pointedly.

I nearly spat my drink out.

"That's pretty presumptuous don't you think?" Or cocky depending on who you ask, I added silently.

He grinned at me as he lifted his hand and ran his index finger down my cheek.

"Watch and see, Gracie," he promised, dropping his hand but keeping his gaze locked on me. "The name is Victor, Victor Pastore."

It is so easy to forget those first blissful moments when you meet the person you're meant to spend the rest of your life with. Instead, we harbor the resentment life has brought upon us and lose touch of the magic that brought two unsuspecting strangers together.

Sitting across from the man I love for the final time I wonder how I ever let myself become so jaded by the trials and tribulations we stumbled upon in our years together. Why did I let the heartache trump the happiness? Why couldn't I hang on to all the times he made me smile, all the times I looked into his eyes and knew I was his one and only. Why wasn't the love we created enough to outweigh the torment of the mob?

I foolishly thought we had years to figure it out, to mend the broken parts of our love. I never expected thirty years to go by in a flash. I never expected a judge to slam down the gavel and sentence him to life in prison. I never expected for him to become fatally ill. I never expected to be sitting here wishing for more time.

I glance down at his hands and my heart breaks at the comparison. His hands are twice the size of mine just as they were thirty years ago but instead of his olive skin matching mine, there is a stark contrast. His skin pales compared to mine.

"I dreamt of you last night," he breathes. I peel my eyes away from our hands and lift them to his. "I always dream of you but last night was one of my favorites," he struggles, breathing heavily. "Give me a moment," he requests.

"You don't have to speak," I tell him.

"But I do," he argues. "It's now or never, Gracie."

I nod sadly, glancing down at our hands again, watching as his thumb draws circles over my palm.

"It was the grand opening of my first night club," he starts, smiling nostalgically.

"Eternity," I recall. I teased him mercilessly over the name he chose for his first venture as a night club owner. Victor knew the scene, appreciated it and at the time figured it was a great way to hide the illegal money coming in.

"You remember," he says.

I laugh slightly.

"How could I forget? I was eight months pregnant with Adrianna," I reply. We argued that night, I didn't want to go, figuring I looked ridiculous sitting in a night club with a glass of seltzer and a big belly, but Victor insisted I be there.

There is no one I want by my side but you. This is our night, Gracie.

"You were the most beautiful woman in the whole place," he whispers. "I made Jimmy stand by the bar with you all night in case you went into labor."

"I remember you kept checking in on me," I whisper, a small smile playing on my lips as the memories vividly take over my mind, transfixing me back to a time when we were the happiest in our lives. "You were so worried my water would break," I chuckle. "I think you were afraid I would ruin the fancy floors you had spent a fortune on."

"Probably," he agrees, pausing for a moment. "I wish you would've gone into labor that night, at least I would've been there for you when you gave birth."

He frowns but keeps his eyes firmly planted on mine.

I prayed so hard that he would make it in time to see our daughter being born but God didn't hear me that night and Victor showed up an hour after Adrianna took her first breath.

"That was the first time I disappointed you," he continues. "The first of many."

"Victor…" I cut him off, but he shakes his head as he releases my hand and lifts his finger to my lip.

"If I could turn back time, if I could have one more chance, I'd be there. I'd never leave your side, Gracie. I'd change all the things I did wrong," he says. "I'd always show up, I'd always put you first, and we'd have no regrets, not a single one. As God as my witness I'd give it all up—the mob, the power, the money—maybe I'd be a bus driver. We would still live in the first house we bought after we got married. I'd trade everything I am, everything I ever was if it meant one more chance to make all your dreams come true. I'd be a different man."

Again, I part my lips to speak, but he shakes his head and smiles faintly back at me.

"Let it be," he whispers.

Tears fall from the corner of my eyes as we sit quietly cataloging every detail of one another's aging face to memory. The resentment of the mob fades away and in that moment, we are just Grace and Victor, two unsuspecting strangers in a night club—meeting their eternal love for the first time.

He smiles at me, the lines in the corner of his eyes pinched with the years of our story embedded in his skin, and it all became so clear. Victor was my one and only. The only man I was ever meant to love, the man put on this earth specifically for me. Our life may not have been what we expected, but it was beautiful and it was real. When the end approaches everyone has regrets, maybe they wish they would've done things differently, but now as the end of our story nears, I know all the answers to the questions I've been asking myself lately. I wouldn't change a single thing. If I knew everything I knew now back then, I still would've put that white dress on and made that trip down the church aisle to the man waiting to marry me.

I let go of Victor's hands, pushed back my chair and gripped the edge of the table, I rose to my full height. His eyes narrow in confusion as I hold his gaze and round the table. He leans back in the chair and tilts his head as I lean down and take his face in my hands.

"I can't let it be," I murmured, as he pushes back his chair and grabs my hips, pulling me down onto his lap. I drop my hands from his face and wind my arms around his neck.

"I wouldn't change a damn thing about you, Victor Pastore." I smile, leaning my forehead against his. "Everything you are is everything I fell in love with. If given the chance, I'd do it all again and I wouldn't change any part of our story except one thing…"

He closes his eyes as he splays his palms against the small of my back. I wait for him to look into my eyes before I continue.

"I'd change the ending," I cry, tracing my thumb along his lower lip. "There'd be no ending." I pause, wiping away the lone tear that travels down his cheek. "This won't end, Victor, this love I have for you, it'll never die," I promise.

"Close your eyes, honey, let me paint you one last picture," I cry.

He did as I asked, closing his eyes tightly. I swallow down the lump lodged in my throat, trying desperately to pull myself together as every chamber of my heart cracks and splits wide open.

How do you say goodbye to the love of your life?

You don't.

You give him something to hang on to as he waits for you to join him.

"I'm wearing a turquoise silk jumpsuit, the very same one I wore when you first laid eyes on me. I look the same as I did that night, the lines from my face are gone, my hair is brown, but there is a lost look in my eyes as I wander around. I don't know what I'm searching for but I know the moment I see you with your hand extended toward me, it's you, you're exactly what I've been searching for."

He keeps his eyes closed as tears spill from the corners and I do my best to wipe them away, eventually I resign, allowing them to fall, for they are the tears of the love we will one day find again and I welcome them, adding my own to them.

We will meet again.

"You're wearing that same charcoal suit, with the black turtleneck and gold chain. Your lines have faded, your hair just as dark as it was that first night, and when you smile at me, it's a smile full of promise. You ask me my name and I tell you, waiting for you to repeat it back because this is a familiar dance we're taking," I continue, stopping a moment to clear my throat.

"I ask you who you are and butterflies take flight inside me as I await your answer. You grin at me and I learn you're cocky, you're confident, and more than that you believe wholeheartedly the words you're about to utter." My voice trails off as I watch his lips part.

"Me? I'm the man you're going to spend all of eternity with," he whispers as his eyes flutter open, applying the final touches to the picture I was painting, reminding me this was *our* picture. *Our* life. *Our* love.

"That's right," I reply, holding his face as I lean closer to him. "Forever and always, my love."

"I love you, Gracie," he rasps. His hands travel up my sides, slowly, knowing it's the last journey they'll ever take over me. Finally, he takes my face and I close my eyes as his lips brush across mine.

Soft and endearing.

Painfully heartbreaking.

Lovingly, Victor kisses me one last time. Thirty years of love, three decades of memories and all the lessons we've learned melt into that one kiss affirming the one thing that may have once been lost to us—the beautiful love we created will never die.

We've found eternal love in a sea full of illicit temptations.

"I'll see you soon," I whisper against his lips, pulling back a fraction to stare into his handsome face one last time.

"Goodbye my love, until we meet again," he says softly.

And we would meet again.

He'll be the man in the charcoal suit.

I'll be the woman in a turquoise jumpsuit.

He'll grin at me and I'll take his hand and together we'll be.

Always together.

Chapter Twenty-Seven

VICTOR

It takes a special breed to kill. For me, there has always been a ritual I take part in before I commit the act. In the early days, Val and I would get pissed drunk on a bottle of Dewar's before we took our guns to the streets. When I became the boss my hands rarely ever got dirty, but I had trust issues, never willing to leave room for error, I always took care of the bodies. I'd drive seven hours to the middle of nowhere, blasting Sinatra's 'My Way' with a shovel beside me and a corpse in the trunk of my Cadillac.

The ritual changed as I got older. I took to God before I slit a throat or pulled the trigger; I prayed for the unsuspecting soul that would meet his maker and while I was at it I threw in an Our Father for myself. It was a crap shoot, really, asking our Heavenly Father to relieve me of all the crimes I committed and those I had yet to, but still, if there was a chance he did then why not take it?

It was selfish of me and in some sense, I felt like a coward.

You see, I didn't think twice before murdering someone. I did it with ease and with confidence. Hell, I did it with grace, each hit becoming more of a work of art than the one before. Even as I dug the holes and covered the bodies with the Earth's soil I had no regrets. I was cocky and arrogant in murder just as I was in everything else. It wasn't until I went home with blood on my hands and saw Grace asleep in our bed that I questioned my actions.

I wasn't afraid of dying; it came with the power, with the suit and the gun. I was afraid of leaving this earth and never seeing my Gracie again. Saint Peter will wait for my beautiful bride, not I, my ass was headed straight to the depths of Hell.

There was no way my sweet, innocent Gracie would ever meet Satan.

Grace and I were over. We ended when my bride of thirty years kissed me one final time and walked out of that visitor's room in Otisville. It ended when my shackled legs shuffled onto the bus that dragged my ass here.

There is nothing left to my existence, nothing to look forward to, all that's left is the last hit. I had a vision for my last kill, a premeditated hit that would be just as dramatic as the first one I ever committed. I contemplated reenacting my first hit but my connections were gone and getting my hands on a gun and a bottle of bleach was goddamn impossible.

Along with my connections, my body failed me. I was running out of time and didn't have time to sit on the G-Man. Once that motherfucker's eyes find mine he'll know exactly what's about to go down and if I don't strike first, then I'll be the one in a body bag by the end of the day.

And I'm not going out like that.

Revenge is a beast that's been living inside of me since I watched the life fade from Val's eyes, his body riddled with bullets, each one meant for me. It was finally time for me to lay down my life for his memory, time for me to give the brothers of the Satan's Knights the peace they so badly craved. It was time to avenge the deaths caused by the G-Man running his product through mine and Jack's streets.

It was time for the last hit.

This body of mine may be weak but it does not know defeat.

I will paint the world one last picture; give them one last piece of Victor Pastore. Everyone will learn what happens to a man when he has nothing left to live for. The Victor Pastore you know, the man the newspapers love to write about is about to resurrect the hitman within him, the soldier before the mob boss. I hope the media is ready because this prison is going to become uncontrollable as I get reckless and this vendetta turns lethal.

There is no sharpened bolt under my cot, no guard to hand me a bible and turn his back as I kill yet another. I'm running on nothing but adrenaline and instinct.

Upon my arrival the correctional officers removed the shackles wrapped around my ankles and brought me into the main building to process my paperwork and complete my transfer. I was then escorted to the medical building where they would take my vitals, learn I was a lost cause and send me to my new cell.

My lungs were closing in on me and I gasped for breath.

"The doctor should be here any minute," the young officer said.

I lift my eyes to him, taking in the helpless expression he adorned and the way he fidgeted, glancing over his shoulder to see if the doctor was on his way.

"What's the matter, son," I struggle. "This your first time watching a man die?"

He chose not to answer and instead wiped the sweat from his brow, making me wonder if he was a rookie.

"Do you know who I am?"

"No, sir, should I?"

My lips quirk at his response.

"No, I don't suppose you should," I replied, struggling to breathe and bowing my head to focus on the linoleum floor.

The less you know, the better. The simpler this is for me.

Something shiny caught my eye causing me to narrow my eyes and focus on the silver circle that glistened against the black and white checkered flooring.

"Mr. Pastore?" I hear a soft voice say.

My eyes travel the sound of my name and find the face of a woman. She has innocent brown eyes that speak to me telling me she couldn't be any more than thirty years old. Her brown hair is pulled back from her face, tied into a ponytail at the base of her neck. She smiles softly, cocking her head to the side as she averts her eyes back to my chart and her top teeth dig into her lower lip. I couldn't peel my eyes from her, studying her features that were so like both my daughters but when her eyes find mine again, I decide she reminds me more of Adrianna than she did Nicole. It was the dullness reflected in her eyes that decided for me. I spent three years staring into similar eyes after Anthony went to prison. This doctor, like my daughter, had someone rip the sparkle right out of her eyes.

I wondered if it was her father that took away the shine like I had taken away Adrianna's.

Probably not.

"I'm Dr. Gazelle," she introduced herself, pulling up a stool and rolling closer. "Mr. Pastore—"

"Call me Victor," I hiss before glancing down at the floor again at the object that held my attention before she walked into the room.

"It says here you're not in the greatest of health, Mr. Pastore, I mean, Victor," she says and I tear my eyes away from the floor to glance around the room. The guard was fidgeting again, pacing back and forth before he bumps into the metal tray and sends it rolling right toward us.

"Sorry," he mumbles. "It's my first day and I'm kind of nervous," he admits when Dr. Gazelle turns around abruptly.

"We've all been there," she soothes, pushing the metal tray aside so it rests between us. The tray is lined immaculately with instruments you'd likely see in an emergency room, a small pair of scissors, a pair of tweezers and lastly a needle and thread.

"I'm sorry, as I was saying, you're pretty sick, Mr. Pastore," she continues, frowning deeply as she flips the pages of my chart.

"How old are you, Dr. Gazelle?"

She closes my chart, rests it on top of her lap before she folds her hands neatly and lifts her sorrowful eyes. I wait for her to answer but she keeps her lips closed in a tight line, studying me with the same intensity she did my medical records.

I take a deep breath, the biggest one my lungs will allow and force a smile.

"Twenty-nine," she finally replies.

"I have two daughters, both in their twenties," I tell her. "I saw them a few days ago and though their faces are fresh in my memory, I can't help miss them like crazy."

I brought my closed fist to my mouth and coughed uncontrollably. My chest ached as I abused what was left of my lungs. Dr. Gazelle stood quickly, turning around to the guard.

"Go get him a glass of water," she ordered.

"But—" he stammers.

"Or you can stay and we can both watch him choke to death. How's that for a first day on the job story?" she chastises, pointing her finger toward the door. "Water. Now."

I continue to choke and gasp for air as the guard disappears from his post and the sweet young doctor grabs an oxygen mask. She fits the strap over my head and covers my mouth and nose with the mask.

"Try to relax, Mr. Pastore," she instructs, turning up the dial on the oxygen tank. "That's it, nice and easy breaths," she whispers, holding the mask with one hand as she moves a strand of hair behind her ear.

I stared at her bare ear, the cough easing up as I brush her hand away and lower the mask from my face.

"Your earring," I rasp.

She lifts her hand to her ear, feeling around for the diamond hoop I had spotted on the floor before she walked into the room.

"Oh, no," she whispers, moving her hand to check for its mate. "They were a present from my father before he passed last year," she explains as she frantically pats down her clothes in search of the earring.

And they say history doesn't repeat itself—fools.

I lifted the mask off my face and point to the floor behind her.

"Is that it over there?"

She turns, following my finger as I lift the mask back to my face and casually rest my other hand on the metal tray.

"Where? Oh! There is its," she murmurs, as my hand closes around the pair of scissors resting on the tray. I continue to breathe in the oxygen as she bends down to lift the earring from the floor. With a quick glance back toward the door I shove the scissors into the waistband of my pants, untucking my shirt and pulling the hem over my pants to conceal my weapon.

Dr. Gazelle stands, fitting the earring back to her ear as the guard walks in carrying a Styrofoam cup of water. I drop the mask onto my lap and reach for the cup he offered, smiling weakly at both of them.

"God bless you both," I whisper before taking a gulp of the water, letting the liquid relieve the rawness of my throat.

I glance at the clock on the wall and feel my lips spread into a grin—it was almost time for the *last supper*.

After a few more hits of oxygen I was carted to my new cell. I didn't hang my pictures nor did I remove my personal effects from the brown paper bag, this was just a resting point, a time to gather my thoughts and pray.

Our father who art in Heaven...
I prayed for my wife.
Welcome her with open arms Saint Peter.
I prayed for my children.
Let them be happy and healthy.
I prayed for my grandchildren.
Let them always be safe.
I prayed for Val.
I prayed for a woman I never met...Christine Petra.
I prayed for Danny Parrish.
I prayed for all the innocent victims of the G-Man.
Rest in peace, this ones for you.
Amen.

I didn't pray for myself, not this time, whatever will be, will be. The bell sounds, and another fresh faced correctional officer opens my cell and guides me to the mess hall. I grab an empty tray and get on the back of the line as my eyes scan the room searching for my mark.

Come out and play.

The room was divided, white sat with white, black stuck with black there was no unity amongst inmates, a sure sign that this prison wouldn't survive the chaos I was about to implode.

I shuffled my feet as I inched my way up the line, scoping the room for the face I hadn't seen in years, a face so gruesome only a mother could love. Bet that bitch hated him too.

Father forgive me.

I made the sign of the cross as my eyes zeroed in on the table in the corner of the cafeteria and the lone man sitting at it devouring a pudding cup.

"How do you want to do this," I hear Val's voice say.

I glance at the man in front of me, peer over his shoulder as he loads his tray and smiles.

"You can't be serious, Vic," Val's voice dares.

My grin widened.

Watch me.

I lift my tray over my head and slam it against the inmate in front of me before stepping to my left. He drops his tray, spins on his heel and glares at the man who stands in line behind me. I watch as he rears his fist back, his knuckles colliding with the poor innocent man just waiting for his grub.

"FIGHT!"

We like to think times change but they don't, society is just as fucked as it was before Martin Luther King had a dream, and segregation was just as much alive in this cafeteria as it was on the streets. White attacked black, black attacked white, yellow went for red and so on and so forth.

And me? I, like Moses, parted the sea, holding my head high as I walked through the chaos, through the disruption, straight to the end.

The G-Man didn't flinch as he continued to eat, ignoring the war raging around him and the man headed for him.

I pull my shirt out of my pants, my hands closing over the metal as my form casts a shadow over the man I've been hunting for since he ordered the hit on me.

He calls himself a boss, a fucking leader, but he isn't worthy of the title and *this boss*, is about to strip him from the label he cherishes. A boss doesn't order a hit and miss the mark. A boss doesn't kill the wrong man and never gets a chance to get the right one. A boss doesn't rest until he gets revenge. A boss does things his way—until he's dead and buried.

I'm the boss.

And it's time for me to rest.

The G-Man's tongue takes a swipe across the plastic spoon, licking the remnants of the pudding as he lifts his head.

The flicker of surprise spikes my adrenaline, transfixes me back to the man I was thirty years ago and for a moment, I'm not dying. I don't have fucking cancer and I didn't just say goodbye to the people I love. I am the fucking man who ruled the most powerful organization in New York City.

I am the legend.

I pull the scissors from the waistband of my pants and watch as his lips move. His words are deaf to my ears as he grips the edge of the table and slowly rises. The lights flash around the room alerting me that the prison is on lockdown.

I've created a riot and now before the riot squad comes barreling in here with their guns blazing I've got to do what I came here to do.

He continues to talk with every step I take toward him. In my mind he's begging me not to kill him but my conscience knows better and tries to get me to listen to what he's preaching.

I don't though.

I lift my gaze from his running mouth to his eyes and spot the black ink just beneath the corner of his eye.

Three little dots that resemble tear drops, a trademark for gang members when they take a life. One of those tear drops represents the life and death of my underboss. I pull the scissors out and lift them in the air.

Forgive me father for I have sinned.

He lunges for me as I rear my hand back and push the blunt tip of the scissors right into his jugular. The instant the metal pierces his vein blood squirts from his neck, spraying over my face.

For I have committed murder.

His hands close around his neck as he sputters blood from his mouth and begins to bleed out from his neck. A moment later he drops to his knees and falls face first at my feet, staining my white canvas sneakers with his blood.

Forgive me father for I have performed my last hit.

The scissors fall to the floor as a pair of hands tighten around my neck and drag me to the floor.

I close my eyes and see my Gracie's face before everything fades to black.

Forgive me Gracie

Dear Daddy,

I have never been much for letters. I never kept a diary when I was younger and I can count on both hands how many times I wrote to Anthony when he went away. Yet, writing to you seems almost painless. In fact, it might be the best idea I've ever had.

The beauty of writing a letter is that I have the final say. You can't interrupt me and put your two cents into my conversation, all you can do is listen. Well, not really listen but you know what I mean.

Before my words bleed onto these pages and I profess the truth of our relationship, I want you to do me a favor. I want you to think back; I want you to collect all the memories we've created but only the ones that made you smile. Go on, my words can wait, just do it. Go all the way back, to the day I was born, and you held me in your arms for the first time.

Knowing you, you're skeptical, looking for the catch hidden within my request but I assure you Daddy, there is no catch, no gimmick, this is just a daughter trying to reconnect with her father one last time. I want to see if my memories match yours and I hope I can add to your list, reminding you of some of the great ones I'll always cherish.

I was five years old; it was my first time riding my brand new bike, the one with the pretty pink basket on the front and the little bell I pretended was a horn. You remember the one, don't you? It was my first bike without training wheels and you couldn't wait to teach me how to ride it. With a steady hand, you guided me, balanced me until I got the hang of it and then, and only then, did you let go. I flew down the block, listening to your laughter fade behind me.

I did it! I rode a two-wheeler. All thanks to you.

The next day, I fell off my bike and broke my arm. You met me and Mom at the hospital just in time for the doctor to tell us it was broken and needed a cast for six weeks. I remember being scared, so scared but then you held my good hand as they fitted the cast and promised everything would be okay. You were the first person to sign my cast and I still remember the stick figures meant to resemble you and me that you drew.

I was eight years old, and it was my First Holy Communion. You and Mommy threw me this huge party, and it was the first time you and I ever danced to 'Daddy's Little Girl'. The dance started off with me standing on top of your loafers and ended with me in your arms.

Do you know how many times I've caught you playing that video over and over? Always rewinding the tape after the song is over to watch it again. I lost count how many times but it was many.

I was eleven years old, and we went to Saratoga for the summer. You took me to the track and showed me the racing form and let me pick the horse in the fourth race. Native Dancer came in first and you won a whole lot of money. I don't remember how much but you gave me a cut and told me not to tell Mommy.

We went to the track a lot after that and I grew to love horse racing. I don't know if it was the thrill of winning or the thrill of spending time with you.

I was thirteen when you took me on my first date. I didn't know it was a date at the time. I thought it was just one of our typical father-daughter dinners. You remember those don't you? The nights you would take me to Villa Pasquette restaurant and had the owners Gino and Maria serenade me at the table. Anyway, back to the date, I was thirteen and instead of going to dinner with my father I wanted to hang out with my friends. I didn't want to go, but you insisted I did and promised it would be the last time.

After work you picked me up and handed me a bouquet of flowers. I looked at you like you were crazy but then you told me, "Remember, Adrianna, a good man will always try to remember the little details."

That night you tried to teach me what I should expect from a boy. You told me to set my standards high and never allow a boy to disrespect me. "To some you'll just be a girl, but to one you'll be the world."

I didn't need for you to show me how a woman deserved to be treated because for thirteen years I watched you treat my mother with the utmost respect. And long before that last dinner we had at Villa Pasquette, I knew I wanted to walk in my mother's shoes one day. I wanted the man I married to look at me, treat me and love me just the way you loved my mom.

Even now, at twenty-nine, married to the love of my life and two kids—you and Mom's story is still my favorite one ever written. Thank you for loving my mom.

I was fifteen, almost sixteen and learning how to drive. I had taken lessons, but I was still nervous about failing my upcoming road test. You had a Lincoln at the time, a navy blue one to be exact, and you didn't even let Mommy drive it. But you let me drive it. You took me out every Sunday morning for thirteen weeks, showed me how to parallel park, how to pop a U-turn and when I told you I was afraid of the highway, you tricked me into driving straight onto the Belt Parkway and over the Verrazano bridge. I passed my road test thanks to you. Thank you for teaching me to face my fears.

It was my sweet Sixteen, and we were on our way to the catering hall when you pulled out a tiny velvet box and gave me a pair of diamond hoop earrings. I had wanted them so badly and I remember you telling me in the limo "I never disappointed you yet and I'm not about to now."

I cherished those earrings. Still do and when Victoria is sixteen, I will pass them down to her.

Even when things got tricky for us, and I started to date Anthony, the dynamic between us, that incredible bond a daughter only has with her father, well, it shined through, allowing us to still build great memories.

Like the subway series tickets, you surprised me with. You wore your Mets gear, and I wore my Yankee gear, we ate hotdogs and rooted for our separate teams, never truly allowing our differences outweigh the bond we created throughout the years.

And differences we had.

I wish we would've done things differently. I wish you would've talked to me about how you were feeling instead of acting out of fear. I wish you would've remembered that before everything, my first role in life was your daughter and I'd always be your girl.

The years Anthony served in jail, I wish I would've been courageous enough to tell you how much I missed you. I wish I would've found the strength to tell you how much I needed one more memory. Maybe a trip to the racetrack would've reminded us of all the memories we made and the ones we still had to make.

We lost three years of our bond to fear and resentment when all we needed to do was be honest with one another.

If you would've come to me, I would've told you all the things I am now about to say.

I will always be your little girl.

I took your advice and found a man who always remembers the little details.

A man who is a lot like you.

I found someone to live up to the great man that is my dad.

And to him I am his whole world.

I found that one person just like you said I would.

And I am now Anthony's wife.

I am a mother to two amazing children.

But at the end of the day I am also your daughter.

I will always be your daughter and you will always be my father. The man who taught me to expect greatness, to never settle for less than I deserve and to conquer my fears.

Three great lessons that I will teach my children.

But there is one lesson I'd like to teach you and that is to know life may end but love doesn't. I'll always love you, Dad. I'll think of you every time I drive pass the boarded up restaurant we used to go to. I'll think about you whenever I wear the earrings you bought me. I'll smile as I speed down the Belt Parkway and imagine you're right beside me in the passenger seat and when the Belmont stakes come around, I'll always bet the fourth race.

I'll miss you.

But you'll always be in my heart.

Thank you for loving me.

Love Always,

Your Little Girl

Chapter Twenty-Eight

JACK

There used to be a time when partying entailed a clubhouse full of whores, a never-ending supply of booze and a brick of the finest weed. A time when the only things the Satan's Knights MC knew was mayhem and grief, blood and death. The days when their president lived for the darkness and craved a little bit of light. The days before I found my Sunshine.

We used to live only to ride, party and fuck, but now some of us, myself included, have found there is more to life than a clubhouse full of cheap pussy. We found our heart, and passing blunts around isn't as appealing as it used to be. I love my club, still live to ride, but I've got a woman to go home to night after night and her pussy is the only one I crave. In fact, as I stare at the menu the only thing I've got an appetite for is Sunshine, not a porterhouse at some swanky restaurant in the city.

It was Wolf's idea, a night on the town to celebrate Stryker's homecoming, and though I'd rather be in bed with Reina wrapped around me, I have to agree with my bat-shit crazy brother, Wolf, Stryker deserves a night out. He probably needs more than a steak though, poor bastard spent eight months in Rikers, more than double the time he was sent in there for, all because he kept getting his ass thrown in the hole. Don't know much about any of the nomads but it's obvious our boy Stryker has a temper.

Closing my menu, I reach for my drink and try to pay attention to the conversation. Wolf has gone all out, setting us up in a private room at Smith and Wollensky's steakhouse and everyone has made it their business to show up. It was like we had moved church to the overpriced joint, taking our respective seats around Wollensky's table just as we do at my table, and as usual the conversation turns to Pipe's wife's tits.

"A fake rack never did it for me," I chime in, lifting my beer bottle to my lips before pausing to point a finger at Blackie. "If you put your two cents into this conversation, I might shoot you."

Leaning back against his chair, Blackie shakes his head and tries to hide the grin spreading across his face—bastard.

"Well, well, if it isn't the man of the hour," Blackie announces as his eyes zero in on a Wolf and Stryker as they walk into the room.

"And his party planner," Riggs notes, raising an eyebrow toward Wolf as he glances around the room. "Fancy place, Wolf."

"You're used to fancy aren't you, Richie Rich?" Pipe quips. He's relentless with the rich boy jokes, especially after Riggs brought it to our attention that the oil diggers are in town looking to make nice with their boy.

I stand from my chair at the head of the table and walk over to Stryker.

"Welcome home, brother," I say, glancing toward the waiter standing in the doorway. "Get this motherfucker the finest bottle of whiskey," I demand, wrapping an arm around Stryker's shoulders.

"Thanks, Prez," he says as I lead him toward the table. As he stands as still as a soldier, Blackie pushes his chair back and rises to his feet to greet his former cellmate. He sizes him up before tipping his chin and biting his cheek.

"How's the nose?"

Stryker shrugs his shoulders, taking the glass, the waiter offered and knocks back the shot before peering at Blackie. As per my orders, Blackie staged a fight with Stryker, broke his nose and got his ass carted to Otisville where Vic was waiting for him. Yeah, I owed Stryker big time.

"It's good, gives me character," he replies.

Blackie smirks and wraps an arm around Stryker's shoulders just as I had.

"Thank you," he says, his face growing serious. "Appreciate what you did," he adds.

"No sweat," Stryker shrugs, pulling up a chair at the table. "I needed the fucking vacation."

"Yo, bro, we've missed your ass," Linc calls from across the table.

"You missed him hustling pool," Deuce states. "Kid's broke."

"Kiss my ass, Deucey," Linc replies, before turning his attention back to Stryker. "They have a table outside if you feel like making a quick buck," he antagonizes.

"Fuck pool," Wolf says, opening his menu. "I've got this room for the next four hours."

"You really went all out," Pipe proclaims as he butters a piece of bread. "I hear The Knot is hiring if you're looking to hang up your cut and plan weddings and shit."

I chuckle, reaching for my beer, finishing it and signaling the waiter for another.

"Fuck you," Wolf hisses. "You should thank me, if it was up to the rest of these clowns we'd be having cherry pie and fake beer while Blackie and Lacey play footsies under the goddamn table." He points his finger toward Riggs, "And this guy would chase his kitty all over the fucking place."

Wolf drapes an arm around Stryker and reaches for the whiskey again. "Don't you worry, man, Uncle Wolf knows how to throw a party. Part of the reason I reserved the room for four hours was because the girls are due to arrive soon."

"What girls?" Blackie asks.

"My man, Stryker has seen nothing but dick for months. Got him some top notch girls. The pussy on tonight's menu is as prime as the cuts of beef are. You are all pussy whipped fools," Wolf mutters, throwing his other arm around Linc. "Not us. Shit, we ain't going down like that, right boys?"

"Fuck no," Linc agrees.

"Yeah," Stryker mutters, refilling his glass.

I laughed to myself, recalling a time when I said those exact words. It takes just one woman to make you eat those fucking words. I can't wait to watch the other half of this table chow down on them.

Wolf wasn't bullshitting, the cuts of beef were prime and by the time our bellies were full his girls showed up. That was my cue to leave. I grabbed the waiter and gave him my credit card before saying my goodbyes. Blackie and Riggs followed me out of the steakhouse but once we straddled our bikes, we went our separate ways.

With the wind at my back I rode my Harley home to my woman. I miss having Reina on the back of my bike, her arms wrapped tightly around me, her thighs molded to mine as her tits press against my back but there was no way I would let her ride while she was pregnant. I'm not taking any fucking chances. Way too much precious cargo.

I pull into the driveway, kill my engine and turn off the lights. I hang my helmet on my handlebars before striding toward my house. I stare at the front door, waiting for Reina to pull it open and greet me with a smile like she usually does when she hears my pipes wake the neighborhood. I reach the top step but the door doesn't open causing me to pick up my pace and reach for my keys.

"Reina," I holler, kicking open the door.

I followed the sound of the television and step into the living room just as she stands from the couch and turns to face me.

"Jack," she murmurs, swallowing as her eyes work me over. Her teeth dig into her bottom lip as she cautiously steps to me.

"What's going on, Reina?" I question, sensing she's off. The woman is as jittery as a fucking virgin on her wedding night. Her fucking hormones have got her head spinning all the time and I'm the one getting whiplash. Then there's the wedding, she's breaking my balls left and right to keep things simple but drags my ass to a cake tasting thing.

I follow the path her eyes take as I close the distance between us and focus on the television.

"It's on every channel," she says, taking my hand and lacing our fingers together. I stare at Vic's mug shot on the screen and reach for the remote, raising the volume as my eyes follow the ticker on the bottom.

If you're just joining us, a riot has broken out in Bennettsville Federal Prison. The prison is on lockdown and the riot squad is trying to get control of the situation. We have confirmation that several inmates have been injured and at least two fatalities. Earlier this morning, New York City's convicted mob boss, Victor Pastore, transferred to Bennettsville from Otisville. We have since learned the infamous mobster has been battling lung cancer. There has been no word on whether Pastore was involved in the riot.

"Jack?"

I slump down, dropping onto the coffee table as I stare at the chaos on the television, I feel Reina behind me. She places her hands on my shoulders and begins to knead them with her fingers, her eyes glued to the screen like mine.

"You don't think..." her words fade as the screen changes and another mug shot fills the frame.

Motherfucker.

We just got word in that another inmate in Bennettsville is a rival of Pastore's, the notorious gang leader, Thomas Gregorio, who is known by most as the G-Man.

Staring into the eyes of the G-Man, I realize how long it's been since I've seen a photograph of the man who took so much from all of us, mainly our dignity. Like the rest of us he has aged, but instead of focusing on the lines that mark his skin I stare at the three tear drops strategically placed beneath his eyes.

I clench my fists as I lean forward, lost in my head as I stare into the eyes of the enemy.

"Who is that?" she asks. I don't answer until she steps in front of the television and presses her finger under my chin, forcing me to meet her worried gaze. "Jack, who is that man on the television?"

I shake my head trying to clear the cloud of anger invading it and stand on my feet.

"Nobody, I've got to get to the clubhouse," I tell her, my eyes finally finding hers and I can see the storm brewing inside them.

"I'm coming with you," she insists, crossing her arms under her chest. Woman's going to be my death—not a bad way to go. I take her face in my hands, her lips purse and I slam my mouth down on the perfect little 'O' they form, erasing it from my view. My tongue glides across her lower lip as she works her pout into a tight line, denying me her mouth until I give into her. She pushes against my chest but I hang onto her face and reel her mouth back to mine, pushing my tongue into her mouth and claiming the lightness she possesses, knowing that shit's about to get dark for me.

She snakes her arms around my neck, leans on her tiptoes as the swell of her belly presses against mine.

"I'm coming with you, Parrish," she murmurs against my mouth. "Those eyes of yours are raging," she whispers, inching further away from me.

I drop my hands from her face and my fingers pinch her hips before gently sliding my palms over her stomach. I'm about to argue, tell her I need her home where she is safe, but the truth is the only place Reina is safe is in my arms.

"Fine, but we're taking the truck," I say sternly.

"Whatever you want, Bulldog," she purrs, kissing my lips quickly.

RIGGS

First, I'll take Kitten quick and hard against the wall or maybe the door, depending on where she is when I get home. If she's in the kitchen, I'm getting all Godfather on her ass and flinging everything off the kitchen table and spreading her out like an Italian Sunday dinner.

The Italians are rubbing off on me.

I'm about to park my bike in front of our building and my phone buzzes inside my jacket. I throw one leg over the seat, adjust my aching balls, before reaching inside my pocket for my phone.

"Kitten, I'm coming, well, not yet but why don't you save us some time and strip. I'm walking into the building."

"Riggs, I'm coming down the stairs. We need to get to Anthony's," she says in a hurry. "Come on, baby, Mommy's got you," she purrs to our son, shifting the phone as she comes bounding down the stairs, holding him at her hip.

Color me stupid, but I stare at her dumbfounded as I disconnect the call.

"What? No sex?"

She blows the hair away from her face as she narrows those baby blues at me.

"Shit, did I say that out loud?"

"Yeah, yeah, you did," she sneers. "You don't know do you?"

"Know what?" I ask, taking Eric from her arms as she pushes her sexy as fuck glasses up the bridge of her nose. I know I'm fucking horny and if Kitten keeps taunting me with her glasses, she's going to know too. Oh, fuck, who am I kidding? She fucking knows.

"Victor's all over the news," she explains, pulling open the door. "There is a riot in his prison and no one knows if he's dead or alive," she continues, lifting her eyes to mine. "I called my brother, Adrianna was hysterical."

Fucking, Victor, always ruining my good time.

I take Lauren's hand, pull her against my side as I balance Eric on my hip with my other hand and level her with a knowing look.

"And you want to go over there to see if there is anything we can do," I surmise.

"Yes.".

Then, let's go, Kitten." I press my lips to the top of her head.

Family's important to Lauren, it's everything to her and she is everything to me. My dick can wait. Not long, but it can wait. Here's to hoping this shit with 'Tony Soprano' doesn't drag all night.

Who was I kidding?

This shit's just getting started.

Chapter Twenty-Nine

BLACKIE

I flick the switch, lighting up the empty clubhouse as my gaze travels around the room and lingers on the stocked shelves behind the bar. I shove my hands into my pockets and pull out the sobriety chip burning a hole against the denim. Dropping the chip from one hand into another, my boots pound against the wooden floor and drag me straight to the hell that's taunting me. Methodically, I reach under the bar for a clean glass and a handful of ice I dump into the glass, filling it to the rim. I turn around and lean my back against the bar and stare at the shelves, my eyes travel from bottle to bottle, skipping the glimpses of my reflection that shine in-between the bottles before I settle on a bottle of Jack.

I unscrew the top and pour the amber liquid into the glass before setting the bottle back in its rightful spot. With the glass in my hand I walk around the bar, take a seat at one of the tables and lift my eyes to the empty chair across from me.

Not that long ago I sat in this very seat across from Jimmy Gold with a needle full of heroin and threw my sobriety to the gutter, yet it seemed like it was a lifetime ago. I twirl the glass watching as the alcohol dances over the rim and drips onto my hand. Placing the glass down, I swipe my hand along the front of my shirt before leaning against the back of the chair.

Pieces of a puzzle taunt my mind. Charlie's face, the Corrupt Bastards, Ronan, fucking Brantley, they are all part of this thing I'm trying to put together. I've been beating myself up for days but no matter how much I rack my brain to figure the common thread, I come up empty.

The last time we flew blind all hell broke loose.

I got hooked on the shit, turned into the devil himself and along with hurting myself I hurt Lacey.

Reina got kidnapped and Jack lost his fucking mind.

It all spiraled out of control, with no end in sight. Even with Jimmy rotting in jail, our club was still hurting with a threat we didn't foresee. We lost Bones, Riggs watched his girl nearly die and his kid fight for life, all while knowing we were burying his brother.

I won't let that shit happen to us again.

I've got too much to lose, a precious life to protect—I've got Lace.

For the first time we all have something to lose, something that means more than the reaper on our backs, and that scares the fuck out of me.

I didn't hear the door open, but I knew I was no longer alone. The scent of Lacey cut through my senses like a razor, pulling me out of my head and the devilish whiskey I was staring at. I turn my head, listening as her boots tap against the floor.

Always saving me, girl.

Her leather boots come into my line of vision and slowly I let my eyes sweep over her. First, I see the knee-high boots, my favorite thing she owned. Then I take in the pants painted onto her legs, pausing at the piercing that dangles from her belly button before allowing my gaze to linger over the Rolling Stones tank she wore knotted under her tits.

Goddamn girl.

Whiskey doesn't compare to the high that sinking into Lace takes me to.

Nothing compares to her.

"I thought I'd find you here," she says, taking a step closer, then another. Three until she has me pushing back my chair and climbing onto my lap.

My hand closes over her knee, sliding up her thigh as I peer at her through the hair hanging over my eyes. Her dark eyes, full of life and light find mine as she threads her fingers through my hair and away from my face.

I silently vow to keep that light in those eyes.

I won't let anyone dull her shine.

No threat, no enemy and sure as hell not me and my addictions.

She averts her gaze toward the glass sitting offensively on the table, threatening to ruin our rewrite.

"Plot twist?" she questions softly.

I wrap both my arms around her small frame, joining her as she stares at the glass and the watermark forming around the bottom of it.

"I wouldn't have drunk it," I admit.

"Then why pour it?"

She unravels my arms from her waist, reaching for the glass. She stands up and walks to the bar, emptying the glass into the sink. I draw in a ragged breath, my emotions a jumbled mess. I don't need her babysitting me, worrying I'm going to fuck up and tear this thing we got to shreds. I poured the drink hoping if I stared at it long enough, hard enough, I'd remember the pain she's made me forget. I need to remind myself of what it feels like to be at the end of my rope so I can keep climbing it, fitting the pieces of the puzzle with each inch I climb.

I hoped the pain would scare me into discovering the link I was missing, the tiny detail that ties this shit together in a neat little package before it falls, without warning, on our doorstep.

She disappears under the bar, popping her head up a moment later holding two bottles of that non-alcoholic beer Reina keeps stocked in the fridge and makes her way back.

"Keys," she demands, standing in front of me, leaning her ass against the table as she places one bottle on the table and holds out her hand. Lifting my hips, I tug the chain from my belt and hand her the bottle opener attached to it. She pops off the top of the beer she's holding and hands it to me before opening the other for herself.

"Here's to you," I say huskily, touching the neck of my bottle to hers.

"Blackie," she breathes as her hand pauses before the bottle touches her lips. "Do you need to go to a meeting? Why don't you call your sobriety coach?"

I take a gulp of the bitter drink, curling my lip in disgust as it works its way down my throat before placing the bottle on the table beside her. My hands take hold of her hips, my fingers drum across her midriff as I rest my head against her chest.

"Girl, you have no idea, do you?" I mutter against her, pressing my lips against the knot of her shirt and jerk my head back to stare into her confused eyes. "You don't have to worry about me, or my choices, because there is only one choice for me and that's you. Drugs or you—it's you. Booze or you—it's still you. Name any lethal temptation and the answer will be you. Your life or mine—always yours. I choose you, Lace."

Her fingers glide through my hair as she bends her head, rubbing the tip of her nose down the bridge of mine before she showers me with Eskimo kisses.

"Leather and Lace," she whispers, a small smile blossoms across her pouty mouth and instantly I picture those lips around my cock. I grow hard, my dick straining against the zipper of my jeans painfully as her tongue traces her lower lip and her eyes travel mischievously around the empty clubhouse.

"Are we alone?"

"Cobra is floating around here somewhere," I mutter, keeping my gaze pinned to her mouth.

"It's been a while since you bent me over that desk in your room," she teases.

"Never bent you over my desk, Lace, I fucked you right on top of it," I growl, pulling back from her. I stand tall, towering over her as I brace my hands against the edge of the table and box her into my arms.

"You want to rewrite that scene too, girl?"

"I don't know," she says quietly, gnawing on her lip. "You're looking kind of tired," she goads, knowing exactly what buttons to push. When your girl is thirteen years younger than you, you make sure your stamina is on point. I take the beer bottle from her hand, set it down beside mine and in one quick motion I lift her over my shoulder.

"Not even a little, and you're keeping the fucking boots on," I order as I climb the stairs and my hands glide over her ass, squeezing it.

"Why do you think I wore them?" she taunts.

All my worries fade away, consumed by the feral need burning inside of me to be one with my girl. I open the door to my room, kick it closed, and as I walk us to my desk I try to remember the last time I stayed here, but for the life of me I can't.

I gently set Lacey on top of the old wooden piece of furniture, grab one of her legs and extend it, resting the sole of her boot against my chest as I work the zipper down the leather covering her leg. She braces her hands on the edge of the desk as she watches me remove one boot and then the other. Clutching them in my fist I jerk my chin and eye the leggings she's wearing.

"Undress for me, girl," I coax. "Show me what you got."

"What about the boots? I thought you wanted me to keep them on," she says coyly, looping her thumbs under the waistband of her pants.

"Undress for me, girl," I repeat, pulling out the chair in front of the desk flipping it over so I straddle the back of it. Still holding onto her boots, I prop my chin on the back of the chair and watch as she slides off the desk, peeling the pants off her legs.

"Goddamn, girl," I groan as she kicks off her pants and spins around. Her lingerie game is on point as she shows off the little number she was hiding under her clothes. I watch as she grabs onto the desk, glancing over her shoulder as she bends over and gives me a view of the G-string tucked between the cheeks of her ass.

"Take it off," I growl.

She turns around again, eyes on me as she pushes the lace down her legs.

"This what you want, Blackie?" she asks, her breath hitching as she leans against the desk.

"It's a start," I rasp, handing her the boots. "Now, girl, dress for me," I say, swallowing as my dick rubs painfully against my jeans, begging to be free. I reach down and run my palm over myself as she extends one leg, slides her foot into the boot and works the leather over her calf. She's got that gleam in her eyes, that look she gets when she's feeling brazen.

That look that brings me to my fucking knees every goddamn time.

With one boot on, the other in her hand, she widens her legs, exposing her sleek pussy to me, teasing me, taunting me—fucking testing my control.

Careful, girl.

She snaps her legs shut, her thighs clench, and she closes her eyes for a moment before they open wide and she fixes me with a look.

Control still intact, hers teetering, she pulls on her other boot and quickly draws the zipper up her leg. Placing both hands on her knees, she opens and closes her legs as she peers at me through her eyelashes.

"Now what, Leather?"

I rise from the chair, reach behind me and pull my shirt over my head and toss it across the room. I shove the chair to the side as I unbutton my jeans, carefully unzipping them, all the while I keep my eyes on her beautiful face.

"Now, I fuck you, just as hard as the first time I had your legs spread on this desk. The only difference this time is you'll be coming just as fucking hard as I do." Kicking off my jeans I close my hand around my shaft. My cock twitches as I watch her lick her lips and her eyes dip below my waist.

I run my thumb over the head, wiping away the wetness from the tip as she reaches out and grabs a hold of my wrist. Tugging me toward her, she presses my wet thumb between her legs and grinds against me.

My control snaps and I stand between her legs. Taking a fistful of her hair I urge her head back and her body arches against me, dark eyes bore into mine.

"Wrap those legs around me, girl," I rasp. "Dig those heels into my back," I ground out.

"Pain," she whispers.

I press my lips to hers, take her lower lip between my teeth and tug gently before swiping my tongue over the sting easing the ache.

"Just pleasure," my words whisper across her lips, reassuring her, reminding her where there is pain there is pleasure. For she is the one who showed me— wherever there was pain in my life, she came and brought me pleasure.

Her legs wrap around me as I move my hips back and slam forcefully and deeply inside her, touching her in places she didn't even know existed. Hearing her gasp, I pause, gathering whatever control I have left and give her a moment to adjust to having me completely invade her. Her heels dig into my ass as her body arches. Her ass slides to the edge of the desk, urging me to continue, to stretch and fill her, to fuck her hard and deep, to rewrite the first time I had her on this desk and feel her come all over my cock.

Sweat drips from my forehead onto her shoulder as I work my hips, gliding my cock in and out of her tight pussy. I struggle to control my rhythm but she makes it hard, clawing at my skin, grinding herself against me, desperate for the high I'm going to give her. There are no words spoken between us, the only sounds are our ragged breaths and the slap of skin on skin.

"Give it to me, Blackie," she cries, grabbing my face. She peers at me through hooded eyes, through the hair that hangs wildly over my eyes, finds my soul and soothes it like only she can.

One look.

That's all it takes for her to take the reins and make me hers.

I thumb her clit, stroke it to the beat of our song playing inside my head, ringing in my ears.

Knew with you to light my night.
Somehow, I'd get by.

"Get it, girl," I ground out, thrusting myself as deep as I can, watching in awe as she throws her head back. My name sounds like a prayer when it escapes her lips.

"So fucking pretty," I murmur as I push deeper, her body clenches all around me and I lose myself buried deep inside the sweet nirvana that is Lace.

Pleasure blinds me as I chase the high she brings, dragging me to bliss—a peaceful place where she's all I need in this world to get by.

A place I never want to leave.

A place where nothing else matters.

Not even mayhem.

Not even the reaper.

Chapter Thirty

ANTHONY

"*This is Ben Lithmore, and I am live in front of Bennettsville prison where a riot has broken out resulting in the prison being placed on lockdown. We have just received word that two of New York's most notorious criminals were recently transferred to Bennettsville. Convicted mob boss, Victor Pastore, and gang leader, Thomas 'the G-Man' Gregorio, both serving life sentences are inside the prison. We learned earlier that Pastore has been suffering from cancer and was transferred here to Bennettsville for medical purposes. There is no information on why the G-Man was transferred or his condition at this time. There are reports that several inmates and correctional officers have sustained injuries and at least two fatalities. At this time, we have no confirmation of bodies.*"

"Shut it off," Grace demands, her tear stained face frozen as she stares at the television.

I walk over to the television, bend down and power it off before rising and glancing around Vic and Grace's living room. My mother-in-law continues to stare at the blank screen in shock. Watching the usual poise my mother-in-law portrays diminish from her was torturous and nerve-racking all at the same time.

She knew about the transfer, she knew what her husband was going to do, we all did, but none of us expected this. I figured it would be quiet, like when he whacked Jimmy inside Otisville, not a fucking media frenzy. I didn't think we'd be sitting here watching the news waiting for a reporter to declare him dead or alive.

Grace stood, but before she could make a move, Nikki stood in front of her and grabbed her hands.

"Let go," Grace orders. "I'm fine."

"You're not," Nikki argues as Adrianna walks into the living room with the phone glued to her ear.

"Okay, thank you," she says before disconnecting the call. "That was daddy's lawyer," she announces to the room. "He still hasn't heard anything, but he promises to call as soon as he does."

"So what're we supposed to do until then? Sit here like a bunch of idiots waiting for some stiff in a suit to call us and let us know if we call the funeral home or not?" Gina shouts.

"You really think that's helping?" Mike fires back.

"Nothing is helping! We're sitting here while the media plays games with us," she argues back. "My ninety-five-year-old mother has to watch this shit and wonder if her son is dead."

"Take her upstairs if it's too much for you people," Nikki sneers.

"Princess—"

"No, Mikey. Everyone wants to feel some kind of way but they forget we're his family too." She averts her eyes to her aunt. "That's my mother's husband, our father," she adds, pointing between her and her sister. "And while Nana may be upset so are we, we're the ones who will call a funeral director—not you."

"No one's calling anyone," I interrupt. "You all need to have faith in the man who's hung onto life this long," I clip, lifting my head as the doorbell rings. "Think about Vic, do any of you really think for one second he will go down like this? At the mercy of another man?" I shake my head. "Have faith in the man who only does things one way—his."

I point a finger to Grace.

"You know better than anyone," I remind her as I start for the door. It rings again as I pull it open and my sister throws her arms around my neck. I wrap my arms around her and turn my gaze to the leather clad man standing behind her.

"Any word on the big guy?" Riggs asks.

"No, and they're all losing their shit in there," I mutter, glancing over my shoulder.

"Have no fear, Riggsy is here," he says, stepping around Lauren and raising his hands holding a box from the bakery.

"What's he doing?" I question my sister.

"We brought cannoli's." She winks, taking my hand and pulling me into the house.

"How you doin' 'Mrs. Soprano'?" Riggs asks, bending down to take Grace's hand and kisses her ring, mimicking a scene from *The Godfather*.

"Who's this?" Gina curiously croons.

"She's all yours man," Mike says, getting the hell out of dodge.

Returning Lauren's embrace, the phone Adrianna is holding rings, forcing them apart.

"It's the lawyer," she says glancing at the screen.

Noting the fear working across her features, I close the distance between us and take the phone from her trembling hand and swipe my thumb across the screen.

"It's Bianci," I answer.

"He's alive."

"And?"

"He did it."

"How?"

"With a pair of scissors and apparently a riot."

"Thank you," I say, closing my eyes briefly.

"He's in solitary. Give the media twenty minutes and that shit will be all over the news," he sighs. "It's over, that's it, Bianci. Vic ain't going to see the light of day anymore. The next call is the one we're dreading."

"I know." I clear my throat, lifting my eyes to the room and the expectant glances of the people who loved Victor Pastore. "Thanks for calling," I say, ending the call.

"Well?" Grace croaks.

"He's alive."

"Thank God," she cries, grabbing a hold of her daughters and hugging them to her. "He's alive," she smiles, closing her eyes.

A phone rings; I glance at the one I'm holding not realizing the sound is coming from across the room. Riggs lifts his phone to his ear, walking toward the kitchen and away from everyone to take the call.

Mike turns the television on again and the scene outside the prison fills the screen. The SWAT team pulls correctional officers and medical personnel from the building before charging in with machine guns. It didn't take twenty minutes for the media to get the information and the reporter's voice booms over the images.

"We can now confirm that the G-Man is one of the casualties. Wait a minute," he pauses, lifting his hand to the earpiece, he remains silent until his eyes widen and he tells the world what we already know. *"We can also confirm that mob boss, Victor Pastore, is alive. I repeat, Victor Pastore is alive. However, we don't know what started this riot here in Bennettsville or the cause of death of the G-Man."*

"Kitten, give me a kiss, I gotta' go," Riggs announces, tucking his phone into his cut before lifting his eyes to mine and tipping his chin. "You coming, Bianci, or what?"

Adrianna pulls out of her mother's arms, spinning around to pierce me with a worried look. I avert my eyes to Riggs, watching as he squeezes my sister's ass in front of everyone, kissing her quickly before lifting his head and snapping his fingers.

"Chop, chop, bro, Jack's waiting," he orders, pausing in front of Grace. "Keep the cannoli's." He winks at her.

"Be careful, Riggs," Lauren calls, biting her lip nervously as her eyes find mine.

"Mike," I ground out. Frustrated, I ran my fingers roughly through my hair, torn between sitting vigil like I probably should and running with Riggs to see where Jack was at with this.

"Yeah," he says, stepping beside me.

"You got this?" I question pinning him with a stare, watching intently as he glances over his shoulder at the women I was asking him to watch over.

"I've got Grace, Nikki, Adrianna and your sister but I ain't making promises about Gina." He narrows his eyes glancing around. "Where'd the old lady go?" he shrugs his shoulders and meets my intense gaze. "I've got this, they're just as much mine as they are yours," he declares.

"Good answer, Mike," I tell him, patting him on the back as I brush past him and pull Adrianna toward me.

"You still going to deny wanting a Harley and a leather jacket?" she whispers, staring up at me, cocking one perfectly sculpted eyebrow.

"I'm going to tell Jack what he's been waiting to hear then I will take you home." I covered her mouth with mine. "Make sure the kids are sleeping when I get back and I'll give you a better ride than any Harley ever could."

"Promise?"

"Reese's, I swear it." I promise her.

"You mob folk move too slow," Riggs complains, rolling his eyes as he waits for me by the front door. I let go of my wife, turn my gaze to Riggs and stab him with a glare.

"Let's go, badass," I hiss, slapping him upside the head as I walk past him.

It wasn't until we were in Riggs' truck, peeling out of Grace and Victor's driveway, when he broke the news to me.

"Jack's in Bulldog mode," he says, stepping on the gas.

"Did you tell him Vic was alive, and the hit was done?"

"Couldn't get a word in between the growling, cursing and the seven times he asked me where the fuck Blackie was. Like I'm that son of a bitch's keeper or something," he sneers. "Why the hell do you think I brought you along? You can give him the news about Vic while I go find Blackie and pull him off Lacey before Jack shoots him and I have to bury his body."

Ten minutes later we are pulling into the Dog Pound, parking the truck next to the ten or so motorcycles that line the front of the building. The overhead lights are on illuminating the property, signaling the clubhouse was very much alive and on high alert.

"Remember the plan," Riggs hisses, pulling open the door.

"Riggs, it's all over television, they gotta know by now…" My words trail off as we enter the clubhouse and the television is blasting the confirmation that Vic was alive and the G-Man was dead.

"Shit," Riggs mutters.

Jack turns his gaze to us, looking over Riggs' shoulder.

"Looks like our man Vic got the job done," Jack says pointedly.

"Did you have any doubt?" I counter, shoving my hands into my pockets. There is a lot to be said about Vic. I myself, have put labels on the man but no one can deny he was a man of his word when it came to business.

Like everything else, Vic's last hit was just as epic as his life.

"Church," Jack bellows. "Now."

Staring at Jack, another powerful ruler, I cross my arms against my chest, watching as his men, dressed in leather, file into their chapel on command. I took in the way his jaw was clenched, the storm plowing through his eyes and his hands balled into tight fists.

The difference between him and Vic was obvious to my eyes. Vic was a mystery, you never knew which way he was going, what he was thinking, he was calm and cool always, but Jack wore his torment on his sleeve. When the shit was about to hit the fan, everyone knew because he morphed before your very eyes into the Bulldog. His anguish, his anger, his torment was just as visible as the patch sewn into his cut, declaring him the president.

Riggs reappeared, coming down the stairs with Blackie following behind him, fitting his arms through the sleeves of his shirt.

"Fucking hell," Jack seethes.

"Jack," Reina scolds, giving a slight shake of her head.

"What happened?" Blackie questions, ignoring Jack and looking to the plasma screen hanging over the bar.

"We are live in front of Bennettsville Federal Prison with the warden, Richard Olsen. Warden, can you give us an update on the situation?"

"As you have already reported there have been two casualties. I can now disclose the names of the two inmates who have died. One is, Owen Richards, and the other is Thomas Gregorio also known as the G-Man. The riot squad is

diligently working to secure all inmates back to their cells and safely remove the correctional officers that were on active duty when the riot broke out."

"There is a lot of talk about Mr. Pastore and the G-Man being rivals, can you comment?"

"We have apprehended Mr. Pastore and have brought him into solitary. That is all the information we have at this time."

"It's over," Blackie says, eyes glued to the screen.

"It's just getting started, brother," Jack corrects. "Chapel. Now," he orders, before pointing a finger at me. "You. Stay here. Don't fucking move, Bianci."

I glance around the room, spot Reina and Lacey in the corner.

I left my women to sit with Jack's women.

What the fuck?

I step around the bar, snatch a bottle of bourbon and take a seat at the bar. Lifting my eyes and my glass to the mug shot plastered on the television.

"Here's to you, Vic," I toast, throwing back the shot.

Victor Pastore.

The mobster.

The legend.

Chapter Thirty-One

JACK

"He's fucking gone," Blackie comments beside me, glancing down at his left hand, rubbing his thumb over the spot on is finger a wedding band once lived. Slowly, cautiously, his eyes lift and turn to me. "It's over," he repeats. "That motherfucker can't touch another soul."

I bit the inside of my cheek as I studied him, trying to figure out if he was asking me or telling me. Not having the heart to burst his bubble I let him hang on to the retribution Vic has given him by killing the G-Man a little longer and turn my gaze to the other end of the table.

If they were still drunk from the restaurant, they hid it well with the attentive stares they fed me.

"Where's Stryker?" I question, tipping my chin to the empty chair in the corner.

"He went home with some broad," Linc answers. "Been calling him but his phone is off."

"He didn't have a chance to charge it. I took it from him from the can to the restaurant," Wolf explains, averting his eyes back to me. "We'll clue him in but why don't you do us all a favor and clue *us* in."

"Riggs, pull up the G-Man's mug shot," I order, leaning back in my chair, stealing a glimpse of Blackie out of the corner of my eye. His eyes were still transfixed on his ring finger but slowly he comes around, turning those tortured eyes onto me.

"You're fucking kidding me, right?" Riggs screeches, sliding his phone across the table at me. "That ain't no coincidence, Prez."

Leaning forward, I reach for the phone but Blackie beats me to it, closing his paw over the iPhone, flipping it over to stare at the G-Man's photo. Many of us had a lot riding on Vic getting the job done, we were banking on it to clear our consciences, but for Blackie it was closure on Christine's death. With the G-Man gone, Christine could finally rest easy in his eyes and the burden of guilt would lessen for him too.

"I fucking knew it," Blackie spits, dropping the phone onto the table before viciously raking his fingers through his hair. "I've been beating myself up, driving myself mad trying to figure out what the fuck Charlie had up his sleeve."

"You two assholes better start talking," Pipe grunts.

"We've been trying to piece together Charlie Teardrop's connection to Brantley and where his bank roll has been coming from," I recap.

"Sending that schmuck into the Bastard's clubhouse turned out to be a dead end," Riggs adds. "He cries as much to them as he does to us, always looking for a handout."

I turn the screen toward everyone sitting at the table and enlarge the image of the G-Man's mugshot.

"Three teardrops," I reveal, passing the phone to Pipe for a better look. "Just like Charlie's."

"What're you saying, Bulldog? This motherfucker built his club while being backed by the G-Man?"

"That's exactly what he's saying," Blackie answers for me. "The G-Man funded the rebirth of the Corrupt Bastards which means he planned something with Charlie, something big, something that would give him control over every operation we've taken from him."

"This can go one of two ways," I begin. "Either Charlie will pull a Jimmy Gold, and take control over all the G-Man's assets and operations, go buck wild and get high on power, trying to turn these streets into his. Or, he will avenge his ally's death because the G-Man dying wasn't part of his plan."

"Either way, we're fucked. Charlie and his club will be pushing in on our territory," Pipe finishes.

"Everything we've buried over the years working with Vic will be resurrected. The drugs will pollute the streets, our streets, and the body count will double in size. I've lost one woman, got the blood of a bunch of innocent kids on my hands, not looking for anymore grief, Jack," Blackie protests, clenching his fists as he closes his eyes and tries to gather his composure.

"Wait a minute," Wolf demands, slapping the palm of his hand against the wood of the table. "Wait just a goddamn minute. The mob took out the G-Man, Pastore whacked that son of bitch, not us. How can we be so sure this cocksucker will retaliate against the club? This shit ain't our gig."

"You're forgetting, Vic didn't just avenge his underboss' death by killing the G-Man, he avenged Christine's too. He made that motherfucker pay for every fucking funeral we were responsible for under Cain's ruling," Blackie rasps, pushing his hair away from his face.

"Even if we're not the target Vic's family most definitely will be," Pipe says pointedly. "And as much as I hate playing nice with them Italians, Vic did what he promised he'd do. He was as loyal to our club as any of us that wear a patch," he huffs, turning his gaze back to me. "So is that poor bastard outside this door."

"You're giving Charlie too much credit. I don't think the cocksucker knows jack shit about us being in cahoots with Vic on the hit."

"If I was Charlie, I'd want to make a play, a move that both avenged the G-Man's death and gained me control," Blackie says, not paying attention to anyone as he works out the thoughts in his head. The room grows silent and we all watch as his eyes narrow and stare blankly at the table. "I'd look for the common link between the club standing in my way and the organization that killed my ally," he continues, raising his head and piercing me with a look.

Glancing around the table, Blackie's words slowly sink in, not only for me but for everyone sitting around this table, everyone except Riggs.

"Why don't I go grab our boy Ronan, send him into the clubhouse to see what the fuck is going on?" Riggs starts as he fiddles with his phone. "Throw that bitch into the fire and see if he comes back with any intel. If the Bastards are looking to strike, their clubhouse will be up in arms with the news coming in that their boy was murdered."

We remained silent, causing his head to lift and his eyes to scan all of our grim faces.

"What? Did I miss something?"

"If I was Charlie, I know exactly who I'd go after," Blackie continues gravely.

"Me?" Riggs screeches. "What the fuck do I have to do with any of this? No offense guys but this shit you're talking about went down before my balls even dropped!" He shouts incredulously.

"You married the mob, boy," Pipe mutters. "Black's right, this is all you, brother."

Riggs' shoulders slump as he shakes his head in disbelief. It doesn't take him long to snap, something wild born in his eyes as he glares at me.

"Tell me what to do," he growls.

"Relax, brother," I try to calm him down, but he slams his fist against the table and rises to his full height, knocking over the chair he was sitting in.

Don't fucking tell me to relax," he shouts, pointing a finger to Blackie. "You lost your wife over this shit and I'm sorry, man, real fucking sorry but I almost lost my Kitten and my kid too. I lost fucking Bones. My people did their fucking time for this club. I won't let anyone else I love hurt over the fucking patch on my cut."

He swallows hard, his jaw ticking with anger as he glares at me.

"Tell me what to do, Jack," he insists. "Tell me how I keep them safe from this hell we all chose."

Leaning forward, I plant my elbows on top of the table and rub my hands along the scruff covering my face.

"Tell me!" He shouts. "Or so fucking help me, Jesus, I will just start fucking shooting them motherfuckers until their threats don't exist, until their blood pours out and their bodies turn cold. Tell me!"

"Time to make nice with the oil diggers, Richie Rich," I mutter, pulling my hands away from my face. "You pack up Lauren and the kid and get the fuck out of here until I or any one of the men at this table tell you it is safe for them to come back here."

"Are you serious?"

"Dead serious." I nod.

"And the rest of them?" He questions. "Bianci's family, what about them?"

Pulling off his hat, he throws it onto the table and points to the door.

"You put me on that man out there, told me to protect him and his family," he argues.

"I will handle it," I say, giving him my word, turning my attention to the nomads across the table. "One of you go grab Ronan, send him to the Bastards and see what he comes up with. The rest of you, eyes open—wide fucking open," I grunt before looking back at Riggs. "Call the folks, Riggs, and whatever you need to do to get your family out of here you let us know and we'll make it happen. But before you do that, go get your brother-in-law so we can fill him in." I slam down the gavel.

The chairs scrap against the floor as everyone, except Blackie, solemnly move to file out of the room.

"Bianci," Riggs calls from the doorway. "Get your ass in here."

Bottle in hand, Bianci strolls in and takes a seat across the table from me.

"You rang?" he questions, narrowing his eyes as Riggs sits to his left and swipes the bottle out of his hand, guzzling bourbon as if it would erase everything we told him.

Bianci keeps his concentration on Riggs as I proceed to tell him what we suspect will happen with the Corrupt Bastards, and to my surprise he doesn't even flinch at my words.

He grabs the bottle from Riggs and taps his hand on the table, demanding his brother-in-law's attention.

"You do as he tells you, take Lauren and Eric to your parents' house and you wait it out. You stick to her and that boy like glue and don't let anyone fucking near them," he says, not as a threat but as his brother-in-law, as his family.

"You hear me?" he questions.

"I hear you," Riggs assures, taking another swig from the bottle.

I watch as Anthony nods his head, accepting Riggs' vow to keep his sister and nephew safe before he turns his cold blue eyes to me.

Fucking Ice, no, glaciers, stare back at me like this is my fucking fault.

"Appreciate the heads up but I ain't the one who should be sitting at this table with you and we both know that."

I hold his gaze as I pull a toothpick out of my cut and shove it between my teeth.

He's right but I'm not ready to break bread with Rocco Spinelli.

"Victor knew this would happen, he prepared for it by putting Rocco in charge of his organization. Now, you need to respect that and get on board before you have a blood bath on your hands, one you can avoid," he informs, leaning back in his chair as he shrugs his shoulders. "Since, I'm so good at being the go-between, I'll take you to the boss."

Leaning into Riggs, he pulls the bottle from his hand and takes a hefty gulp of the poison, cringing as it burns his throat. He tips the bottle toward me and swallows.

"But motherfucker you're driving because I'm wrecked," he declares, throwing back his head as he takes another shot.

Blackie turns to me.

"This how we gonna play this?" he whispers harshly. "I know I said I was all for you giving this guy a chance, but now, at this particular moment, I'm not sure I want to entrust this to him," he admits.

"Rocco may have learned how to be a boss from Victor but he's going to learn how to lead from me," I declare, pushing back my chair and standing up. "Let's go, Bianci," I order, pointing to Blackie. "You take Reina and Lacey home," I say then turn to Riggs. "Make the call, pretty boy," I tell him one last time before following Bianci out of the chapel.

Reina's worried glance is the first thing I see when I step into the common room, followed by my daughter's fearful eyes that are pinned to the man behind me.

I grab Reina's hand, pull her against me and snake my arms around her waist.

"I've got to head out. Blackie is going to take you and Lacey home and when I'm done I'll come home," I tell her, pushing her blonde hair over her shoulder. "Don't look at me like that, Sunshine…everything's all good," I lie.

"Parrish, I know that look and *you*…it's not fine."

"It will be, I promise."

Reluctantly she stares back at me as I bend my head to kiss her but her mouth doesn't respond and I lean back to better assess her, watching as she chews on her lower lip nervously.

Oh, hell.

"Maybe we should postpone the wedding," she suggests, biting back the frown that's fighting her mouth.

Without hesitation, I take her face in my hands, bending my knees to be eye level with her, I shake my head.

"Listen here, Sunshine, ain't nothing stopping me from marrying you," I vow, determination laced heavily with every word. "Not a thing," I repeat.

"As long as you're sure," she says softly, closing her hands around my wrists before touching her lips to mine.

"Never been sure of anything in my life but I'm sure as hell marrying you."

And I was.

Come hell or high water.

I was marrying Reina DeCarlo.

Nobody, no war, nothing would stop me from making her property of Parrish.

Except death.

And I'm not dying anytime soon, there's a lot of life left inside this body, a lot of good buried under the bad and I want the chance to give the good to the people who deserve it. Reina, Lacey and that baby I'm going to love, that baby is my second chance.

I kiss Reina again, putting a sliver of that good into it, hoping it's enough to ease her fears. I give Lacey a hug, promise her both men in her life will stay safe and finally, I lock eyes with Blackie.

We got this, brother.

Riggs, Anthony and I drive over the Verrazano Bridge to the Todt Hill section of Staten Island. Bianci instructs me to turn onto Circle Drive and the gated mansion comes into view. Conveniently the front gate is open leading to a winding cobblestone driveway and a massive entryway. I park my truck haphazardly next to the Maserati, leave the engine running but throw it into park before I jump out of the truck.

I slam the brass knocker against the door and ring the bell three times. I count because it's taking forever for Riggs to drag a drunk Bianci out of the truck. The door opens as Riggs gets Bianci to stand upright and I am greeted by Rocco.

"What can I do for you Parrish?" he questions, tugging on the knot of his tie. I study him for a moment, take in the draining look in his eyes, the dark circles beneath them and five o'clock shadow outlining his features.

"Rough night, boss?" I taunt.

"What do you think?" he clips, glancing over his shoulder at Bianci. He's got his eyes pinned to Rocco as he snarls.

"Better be up for the challenge, cuz," he sneers.

"Yeah? What challenge might that be?"

"The one I'm here to deliver to you," I say, interrupting their pissing contest. "Vic put you in charge for a reason Spinelli, more importantly he sent you to my doorstep for one purpose and now that purpose is clear. Vic knew the consequences, fuck, he expected them that's why he made Bianci bring you to my club, it's why he asked me to stand with you and not against you. Vic wanted me to deliver my new ally a message and so, here I am. This city, *my* city, is about to become a fucking war zone now that the G-Man is off the streets. You want a place in my streets, do as I say. Your only job now is to protect Vic's family, not his organization. Nothing else exists except for his wife, your aunt, and your cousins. Forget making scores, climbing the ranks and ordering hits. I'm telling you that shit don't matter. Your sole purpose, your number one priority is making sure everyone in Vic's circle keeps breathing."

He opens his mouth to speak but I lean into him, get in his face and shake my head.

"Nuh uh, boss. You don't get a say. You do as you're told until I tell you otherwise. You want to be the boss then you need to learn what comes first in this world. You need to learn that without heart you ain't worth shit. Your family is your heart and you keep them safe, Spinelli, you keep them fucking breathing or I'll rip you from the streets and send you back to Miami," I seethe. "Welcome to *my* city, Spinelli. If you're a good boy, I'll share it with you."

I don't give him a chance to argue, I don't give him a chance to even respond. I want his actions not his words. Turning around, I grab Bianci's elbow and shove him toward the truck.

"Your wife is going to kick my ass," I mutter.

"Probably," he agrees.

Not probably, Adrianna definitely will have my balls in a knot, that's why Riggs was bringing his brother-in-law to the front door and I was staying in the truck.

Fuck that.

Chapter Thirty-Two

RIGGS

This blows.

I'll say it again, standing here, staring at a fucking stone imagining my best friend is standing in front of me and not in a box six feet under. This fucking blows. I picture him leaning against the stone, his leather cut fitted to his upper body. Rolling a toothpick between his teeth, he crosses his arms against his chest and grills me with his eyes. I vividly see him in my mind shake his head, biting back a smug grin, everything about his demeanor says he is itching to tell me I've gotten myself into another fine mess. But the words never leave his mouth, just like they never did while he was here with me and not living within my head.

No matter how bizarre the situation he never laughed in my face, never so much as judged me. Instead, Bones worked through my shit with me. He talked to me, listened and asked questions. He didn't give me the answers; he gave me his advice, put himself in my shoes and told me what he would do if he was in my situation.

"I fucking hate this," I admit, pulling the baseball cap from my head to drag my fingers through my hair. "I hate that you're not here. I need you to make sense of what the fuck is going on. I need you to help me figure out if I'm doing the right thing...*for them*. Because, I gotta tell you, brother, it doesn't feel right. It don't feel right fleeing town with Kitten and Eric. I'm supposed to trust the club to handle this shit but it should be me. I should be the one slaughtering anyone threatening my family. Fuck," I growl, clenching my fist and punching the palm of my other hand. "I don't even know how the fuck we're involved in this shit. Why my family? Why are they the fucking bullseye? It made sense with Sun Wu, I fucked up but I don't even know this gangbanger. They say it's because hurting Lauren hurts the club and the Pastores, mainly Bianci. I suppose it makes sense." I pause, shaking my head. "It's amazing I used to laugh in the face of fear until that day, the day you went away, the day Eric was born and I almost lost both of them too. I can't fucking lose them. I can't go through that again, wondering if they're going to make it or not, stand by helplessly as some mythical god decides if I'm worthy of having them in my life. No fucking way, man. I'm scared as fuck because you're not here to jump in front of a bullet this time. This time it's all on me to keep them safe. I know I need to own that shit. I know wherever the fuck you are you're calling me a pussy right now and maybe I am. I'm fucking scared. What if I'm not quick enough? What if I unintentionally fuck something up, make a mistake and cost them their lives and me my heart."

I bow my head, staring at the ink on my fingers.

"Do me a solid?" raising my head, I stare at the headstone and clear my throat. "I will do everything in my power to keep Lauren and Eric safe, gonna make you real proud, brother." I pause, swallowing down the lump in my throat. "But, if you could look out for them too, man, well, I'd appreciate it."

Drawing in a deep breath, I fit the baseball cap back onto my head about to shove my hands into my pockets when my phone rings. I pull it out, not recognizing the number and accept the call.

"Talk to me," I say, reaching out to run my fingers over the words carved into his stone, the same words tattooed to my hand.

"Son, I'm glad you called," my old man's voice booms in my ear, causing me to roll my eyes. Fake ass shit.

This morning I called the number on the business card he left behind and when the call went to his voicemail, I hung up. Then I walked into Eric's room, watched him sleep peacefully and fucking dialed my old man again, leaving a message the second time.

"Yeah, listen, why don't we skip the pleasantries and all that bullshit," I clip. "I got a proposition for you, old man. You like propositions, don't you?"

He doesn't answer me right away and I struggle not to hang up on him.

"I'm listening," he says finally, his voice laced with control as if he was talking to another one of his associates and not his estranged son.

"Time for you to prove if you and that Botox loving mother of mine are sincere," I start, grimacing at the thought of bringing Lauren and Eric near these people. I remind myself of the alternative and continue. "I need to get out of town for a while. I don't know how long but I need a safe place to bring Lauren and Eric."

"Are you in some kind of trouble?"

That's how much he knew about me. Trouble didn't find me; it wasn't something I stumbled upon by mistake, it was my fucking name. He wouldn't get it though and it wasn't worth my spit explaining.

"Nothing I can't handle. I just need to get away with my family for a little bit and figured if you had a genuine bone in your body, this would be the perfect time for you to prove it."

Silence.

How did this guy make multimillion dollar deals when he didn't fucking speak?

"Your mother and I left the city, we're in Martha's Vineyard on a holiday. I will send a car for you, Lisa, and the child."

"Lauren. Her name is Lauren and your grandchild has a name too. In fact, I want you to grab one of your fancy pens and scribble their names on your palm. You know what? Forget it. I'm bringing a fucking Sharpie with me," I snarl.

"Very well…I'm glad you called. I know you didn't want to and whatever is pushing you to do so must be very troublesome to you or you wouldn't have reached out. Still, let's try to make the best of it. I'm excited to spend time with my grandson."

I think about his words for a moment, wonder if they're sincere as a part of me wishes they were. Not for my sake, but for Lauren's. Family is everything to her and even though she doesn't bust my balls to give my folks a second chance, she secretly wishes I do. She thinks I'm missing something, she hasn't realized that the only thing I was missing in life was her and Eric.

"I'll have the car pick you up this afternoon, say, three?"

"Fine, see you," I say, disconnecting the call abruptly, having had enough of the conversation and the thoughts that came along with it.

I step closer to the stone marking Bones' grave and rest my hand on top of it.

"Looks like I'm headed on another detour," I mutter, recalling the day I left my parents' swanky mansion. Bones was sitting in his old beaten and worn pickup truck when I stormed out of the house. His eyes found mine, and he jumped out of the truck, lowered the lift-gate and helped me shove my shit into the bed of the truck.

"You ready?"

I stared at him expectantly, unsure what I was ready for, feeling like a fish out of water.

"Come on, time for you to take a detour," he said with a grin, patting me on the back.

That detour changed my life and took me to the Satan's Knight's clubhouse. The next detour I went on would lead me to my Kitten and Eric. Facing another detour, I couldn't help but wonder what I'd find but, whatever it is I find, I pray it's not grief.

Lauren

"The itsy bitsy spider crawled up the water spout," I sing to Eric as he sits in my lap trying to mimic my hands. "Down came the rain and washed the spider out," I continue watching him drop his hands and shake his head.

"Uh oh, mama!"

Smiling, I stare at my little man in awe, his laugh is intoxicating and I wonder how I ever lived without him. Watching him turn his head to look at me, I don't understand how being a mom was never part of my plan. I always thought I needed a plan, a calculated course of action but the unexpected detour was so much more rewarding. It gave me purpose. Riggs talks about finding heart since he's found me but he's not the only one who found their heart.

"Again, mama!" Eric demands, clapping his chubby hands excitedly.

I laugh, squeezing him a little too tight before I sing again. The door opens and I lift my eyes to see Riggs, watching as he leans his back against the door and stares back at me and our son. The grin I love so much spreads across his lips while his eyes focus on Eric as he tries to make his hands climb the imaginary spout.

Eric's hands drop to his lap as he spots his daddy and scrambles off my lap.

"Dada," he cheers, wobbling his way to Riggs.

"Hey, buddy," Riggs says, bending down to swoop Eric off his feet and raise him high above his head. "How's my boy?"

I love watching them together. An overwhelming sense of pride envelopes me knowing I gave them to one another. Me, I did that, and that's better than any nursing gig I ever could've dreamt of.

"Did you hear me, Kitten?"

Drawing him into focus I lift my eyes and shake my head.

"What did you say?"

"I said," he starts, holding his free hand for me to take and pulls me to my feet. "Pack a bag we're going on a mini vacation."

He laughs when I stare at him like he's lost his mind, for real this time.

"Hurry up, the car will be here within an hour to pick us up."

I stare at him, watching as he calmly strolls around the apartment, pulling the phone charges from the outlet by the counter all the while holding Eric. He moves to the cabinet and pulls out sippy cups, toddler spoons and forks, Eric's favorite Mickey Mouse bowl and places everything alongside the chargers.

"Where is your contact solution and case?"

"You're serious," I accuse.

"Kitten, don't make me light a fire under that tight ass. I won't have you ruining the surprise."

"The surprise," I repeat. He places Eric on his feet and closes the distance between us, cupping my chin with his hand and tilting my head so my eyes are level with his.

"Go with it, Lauren," he says softly as his eyes fall to my lips. "Take the detour," he whispers. His eyes travel back up to mine and he winks. That's all it takes.

"Where are we going?" I question.

"Now, it wouldn't be called a detour if you knew where we were headed, would it?" he bends his head, brushes his lips across mine. "Run away with me," he whispers huskily against my mouth.

He didn't have to ask, I'd always run with him.

Anywhere and everywhere.

An hour later, a chauffeur piled our bags into the trunk of a limousine while Riggs secured Eric's car seat inside. I don't know what brought on the unexpected getaway but I was going to take the detour. Just me and my boys.

Chapter Thirty-Three

Lauren

Just me and my boys—and Mr. and Mrs. Montgomery. The polished couple or former couple, whatever their status, greet us, pulling open the door to the limousine after arriving at their house in Martha's Vineyard.

As far as surprise go, Riggs nailed it. I never saw it coming and I'm not quite sure why we're here since Riggs became tense the moment he stepped out of the car, ignoring his father's hand he extended to him.

"Lauren, welcome," Mr. Montgomery greeted, pinning his son with a sarcastic look as he raised his hand, turning over his palm to reveal my name scribbled on his skin.

Narrowing my eyes, I glance over my shoulder at Riggs, watching as he bites the inside of his cheek and stares daggers at his father. He moves Eric to his other arm and reaches behind him pulling a black Sharpie from the back pocket of his jeans.

"Well played, son," Mr. Montgomery says amused.

"Roger will bring your bags to your room," Lenore announces, making her son turn his gaze to her and lift an eyebrow.

"Roger still works for you? He's gotta be close to eighty, right?"

"It's impossible to find help like him anymore and your mother does love the way he makes a Bloody Mary," Mr. Montgomery adds, smiling at his estranged wife who was sipping on a peppered rimmed glass with a stalk of celery as big as her head popping out of it.

"Please, he can never retire," Lenore admonishes, glancing at Eric for the first time. "Hello there," she fusses. I couldn't tell if it was forced or genuine and neither could my son, turning his face to bury it in Riggs' neck.

"He doesn't like me," she says.

"He doesn't know you," I reply, offering her a small smile when she frowns. "I guess this little getaway will change that though."

I elbow Riggs as he grunts and mumbles under his breath.

"Come on, Eric, I'll show you where Uncle Bones and I used to build forts and pretend we were soldiers," he tells our son, walking past his parents. Reaching the door, he pauses and turns to me. "You too, Kitten."

"Dinner will be at seven," Lenore calls to us as Riggs grabs my hand and pulls me away from his parents.

Dragging me through the mini mansion, Riggs takes off like a bat out of hell. Everything about him screams that he wanted to be anywhere but here, yet this was his idea—his surprise. The fun, easy-going guy I love disappeared and I was left with the part of him I knew very little about.

I dig my heels into the grass once we reach the backyard and force him to turn around and look at me.

"What are you doing?"

"What am I doing?" Widening my eyes, I questioned him. "What in God's name are you doing?"

"Hanging onto what's left of my sanity?" he offers, sighing as he repositions Eric in his arms. "This fucking place makes my skin crawl," he admits, dropping onto one of the lounge chairs and placing Eric on his lap.

"Then why are we here?"

"I thought it would be nice to get away," he says quickly.

Too quickly.

"The truth, Riggs," I demand softly, crossing my arms under my chest as I take in the scenery, the rolling greens, the pool that sits gated to the left of the property and the custom built bar and grill area across from it. It's beautiful here, the perfect getaway for a family yet the memories I can see us making aren't the type of memories Riggs has of this place.

"We used to come here every summer," he starts. "My father would lock himself away in his office and my mother would bang her tennis coach," he sneers. "She'd come home from the country club and they'd fight. He'd accuse her, she'd deny it—they'd scream for hours. Bones' mom would take us out here and we'd play for hours, pretend we were soldiers fighting against the bad guys. By the time the sun went down, my father was gone and my mother was sitting in her room nursing one of those Bloody Mary's she likes so much."

"I'm sorry," I say, sitting beside him on the chaise lounge.

"Seeing them like this, pretending the last twenty-five years didn't happen is fucking driving me insane," he grimaces, placing a kiss to Eric's head. "Sorry, I meant to say ducking."

"They don't seem at odds now," I say thoughtfully. "Maybe they've made peace."

His gaze turns soft as he props his chin on Eric's head and stares at me. There was so much in his eyes—adoration, love, forever.

"Never change, Kitten," he pleads. "You're all the good left in the world."

He wraps his arm around my shoulder and pulls me into the crook of his arm.

"I hope our kids all have your heart," he declares.

"Are we interrupting?" Lenore questions, holding a tray full of empty glasses and pitcher of what looked like lemonade.

I smiled, leaning closer to Riggs.

"Be nice," I warn through clenched teeth.

"Did you spike that?" he asks his mother as she fills the glasses.

"No but I can if you'd prefer that," she lifts her eyes to his and raises an eyebrow.

"Might not be a bad idea," he says, holding her gaze.

Riggs' hold on me loosens a bit, and I swear his mother smiles at him. Mr. Montgomery sits across from us, waving playfully at Eric as he averts his eyes back and forth between me and Riggs.

"So how did you two meet?"

"Lauren was dancing on top of a bar when I first met her," he says proudly.

"He kidnapped my mother," I blurt simultaneously, before we both burst out laughing and his parents gawk at us.

"I think spiking the lemonade is a great idea," Lenore states.

"I'll get the Goose," Mr. Montgomery offers, rising to his feet. Eric raises his hands as his grandfather stands, causing the man to freeze in his tracks and Riggs to wrap his arms protectively around our son.

"I'm not a vulture," Mr. Montgomery says, smiling at Eric. "How about an ice pop?" he turns his gaze to me. "We sent Roger to the store for a couple of things, unsure what he might like. We have all different flavors of those natural fruit bars. Is he allergic to anything?"

"Who are you?" Riggs mutters.

"No, Mr. Montgomery. Eric doesn't have any allergies why don't you bring him out your favorite and we'll see if he likes it."

"Call me, Robert, please," he requests before looking back at his son. "And to answer your question, I'm your father. I might not have been a great one, even a decent one, but you are my son and I'd like the chance to be some kind of father."

Riggs was speechless.

Somewhere pigs were flying and hell was freezing over.

Lenore pours half a bottle of Grey Goose into the lemonade, refilling the pitcher after we finished the first one. Once she lost the uptight act, she wasn't all that bad. She told me stories about when Riggs was little. There weren't many but the few she told had me smiling. My favorite was the one she told about Riggs and Bones lighting the garbage cans on fire.

Robert watched off to the side as Riggs chased Eric around the grass, building his courage to join in before three generations ran around the yard chasing a soccer ball. It wasn't perfect, there was still tension between Riggs and his parents but they were trying and in turn so was he.

Later that night, I left Riggs and Eric on the bed and drew myself a bath. The bathroom connected to our room was almost the size of our apartment. The minute I sank into the bubbles I felt like Julia Roberts in *Pretty Woman*, the only thing missing was Prince singing in my ear.

Relaxed, I close my eyes and rest my head against the back of the tub. My fingers shrivel but I continue to stay buried beneath the bubbles when the door creaks open and I force my eyes open. Leaning against the door frame, wearing nothing but a fitted pair of boxer briefs, Riggs fixes his hungry eyes on mine. I try to hold his gaze but my eyes wander down his tattooed body. Every piece of ink tells the story of who he was and who he became. Today, I learned a little of who Riggs used to be before the Satan's Knights MC and I love those broken pieces just as much as the colorful package he's become.

"Eric's sleeping," he says, pushing off the frame of the door, casually striding toward me. "How's the water?"

"Cold now," I hoarsely reply, cocking my head to the side as he kneels in front of the tub. Nonchalantly he dips his hand under the lukewarm water and touches my thigh.

You feeling frisky, Tiger?" I ask as he caresses my leg brushing away what's left of the bubbles so I'm exposed to his hungry eyes.

"Why, Kitten?" he smirks, lifting his gaze as his hand curls around my thigh. "You wanna play?" he asks mischievously as his fingers tickle the inside of my thigh, trailing higher and higher. I open my mouth to speak but the words get lost on my tongue as his fingers glide over my pussy.

"Hmm." He probes, his infamous grin slyly displayed across his face as he continues to stroke me.

"You don't play fair," I hiss as he slides two fingers inside me. I close my eyes, loving the feel of him and arch my body against his hand making slight waves around me.

"Maybe not," he says thoughtfully. "But I always get you off first. Sounds like a win-win to me," he counters, expertly moving and curling his fingers inside me. "You want to get off, Kitten, don't you?"

"Mmm," I murmur. His fingers leave me as he swirls his thumb over my clit. Water splashes as I widen my legs as much as I can, throwing one over the edge of the tub. My eyes shoot to him as he slams his fingers back where I want them and smiles cockily.

"Yeah, you want to get off," he states. Leaning over my leg he turns his gaze beneath the water to his hand. "Fuck, that's hot," he groans or maybe he whimpers.

Actually, it's me. I'm the one whimpering because he's right, it is hot and incredible, and not enough. I close my hand around his wrist and stare into his eyes. He knows the look I'm giving him, he's real familiar with it. It's the look I give him when I'm desperate for his dick. The look that tells him this Kitten wants to get fucked hard.

"Up you go," he says, pulling his hand away. He slides his hands under my arms and lifts me out of the tub, water splashes everywhere as I wrap my arms and legs around him. Carefully he walks across the wet tiles being sure he doesn't slip and send us both flying, he makes his way to the counter. Setting me on top of it, he removes my arms from around his neck and places my palms flat against the counter.

"Don't move," he warns. I lick my lips as his hands move from mine and he works his boxers down his thick, muscular legs. Stepping between my legs, he grabs my thighs and secures them around his waist, pressing his thickness against my core.

"You going to scream for me?" he growls against my ear, taking my earlobe between his teeth and tugging slightly.

My ass slides further against the counter, craving the friction of his dick rubbing against me.

"Loud and proud, Tiger," I say reaching for him.

"Didn't I tell you not to move?" he grunts, reaching between us to wrap his fist around his cock.

"Don't you know by now I don't follow instructions?" I counter breathlessly. He rubs the swollen head of his cock along my entrance.

"Tell me how you want it? Talk to me, Kitten, give me the good stuff," he says, continuously stroking himself with one hand. His free hand reaches behind me and squeezes my ass, pushing me forward, I think he's going to finally give me what I need but all he does is tease me more.

"You going to hold your cock or you going to fuck me with it, Tiger?" I taunt.

"Fuck me nice, fuck me good, fast and hard on this counter, up against the wall, bend me over and do what you do best but for the love of God just do it," I rasp, peering up at him through hooded eyes.

He releases his hold on his cock, wrapping both arms around me and lifts me off the counter by my ass. He takes a couple of steps before slamming my back against the wall, lining his cock with my entrance.

"I love it when you talk dirty," he grits, thrusting deep and hard inside of me.

I wrap my arms around his back, my nails dig in as he takes me fast, hard, mercilessly. With every pounding thrust, the back of my head slams against the wall. Neither of us care as the fancy framed art work falls off the wall crashing onto the tile. We don't stop, we don't slow down, if anything he fucks me harder and I take him deeper.

"Riggs," I growl, feeling my orgasm take flight. I frantically rock my hips, chasing it, demanding it until his mouth closes over mine and his tongue mimics the actions of his cock. He fucks my mouth softly, gently, but continues to fuck me hard and recklessly with his cock.

"Come for me, Kitten," he grunts against my mouth.

I scream his name as my body goes over the edge. Clenching my legs tightly around him, my pussy squeezes his cock, insisting we do this together, desperate to feel him unravel.

"Fuck," he cries as he drops his head to my shoulder, groaning as his dick jerks inside of me and he fills me with his release.

Our breaths are ragged as he comes down from the high and I wonder how he has the strength to stand, much less hold me up. My legs are like Jell-O, my body hums with relief as he kisses my shoulder. Finally, he lifts his head and stares at me.

"We broke the picture," I say, glancing over his shoulder at the shattered glass.

"Fuck the picture," he mutters, grinning widely. "Give me twenty minutes and we'll break another."

I laugh, wrapping my arms around his neck and lean in to brush my lips across his. I frown against his mouth as he slowly pulls out of me.

"Don't worry, baby, the Tiger isn't finished with you yet," he assures me with a wink. "Going to fuck you until my dick don't work no more and you can't walk," he says before bursting out laughing. "Should make for good conversation with the oil diggers over breakfast."

I feel my cheeks redden as he reminds me that Lenore and Robert probably heard their son fucking me senseless.

I drop my head into my hands and groan.

"Aren't you happy you brought me home to meet the folks?"

"Actually, I am," he admits, pulling my hands away from my face. "Come on, MIJF Let's take a shower."

I furrow my eyebrows at the initials.

"What did you just call me?" I ask as he slides me down and steadies me on my feet. Rolling his eyes, he laughs and leads me to the glass showers.

"Mom I just fucked," he says cheekily, biting the inside of his cheek as he pulls me into the glass enclosed shower. His eyes travel the length of my body as he turns on the water. "I take it back. You're the hot as fuck mom I just fucked."

Chapter Thirty-Four

RIGGS

Three days without my club, my bike and my brothers felt strange, unnatural—wrong. Three motherfucking days on the lam like I was some snitch in the witness protection program, it was driving me mad and that was putting it mildly. A more accurate description would be I was fucking losing my mind. It's not that I wasn't enjoying my time with Lauren and Eric. I couldn't even blame my insanity on my parents, as fucked as they are, they were genuinely trying. My mother stopped looking at me like I would pocket her silverware and my old man was trying, real fucking hard, to get to know me. He was even putting in a real effort with Eric and Lauren which made me smile more times than I care to admit.

I was losing my shit because I had no idea what was going on back home, and fucking lying to Kitten sucked balls. I spoke my mind freely without worry, without consequence, there were no lies between me and my girl until the fucking mob folk fucked with us. Again.

I finally heard from Blackie yesterday when he texted me on my burner phone, informing me they were working on figuring out how to get me back home with my family. Ronan, that useless piece of shit, was a dead end. Even the Corrupt Bastards think he's a shady motherfucker and want nothing to do with him. I've been doing some work on my end whenever I can steal a moment away from Lauren and the fucking *Partridge Family,* but it's hard. Yesterday I took my laptop into the bathroom with me, faking a case of the shits so I could tap into the Federal Bureau of Prison's database and get an extensive report of all names approved to visit the G-Man. Forty-seven fucking names. I don't even know if that's a legit thing, could a prisoner really have that many approved visitors? Whatever, all I know is I'm going to have to fake a stroke to get background information on all those names.

Sitting on the veranda overlooking the water, I take a long pull of the blunt I snuck away to smoke. I close my mouth, hold the smoke in until my lungs feel heavy and my throat burns. Puffing out a ring of smoke, I reach for my burner phone and dial Jack's number. The Bulldog is getting married today and instead of getting my fill of cherry fucking pie, I'm playing charades with my drunk mother, talking shop with my pops and fucking Kitten senseless. Shit, we've been going at it like rabbits since we've been here. I think subconsciously I believe I can fuck her into forgetting that the wedding is today.

I'm sure she's skeptical as to why we're here playing like we're on an episode of *Lifestyles of the Rich and Famous,* but she hasn't asked many questions. She didn't bust my balls about leaving so abruptly and the more time goes on I think she believes I genuinely wanted to surprise her. At least that's what I hope. Kitten will get all mafia princess on my ass if she finds out I'm lying or that there is a threat against us. After thoroughly scoping out the house I didn't find any baseball bats, but papa dukes does have a fancy set of golf clubs that are accessible to Lauren. I'm fucking done, good as dead if the little Yankee gets her hands on one of those and starts swinging, no Bastard or goon of the G-Man would stand a chance—she'd take me out with one shot.

I take another drag as the phone rings in my ear and I wait for Jack to answer.

"Parrish."

"Well if it isn't the fucking groom," I say, choking on the smoke as I exhale.

"Brother," he starts then pauses for a moment. "How you holding up?"

"Peachy," I say. "No 'Al Capones' lurking around this place just uptight rich folk."

"Pipe's working on neutralizing our situation. We're going to meet with our friends in Boston this week and hopefully get your ass back to Brooklyn by Friday."

"No honeymoon then?" I question, as I crush the tip of my blunt with my fingers.

"Nah, after the baby is born I'm going to take her somewhere nice," he says. "Now isn't the time for me to go off the grid."

"Yeah," I sigh.

"We will make it right, Riggs," he states.

"I know that," I reply, pulling off my baseball hat and running my fingers roughly through my hair. "But listen, I called to wish you luck. It ain't every day the Bulldog takes a wife. Fuck, wish I was there to see you in a monkey suit."

"No monkey suit here, brother," Jack says laughing.

"You're getting married in your leathers?"

"Fucking, damn right, boy."

"Take a fucking picture, please," I laugh.

"I'm pretty sure I dished out a few G's for a photographer. That motherfucker better take pictures of everything, someone sneezes he better capture it."

"Well, I won't keep you I just wanted to call and congratulate you. Reina's great man, perfect for you, and we're all lucky to have her around the clubhouse."

"Thanks, brother, means a lot. Take care of you and yours."

"Always," I vow. Standing up, I turn around and face Lauren.

Shit.

Quickly, I disconnect the call and shove my phone into the pocket of my jeans and stare at a very pissed, very ferocious Kitten.

"Funny thing happened," she starts, stepping toward me.

"Oh yeah?" I say, taking a step back trying to put some distance between us. She appears to be unarmed but I wasn't a hundred percent positive, we were talking about Lauren, the girl who carried a can of Mace in her bag at all times.

"Hmm," she hums, eyes bulging a little. "I don't know who I am mad at most, me or you. Me, because I've been so distracted that I didn't realize what today is or you for purposely lying and avoiding what today is."

"What're you talking about? It's not your birthday. We didn't get hitched yet so it can't be our anniversary, wait, is it one of those fucking anniversaries that women make up just to torture a guy. You know, like the first time we fucked, or the first time we spoke on the phone. It's one of those crazy fucking things, isn't it?"

If I have learned anything hanging around mobsters it's that you deny, deny, deny until the end.

"The first time we took a ride on my bike?" I offer, raising an eyebrow at her as she fists her hands and glares at me. "Okay, it's not that."

This shit so wasn't working. I was fucked. No, I was motherfucking fucked.

"Cut it out, Riggs," she warns through clenched teeth. "You know exactly what today is. I heard you on the phone just now," she hollers.

I groan, forgetting all about the phone call I literally just made. Kids, don't smoke pot, it fucking fries your brain cells. It's a shame Nancy Regan died, with my handsome face and her catchy slogan we could've resurrected the 'Just Say No' campaign.

"It's Jack and Reina's wedding and we're here visiting with parents who you can barely tolerate," she accuses, narrowing her eyes into tiny slits as she pokes her finger into my pecs. "And don't you dare say you were trying to surprise me."

"Weddings aren't really my thing," I lie, hoping to buy myself some time. Reaching for my temples I rub them, willing my brain cells to return and come up with a way to break it to Kitten we had a possible target on our backs.

"If you don't give me a fucking explanation, then I am going back to that house, grabbing our son and crashing Jack's wedding. Don't fucking dare me, Riggs, *Wedding Crashers* is my favorite movie. I'll ace that shit."

God, she's fucking sexy when she's pissed. Did I mention how much I love her taste in movies too? I mean movie night at Casa Kitty is a damn good time, just last week we went on a *Rush Hour* marathon. Chris Tucker is my hero.

Focus Riggs!

"Wait a minute, where is Eric?"

"I sold him to a bunch of gypsies. Where do you think he is? With your parents!"

"Shit, Kitten, are you off your rocker? We're going to go back there and he's going to be wearing an ascot!"

She grabs my shirt with her fists and shakes her head.

"Why are we here, Riggs? The truth."

"I can't get into it, Lauren," I say truthfully. The less she knows the safer she'll remain, I hoped. "It's club business but know that I've got it under control—Jack and the guys have it under control and us being here is just a precaution."

Wrong fucking answer.

Releasing my shirt from her hands she takes a step back and her eyes go as wide as saucers.

"Club business?" she screeches.

"Yeah, but like I said I've got it under control."

She stares at me bewildered, traces of hurt and confusion reflect in her baby blues I loved so much. Taking a step closer to her, she shakes her head insisting I don't advance any closer. I watch as she grabs the neckline of her tank top and inch it down, revealing the offensive scar marking where the bullet entered her body. My eyes fall to the scar, anger boiling in my veins just as it always does whenever I see it.

"I think I deserve more than an elusive answer not only from your club but from you. Look at this scar, go on, Riggs, take a good look," she demands. "I stare at this scar every day. Every day I am reminded that I was shot, remained in a coma for days, that our son was born premature because of a bullet. I almost died, Riggs, our son could've died too and Bones did die. Now, I have never thrown that in your face, not once because I know that you would have died right along with us if that bullet succeeded in what it set out to do. You're not in a relationship with someone who is ignorant and naïve to the life you lead; I am Anthony Bianci's sister. I have lived this shit since before you knew it existed, when you were Robert Montgomery and not Riggs. I know better than to demand inside information on what it is you do and what goes on behind the scenes of your club and I'm not asking. I am asking you to remember that you and I are a team and this is our family. If we are hiding out because something is going on with your club, then I deserve to know we are vulnerable. I deserve to know so there are two of us on high alert, protecting that innocent boy we brought into this world." Her voice cracks as her lip quivers. With trembling hands, she reaches for mine and lays them over her stomach. "And the brother or sister we're going to give him."

My eyes immediately drop to her flat stomach covered with our hands, widening in shock as they lift back to hers. The blues of her eyes fill with tears as she answers the questions reflected in mine by nodding her head.

Still, I ask the question, needing the words.

"You're pregnant?"

"Yes," she cries. "I took a test before we left but I didn't have time to make a doctor's appointment because you came home and brought us here," she explains, squeezing my hands tightly. "I can't have history repeat itself, Riggs—"

I cut off her plea with my lips, gently covering hers with mine. It was an attempt to prove to her I wouldn't let history repeat itself. The last time she told me she was pregnant I had an anxiety attack, lost my fucking shit at the thought of becoming a father. I didn't kiss her; I didn't give her all the words she needed to hear. Starting now, this very moment, I would prove to her everything would be different this time around. I'd be at every goddamn doctor's appointment and I'd hold her damn hand as she delivered our kid. There was no way in hell history was repeating itself, no way I would let anyone take that from us—not this time, never again.

"Nothing will happen to you or either of our kids," I declare, my voice rougher than usual. "We're going to stay here until this shit dies down and Anthony and Jack can assure us both it's safe for us to go back to Brooklyn."

I lift my hands to her face, bend my knees as I cradle her face and stare into her framed eyes.

So ducking gorgeous my Kitten was.

Yeah, I said ducking.

We were having another Pea.

"I asked you to take a detour, you took my hand and ran. I asked you to fight your way back to me and Eric, you did it with vigor. I asked you to marry me, you said yes. I asked you to make another baby with me, you gave me another Pea.

Now, I'm going to ask you to trust me, trust me with your life and the two we created together. I swear on everything I give a damn about, everything that matters, I will keep you safe. Are you going to take my hand and run with me one more time, Kitten?"

She lifts her hands to mine, her small hands close around my wrists.

"I'll always run with you. I'll hold on and swing right when there is an unexpected turn—"

"Detour," I correct her, smiling back at my baby mama.

"I'll run through every detour with you as long as you're real with me. I promise you I can take it, I can handle everything you are and everything that's thrown at us, but you need to trust that as much as I need to trust your capabilities of keeping us safe."

"You got yourself a deal, babe," I answer, brushing my lips across hers. I pull back, taking her hands in mine, placing her at arm's length to fully take her in. "Fuck, I'm lucky."

"Yeah, you are," she laughs, dropping one of my hands to wipe at her cheeks. I tug her to my side and wrap my free arm around her, placing it on her belly.

"Well, that didn't take long." I pondered. "I think I have super sperm."

She chuckles, turning her face into my chest, her laughter vibrating against my heart.

Music to my fucking ears.

I wanted more.

More laughter, less tears.

No fucking tears.

"Come on, Kitten, let's shake things up at Casa Montgomery."

"What did you have in mind?"

"Let's tell Lenore she's going to be a grandma again," I laugh. "Shit, she'll probably deplete the liquor supply but it'll be fun to watch," I kiss the top of her head before placing my index finger under her chin and cocking her head back so her eyes met mine. "I love you, Lauren Bianci."

I grinned to myself.

I knocked up Kitten again.

I was going to have two little rug rats.

If I was a believer, I'd look up to the heavens and ask Him to keep sending the detours my way because they keep getting better and better.

With my baby mama tucked into my side, the threat of doom somewhere flapping in the wind, we take off to the main house to rescue our ascot wearing toddler and break the news to the oil diggers that there would be another Montgomery heir to spoil with their millions.

Life was good.

Nah, it was fucking great.

I dare someone to take this from me.

I fucking dare them.

Chapter Thirty-Five

JACK

I glanced down at the photo staring back at me on top of the bar. It had seen better days; the edges were frayed and there were thick creases in it from folding it so many times throughout the years. It was my favorite photograph of my son. His innocent smile was as bright as the sun and his eyes full of joy. I used to carry it everywhere with me hence the tattered condition it currently was in, but as the edges wore I realized it was too precious to take with me everywhere I went. It felt wrong bringing him along with all the illegal shit going on, exposing him to the grit and mayhem. He was pure and innocent when he left this earth and that's how he shall remain. Then there was always the nagging in my head that I'd drop the fucking picture, forget it somewhere and I'd lose him all over again.

These days I keep the photograph on top of my dresser and it's the first thing I see in the morning but today was different. I made a promise to my boy at his grave, told him I'd bring him with me for all the good, and today was the start of the good. Today, my ass was marrying Reina, and it didn't get any better than that.

I pour myself a shot, knock back the whiskey before folding the photo delicately in half and sliding it into the inside pocket of my cut, covering my heart. All my kids will be with me when Reina becomes my wife. Lacey would stand across from me, alongside my wife, and my boy would be in my heart. Then there was our kid tucked safely in Reina's belly. Seemed like a perfect fucking union if you asked me.

I turn around, taking in the transformation of my clubhouse and the clowns behind it. The prospects, Mack and Bosco, were lining up folding chairs, leaving a walkway in-between to make an aisle for Reina to walk down. Pipe was stringing Christmas lights around some sort of gazebo looking thing they brought in and placed in front of the reaper mural. Wolf, fucking Wolf, he was turning blue blowing up white balloons. Amused is what I was as I watched his cheeks fill with air as he blew into the white latex until his lungs threatened to collapse. He angrily ties a knot at the end and smacks the balloon away from him.

"Deuce, go hang those fucking things somewhere," he orders breathless. "Hey, Pipe, you bastard, you still don't know where the fucking air pump is?"

"I know where it is," Pipe yells. "It's at the garage where it fucking belongs."

"When I have a fucking heart attack and drop dead, it's your ass I'm haunting," Wolf grounds out as the door opens and Linc walks in with a man carrying a box.

"Who the fuck is that?"

"The florist." Linc points his thumb toward the man staring at the clubhouse in horror." I checked him out, the only thing this motherfucker has is wire and a fancy pair of sheers. Says he needs them to cut the stems and all that shit, isn't that right?"

"What the hell did you people do? Balloons?" he drops the box onto one of the tables and grabs one of the balloons off the floor, popping it with his hands.

"Is this fucker kidding me?" Wolf bellows. "You got any idea how much wind was in that thing?"

"Who hired you?"

"Clearly, the bride," the florist deadpans. "Is that a trellis?" he questions pointing to the thing Pipe was stringing the lights on. I should mention that the lights weren't those little white lights people hang on everything, these were the old school Christmas lights. They were the colorful, big fat ones we hung from the gutters when we were kids.

I shrug my shoulders, pushing off the bar and make my way toward the man. I place my arm around his shoulders and pat him on the back.

"Reina hired you to make this place look nice, you do that, make it look real pretty in here," I say, reaching into my pocket, pulling out a couple of bills, and shove them into his hands. "And add some sunflowers to the place."

"But that isn't on the order," he argues.

"Make a new order," I demand, smiling at him. "Make it happen flower boy."

Turning back to the bar I pour myself a drink, I lift my eyes as the door opens again and Lacey strolls in with Blackie on her tail. I pause, hand wrapped tight around the neck of the bottle as I drink my little girl in. Her heels had to be at least six inches, strappy things that decorated her calves. She was wearing an off the shoulder, black lace, cocktail dress and her hair was windblown—wild from being on the back of Blackie's bike. My eyes dart to him and I catch him staring at her ass.

"For fuck's sake, you put her on the back of your bike dressed like that?" I seethe, shaking my head. To hell with the fucking glass, I take a swig straight from the bottle. My daughter smiles widely as she reaches for the bottle and wraps her arms loosely around my neck.

"You're not allowed to be a grump on your wedding day," she says, pressing a smacking kiss to my cheek as I wrap my arms around her and hug her tightly, keeping my eyes on Blackie.

"I'm with Lace."

"Of course you are, you don't want me to strangle you," I tease.

"Then you'd have no best man," he retorts, smiling back at me.

Lacey pulls back, turning slightly, so she is standing in between me and Blackie.

"First of all, I insisted we go on the bike and I also insisted I get dressed before we leave so I can help Reina," she points out. "He just goes along with what I say,"

"She wears the leather around here," Blackie jokes, grabbing her around the waist and pressing her back against his front.

"Lost your balls, did you?" I raise an eyebrow and turn my gaze toward Lacey. "Anyone ever tell you you're hard headed?"

"I wonder where I get that from," she laughs.

"Have no idea what you're talking about, Lace," I say innocently, winking at her before turning my attention back to Blackie. "You have the ring, right?"

"Shit," he mutters.

"You had one fucking job—"

"I've got the ring," he interrupts, flashing me a smile as he runs his hands over his cut, patting his pockets before reaching inside and producing a tiny, black, velvet box. I take it from his hands, flip up the top and stare at the custom wedding band designed with two rows of canary yellow diamonds.

Sunshine.

Always.

Lacey leans over my shoulder to get a peek at the ring, a smile spreading wide across her face as she stares at it.

"Wow, it's beautiful Dad," she says, placing a hand on my shoulder. "Reina's going to love it."

I hope so.

I take the ring between my fingers, pull it out of the box to turn it over to inspect the band. There engraved into the gold are the two words that sum up our relationship.

You.

Me.

Lifting my eyes to Blackie, I crack a smile and tip my chin.

"Thanks for getting it done," I say.

"What's a best man good for if he can't pick up a ring?" he slaps my shoulder, leaning forward to press a kiss to Lacey's cheek. "I'm going to make a quick run, check things out and get a handle on this hair," he points to his wild locks, looking to me and giving me a look. Words may not have been spoken, but they were reflected in his eyes.

Going to check out the security on the property.

I got you, brother.

"Don't you dare touch the hair," Lacey orders, cocking her head to the side. "I mean comb it, maybe tie it back but if you so much as cut a centimeter of it—"

"Don't you worry, girl. I know you like it…" His eyes turn to mine and he smiles sheepishly leaving the rest of his answer on his tongue. Smart fucking man.

Silently, I hand him the ring to keep safe until the ceremony and watch him walk out the door to check the perimeter of the building. I turn toward Lacey, noticing her eyes are still pinned to the door Blackie just walked through.

"Hey, pretty girl, where are you?" I question, stepping in front of her to draw her attention back to me. "Lace?"

Shaking away whatever thoughts took her mind hostage for a brief moment she averts her gaze back to mine and forces a smile.

"Sorry, I was daydreaming," she explains.

I wanted to believe that Lacey was capable of the simple things like daydreams but knew it wasn't likely. That bitch of a maker was planting seeds of fire in her brain but this time she was able to fight against it. Ignore the voice dragging her down. Wish like hell she fought and won every damn time. Wish like hell, I didn't have to watch her battle her mind like I do.

The hyper florist stood alongside me, dropping a box on the bar before firing instructions at me and Lacey.

"Boutonnieres and bouquets are in there." He points at Lacey. "Are you part of the wedding party?"

"I am the wedding party," she laughs at the frazzled man in front of her, leaning over the box to inspect the contents. "I'll take care of it," she confirms, lifting a boutonniere.

"Are you ready to get married?" she questions, opening the clear plastic container holding the flowers.

"I'm ready," I assure her, watching as she lifts the delicate flowers and pulls out the pin in the back of the arrangement. I angle my head to the side as I study her. I take a step back as I envision my little girl dressed as a bride and I am the one holding the flowers, handing her a bouquet before walking her down the aisle.

Shit, that will happen one day.

Probably a lot sooner than I'd like.

"One day it'll be you," I rasp, as she closes the space I put between us and touches the worn leather of my cut. She stares up at me through her long eyelashes, smiling as she pins the boutonniere beneath my patch declaring me the president of my club. "All dressed in white, you'll probably want to make your grand entrance on a bike…"

"Will you take me to church on your bike with my big pretty dress?"

"If that's what you want."

"What if I asked you to wear a tux?"

A fucking tuxedo. Shit, I glance down at what I considered dress attire—black jeans, new so they still looked black and not gray, a white dress shirt and my leather cut. Oh, and the new leather moto boots that Reina insisted I buy for the wedding.

Reina was good with the biker wedding. As long as she got to pretty herself all up she didn't care what I wore, aside from the worn boots. She wasn't having it. Glancing around the clubhouse, taking in how the florist was making this place take shape for a wedding, I knew it was perfect for me and Reina but not Lacey.

Lacey would be the one to stuff me into a monkey suit.

They say a daughter is a man's weakness. It's the fucking truth.

She laughs as she smooths down her hand over my vest.

"I'm kidding," she teases, kissing my cheek before stepping back and giving me a once over. "Okay, big guy, my job here is done. You look ready to marry the love of your life. It's time for me to go primp the bride," she declares, pressing another noisy kiss to my cheek. "I'm really happy for you, Dad."

"Thanks, sweetheart, means a lot," I reply, bringing her against my chest one more time.

"You're going to squash the flowers!"

"Fuck it, we'll get some more," I kiss the top of her head. "Love you, Lace."

"Love you too."

After a few moments I loosen my grip on her, watch as she balances herself in her heels and grab the box of flowers on top of the bar.

"Where is the blushing bride, anyway?"

I grunt, shaking my head at the ridiculousness.

"She's upstairs in my room, refusing to let me see her. I had to sleep here last night too and snuck out this morning so she could shimmy her ass in here," I growl. "Woman is superstitious as all hell," I say, taking another swig of the whiskey as Lacey's laughter vibrates through me and her heels click across the floor.

Lacey disappears up the stairs to tend to Sunshine, leaving me with the florist and the baker that had arrived with the cake. All we were missing here was the fucking candlestick maker. Pipe and Wolf took to my sides, the nomads too. Except for Linc, who walked around the bar and pulled a few clean glasses out and filled them with the whiskey I was hogging.

"Think this day deserves a toast." Pipe begins. "Never thought you'd take an Old Lady, much less marry one," he says, handing me a glass.

"Fucking threw me for a loop too," Wolf admits, raising his glass.

"And she's hot," Linc adds, earning a glare from me.

"The woman can cook too," Wolf chimes in. "Not just a pretty face and smoking piece of ass."

"Wolf," I growl.

"Calm your tits, Parrish. Can't help a man for appreciating beauty." He lets out a huge belly laugh.

"To Jack and Reina," Pipe cheers. "Here's to health, wealth, and the little biker that's going to be running around this place."

raise my glass, tipping my chin to my brother in appreciation.

"To Reina," I add. "And all the sunshine she brings to this place."

"To Sunshine," everyone cheers.

The Bill Wither's song, *Ain't No Sunshine*, always reminded me of Reina, especially after Jimmy Gold kidnapped her.

She was young, a bit shy, a whole lot sheltered until I came storming into her life.

I should've let her be.

But she had me from the very first time I set foot inside Dee's Diner.

Now, I'd never let her go.

Because…

Ain't no sunshine when she's gone.
Only darkness every day.

Chapter Thirty-Six

Reina

Standing in front of the mirror, I tie a knot in my white silk robe, my stomach twisting in knots. My anxiety spiking to levels I have never experienced. Today is my wedding day, a day I wasn't so sure I'd ever see. I was going to marry the love of my life, promise to share all of me with all of him. I was going to be Jack Parrish's wife.

It was everything I ever wanted and nothing I knew I needed. The crass biker who strode into the diner, night after night, for five weeks. The man I barely looked at, hardly spoke to. The man I never wanted to give a second glance was the man who rescued me from my own hell, my own torment and breathed life back into my soul. He healed me and in the process, I healed him too. We were broken, lost, two fractured souls who found one another in a sea of grief and despair.

Piece by piece, brick by brick, we built one another up and then he asked me to marry him. Of course I said yes, I *wanted* to marry Jack Parrish more than I wanted to breathe. But as much as I wanted him, I was frightened to have him.

It all goes back to having everything and having everything to lose.

I've been there before.

My relationship with Danny may have been a farce. I still don't know if he truly loved me. How could I? There were so many lies between us it was impossible to decipher the truth. At the time of the fire and his death I didn't know about all the lies. After the fire I found myself in a hospital, covered in burns, listed as a Jane Doe, grieving for a man I knew nothing about. I grieved for the woman lost in that fire, the man I thought was my forever and the deceit our forever was built upon. I lost everything I thought I wanted.

Now I have everything I want but everything I need too. I have a real forever. True love. I have Jack Parrish and I am so afraid of losing him. My fear is consuming me, turning the happiest day of my life into a nightmare full of anxiety. I can't shake the feeling lurking in the pit of my stomach. The strange sense that something terrible is about to happen. Call me crazy, but it's not like doom doesn't fall on the Satan's Knights doorstep frequently. In fact, it's more common than not.

I was too wrapped up in my head to hear the door open but I heard Lacey call for me as she walked around Jack's room.

"In here," I rasp, lifting my hand to my throat, swallowing down the fear and forcing a smile on my face, one that didn't reach my eyes.

"Happy wedding day," Jack's daughter cheered. Standing in the doorway of the bathroom, her smile falters when she takes in my reflection in the mirror. "What's wrong?"

"Nothing," I lie, spinning around to face her.

Her eyes widened, and she takes a step closer, placing her hands on my shoulders.

"Reina, everyone is arriving, you need to get dressed," she whispers, lifting a hand to my hair which still tied back in a ponytail.

"I just lost track of time," I insist, drawing in a deep breath as I reach for her hands and give them a reassuring squeeze. "I'll hurry up."

Her dark eyes skeptically stared back at me, assessing me, probably trying to figure out why I looked so fucking scared on my wedding day.

"Okay," she says finally. "Is there anything I can do to help?"

"Can you go downstairs and tell everyone I need a little more time?" I ask, turning around to face the mirror. Grabbing my make-up bag off the counter, I rummage through it, busying myself so I didn't have to look at Lacey and have her discover how nervous I was. I didn't want her to think the worst, that I didn't want to marry her father.

"Sure," she says, pausing a moment. "I'll go do that and be right back."

"Thank you," I mutter, keeping my head down, pretending to dig in the bag, for what, I don't know. I hear the door close behind me and finally lift my eyes to stare at myself in the mirror.

"Snap out of it, Reina," I hiss to my reflection. "Everything will be fine. Nothing will stand in the way of you marrying the love of your life."

Please God, let it be true.

JACK

"Bulldog, looking sharp," Nikki Pastore greets, working her way in-between the band of brothers surrounding me.

"Well if it isn't my favorite Pastore," I grin, taking her and pulling her into a hug.

"It's Valente now," she corrects, returning the embrace.

I had a soft spot for Vic's youngest daughter, took a liking to her the moment she and Mike jumped into my truck and she robbed my cigarettes.

Pulling back, I avert my eyes back and forth between her and her new husband. Mike Valente, dressed in black dress pants, a white V-neck t-shirt and a sports jacket that matched the tailored pants. Taking another look at Nikki, I notice she matched his attire with a black and white dress. They were the perfect fucking couple, made me real proud to have a hand in saving their asses.

"You two get hitched and didn't tell anyone?"

"It was a spur of the moment thing," Mike replies.

"We got married in prison in front of my father. We went to the courthouse yesterday to get our marriage certificate."

"Bet you made your old man the happiest he's been in a long time." I wink at her. "How's your mom doing?"

"She's okay, hanging in there," Nikki sighs, before smiling sadly. "Sits by the phone day and night."

"Dad!"

I peel my eyes away from the newlyweds and turn to face my daughter.

"Hi everyone." She waves before grabbing a hold of my arm. "Excuse us one minute," she adds, dragging me off to the side.

"What's wrong?"

"It's Reina," she huffs. My face must have dropped because she quickly adds that she was fine physically. "I think she has a case of wedding jitters—" I didn't wait for Lacey to finish explaining. Leaving her in the common room with the guests I start for the stairs, superstitions be damned. Climbing the stairs two at a time I reach the door to my room and pushed it open.

"Sunshine?" I call, stepping inside the room, my eyes falling upon the wedding gown lying across my bed causing me to freeze in my tracks and imagine what she's going to look like in it. Fucking beautiful. Stunning.

The bathroom door slams shut pulling me out of my trance.

"Jack! You can't be in here. It's bad luck to see me before the wedding."

I walk to the door, leaning my forehead and splaying my palm against the wooden door I drink in her scent.

"Reina, what's going on?" I question.

"Nothing, I'm getting dressed," she answers in a high-pitched tone.

"Open the door, Sunshine," I coax. "I promise to keep my eyes closed, I want to feel you, touch you..."

"It's not locked," she whispers behind the door.

I turn the knob, closing my eyes as I promised and open the door.

"Where are you?" I ask, holding my hand out as I keep my eyes closed. She fits her hand into mine and I take a few steps further into the bathroom.

"Turn around," I demand. "I want you facing the mirror."

It wasn't that long ago we stood in this very position. It was the night I claimed her to my club, the night I confessed all my sins to her and the night she gave me her scars. It was an act of self-control, keeping my eyes straight toward the mirror, not allowing them to travel across the body I worshiped as she undressed for me and exposed me to her secrets. I remember thinking she ruined me, then realized all she did was fix me and how badly I wanted to fix her.

Like now, whatever is bothering her, I want to fix.

"Are you facing the mirror, Sunshine?"

"Yes," her voice cracks with the simple word.

My hands roamed the air searching for her. Finding her I drop them to her shoulders as I stand behind her.

"What do you see when you look in the mirror?" I probe, my voice husky against her ear.

"I see you," she whispers. "I see me."

"You and me."

"Us."

"Look lower," I command gently, pressing my lips to her ear as I glide my hands down her sides and wrap them around her, splaying both hands against her bump. "Now what do you see?"

"I see love," she whispers. "I see so much love."

"What else?"

"The future. You, me, him or her. I see Christmas mornings and birthday parties. I see you standing behind our child waiting for him to blow out his candles on every cake you put in front of him. I see Lacey and Blackie, their wedding, their kids, their life we get to be a part of. I see visits to Jack, sharing with him all the stories he's missing. I see rides, long rides to nowhere particular. Dinners with a table full of your brother's, big family dinners."

"I see all that too," I admit, eyes still closed tightly as my lips trail down her neck. "It's called forever, Sunshine."

She places her hands over mine.

"You," she whispers.

"Me," I reply, brushing my lips across her shoulder. "Marry me, Reina. Let me spend the rest of my life seeing forever through your eyes."

"You think I don't want to marry you? Jack there is nothing, not a thing, I want more in this lifetime, in this crazy world than to marry you. I told you before I was scared and that's no lie. I'm so scared of losing you. It was never a question of whether I want to be your wife, it's a question of whether or not I'll get to be. I have such a bad feeling that something will happen, something terrible and it'll all be over before it began. Our perfect forever gone before we even get to say I do."

I growl and something feral explodes from my mouth as frustration gnaws at me. I promised I'd keep my fucking eyes closed because all I want to do is spin her around, force her to look me in the eye when I tell her there isn't a goddamn thing in this world that will stop this wedding from happening.

I may not know much.

Might not be worthy of anything at all.

But I know for sure that Reina was put on this planet to be Mrs. Jack Parrish. She was born to wear my patch, born to be my old lady.

And me?

I was put on this earth to love her.

To heal her as she's healed me.

To protect her and chase away her demons.

"Reina, I can't promise you we won't face times that are ugly. I can't promise that club business won't fall into our laps, at our doorstep or even at special times like the one we're about to share but I can promise you I protect what is mine. I can give you my word, I always fight for what is mine, and you, you're mine, this forever is mine, it's Property of Parrish." I smile at her. "And you know how serious I take my property."

"That scares me, Jack, because I know you'll lay down and die before you let anything ever touch me, this baby, Lacey. You'll always choose us over you. Don't you get it? I choose you. I choose your life."

"We all gotta die sometime. When our time is up, it's up, but I'm not dying anytime soon, Reina. I'm going to live to a ripe old age. I promise you that," I say with conviction.

I believed it or I wouldn't swear it. God didn't want me, Satan didn't either, the only way my existence will end is when this body of mine grows old and tired, worn like the boots she wouldn't let me wear today.

I feel her turn around in my arms, her hands on my face, inching up to my eyes.

"Open your eyes," she whispers softly.

"You sure?" I ask, respecting her beliefs, even if I thought they were nuttier than a fucking fruitcake.

"Open your eyes," she demands.

On command my dark eyes bore into hers

"Tell me what do see," she says.

"I see a beautiful woman who is far stronger than any I have ever known. I see beauty. I see light. I see promise. I see her. I see me. I see a full life full of love. If I look closer, I see the answer to every question I have ever asked myself. I see relief from the darkness that has consumed me for most of my life. I see Sunshine. I see Mrs. Parrish," I say huskily.

She grabs my face, rises onto her tiptoes and covers my mouth with hers. A kiss to seal the moment. I knew the moment I laid eyes on her, she would ruin me, wreck me, heal me and fix me. She would force me to feel. She would love me, accept me and honor me all the days of my life.

"Whose property, are you?" she asks softly against my mouth.

It was a familiar question, one she asked me that same night she gave me her scars.

"Whose property are you then?" She asked, her eyes flickering with something I couldn't name.

"No one's," I answered, taking her hands and pulling her toward the bathroom.

"Whose property are you, Parrish?" she repeats.

I pull back an inch, cup her face in my palms as I lean my forehead against hers and stare into her eyes, into her soul.

"Yours."

Always yours, Sunshine.

Forever yours.

Chapter Thirty-Seven

VICTOR

Alone.

Darkness, my only friend.

My mind, my only companion.

I am confined to four walls, never to see the light of day again. The only time my body will touch the Earth's soil is when it is buried beneath it.

Seconds feel like hours, hours feel like weeks, and days feel like years. I have no idea what day it is or how long I've been trapped here. By the scent of me I'm guessing it's been a damn long time. I'm filthy, my throat is parched, and my stomach is empty. My already failing lungs are collapsing, disintegrating from the cancer and I feel as though I am suffocating. I have no strength left, not even to stand and walk to the toilet and I faintly feel the warmth flood my pants.

The pride I hung onto with all my might is gone.

I have nothing left.

I pray for God to take me but He continues to make me suffer and pay for my sins.

I close my eyes, tears fill them and leak out of the corners onto my dirty face, still caked with the G-Man's dried blood.

They locked me away in this dungeon and threw away the key. Once a day a guard slides the square opening in the center of the door, peers inside my dark cell with one eye and checks if I'm alive. He closes it as quickly as he opens it, leaving me to die.

It's not a peaceful death.

It's a nightmare.

I'm haunted by those I love; those I miss. The beautiful faces I'll never see again. The memories are so real it's hard not to believe Grace and the girls are here with me but while my mind may not know the difference, my heart does. My heart knows they are too pure, too good and far too beautiful to be in the depths of Hell with me.

Still, I close my eyes and ignore my heart, pretending my girls are here. My senses shut down, the foul scent of urine, body odor and feces disappear. The darkness turns to light and I see my Gracie.

"Gracie?" I called, shrugging out of my tuxedo jacket, carefully hanging it over the back of the lone chair in the corner of the hotel room. I glanced around the room, spotting the candles I requested the hotel have on hand and began to light the wicks.

The soft bask of candle light sets the perfect ambiance for our wedding night. I averted my eyes back to the bathroom door that was still closed and moved to the silver ice bucket in the middle of the room. Popping the cork, the champagne pours over the neck of the bottle as the door creaked opened and the most beautiful women shyly crept out of the bathroom, wearing nothing but yards of white lace and silk.

"Wow," I whispered, mesmerized by the beauty who was now my wife. I smiled widely, placing the bottle back in the bucket before walking toward her.

"I didn't think it was possible but you're even more beautiful than when you walked down the aisle."

"I feel ridiculous," she admitted, taking a step closer. I took her hands in mine and pulled her close.

"Why?" I asked softly, tucking a strand of black hair behind her ear.

"You know why," she whispered as I leaned over her shoulder and pressed my lips to the skin just below her ear, softly peppering kisses along her neck to the silk strap of her nightgown.

"We'll go slow," I promised, lifting my head from her shoulder and turning my head a fraction to stare into her brown eyes. "I knew one day I'd marry you."

I bent my knees, lifted her into my arms and spun her around, her laughter filled the air like a soft melody.

What I wouldn't give to hear her laugh again, hear her soft voice whisper against my ear, feel her body against mine just one more time. Instead, I relive the memories and thank God they are so clear and vivid.

Then I think of my girls.

And like their mother, they too come alive within my dreams.

"I have a date tonight," Adrianna said, sitting across the breakfast table, nonchalantly eating her cereal.

I lowered the newspaper, folded it in half and placed it on the table, lifting my coffee mug to my lips as Grace set a plate of pancakes in front of me.

"Michael?" I questioned, drenching the pancakes in syrup as I glance across the table at my sixteen-year-old daughter.

"No, not Mike," she said, smiling sweetly. The little vixen was up to something and one look at my wife, nervously flipping pancakes as if she was feeding all of Bensonhurst, it became clear she knew what that something was.

The doorbell rang and Nikki jumped to her feet.

"I'll get it," she offered.

"Are we expecting someone?" I looked between the mountain of pancakes and my daughter who decided to make her lower lip part of her breakfast.

Nikki came back into the kitchen with our visitor. Anthony Bianci, the eager enforcer looking to make a name for himself within my organization stood in my kitchen, making the oversized room seem small. Anthony had potential to go places. He was loyal to the core, dropped everything at my command and did as he was told, no questions asked. However, that was about to change.

"What are you doing here?" I questioned the man staring at my eldest daughter. Adrianna pushed her chair and stood, facing Anthony. Her smile lit up the kitchen and I watched as he tried his hardest not to be affected by it.

"I came to ask you a question," he muttered, never taking his eyes off my daughter.

It was a strange feeling watching them together, one mixed with sorrow and relief.

"What question might that be?" I asked, reaching for my coffee mug again as they continued to ogle one another. I knew what he was going to ask. I knew they had been sneaking around behind my back for months, but what I thought was a mild crush became serious over Grace's pancakes. Anthony Bianci wouldn't have risked his position with my organization if he wasn't head over heels in love with my daughter.

It was that morning; I knew that they were the real thing. It was scarier than anything I had ever experienced before, knowing the man you never saw coming was standing in front of you, next to your daughter and, that he would be the man in her life for all of eternity.

My wild child, Adrianna, the rebellious little girl who grew to be such a strong woman.

And then there was my Nicole.

"Daddy, I baked you a cake!" she exclaimed, pointing to the lopsided cake on the kitchen table.

"Did you make this all by yourself?" I asked, lifting her high on my hip as I brushed the tip of my nose across hers.

"Yep! Mommy said you love chocolate cake," she said excitedly.

I walked her to the kitchen drawer, pulled out two forks and set her on top of the table next to the cake.

"Mommy's right. It's my favorite," I smiled at her. "Should we dig in?"

"What about plates?"

"What about them?" I winked, handing her a fork before I dug into the cake with mine. Her giggle caused my heart to grow ten times in size as she followed my lead and dug into the lopsided cake.

Those days, when the girls were young, were my favorite. They were the precious moments I took for granted and if I could do it again I'd be home more, spend more time with them because those years flew by.

My memory betrayed me, pulling the beautiful memories I cherished away and replacing them with the ugly ones. I was transcended to the cafeteria, stalking my way through the riot to the G-Man, watching as he licked the chocolate pudding off his spoon and locked eyes with me.

The flicker of surprise in his eyes had my pace quickening and I realized I did what I set out to do. I saw my plan through without exception. He never suspected that this would happen. That we would meet like this and I would take his life.

He stared at me, watching as I pulled the scissors out and close the distance between us.

"It's about time, Pastore," he goaded, gripping the edge of the table as he slowly stood. "You took long enough to get yours. I was thinking you would let me get away with everything."

I didn't reply, truthfully, I didn't even hear his words at the time but my conscious did. My conscious remembered every fucking word he uttered.

"Come on motherfucker, kill me, but it won't make you the winner." He shook his head. "I may have thought you gave up on revenge but that doesn't mean I didn't prepare for it."

Lights flash, sirens sound, men scream but I'm ignorant to it all.

It's a war zone around us but for me and him we are the only two who exist.

"No one will stop what I have planned. Not you, not your organization, and not your friends over at the Satan's Knight's clubhouse" He smiled eerily at me. "This is bigger than the rivalry between you and I, me and Jack Parrish, this is international and it doesn't stop with me. The clock is ticking, Pastore, the plan is set, and no one is safe. A blood bath is coming. If you believe in God, then I suggest you pray for those tied to you and those tied to the Satan's Knights."

I open my eyes; the darkness blinds me as I try to focus and make sense of my dream. Confused, I don't know if it's real or my mind playing tricks on me. His words repeat over and over in my head as I stand on wobbly legs.

A blood bath is coming.
Pray for those tied to you and those tied to the Satan's Knights.
The plan is set, and no one is safe.

"No!" I scream into the darkness.

No one hears me.

My voice echoes off the walls.

Alone.

Darkness, my only friend.

My mind, my only companion.

My memories, my enemy.

A blood bath is coming.

So real.

So vivid.

So true.

Chapter Thirty-Eight

ANTHONY

I lift the sleeve of my black suit and stare at the Breitling watch on my wrist then toward the staircase. We were late for the wedding and Adrianna was taking her sweet time getting dressed.

"Reese's!" I shout up the stairs.

"Daddy, Grandma Maria said I can stay up late tonight," Luca announces, walking into the living room tugging my mother's hand.

"And that I can have ice cream," he adds innocently.

I turn my gaze to my mother who shrugs her shoulders.

"Grandma's have free control to spoil their grandbabies," she answers. "Hasn't that hooligan's wedding started already?"

"Jack isn't a hooligan."

"Right, excuse me, I forgot he was the big cheese of a lovely motorcycle club," she corrects, rolling her eyes. "Blue collar criminals, different from the classy ones we're used to," she sneers, shaking her head. "One kid married the mob the other married the biker club. Where did I go wrong?"

"Reese's," I holler again, desperate to escape my mother's shenanigans.

"I'm coming!" She calls, her heels clicking across the cherry wood steps, causing me to turn around and lift my eyes in her direction.

She wore a skintight, red dress that hugged her in all the right places and stopped at her knees. After a quick glance, I treated myself to a slow perusal of her body, starting with her shoes. Those fucking things cost me a fortune when all I really had to do was grab a pair out of her closet and paint the bottoms red. Looking at them now, they were sexy as hell and worth every red cent. Her legs, tan and toned, hidden beneath the red fabric that started at her knees, hugged her thighs, accentuated her hips and pinched her waist. I couldn't wait to run my hands up those curves and bury my face between her breasts. Shit, they were everywhere, spilling out the top of the dress that tied around her neck.

Finally, I find her eyes, full with amusement. She winks at me and spins around so I get the full effect and a glance of her round ass.

"Close your mouth, Bianci," she laughs, stepping toward me. "Everything you see is everything that is yours."

Ain't that a fucking fact.

I grab her hands and pull her against me, pressing the bulge in my fitted pants to her stomach. I want her but that's no surprise, she does it for me. She did it for me when she was just a girl and she really fucking does it for me as a woman.

A grin spreads across her face as she tilts her head back and brushes her lips across mine.

"You look good enough to eat," I growl against her lips.

"Maybe we should skip the wedding," she says, tugging on my tie. I bitched when she brought it home but now I get it—it matched her dress.

"No, but we're already late what's a few more minutes?" I say as my teeth graze her red lips teasingly before I pull my mouth from hers and look over my shoulder. "Give Mommy and Daddy a kiss, Luca," I say, turning around and crouching to my knees to catch him in my arms.

Lifting him into my arms, both me and Adrianna shower his face with kisses as my mother lifts Victoria out of her swing and cradles her in her arms. I set Luca down on his feet and kiss my daughter's head, watch Adrianna do the same then take her hand and lace our fingers together.

"You two get going, I have it under control," my mom says, winking at Luca.

"We won't be too late," Adrianna reassures her as I drag her to the door. Barely closing it I push her up against it and take her face in my hands as I slam my mouth over hers. I swallow her gasp as I work her lips apart and slide my tongue over hers. The taste of her awakens the beast inside me, one that won't ever be sated. I kiss her deeply, frantically, feverishly tasting every sweet crevice of her mouth.

Breathless and harder than a fucking iron horse I tear my lips from hers, watch as her eyes flutter open and her lips part, releasing a soft pant.

"Car. Now," I growl, pulling my keys out of my pocket and taking a step back giving her room to pass. She pushes off the door, smooths down the front of her dress causing me to laugh.

"What're you laughing at?" she asks, still a little breathless.

I lean forward, blow the hair away from her ear and whisper.

"You fixing yourself. It's a waste of time. I'm only going to mess you all up the second we get in the car," I rasp, slapping her ass playfully sending her jumping in her seven hundred-dollar shoes. "Go on, Reese's strut for me," I croon as she starts for the car, sashaying her hips with every step.

I bite the inside of my cheek as my eyes drink her in and I unlock the car, reaching over her to pull open her door and usher her inside the truck. I painfully walk around the front of the truck to the driver's side and climb in.

"Now what?" she asks huskily, as I start the car. I glance in the rearview mirror and back out of the driveway. I didn't bother answering her, driving to the corner of our block and pulling into the spot in front of the Johnny pump.

I turn to her, pressing the recline button on my seat and with my other hand I tap my lap.

"You're kidding," she accuses, undoing her seatbelt.

"Try me," I dare.

She arches her hips, rolling the silk of her dress up her thighs so it pooled around her waist, revealing a black lace thong.

I groan as she slid the thong down her legs, pulling it off at the ankles as I unbuckle my pants. She was about to remove the shoes when I reached for her hand.

"Don't," I order.

"Want to get your money's worth?" she laughs, raising an eyebrow teasing me.

"Damn straight," I say, dragging my pants to my knees. Her eyes zero in on my cock as I wrap my hand around it, stroking it as she chews on her lip. She was some sight. Sexy as all hell, and all mine.

"Come on, Reese's, show me what you got," I dare, pumping my swollen dick, watching as she straddles the console between us then finally me. She grabs onto the leather headrest behind me, throws her hair over her shoulder as she works her hips, grinding her pussy against me working her clit over the head of my cock.

I reach up, untying the bow at the back of her neck and pull the neckline of her dress until I expose the most perfect set of tits. I take them in my hands, squeeze as much as I can. They used to fit in the palm of my hand but now they were more than a handful. Her nipples were bigger too, darker and when erect even more sensitive than before.

They were perfect.

Like everything else about Adrianna.

I bend my head, take one nipple between my teeth and tug, loving the effect it has on her as she grinds herself harder against my cock. I soothe the sting with my tongue and repeat the action over and over causing her to quicken her pace.

The windows fog as my control teeters. Threading my fingers through her hair, fisting the ends, I force her head back and close my mouth over her pulse point on her neck.

Time to mess you up, Reese's.

I untangle my hands from her hair and slide them down to her hips.

"Up," I order, my mouth still firmly planted on her neck, sucking, nibbling, devouring every inch of her smooth skin.

She lifts her hips as I grab my cock and slide the head over the seam of her wet pussy. The breathy moan that escapes her lips has my dick twitching with need as I position myself and arch off the seat. She slides onto my cock, taking me deeper and deeper until she sits fully on my lap.

I lift my hands back to her face and turn her gaze to me, claiming her mouth with my own as she works me, slowly at first, finding a rhythm that suits both of us. Sweat drips off her face onto mine, skin slaps skin, clothes pushed and shoved aside as she rides me—just like I taught her all those years ago.

My lips are everywhere; her mouth, her neck, her tits, her shoulders and back to her mouth, bruising every part of her. I take hold of her hips again, pushing off the back of the seat and slide into her as deep as I could possibly go.

"I can't hold it back anymore," she pants, reaching between us, her fingers caressing her clit. She throws her head back; brown waves fall over the steering wheel as I have front row seats to my favorite show. I watch as Adrianna gets off. Her sleek pussy clenching around my cock, holding me in place as her fingers work vigorously to see her through her orgasm.

"That's it," I urge, gritting my teeth. "Come all over me, Reese's," I say, grabbing onto her tits as I thrust inside her sensitive pussy. Her eyes roll behind her head as I feel my balls tighten and my dick swell. "Fuck," I roar, shuddering as her pussy squeezes my release right out of my cock.

Moments later she collapses on top of me, breathless and messy.

"We're so late," she mutters against my chest.

"But it was so fucking worth it," I reply, palming the cheeks of her ass before giving one of them a light smack. "If we leave now, maybe we'll make it in time for the priest to pronounce them husband and wife."

"There's a priest?" she says laughing, leaning back to question me with her eyes.

"Reina's a holy roller," I explain as she crawls over the console and drops the visor down.

"Oh my God!"

"He's a popular guy," I tease, zipping up my pants. I start the car, roll down the windows to let the steam out of the car before I glance over at her.

"I look like I was just fucked," she complains. I grin as I drive out of the spot, watching out of the corner of my eye as she tried to straighten out her wrinkled dress.

I love it when she lets me mess her all up.

Twenty minutes later, I turned the truck onto the street of the Dog Pound. Adrianna was still trying to fix herself, giving up on smoothing the wrinkles out of her dress she concentrated on her hair.

"You look beautiful," I tell her as I pull up to the gate.

She screams as a reply to my compliment, stopping my heart as I slam my foot against the break. Turning to face her, my gaze travels out the window in the direction she stares at in horror. The glass security booth that mimics a parking attendant's booth is splattered with blood.

"Don't move," I shout, opening the console. I pull out my revolver, knock back the safety and jump out of the car. The arm that lifts to let cars through is hanging off by the hinge and is riddled with bullet holes. I walk alongside the truck, with my weapon drawn and stand in front of the window Adrianna is still staring out.

"Get down," I whisper harshly, waiting for her to do so before I take a few steps closer to the glass booth and enter it. The body inside the booth is slumped over. Forcefully I push his chest back so he leans against the chair and I can inspect who it is.

"Shit," I hiss, wiping his blood down the front of my shirt as I peer into Mack's lifeless eyes.

"Anthony," Adrianna cries, causing me to turn around and watch as she points straight ahead. I avert my eyes in the direction she's pointing and I see an unfamiliar man walking toward the clubhouse. His arms are extended at his sides and his feet shuffle with every step he took, appearing as if there were cinderblocks weighing down his feet.

I race out of the booth and hurry to the car.

"Anthony, Nikki and Mike are in there," Adrianna shouts.

Fuck. I kept my hand firmly on the shifter and contemplate my next move, my eyes never wavering from the man making his way toward the clubhouse. My first instinct is to drive my truck over the fucking guy who killed one of Jack's men but I had my wife next to me and this wasn't some Bonnie and Clyde bullshit.

I narrow my eyes, looking for weapons and notice the vest wrapped tightly around his body.

"Anthony!" She shouts.

I ignored her as I continue to concentrate on the vest. Little red and blue threads wrap around his torso and his back connecting to something on his chest. I shift the car into drive and roll toward the clubhouse to get a closer look when Adrianna grabs my arm.

"Are you listening to me? We need to get Nikki and Mike out of there," she orders, desperately.

I run my fingers through my hair, glancing at the gun on my lap before lifting my eyes back to my wife's.

"There's a gun under your seat. The clip is in the glove box," I instruct, turning my attention back to the man who stands in front of the door. "You stay behind me and do as I say, you hear me Adrianna? I'm not kidding this time. I tell you to stay put, stay fucking put."

"And if someone holds a gun to your head?"

"Shoot the motherfucker like you shot Rico," I say, slamming my foot against the gas as the man pulls open the front door of the Dog Pound and disappears inside.

I turn to face her, watch as she pulls back the safety and stare at the door.

"Hey," I say, reaching over the console to squeeze her knee. "I love you."

"I love you too," she replies, turning her gaze to me.

I lean over the console and kiss her quickly. I didn't pull away, and neither did she but the kiss ended as we were thrown from the car and the Dog Pound exploded.

Chapter Thirty-Nine

JACK

I took my place beside the priest, offered him my hand and to my surprise, when he shook it, I didn't turn to ash. Maybe there *was* hope for me.

Blackie walks up behind me, pats me on the shoulder before tipping his chin toward Linc who sits on top of the bar strumming a guitar.

"You knew he could play?"

"No idea," he replies as Linc lifts his head. His eyes remaining closed as he hums along to the familiar tune. Finding the beat, he begins to sing.

If I could then I would.
I'll go wherever you will go.
Way up high or down low, I'll go wherever you will go.

Our attention diverted from Linc to the end of the makeshift aisle where Lacey stood smiling from ear to ear. I return her smile as she starts down the aisle to the sound of Linc's smooth voice surrounding us. Clutching her bouquet, her gaze locks on the man standing to my left and she continues toward us. Pausing in front of me she presses a kiss to my cheek before reaching for Blackie's hand. Winking at her, he lifts her hand to his lips and places a quick kiss to her knuckles. Lacey winks at him before she turns and takes her spot across from me. I take in a deep breath as I turn, knowing I was about to lay eyes on the light of my life.

To watch you, to guide you through the darkest of your days.
If a great wave you shall fall and fall upon us.
Then I hope there's someone out there who can bring me back to you.

Even with a mind that fails me, there are moments in my life that have stuck with me. The day my parents died. The day I received my patch. Both days my kids were born. The day I took the gavel as president of the Satan's Knights. The day I walked into Dee's Diner and ordered a slice of cherry pie. They all float around in my head.

But this day, this moment, this one will stick with me even after I'm buried. Seeing her at the end of the aisle, smiling at me with love radiating from the depths of her soul and shining through her eyes. This moment will be engrained in my heart. The moment my bride walks to me and offers me a future.

Pairing her wedding gown with a black leather jacket, she was a vision of white silk and worn leather. The dress beneath the leather was simple, fitted across her chest and flowed freely from under her bust, accentuating the swell of her stomach and trailing behind her with every step she took toward me. She lowers the bouquet of sunflowers and places her hand over her stomach as she takes the final steps.

She hands Lacey her bouquet before turning to me and placing her hands in mine.

"Dearly beloved, we are gathered here today on this beautiful day to join this man and this woman in holy matrimony," the priest begins as I lace our fingers together, squeezing her hands slightly as I swallow the lump in my throat.

"If anyone can show just cause why this couple cannot lawfully be joined in matrimony, let them speak now or forever hold their peace," the priest continues.

I tear my eyes away from Reina and glance around the room, daring anyone to fuck with me, but all I see are smiling faces. A room full of people near and dear to both me and Reina, people who respect the both of us, all of whom are part of our new family.

I'd remember their faces and this moment too.

And the one that came next.

The door opens, sunlight streams from behind the figure shuffling through the door, blinding the view of the man's face. When the door finally closes behind him I see Ronan clear as day, gagged with duct tape, arms extended out to his sides mimicking Jesus on the cross and enough explosives strapped to his chest to blow up an entire neighborhood.

Frozen in place, his eyes meet mine and I watch the tears spill down his cheeks.

That was the final moment engrained in my memory.

The moment my eyes met the man the enemy sent to deliver us our fate.

My life and love might still go on.

In your heart, in your mind, I'll stay with you for all of time.

BOOM.

Chapter Forty

Adrianna

My eyes flutter open, fighting for focus through a thick cloud of smoke and dust, reminding me why I was face down against the concrete. Lifting my cheek from the ground, I open my mouth to call for Anthony but it feels as if there is something in my throat, suffocating me. I swallow hard, trying to scream but only managed to whisper. I close my eyes, swallow again and try one more time. This time, I push myself up off the ground and allow my eyes to roam over the destruction surrounding me. Bile rises in my throat as I see the orange and amber glow of flames through the thick fog of smoke.

"Anthony," I scream, hysteria coursing through me as I twist my head from side to side hoping to spot my husband. Kneeling, I groan in pain, my stomach aches with every slight movement I make. I stay hunched over, clutching my ribs that are probably broken from the impact of being tossed from the truck. Coughing, I cover my mouth and slowly stand on my bare feet.

My shoes are gone.

"Anthony," I cry frantically, walking through the fog over the glass and debris. In the distance I can hear the faint cries of others pleading for help but none of them match the voice I'm searching for, desperate to hear.

"Oh God," I whimper, climbing over the truck. "Anthony!"

"Reese's," he mumbles.

"Yes, baby it's me. Where are you?" I ask, squinting as I ignore the burn of my eyes and try to locate him. "Keep talking so I can follow your voice."

"I'm over here," he says, sounding more coherent than before. "Shit," he groans. "My arm is fucked."

I follow the sound of his voice, finding him leaning against a piece of what I think is our truck, one arm crossed over his chest, clutching his bicep that is pouring blood. I run to him, crunching glass beneath my feet. I'm reminded of the pain in my stomach when I drop to my knees in front of him. Wincing in pain I grab a hold of his face and touch my lips to his.

"Thank God," I cry, leaning my forehead against his as he snakes his good arm around my waist.

"Are you okay?"

"I think I may have a broken rib or two but I'm okay," I assure him, leaning back to take a look at his arm and stare at the offensive piece of metal piercing his bicep. He grunts through his teeth, forcing my focus back to his face.

"It's nothing," he grumbles.

It's not nothing, but glancing over my shoulder, following the sounds of the people inside the demolished clubhouse, I know it's the lesser of the injuries we're about to face. There's death waiting on the other side of the cloud of smoke and I pray it's not my sister.

"Adrianna," Anthony shouts, dragging my focus back to him. "Listen, I need you to pull this piece of metal out of my arm."

His blue eyes are dead serious as mine widen, shifting to the dagger.

"If I take that out of your arm you will bleed out."

"If you don't then I'm useless and there are over two dozen people trapped in those flames that need us," he protests through gritted teeth. "Pull the metal out of my arm, Reese's."

My hands trembled as they move toward his arm.

"Do it," he shouts.

I shake my head, glancing around then back at him and the red tie that hangs loosely around his neck covered in ash.

"Do it!" he repeats.

I loosen the knot, pulling the tie from his neck before I stand and close my eyes. Forcing myself to stay calm I close my hands over the metal.

"On three," I say. "One. Two."

"Three," he grunts.

He curses as the metal slides out of his body, slowly torturing him until I drop it to the ground and quickly wrap his silk tie around the wound. It instantly becomes soaked with his blood but I continue to wrap it, pulling it tight with all my might before double knotting it and praying it controls the bleeding.

"I'm sorry," I cry watching his face contort with pain. He takes a deep breath and grabs my hand, slowly hoisting himself up until he stands on unsteady legs. He drops a kiss on my forehead before fixing his eyes to mine.

"Don't leave my side," he orders.

"I won't," I say, rubbing the ache beneath my breastbone.

We walk through the smoke, bypassing the flames crawling around parts of the ground. It was hard to decipher what was the parking lot and what in fact were the remains of the clubhouse.

"Hello!" Anthony calls into the devastation. "Call out if you can hear me."

"Nikki!" I shout. "Mike!"

Nothing.

"Bianci, you bastard, I've never been so happy to hear your voice."

"Pipe?" Anthony questions.

"Aye," he replies.

"Keep talking," my husband instructs Pipe. I stay close behind him as he follows the sound of Pipe's voice but the arch of my foot pulses, forcing me to stop. Balancing my weight onto one foot, I turn around and spot a body face down on the floor. I glance over my shoulder, making sure that Anthony wasn't too far behind me before I start toward the body.

I freeze when he crawls across the debris.

"Hey," I call out, unable to make out who it is but my voice is mute to him. He's crawling straight toward the fire with no regard. "Hey," I shout again but he continues to ignore me.

Taking the few steps remaining between us, I bend down and grab a hold of his shoulder.

Big fucking mistake.

His hand closes around my wrist and snaps it back as he rolls over onto his back and glares up at me.

"Don't fucking touch me," he sneers. The pain vibrates through my whole body and blurs my vision as he snaps my wrist before releasing it. "Johnson! Rogers! Diaz!"

I blink through the pain, push my eyes to focus and take in the man before me. His eyes are blank as he continues to search frantically for the three names he calls over and over again. I think he's in shock and for a moment I remember what it feels like. I remember pulling the trigger on my sister's boyfriend and losing my bearings. I glance down at his cut, squinting to try to and make out the name sewn to the leather.

"Stryker," I say, dragging his attention back to me. "Stryker, it's okay we'll find them," I plead, trying to soothe him.

"They were fifty yards out where the Afghan post is," he rambles.

I'm about to answer, talk him through it when I close my eyes as the pain shoots through my wrist sending tingling sensations up my arm.

"Adrianna!"

"Over here," I whimper, tears filling my eyes. I blink through them and find Stryker staring back at me shaking his head as if he wishes he can erase what just happened.

"Shit," he grits, taking in our surroundings, realizing he's not overseas and the war zone we're in the middle of has nothing to do with terrorism and everything to do with the club he's a part of. He turns his gaze back to me.

"Are you okay?" he asks.

"Stryker, you're okay, man?" Pipe says, limping alongside my husband. "I've got to find Oksana."

Stryker doesn't pay Pipe any attention and continues to stare at me, averting his eyes to my wrist, he swallows.

"What happened to your arm?" Anthony asks.

I open my mouth to answer when I hear my sister's scream echo through the devastation.

"Nikki!"

"Where are you?" Anthony shouts into the smoke, coughing as his lungs fill with dust.

"I don't know," she cries. "Please help! Mikey is trapped."

"What do you see around you?" Pipe shouts.

Nikki remains silent as we start to move. I can feel Stryker's gaze burning a hole into me but I ignore the mentally anguished veteran and wait for my sister's reply.

"He's trapped underneath the bar," she calls back to us.

"This way," Pipe instructs.

"Linc," Stryker mutters. "He was sitting on top of the bar before the blast."

"Is Mike conscience?" Anthony asks.

"In and out. Please help!" Her voice is frantic and my heart breaks at her plea.

"Do you see anyone else trapped?" Stryker questions over Pipe's shoulder.

"We've got a problem," Pipe announces.

Following his gaze, I see the violent flames swirling in our path.

"There are two people trapped but I can't tell who they are, one is wearing cowboy boots and the other is…oh my God," she shrieks.

"What! What is it?" I scream back to her, watching in horror as the three men try to figure a way to get passed the flames.

"It's a woman, but she's all the way at the other end. I only see her shoes."

"What color are they?" Pipe asks.

"They look red but I can't be sure," she chokes. "The smoke is so thick over here. Are you guys close?"

"Oksana was wearing red shoes," Pipe says to himself, raking his fingers through his thinning hair.

"Help me with this," Stryker orders, walking over to the metal door lying haphazardly amongst the debris. He bends his knees and grabs one end while Pipe reaches for a corner and Anthony grunts through the pain to grab the other end. The three men quickly shuffle their feet toward the fire and throw the metal door over the flames. It takes a few minutes before some of the fire is contained but not all of it.

"I need to get to my sister," I shriek, hope diminishing inside me as I watch the flames continue to dance, separating us from saving her and Mike. "Nikki," I cry, my body writhing with sobs as I feel Anthony slide one arm around me, pulling my back toward his chest.

"I'm going in," Stryker announces. Before any of us can say anything he pulls his leather over his face, bows his head and charges across the metal door into the flames.

It's my breaking point and I crumble. The sound of my sister begging Mikey to open his eyes, the fire crackling around me as I watch Stryker disappear into the amber lights. He's one man fighting flames trying to rescue three people trapped beneath destruction. Even if he's able to get one of them free he won't be able to carry them through the fire to safety.

Dread fills my soul.

Panic runs through my veins.

The stench of death is heavy in the air as we become helpless to those trapped amongst the devastation.

How do you choose who lives and who dies?

How do you save everyone?

How do you live with yourself if one can't be saved?

"Adrianna," Anthony shouts, shaking me as he turns my chin left of the flames. I narrow my eyes, push through the tears and watch as Stryker emerges stomping over a mountain of rubble carrying my sister.

"Mikey," she screams over his shoulder, pounding her fists over and over against his shoulder. "Put me down! I told you to leave me if you couldn't get him out."

Stoically, he drops my sister in front of me and grabs a hold of Pipe. I bend, ignoring the aches shooting through my body and wrap my arms around my sister.

"Thank you," I whisper to him. I'm not sure if he hears me because he grabs a hold of Pipe's arm and turns his gaze to Anthony.

"I need help getting the bar off them."

"Anthony, please, you have to save him. Please!" Nikki cries in my arms.

Another shrill voice screams, tearing my attention away from the three men staring back at me and my sister.

"Lacey," Pipe screams, looking between the direction of Lacey's voice and the other where his wife, Mikey and God knows who else is trapped.

Who do you save?

Who do you choose?

Chapter Forty-One

Lacey

Wake up!

But this isn't a nightmare and I'm already awake.

Creating deep scratches, I drag my nails back and forth across my arms and draw blood. Despite my hopes and prayers, the crimson stares back at me antagonizing me just like my mind is and confirms this is real.

Hysteria ripples through me as my eyes dart around searching through thick smoke and fire for the people I love.

Blackie.

Dad.

Reina.

I was standing right beside Reina when the man came into the clubhouse. Right beside her. She has to be somewhere close. And Dad, I remember him throwing himself over her before the blast. I remember that because when they went down I locked eyes with Blackie and saw the terror in his face, the unmistakable look of defeat.

"GET DOWN!"

There wasn't enough time for him to get to me and the look in his eyes, accompanied by the pain in his voice, solidified my knight cloaked in leather wouldn't be able to save me.

Not this time.

I fought my mind believing the destruction was all in my head but another glance at the track marks my nails are making on my arms and I know that this time it's not the maker inside me wreaking havoc but one we don't know.

"Blackie!" I scream, not sure my voice is even making a sound. There is something lodged in my throat suffocating me. I try to pull whatever it is out with my fingers but nothing is coming out. I swallow but it doesn't help. I force myself to cough, hoping to hack whatever it is up but wind up spitting into my hand, covering my palm with my saliva and blood.

Wiping my hand down the front of my dress I hear people screaming and crying. My eyes widen with hope and my heart rate picks up. There are survivors out there in the fire, in the rubble there are people alive begging for help.

Not your people.

Listen closely, those aren't the voices you want to hear.

Covering my ears, I press my palms down as hard as they can go, squeezing my maker out of my head as I crawl out from the corner I seem to have land in when the explosion occurred.

They didn't survive.

Your father is dead.

Blackie is dead.

Reina and the baby won't make it.
You'll live the rest of your life alone wishing you died too.
"No," I yell. "Shut up! Just shut up!"
But my maker doesn't stop and every step I take, the voice becomes louder. Through my tears, through the torment of my mind, I see the familiar reaper. I drop my hands from my head and with a belly full of dread I walk toward the body. My hands tremble as I roll the body over and stare at the familiar face. Bosco. I bring my fingers to his neck, pray for a pulse but the moment my fingers touch his skin I know I won't find one. The life is already drained out of him.
"Lacey!"
Rocking back on my heels, I drop my hand from Bosco and search for the voice calling out my name.
"Blackie?" I shriek, fisting my hands in frustration as the smoke fills my lungs and burns my eyes. "Where are you?"
Struggling, I climb over Bosco's body in the direction I think his voice is and fight to keep my eyes open.
"I'm coming for you, girl. I'm going to get you out of here," he yells. "I need you to look around and tell me what you see. Can you do that for me?"
Bracing one hand against a piece of steel, I clear my throat and swallow the grainy particles choking me. I lift the hem of my dress and wipe my irritated eyes, blinking several times before scanning the area. I narrow my eyes as I see a doorway but I'm not sure where it leads. Stepping closer, I hear another person groan.
"Hello?" I call out. "Who's there?"
"Lacey, you need to name your surroundings. Something. Anything," Blackie shouts.
A large frame fills the doorway and my eyes clash with Wolf's strained face.
"Wolf!" I holler, relief filling my voice. "Blackie, I see Wolf!"
Wolf doesn't pay any attention to me, he's to enthralled with the object he's struggling to drag through the door way. I hurry toward him, climbing over thrown objects until I'm standing in front of him. He lifts his eyes, sweat pouring from his face as he drags the beloved table out of the chapel.
"We're near the chapel," I shout back to Blackie.
"Don't move, I'm coming for you."
"Okay," I cry out, turning back to Wolf. "Did you hear that, Wolf? Blackie's coming, he will get us out of here."
Lifting his right hand to his left arm, Wolf hunches over the table as his face contorts with pain.
"Wolf?"
"Tell the Bulldog I tried to save it," he grunts, losing his grip on the table as he collapses in pain before my feet.
"No, no, no. Wolf!" I cry, dropping to the ground as I reach for him. "Stay with me," I plead, watching as all the strength drains from his body and he continues to clutch his arm.
"Lace, I'm almost there," Blackie calls.

"Please hurry! I think Wolf is having a heart attack," I shriek, taking his left hand. "Hang on, Wolf, hang on for your sons, they need you," I tell him but as the words leave my mouth his eyes close in defeat.

A crash sounds in the distance, forcing my eyes to lift and watch as Blackie appears, swinging pieces of metal out of his way, clearing a path straight for me. There are several lacerations marking his face, blood drips from his brow, a gash under his eye and his bottom lip is split in two. He turns his head, his eyes finding mine, and he tear escapes his eye.

There is so much reflected in his eyes but the most evident is love and relief. It mirrors what shines in mine as I look at him.

Face to face.

Leather and Lace.

"Thank fucking God," he says, rushing toward me.

His arms wrap around my trembling body and the nightmare we're a part of fades away. It's just him and I, two people who never stop fighting for each other.

His lips brush my temple as he pulls back, holding my face as he examines me.

"Are you okay?" he asks as he tucks a strand of hair behind my ear and winces when he gently touches the gash on my head.

"I am now," I whisper through my tears.

He brings me against him again, crushing my bruised body in his arms before he kisses my lips lightly.

"I thought I lost you too," he admits. "Shit, Wolf..."

He releases his hold on me, moving around me to check Wolf's pulse.

"Is he..."

"He's alive," he confirms, throwing one of Wolf's arms around his neck. "Come on, Wolf, we're going to get you out of here. Lacey, grab his other arm," he says, struggling to lift him. Quickly, I move to his other side and mimic Blackie's stance. Together, we move Wolf into an upright position. His body like lead, we pull him up, balancing his weight between us.

Blackie leads the way and we walk in the direction he first appeared. I glance around the destruction; my eyes fall to the wooden table that Wolf tried so hard to salvage. The table my father held dear to his heart.

"You with me, girl?"

"My dad," I murmur, turning my eyes to Blackie's. "What about him and Reina?"

"We'll find them," he reassures me.

No you won't.

It's too late.

I close my eyes, fighting back the voice I fear is true and pray Blackie is right. I pray they are together.

And more than anything I pray they are alive.

Reina

There is something solid on top of me, pinning me down, something heavy that acts as a shield. Opening my eyes, I realize it's a body that is protecting me from the building that has exploded and continues to collapse around us.

The body of the man I was supposed to marry.

There are certain things that resonate with you, unforgettable situations that stick with you, like, being trapped in a burning house with your fiancé. For a moment I feel as if I'm transcended back in time. The sounds are the same, the scents too, and so is the suffocating feeling of dust and debris trapped in my lungs. The flames crackle and sizzle, threatening to melt the layers of skin as they once did before. And like before, I don't care. I am not frightened by the fire but terrified of losing the man I'm with.

However, amongst the similarities there are also differences.

Jack is unconscious, but he's breathing, he isn't dead.

And there is a life inside of me, a fragile life who is relying on me to keep it safe.

This time I won't lay down and die.

This time I'll fight.

I swallow, easing the dryness from my throat and lift my hand to Jack's ash covered face.

"Jack."

He doesn't respond but I feel his shallow breaths against my neck and hang on to hope. He's heavy against me and my body aches as I slide out from under him. I clutch my stomach the minute I'm free as I feel a painful tightening across my stomach. Grinding my teeth through the pain, I try to move closer to Jack.

"Jack, please wake up," I cry, glancing down at my stomach. Closing my eyes, I take a deep breath, hold it and blow it out as the pain eases.

I turn back to Jack, crawl toward him and roll him onto his back before taking his face in my palms.

"Jack!" I shriek, desperate for him to wake. "I need you," I plead, fearing the worst, knowing that another pain will shoot through my stomach and every minute that passes is crucial to the survival of our child.

I lift my eyes as I hold his face and stare at the violent orange, yellow and red swirls dancing around the room. There is no life to be found amongst the ruins. There is only us. The cramps spread across my abdomen as I lay my head against his chest and my body shudders with sobs.

I don't know how long I lay there, staring at the flames as I clutch Jack's leather vest and pray for a miracle. I think about the baby inside me, the man beneath me and how I'm slowly losing everything I've ever wanted. Any pain, heartache or suffering I've experienced in my life is insignificant compared to what I feel right now.

"Hail Mary full of Grace, the Lord is with thee," I murmur as the tears roll down my cheeks and disappear somewhere onto the man I planned to promise to love and honor until death do we part. "Blessed art thou among women and blessed is the fruit of thy womb, Jesus. Holy Mary, Mother of God, pray for us sinners, now and at the hour of our death."

I close my eyes, lay one hand on my belly and the other on Jack.

"Amen."

My hair catches on something but I ignore the pull until it becomes a persistent tug. Opening my eyes, I slowly lift my head and my eyes stare into Jack's.

He unwinds the lock of hair wrapped around his fingers and continues to keep his eyes on me. I open my mouth to ask him what hurts when another pain shoots through me. Instantly, his eyes darken and I try to mask the pain contorting my face.

"What's the matter?" he questions.

His eyes narrow in confusion and he opens his mouth again to speak but closes it as I shake my head.

"Nothing," I say through clenched teeth as I try to sit up.

"Reina," he shouts, forcing my gaze back to him as I clench my jaw and try to breathe. I watch as he lifts a hand to his ear and tries to shake his head.

"I think…oh boy," I hiss, watching as his eyes move to my lips. "I'm having contractions," I groan.

"Speak up," he commands, averting his eyes back to mine.

"I'm having contractions," I shout even louder though he is merely centimeters from me. I watch his face fall. He shakes his head as he lifts both hands to his ears.

He can't hear me.

Not a word.

Silently, I pull his hands from his ears and rest them over my belly.

A storm rages in the depths of his black eyes before he drops his gaze to my belly. His hands never leave me as I watch him cringe and struggle to sit up. I place my finger beneath his chin and tilt his head back so his eyes meet mine.

I love you.

My eyes whisper within the sound of silence.

"You," he replies with deaf ears.

I take his hand, lay it flat against my chest and stare back at him.

Me.

Nikki

I become inpatient waiting for Stryker, Anthony and Pipe to rescue Mikey, knowing every minute wasted is another cut from his life. If they couldn't get him out then I wasn't leaving his side. For better or worse, in sickness and in health, until death do we part. Unable to stand on her bare mangled feet, I watch as Adrianna collapses on top of the rubble before dodging back through the smoke and making my way back to my husband. The smoke is thick, making it hard to see, but I hear Anthony's voice at the other end of the bar.

"What are you doing?" Mike asks hoarsely.

Ignoring him, I continue to move broken shards of glass, steel, and wood. I know it's not making much of a difference and that I can never lift the weight pinning Mikey to the ground but I can't sit still. I have to do something.

"Nikki, we've got it! Go back to your sister," Anthony shouts.

I clear enough space to step between the debris and the woman wearing the red shoes. Before, I couldn't tell who it was because of the large piece of Sheetrock blocking my vision. I grunt, pushing it out of the way just as the three men jump over the scatter of flames contained by steel.

My eyes drift upward and I scream in horror as I stare at the lifeless woman. One of the glass shelves must have come flying at her and slit her throat.

"What is it?" Mike demands.

"Nikki," Anthony hollers.

"She's over there! Fucking leave me, get her. Go to her!'

I close my eyes, open them and she's still there, dead, her head hangs onto her shoulders by a thread.

"No! No! No! Oksana," Pipe screams, knocking me out of the way as he reaches for her. His hands hesitate as they close in on her body, unsure where to touch her.

Anthony pulls me up and spins me around, wrapping his arms around me and pushes my face into his chest, shielding my eyes from the brutal scene. I cry for the woman I never met and the man who collapses over her body and mourns.

My brother-in-law guides me away from the tragic couple and back to my husband.

"On three," Stryker orders and Anthony releases me, pulling back to stare at me.

"You're okay," he assures. "Mike will be okay. It'll all be over soon. I promise."

I don't respond as he lets go of me and moves to the other side of the beam trapping Mikey's legs. The voices fade as the men count, grunt and struggle to free my husband and then I hear the muffled sounds of sirens.

"Help is here," Adrianna calls out to us.

I close my eyes and thank God.

But for some it is already too late.

For some this is the end.

Chapter Forty-Two

RIGGS

I lean my elbows on my knees and stare at the glass doors as the sirens draw closer. After the call from Maria informing us of the explosion Lauren and I chartered my parents' jet and hauled ass to the hospital. From take-off to landing we took two and a half hours to arrive. We've been waiting for a little over an hour now with still no word of anyone being brought in from the Dog Pound. Every time the doors open and they wheel in another stranger I lose my fucking shit. I've been here before. Sitting here helpless, waiting for word of those that matter and I swore I'd never do it again.

The only silver lining is Kitten is beside me and not on a gurney speeding through the emergency room.

"Look," she says beside me, wrapping her arm around mine as she leans her head on my shoulder and points toward the dozen doctors running straight to the emergency room entrance.

"That's gotta be them," I reply.

Together we stand and make our way to the entrance, catching sight of the first ambulance that pulls in front.

"Thirty-year-old female. Thirty weeks pregnant, contractions are seven minutes apart but her water hasn't broken," the paramedic shouts as the team of doctors wheel Reina through the doors.

"Jack! Where's Jack?"

"Ma'am, I already told you we've got him. He's in the next ambulance," the paramedic assures her.

"Reina!" I shout, trying to make my way over to her but I'm quickly pushed back as the doctors' race away from the door. I spin around as another gurney is pushed through the doors.

"Second-degree burns to his back and he can't hear out of both ears," someone says as they wheel Jack into the hospital.

barely process my president lying helpless on a stretcher.

"We've got a massive coronary over here," another paramedic hollers from the street, lifting Wolf from the back of the ambulance.

"Oh my God," Lauren cries next to me, covering her face with her hands as the parade of injuries continues all at once.

"Kitten," I murmur, peeling back her hands as Anthony appears. A nurse pushes him in a wheelchair as he holds an oxygen mask to his face. His other arm is fucked up, covered in blood and wrapped with a tie.

Lauren locks eyes with her brother and takes off running for him.

"You're okay," she cries, bending down to throw her arms around him. I watch as he removes the mask and wraps his good arm around her. "Where's Adrianna?"

"Right here," she calls from behind him.

If the circumstances were different, and I wasn't so fucking relieved to see the Biancis, I'd bust their balls over the *his* and *her* wheel chairs they were sporting, but fuck, I was just happy they were breathing.

I tried to keep tally of everyone and their injuries, silently breathing a sigh of relief each time another wounded victim was brought in through the doors.

So far no casualties.

The doctors were working to stop Reina's labor. Jack was being treated for first and second-degree burns and they feared he may be deaf. Wolf needed emergency surgery after suffering a massive heart attack. Anthony needed thirty-seven stitches for that injury to his arm and a pint of blood. Adrianna broke her wrist and the soles of her feet needed stitches. Mike broke both his legs and suffered a concussion. Nikki needed sixteen stitches to close the gash in her arm. Blackie and Lacey were both treated for minor lacerations.

Pipe was still missing.

So were the nomads.

Another ambulance pulls up and Stryker jumps out the back, stepping aside as they wheel in Linc. He was in bad shape and they needed to get him into surgery immediately. The doctors hollered all sorts of medical mumbo jumbo but the one word that stuck with me was paralysis.

Insisting he was fine, Stryker refused medical treatment, but the man was badly burned on one side of his arm. I tore my eyes from him as Cobra walked in covered in blood and froze. The past hit me like a ton of bricks and for a split second I remembered being in his shoes, only the blood I wore was Lauren's and Bones'.

I watched as he stepped aside, and Pipe came into my sight, walking alongside a stretcher carrying a black body bag.

"Sir, you can't come with us," the paramedic told him.

"The fuck I can't," he growled, his eyes staring daggers into the man denying him.

I glanced back at Cobra, looking for answers as to who the victim was and notice the pair of red shoes he carried in his hands.

"We're sorry for your loss, Sir, but you're not allowed in the morgue," a policeman informed him.

"Pipe, you have to let her go, man," Deuce says from behind him.

Every single one of us gave Pipe grief over marrying Oksana, called their marriage a joke and every single one of us were fools. Pipe loved that woman and he loved her just as hard as the rest of us love ours.

His grip loosens from the stretcher and he takes a retreating step back. Changing his mind, he takes a step forward and reaches for the bag but the paramedics quickly roll her away from him.

Oksana wasn't the only one who lost her life.

Prospects, Mack and Bosco were both murdered too.

Lauren wraps her arms around me, burying her face against my chest as I hold on tightly with everything I am. I glance over her head toward Pipe and watch as he stares at the closed doors they wheeled his wife through. He turns his head, his gaze travels over me and Lauren and I open my mouth to offer my condolences but he quickly looks away. Solemnly he takes the shoes from Cobra's hand and walks out of the hospital without a word.

Some stand, others fall, in the end we all bleed.
And we're all bleeding for Pipe.

ANTHONY

Leaning back against the cot, I close my eyes as the attending doctor stitches my arm. I'm fucking exhausted but adrenaline is coursing through my body making me antsy. I want to get the fuck out of here, go home, kiss my kids and sleep for a month.

"You about done, doc?"

"Almost," she says, pulling back the needle.

The curtain slides open and Adrianna comes into my view. She's in a wheelchair; her feet propped up and covered in bandages. Her right arm is also bandaged from her wrist to her elbow with a fiberglass cast. There's a butterfly stitch over her brow and a nasty bruise forming under her eye. She's still the most gorgeous woman I have ever laid eyes on.

"That should do it," the doctor announces. "I'll be back to check on you."

Tearing my eyes from my wife, I turn to face the doctor and narrow my eyes.

"Check on me? Come on, doc, you stitched me back together, isn't it time to cut me loose?"

"Sorry, Mr. Bianci, but it says on your chart we're keeping you for observation," she informs me before pulling back the curtain and disappearing out of my view. I grunt and turn to my wife as she wheels herself over to my side and struggles to stand on her injured feet.

"Why don't you let Riggs take you home?" I question as she climbs into the tiny bed with me.

"Looking to get rid of me?"

"Never," I answer, wincing as I lift my injured arm, making room for her, careful of her own injuries. "But, I know you'd rather be home in our bed with the kids."

"Lucky for us, I snatched Riggs' phone," she says, producing the phone she had tucked between her breasts.

"Lucky phone," I tease as I place my finger under her chin and tilt her head back. "Hey," I started.

"Hmm?"

I search her eyes for signs of despair, recalling how closed off she became after the shooting at Temptations, but there are no traces of shock or PTSD like last time. I don't know if this is the calm before the storm, if she'll break once she's home and the dust has settled or if her skin has grown thicker since the last time we faced certain death.

"What's going on inside that head?"

"I lost my shoes," she replies flatly. I follow her gaze to the gauze wrapped around her feet.

"I'll buy you a new pair," I tell her, kissing the top of her head. "Now…the truth, what are you thinking about?"

"What happens now?" she asks softly, lifting her eyes to mine.

I stare at her silently, deciding how to answer her since I'm not sure what happens from here. I don't want to frighten her and tell her there will be a motherfucking war, one that will likely make the shit we've been witness to in the past look like a church picnic.

"I mean whoever the fuck did this will pay for this, right?" she questions, surprising me.

"Come again?"

"You can't get up but I did, and this emergency room is full of everyone we know and love. If my father was here, he'd be on the streets already, looking for mercy. So, again, whoever did this, whoever ruined Jack and Reina's wedding, jeopardized their baby, and scarred the lives of all of us, they will pay, right?"

"You offering to take them out?"

"We could've died and left our kids orphans so yeah, if it came down to it, I'd be the first in line," she says, her face set in stone.

Another man may have laughed at his wife's offer to take out the people responsible but not me. I didn't doubt, given the opportunity, Adrianna would take out the enemy. She's a fighter, been fighting for what she loves since she was fifteen years old, since she met me.

What I'm saying is I know you will have a part in this and I'm okay with it, just as long as you raise all sorts of hell and get every last one but you come home to me. You come back and you tuck our kids into bed and love me because if I ever lose you I'll lose me too."

I open my mouth but she silences me with a finger.

"Just need your promise, Bianci," she whispers softly. "No explanations."

"I promise," I say against her finger and watch her nod in satisfaction. She drops her hand and a smile forms across her perfect mouth. A little chuckle escapes next and I think it's happening—she's going to lose her cool.

What's so funny?" I cautiously ask.

"I was just thinking back to that night I went looking for you, the night I found you in the gym...do you remember?"

"Yeah," I say, wondering where she's going with this.

"We were so worried about simply being Anthony and Adrianna but we'll never just be Anthony and Adrianna, will we? I'll always be the mobster's daughter and you will always be his enforcer. We can be parents, we can be gym owners but at the end of the day we will always be Anthony and Adrianna and the mob will always be the foundation our family was built upon."

If today was any indication, she was right There will always be something that pulls us back, reminding us who we are and what we're capable of. Today it was a bomb, tomorrow it'll be when the mailman forgets to deliver her Amazon package and twenty years from now it'll be when Victoria brings home a boyfriend.

I press my lips to hers gently, sealing our fate and the truth. We'll never be ordinary.

"Now, let's call our kids," I say against her mouth.

She pulls back and dials the house, placing the call on speaker. My mother answers and instantly praises Jesus, cursing Jack, going through the whole spiel on how everyone I'm associated with has a death wish. Finally, she puts Luca on the phone and everything is right with the world again.

he terror we survived fades.

Revenge does too.

All that exists is the two innocent people who don't know how ugly the world truly is.

And I hope they never do.

Chapter Forty-Three

BLACKIE

"Mr. Petra, the x-rays show you have five broken ribs. As I'm sure you know there isn't much we can do but give you something for the pain—" the doctor says, reading the films.

"No," I say, cutting him off as I throw my legs over the side of the bed. "I don't need anything," I grunt, cringing as I slide off the bed.

"We'll give you Motrin—" he begins again.

"I said no. I'm a recovering addict so if all I got is a few broken ribs I'll survive. Now, I need to get out of this bed," I tell him, pushing the hair away from my face so he can see the sincerity in my eyes. "I'll deal with the pain by not being kept away from the people who need me so how about you go get my discharge papers and stop wasting my time," I say, my patience running thin.

"Do you realize you've suffered a traumatic experience? You survived a bomb," he replies incredulously.

"I'm well aware of what I survived, and the bomb is one of many on a list of lethal things," I tell him as I grab my blood stained shirt and try to put it on. "If you won't discharge me, I'll sign myself out."

Giving up on the shirt, I toss it onto the bed and grab my leather jacket. I mask the pain in my ribs as I shrug it on and tip my head to the doctor.

"If you've got some time on your hands, there's a pregnant woman who's in labor, a deaf man with burns, another one with two broken legs, should I could continue?"

I didn't give him the opportunity to answer, pushing back the curtain of the triage cubicle. I walk past him and straight into the chaos of the emergency room. And chaos it was. I don't know if they were understaffed or if collectively we had too many injuries, but doctors, nurses and attendants ran around from cubicle to cubicle, treating the victims.

At the compound I was too consumed with making sure Lacey was okay to take in the destruction, but seeing the magnitude of devastation antagonized me, planting the seeds of revenge in my mind.

Images of Ronan flash in front of my eyes, the bomb strapped to his chest, the horror reflected in his eyes as he steps further into the clubhouse. The sound of the explosion rings in my ears and I fight against my natural instincts to flee the hospital and go hunt for the men responsible for this.

"Blackie," Lacey calls, pulling me out of my vengeful thoughts. I blink to clear my vision and focus on my girl. Staring at her doesn't alleviate the dire need for revenge, if anything it broadens it. She looks exhausted, a million miles away and hanging on by a thread. The stitches on her eyebrow and the dried up blood along her hair line doesn't help matters.

I lift my hands to her face, run my thumb over that pouty lip of hers and lean my forehead against hers.

"You see your father?" I ask as her hand travels down the front of my jacket and her fingers graze the gauze wrapped around my midsection.

"Barely, I've been with Reina the whole time," she lifts her gaze to mine. "My dad can't hear, Blackie. The doctor's say its temporary but aren't a hundred percent sure." She pauses to assess my features. She informed me of Jack's diagnosis but her eyes are looking to me for answers.

"You got something you want to ask me, girl?"

he shook her head.

"The answer is in your eyes," she whispers as she grips the ends of my jacket and diverts her eyes downward. "My dad won't be able to ride with deaf ears. He will step down until he's better and someone else will step up. That someone else is you. Even if you weren't the vice president, it'd be you, you're already plotting how to make this right. I see it in your eyes." She lifts her head and stares back at me.

She was right and there was no sense in denying it or making excuses. When I accepted my role within the club, I knew one day this could happen. At one point I even wanted it—to be next in line for the gavel. It wouldn't have been a forced decision like it is now, ideally, my brothers would've voted me into the head of the table after Jack retired.

The Satan's Knights haven't gotten this far in the game by letting our enemies win. Our creed isn't one that accepts defeat. They strike, we strike back. They kill, we extinct. If Jack is in as bad a shape as Lacey is saying he is, he won't be able to lead our club and it will be my duty to do so in his place.

Glancing around the emergency room I decide it would be my fucking honor to take down the motherfuckers that did this. But, looking back at Lacey I question if retribution on this disaster is worth her sanity. As strong as she is there is only so much her mind can withstand.

I'll take the gavel, lead the ride in our quest for retribution and leave Lacey back home with her demons. I struggled back there for a minute, denying the drugs the doctor was ready to feed me because I have a handle on whether I succumb to a relapse. Lacey is different. She can take her meds daily but they won't always silence her maker. She's fragile and sitting home, knowing I'm risking my life to pay back the people who took life from our club, well, I fear that'll send her over the edge.

I won't be there to comfort her, won't be there to turn on the radio and dance with her under the porch lights. Her mind will feed her lies and she'll believe them. not because she wants to, but because I'm not there to prove her maker wrong.

"I get it," she says, dragging me out of my won head. "It's part of the package." She forces a smile.

"You remember what I promised you?"

"You promised me a lot of things."

"Gonna make good on all those promises, girl," I say as I bend my knees, grinding my teeth through the pain as I stare into her dark eyes. "Gonna marry you. Gonna fill that house with a bunch of babies. Gonna grow old long before you but with you right by side, keeping my ass young." I wink at her. "But the promise I will keep before all of those is the one I keep telling you."

I pause, watch the flicker of hope spark in her eyes and know that she's on the same page. She knows the words I'm about to say. She lives by them. Just as I come alive when I say them.

"Girl, I'm coming back for you," I confirm.

And I will.

I'll always come back for my girl.

"Reina!" Jack's screams echo off the walls of the hospital, shrill and unnerving, demanding attention.

Lacey's body grows rigid and I force her eyes back to mine.

"Go back to Reina," I watch her struggle, biting her lip as she decides whether she will listen. "I'll go to him," I assure her, prying her hands off my jacket and kissing her quickly.

Hesitantly she starts for Reina's room and I question why the fuck I denied Motrin, knowing that dealing with Jack ain't going to be any kind of easy.

JACK

I've been poked and prodded and still I can't hear fucking shit. It feels like someone is holding my head under water and I don't fucking like it. Not one fucking bit. I need to get to Reina. I need to make sure she and the baby are okay. Without a fuck left to give, I maneuver myself off the stretcher, leaving the plastic surgeon working on my back behind me.

Swiping the curtain back, I stumble out of the cubicle and into the chaos of the emergency room. Doctors try to grab me and usher me back to my stretcher but I push them out of the way.

"Reina!"

I know her name sounds like a scream because of the burn in my throat but to my ears it's less than a whisper.

Another doctor steps in front of me and before he opens his mouth, I fist his scrubs in my hand and glare at him. Ignoring his moving lips, I shove him to the side as a hand closes around my arm. I go to shrug the person off me, no one will stop me from getting to my woman. Forcefully, I'm spun around and meet Blackie's worried eyes.

He says some shit I don't comprehend and I lift my hands to my ears.

"Can't hear shit. I'm fucking deaf," I growl, well I think I growl...

I follow his eyes as he glances over his shoulder and points to the cubicle behind him where Lacey is sitting with Reina. My feet take off, leaving Blackie and whatever words he's blabbing behind me and head straight for my girls. My eyes dart between them and the monitor that Reina is hooked up too. I can't hear the familiar sound of our baby's swooshing heart beat but I spot the steady numbers flashing next to an image of a heart. The wedding dress she was wearing has been cut off her and she's in a hospital gown with a big strap across her belly. Her eyes find mine and I can tell she's both exhausted and in pain.

Ignoring the burning sensations rippling over my back, I make my way to her bedside. I kiss Lacey's cheek, trading spots with her and turn my eyes back to Reina.

"Someone tell me what's going on," I say, lacing my fingers with Reina's and turn to my daughter. I draw in a deep breath and try my hardest to remain calm and patient as she speaks and I try to read her lips.

"Slow down," I tell her as I continue to concentrate on her mouth and each word she enunciates I try to read from her lips.

Stopped labor for now.
Continuing to monitor.
Bedrest.

I lift her hand to my mouth and hiss in agony as the skin on my back feels as if it's being torn apart. My eyes zero in on the bracelet on her wrist and the name it reads.

DeCarlo, Reina.

That's not supposed to be.

Turing my eyes back to hers I shake my head.

"We're supposed to be married," I say, not giving a fuck if my voice is loud or low. I may not have taken my vows today, but I made a promise to Sunshine, told her there wasn't anything that would keep me from marrying her.

Some fucking wedding, I gave her.

"Can't hear shit, Reina. Don't know if it's permanent or some fluke shittin' thing but my heart still works and that thing beats for you, always will. Made you a promise and I like to think I'm a man of my word. If you don't mind marrying someone who can't hear you but someone who'll always love you, then let's do it."

She opens her mouth in a perfect little 'O' and her eyes widen through their exhaustion and I see the inner struggle she's battling. She thinks I'm crazy, knows I am but, there's a piece of her that wants to believe what I'm saying isn't the crazy talking. She wants to believe this beaten down man's heart is the one asking her to marry her.

Believe, Sunshine.
Keep believing in me.

Squeezing her hand tight, I turn to Blackie and Lacey.

"Where's the priest?"

I feel Reina squeeze my hand to bring my attention back to her.

"Jack," she says slowly.

Blackie rips the curtain next to us down off the clips and the priest Reina hired is in the bed next to her.

"You believe in signs, Sunshine?"

Nodding, she smiles at me and mouths the words that completely undo me and put me back together all the same.

"I believe in *you*."

Words to heal the soul.

Blackie lays a hand on my shoulder and looks between me and Reina then settles his gaze on me and points to his lips.

"He'll marry you."

More healing words.

I glance over at the priest and watch as he lowers the oxygen mask from his mouth and speaks. I don't know what he's saying, he's too far away for me to read his lips but I know the words he's saying are more for Reina than they are for me. There are only two words that need to be said to make this union official.

I stare at Reina, remembering how stunning she looked walking toward me before the mayhem exploded and I can't spot the difference, even in a hospital gown she's the most beautiful bride.

Lacey moves across from us and stands at Reina's bedside, next to the baby monitor where our baby's heartbeat is singing strong. I don't need to hear it to know that kid's a fighter, just look who his parents are.

The priest continues to talk, taking a break for oxygen here and there while Reina hangs on his every word. The doctors I ditched stand close by, once this marriage is official I'll make them play with my back and these burns some more, but for now they can stand there and wait for me to collapse in pain. Blackie pats my shoulder and I turn to him to see him holding Reina's ring.

Talk about signs.

That yellow diamond weathered a bomb.

It almost makes me want to be a believer.

I take the ring from his hand and look back at Reina. This isn't my first rodeo and I vaguely remember the words I'm supposed to say when I slide the ring on her finger. The priest is instructing me on what to say but I don't even try to read his lips.

Instead, I go with what's inside. I speak from the heart and give her my solemn vow.

"You."

I say as I slide the ring onto her finger and stare into the eyes of the woman that saved my soul and my mind. The woman who holds my future. The woman this heart beats for.

"Me," she replies.

Nothing else matters.

It's that moment when we become Mr. and Mrs. Jack Parrish and I become property of Sunshine. Deciding I don't need a priest to give me permission to kiss my wife, I fight through the pain in my back and lean over the rail of the bed to press my lips to hers.

It's not perfect, nowhere close, but in a Jack and Reina way it is.

Chapter Forty-Four

Lauren

On the ride back to his parents' house in Martha's Vineyard, I lay my head on Riggs' shoulder and he threads his fingers through my long hair. The last twenty-four hours have been a nightmare, making us relive a memory we are so desperate to forget. I watched as Riggs he stood by helplessly waiting for someone, anyone, to tell him what was going on with the men he called his brothers. It was a glimpse of the Riggs that suffered when I was in a coma and our son was fighting for his life. For me it was a little different, I don't remember much after I was shot but I learned how much I don't like being on the sidelines, how much I don't like sitting in a hospital waiting to find out if the people in our lives survived. All I kept thinking was how lucky we were to have escaped that bomb. I don't know who decided we would be hiding out in Martha's Vineyard with Riggs' parents but whoever was responsible would always hold my gratitude.

I spent a good part of my life worrying about my brother's well-being, wondering when the day would come that he'd be a victim and not a survivor. It sucked, and I never understood why Adrianna stuck with him. How could she live life worrying if the man she loved would live or die the moment he stepped out the door? Then I met Riggs, and I understood. As crazy as it sounds, loving Riggs is worth living in fear. I can't imagine my life without him and as much as it kills me to know that as long as he has the reaper on his back he'll always have a price tag on his head, I wouldn't trade him for all the straight and narrow guys in the world.

"Kitten, you're thinking too loud," he murmurs.

I lift my head from his shoulder and stare at his face, watching as he looks at me with one eye.

"We're almost there," he says, folding his hands behind his head as he tips his chin toward the driver his parents sent for us. "You'll get a dose of Eric and everything will be right with the world."

"What happens now?"

I watch as he opens his eyes, stares straight ahead and filters through the truth and what he can actually admit.

"Now, you and Eric will stay with my parents," he states.

"You're not staying with us?" I torture us both by asking the question he doesn't want to answer and the one I already know the answer to.

"Kitten, you saw what I saw, the club needs all capable hands on deck. I want you and Eric back home with me in our little apartment, filling the front of our fridge with pictures of him and sonogram pictures of that little pea inside you. But I won't do that unless I know it's safe, and knowing means seeing, it means doing it myself with my own hands and mind."

"I get it," I say softly as he turns his gaze and assesses my features to see if my words are truthful. "I don't like it," I add. "But I get it and I'll go along with whatever you think is right for now but you have to promise me something."

"Anything," he replies quickly.

"You'll stay safe. You'll think before you act and when you feel like jumping into the line of fire, remember me and our babies and take two steps back. Bones isn't going along for the ride; he won't be there to step in front of a bullet, he's not here to make sure our little family stays intact. It's all on us now."

"I promise you," he says, throwing an arm around me and pulling me closer to him. "You're pretty fond of your Tiger aren't you, Kitten?"

I shake my head as I clutch his leather jacket with my fingers.

"Fond doesn't even begin to describe it," I admit. "I love you, Riggs. I finally understand what you went through after the shooting. When I first woke up and I looked into your eyes I couldn't explain what I saw reflected at me, but after sitting in that waiting room tonight with you and feeling helpless as we watched our friends and family being brought in with all those injuries, I tried to imagine how you felt. I put myself in your shoes and I don't think I could do it. I couldn't sit beside you and beg God to let me have you. I couldn't look at Eric and wonder how I'd raise him without you. I need you, Riggs, I need you to keep me believing that dreams come true because no dream is worth having if you're not in them," I whisper.

He moves his hands up to my face and drags my mouth down to his, kissing me softly at first before his lips and tongue turn into a frenzy of desperation.

"Luckiest guy in the world," he mutters against my mouth. "I love you, Lauren Bianci," he adds, pulling back his mouth to stare at me as I push my black-rimmed glasses onto the bridge of my nose. A smile spreads across his face and he winks at me. "I'm so fucking glad they chose me to kidnap mama Bianci."

I roll my eyes and try not to laugh as he wraps his arms around my waist.

"Hey," he says, tipping my chin with his index finger. "I will be fine and you know what we're doing as soon as this whole thing is over?"

"Well you can't say make a baby," I tease.

"You're going to marry me," he says confidently.

"Oh yeah? You're going to make an honest woman out of me?"

"Yeah, I am," he agrees, then furrows his brow.

"What is it?"

"We can't be Mr. and Mrs. Tiger," he mutters, actually looking scorned.

"No, babe, we can't. It would be Montgomery," I say, holding back the chuckle as I lift the knit beanie from his head and run my fingers through his hair. "Is that such a bad thing?"

He glances out the window as the limo pulls up in front of the mini mansion.

"I guess not," he murmurs. "Let's go see our boy."

The driver opens the door and Riggs slides out of the limo first, holding out his hand for me and together we walk to the front door. He raps his knuckles against the large oak door and rings the bell like an annoying child, laughing to himself as his mother calls from somewhere in the house that she's coming.

I glance over at him, studying his strong profile and while it's still a mystery as to why he is not wearing a suit and tie, walking in his father's shoes instead of the leather boots of a Satan's Knight, I wouldn't change a thing about the colorful man who I'm in love with. He's eccentric as the day is long but he's got tons of heart.

The door opens and I watch Riggs' eyes widen in shock before the laugh escapes his mouth and I let my eyes travel the path of his and my mouth drops open.

Lenore is standing at the door with a naked Eric on her hip, spaghetti in her hair and tomato sauce splattered across her white silk shirt. My baby grins widely, displaying his top tooth as he snuggles against his grandma. I extend my hands, expecting Lenore to throw Eric into them like he's a fireball but instead she wraps her arms tightly around him and laughs.

It's a laugh that resonates through her eyes. She winks at me before settling her eyes on her son and I can't help following her gaze. Riggs' laughter subsides, but the smile stays planted on his lips as he crosses his arms and nods in appreciation.

"Well played, Eric. Well played," he whispers and then surprises both me and his mother when he leans forward to kiss Eric's cheek but plants a pec on his mother's first.

Robert 'Riggs' Montgomery is the complete package.

Colorful.

Eccentric.

Full of heart.

RIGS

After spending quality time with Eric and Lauren, making sure they're settled before I leave, I search the house for my father. I tell myself it's because I'm entrusting my old man with my family, I'm giving him my most prized possessions and he needs to know that's a big fucking deal. It's bigger than his millions, his mansions, it's more than any oil rig.

I stand at the doorway of his office, listening as he speaks with one of his employees.

"Everything goes," my old man says.

"Where are you going to conduct business?" The employee questions.

"I'm not worried about it and neither should you. Now, make sure it's all cleared out by the end of the week. Get the contractors here to paint as soon as possible." He pauses and I watch from the door as he strokes his jaw in concentration. "Something neutral, in case my new grandbaby is a girl. I want them both to be comfortable."

"Very well Mr. Montgomery."

"Yellow or green," my dad decides. "And maybe we can get animals painted on the walls. I want it bright and cheerful."

"Whatever you wish."

Stepping into the room, I knock on the door and watch as my father's lackey sizes me up, his eyes gawking as they take in my worn boots, ripped jeans and the tatts decorating my arms. I walk to him, take the phone out of his hands and flip the camera, lifting my middle finger I smile and take the selfie before handing the phone back to him.

"That should hold you over. Don't jack off to it though, that shit's just wrong," I say purposely as his eyes bulge out of his head and his mouth drops to the floor.

"Arnold that will be all for today," my father says, dismissing the jaw slacker.

"Don't post that shit on Facebook and shit. Kim K may have broken the internet with her ass but people are dying to get their hands on the Tiger. You'll destroy the internet with that bad boy," I tell him as I take a seat on top of the mahogany desk.

I chuckle as Arnold hurries out of the office and my old man crosses his arms and looks at me bemused.

"You love to bust chops don't you?"

It's more of a statement than a question so I shrug my shoulders and glance down at the desk.

"I couldn't help but overhear you tell him to clear this place out," I begin, taking a stress ball off the blotter on his desk and squeezing it in the palm of my hand.

"Yes, well, your mother and I were talking and we want a place for the kids to feel comfortable when they visit."

"What's going on with you two?"

"Your mother and I?"

I nod as he shrugs his shoulders and walks toward the French doors and looks out toward the pool.

"To be honest, I'm not sure. It started off as two parents banding together to get in touch with their only child and now, well, I suppose I'm becoming reacquainted with the woman I first met." He turns to face me. "I didn't realize how much I missed her or the early years of our marriage, but watching her with your son has reminded me of all the things we wanted when I first met her. Money ruined us. It's funny, most people think money will solve all their problems yet money caused all of ours."

I watch as he pauses for a moment and steps around the desk and opens the top drawer producing a framed photograph. He walks back around and stands in front of me, staring down at the picture before handing it to me.

I thought seeing my mom with a smile and Eric on her hip shocked me but the photograph in the frame completely throws me, mind fucking me as I make out the young faces of my parents standing in front of a Harley.

"You're shitting me!" I accuse, lifting my eyes to his.

"There's a lot you don't know about your parents, Robert," he smirks.

"Clearly," I reply, averting my eyes back to the photograph. "Were you part of a club?"

"No," he says with a chuckle. "Not for lack of trying though," he adds, taking the photograph from my hand and standing it upright on his desk. "I understand you better than you think I do."

"Maybe," I say finally. "I'm heading out and I'm not sure when I'll be back. There are some things that need to be taken care of back home. My club needs me and in order for me to bring my family back home I need to concentrate on making them safe again."

My father nods his head in understanding.

"Lauren and Eric will be safe here," he assures me.

"Promise me," I plead.

"I swear it," he says, patting me on the shoulder. "They're our family now too."

"You really mean that, don't you?"

"Of course I do."

Holding his gaze, I can spot the sincerity in his voice.

"Can I ask for something in return?"

A couple of days ago I would've rolled my eyes but I find myself nodding and waiting for him to speak.

"Stay safe, son," he hoarsely asks of me.

I raise an eyebrow as his eyes plead with mine and for the first time since they showed up on my doorstep I actually start to think about him and my mom having a place in my life, in my family. I think of the future and I can see them fitting in.

"Haven't you heard? Safety is my middle name," I say, sliding off the desk before I return the gesture and pat him on the back. "Just ask, Kitten."

He chuckles as I start for the door with a smile on my face. Reaching the hall, I turn and glance over my shoulder at my dad. He leans against the desk, mimicking the stance he held in that old photograph and I smile at him.

"Thanks, Dad," I call before striding down the hallway, confident Lauren and Eric will be just fine here. My parents may have made a bunch of mistakes throughout my childhood but I couldn't deny the change in them and how genuine their newfound love for their grandson was.

My phone rings, pulling me away from my thoughts and I swipe my thumb across the screen to answer the call.

"The Tiger speaking," I answer.

"You take care of the family?" Blackie asks.

"Yeah, they're good," I reply, closing the door behind me and stepping toward the car waiting for me. "I'm on my way back," I tell him as I climb into the car.

I stare out the window at the house that holds my family until the limo drives away from the safe haven and whisks me away to Hell.

Chapter Forty-Five

BLACKIE

Three days later I got a call from Jones giving me a heads up that Brantley was sniffing around the clubhouse—whatever the fuck was left of it. Technically, it was a crime scene, and we weren't allowed passed the compound gates but after a call to the club attorney I got us access. The nomads were living at the clubhouse before the explosion, everything they fucking owned was inside and if anything could be salvaged they needed to get to it. Poor bastards came to Brooklyn, got their shit blown to bits, and their asses thrown in some fleabag motel. Stryker got off easy doing a bid in prison, poor Linc needed six surgeries, a metal rod put in his back and fuck if I know how many screws, pins and bolts to keep his fucking spine intact.

Pulling my truck into the compound, I pass the glass enclosure, still splattered with Mack's blood, and the gruesome reminder we'll be burying him tomorrow. Disgusted, I throw it into park and climb out before stopping in my tracks and staring at the damage.

The yellow caution tape obnoxiously stares back at me, taunting me, reminding me how fucking hopeless this whole thing is. Jack's out for the count, leaving this shit on my shoulders, and I don't know where to begin. This attack differed from the others. This wasn't anywhere close to the shootout at Pops' gun range, or the sneak attack drive-by that pussy, Wu, played on us. The Bastards left us in ruins, without a home, half our club in the hospital, some in the morgue and all our bikes blown to smithereens.

Tearing down the tape, I climb over the rubble and debris and stand in the center of what used to be the Dog Pound. I bend down, pushing aside pieces of glass and Sheetrock and pull the corner of a tattered American flag to the surface.

"Yo, Blackie's here," Deuce calls out, forcing me to divert my eyes away from the flag in my hands to the three men walking toward me.

Stryker, Deuce and Cobra look similar to the way they did after the bomb exploded—sans the blood—covered in dust, dirt and soot. I watch as something flashes over Stryker as his eyes drift down to the flag I was holding.

"Think this belongs to you." I offer the flag.

"Shit," he mutters, taking the worn fabric from my hands, running his fingers over the stars and stripes. Lifting his head, he nods in appreciation. "This flag survived Afghanistan and now this. It's indestructible," he says thoughtfully, folding it expertly into a triangle, like they do at a soldier's memorial. Tucking the final corner away he hands it back to me. "Fix this shit, Black and show every motherfucker from here to the West Coast the Satan's Knights of Brooklyn are just as resilient as that flag."

"Deep shit, bro," Deuce comments.

"And if that's not enough incentive," Cobra begins as he glances over his shoulder. "There's a man hurtin' over there that is desperate to make that message clear."

I follow his eyes and spot Pipe sitting on top of what's left of the bar. Without hesitation, I nod to the three men new to our charter, ready and willing to ride to their death, and it becomes clear, whatever it takes, however it can be done, I will make it right. With a tip of my chin, I leave them behind to continue recovering whatever they can and I make my way to Pipe.

Lifting a silver flask to his lips he notices me standing close but says nothing. He tips his head back and guzzles the alcohol unfazed by presence. I know that look. I've seen it in the mirror a thousand times. I know everything Pipe's feeling, the regret, the anger, the loss, the ache ripping through his heart. The dire need for revenge pulsing through your veins. I felt all of that and more after Christine died and there are days I still feel it.

"Found her body right there," he slurs, using the tip of the flask to point to the end of the bar. "Her head hanging on by a thread."

Shoving one hand into my pocket, I step closer to him and bow my head to collect my thoughts. We're supposed to say we're sorry, it's what society deems right when someone loses one they love, but that shit don't work. It's not what you want to hear. You want to hear the voice of the one that's left you broken and alone.

"Pipe, I've been where you at," I start. "Felt everything you're feeling, brother, and I ain't going to give you my apologies because it won't bring her back. It won't fix you."

He takes another gulp from his flask, dangling it over his mouth to catch the last drops before he tosses it into the rubble.

"Finally a piece of truth," he mutters, lifting his beady eyes to mine. "You people all thought my marriage was a joke."

"That ain't true," I argue. "We busted your balls but only a man who knows love could see how much you loved Oksana. I saw it."

He swipes a hand over his face and I think he's probably debating on whether I'm being sincere.

"The men who did this will pay," I vow. "We will torture them with our bare fucking hands, Pipe."

With a groan he stands.

"The Bulldog ain't got his ears, and it's my understanding he won't be riding," he says, settling me with a stare. "You got Wolf in ICU, Linc in a goddamn full body cast and two dead prospects. No fucking clubhouse and the only one who still has a bike is Riggs. Don't be making promises, Black. This shit is over. The Satan's Knights are done."

"So, that's it?" I question, watching as he moves to walk past me. "We throw in our cuts and call it a day? Let the Bastards get away with murdering your wife? You disappoint me, Pipe."

"Fuck you," he hisses, grabbing the ends of my cut. "Don't need the club to take care of what's mine, Black."

"You're not doing anything without the club," I warn.

"And who the fuck is going to stop me?"

"You really want me to answer that, brother?"

Stumbling backward, he releases my cut and narrows his eyes at me.

"You're done, Black, accept that shit and move the fuck on. Be happy you got your life and your woman has hers," he sneers, his boots crushing the debris as he stalks away from me.

I fist my hands at my sides, itching to punch a fucking wall but there aren't any left standing. I glance over my shoulder at the nomads, sifting through the dust, maybe Pipe's right.

"One of you stay with him and make sure he doesn't do anything stupid," I order.

"Can you define stupid?" Deuce asks.

"Don't let him fucking kill anyone," I growl. "Including himself," I add. Turning around to I stomp through the grit toward my truck. I pause mid step and divert my attention back to them. "Did you happen to find the table?"

"He's kidding right?" Deuce asks absurdly.

"Smartass," I sneer. "It's there somewhere. Wolf was dragging it before he collapsed."

"We'll keep looking," Cobra says.

I nod before continuing for my truck. Once I reach the car, I toss the flag into the passenger seat and stare at it for a moment, wishing the table was as indestructible as the red, white and blue cloth staring back at me, desperate for a sign that the club engrained into my soul wasn't dead too.

JACK

Sitting still, lying low—it's not me. But what choice do I have? If I want to hear that baby's cry I need to heal and as much as revenge is a priority, hearing that baby means more. Seeing Reina through the last leg of her pregnancy, making sure she obeys her doctor's orders and stays on bed rest—that's my fucking job.

That doesn't mean I will allow the Corrupt Bastards to reign over my city and it sure as shit doesn't mean I will let them get away with fucking with my club. That tear drop sporting prick will pay for what he's done. He will cry, bleed and wish his mother swallowed him.

Reina stands from the couch, jolting me away from the sadistic thoughts of revenge and how I will cut Charlie's balls off and feed them to whatever whore is currently sucking his dick.

"Where are you going?"

"The bell rang," she answers, loud enough for the neighbors to hear.

"Sit," I bark, standing and pointing back to the couch.

The one good thing about this hearing loss thing is I can't hear her curse me under her breath as she reluctantly sits down with a huff. Guess who has trouble sitting still too? We're fucked.

I pull the door open and find Blackie looking all sorts of haggard on my door step, running his fingers through his hair.

"Shit," I mutter.

"Yeah," he agrees, holding up a pad and pencil. "We need to talk," he drawls, waving the pad.

"Cute," I growl, knocking the pad out of his hand before spinning back around and leaving his ass on the front porch.

As I head for the kitchen, Reina says something I can't make out and Blackie slams the door. I know he slams it because the whole fucking house vibrates. It's true what they say, when one of your senses fail you, the others work overtime.

I grab a beer from the fridge, lean against the counter and pop the top off the bottle. I'm guzzling the ale when Blackie stomps through the kitchen and lays his pad on the kitchen island. He shrugs his jacket off and drapes it over the back of the stool, twisting his neck from side to side before he rolls up his sleeves and grabs a pen. Angrily I watch the ink bleed onto the paper as I drain the rest of the bottle down my throat. Lifting his eyes to glare at me, he throws down the pen and pushes the pad toward me.

"Read," he says, and by the way his jaw tightens I know it's not a request but a demand.

Holding his gaze, I push off the cabinets and walk to the island. I grab the pad and see the three underlined words.

THE FINAL RIDE.

Arching an eyebrow, I slide the pad back to him.

"What kind of bullshit is this?"

He grabs the pad, starts scribbling words but I lean over the island and knock the pen out of his hand.

"Talk slow and loud," I demand.

"Fine," he starts, sighing heavily. He explains our situation, some words I catch others are difficult, and he uses the pad to jot them down. Piecing together both, I understand what the three underlined words mean. No one expects us to prevail from this, in fact, I'd bet the house the Corrupt Bastards are confident we won't even retaliate because they have left us on the balls of our asses.

"I rented six rooms at the Motel Six for Stryker and the boys who are temporarily staying there until we figure out what we will do with the Dog Pound. I can't get a look at the books and where our numbers are because Pipe is in bad way. I don't know how long I will keep him at bay. The man is thirsty for blood and doesn't give two shits about consequences. I need to get this plan in motion quickly or else he will tear into the Corrupt Bastards with no one behind him."

"Riggs can get you hard copies of the club's finances, make sure you get him put a call into the insurance company. It will take time to get everything up and running so you will need a temporary place to congregate. Pops' shooting range will do for now, and while your ass is in Jersey, you will need to pay a visit to our friends at the Bergen County charter."

"I was thinking that," Blackie says. "I was going to see if they'd lend us their pipes."

"Fuck that, we're not showing up at Charlie's door with a bunch of loner bikes. I was working on a gun deal with Rocco Spinelli, go to him tell him the deal is off the table unless he comes up with the money now, and you replace our pipes with that money."

"So why am I going to Bergen County?"

"Black, they blew us up, with every intent to wipe us off the grid. Who you going to ride with? Riggs? You two going to be the dynamic duo? You need more man power. You want to avenge this shit then you need an army or this final ride will be *our* final ride and not theirs. You need to roll up to those gates in Boston, deep and wide, headlights for miles."

I watch as he absorbs my words and nods his head as he takes the pen and makes a list of our men. He's first on the list, then Riggs, Stryker, Cobra, Deuce and five prospects.

"Pipe," I add, watching as he hesitates before writing his name.

"I'm worried about him," he admits.

"I've known Pipe for many years," I start, taking the pen and circling my Sergeant of Arms' name with the ink. "That motherfucker will be your most lethal weapon." I cross my arms against my chest and glare at him. "Call Jones and tell him we're done, not to expect any pay offs. I don't trust that prick Brantley and we can't be sure he doesn't know Jones is on our payroll. You rebuild and you bide your time, make everyone believe what they want. Charlie didn't do this to avenge Boots' death he did it to push through our streets. Let him think he can. Let the whole fucking world think Jack Parrish and the Satan's Knights are finished."

"Then we get them," Blackie confirms.

"Then we fucking get them and we hit them hard. They didn't just go after our club; they went after our families too, no one is safe. Not this time. This time we don't give a fuck who is innocent and who isn't. You go in guns blazing, vicious and hungry. When you start to feel your conscience creeping up on you, remember the faces of everyone in that room before the bomb went off. Remember that feeling in your gut, that hopeless feeling when you knew you wouldn't be able to get to Lacey quick enough, and you fucking shut down that little voice in your head and you do what has to be done. You hear me?"

He takes the pen and paper and writes his reply.

I hear you.

"You're a dick," I say, ripping the paper in half before throwing it back at him.

Blackie smirks as he shrugs on his leather jacket.

"Black," I call out and watch his eyes turn back to me.

"You got this, brother," I tell him.

I should be leading my club to retribution but if I can't, there is no one better suited than the man standing before me. I won't hold the gavel forever, someday I will pass that shit down, someday it'll be Blackie sitting at the head of the table. It will be his job to bring Satan's law to justice and now is the time to see if he's capable.

We might plan the final ride for the Corrupt Bastards but this shit right here, this was Blackie's test drive, riding front and center, leading the pack of Knights straight to Hell.

Where did that leave my daughter?

I suppose on a test drive of her own.

Could my sweet girl stand in the shadows of the acting president of the Satan's Knights?

We're about to find out.

Chapter Forty-Six

BLACKIE

Sitting on an empty oil drum in the middle of Pipe's garage I turn to Riggs, watching as he pulls his hat off and runs his fingers roughly through his hair.

"Bro," he starts, fitting the hat back to his head. "Where the fuck is everyone?" he asks tapping his fingers on the rolling tool chest in front of him. "I mean it's not just me and you on this suicide mission, right?"

I sure fucking hope not.

Pulling a toothpick out of my jacket, I roll it between my lips and try not to dwell on the urge burning inside of me to seek something out and alleviate the itch to drink this whole fucking ordeal away.

"We've got company," he announces as he jumps off the hood of the car he was sitting on and heads out to the lot. I follow him and watch as the flatbed truck, loaded with Harley's, backs into the lot, stopping right in front of us.

"Merry fucking Christmas to us," Riggs mutters, jumping onto the flatbed to inspect the brand new bikes as I walk around to greet the trucker opening the driver's door.

"Either one of you Blackie?"

"Who's asking?" I question as he waves a clipboard at me.

"Delivery from Jack Parrish," he grunts, picking up his pants that hang beneath his belly and shoving his clipboard into my hands.

"You're shitting me," Riggs calls.

"Sign," the trucker orders as he waddles to the back of his truck.

I glance down at the invoice for twelve new bikes and notice the make and models of them. These broads were beauties and cost twice the amount of our old ones. Placing the invoice on the hood of the truck, I pull out my phone and dial Jack's house to confirm with him. Reina answers the phone since his hearing is still sketchy.

"Hey, Reina, do me a favor and ask Jack if he had something delivered to Pipe's garage?"

"Sure, give me a minute," she says and I hear her shuffle around and Jack's loud muffled growl. Riggs and the trucker start unloading the bikes as a van pulls into the lot and parks right beside the bikes.

"Give me the phone," I hear Jack call.

"Blackie, you're on speaker," Reina adds with a huff.

"Told you my club won't be ridin' with borrowed pipes and I meant it. Break them bitches in and make them sing pretty for me," he says.

"You hear that, Blackie?" Reina questions.

"Loud and clear," I respond. "Take care of the big guy, Reina. I'll be in touch," I add before disconnecting the call. Stryker, Deuce and Cobra climb out of the van and curiously stare at the bikes.

"A present from the Bulldog," I explain, signing the invoice on the clipboard.

"Guess today is a good day for the Satan's Knights," Cobra mutters as the three of them open the back doors of the van and pull out a piece of wood. Turning it over, they prop the wooden slab against the side of the van and the reaper carved into the center stares back at me.

"We need to put some legs on it and sand this beast down but next time you speak to the Bulldog, tell him we dug his fucking table out of the rubble," Stryker says, running his hand carefully along the splintered edges.

"You called church didn't you?" Deuce questions, reaching into his pocket and producing a meat mallet.

"It's not the original but it'll do," he adds as I stare at the silver mallet with the *Bed Bath and Beyond* ticket still attached to it.

Fighting back a smile, I take the mallet from his hand and tip my chin toward the table.

"That's it, go on, you know you want to," Riggs encourages as he steps behind me and the trucker peels away from us, without twelve new motorcycles. I tighten my grip around the silver kitchen utensil and bring the head down to the table top and bring my first meeting as acting president to order.

Riggs clasps his hands over the back of my shoulders.

"Let's tag some toes, motherfuckers," he cheers.

I'm about to order them to drag the table into the garage when I hear the distinct sound of engines blaring. Without hesitation I reach behind me and draw my gun out of the waistband of my jeans and aim it at the gates. Riggs, mimics my stance and together we start for the gates. Stryker, Deuce and Cobra are right behind us, the adrenaline vibrates through the air as the bikes draw closer.

My finger steady on the trigger I watch the first bike turn into the lot.

"What the fuck?" Riggs says next to me, keeping his gun just as cocked and ready as Pipe leads a pack of at least ten bikes. I narrow my eyes as Pipe breaks in front of me and throws down his kickstand.

Lifting his helmet from his head, he turns to face me, bloodshot eyes peer back at me. There is nothing left of the man, his eyes are as dead as his soul and his body is just a shell, just a place to house the vengeance pulsing through his veins.

I avert my eyes to the men pulling up behind him and zero in on the Satan's Knight's patch sewn into their leathers.

"Brooklyn meet Bergen County," Pipe introduces, tipping his chin to the gun in my hand. "You going to shoot the men here to help us or are you going to invite them to your table?"

Lowering my gun with one hand, I size up the president of the Bergen County charter, a man who goes by the name of Smoke.

"Word on the street is there is no Brooklyn charter," Smoke says, dismounting from his bike.

"Didn't anyone ever teach you not to believe everything you hear?" I retort, tucking my gun into the front of my jeans.

He shrugs his shoulders.

"Better off letting them believe you're dead that way they don't expect to see your ghost," he counters, holding out his hand. "Time for you to put those rumors to rest and show everyone what you're made of, Blackie."

I've been Jack's right hand for years, been the talk of many, on the outside I'm nothing but a recovering junkie, a hothead who lost his way when he lost his wife. No one speaks of my loyalty to the reaper on my back, or the men I stand with. They don't know what I'm capable of, what happens when I've been pushed too far. They don't know the reason my road name is Blackie, they don't know it's because I've faded more lives to black than most—without consequence, without regard.

They tried fading us to black and now it's their turn to fade. There won't be any mishaps. There won't be anyone left standing, not a fucking fly on the wall of their clubhouse will survive what we're going to do. It's not a test of physics, there won't be some little prick in a basement making a bomb to strap to an unsuspecting asshole. No, revenge will be at the hands of the men surrounding me and it will be executed the old fashioned way, where we take life with our bare hands.

I lead my men and the men of the Bergen County charter into the garage and brief them on what I plan to do. An operation that seemed hopeless a few days ago springs to life and retribution is so close I can taste it. With the help of the other charter, the new bikes and enough ammo to take out a village we have a strong chance of wiping them out, especially if they don't see us coming.

Surprise them.

Introduce them to the ghost of the Satan's Knights.

Make them fade to Black.

JACK

My body is here lying on the couch next to Reina's but my mind isn't, my mind is out there, with my brothers fighting to take back what is ours. Even before I was the president, as long as I've held my patch I've been on the front lines. I don't know what it's like to be left behind while my boys are off riding and avenging.

I glance down as Reina reaches for my hands and rests them on top of her belly. I bury my face in the crook of her neck as the baby kicks against my hand. It's my kid who reminds me that sometimes we all need to take a step back and appreciate the little treasures in life. The blessings.

She lifts her head from my chest and I stare at her lips as she says another name.

"Chloe," she suggests.

I recite the name in my head and shrug my shoulders, not sold on the name. We've already decided on the name if the baby is a boy but this girl thing is rough. I don't remember doing this with Connie when she was pregnant. I'm not sure if it's because I didn't have an interest back then or if it was because I was out on the road for most of her pregnancies. Probably a bit of both.

"What about Dana?" I say.

"I think we should just keep praying for a boy," she replies and I actually hear every other word clearly. I'm noticing that I favor my left ear more so than my right.

The bell rings and Reina crawls off me and tries to lift herself off the couch but it's a losing battle. I feel the smile tug at the corners of my mouth and lean forward to kiss her. Pregnancy suits Reina, makes me wish I was a little younger—we wouldn't stop at one.

"I'll get it," I tell her, patting her knee for her to stay where she is on the couch. I grab my shirt off the back of the couch and pull it over my head as I walk to the front door, never expecting Grace Pastore to be on my door step.

"Hi, Jack," she says, forcing a smile on her worn face. Vic's wife is a looker but these days she looks so damn tired, so damn heartbroken.

"Come in," I say, moving aside for her to enter before kicking the door closed and ushering her into the living room where Reina can help me communicate with our guest.

"I hope I'm not interrupting," she starts as Reina holds out her hands to me and I help her onto her feet so she can greet Grace.

"Of course not," Reina says. "Can we get you something? Coffee maybe?"

She shakes her head and turns to me.

"I came to congratulate you on the wedding," she pauses, cocking her head to the side. "But now that I've said it, it sounds ridiculous. I'm so sorry about everything that transpired on what should've been such a beautiful day."

I didn't even notice the present in her hand until she handed it to Reina.

"Thank you, Grace," Reina says, taking the present from her.

"Have you heard anything from Vic?" I ask and I immediately regret the question when her smile falters and she shakes her head.

"I don't expect to either," she answers, instantly wiping a tear from the corner of her eye. "No news means he's still alive, so I hang on to that and hope he's not suffering," she says, turning to Reina who is staring down at a silver serving platter that has our names engraved on it. "Vic's mother gave me one of those when we first got married and when the girls were born we added their names to it. We thought it was silly at first but after we had the girls we used that platter every night we ate dinner together as a family."

"It's beautiful," Reina says, laying it on the coffee table. "And if we ever decide on a name, we'll be sure to add it to the platter."

"Grace," I say, reaching out for her hand. Her tearful eyes lift to mine and I squeeze her hand. "Vic's a lucky guy."

"We were both lucky. It wasn't just one sided," she argues and then smiles sadly. "Love is precious, its frail, and it's gone before some even have time to appreciate it."

Her eyes drift between me and Reina before she continues.

"Enjoy these times, they may be bumpy, they may be hard but they'll be a memory quicker than you realize." She sighs wistfully, pulling me into her arms to embrace me. "If I know my husband as well as I think I do, I know he'd want me to come here today and wish you and your wife the best of luck and to tell you that."

I wrap my arms around her and look at my wife, her face says it all, she doesn't want to ever be in Grace's shoes. I'm an outlaw, albeit an out of commission one, but none the less a man who lives to tempt fate. If I had any sense whatsoever I'd take this injury and run. I'd give her and that kid everything they need, I'd give them me. But I've already been dealt these cards, and this patch isn't just sewn to my cut but it's branded to my soul.

"I should go," Grace says, breaking our embrace and moving to kiss Reina goodbye.

"Thank you for the gift and for stopping by," Reina replies. "Our door is always open."

The smile on Grace's face is genuine as she nods and I walk her to the door.

"Anything you need—" I say but she interrupts me.

"I know," she whispers, cocking her head to the side as her warm eyes pierce mine. "Be safe, Jack Parrish, be smart and be attentive. That woman inside accepts you as you are, loves you as you are but her heart will only take so much. It takes a special kind of woman to live the life you and my husband chose. Respect her for trying."

She leans in and kisses my cheek before turning on her heel. Her words ring in my ears as she walks to her car, reminding me I am a husband and a father first. Quickly her voice fades and is replaced with another familiar voice.

Ride or die.
You are Satan's Knight.
You are the devil's disciple.
And there she is, that bitch of a maker.

Chapter Forty-Seven

Lacey

Frustrated, I drop the pen onto the open textbook sitting on the coffee table and reach for the banana clip next to it. I twist my hair into a bun and clip it in place as the front door opens. I'm used to hearing Blackie's bike pull onto the street minutes before he walks through the door but with him driving his truck I never know when he's coming home. Not that I mind, I'm just happy he actually comes home.

Since the hospital discharged us he's been out a lot, bouncing between the Dog Pound, my father's house and wherever the rest of the brothers are temporarily staying. It's only been a couple of days but my heart doesn't know that and neither does my mind. I'm lonely, missing him and worried sick. It's different being the girlfriend versus being the daughter. I love both men but it's different with Blackie, my love has no bounds; it completely consumes every fiber of my being. Without Leather there is no leather and lace.

He throws his leather jacket on a chair and steps into the living room. Silently he walks over and drops down onto the couch behind me, leaning forward to unclip my hair he watches it cascade down my back.

"Come here," he says huskily as I turn to face him. Unfolding my legs from under me I crawl on my knees and move between his legs. He pushes his fingers through my hair as I angle my head and look up at him.

"Miss you, girl," he murmurs as he continues to stare at me thoughtfully before his gaze wanders to the books behind me on the coffee table. "Do you have a test?"

"Finals are next week," I say with a nod. "Since you haven't been around much, I figured I'd get a jumpstart on studying."

"You feel like taking a break?" he questions, turning his attention back to my face. He cocks his head to the side, the tip of his index finger travels down my neck to the buttons on the front of my shirt.

"Does that mean you're taking a break?" I reply, watching as his fingers play with the first button of my shirt.

"Yeah," he nods, dropping his fingers from my shirt and meeting my gaze again. His tongue slips out and wets his lower lip before both lift into a smirk. "Need a fix of my girl."

The way he looks at me has the butterflies that have been dormant over the last few days taking flight, their wings flutter around inside me causing me to hang on his every word.

"What did you have in mind?"

"I need time away from this shit sitting on my shoulders," he explains pulling me off the floor as he leans back against the couch and drags me onto his lap. Cradling my face with his hands, he runs the tip of his nose down the bridge of mine and stares into my eyes. "I need to be with you, had nothing specific in mind, whatever you want to do, we'll do. I'll take you anywhere you wanna go, girl."

"Anything?" I ask, raising an eyebrow.

"I know that look, girl," he sighs, pulling back, leaning his head against the pillows as I straddle his lap. "So damn pretty," he hisses, shaking his head. "Yeah, anything you want," he agrees finally.

I push the hair from his face and dip my head to press my lips against his. The groan that instantly escapes his mouth excites me and has me grinding my hips against him as his hands slide into the back pockets of my jeans and he arches off the couch and I feel his thick erection beneath me.

"Later," I promise, taking his lower lip between my teeth. "All night," I state, releasing his lip and untangling his hands from around me. I climb off his lap and give him one last glance, watching as he palms the bulge in his jeans and hangs his head miserably. He's so fucking hot when he's horny.

"Hurry up," he grunts as I head for the stairs.

Ten minutes later I'm dressed in a pair of Victoria's Secrets Pink yoga pants and a hoodie with a zipper up the front. I come bounding down the steps and Blackie is sitting on the couch where I left him, flipping through my textbook.

He lifts his head and narrows his eyes as he takes in my casual appearance.

"Keys," I say, holding out my hand as I smile at him. He pushes off the couch and walks toward me, digging into his pocket and producing his key ring. I go to snatch them from his hand but he pulls back, wraps his arm around my waist and pulls me against him. His breath is hot on my ear, his scent intoxicating making me question why we're even leaving the house.

"What you up to girl?"

"You'll see," I murmur, rising on my tip toes to grab the keys. He swats my ass playfully and follows me out the door. Once we're in the car, he reclines the passenger seat back and keeps his eyes on me. I don't need to turn around to know he's smiling, I feel it down in my bones, deep inside my soul. It's the smile that makes everything right, the smile that erases the doom that's headed straight for us. It's the smile I want to hang on tight to and never let go.

Enjoy it while it lasts.

I want to believe they are the words of my maker but they are our truth. I don't know what tomorrow will bring for us, I don't know what Blackie has been spending day and night planning. I probably won't know until it's over but whatever it is, it's dark and ugly, cold and uninviting.

"Stop that," he says softly, reaching over the console and cupping my knee. I tear my eyes away from the road and look at him from the corner of my eye.

"What?" I ask innocently, my voice cracking slightly.

"You got that look on your pretty face you get when your mind is working you over," he says, with a shake of his head. "It's just you and me tonight, girl. The rest of the world doesn't exist. Tonight, we're just Lacey and Dominic," he says with a wink and an affectionate squeeze of my knee.

I love that so hard. There aren't many times I get the man and not the knight but when I do, well, those moments are everything. They're the moments we're two ordinary people in love. There is no club, no illness or addictions, just a girl and a man who love one another despite everything weighing them down.

With no more thought to the storm heading our way I pull up to our destination and kill the engine on the truck. Blackie's eyes lazily glance out the window at the tattoo parlor and I reach for my phone, snapping a photo to capture the smirk on his face with every intention to stare at the photo when I'm lonely and he's off riding.

"You finally going to tattoo my name to that ass of yours?" he asks slyly as I turn the camera around and lean in close to him and snap a selfie.

"You'd love that wouldn't you," I reply, snapping another photo, this time my tongue sneaks out the corner of my mouth and touches his cheek.

The next selfie is snapped as he pushes my hair away from my face and presses his lips to my cheek. Next, he grabs my face and the phone slips from my hand as his mouth crashes against mine and his tongue works its way into my mouth and over mine. I could easily get lost in the kiss just as easy as I can get lost in his scent or the way his body feels next to mine. The moan escapes my lips and melts against his as he slowly breaks the kiss and swipes his thumb over my lower lip.

"Girl," he whispers.

"Don't even try to talk me out of it," I warn.

"Fuck that, never," he laughs, dropping his finger from my mouth. "Nothing sexier than having my name on you," he says, reaching for the door handle.

"I never said I was getting your name," I laugh as I get out of the car and meet him around the front of the truck. He takes my hand and laces our fingers together, leading me toward the tattoo parlor.

"You didn't have to." He grins at me.

Three hours later I had a beautiful rose wrapped in rosary beads inked to my right shoulder blade. Blackie stopped me from adding his name to the tattoo, insisting he wants me to take his name in marriage not in ink.

"After you marry me, you can ink my name to every inch of your body but the first time you take my name will be when you're my wife," he said, whipping out his phone and snapping a picture of my face after he said the words.

There are some moments too good not to capture. Moments that are too good not to treasure.

BLACKIE

I don't tell her I'll be on the road for the next three days, instead I pretend like everything is fine and I'm not about to declare war on the Corrupt Bastards. Ignorance is bliss and for tonight all I want to be is blissfully buried inside Lacey, drowning in the sweetness she possesses.

Holding her hand as the needle pricked her skin and marked her flesh provided the perfect distraction for a while but now we're home and the only thing I want distracting me is her body. I watch her unzip the hoodie she's wearing, glancing over her shoulder as she lowers it down and checks to see if the gauze is still taped to her back, covering her new tattoo.

She's not trying to be seductive but every fucking move she makes has me hard and craving her. Poor girl, I will demolish her tonight so that when I'm on the road, the ache in between her thighs keeps her company, reminding her I'm never too far from her.

She turns around and peers at me from under her eyelashes, slowly reaching behind her to unclasp her bra as I lean against the wall and drink in the show she's about to treat me to.

"Go on, girl," I urge, crossing my arms against my chest as I bite the inside of my cheek and watch the straps slide down her arms and expose her to my hungry eyes.

Her thumbs slide into the waistband of her pants, dragging them down her legs before she steps out of them.

"No panties?"

"Not tonight," she says, reaching behind her to pull her hair out of the clip. Her back arches and her perky tits salute me. "Give me your phone," she says, shaking out her long hair so it falls down her back and over her shoulders.

Fucking gorgeous.

Curiously, I pull my phone out of the back pocket of my jeans and hand it to her, watching as she pushes her breasts together and snaps a photo of herself. Bending over, she angles her phone and snaps another photo of her heart-shaped ass.

"Damn, girl," I groan.

She straightens up, eyes on me as she takes two steps closer and spreads her legs. Holding the phone with both hands she lowers it so the lens is level with her pussy and snaps another picture.

"Don't say I never give you anything," she teases as she tosses the phone back, clarifying I'm not the only one leaving reminders behind.

I catch the phone, place it down on the dresser before closing the distance between us. With one hand I reach behind me, my ribs are still bruised but I don't react to the twinge pulling across my midsection as I pull my shirt over my head.

"You want something in return, girl?"

"Depends what you're offering," she says coyly, placing both hands on her bare hips as she winks at me.

I don't offer anything instead I drop to my knees and take what I want and give her what I know she needs, placing my open mouth over the lips of her pussy and pushing my tongue between them. Her hands fall from her hips to my shoulders and her nails dig into my skin as my tongue lavishly strokes her.

Starving.

Insatiable.

I feed off her, lapping at her clit, sucking on it until her hands are in my hair, pulling it begging me to take her over the edge.

Not yet.

Girl needs to squirm a little. That's right, grind on me girl.

"Blackie…" She shrieks as I slip two fingers insider her.

"Give it to me, girl," I grunt against her pussy, pumping my fingers to the same beat my tongue is playing.

Give me something to dream of when I'm off the grid.

Give me something to remember in case I break my promise to you and can't come back.

I feel her tighten around my fingers, hear her cry out in ecstasy as I continue to selfishly take my memory from her, ingraining it to my mind, body and soul as she loses control over my mouth. Her body goes lax after the tremors subside and I slowly pull my mouth away from her. I lift my eyes to hers and lick my lips, savoring the taste to my palette.

"Fuck, Blackie," she says breathless, dropping to her knees as she takes my face with her hands. Leaning forward, her tongue sneaks out tasting what's left behind of her on my mouth.

"You like that don't you? That's all you, girl," I speak against her mouth. Taking hold of her face I pull back and stare into her dark eyes, only they're not dark with demons but dark with lust.

On our knees, arms wrapped around one another, mouths fused together, the both of us wishing tomorrow never comes.

But it does.

And I kiss Lacey goodbye, promise to come back to her and pray that I do.

I love you, girl.

Chapter Forty-Eight

CHARLIE TEARDROPS

The bitch sucking me off has a mouth like a Hoover vacuum, thank Christ because her face is brutal. I try to thread my fingers through her over processed red hair but the knots make it a chore. Instead, I arch my hips and bury my cock deeper into her mouth—the head hits the back of her throat and she gags.

"Prez, someone here to see you," Dipstick says, dropping onto the couch beside me. The prospect watches on as the red head continues to choke on my cock. "I'd be happy to take your place while you handle business."

"Fuck that," I sneer. "Tell whoever it is I need five minutes," I grunt, pumping my hips faster, ignoring the bitch choking on her knees.

"You don't have five minutes."

I know that fucking voice. It grates on my nerves like nails on a chalk board. I think it's the fucking accent. I never cared for the Russian tongue, I wonder if ginger over here is a Ruski. That would explain why I haven't splattered my shit across her face yet.

I stare up at the impeccably dressed Russian gangster as his eyes take in the bitch slurping my dick.

"Jealous? Don't you worry, Vladimir, I'll give you a turn."

His blue eyes pierce me with a lethal gaze and I swear my cock goes soft.

"Not my type," he declares.

That's right. Stupid Charlie. Vladimir Yankovich likes his girls young and naïve, easy to charm and make them believe he's one of the good guys sent to sweep them away from their boring lives. He takes them away from their families, hooks them on drugs and when they're so far gone, he sells them to the highest bidder.

Yeah, this creepy motherfucker that the G-Man saddled me with isn't into selling dope on the streets of New York. He sells girls. Vlad's no pimp though, —he ain't selling five-dollar hookers under the Brooklyn Bridge, he's carting them in containers and shipping them overseas, selling these girls to twisted foreign millionaires.

I'm down with a lot of shit but I ain't down with that. The G-man blindsided me, paired me with a fucking glorified pimp and made me promise to destroy Pastore's power over the New York harbors. He then promised me I could move in on the Satan's Knight's territory. Vlad would take over the docks and I'd get the streets. If I eliminated Jack Parrish and his club, the new gangster taking over Victor's territory wouldn't have a leg to stand on; he'd have no choice but to relinquish control to Vlad.

I've been biding my time, working with some shady as fuck cop named Brantley to bring these fuckers down and I had a plan all set in motion but someone beat me to the punch and tried to wipe out the Knights and Pastore's family all in one shot.

I wish I could take the fucking credit for the explosion that mangled the club responsible for murdering my predecessor but I can't.

Vlad grills me as I push the ginger off my lap and shove my limp dick back into my jeans. That brutal face stares up at me like a lost puppy and I roll my eyes, slapping Dipstick upside the head.

"Give her a hit of something and send her on her way," I command.

"Oh I'll give her a hit all right," he replies sleazily.

Drawing my attention back to the Ruski and the posse standing behind him, I lift an eyebrow and reach for my beer bottle.

"What're you even doing here? I thought our business was finished."

"Why would you think that?"

Sure he had heard, every outlaw on the east coast knew the Satan's Knights of Brooklyn were fucked. They might not all be dead but they were fucking disabled, the fucking president was deaf, their clubhouse was a mountain of dust and their bikes were a fucking scrappers dream.

"Parrish and his club are crippled, off the grid. The Brooklyn charter of the Satan's Knights is finished. You can move whatever the fuck your heart desires through that harbor, Spinelli doesn't have the power to stop you."

"We had a deal, and you didn't deliver," he says calmly, pulling out a gun and aiming it straight for my limp dick. "I don't give second chances but I'm feeling generous," he says pulling back the safety on his gun.

Second chances? I didn't even get a first chance and now my dick would pay the price for some negligence I wasn't even responsible for.

"Fine," I agree, shielding my cock with my hands. "I'll do it. I'll finish someone else's job."

"No, you'll complete your job and while you're at it, you'll add Spinelli to that long list of casualties. If you don't succeed, it'll be your head." He pauses and a mischievous smile spreads across his face. "I'll let you decide which one gets the bullet." He lifts the barrel from my cock and targets between my eyes.

A moment later he drops his weapon and stares at his watch.

"It was nice knowing you, Charlie," he says eerily before turning around and leaving me with both heads intact.

"It was nice knowing you, Charlie?" I repeat. What the fuck did that mean?

Pulling up my zipper, I stand on my feet. I slide back the curtains leading to the common room and make my way to the stash of coke on the bar. Pretty soon this powder will decorate Brooklyn and make me a shit ton of money.

But first I had to kill anyone with a reaper on their back.

I cut the coke and push it into a fine line. One rip and I'll be good, then I'll call church and we'll finish the job these faceless pricks started, and when I'm done wiping out the Knights, I will hunt down whoever the fuck blew their shit up and make them my bitch too. Fucking amateurs.

"Shit! Incoming!" I hear my vice president shout as I snort the coke. The motherfucker is probably hallucinating again, goddamn junkie.

He grabs my cut and spins me around, throwing a rifle into my hand and to my surprise he looks straight. I fight for focus but I'm too distracted by the blaring engines approaching the clubhouse. I glance at the security footage and all I see are headlights, the whole fucking screen is lit up like the tree in Rockefeller Center.

I order my club to spring into action and collect their weapons but we're not quick enough. The ginger that sucked me off shrieks in horror causing me to turn around and watch as the Molotov cocktail flies through the glass window and lands on her lap. The flames crawl up her skin and the message is clear.

Satan has arrived.

Chapter Forty-Nine

BLACKIE

Like the night before, I let my mind wander back to the night before I left for Boston. I see her face, flushed, a fresh sheen of sweat glistens over her creamy skin and her lips are swollen from the desperate assault my mouth played on hers. Her limbs weak as they wrap around me, and though she's fucking exhausted, she arches for me one last time, drawing me into her until we become one. She whispers my name, tells me she loves me and makes me promise to always love her.

And I will.

I'll always love Lace.

The Corrupt Bastards' clubhouse comes into sight and I push back the sweet face of my girl and bury Dominic Petra. Leading what we've dubbed as the final ride, the devil resurrects in my saddle and Blackie emerges. I lift my hand off the handlebar and circle my index finger in the wind.

Round up boys.

Satan's ready to fade these motherfuckers to black.

My brothers flash their headlights behind me.

Ready, all we see is red. We're broken down, battered but we're ready to crawl our way back to the top. They tried to break us but they don't know we're made of concrete skin—it's time they learned. Thirty bikes deep we roll through the gates, Stryker and Cobra come up alongside me, each steer with one hand and fire with the other, shooting at any living thing in the parking lot. I pull in front of the clubhouse, drop my kickstand and pull the glass bottle out of my saddlebag shoving the rag inside of it. I pull a lighter from my jacket and watch the flame travel the length of the fabric before rearing my hand back and tossing the bottle into the glass window. I don't care where it lands or who it hits. Burn motherfuckers.

Pulling the machine gun over one shoulder and fitting the magazine of bullets to the other I dismount my bike. The sea of headlights illuminates the path our boots pound as we race toward the clubhouse. Three Bastards emerge from the shattered glass, guns blazing, but Riggs skids to a stop and sprays them with bullets, waving me to go ahead.

I shoot my way through the front door and catch sight of the woman dancing in the fire, but before I can put her out of her misery, Deuce does. They creep out of the corners like cockroaches, whores and Bastards, but our bullets don't stop. We have no regard for human life; we pump them all full of our lead and won't stop until every last one is dead.

With another twirl of my finger in the air I let my boys loose and let them do whatever the fuck they want. I've got my sights set on the leader, ready to cut him to the marrow and watch the life fade from his eyes. I crave it like the drugs that used to haunt my dreams.

Charlie lifts his head from the bar, aims the barrel of his rifle at me and fires off a round.

Come at me motherfucker.

Let's go.

"Promise me you'll come back to me."

"I'll always come back for you, girl."

I take cover behind a wall, close my eyes for a second and she's back, miles of dark, wavy hair that match her dark eyes. I can almost see the tortured expression reflected at me when they tell her I'm gone. I want to make it better, I want to dance with her and make it all go away but the only way I can do that is if I keep my promise and keep coming for her.

I reload my clip and step out from behind the wall. My eyes do a quick sweep of the room and watch as Bergen and Brooklyn destroy and rob the lives of the men responsible for the destruction of our club.

Pipe crosses his arms, a gun in each hand, and fires away, screaming out in agony as he keeps his index fingers firm on the triggers.

That's for Oksana.

Riggs jumps on top of a chair and spins around in a full circle shooting six Bastards. Repeats the act, shooting the same targets, making sure they're dead.

That's for Mack and Bosco.

A bullet pierces Cobra's shoulder and he screams through the pain continuing to shoot, lining up a clean shot and shoots the ear off one of the Bastards.

That's for Jack.

Smoke and his men drop bodies as quick as they appear, we've got this.

Out of the corner of my eye I see the barrel of Charlie's gun. I cross my left arm over my right and pull the trigger before he can. I pull it again. And again, once more.

Spinning around, I watch as Charlie clutches his chest with one hand and raises his other with the gun and struggles to pull the trigger.

"Go on, I'll give it to you," I dare him.

His finger closes around it as my bullet whizzes through the air and blows his finger off. The shots begin to die down, the gun powder is thick in the air and the bitch is still burning on the ground. Smoke throws his gun over his shoulder and walks over to the unfortunate club whore and whips out his cock and takes a piss on her.

Charlie squeals like a pig, drawing my attention away from Smoke and his attempt to put out the fire. With my gun still poised I make my way toward him and stand over him as he slithers across the floor like a snake.

I arch my shoulders and pull the trigger again. His body stills and I bend over to stare into his eyes and watch as the life spills out them. He hangs on by a thread, suffering through his death. I sling the gun over my shoulder and turn around. My eyes struggle to search through the smoke for my brother that deserves to take this man's life and fade him to black.

"Pipe," I shout, pulling the utility knife from my belt. I hear his boots creep up behind me and I straighten my back and hand him the knife as he stares at Charlie.

"He's going to die, make it be from your hand," I tell him. Pipe diverts his eyes to the knife I'm offering and then he looks back at me as his hand takes the weapon.

After Christine died I struggled for years, let my temptations become my demons all because I was desperate for retribution. I got mine and now it's time for Pipe to get his.

I watch as he kneels beside Charlie and presses the blade against his cheek, the sharpened point touches the outline of one of the teardrops inked beneath his eye.

"Your tears belong to me now," he seethes, as he traces the drops of ink, carving the tattoo from his cheek. Charlie's body jerks but he can't fight. He can't scream. He can only lay there and be at the mercy of the knife.

Like Oksana.

Pipe flicks the pieces of bloody skin off his fingers before he drags the knife across Charlie's neck and slices it wide open.

Retribution.

It has a color.

Its color is *black*.

Chapter Fifty

Lacey

Three days feigning off the sadistic voice inside my head that tells me the long languid kiss Blackie gave me before he slipped out of our bed, was the very last one he'd ever give me, has left my heart in a million tiny shattered pieces. I did everything I was supposed to do. I woke up and routinely took my dose of lithium, replayed his promise over and over in my mind but nothing worked.

I'm coming back for you, girl.

In a last ditch effort to pull my sanity from the ruins Blackie's departure left me in I went to my father's house. My father knew I was being worked over by my treacherous mind the moment he opened the door. Either he spotted the familiar signs reflected in my eyes that he sees every time he glances in the mirror or I am more transparent than I thought. Whichever the case maybe he was trying his hardest to pull me from the depression dragging me down.

He didn't need my stress added to the mountain sitting on his shoulders but he took it, anyway. He acted as if it wasn't severing his soul that he wasn't with his club or that they were on the road facing peril without him. And after he cooked me and Reina dinner he and I went upstairs and painted the nursery.

"He will come back, right?" I ask, rolling the green paint on the wall. I couldn't avoid the question anymore. I know I'm not supposed to ask, that a better, wiser old lady would just sit idly and wait for her man to come home, but I couldn't help myself.

He doesn't answer me straight away and for a moment I wonder if he heard me, forgetting his ears were still on the mend. But my father heard my words, maybe not as loudly as I spoke them but he heard my question. He thought before he actually answered, not something Jack Parrish usually did. The man doesn't have a filter.

He places the roller into the tray and turns to me taking a deep breath as I continue rolling the paint on the wall.

"Careful how you answer, Bulldog, wouldn't want to make a liar out of you."

The roller falls from my hand as that deep voice vibrates through me, awakening all the dormant parts of my body and finally ending the torment.

My dad's face comes into view first, the cocky smile, wide and proud on his face. My eyes follow the direction of his and I see Blackie casually leaning against the frame of the door. His smile matches my fathers, arrogant and victorious. But everything else about him screams exhaustion, everything except his eyes. Those bad boys are feral, primal, outright hungry.

"Whatcha waiting for, girl?"

Pushing off the frame, he crooks his finger and beckons me.

"Jack, with all due respect, you might want to get your ass out of this room. Pipe's downstairs waiting for you anyway," he says, his long legs swallowing up the space between us.

"Wish I lost my fucking vision not my hearing," my father grunts as he pats Blackie on the back and disappears out the door.

"Get over here," Blackie whispers.

He doesn't have to say it twice. Like so many times before, I jump straight into his waiting arms and throw mine around his neck. The familiar smell of gasoline assaults my senses and I bury my nose in his neck, breathing in his scent. My fingers slide over the leather covering his shoulders as his slide into the back pockets of my jeans and squeezes my ass.

Blackie's back.

I lift my head from the crook of his neck and stare into his eyes.

"You kept your promise," I whisper.

"I did," he agrees, leaning his forehead against mine. "Now it's time to keep all the others," he says huskily as his gaze lowers to my mouth. "How quickly can you finish your degree?"

I open my mouth to question what he means, but he doesn't give me a chance.

"Take another class, do whatever it takes, girl," he murmurs against my mouth, softly sucking on my lower lip. "As soon as you get that degree I'm putting a ring on that finger and then you're gonna get that tattoo you want so bad," he rasps before covering my mouth with his.

I thread my fingers through his hair, pull on the ends and wait for him to say the words I've been waiting to hear.

"I'm back, girl."

Yeah, Blackie's back.

And he'll keep coming back time and time again.

And these arms of mine will always be waiting.

JACK

Pipe's standing in the kitchen, his hands braced against my counter, his eyes trained on the knife laying on top of it.

"Brother," I say, jolting his gaze from the pocket knife. Beady, drained eyes stare back at me and the cockiness I felt upstairs when I saw Blackie alive and well disappears.

"Mission accomplished," he says solemnly. Two words. Two words that declared victory for our club but they were lack luster coming from Pipe. "The insurance adjusters will assess the compound this week, if there isn't enough to cover the rebuild you have plenty of equity in my garage—pull it out and rise up."

"You talkin' like you're going somewhere," I accuse, crossing my arms against my chest as I continue to stare at him, dreading the words he's about to say.

"I'm done," he declares, shrugging off his cut. "Riggs would be good in my position; the kid is a whiz."

"Pipe, brother, I know—" he cuts my words with a glare.

"You don't know," he spits. "Like I don't know what it's like to watch my kid die you don't know what it's like to find your wife with her neck slit."

I snap my mouth shut and grind my teeth. Another man would've been dead for bringing up my boy but I know Pipe's just hurting. He was there for me when I buried Jack, stood by my side and reeled me in every time I tried to join my boy in eternity. He gets a pass.

He turns his cut over and picks up the knife, inching the blade under his patch and cuts stitch after stitch.

"You're right, I don't know what you're feeling but I know whatever it is it's made you raw and you need to heal."

My words are ignored, and he continues to pull the stitches out until his patch is free. I watch on as he shrugs his cut back onto his shoulders, pockets the knife and hands me the patch.

"That patch is who you are," I argue.

"That's not who I want to be anymore," he sneers. "Take the fucking patch, Parrish," he seethes, extending his arm. "TAKE IT!"

I snatch the worn patch from his hand and grab his cut with the other, stepping to him as I set my eyes on his.

"I'm taking the fucking patch, Pipe, but you're coming back for it. Clear your head, get your shit figured out but you get back on that bike and you come home. Your patch and your chair will be waiting for you. I will be waiting for you."

Without another word he pulls out of my grasp and glares at me before charging out of the kitchen like hell was on his tail—maybe it was.

Reina steps into the kitchen as I throw Pipe's patch on the counter and fight the urge to throw something.

"Jack," she shouts, demanding my attention. Turning my narrowed eyes on her I see the phone she's holding against her chest. "It's Bianci."

Of course it is.

"Victor passed away," she says solemnly.

I heard the three words.

Read them off her lips too.

And wished I did neither

Chapter Fifty-One

Grace

The call came from the warden. Thinking back now I don't remember what he said but I know there was no remorse in the deliverance of his words. And why would there be? To him he was just a number, just a problematic inmate, a criminal who turned his prison upside down. He was happy to be rid of him.

I had been preparing myself for the inevitable and I think that's why I didn't react at first. I held my composure and called my son-in-law, Anthony. Bless his big heart, the man brought my daughters, and together we told them that their father had passed.

I was sure watching my children mourn their father would be my undoing but still I didn't shed a tear and was able to be the rock they both needed. The girls stayed with me that night and just like when they were small, and Victor would work through the night; they crawled into the king-sized bed I shared with their father and snuggled close.

Victor's body was released and flown back to New York, Anthony and I went to identify his body. I wish I never stepped foot into that morgue because the man beneath the sheet was not the man I married; he was not the handsome, dapper man I met at Studio 54. He was skin and bones and all the suffering he did in the last few weeks of his life stared back at me and it became evident that my husband died a miserable death. A man who was loved beyond measure died alone and imprisoned with a failing body and broken heart.

I left Anthony in the morgue and ran out of there as quickly as my weak legs would allow and desperately tried to erase the image from my mind. I closed my eyes and begged Victor's soul to paint me one last picture and envision the young man with the charcoal gray suit and the black turtleneck. The man who promised to marry me and make a life with me. I closed my eyes and remembered our last visit and the way we promised one another we would remember the other.

Still, I didn't cry, not a tear.

At the funeral parlor I picked out the most lavish casket, the final throne for the king. Anthony gave the funeral director Victor's favorite suit, and he assured us he would pin it to look like it was tailored to fit. We matched the handkerchief to the tie just as he always did and included a pair of his Italian loafers. Some might say I was being foolish since I had kept the casket closed but I wanted my husband to be impeccably dressed for his final sleep just as he was in life. He would want that too.

Once his wake was settled, it was time to pick a burial plot. The ride around Green-Wood cemetery to decide on where we would both rest eternally, that broke what was left of my heart. He tried so hard to give me what I wanted in life, bought that huge house because he thought it would make me happy. We made that house our home and now I was left choosing our final home. And still I didn't cry.

The girls met us at the florist and we ordered the traditional pieces. A bleeding heart from me, a broken heart from Nicole and Mike and a piece the florist called the Gates of Heaven from Adrianna and Anthony. We also ordered the rosary beads for inside the coffin and made that from his grandchildren. So along with their pictures, Victor would be buried with remnants of Luca and Victoria.

The night before the wake the girls came over, and together with my in laws, we went through old photo albums to display around the funeral parlor. My daughters marveled over one photograph in particular, one of me and their father. The year was 1984, and it was one of a few where my husband was dressed casually in a pair of jeans. I stared at the photo and the outfit I was wearing, white fitted pants and a turquoise blouse. I wore a lot of that color in the early years and I remember why, Victor loved the color on me, told me it reminded him of the first day we met.

I wound up slipping that photo into Victor's folded hands the morning of the wake when they allowed me to view him before they closed the casket for the final time.

Victor's wake reflected his life. It seemed anyone Victor ever met throughout the duration of his sixty-six years showed to pay their final respects. Some of the faces I remembered, some I didn't. All I thanked for coming and told them how grateful Victor would've been. The old time gangsters competed by sending extravagant floral arrangements and stood in the back of the viewing room sharing stories of all the illegal activities they conducted with my husband. The younger ones, the fresh faces like my nephew, sat vigil, quietly taking in the death of a mobster. Whether they were young or old, veterans or new blood they showed up, but I knew that once the dirt settled over my husband, they would fight tooth and nail for everything he built.

Then there were the loyal men who never wanted a piece of my husband but were always there to lend a hand when rough times fell upon him, those were the men in leather. Jack Parrish stood the left of my husband's casket and his vice president stood to the right. They never left his side, not once, stood like two soldiers guarding his body until it was time to head to church for the final mass.

And even then they didn't leave his side.

As the hearse pulled away from the funeral parlor, they straddled their bikes and rode alongside him, accompanying him to the church we were married in. But their loyalty didn't stop there, the Satan's Knights respectively removed their cuts and carried my husband's casket into the church.

It wasn't until I entered the church and the choir sang *Amazing Grace* as I walked behind my husband's casket that I lost myself and the tears fell uncontrollably down my face.

Amazing Grace, how sweet the sound,
That saved a wretch like me...
I once was lost but now I'm found,
Was blind, but now, I see...

I stared at the coffin as the priest prayed over Victor's body, begging our Lord to relieve him of his sins and welcome him into his arms. As he continues the mass I continue to beg and bargain with our Lord for a chance to be reunited with my love.

Forgive him Heavenly Father.
Please don't take away my eternal love.

The mass ended, it was time to take Victor to his final place of rest, the home where he'd wait for me to join him. A funeral procession of fifty cars, two limousines, three flower trucks and hearse guided by a dozen bikers stopped traffic along Fort Hamilton Parkway.

Wherever Victor was, I knew he had a grin on his face, loving that his send-off was as big as his personality.

The media were waiting outside the cemetery gates hoping for one last headline, snapping photos of us as we cried over his grave. One by one, everyone laid a rose on his coffin until there was only five of us surrounding him. Michael and Nikki said their goodbyes first, followed by Anthony and Adrianna.

Then it was just me.

Me and Vic.

I stepped to the coffin and placed my rose on top of all the others.

How do you say goodbye to the love of your life?

You don't.

I'll never say goodbye to my Victor.

I leaned over the coffin and pressed my lips to the top of it.

"Until we meet again my eternal love…I'll be the girl in the turquoise jumpsuit."

The End.
For now.

Epilogue

JACK

I ease Reina into the passenger seat of Lacey's car after the cemetery. The two of us defied doctor's orders, she took herself off bedrest and I damned my hearing to hell by riding, neither of us willing to give up the opportunity to pay our final respects to Vic and his family.

"Lace, take her straight home," I tell my daughter as I buckle Reina's seatbelt and turn my eyes to her. "You feel okay?" I ask, narrowing my eyes as she shifts uncomfortably.

"I'm fine," she insists. "I'm just tired," she adds as she kisses me.

"I'll meet you at home and we'll take a load off, watch one of those sappy movies you love so much."

She smiles widely, and I laughed. Sunshine loves torturing me with the Lifetime Channel. I press another quick peck to her mouth before closing the door and tapping the hood of the car.

"Jack, I need a word," Rocco Spinelli calls from behind me and the smile instantly falls from my lips. I turn, rolling my neck from side to side as I size up the boss of the Pastore family. The threads are the same and I'm sure Vic's smiling down on his protégé. On second thought, maybe not, the kid seems to have forgotten the silk tie and matching handkerchief. That shit wouldn't fly with Vic.

"We have nothing to discuss," I say finally, lifting my gaze to his. Standing beside Vic's coffin I observed a lot over the last few days and I decided on a number of things on behalf of myself and my club.

Victor Pastore wasn't anything like the mobsters that flooded that funeral parlor. Not even the man he trained to take his place could ever fill his shoes, and I didn't have a desire to join forces with any of these mutts.

"It's about the bomb," he mutters, undoing the top button of his collared shirt.

Rolling my eyes, I let out a sarcastic chuckle, he knows shit about that bomb. He wasn't there when everything turned to dust. He didn't lift a finger to help rebuild. He sat his pretty boy ass down, kicked up his legs in his mansion and barely checked in on his aunt.

"Thanks, but we've got everything under control." I dismiss him, turning back around to head for my bike but he grabs a hold of my arm and holds me back.

Snatching back my arm, I step to him, narrowing my eyes as I drill him with a deadly glare.

"Don't you ever put your fucking hands on me again, not unless you want me to cut them off—" I threaten but he quickly cuts me off.

"I don't think the Corrupt Bastards sent that guy into your clubhouse with the bomb. There's another enemy moving into our harbor and our streets and his name is Vladimir Yankovich. I have reason to believe he was working with the Bastards. Now, I think we can shut him—"

"Hold it," I order, cutting him off and holding up my hand to stop the bullshit spewing from his mouth. "First, what happened to my club isn't your concern. I don't give a fuck about your theories and I sure as hell didn't ask for them. Second, you made a mistake assuming there is a *we* here," I growl as I wave a finger between his chest and mine. "My alliance was with Victor," I clarify, pointing behind his shoulder to his fresh grave and his wife standing over his casket saying her final goodbye. "That alliance follows that coffin into the ground today. The Satan's Knights are done with the mob."

"But—" Rocco argues and I shake my head.

"And they say I'm the one with failing ears," I grunt. "We're done here," I continue. "Good luck, boy, you're sure as hell going to need it."

"Dad!"

I turn around at the sound of my daughter shouting.

"Reina's water broke!"

There was no mistaking those three words, and I took off as quickly as my feet would carry my ass down the hill to the curb where Lacey's car was parked. Pulling open the passenger door, my eyes roam over Reina, watching as tears stream down her cheeks and she clutches her belly.

"I'm sorry," she cries.

"Woman, what're you sorry for?" I question, taking her hands in mine.

"The car, it's a mess!"

I glance down at the stains setting in Lacey's mats and let out a low chuckle as I turn my attention back to my wife.

"Damn, Sunshine," I shake my head, taking her face in my hands and touch my forehead to hers. "Who gives a fuck about the mats? We're about to have a baby," I rasp as I smile at her, my thumbs work at drying her tears. "You ready to meet this kid of ours?"

"I'm more than ready," she whispers. Leaning in to kiss me, she pauses and her eyes go wide. "Oh God," she groans as she clutches her belly.

"What? What is it?"

"I think I'm having a contraction," she says, through clenched teeth.

"Is it true? Oh dear, it's true!" Grace says, coming up behind me. I turn to her, relieved to see someone who probably knows what the hell is going on.

"She thinks she's having a contraction," I explain.

"She most definitely is. Give me your watch," Grace orders, pulling open the back door and climbing into the car. I hand her my watch and run around the front of the car and switch places with Lacey. Grace has one hand planted on Reina's shoulder, caressing her arm as she tells her to breathe and eyes the watch in her hand.

"We'll follow you," Lacey says, pressing a kiss to my cheek. "Good luck!"

"Love you," I call out the window and start the car. "Hang in there, Sunshine, we'll be at the hospital in no time," I tell her, steering the car with one hand and placing the other on her knee.

"It's still early," Reina cries.

"It's okay," Grace assures her. "This baby will be just fine, Reina."

My eyes meet hers in the rearview mirror, they're red and blotchy from the tears she shed over her husband but still they shine back at me as she smiles.

"Drive, Parrish, or we're going to deliver this baby ourselves."

She didn't have to tell me twice. I accelerated on the gas, maneuvered in and out of traffic with a brigade of Harley's following me.

"Is it supposed to hurt this much?" Reina wails in pain.

"We're almost there," I tell her.

"Shut up! You're never touching me again, Jack Parrish. Never," she shrieks, squeezing my hand and crushing my fingers with all her might.

My lips quirk at the threat and she squeezes my hand harder.

"I'm serious," she says through her clenched jaw.

"Sure you are, Sunshine."

From the moment I pull up in front of the hospital everything seems to happen in a blink of an eye. We're ushered into a labor and delivery unit where I trade my leathers for a pair of scrubs. Reina's doctor informs us she's progressing fast, too fast for an epidural, and for a moment I believe Sunshine truly may never let me touch her again.

I try to process everything, ingrain it to my memory, for this time I don't want to forget a single moment of this child's birth. I stare at Reina, brush her blonde hair away from her face and continuously kiss the top of her head as she clutches my hand and grips down.

Her screams are muffled but I feel them down in my soul as our baby makes its descent into this world.

"You're doing great, Sunshine," I soothe as the doctor and his staff work diligently to prepare for our baby's entrance into the world.

The incubator is turned on.

With a clean blanket draped over her arm the nurse moves next to doctor.

The doctor lifts his eyes to Reina, holds up one finger, then another and finally a third and commands her to push.

I swallow the lump in my throat, knowing the next noise that'll fill this room is the voice of my child's first cry. I pray to whatever God hears me I can hear it loud and clear.

I'm not one for prayers but while I'm at it I pray for the child that is about to be born.

I pray he or she is healthy.

Please be born free of a troubled mind.

I pray he or she lives a long beautiful life.

Please go on to live way passed me.

I pray he or she never knows the ugliness of the world.

Please don't follow in your Daddy's footsteps.

Live.

Love.

And always find your sunshine.

I'm just about to turn my attention to Reina and thank her for the gift she's about to give me when the doctor lifts the tiny miracle Sunshine and I created together into the air.

A strong pair of lungs lets out a shrill cry that echoes through the room.

"It's a boy!" The doctor announces.

I hear him.

My boy, I hear his cry.

"That's it boy, sing for Daddy," I say with a smile, tearing my eyes away from my perfect boy to his perfect mother. "Sunshine," I rasp.

"We have a son," she cries into my chest.

"Dad, would you like to cut the cord?"

I lift Reina's head from my chest and press my lips to hers.

"Thank you," I whisper against her mouth. Two words.

I wink at my wife and turn to the doctor, taking the scissors from his hand and cut the cord. They clean him, wrap him tightly in a blanket and place him into Reina's waiting arms. I move to stand beside her and lean close to them. He's perfect, absolutely perfect.

"Welcome to the world, Daniel," Reina tells our boy, rubbing the tip of her nose against his tiny one. I watch as mother and son bond for the first time and I feel a pang in my heart, the familiar dull ache for the boy I lost.

Don't you worry Jack; your old man won't ever forget you.

I bend my head and press my lips to my son's bald head and stare into his precious face, watching as he yawns and struggles to open his eyes.

"You," I whisper to him as his eyes flutter open and he stares back at me.

I don't know how long the three of us stayed like that, wrapped up in each other's arms blocking out the rest of the world, but I wouldn't have minded staying like that for the rest of my life. The doctor had a different plan though, insisting they take Danny to the nursery as they moved Reina into a regular room. I guess it was a good thing they kicked me out or else I would've forgotten all about the people in the waiting room

've done a lot of shit in my life, committed a ton of sins and probably don't deserve to be smiling like I am, but hell if it doesn't feel good. I push the doors to the waiting room wide open and watch as every pair of eyes turn to me.

My daughter.

My right hand, best friend and future son-in-law.

Grace Pastore.

Her two daughters.

Michael Valente.

Anthony Bianci.

Riggs and his Kitten.

The three new brothers patched into my club.

My family.

Every person in this room is mine. They are all Property of Parrish.

"It's a boy," I beam as the smiles spread across their faces.

Together we mourned and now together we'll rejoice.

We buried one of our own today but gained another.

God works in mysterious ways, he makes sinners become believers.

Bonus Epilogue

JACK

My boots pound the pavement of the seedy motel's parking lot. I can't wait for the construction to be complete on the clubhouse. I don't know how the fuck Stryker and the boys have been living in this fleabag motel for the last five months.

Resolving to fix their living conditions, I shake the thought from my head and focus on the reason I was pulled away from Reina and our son at four in the fucking morning. Just when Danny started sleeping through the night the phone rang and Stryker's frantic voice filled my groggy head.

I didn't know what the fuck he was saying at first but then he calmed down and told me he found the girl he's been banging in an alley way. I've been too wrapped up in my own life to pay much attention to my brother's but after placing a quick call to Wolf I found out the girl, Stryker's girl, isn't just some tight piece of ass he hustled pool with, nah, our boy Stryker opened a whole fucking can of worms I tried real hard to bury.

I don't know what the fuck goes on with my men but they love that mobbed up pussy.

"Parrish," the cocky voice greets me as the man it belongs to steps out of the Maserati.

"Spinelli," I sneer.

"I'm surprised you called," he says, unbuttoning his suit and sliding a hand into the pocket of his tailored pants. Vic would be proud, his little protégé is fitting the bill of a mob boss. "But I'm happy you finally came around."

"I didn't call you here to break bread," I say, tipping my chin to the dingy motel. "One of my brothers found something that belongs to you."

His eyes narrow suspiciously as I lead him to the room Stryker occupies.

"What could one of your men have that belongs to me?"

"Your sister," I reveal, closing my fist and pounding it against the door. I don't have to turn around to know the air deflates from his lungs, I hear it.

Stryker pulls open the door and I take in Satan's soldier. I knew the minute I met the veteran turned biker, he was a force to be reckoned with. I pity the motherfuckers overseas he took down, almost as much as I pity the man responsible for the look in his eyes now.

"Where is she?" Rocco demands from behind me. I watch as Stryker's cold eyes turn to him. Stryker crosses his arms against his chest and barricades the door, sizing up the gangster before he turns that glare back to me.

"What the fuck is he doing here?" he hisses.

I open my mouth to explain when a guttural shriek sounds from the motel room. Rocco shoulders his way past me and grabs a hold of Stryker's cut. Shoving him out of his way he enters the room and runs to his sister's side.

Stryker moves to lunge for Rocco but I reel him in by pulling on the back of his cut.

"Get off me," he shouts.

Forcefully, I tug him back, my patience wavers as I lean over his shoulder and clench my jaw as I hiss the words that come out of my mouth next.

"That woman wrestling her demons in your bed is Rocco's sister."

So much for Satan's Knights steering clear of the mob.

Here we fucking go again…

*Turn the page for
Bonus Chapters*

Reckless Temptations: Lauren & Riggs
Chapter One

Lauren Bianci

Before there was the movie franchise, Bad Moms, there was me, Lauren Bianci. The ex-nursing student who took a detour to the Satan's Knights clubhouse found her tiger and got knocked up in the parking lot. Three kids later and another on the way, I am the OG mom, the fucking inspiration behind those blockbuster hits.

Like Mila Kunis, I too have an overbearing mother and while she might not point out all my parenting fails, she does like to remind me that I'm breeding out of wedlock. Yes, I said breeding—her words, not mine.

Insert eye roll.

Now, I know what you're thinking…you think the reason I'm an unwed mother of four is because my baby daddy won't marry me. Wrong. In fact, marriage might be the one and only thing my mother and Riggs agree on. For someone who was scared shit over becoming a father and engaging in a monogamous relationship, Riggs is the most devoted father and wannabe husband a woman could ever hope for.

The reason we're not married is all on me.

For as long as I can remember, I've always had a vision of what my wedding would be like. I would wear a big white gown with a twenty-foot train just like Mariah Carey wore when she married Tommy Mattola and my bridesmaids would be decked out in the lavender silk. There would be flowers everywhere and those fancy candelabras on every table. My brother would give me away and there would be a grand reception after an epic kiss declaring us husband and wife.

The plan has changed some.

Instead of picturing Luke Perry as my future husband, it's always Riggs that's waiting at the altar for me and we're not surrounded by a fleet of lavender. Now, when I think of our wedding, it's our kids that are beside us. Our three boys and this little girl I'm carrying.

So, yes, I want to marry Riggs but not until this little girl makes her big debut. We've waited this long, a few more months won't hurt. It may not be conventional but, Riggs and I were never the traditional type. We're Kitten and Tiger and when we take our vows, I want all our cubs to be there. All the little peas we created because we took a detour.

They'll be chaos.

The cake will probably go flying.

One of the boys will likely break something very valuable.

Another will likely tie my mother-in-law to a chair and my father-in-law will probably assist.

Our daughter will fuss.

My mother will nag.

The Satan's Knights will surround us, all wearing a patch in memory of Bones. It will be perfect.

The phone rings pulling me away from the wedding of my dreams and forcing me back to reality. Instinctively I cringe as my eyes dart around the room, realizing it looks like a tornado took root in my living room. Aside from the playpen, the walker and the vast variety of baby stuff, there are toys everywhere thanks to Riggs. The moment he found out Toys R Us was closing, he took the boys to the beloved toy store and cleaned the place out. I shit you not, there is one of those plastic cottages in my living room—you know the ones that normal people put in their backyard—yep, right smack in the middle of the room.

Realizing there's no point in physically searching for my phone, I follow the sound of the ringtone. As I reach for the cushions on the couch a baseball flies past my head.

"Eric, you can't play ball in the house!"

Turning to my first born, I narrow my eyes and watch him grin deviously as he whacks another ball into the air.

From his rebellious streak to the sunglasses he refuses to take off, he's a clone of his father.

A horn sounds and my eyes widen as my second oldest, Anthony, whizzes past me with his new wheels.

"Didn't I say you couldn't ride your Power Wheels inside the house!?"

"Daddy said it was okay," Anthony argues.

"Of course he did," I growl.

Baby Robert starts to cry as he lifts himself to his feet and reaches over the edge of the playpen for me.

"Just a second baby," I soothe. Finally finding my phone, I glance at the screen. Seeing it's my mother calling, I accept the call and lift the phone to my ear.

"Eric," I shout as he swings the bat again. "Hi, Mom, sorry—"

"Lauren, I hate to do this to you sweetheart, but, I can't watch the kids tonight."

The tip of the bat collides with the ball and I watch as it crashes into a vase. My mother's words register as the porcelain cracks and the dirt filling it pours freely all over the beige carpet.

"What? No, you can't cancel on me. Mom, I need you to watch them. It's parent-teacher conferences at Eric's school."

"I'm sorry Lauren but, I'm not feeling well. You know I wouldn't cancel on you."

"What am I supposed to do with them?"

"Maybe Anthony and Adrianna can watch them?"

"Grace is watching Luca and Victoria so, they can go to the conferences too."

"Well—"

"It's fine," I snap, blowing out a breath as Robert screams at the top of his lungs. "I'll just have to take them with me."

"Where's that scoundrel you procreate with?"

"And, this conversation is officially over. Feel better Mom," I say before ending the call.

"I'm hungry," Eric groans, tossing the bat onto the floor.

"Mommy, I have to go pee-pee," Anthony whines.

"Mama!" Robert cries, snot dripping from his nose.

"Have kids they said…." I mutter as I make my way to the playpen. Lifting him into my arms, he buries his face in the crook of my neck and rubs his snot all over me.

"Mommy! I'm hungry!"

"Mommy! I need to go pee-pee!"

"It'll be fun they said…"

They clearly didn't have a fleet of boys with the self-proclaimed Tiger.

Reckless Temptations: Lauren & Riggs
Chapter Two

Riggs "The Motherfucking Tiger"

Pulling in front of the elementary school, I kill the engine on my Harley and drop down the kickstand. Without turning my attention toward the front of the school, I can feel the parents gathered at the doors glaring at me. They're just salty because they had to park their minivans seven blocks away. It's not their fault no one told them to join an MC.

Removing the helmet, I fit my signature aviators to my face and throw my leg over the bike. The sun has been down for hours but, all the cool kids wear their sunglasses at night. Another thing no one told these stiffs.

Fixing a grin to my face, I stride through the front door like the tiger I am and make my way to the security guard at the desk.

"Can I help you?" she asks without bothering to look at me.

"Hello, beautiful," I croon, flashing her a smile.

Lifting her head, she stares at me over the rim of her glasses. Taking her in, I decide she's about the same age as my granny back in Texas. I love my granny and all but, she's not equipped to be a security guard, and neither is this lady. Calling the numbers at a Bingo tournament is where this lass belongs but, I'm too much of a gentleman to tell her that. Instead, I lay on the charm, ask her to point me in the direction of Eric's class and make a mental note to write a letter to the Board of Education requesting they beef up the security in the public schools. Maybe, while I'm at it, I'll offer my services.

Picture that.

The Satan's Knights standing guard in front of schools near and far.

We'd have to curb the curses some and maybe regulate Jack's medication. I don't think the parents would be too fond of Parrish going bonkers in front of their children. Still, it's a thought and as I reach Eric's classroom I decide to bring it up at the next PTA meeting.

Yes, I sometimes attend those.

Don't fucking judge.

The bake sales are fucking epic.

As I prepare to enter the classroom a smile works the corners of my lips knowing Kitten is waiting for me and the kids are with her mother. You know what that means right? Kitten and I are totally getting frisky in the back of the Suburban after the conference is over.

Fuck yes.

I hope she parked close to the school that way we can give those minivan driving parents a fucking show they'll never forget. My dick twitches with excitement as I start to picture the truck rocking as I bury my face in Kittens ginormous tits while she rides my cock.

Have I mentioned how well pregnancy agrees with my little lioness? Not only is she always hungry for my anaconda but, her tits—Jesus fuck, they're like globes now.

"Daddy!!"

The sound of Eric's voice filters through the air as I step into the classroom and the boner I was sporting a second ago vanishes. I love my kids. I truly do but, I had my hopes set on rocking Kitten's world. I even wore my favorite pair of boxer briefs for the sex fest. The black pair with a tiger's open jaw screen printed over my cock.

Bending down I lift Eric into my arms as I find Lauren's eyes.

"Surprise," she offers, bouncing Robert on her knee. "Anthony get down from there," she scolds, tearing her eyes away from me. Following her gaze, I watch my son hop from one desk to another.

"Jingle bells, Batman smells, Robin laid an egg," he chants.

"I'm really sorry about this," Lauren says to the teacher. "My mother got sick at the last minute."

Dropping Eric onto his feet, I bend my knees making us eye level.

"Do me a favor? Keep your brother occupied so me and your mom can talk to your teacher."

"What's in it for me?"

"Five bucks," I wager.

"Make it ten and you got yourself a deal," he counters.

"Anthony!"

"Fine, ten dollars," I grunt, reaching into my back pocket. Pulling out a ten, I slap it into Eric's open palm before rising to my full height. I watch Eric run toward Anthony and make my way next to Lauren. Bending my head, I press my mouth to hers in a quick kiss and take Robert from her lap.

"Sorry, I'm late," I offer. "Traffic was a bitch."

"Riggs," Lauren hisses. "Language."

"Oh, stop it, you love it when I talk dirty."

"Riggs!"

"Mr. and Mrs. Montgomery—"

"Oh, no, we're not married," I correct Eric's teacher. Stealing a glance at Kitten from the corner of my eye, I watch as she scowls. Every time the topic is brought up, Lauren skates around it. I'm starting to think she doesn't want to be Mrs. Montgomery after all.

"Really, Riggs? Now, isn't the time," Lauren argues, forcing a tight smile. "We're here to discuss Eric's progress."

"Progress? He's in kindergarten," I argue, winking at the teacher. "No offense, lady, I donate to the United Federation of Teachers or whatever it's called but, he plays with blocks all day," I say, leaving out the fact he probably learns more life lessons coming to the clubhouse with me on a Saturday morning then he does the six hours a day he's here singing about a muffet who sat on her tuffet.

I mean check out his bargaining skills. They probably don't teach that kind of shit until the third grade.

"Actually—"

Turning back to Lauren and the problem at hand, I hold up a hand and interrupt the teacher.

"And, while we're at it," I continue, bouncing Robert on my knee. "If I had a dollar for every time I brought up getting married and you replied with 'now isn't the time', I'd be even richer than I already am."

Kitten rolls her eyes as she pats her protruding belly.

"Maybe if I wasn't pregnant every time you brought it up, I'd have a different answer," she turns to the teacher. "We have three boys, Eric being our oldest and I'm pregnant again, you do the math."

"Go play with the blocks," I tell Robert before setting him on his feet.

"Oh, here we go," Lauren mutters, crossing her arms over her tits.

Tits I'm going to motorboat so hard when this is over. Kids be damned.

Lifting my hips, I reach into my pocket and whip out my phone. Quickly I punch in my passcode and swipe through my photos, finding the perfect one. Dropping it on top of the teacher's desk, I nudge it closer to her.

"Look at her, that was roughly seven months ago," I declare, calculating the date I planted another little pea inside my ferocious kitten. "She's hot as fuck and then wonders why she's pregnant all the time."

"Mr. Montgomery—"

"Call me Tiger," I say with a wink.

"Oh, you're a tiger, alright," Lauren says, twisting in her chair to face me. "All hail to the king of the jungle."

"Actually, I think that would be a Lion but, I'm cool with you call me a king baby."

"Mr. Montgomery and Miss—"

"Bianci."

"Montgomery sounds better," I point out.

Sighing, Lauren looks at me pleadingly.

"Can we not do this here?"

"I've got plans for you later," I retort. Leaning forward, I take both her hands and shuffle my chair closer to her. "Why won't you marry me?"

"Riggs."

"I want to marry you," she whispers. "Probably more than you want to marry me."

The teacher clears her throat causing me to glare at her.

"Do you mind? We're kind of having a moment here."

"By all means, go ahead," she replies. "But, maybe one of you would like to tell the little boy he can't write on the smart board with crayons!"

"Anthony!" Lauren shouts, pulling her hands out of mine and springing to her feet.

"Eric, give me back my ten bucks," I groan, hanging my head.

Grabbing Anthony's hand, Lauren turns to the teacher.

"Maybe we can reschedule?"

"Yes, I think that would be best. Maybe after you marry Mr. Montgomery."

My eyes flit to the teacher and I grin widely at her.

"You, my friend just made next year's donation ten percent higher than this years."

"Let's go Riggs," Lauren orders.

With another wink to the teacher of the year, I lift Robert into my arms and follow Kitten and our cubs out the door. My eyes drift to her ass and I wonder if the good teacher wouldn't mind watching the boys for ten minutes so, I can take Kitten into the teachers lounge and fuck her from behind. Maybe, just maybe, while I'm buried balls deep inside her and she's screaming my name, she'll tell me why she hasn't set a date.

Before I can turn around and make my way back to the classroom, Lauren stops in her tracks. Facing me, she closes the distance between us and releases Anthony's hand. Her hands reach for my face and, she surprises me by placing her lips firmly over mine.

"You want to know what I'm waiting for?" she questions against my mouth.

"Fuck, yes," I growl, nipping at her lower lip.

"Our daughter," she whispers against my mouth.

My mouth pauses and, my eyes widen as her words register.

"Are you saying what I think you're saying?" I ask, searching her eyes.

"I know you wanted to be surprised but, you keep asking me to marry you and I thought you should know the real reason."

"It's a girl?"

"Yes," she whispers. Her lips curve as she slides her black framed glasses up the bridge of her nose. "Riggs?"

A daughter.

I'm going to have a daughter.

A little girl who if she looks anything like her mother will be a stunner.

"I need to go to the shooting range," I blurt, focusing my attention back to Lauren. "And we need to move."

"Riggs—"

"I saw on the news that Trump went to inspect the prototypes of the wall he wants to build. I need to see those things. Get one for around the house."

"You want to build a wall?'

"You just told me we're having a daughter, of course I want to build a wall. A great big wall," I say, spreading my arms wide and doing my best Donald Trump impersonation. "Huge."

"Tiger…"

"Kitten, we're having a daughter," I say, wrapping my arms around her waist.

"Yeah, we are," she says wrapping her arms around my neck.

"Oh my God, I can't wait to tell my Instagram followers!"

Lethal Temptations: Blackie & Lacey Petra
Chapter One

Blackie

Rounding the front of my truck, I reach the passenger door just as Lacey slams it shut. When we first got married, she rode on the back of my bike and opening the door for her was never a problem. Then she got pregnant and adding a sidecar to my Harley wasn't an option. I bought her the safest crossover on the market and whenever we had someplace to go, I got behind the wheel. It took some time getting used to but, I sucked it up. Lacey, however, still hasn't wrapped her head around me wanting to open the door for her and always beats me to the punch. It's little things like that where our age difference comes into play and I have to remind myself I robbed the cradle.

Reaching for her hand, I follow her gaze and watch as our girls run toward Jack and Reina's house. If someone would've told me fifteen years ago, I'd be married to Jack's daughter and we'd have two little girls of our own, I would've laughed in their face. I would've reminded them I was nothing more than a junkie who didn't deserve to live. A man with a longstanding love affair for poison, someone with an expiration date. But by some miracle of God, I got clean and though there have been times when I craved the temporary high, I've remained sober.

It took the girl with the sad eyes to show me there was more to life than empty syringes and a bottle of booze. She gave me another chance at life. The love she gives me and the life she's made with me, heals me. It gives me the strength I need to battle my addictions and be the man my girls deserve.

"They're getting so big," Lacey says softly, causing me to glance down at her. There's a sadness to her tone and I know the source of it.

She wants another child.

While she loves Dominique and Jacqueline to pieces, Lacey is itching to give me something I never asked for.

A son.

I suppose having a boy would be nice but, we've got two perfectly healthy daughters and that's more than I could've ever hoped for.

One was a blessing.

Two was a gamble.

Being a manic depressive forced Lacey off her meds and made pregnancy brutal for her. You hear of women getting postpartum but what Lacey experienced after Dominque's birth was worse.

It was downright crippling.

Lacey had barely had a chance to bond with the baby before she was admitted into the psych ward after suffering a nervous breakdown. Having my wife in the hospital while I cared for our newborn baby at home made some of my old temptations surface.

The lethal kind of temptations.

The kind that almost sent me off the wagon.

If it wasn't for Jack and Reina, I'm not sure I would've survived. Reina stayed at the house with me and helped me take care of Dominique and Jack took me to my meetings. He got in touch with my sobriety coach and he and I took turns sitting with Lacey.

Even after she was discharged and her meds were regulated, we struggled. She felt lost around our daughter and part of her resented me for being able to bond with her while she was being treated.

It wasn't until Dominque was six months old that my Lace finally came back to me and I vowed never to put our little family through that pain again. Then two years later, my wife started talking about babies again. She didn't want Dominique to be an only child and she even tossed my own words back in my face, reminding me of a time when I told her I wanted to fill our house with babies. She begged and pleaded, explained that she wanted a second chance to enjoy pregnancy. She wanted to be able to bond with her child and be locked in a padded room after giving birth. Still, I stood my ground, knowing I couldn't go through that again. I couldn't lose Lacey to her maker.

It was every bit as selfish of me as it sounds and eventually she wore me down.

Jacqueline was born and this time, when our little girl was discharged, it was her mama who carried her into our home.

God was good to us.

Or so I thought.

Jacqueline was colic and never slept. Between both girls, Lacey ran herself ragged and at the time, I was tied up with the club and not much help to her. She stopped taking her pills and soon after she had another breakdown. It was the final nail in the coffin and after she recovered we decided our family was complete. Lacey got an IUD and still, I wrapped my shit tight.

Things got back on track for us and it wasn't until Lacey's brother, Daniel, started taking an interest in baseball and I volunteered to coach his team that Lacey let her desires to give me a son be known. I suppose she thought I offered my time to the league because something was lacking but, I did it for Daniel. I did it for Jack knowing he was slipping. His battle with mental illness was inching to the finish line every day and if he was well enough, he would've been on that field not me.

"Before you know it, they'll be dating and we'll—"

"Lace," I growl, pulling her small body against mine. "Don't go there."

"It's going to happen," she teases, turning in my arms. Rising on her toes, she lifts her hands and runs her fingers through my long hair. "They're going to fall in love and if we're lucky they'll find a man who cherishes them like their daddy cherishes me."

My hands find her hips as my eyes drift over her shoulder to the front door. For a moment I watch as the girls greet Jack before looking back at Lacey.

"You caught onto that, yeah?"

"It's hard not to," she whispers, winding the ends of my hair around her fingers. "You've always made me feel like the most loved girl in the world."

"Good, then I've lived up to the promises I made to myself," I say before dipping my head and taking her mouth. The kiss starts slow until she parts her lips and invites me into heaven and just like the first time I tasted her, I'm hooked.

"Do you think they'll notice if we go back to the car?" she asks in between kisses.

"You leave something behind?" I retort, tugging her lip between my teeth. Sliding my hands down her back, I squeeze her ass and press her into me. My cock painfully strains against my jeans and I rock against her. A moan escapes her throat as she pulls at my hair.

"Damn, girl," I growl. "You got me all riled up."

"Just the way I like you," she pants, peppering my jaw with kisses. "Ask me how I want it, Blackie," she demands, trailing her mouth down my neck.

"Oh, girl, I know how you want it," I tell her as I start walking backwards to the truck. "My woman likes pleasure and pain."

Lucky for her, I'm an expert at delivering both.

Lethal Temptations: Blackie & Lacey Petra
Chapter Two

Lacey

Climbing onto Blackie's lap, our eyes lock as I push his leather vest off his shoulders. Before I can reach for his thermal, he leans forward and pulls the front of my shirt down with one hand, revealing my bra. In one swift move, he lifts one breast from its cup and then the other.

"So fucking beautiful," he growls, squeezing my tits. His thumbs gently caress my nipples until they harden into sharp peaks and he pinches them.

Pain.

Exquisite pain that shoots straight down to my core. Desire pools between my legs and I rub myself against his erection as he dips his head and sucks my puckered nipple into his mouth. My fingers thread through his hair and a smile spreads across my lips. Fifteen years later and though there is some gray sprinkled throughout, I'm still as infatuated with his long locks as I was when I was just a girl crushing on the vice president of her dad's motorcycle club.

Pulling away, he releases my nipple with a pop and reaches for my face. Dragging my mouth to his, he slides his tongue between my lips as I unravel my fingers from his hair. My hands slide down his front and find the button to his jeans. Making quick work of it, I drag the zipper down next and pull his raging cock from his boxer briefs. My fist closes around his shaft and I groan into his mouth as my thumb grazes the crown, swiping away at the precum covering it.

He raises my hips, forcing me on my knees and peels away my pants. Kicking them off the rest of the way, I maneuver myself back onto his lap and wrap my arms around his neck.

"How hard you want it?" he pants, shoving a finger under the lace covering my pussy.

"As hard as you can give it," I hiss as he drags his fingers between my swollen lips.

"Damn, girl," he growls, pulling his fingers out. Lifting them between us, I can't help but notice how wet they are. Before I can point it out, he brings the glistening digits to my tits and paints my nipples with my come. Bending his head, he sucks one nipple into his mouth and I lose my patience. The need consumes me and I position myself over his cock. Without warning, I slide onto him, taking him deep with one move. My body stretches until I'm fully seated on him and his balls rest between us.

"You think you're in charge?" he questions, lifting my hips.

"Stop complaining," I order as I push down again. "Fuck me, Blackie. Fuck me like it's forbidden. Like we're two lost souls sneaking around. Hard and fast like our first time. You remember our first time, don't you?"

A curse escapes his lips as he threads his fingers through my hair and pistons his hips. Pulling at my locks, he lifts off the seat and fucks me thoroughly. His thick shaft sliding in and out of my wet pussy.

"Fucked me in your room at the clubhouse," I pant. "On your desk."

"Took your virginity," he grunts, as I clench around him.

"Made me yours right then and there."

"You were mine before that, girl," he says against my mouth. "You were mine the moment I laid eyes on you. I just didn't know it."

"Do you know it now?"

"Come for me," he demands.

"Do you know it now?" I repeat, bouncing up and down on his cock. "Do you know I was born to be yours?"

"With every fiber of my being," he hisses. "Now. Fucking. Come."

"Say please."

"Lace…"

"Blackie."

"Girl—"

That's all I needed to hear…

Holiday Shenanigans

Halloween with Kitten and Tiger

Bringing the phone away from my face, I stare at Lauren and raise a single eyebrow.
"Come on, Kitten, pose for me," I encourage as she rolls her eyes at me.
"After the third kid is it really necessary to make an announcement?"
"Of course it is," I retort, dismissing the ludicrous comment. "My followers are waiting for this," I add for extra emphasis.
"Your followers?"
"Yeah, some people got hoes in different area codes, I got fans in different zip codes. All over the world, people are following me on social media."
"You mean Facebook?"
"Babe, I'm bigger than Facebook. I'm neck and neck with Bruce Jenner when it comes to Instagram followers—"
"You mean Caitlyn Jenner."
Who?
What?
No.
Scratching my head, I stare at her perplexed.
"Who's that?"
"There is no Bruce Jenner, he's now Caitlyn. Riggs, he became transgender years ago," she explains, seemingly concerned over my lack of knowledge when it comes to celebs. I'm about to argue with her and tell her my Twitter stats when it dawns on me--all this time I thought I was comparing followers with an Olympic medalist who is probably a fake. An imposter! Will the real Bruce Jenner please stand up?!
"Daddy! Can we go now!?" my youngest son asks, tugging my leg and interrupting my epiphany. Staring down at him, I can't help but smirk. Dressed as a classic gangster, complete with a fake cigar and fedora on his head, he takes after his uncle.
"Just a second, Anthony. As soon as I get a picture of your mother we'll go trick or treating."
He turns his head and looks curiously at Lauren.
"Why is daddy taking your picture you don't even have a costume on?"
"Because he's crazy," my oldest, Eric, answers.
"Watch it, kid, or I won't let you egg the neighborhood tonight."
"What!?" Lauren shrieks. "You told him he could vandalize people's property with eggs?!"
"Not people we like," I defend. "I gave him a short list of assholes. Like, the dickhead who lets his poodle piss on our lawn, he's getting creamed. Now, say cheese, I still have to finish applying the fake blood to Robert's face."
The odds of Kitten giving me a smile are pretty slim considering she's pissed so I snap the picture, focusing on her bump and the cute little skeleton baby on the front of her shirt. I crop out the middle finger she throws up and get to work on posting my Halloween/we're expecting another kid post. While the fake Bruce

Jenner may have gotten one over on me, I'm no stranger to the social media game. I know hashtags are important when trying to make something go viral. It's like your calling card! With that in mind, my fingers go to work...

#myhumpinputthebumpin #icame #sheroared #babynumberfour #magicsperm #myswimmerareolympians #takethatfakebruce #teamboy #teamgirl #wheelsorheels

Trick or treat! Baby number four is on the way! Follow me on Facebook, Twitter, YouTube, Snapchat, your sister's ass and the pony express!! @themuthaeffintiger

Independence Day with the Knights

A hand closes over my shoulder as I man the grill, flipping burgers and dogs for forty people. Glancing over my shoulder I look at Jack. "Why don't you take a break, Wolf?"
"And let you take over? No way man, I've had your burgers," I argue. Jack Parrish may be a lot of things but he can't grill for Shit. "Real nice thing you did here today, getting everyone together."
Wiping my brow, I close the lid of the barbecue and turn around. My backyard is full. My brothers, their wives and kids even my own sons are here. Family—one big happy family, that's what we are.
"Wish Pipe was here," I mutter as I take the beer Jack offers me and guzzle down a few gulps.
"Yeah, me too, brother, me too," Jack says.
"Motherfucker is stubborn," I add, lowering the beer from my mouth. As I'm about to reveal Pipe came to the garage, my middle son walks up next to me.
"Hey, kid," Jack greets. "Jesus—when the hell did you get so big? I remember when you were little and your old man would bring you around the clubhouse and you'd hide my smokes."
"I used to rob your weed too," my son deadpans, earning a slap upside his head. So what if the kids twenty-two years old and five inches taller than me.
"What'd I tell you about revealing too much, boy?"
"I thought it would be good to get everything out in the open," he replies with a shrug. "Especially since I want to ride with the Knights."
Jack's beer sputters from his lips as my son glances between us both.
"Have you lost your fucking sense?" I question. "I had to sell a fucking kidney to pay for that fancy fucking college you and your mother insisted you go to."
"I dropped out," my son reveals.
"Have kids they said," Riggs whispers as he steals a hotdog from the grill. "It'll be fun they said..."

Happy Fourth of July from the Satans Knights.

A Pipe and Wolf Thanksgiving

#Pipe #SatansKnights If someone would've told me all those years ago when we were in juvie that I'd be standing in Wolf's kitchen on Thanksgiving, crying while this motherfucker makes me slice five pounds of onions—I would've told them to fuck off. "Where is the apron I got you?" Wolf questions, taking a break from the tedious task of slicing garlic.
"Fuck you and your apron," I growl. Dropping the knife onto the cutting board, I lift my shirt and wipe my watering eyes.
"Suit yourself you bastard, I was just concerned your fancy plaid shirt would get dirty."
"Layla and the girls picked it out," I grunt as I glance down at the brown and yellow fucking get up I'm wearing. Jesus Christ.
Sensing my disgust, he tosses me the apron. One that reads, This Guy Needs A Beer.
At least he didn't get us matching ones.
"Put the fucking apron on and stop being a bitch."
Taking it from his hand, I glance at the apron he's wearing...an apron that reads, May I Suggest the Sausage.

More to come 🌝😊

About the author

Janine writes emotionally charged novels with an emphasis on family bonds, strong willed female characters, and alpha male men who will do anything for the women they love. She loves to interact with fans and fellow avid romance readers like herself.

She is proud of her success as an author and the friendships she's made in the book community but her greatest accomplishment to date would be her two sons Joseph and Paul.

˛.•´✶CONNECT WITH JANINE˛.•´✶
Website: http://www.janineinfantebosco.com/
Facebook: https://www.facebook.com/janineboscoauthor/
Twitter: https://twitter.com/JanineBosco
Pinterest: https://www.pinterest.com/grassking205/
Goodreads: http://bit.ly/1FJa8S3
Newsletter: http://bit.ly/29Dfru4
Amazon Author Profile: http://amzn.to/2b98hQM
Book Bub Author Profile: http://bit.ly/2kXDpo1

Other books by Janine

The Nomad Series: *all can be read as standalone*

Drifter (Book One)
Wanderer (Book Two)
Roamer (Book Three)
Loner (Book Four)

Satan's Knights novels: *all can be read as standalone*

From the Ruins
The Devil Don't Sleep – Coming Soon
Riding the Edge – Coming Soon

Stand-alone novels

Raging Inferno – From the Burn Me Anthology – Full novel Coming soon

The Riverdale Series: *should be read in series order*

Pieces – Book One
Broken Pieces – Book Two
Fitting the Pieces – Book Three
Jake's Journal (Book 3.5) novella – companion to the series

Printed in Great Britain
by Amazon